'THE FOURTH BOOK IN THE RED GAMBIT SERIES'

# IMPASSE

## COLIN GEE

# 'Impasse'

## The fourth book in the 'Red Gambit' series.

1st NOVEMBER 1945 TO 24th DECEMBER 1945.

### WRITTEN BY COLIN GEE

Warning! This book contains some scenes of a sexual nature that could cause offence and upset. That is not my wish and I have written them only because I felt they were necessary to convey the full story in a proper manner.

I have included a warning at the beginning of the phase so that those who do not wish to read it may bypass it without being exposed.

Apologies to anyone who reads the piece and is subsequently offended.

It is not my wish to offend, but I felt that I could not gloss over the events of which I write, so gave them my best efforts without wishing to be gratuitous. I can assure you that it was not easy to write.

Please note that the book is written in, and checked in, English. There are fundamental differences between US English and English that have been highlighted by comments regarding poor spelling.

In many, many cases, that would appear to be because an Englishman sees an Americanism, and vice versa.

In general, I will use the American version solely when it is in regard to something American.

By way of example, Armor [US] and Armour [UK], Honor [US] and Honour [UK]. Whilst I accept that there will probably still be basic spelling errors, please try to remember the national differences. Thank you.

# Series Dedication

The Red Gambit series of books is dedicated to my grandfather, the boss-fellah, Jack 'Chalky' White, Chief Petty Officer [Engine Room] RN, my de facto father until his untimely death from cancer in 1983, and a man who, along with many millions of others, participated in the epic of history that we know as World War Two. Their efforts and sacrifices made it possible for us to read of it, in freedom, today.

Thank you, for everything.

# Overview by Author Colin Gee

If you have read the books leading up to 'Impasse' then, I hope, you will already understand the concept behind 'Red Gambit'. Therefore, my words now will be mainly for those who have come in at this moment.

After the end of the German War, the leaders of the Soviet Union found sufficient cause to distrust their former Allies, to the point of launching an assault on Western Europe. Those causes and the decision-making behind the full scale attack lie within 'Opening Moves', as do the battles of the first week, commencing on 6th August 1945.

After that initial week, the Soviets continue to grind away at the Western Allies, trading lives and materiel for ground, whilst reducing the combat efficiency of Allied units from the Baltic to the Alps.

In 'Breakthrough', the Red Army inflicts defeat after defeat upon their enemy, but at growing cost to themselves.

The attrition is awful.

Matters come to a head in 'Stalemate' as circumstances force Marshall Zhukov to focus attacks on specific zones. The resulting battles bring death and horror on an unprecedented scale, neither Army coming away unscathed or unscarred.

As the war progresses throughout the three books preceding 'Impasse', other agencies are at work across the continent and, sometimes, beyond.

Soviet organisations, such as the NKVD and the GRU [Soviet Military Intelligence], come together or clash, depending on their masters, and their agents reach far and wide.

Across no-man's land, their rivals, SOE, OSS, the FBI, MI5, and the Deuxieme Bureau retaliate, seeking out advantage over their clandestine enemy.

In the Pacific, the Soviet Union has courted the Empire of Japan, and has provided unusual support in its struggle against the Chinese.

In the three previous books, the reader has been presented with the facts of the matter, all the way to November 1945. That has taken him or her on a journey from Moscow to Alamogordo, the Haut-Kœnigsbourg to Hamburg, Ireland to

Greenland, and brought them to other places that have since become synonymous with the horror and pain of those years, such as Trendelburg, Reichenberg, and Bloody Barnstorf

We all know that what came to pass was known as the 'Cold War'.

This series is written about the alternative that our forebears could have faced.

From this point forward, the writing will be done in such a way as to reflect an historical record of events.

Much of what has been written before is factual, and sometimes, in the research, I wondered why it was that we did not come to blows once more.

We must all give thanks it did not all go badly wrong in that hot summer of 1945, and that the events described in the Red Gambit series did not come to pass.

Again, I have deliberately written nothing that can be attributed to that greatest of Englishmen, Sir Winston Churchill. I considered myself neither capable nor worthy to attempt to convey what he might have thought or said in my own words. The pressure to do otherwise is mounting.

My profound thanks to all those who have contributed in whatever way to this project, as every little piece of help brought me closer to my goal.

[For additional information, progress reports, orders of battle, discussion, freebies, and interaction with the author please find time to visit and register at one of the following:-

www.redgambitseries.com, www.redgambitseries.co.uk, www.redgambitseries.eu,
Also, feel free to join Facebook Group 'Red Gambit'.]
Thank you.

I have received a great deal of assistance in researching, translating, advice, and support during the years that this project has so far run.

In no particular order, I would like to record my thanks to all of the following for their contributions. Gary Wild, Jan Wild, Jason Litchfield, Mario Wildenauer, Loren

Weaver, Pat Walshe, Elena Schuster, Stilla Fendt, Luitpold Krieger, Mark Lambert, Simon Haines, Greg Winton, Greg Percival, Robert Prideaux, Tyler Weaver, Giselle Janiszewski, James Hanebury, Jeffrey Durnford, Brian Proctor, Steve Bailey, Paul Dryden, Steve Riordan, Bruce Towers, Victoria Coling, Alexandra Coling, Heather Coling, Isabel Pierce Ward, Hany Hamouda, Ahmed Al-Obeidi and finally BW-UK Gaming Clan.

One name is missing on the request of the party involved, who perversely has given me more help and guidance in this project than most, but whose desire to remain in the background on all things means I have to observe his wish not to name him. None the less, to you, my oldest friend, thank you.

The cover image work has been done by my brother, Jason Litchfield and, as usual, his skill has produced a cover of excellent quality. Thanks bro.

Quotes have been obtained from a number of sources, which have included brainyquote.com and quotegarden.com. I encourage the reader to visit and explore both sites.

Wikipedia is a wonderful thing and I have used it as my first port of call for much of the research for the series. Use it and support it.

My thanks to the US Army Center of Military History and Franklin D Roosevelt Presidential Library websites for providing the out of copyright images.

All map work is original, save for the Château outline, which derives from a public domain handout.

Particular thanks go to Steen Ammentorp, who is responsible for the wonderful www.generals.dk site, which is a superb place to visit in search of details on generals of all nations. The site has proven invaluable in compiling many of the biographies dealing with the senior officers found in these books.

I should also thank the website redbrick.dcu.ie for the Irish Republican quote.

If I have missed anyone or any agency, I apologise and promise to rectify the omission at the earliest opportunity. This then is the fourth offering to satisfy the 'what if's' of those times.

Book #1 - Opening Moves [Chapters 1-54]
Book#2 - Breakthrough [Chapters 55-77]
Book#3 - Stalemate [Chapters 78-102]
Book#4 – Impasse [Chapters 103 – 125]

# Author's note.

The correlation between the Allied and Soviet forces is difficult to assess for a number of reasons.

Neither side could claim that their units were all at full strength, and information on the relevant strengths over the period this book is set in is limited as far as the Allies are concerned and relatively non-existent for the Soviet forces.

I have had to use some licence regarding force strengths and I hope that the critics will not be too harsh with me if I get things wrong in that regard. A Soviet Rifle Division could vary in strength from the size of two thousand men to be as high as nine thousand men and in some special cases, could be even more.

Indeed, the very names used do not help the reader to understand unless they are already knowledgeable.

A prime example is the Corps. For the British and US forces, a Corps was a collection of Divisions and Brigades directly subservient to an Army. A Soviet Corps, such as the 2nd Guards Tank Corps, bore no relation to a unit such as British XXX Corps. The 2nd G.T.C. was a Tank Division by another name and this difference in 'naming' continues to the Soviet Army, which was more akin to the Allied Corps.

The Army Group was mirrored by the Soviet Front.

Going down from the Corps, the differences continue, where a Russian rifle division should probably be more looked at as the equivalent of a US Infantry regiment or British Infantry Brigade, although this was not always the case. The decision to leave the correct nomenclature in place was made early on. In that, I felt that those who already possess knowledge would not become disillusioned, and that those who were new to the concept could acquire knowledge that would stand them in good stead when reading factual accounts of WW2.

There are also some difficulties encountered with ranks. Some readers may feel that a certain battle would have been left in the command of a more senior rank, and the reverse case where seniors seem to have few forces under their authority. Casualties will have played their part but, particularly in the Soviet Army, seniority and rank was a complicated affair, sometimes with Colonels in charge of Divisions larger than those commanded by a General. It is easier for me to attach a chart to give the reader a rough guide of how the ranks equate.

Fig#1 - Comparative ranks.

| SOVIET UNION | WAFFEN-SS | WEHRMACHT | UNITED STATES | UK/COMMONWEALTH | FRANCE |
|---|---|---|---|---|---|
| KA - SOLDIER | SCHUTZE | SCHUTZE | PRIVATE | PRIVATE | SOLDAT DEUXIEME CLASSE |
| YEFREYTOR | STURMMANN | GEFREITER | PRIVATE 1ST CLASS | LANCE-CORPORAL | CAPORAL |
| MLADSHIY SERZHANT | ROTTENFUHRER | OBERGEFREITER | CORPORAL | CORPORAL | CAPORAL-CHEF |
| SERZHANT | UNTERSCHARFUHRER | UNTEROFFIZIER | SERGEANT | SERGEANT | SERGENT-CHEF |
| STARSHIY SERZHANT | OBERSCHARFUHRER | FELDWEBEL | SERGEANT 1ST CLASS | C.S.M. | ADJUDANT-CHEF |
| STARSHINA | STURMSCHARFUHRER | STABSFELDWEBEL | SERGEANT-MAJOR [WO/CWO] | R.S.M. | MAJOR |
| MLADSHIY LEYTENANT | UNTERSTURMFUHRER | LEUTNANT | 2ND LIEUTENANT | 2ND LIEUTENANT | SOUS-LIEUTENANT |
| LEYTENANT | OBERSTURMFUHRER | OBERLEUTNANT | 1ST LIEUTENANT | LIEUTENANT | LIEUTENANT |
| STARSHIY LEYTENANT | | | | | |
| KAPITAN | HAUPTSTURMFUHRER | HAUPTMANN | CAPTAIN | CAPTAIN | CAPITAINE |
| MAYOR | STURMBANNFUHRER | MAJOR | MAJOR | MAJOR | COMMANDANT 1 |
| PODPOLKOVNIK | OBERSTURMBANNFUHRER | OBERSTLEUTNANT | LIEUTENANT-COLONEL | LIEUTENANT-COLONEL | LIEUTENANT-COLONEL 2 |
| POLKOVNIK | STANDARTENFUHRER | OBERST | COLONEL | COLONEL | COLONEL 3 |
| GENERAL-MAYOR | BRIGADEFUHRER | GENERALMAJOR | BRIGADIER GENERAL | BRIGADIER | GENERAL DE BRIGADE |
| GENERAL-LEYTENANT | GRUPPENFUHRER | GENERALLEUTNANT | MAJOR GENERAL | MAJOR GENERAL | GENERAL DE DIVISION |
| GENERAL-POLKOVNIK | OBERGRUPPENFUHRER | GENERAL DER INFANTERIE' | LIEUTENANT GENERAL | LIEUTENANT GENERAL | GENERAL DE CORPS D'ARMEE |
| GENERAL-ARMII | OBERSTGRUPPENFUHRER | GENERALOBERST | GENERAL | GENERAL | GENERAL DE ARMEE |
| MARSHALL | | GENERALFELDMARSCHALL | GENERAL OF THE ARMY | FIELD-MARSHALL | MARECHAL DE FRANCE |

' OR ARTILLERY, PANZERTRUPPEN ETC

1 CAPITAINE de CORVETTE    2 CAPITAINE de FREGATE    3 CAPITAINE de VAISSEAU

ROUGH GUIDE TO THE RANKS OF COMBATANT NATIONS.

# Book Dedication

My best friend and I have often discussed what we would have done, or where we would have chosen to serve, had we been called to arms in World War Two.

As you might expect, personal safety plays a huge part in our discussion, and he and I agree totally on the place we would least like to have served.

In a number of conflicts, struggling over the same lands, and confronting the same terrible enemies, both man-made and those created by nature, man endured the unendurable in one corner of the planet; one that, in regard to 1939-1945, still seems to be ignored in favour of its more well-known and more overtly dramatic cousins.

From the days of the 1941 Japanese invasion to the struggle of the Fourteenth Army in Burma, men, more often than not forgotten by those for whom they fought, endured the unendurable.

When silence fell in May 1945, it was not long before others were called to serve over the same battlefields, such as the French Army, whose soldiers and Foreign Legionnaires fought and died in Indo-China.

The fighting and the dying only ended when the last US marines and soldiers came home in 1975 or, in some cases, later.

Even then, the suffering was incomplete, something I remember seeing on newscasts, a final ignominy visited upon some returning US veterans, all of whom were worthy of an honourable reception; soldier's welcome from a grateful homeland.

Some were solely greeted with derision, others were abused, sometimes spat at, and many were simply ignored.

I, even at that young age, was horrified, and I take this opportunity to say my piece now.

To those that did such things to your military, you are forever shamed and I offer you nothing but my utter contempt.

Therefore, it is with due deference and admiration, that this book is dedicated to those soldiers who, from 1940 to 1975, earned their spurs in the 'Big Green', the Boonies, or whatever expression is used to describe the awfulness of the jungles of Asia.

Although I never served in the Armed forces, I wore a uniform with pride. My admiration for our young service men and women serving in all our names in dangerous areas throughout the world is limitless. As a result, **'St Dunstan's'** is a charity that is extremely close to my heart. My fictitious characters carry no real-life heartache with them, whereas every news bulletin from the military stations abroad brings a terrible reality with its own impact, angst, and personal challenges for those who wear our country's uniform. Therefore, I make regular donations to **'St Dunstan's'** and would encourage you to do so too.

---

As 1945 draws to a close, I found myself thinking more about the innovations and advances that would have been made, given the continuance of war.

Some weapons that progressed slowly out of the war years might well have been developed a lot quicker, had combat been shouting its needs in the ears of those working on engineering and design.

To that end, from this point forward, it is possible that the reader may find equipment appearing before its rightful time.

At no time will it appear before a time that I consider wholly feasible or, I hope, that is unacceptable to the reader.

# Table of Contents

14

20

23

# Fig#72 - European locations of Impasse.

## MAP OF EUROPE - IMPASSE

| | | | | | | | |
|---|---|---|---|---|---|---|---|
| A1 | ARNOLDSTEIN | O1 | OSTERKAER ISLAND | T1 | TORUN | | |
| A2 | ARDENNES | O2 | OTTWILLER | T2 | TRELLEBORG | | |
| B1 | BADEN BADEN | P1 | PFALZBURG | V1 | VERSAILLES | | |
| B2 | BALTIYSK | P2 | PRUM | V1 | WURZENPASS | | |
| B3 | BARANOVICHI | P3 | PUCH | Z1 | ZITTERSHEIM | | |
| B4 | BRUMATH | R1 | RHEINE BENTLAGE | | | | |
| C1 | CHISELDON | R2 | RINGENDORF | | | | |
| C2 | CIERPICE | R3 | ROTTELSHEIM | | | | |
| D1 | DAHLEM | S1 | ST KILDA | | | | |
| D2 | DUBLIN | S2 | STAKHANOVO | | | | |
| D3 | DOSSENHEIM | S3 | STRASSFELD | | | | |
| E1 | EBSDORFERGRUND | S4 | SULINGEN | | | | |
| E2 | EICHERSCHEID | | | | | | |
| G1 | GOUGENHEIM | | | | | | |
| H1 | HATTMATT | | | | | | |
| H2 | HINTEREGG | | | | | | |
| J1 | JADERKREUZMOOR | | | | | | |
| K1 | KARUP | | | | | | |
| K2 | KLAGENFURT | | | | | | |
| K3 | KLUCZEVO | | | | | | |
| K4 | KUNTSEVO | | | | | | |
| M1 | MOSCOV | | | | | | |
| M2 | MUGGENHAUSEN | | | | | | |
| N1 | NEUWILLER-LES-SAVERNE | | | | | | |
| N2 | NORDHAUSEN | | | | | | |

*You cannot run away from weakness; you must some time fight it out, or perish; and if that be so, why not now, and where you stand?*

Robert Louis Stevenson

# Chapter 103 - THE CHANGE

<u>1033 hrs, Thursday, 1st November 1945, Headquarters of SHAEF, Trianon Place Hotel, Versailles, France.</u>

Eisenhower could feel for the man, they all could, but the mantle of failure had to be laid somewhere and, in this instance, it lay fully on the shoulders of Group Captain James Stagg.

His information, received from civilian and military sources across the spectrum of agencies, had been misinterpreted.

Gathered in the room were the heavyweights of the Allied Command Structure, initially brought together to discuss the changes in the Soviet hierarchy, but now all were overtaken by a new priority, equally afflicted by the meteorological prediction error.

"Well, Jim, it's done and no use crying over it now. It doesn't happen again. We can't afford to get caught like this a second time."

Stagg took his leave, intent on reviewing the situation to discover where the errors were made.

Ike watched him go and then returned his focus to the group.

"Right. We move on."

He brought them back to the moment.

The men edged forward to examine the map but were distracted by the sound of laughter from outside the room.

Their eyes were drawn to the window and a group of military policemen, playing hard as soldiers do, firing missiles at each other at breakneck speed, stopping only to scoop up more handfuls of the snow that covered the landscape for as far as the eye could see, and whose arrival had caught the Allied forces unprepared.

Patton moved briskly to the window but Eisenhower stopped him with some quiet words..

"Let 'em be, George, let 'em be."

Reluctantly, the Commander of the US Third Army moved back, sparing a moment to scowl at the soldiers, oblivious to their seniors as they cavorted in fifteen inches of pure white snow.

"Now. Let's sort this mess out."

That work was in progress when a simple message arrived.

The Italian Government had declared its neutrality.

---

To be fair to the Meteorological Department, they had forecast snow to fall as of the night of the 30th. The issue was in its quantity and the dip in temperature that ensured it remained.

On the morning of the 30th October, the temperature stubbornly refused to break 0°, dropping to -9° as November arrived.

November 1st had seen better temperatures at the southern end of the line but, in the centre and the north, 0° became but a pleasant memory.

Stagg had presented them with a revised forecast that morning; one that did not cheer them.

More snow was on its way and with it would come a further drop in temperature, partially because of the presence of a huge cold front and partially because of the winds that would accompany it.

He added widespread freezing fog to his glum forecast.

Now the Allied Armies would have to battle the elements, as well as the Russians.

### 1251 hrs, Thursday, 1st November 1945, Rheine-Bentlage Airfield, Germany.

The three men sat quietly, well apart from all the others, mainly wounded soldiers and furlough men waiting for the arrival of their ride home.

The threesome drew a number of looks, as much for their disparate proportions as the fact that they were clearly combat veterans who had been through some sort of hell on earth, which, in truth, they had.

A cigarette moved steadily between the smallest man, seated on the left end of the barrier that the three had made their personal seat, travelling to the man seated in the middle, and back.

On the end, nearest what had been decided had once been an Opel Blitz lorry, sat the largest of the men. He did not smoke, but shared the canteen doing steady business on all three sets of lips.

A brazier, constructed by the airfield guards for their own comfort, produced both heat and smoke, warming bodies and stinging eyes.

The steady drone of an approaching aircraft broke into their comfortable silence and three sets of eyes were suddenly wide open and scanning the sky for threats.

An RAF transport aircraft descended through the gently falling snow, landing harder than the passengers or the pilot wished for.

A door flew open on the temporary structure that was presently the operations centre for the small field, yielding a weasely faced British MP Captain, whose voice broke the silence as he shouted the waiting passengers into some sort of order.

The moment had come, one the three had simply ignored.

They stood as one and hands were extended.

Bluebear ignored both hands and swept his two friends up in his massive arms, crushing them close.

From under his left armpit came an unmistakeable voice.

"Oi Vay Chief! Leave me shome breath already!"

With a laugh, BlueBear tightened his grip on Rosenberg and then released both men.

The diminutive Jew drew air into his recently crushed chest and proffered his favourite suggestion one more time.

"You shure you don't wanna batman like the Limeysh do? You'd be doin' me a favour, Chief."

The Cherokee looked the small man up and down, feigning disdain.

"No pets allowed on the aircraft."

Hässler laughed, as much at Rosenberg's inability to immediately respond as at the humour itself.

Rosenberg rallied.

"And fucking shquaws ride on the roof!"

Their intimacy was broken as the MP Captain appeared magically in their midst, his clipboard held firmly as a pencil hovered expectantly.

"Names."

"Rita Hayworth, Hedy Lamarr, Betty Grab..."

The British MP poked Rosenberg in the chest with the clipboard.

"Don't try to be funny with me, Yank."

"You asked for namesh, you got namesh, wishe-assh."

The clipboard seemed to develop a mind of its own, firstly moving back, almost as if to strike the recently promoted Jewish Sergeant. Secondly, it jerked upwards as it left the British officer's grasp, snatched away in the mighty paw of a Cherokee who was not going to watch his friend messed with by the Limeys.

"My name's BlueBear.... Lieutenant BlueBear... I'm on the list... here, Captain."

A strange silence followed.

One in which the MP was clearly assessing his next move.

One in which he realised the precariousness of his position.

One in which he decided that valiant retreat was the order of the day.

"Well, hurry up and get yourselves on the 'plane. The weather's going to close in shortly and there won't be any more flights for some time."

This time the three shook hands in silence, exchanging smiles and nods, everything having been said on the journey to the airfield.

BlueBear mounted the steps to the DC3 and turned to wave at his two friends.

The wave was returned and then they went their separate ways.

[Charley BlueBear was being flown back to the States to receive his Medal of Honor from the hands of President Truman. As the first Native American to be honoured in the new war, the propaganda value was immense and, as with others before him, BlueBear was to be used to raise the capital with which to grease the wheels of war.]

## 2357 hrs, Thursday, 1st November 1945, GRU Commander's office, Western Europe Headquarters, the Mühlberg, Germany.

A week had passed and passed quickly.

There was plenty of work in which to immerse a troubled mind and Nazarbayeva had committed herself fully to the new challenge ahead. The pain of the wound had eased and her recovery was assured.

Some minor irritations had surfaced, men who had felt they were more qualified than the woman who had pulled the trigger on Pekunin, men who started agitating, whispering, and plotting behind the scenes.

Nazarbayeva had been put in her new position by events, that was clearly the case, and some wondered whether her obvious ambition either had engineered those events or pushed her into precipitous action. After all, there was no evidence against Old Pekunin.

*'Was there?'*

On Stalin's personal order or, more likely on Beria's suggestion, NKVD General Dustov had remained at hand, supported by a contingent of his troops.

The whispering and plotting gradually died away, as did the presence of the two senior GRU officers mainly responsible for it, neither of whom welcomed their transfers to other distant and much cooler climes.

Poboshkin, newly promoted to Lieutenant Colonel, stood smartly as GRU Major General Tatiana Nazarbayeva opened the repaired office door, her work for the night complete.

"Good night, Comrade General."

She smiled a weary smile to her loyal aide.

29

"And to you, Comrade Poboshkin. I wish you every success. Safe journey tomorrow."

Nazarbayeva strode over the crisp snow, her thoughts mainly on the special mission that she had entrusted to her Aide.

Poboshkin reseated himself, anxious to keep on top of the fine details of his first presentation to the GKO, intended for Moscow the following Sunday. But his thoughts also strayed to the mission he had been given by his new General, the reason he was returning to the seat of power two days earlier than needed, a mission that was intended to delve into certain aspects of the life and death of the dearly departed GRU Colonel General Roman Samuilovich Pekunin.

---

In her private quarters, Nazarbayeva sat with a glass of water and completed the now ritual examination of her breast wound.

Satisfied with the healing process, she settled into the leather chair and again commenced the mental exercise that tried to make sense of the past week. Part of that process was to attempt to solve the puzzle box that Pekunin had wanted her to have but, for now, its secrets remained hidden.

She recalled his words.

*'It is my personal gift to you. Use it how you wish. Believe it and believe nothing else.'*

Thus far, it had denied her entry, its inner workings conceived by the most cunning of minds.

She had felt almost taunted by its presence; so close but yet the contents were so far from her reach.

At times, her mind had strayed to other options. She had contemplated using her boot as a hammer and once had even picked up the grenade she had found by the river bank that summer's day, thinking to use its metal case to break the box open.

She always resisted the temptation of force, although the defiance of the twelve centimetre square box pushed her to the limit.

*'Who knows what old Pekunin put inside that could be broken?'*

But tonight, as she relaxed in her chair, a visual memory stirred, one that had remained hidden or forgotten, perhaps obscured by the gravity of the conversation that took place at the time.

'*Mudaks! You old devil!*'

Clear as day, the image came. As he talke, Pekunin had shown her the first stages; very deliberately.

The simple box had few markings and, in any case, each side was the mirror of the others.

Her mind's eye recalled the moment, seeing the two thumbs on the leading edge, easing one of the sides across a few millimetres.

Taking up the box, Nazarbayeva pressed and found nothing but resistance. She tried each facet in turn, the seventh attempt yielding some movement.

Her memory was hazy and the image now indistinct, so she worked the box, pressing in all directions without reward.

'*Think, woman, think!*'

The slightest scuff on the wood shouted at her, its presence almost imperceptible but, in itself, a pointer to stage two.

Pressing down and right, the next section moved to one side with ease.

The two stages together brought the third part of the unlocking process to mind and she found the correct panel first time.

Now she was on her own, without Pekunin's hand to guide her, but her mind was equal to the logic of the box and the fourth stage fell quickly to her assault.

Within ten minutes, the box had yielded a small piece of paper.

The words written on it were simple.

'*My loyal Tatiana, I am sorry to burden you. Do what is right for the Rodina and remember that your duty lies to her above all other things, come what may. Please accept my copy of 'The State and the Revolution' as a memento. With affection, Roman.*'

Written at a different angle, in a different pen and in a seemingly different hand, almost as if the shred had been ripped from another larger piece, were apparently unconnected words.

*'Ref C5-C dated 130644 ref Theft of utensils from 22nd Army Stores'*

The note was directing her towards an old GRU file.

---

Ten minutes later, Poboshkin was surprised to see his boss back in the headquarters.

"Relax, Comrade Poboshkin."

"May I assist you, Comrade General?"

"Not necessary, Comrade. I just want to pick up an old file that I need to remind myself of. I'm still capable of opening a filing cabinet by myself."

Her smile disarmed him but he still rallied.

"Perhaps I can get a clerk to fetch it for you, Comrade General?"

"No, leave them to their rest. It's no problem."

To mark the end of the exchange, Nazarbayeva moved off quickly towards the archives.

Given the age of the file, she surprised herself by finding it quickly, strolling past Poboshkin no more than four minutes after she had walked away.

"Tea, Comrade General?"

"Excellent idea. I shall be in my office, Comrade."

The file was face down on the desk when the orderly brought Tatiana her drink, his presence barely acknowledged by Nazarbayeva, who was sat holding a first edition of 'The State and the Revolution', one of Lenin's most influential works, in one hand, and the photograph it had relinquished in the other.

The family pictured in it needed no introduction as she had seen a similar larger print on Pekunin's desk day in, day out; it was the old General's son and his family.

Finally alone, she explored the folder and found efficient reporting of a GRU investigation into the thefts from 22nd Army Central Stores. The culprits were probably long dead, transferred to penal mine clearing units.

Contained within the official paperwork were a few sheets of paper with meaningless sequences of letters and numbers, all in the same hand, a hand she didn't recognise but instinctively knew to be Pekunin's disguised.

Taking a pencil and a fresh sheet of paper, Nazarbayeva selected the first document, arranged Pekunin's literary bequest in front of her and, with a deep breath to calm her growing worries, opened the book on the page where she had found the photograph and commenced decoding.

---

One hour and forty-seven minutes later, Nazarbayeva's tears slid gently down her face as she finished the last sequence

She was now in possession of six decoded documents.

Her first effort had outlined the execution of Pekunin's family, on Beria's orders.

*'Poor Pekunin.'*

The second had pointed at possible evidence of the betrayal of the Spanish mission that resulted in the death of her son, on Beria and Stalin's orders.

*'If this is true, there will be a reckoning.'*

Sheet three revealed that the premises for going to war with the Allies were either exaggerated or contrived, again on the specific direction of Stalin and Beria.

*'So they brought all of this on the Rodina for what?'*

The very thought had left Nazarbayeva cold.

The fourth revealed Beria for what he was; rapist and sexual predator, listing a few times, dates, places, and names.

*'Some people are truly evil.'*

Number five was a personal record of a conversation to which Pekunin had been privy, when Stalin and Beria had agreed the sacrifice of the airborne troopers in the four attempts on the Allied symposiums. Both had apparently acknowledged the lack of real significance but insisted that the missions went ahead regardless of cost, despite the GRU General's pleas. Beria had apparently produced an informer's report on a less than complimentary exchange between Makarenko and Erasov, during which their belief in the shortcomings of the political leadership was top of the agenda. In Pekunin's considered, yet unbelievable estimation, whilst possibly justifiable militarily and psychologically, personal revenge also played a part in the fool's errands that were the Zilant missions. It also spoke of the exchange in Beria's office and the GRU General's belief that Beria found pleasure in Nazarbayeva's loss.

*'Not even the Chekist swine would do that! The Rodina is all-important!'*

Another part of her brain contributed to the silent debate.

*'This is Beria, Tatiana. He has no soul, no honour, no decency.'*

She pondered that a moment and found no argument to oppose the little voice.

*'He's capable of anything that preserves his world and keeps his power.'*

Tatiana Nazarbayeva, GRU General, Hero of the Soviet Union, shuddered.

She moved on, pushing the growing voice back into the recesses of her mind.

Smallest of all the messages was number six. It was also the most confusing, with no apparent meaning.

*'There is nothing like Christmas in Krakow.'*

*'Except May Day in Moscow.'*

Undoubtedly, Pekunin would not have included it if it were not important, but the purpose of the message was unknown.

The seventh and final decode contained a few words, albeit powerful ones. They were the names of people that Pekunin had spoken to in the last few weeks, the dates he had approached them, all of them men who knew what was going on in Mother Russia and who, for the most part, according to Pekunin's brief notations, were prepared to risk all to protect her from the enemy within.

Nazarbayeva slipped into bed after destroying the decodes and reassembling the GRU file to its original state, the contents of the messages safely kept in her mind.

The night brought her little sleep or rest as her mind toyed with the awful truths she had been presented with.

Yet, in spite of the awfulness, personal tragedy even, of some of the messages, she kept returning to the seventh decode and the last entry on the list.

*'23/10/45 Molotov - declined.'*

What Tatiana did not, could not, know was that Molotov had acquired a debt when the indiscretions of his nephew Skryabin had fallen under Beria's gaze before the war commenced. That debt had been discharged, as it was the Foreign Minister that had supplied proof of the last elements of Pekunin's 'treachery', revealing to Beria the details of Pekunin's approach.

---

Her dreams kept her from proper rest, her sharp brain reminding her that by the very act of not revealing the names in the seventh message was, in itself, an act of treason against the state. Waking from her fitful sleep, Tatiana's brain again presented her with the quandary; the unknown meaning of an entry in the last document.

*'15/10/45 VKG -?'*

Her mind worked the possibilities, as it had done since the first moment she read the entry.

'Kuzma Galitskii... no.'

Her mind clicked into place, throwing up a solution.

'Vladimir Konstantinovich Gorbachev? Where is he now?'

She woke and wrote the name down and went back to her broken sleep.

---

In the morning, Nazarbayeva established that Major General Gorbachev was in command of the 346th Rifle Division, part of the 1st Guards Rifle Corps, the major fighting unit of 22nd Army of the 1st Baltic Front.

In the mid-afternoon, that information was flamed by one of her aides, who reported that the GRU file on 22nd Army was dated and inaccurate.

The 346th had seen some modest fighting in September, enough to cause casualties, amongst whom was Gorbachev. His injuries were serious enough to send him back to the Motherland to recover.

The latest report had the General in the hierarchy of the Moscow Military District.

The Deputy Commander of Military Training for the MMD, Dmitri Kramarchuk, had been killed in a car accident and the recuperating Gorbachev was immediately put in his place.

Nazarbayeva checked the dates and found that Gorbachev was in the MMD ranks on the 3rd October.

His position gave him control over new army formations being put together in and around the capital city, which immediately suggested to Tatiana that she had been right in her assumption and she had her man.

### 0400 hrs, Sunday, 4th November 1945, Frontline position, the Jade River, west of Jaderkreuzmoor, Germany.

"Thank you, Sarnt."

Ames accepted the enamel mug and its scalding hot contents as if they were gifts from the Gods.

"My pleasure, Sah. They Welsh boys's ok. They'm took a shine to you, by all accounts."

Ames took a tentative sip of the strong brew and shrugged, attempting humour to downplay the moment.

"We've spent some quality time together, Sarnt. They're good lads."

Sergeant Gray was a recent arrival with the 83rd Field Regiment, Royal Artillery, yet another of those men who had spent time behind German barbed wire.

Placing his mug on the snow, he spared a look at his surroundings, the combination of the moon and the steadily falling snow creating a relaxing, almost Christmas-like feeling to the land.

He pulled out his large pipe and had it loaded in record time.

The awesome object had already acquired the nickname of 'The Funnel', its bowl constantly belching something indescribable that bore scant resemblance to the aromatic products of pipe tobacco.

Theories abounded, starting with shredded tyre rubber and ending with old unwashed socks.

The Sergeant quickly checked the radio and found it satisfactory, rewrapping it in the army blanket used to insulate it from the elements.

His desires kick started by the sound of Gray sucking greedily on the Funnel, Ames was soon puffing on a Woodbine.

The Artillery officer had acquired a heavy smoking habit since the fighting in and around the Hamburg Rathaus in August, which now neared forty a day, if supplies were sufficient.

"One of they Welshies was telling me bout 'Amburg, Sah. Sounds like 'er was a right bastard, fair 'nough."

Ames' eyes softly glazed, as his memories took him back to those few bitter days, fighting with the Royal Welch, the Black Watch, and even those German Paratroopers.

"To be honest, Sarnt, it was pretty horrible... and we were extremely lucky to get out of it. Many good lads didn't."

His mind presented the awful image of the young Lieutenant Ramsey, thrown into the masonry of the Rathaus by an high-explosive shell with such force that his body adhered to the surface, and only reluctantly relinquished its grip after the main battle was over.

He shuddered.

Gray understood, and left the younger man to his memories.

Both men enjoyed the peace, until the light rattle of the simple warning device forced Gray into action.

"Chalky, I told yer to watch the cans, you bloody idio..."

Gray turned his head, just in time to catch the stale breath of a Soviet soldier.

Ames also turned, alarmed as much by the rapid end to Gray's words as the sound of an enamel mug falling to the bottom of the foxhole.

He fumbled for his Sten, finding only another enemy soldier, and then another.

Cold hands pressed themselves to his face and caught his flailing arms.

**0433 hrs, Sunday, 4th November 1945, Frontline position, the Jade River, west of Jaderkreuzmoor, Germany.**

Lance-Bombardier Chalky White knew he was in trouble, in more than one way. His hands were full of the bacon sandwiches that were to be the breakfast of his officer and Sergeant, but they were now needed to prise his greatcoat away from the snagging barbed wire.

His efforts were accompanied by the constant rattle of the old tins, all filled with pebbles, noisemakers that danced and announced his every movement.

*'Sod it!'*

He moved backwards, reasoning that the barbs would give up their hold more easily.

They held the greatcoat fast until, in an instant, they relinquished their hold and the wire twanged back into place.

The nearest tin taunted him with its audible warning.

A voice boomed out

"Who goes there?"

"The OP's soddin' bacon butties... now shut the fuck up!"

Hardly text book but it had the desired effect. No Russian could have managed it and the owner of the voice knew the early routine. He already had his sandwich in his belly.

White resumed the crouching advance and found the foxhole.

That was pretty much all he found.

No radio, no maps, no Ames.

Just Gray.

Gray was already cold and stiff, his throat cut from ear to ear.

"Stand to! Stand to!"

*Courage is doing what you are afraid to do. There can be no courage unless you are scared.*

*Eddie Rickenbacker*

## __Chapter 104 - THE FEAR__

### __0435 hrs, Sunday, 4th November 1945, Frontline position, 400 metres north of Hinteregg, Austria.__

Up and down the Allied lines, soldiers were woken from their slumbers by cries of alarm, as Soviet raiders visited trenches and bunkers in search of intelligence and prisoners.

Many men simply disappeared into the freezing night, others died at their posts. Yet others were fortunate enough to see or hear the threat before they were overcome, turning the tables on their would-be kidnappers.

Nervous sentries called their units to arms and equally nervous officers filled the sky with magnesium light, or called down artillery to deal with a supposed enemy attack.

Artillery and mortars exchanged their shells and bombs, as ranging shots, then battery, then counter-battery fire escalated the long-range exchange. And then it stopped, as quickly as it had erupted.

Whatever happened, few men on either side of the divide slept that rest of that night.

---

Private First Class Frederick Lincoln Leander, the worst soldier in his platoon, bar none, reluctantly rose up from the bottom of his position, unable to ignore the urgent whispers of the other occupant.

He looked around with an inexperienced eye.

Nothing.

"Oh Lordy, it's cold."

"Can it."

"Sorry, Sarge."

"I said fucking can it, Contraband!"

Silence had descended again, except for the gentle patter of fresh snow falling... and the heavy breathing of the terrified.

The sound of artillery was gone, its intrusion brief, but intense. Its flashes and bangs had added to the decidedly threatening atmosphere, illustrating trees long stripped of their shape, creating almost a gothic horror movie feeling to the frontline positions of the 92nd Colored Infantry Division.

The occupants of the shallow hole were not friends; far from it. Circumstances had brought together Sergeant Clay and Private First Class Leander and placed them in the foremost position of King Company, 3rd Battalion, 370th Infantry Regiment.

Everywhere was white, something that had become a joke to the Buffalo soldiers of the 92nd Colored Infantry Division.

A number of humorous discussions had taken place about the wiseness of using black soldiers in a white environment. The humour of it was soon lost after a few men were lost to sniper fire and a number of soldiers started to cover their faces with anything suitable, from flour pastes to white paint, which brought forth more humour.

In the main, the men accepted their lot and coped with the increasingly bitter temperatures, but some found their prejudices either resurfacing or reinforced, as they perceived some intent on the part of their white superiors.

Clay and Leander came from different poles of the matter; the former, his rank hard earned in the face of extreme discrimination, saw bias in everything, racism in everything, hate in everything, and tempered his judgement with his own beliefs and prejudices, as his father and his grandfather had before him.

Leander came from a privileged, educated background, one in which there was little or no tension between people of different colours, just an acceptance of difference without the fear and vitriol that normally went with it.

He was different, hence his nickname, one that was intended to cause offence, with its roots back in the Civil War. His education and attitude set him apart from the majority and he found himself discriminated against by those who would, should, have called him brother, although it was his lack of soldierly skills that caused most angst amongst his peers and which set him at loggerheads with Clay.

The Sergeant's hand was suddenly raised and a finger marked out a direction down which both men strained their eyes.

Nothing.

*'What's that?'*

Nothing.

*'Ma eyes is playing tricks.'*

Nothing.

*'That moved!'*

Leander brought his own hand up, pointing slightly off to the right of the NCO's, picking out the 'something' that he thought had just shifted slightly.

The snow flurried, driven by a sudden wind.

Nothing.

A sudden single sound broke the reverie, and had Clay taken but a moment to think about it, a sound similar to that of a small stone thrown into the snow.

But he didn't and automatically swivelled to his right, eyes searching out the source whilst his soldierly instincts screamed at him for his stupidity.

His companion hadn't heard it so stayed 'eyes front'.

Those eyes widened.

Something.

*'Oh my lord!'*

"Sergeant!"

The nothing that had become something became more stark and real, subdividing into two then three rapidly moving somethings, white forms on a white background almost on top of the position already.

Clay swivelled back to his front as his hands started to bring up his grease gun.

The short barrel fouled on the iron hard edge of the hole, but his finger had already received the command to pull the trigger and the weapon started to chew the frozen earth as it sent out bullets.

The first white shape was on him in an instant and Clay's own camouflage, a simple bed sheet looted from a

Gasthaus in Möggers, was indelibly marked with blood as a wicked blade slashed at his throat.

The grease gun stopped and was dropped to the floor of the hole as approaching death took precedence, Clay's hands grabbing at the wound in an attempt to stem the flow of blood.

The enemy soldier reversed his blade and rammed it hard into the back of the dying man's neck, killing him instantly.

Leander screamed as the second figure loomed large over him, a similar blade beginning to descend.

He ducked and the knife glanced off his helmet.

Other calls of alarm rose up from nearby positions, as more Buffalo soldiers became aware of the enemy in their midst.

A flare rose and silhouetted a number of Soviet ski troopers in various poses, from grabbing unfortunates for prisoners to plunging their Kandra knives into unprotected flesh.

It was also, for some, a deadly distraction.

Leander, the useless soldier, motivated now by survival, picked up his Garand and sideswiped his attacker in the face.

The Russian went down hard and out for the count.

The third man got his hands on the rifle but without sufficient purchase and Leander jerked the butt into his throat, crushing soft tissue and dropping the would-be kidnapper to the snow.

Shots started to punctuate the night, as attackers and defenders brought more conventional weapons into use.

The Garand jumped in Leander's hands, pointed in the right direction by the trembling soldier but with no accuracy and both bullets missed.

Knife recovered from Clay's corpse, the Soviet ski trooper launched himself at the petrified negro soldier, content that he could easily overpower the man and bring back the prisoner that his Commander so wanted.

He changed direction in mid-air as the Garand barked again, this time putting a heavy bullet through his stomach.

The Russian thrashed about in the scarlet snow, screaming as the agony overtook him, attracting attention from both friend and foe.

Leander turned around on the spot at speed, rapidly jerking into position to defend his hole, seeing nothing, then jumping to another point of the compass.

By the time he looked due west, two more enemy troopers were almost on top of him.

He screamed, not to encourage himself but out of pure fear, the two Russians clearly bearing the bloody marks of kills already made that night.

The Russian with the PPSh took the first bullet low in the groin, the second in the right shoulder. The first bullet slowed him down, the second spun him away, the submachine gun flying at Leander and bouncing back off Clay's inert form. As he went to ground, the Russian's face connected with a tree stump and disintegrated as bone was shattered by the impact. Immediately knocked unconscious, the comatose figure came to rest on his back, in which position the veteran of four years of war silently drowned in his own blood.

Leander's screaming redoubled as his tears froze on his face and ice played havoc with his eyes.

The first shot passed through the camouflage jacket of the last trooper, closely followed by the second, which missed by two feet. The third hit home.

Leander's Garand spat out its redundant metal clip, signifying that the weapon was empty, the metal falling to ground at the front of the hole, coinciding with the thud of the ski trooper's body, left knee destroyed by the passage of the heavy bullet.

The wounded man scrabbled for his own rifle, but it had fallen too distant.

In desperation, he extracted a grenade and primed it, underarming it accurately towards the small hole.

Leander ducked and the deadly missile struck his helmet, deflecting to the rear of his position.

It exploded and brought silence to the man who had killed Clay.

Slipping another charger into his rifle, Leander took deliberate aim on the wounded man to his front, but still needed three shots to put the man out of his increasing misery.

Another grenade, this time better aimed, dropped into the hole at his feet. With reactions previously unsuspected, he picked up the deadly object and tossed it out, ducking his head before it exploded, heaping yet more ignominy upon the living and dead in front of his position.

Standing upright again, Leander felt the products of defecation slide down his legs, his fright causing him to constantly soil himself.

Three Soviet troopers approached, aiding a stumblingfourth man, a comrade, whose injuries were leaking rich red blood, soaking through the white snowsuit he was wearing.

Leander screamed again and discharged his rifle indiscriminately, hitting the wounded man in the calf, bringing him down and, in the doing, causing the others to fall to the ground.

One man recovered himself quickly and brought his PPD into action, the burst kicking up earth and snow all around the petrified black soldier but failing to cause him harm. None the less, the fear caused him to drop the new charger, then the Garand.

The ski soldiers saw their opportunity and rushed forward.

A PPSh is a superb close quarter weapon, capable of a phenomenal rate of fire.

In the hands of a trained soldier, it is a deadly beast and was rightly considered the finest submachine gun of WW2.

It could also be a very forgiving weapon in hands unfamiliar with its traits, and so it proved, as Leander scrabbled for the discarded weapon and brought it to bear.

The sound of his screams disappeared in the rattle of automatic fire as the weapon belted out the remaining sixty-three bullets from its distinctive round magazine.

Seven bullets found targets beyond the immediate threat, wounding two ski troopers and one buffalo soldier prisoner and dropping all three to the snow.

Forty bullets missed any target, finding termination in frozen earth, wood, or snow.

The remaining sixteen spread themselves between the three Soviet attackers.

The middle soldier died instantly as three bullets struck him in a microsecond, smashing his face and turning his brain to mush.

Either side of him white ski suits blossomed with scarlet buds and the other men went down, neither killed but both most certainly out of the fight.

One lay silent but conscious, the blood bubbling on his lips.

The other joined the screaming, his pain equally spread between the eight wounds he had sustained.

Another grenade bounced nearby and exploded, its arrival and detonation simultaneous and not permitting Leander the opportunity to duck.

One piece of metal sliced across his forehead, dropping a two-inch sliver of flesh across his left eye. Another piece smashed into his left elbow and stuck in the ball joint, bringing with it yet another reason for the young African-American to scream.

Movement to his right focussed him and he pointed the PPSh at whatever it was.

"Shit!"

He had not realised that the weapon was empty.

Some clarity descended on his mind and he turned to the body of Clay, grabbing at the pistol holster and the weapon within.

A bullet thumped into his left shoulder, passing straight through without contact with vitals or bone, but jarring the elbow against the body of NCO and causing him to almost faint with the pain.

A second bullet took the dead body in the upper chest and a third struck Clay's forehead, sending parts of his skull and brains flying across the snow behind the position.

The Colt 1911A came free and Leander swivelled, seeking out his attacker.

No obvious enemy came into view but his vision was still restricted by icy tears of fright and pain in equal quantities.

To his right, a shot was followed by a short squeal, signifying another life terminated prematurely.

Again, to the right, the snow seemed to open like a set of theatrical curtains, permitting clear view of a group of four Russians carrying a kicking Buffalo soldier away. The curtains closed as quickly as they had parted and Leander was alone again.

His right hand trembled, the automatic pistol shaking as he pointed it at any and every small sound that followed the end of the Soviet raid.

Nothing.

*'I'm still alive. Praise the Lord! Praise the Lord!'*

A distinctive crack made him jump.

The Colt swivelled and he looked down the jumping sights as the broken branch descended to ground level, bringing snow with it.

A soft thud behind him reminded him of a grenade and he ducked as best he could, not realising that another ravaged stump had surrendered its weighty load of snow.

His wounded elbow banged into Clay's metal canteen.

He screamed, and relieved himself once more.

"Medic! Medic!"

There was no answering call, no repetition of his plea, save that which echoed off the increasing snowfall.

Nothing.

His eyes blurred as temperature, stress, blood loss and tiredness fought for control.

He jumped as his mind sought to fight back and remain alert.

He watched and listened.

Nothing.

"Oh Lordy, it's cold."

Private First Class Frederick Lincoln Leander, only survivor of his platoon, slipped into the bottom of his little hole and passed out.

### 1349 hrs, Sunday, 4th November 1945, the Kremlin, Moscow.

The GRU briefing ended and Poboshkin waited expectantly.

He had not been asked one single question throughout, everything he said apparently accepted without dispute.

"Thank you, Comrade PodPolkovnik. That will be all."

Poboshkin swept up the documentation and stowed it quickly in his case before saluting and turning towards the heavy door.

Beria's voice followed him.

"Oh, and please inform General Nazarbayeva of our concern for her well-being, and that we look forward to the time she'll be able to travel and brief us herself, particularly on her report regarding Pekunin's treachery."

Poboshkin nodded by way of response and left.

Stalin looked quizzically at the bespectacled NKVD Marshal and, with unusual humour, commented on the exchange.

"Very touching, Lavrentiy."

"I meant no more than that, Comrade General Secretary. She's competent and loyal to the Rodina, certainly more competent and loyal than that shit Pekunin."

Stalin grimaced and then pursed his lips, not wishing to be reminded that treachery had dwelt so close at hand but, now that it had happened, turning his mind to the matter.

"How goes the NKVD investigation into the traitor?"

Beria went straight for the glasses and handkerchief routine, betraying his desire to exercise care in answering.

"We have established some unusual activity in the last two months, activity that's now being interpreted in a different manner, given the circumstances. It will take time, as I've ordered my men to be thorough, but I think his betrayal started only recently. He's no family that we can interrogate, Comrade. They died some time ago," Beria studied the gleaming spectacles as he finished his verbal assessment, "And his Deputy also fell by our Nazarbayeva's hand. Extremely efficient... and extremely convenient."

Beria had spoken at length for a number of reasons.

He already knew that Stalin knew much of what he had spoken of, but he knew that Stalin did not know of the circumstances behind the demise of Pekunin's son and family, and he hoped above hope that he never would. The official suggestion had been an overzealous approach by the investigating team. Those responsible had succumbed during their debriefing, as directed by the head of the NKVD, keen to tidy any loose ends.

Beria's attempt to throw some suspicion on Nazarbayeva was his own maskirovka, moving the Dictator on from awkward questions about the demise... 'executions'... of Fyodor Romanevich Pekunin, his wife, and their three children.

47

It worked.

"Convenient, Comrade? Are you suggesting that the woman had some hand in this treachery?"

Beria took his time in answering, forcing himself to return the glasses to their proper position.

He looked through them, feigning reluctance both with his eyes and with his tone.

"I've no evidence to that effect, Comrade General Secretary, but I do know she was very close to Pekunin. There's talk of a relationship between them that went beyond professional limits."

That was true, in as much as Beria had started the talk.

"Is this some criticism of my decision, Comrade?"

Beria knew he was on dangerous ground.

"Not at all, Comrade General Secretary. You promoted on competence... and we've all seen how efficient and competent the woman can seem. This is new information to which you could not have been privy and, in truth, it may yet prove to be nothing of concern for the State. We'll know soon. Her report should give us indication of any issues, particularly if she omits anything that we already know."

Stalin nodded but once, signalling an end to the discussion and the opening of another.

"So?"

The word was not directed at Beria but at the other occupant of the room.

Konev had been stood at attention, patiently waiting whilst the GRU lackey had delivered his reports, with nothing new presented; certainly nothing to change his mind from the course of action he had proposed that morning.

"Comrade General Secretary, I see no reason to change my proposal. Given the weather conditions, the location of the Yugoslavian stocks, and the military situation I've inherited, it makes perfect sense and should yield good rewards for us, both militarily and politically."

That was no less true than it had been this morning.

GRU's briefing had confirmed the Italian position and some excellent successes against Allied supply and infrastructure by communist sabotage groups, particularly the volatile Italian groups who had been stirred up by rhetoric and promises delivered by recently arrived NKVD agents.

"Very well, Comrade Marshal. You may commence Italian operations and the limited attacks as outlined in your Plan Red Two."

And with that simple statement, the pre-war planning was consigned to the bin and Konev's new assault plan was set in motion.

---

As Konev left, a dishevelled civilian stood and accepted the invitation of the still open door; a man the Marshal recognised but could not presently name.

Two further men followed, one clad in the uniform of the NKVD, the other clearly a Red Navy Admiral, bearing all the hallmarks of an experienced submariner.

The door closed on the trio and another audience commenced.

It was not until he seated himself in his staff car, already well warmed for the journey to the airbase, that he recalled the name and, more importantly, the man's purpose in life.

"Ah, Comrade Kurchatov!"

"Sorry, Comrade Marshal?"

Konev had unwittingly spoken aloud.

"Nothing, Comrade Driver, nothing at all. Shall we see what this fine Mercedes is capable of?"

The woman needed no further inducements and the powerful beast surged ahead.

*'Comrade Kurchatov... Comrade Director Kurchatov of the Atomic weapons programme.'*

His eyes narrowed.

*'Atomic scientists, the NKVD and the Navy... all together... with no Army or Air Force presence.'*

His eyes closed.

*'What's being hatched behind our backs, I wonde...'*

No sooner had the thought taken shape than it was expelled as sleep overtook him. The darkness did not relinquish its grip until he was shaken awake at Vnukovo.

*In the absence of orders, go find something and kill it.*

*FeldMarschall Erwin Rommel.*

# Chapter 105 - THE SUNDERLAND

The Sunderland Mk V was a big aircraft, the four American Wasp engines giving her the power previously lacking in the Mk III.

She was called the Flying Porcupine for very good reason, her hull bristled with defensive machine-guns, fourteen in total, manned by her eleven man crew. Such armament was required for a lumbering leviathan like the Short Sunderland, whose maximum speed, even with the Wasps, was a little over two hundred miles an hour.

In the German War, encounters with enemy fighters had been mercifully rare and, in the main, enemy contacts were solely with the Sunderland's standard fare; submarines.

This Mk V also carried depth charges and radar pods, making her a deadly adversary in the never-ending game of hide and seek between aircraft and submersibles.

NS-X was out on a mission, having flown off from the Castle Archdale base of the RAF's 201 Squadron. The men had once been in 246 Squadron but, when that squadron was disbanded, the men of NS-X, all SAAF volunteers, had been one of two complete crews to be transferred to 201 Squadron.

During World War Two, there had been a secret protocol between the British and Éire governments, which permitted flights over Irish territory though a narrow corridor. It ran westwards from Castle Archdale, Northern Ireland, across Irish sovereign territory and into the Atlantic, extending the operating range of Coastal Command considerably, and bringing more area under the protection of their Liberators, Catalinas, and Sunderlands.

The agreement was still in force.

NS-X had followed this route out into the ocean, turning and rounding the Irish mainland, before heading north, past Aran Island and onto its search area around St Kilda.

Fig#73 – Éire, Great Britain, and the Atlantic 1945.

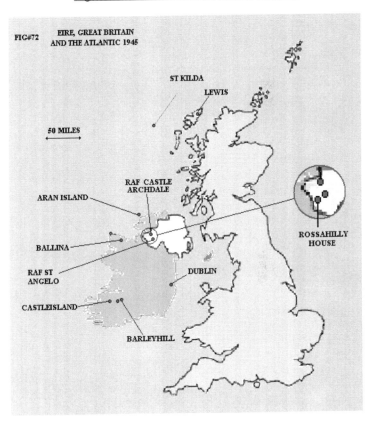

A Soviet submarine had been attacked and damaged the previous day, somewhere roughly fifty miles west of Lewis, and the Admiralty were rightly jittery, given the importance of the convoy heading into the area in the next ten hours.

There was little good news.

The RCN corvette that had found and attacked the submarine was no longer answering; it was now feared lost with all hands. Other flying boats and craft were assigned to the dual mission, all hoping to rescue or recover, depending on how fate had dealt with the Canadian sailors, as well as attack and sink the enemy vessel.

Flight Lieutenant Cox, an extremely experienced pilot, hummed loudly, as was his normal habit when concentrating.

Having just had a course check and finding themselves a small distance off their search pattern, he eased the huge aircraft a few points to starboard, before settling back down to the extended boredom of searching for a scale model needle in a choice of haystacks.

The Sunderland carried many comforts, including bunks, a toilet, and a galley, the latter of which yielded up fresh steaming coffee and a bacon sandwich, brought up from below by Flight Sergeant Crozier.

"There you go, Skipper, get your laughing gear around that, man. I'll take over for a moment."

South African Crozier wasn't qualified to pilot the aircraft, but that didn't trouble the old hands of NS-X. He flopped into the second seat and took a grip, permitting Cox to relinquish the column to the gunner.

He let Cox start into the snack before airing his concerns.

"Skipper, I think Dusty's an ill man. He's wracked up on a bunk, looking very green."

Dusty Miller was the second pilot, and he had disappeared off to sort out a stomach cramp, about an hour beforehand.

"Too much flippin Jamesons last night, that's what that is, Arsey", the words came out despite having to work their way around large lumps of bread and bacon.

Rafer Crozier didn't much care for being called Arsey, but it didn't pay to point that out, for obvious reasons.

"Don't think so, Skip. Dusty was the only one to have the goose, wasn't he?"

The local procurer of all things, Niall Flaherty, had slipped such a beast to the camp cooks for a small consideration. In contravention of standing orders on aircrew's meals, Miller had wangled a portion of the well-hung goose, prior to flight ops.

"Maybe you've a point, Arsey. Best we keep quiet then, eh?"

Another voice resonated through the intercom.

"Contact, Skipper. Starboard 30. One thousand yards. Possible wreckage."

Flight Sergeant Peter Viljoen's crisp and concise report interrupted the great Goose discussion, as Cox wiped his hands clean on his life preserver and took back command of the aircraft, releasing Crozier to crane his neck in the direction of the sighting.

Viljoen's voice came again.

"Contact confirmed Skipper, Starboard 35, One thousand yards. Wreckage, and lots of it too."

Cox spoke to the crew.

"Pilot to crew. OK fellahs, close up now, and keep your eyes peeled. Turning for a low level run over the site now. Sparks, get off a report to base right now. Magic, pass Sparks the position please."

Both radio operator and navigator keyed their mikes with an acknowledgement, as the port wing dipped to bring the lumbering seaplane around in a circle for a west-east run across the wreckage.

Whilst some of the crew used binoculars to probe the floating evidence of recent combat, others remained with eyes firmly glued elsewhere, seeking out the tell-tale plume of a periscope, or the reflection of sun from the wing of an aircraft.

Nose-gunner Viljoen was first up again, professionally and matter-of-factly, at least at first, then rising in pitch and excitement as his eyes worked out the details of what he was seeing.

"Contact dead ahead, 500 yards. Dinghy in the water. Men onboard, Skipper, there's men onboard! They're waving!"

"Roger, Dagga. How many?"

"Hard to say, Skipper. Five, maybe more. Looks like a standard issue navy dinghy, and I'll bet a pound to a pinch of pig shit that they're navy uniforms, Skipper."

The reason behind Viljoen's nickname was lost in time, but he was Dagga to everyone, including 201's Commanding Officer, although, in fairness, that may have been because they were brothers.

Sparks came back with a message, confirming the passing on of the location report, leaving Cox free to concentrate on his fly past.

His first sweep had been at full speed but, with the absence of any adverse reports, Cox turned his aircraft round for a second pass and throttled back to permit closer examination.

He saw the waving men in the dinghy himself, and believed he saw others in the water, whose only motion was caused by the shifting of the sea.

*'Poor bastards.'*

"What's the latest on Dusty, please?"

A slight delay, and the metallic voice of Rawson, one of the gunners, responded with negative news.

The pilot did not welcome being single-handed for the entire flight.

"Bollocks with an egg on top."

His favourite expletive and one that always puzzled those who heard it.

"Arsey, I need a hand up here. Pass your guns onto someone will you."

"Roger, Skipper."

Crozier looked away from his waist guns, and saw Rawson moving forward.

"All yours, Tiger," and Crozier slapped the gunner on the shoulder as he headed towards the steps that rose up to the flight deck.

Rawson had been nicknamed 'Sid' at a young age, for reasons best known to God and his friends in Mrs Oosterhuis' class. That label survived until the first time that 246 Squadron's Operations officer had placed his initials up on the crew roster.

By the time those present had stopped laughing at G.R.R.R., 'Sid' was history and 'Tiger' was born.

"Radar Contact, bearing 010, range approximately 95 miles, heading unknown, possibly south-south-west, Skipper."

Magic Malan's report was delivered in his normal impersonal style. The type VIc Radar set was supposed to be capable up to 100 miles in the right circumstances, and Flight Sergeant Malan always seemed to coax the best out of the equipment.

Cox thumbed his mike.

"Witty, fit in with you at all?"

After the slightest delay, the Navigator replied.

"Position could tie in with the Stord, Skipper."

"Roger."

Stord was a destroyer of the Royal Norwegian Navy, one of the array of vessels converging on the area.

Crozier slipped into the second seat, a place he often occupied. He had failed his pilot's training, not on his ability behind the controls, but more on his inability with the required mathematics.

Lining up on the wreckage, Cox throttled back as much as he dared.

"Ok crew, slow pass. Keep your eyes skinned."

As the big flying boat did a leisurely flyover, Dagga and rear-gunner Van der Blumme confirmed the presence of naval personnel amongst the survivors, as well as many bodies floating on the surface.

"Skipper, radar target has changed course, now confirmed at 90 miles, heading 190. She changed course after Sparks lit up the airwaves."

"Roger, Magic."

Standing orders no longer permitted the Flying Boat to touch down and recover the Canadians, but as the Norwegian Navy was coming to the rescue, it just meant a few more hours on the water for the survivors.

"Dagga, use the Aldis. Let them know we can't stop, but help is on its way. Witty, how long?"

Navigator Jason Witt was already prepared for the question, so his answer was immediate.

"Thanks, Witty. Four hours, Dagga. And wish them good luck. Sparks, send confirmed survivors at this location."

The Sunderland circled slowly, as the signal lamp blinked out the message to the men below.

"Skipper, message sent."

"Roger Dagga. Right, now let's find the bastards who did this."

Generally speaking, one bit of ocean looks much like another, but the piece of the Atlantic they had just flown over and now drew them back displayed something special.

Fuel oil.

On one of the southbound legs of their search pattern, Dagga's sharp eyes had seen the long, thin, glistening streak on the surface below.

Cox gave the matter some thought.

"Pilot. Witty. Pop across to the palace will you."

Within seconds, Flight Sergeant Witt arrived from his navigating station behind the flight deck, or palace as it was known.

"Witty, get a bearing on that slick and plot it in relative to the Canadian sinking will you. I'm going to deviate off our pattern and I want a bearing down which to fly ok?"

The Navigator understood immediately and, with a modest acknowledgement, disappeared.

---

NS-X was flying south-south-west on a course of 192 in search of whatever it was that was littering the ocean with fuel oil. Three more distinct glistening marks had been found, all on a heading of 192, vindicating Cox's hunch.

Whatever they were tracking was hurt.

---

B-31 had been rushed to sea and that sort of haste never paid with submarines. However, the former Type XXI had easily manouevred into a killing position on the Canadian Corvette, without the surface vessel having the slightest idea that it was about to die. The XXI's quality sonar systems had identified the approach of the warship, whereas the Canadian system was built for submarines less advanced than the XXI.

As the computer-guided torpedoes had approached, the corvette's captain got his men moving to action stations and fired off a hasty contact report before two warheads ripped the heart from the small craft.

Forty men died in the twin explosions and the RCN London Pride was doomed, listing immediately.

Off the starboard beam, the B-31 raised its periscope for a fleeting look at the sinking vessel.

A single shot, hastily aimed, left the barrel of London Pride's 4" main gun, thumping into the sea forty yards over target.

The corvette turned turtle before a second shot could be fired, holding on the surface for a few seconds before surrendering herself to the inevitable and disappearing from view.

B-31 dropped her periscope and proceeded at fifteen knots, moving swiftly away from the sinking, south-south-west on a heading of 192.

The 4" shell had missed but there was sufficient water hammer from the explosion to seek out two items of faulty workmanship. The first effect was to shake loose an electrical coupling in the 'Bali' radar detector apparatus. The FuMB Ant3 Bali was used to detect incoming radar signals, and the B-31 had now lost the capability.

The shockwave also slightly unseated one of the fuel intake valves, which intake also lacked a properly functioning non-return valve. All of which meant that the B-31 occasionally vented modest quantities of fuel oil into the ocean as she sought to evacuate the area.

It was not until two hours had passed that the Engineering Officer noticed the fuel discrepancy and reported it to the submarine's commander.

The excellent sonar system showed no threat's nearby, the Bali was clear, and so it was decided to quickly ascend to assess what was happening.

B-31 blew her tanks and rose to the surface of the Eastern Atlantic at precisely 1303hrs.

### 1304 hrs, Monday, 5th November 1945, Eastern Atlantic, 163 miles north of North-Western Éire.

Dagga fired off an excited report.

"Fuck a rat! Submarine dead ahead, Two thousand yards, just surfacing!"

"Pilot to crew. Action stations. Action stations. Surfaced Submarine ahead."

Controlled pandemonium ensued as all the crew, except Miller, prepared for combat.

"Identify it someone!"

57

The pilot accompanied his request with a controlled turn, in order to not overfly the submarine.

"Not seen one like that before, Skipper. Not on my list."

Dagga was referring to an illustrated list of submarine outlines that the crew used to identify types. It was not unheard of for aircraft to send friendly vessels to the bottom for lack of correct identification.

RAF Coastal Command's printing and distribution service had decided to send the full Northern Ireland allocation of the latest intelligence manuals to RAF Belfast, from where they could be easily distributed. That flawed decision, as it was not made clear to those who received them they should be sent on, was about to bear terrible fruit.

NS-X passed on the submarine's port side at eight hundred yards distance, a few figures now obvious on the submarine's wet hull and in the conning tower.

Magic Malan piped up.

"That could be the latest German type XXI they never got to deploy, Skipper. Very streamlined, no gun mounts. It fits."

"Anyone else?"

Rolf Pienaar, the mid-upper gunner chipped in.

"I think Magic's right, Skipper."

The intercom went silent as Cox considered his options.

"I am identifying that as an enemy submarine. It's not an Amphion Class, which we were told was in the area. Agree?"

All those who had examined the sleek vessel agreed.

"Skipper, definitely, **definitely,** not Amphion Class. Conning tower all wrong... no gun mount forward. Bow section's wrong too."

Magic had put his book alongside that of Erasmus the Flight Engineer for comparison.

"Roger, Sparks, get a message off. Attacking confirmed Soviet submarine. Get the location and send it."

"Best you stay here, Arsey. Just in case."

The Sunderland swept around and took up a stern approach position. Cox upped the throttles and adjusted the aircraft's height.

"Pilot. Crew. Attacking. Good luck fellahs."

---

Onboard S-31, the appearance of the large amphibian caused a near-panic. The Soviet Captain called his men to order, knowing that he could not dive without letting the Sunderland attack unmolested.

So he did all he could, which was fight back.

---

The Sunderland crew's knowledge of the Type XXI was incomplete. German U-Boats had traditionally sprouted AA guns all over the conning tower, the more as the war went on and German submarine losses to aircraft climbed.

The XXI stepped back from that, anticipating its superior submersible qualities would keep it out of harm's way most of the time.

However, putting a submarine to see with no close defence would have been mad, and the designers of the ElektroBootes were not in that category.

In sleek sponsons, fore and aft on the conning tower, sat twin 20mm automatic weapons, easily missed by those who had studied the U Boats of the previous war or, in the case of the crew of NS-X, had seen snaps of such things at anchor.

The rear sponson hammered out a steady stream of cannon shells that slowly rose into the air until it seemed that the giant aircraft consumed them.

The Sunderland overflew the B-31, its rear guns lashing out and wiping men off the deck and into the sea where some died before the waters overtook them.

The depth-charges stayed in the racks and the aircraft adopted a steady southerly course.

---

20mm cannon shells are unforgiving things and NS-X was mortally wounded.

Dagga was dead, his position chewed to pieces by explosive shells, his guns silenced without firing a shot.

Also dead were Sparks and Jason Witt, in pieces, along with much of their equipment.

Flight Sergeant Peter Malan had lost his radar but had not been touched by any of the storm of steel that had swept through the Sunderland.

Dead too were Dusty Miller and Tiger, the former ignominiously smashed as he sat on the latrine, the latter decapitated by a direct hit.

Sat in the second seat Arsey started to recover his senses, having temporarily blacked out.

He became aware of a low animal sound near his left side.

As his eyes cleared the bile rose in his throat and he brought up the recent bacon sandwich, his stomach rebelling at the sight of the pilot.

Cox was still alive, and by an extraordinary effort, he had managed to flick the autopilot on, which steadied the damaged bird and took her away from danger.

The pilot had lost his left arm and left leg as the torrent of metal had flayed the palace. Further pieces of metal had emptied his left eye socket.

Erasmus arrived like a drunk, his unsteady gait giving testament to the horrors he had endured in the area he occupied with the navigator and wireless operator.

"Gimme a hand, Aidan... we gotta get the skipper out!"

Grabbing hold of something so ravaged and destroyed was not easy, but they managed, Cox's awful moaning lending both strength and compassion to both men.

Arsey slipped into the sticky pilot's chair and hooked up.

"Crew check. Call in."

Responses came solely from Malan, Pienaar, and Van der Blumme.

'*Oh hell.*'

"Magic, get up to the palace now and give Aidan a hand. The Skipper is hit bad. Chris, Rolf, stay put and keep your eyes peeled. I need to check out the bus."

As Peter Malan arrived to help Erasmus carry the hideously wounded Cox below, Crozier examined the flight deck.

The cold was intense, but not unbearable, ocean air being driven in thru countless holes.

Many gauges were useless, either broken or not registering because of damage elsewhere.

The autopilot, developed for the Mark V's long over ocean flights, was clearly working.

He grasped the control column and flipped off the autopilot, ready to instantly react to any problem in handling that arose.

The aircraft was perfectly trimmed and responded easily to his gentle commands. Using his foot controls, he tested more responses and was satisfied that he could control the Sunderland fully. He ignored the severed piece of Cox's left leg that lay next to the pedals.

"Pilot. Crew. Aircraft is fine. Action stations."

To their credit, none of the survivors of NS-X questioned either the order to attack or the fact that it was given by a Flight Sergeant gunner who wasn't qualified to pilot the aircraft.

Magic's voice broke in his ear.

"Skipper's gone."

Advancing the throttles, Crozier turned the leviathan back towards the enemy submarine.

"OK Magic, take over Dagga's guns. Make them keep their heads down on the run in."

"Roger, Skipper", the words tumbling out of Malan's mouth in spite of himself.

Leaving Aidan Erasmus to cover up the dead pilot, Malan made his way forward, into the charnel house that was the nose section.

At three miles out the Sunderland steadied itself, making a beam approach to what was now clearly a rapidly diving soviet submarine.

Nose and mid-upper machine guns sang out, sending a stream of deadly projectiles at B-31, many of which rang noisily off the casing and plates, unsettling those in the hull. The 20mm shells had damaged the firing system, so the vengeful Crozier could not fire the forward fixed .50's and add to the submariner's miseries.

At half a mile out only the top of the conning tower was visible, and Pienaar could no longer bear. He switched his guns to the rear in case further opportunity presented itself. Malan continued to flay the elektroboote for all he was worth.

Releasing the depth bombs, Crozier accepted the leap as the aircraft gained height and commenced a port turn as both Van der Blumme and Pienaar whipped up the waters.

All four charges exploded, sending a mountain of water skywards.

Damage to the aircraft's monitoring systems meant it was some time before the crew realised the starboard outer engine was on fire and that leaking fuel, similarly alight, was creeping slowly and inexorably along the wing.

---

The Type XXI was innovative for a number of reasons. Hydrogen peroxide engines, high capacity electric engines for unheard of underwater speeds; A superbly efficient schnorkel system and automatic reloading system for its torpedoes.

One unusual aspect of its production was that it was assembled from pieces, with a number of cylindrical component sections brought together and assembled into a whole.

During the previous war, when Allied aircraft looked for anything to bomb, a U-Boat in production made a tasty target. With this system, the XXI could be made in pieces, in small nondescript workshops, and then assembled secretly.

Two such sections had been welded together under canvas in the Gdansk Yards in early July.

Frame six comprised the rear section of the control suite and frame seven, the forward section of the main engine room.

NS-X's bombs were perfectly placed.

Two struck the hull either side of the conning tower and sunk on the port side of the submarine. One ploughed through the periscope stanchion, deflecting it towards the bow section.

The final bomb struck the stern and angled off, ending up on the starboard side of the B-31, perfectly in between the bursts of the other two bombs.

The effect of all three detonating virtually simultaneously on both sides of the hull was similar to placing a cardboard tube on a house brick and then pushing down on either side.

The rupture was immediate and wholly catastrophic.

B-31's engine was instantly flooded and the broached control room uninhabitable within seconds.

The Elektroboote B-31, once known as U-3536 [unfinished] took fifty-eight soviet seamen and six German civilian advisors to the sea floor below.

---

It was Van der Blumme who noticed the smoke and shouted the warning.

All eyes swivelled in the direction of the starboard wing, assessing the danger.

Fire buttons were thumbed and extinguishing media helped a little with the engine, but the fuel leak and external fire were slowly affecting the wing.

"Pilot. Aidan, have a look at Jason's charts. Get a course for the nearest land. Can't be far."

Flying Officer Erasmus made his way up into the navigator's position and tried hard to fathom what he could from the map.

Pienaar and Van der Blumme quickly discussed the likelihood of having killed the Russian.

"Fucking shut up now! Aidan, talk to me."

"Due south, Rafer, head due south. We should hit Ireland."

Responding quickly, Arsey moved the aircraft onto a dead south course, sorting out the engine revs of the three working power plants.

Aidan Erasmus slid the body of Sparks Warner to one side and worked on the radio.

NS-X flew steadily south, carefully nurtured by a gunner-cum-failed-pilot, who looked at the spreading dark stain in his lap with more concern as each minute passed.

A growing whine preceded graunching sounds from protesting metal as the port inner surrendered to friction, the absence of coolant neither known nor suspected, as gauges failed to show the fatal rise in temperature.

The engine seized and immediately affected the characteristics of the Sunderland, even though Crozier reacted swiftly and feathered, reducing the effect of the idle propeller.

"Flight. Skipper."

Erasmus experienced the joy of success as the sound of static over the speaker illustrated he had breathed life into the damaged radio.

"Go ahead Aidan."

"I think I have the radio up. Going to send sitrep and position ok?"

"Good effort, and keep sending. I can't see land yet mind you."

Erasmus keyed the transmit button and spelled out the rough position of NS-X, as well as the condition of the crew.

He managed it for nearly six minutes before a gentle fizz marked the permanent end of communications.

## 1411 hrs, Monday, 5th November 1945, Eastern Atlantic, 8 miles north of North-Western Éire.

"Mid Upper, Skipper."

"Go ahead, Rolf."

Pienaar was too excited and relieved for all the formalities.

"I can see land, manne, Straight ahead. Ireland."

Crozier strained his eyes and then saw for himself.

*'Ireland. Thank fuck'*

Grabbing charts of the Irish coast, Erasmus moved into the palace and looked for landmarks as the forbidding coastline grew clearer. The absence of land to the far west helped greatly.

Looking up and looking down, Erasmus spoke the obvious.

"Fuck man, we only just caught the edge of Ireland. We could have been flying all the way to the Equator."

*'Or not'*, both men thought, knowing they would have crash landed in the Atlantic and never been heard of again,

"Pilot. Crew. I'm going to drop the old girl down soon and we'll sail her into the coast. Don't want to take risks with her temperatures."

A worrying whine from the port outer engine emphasised the decision.

"Aidan is working on our position. We'll find a place to moor up, somewhere sheltered. Then we can decide if we fancy internment or whether we wanna to get back in this war."

The Sunderland dropped closer to the water and made a textbook landing on the light swell.

The starboard wing tank was virtually empty, which meant the external fire died quickly but the remaining engine started to misfire, as it could not draw a steady supply of fuel.

*'A close run thing that.'*

Rafer Crozier, Arsey to his friends, was surprised at how calmly he handled all that the damaged bird could throw at him.

Still engrossed in his map, Aidan tapped a section, drawing Crozier's attention to the headland.

"Go port side of the headland for sure, more protected from the Atlantic, Rafer."

That made sense.

Momentum and the remaining full power engine was all he needed to nurse NS-X in close to shore, round the headland, seeking a suitable place to drop anchor.

Keeping a suitable distance from the starboard shoreline, Crozier ignored the first inlet, rounding a two hundred metre peninsular and deciding it was as good a spot as any.

He suddenly realised that he had not organised the anchor party.

"Pilot. Magic. Pilot, VDB. Stand by anchors."

Both men had prepared themselves and not intended to criticise the man who had saved them, sunk the Russian sub, and avenged their comrades.

Crozier cut his switches, allowing the last vestiges of forward momentum to bring him to perfect position.

"Away forward, away aft."

Both anchors bit and the wounded aircraft lay safely at rest in the lee of the small peninsular.

Crozier closed his eyes and prayed, giving his God full thanks for the mercy and grace he had shown his son that day.

Pienaar arrived with a thermos of coffee and poured Arsey a full measure.

The warm beverage tasted like nectar to the exhausted and wounded man, lifting his spirit as only simple pleasures following extremes of terror and fear can.

"Right then, Aidan. Where are we?"

"Right on the money as it happens. We're a short dinghy ride from civilisation, and I can smell the Guinness already."

The three laughed, aware that sounds of movement meant that Malan and possibly even Van der Blumme were making their way up to the palace.

"And what's the name of this oasis of pleasure?"

Erasmus squinted and confirmed the facts, affecting an upper class English accent.

"Well, if I'm right about where we are, yonder lies the fair Irish hamlet of Glenlara and a welcome fit for heroes."

Their eyes were drawn in the direction he was pointing and they could already see men dragging three boats down a ramp leading to the water's edge.

It was as well that they could not hear.

"English bastards! Not a man, Seamus, not a fucking man."

His number two, Seamus Brown, had already sprinted away, joining the throng of IRA volunteers at the boats.

Reynolds had been christened Judas but no one called him that. Patrick, his second name, was favourite unless seeking a fight and an early grave.

Judas Patrick Reynolds had seen combat on the streets and hillsides of Spain during the Civil War and had revelled in its nastiness. He brought the lessons he learned home and subsequently acquired a reputation within IRA circles as an extremist, in every sense of the word.

Standing out in a group of extremists meant that Reynolds was marked for either an early grave or higher things.

Powerful men believed that the latter was most appropriate and a brief period of posturing and murder commenced.

But he had survived the internal squabbling that left fourteen families grieving, which culminated with his former unit commander on the wrong end of a shotgun. The hierarchy decided that enough was enough and they pulled the 'rabid dog' back into the fold by giving him leadership of the unit he had so recently made leaderless.

Judas Reynolds commanded the IRA Battalion based in County Mayo, a grand title for less than two hundred men, although most of them were to hand right now.

From his vantage point in the little school house, he could see the damaged British Sunderland and a handful of men waving from the now open hatch.

Turning to his companion, he reassured the worried man.

"This is no problem, Captain. We'll dispose of the aircraft and crew down the coast. No attention'll be drawn to our nest."

He turned to the imposing man in the dark blue uniform.

"Trust me, Ilya."

Trusting a man whose life had been spent in deception and treachery did not come easy to Captain-Lieutenant Ilya Nazarbayev, Commander of Special Action Force 27, Soviet Naval Marines.

However, he had little choice.

---

"Word for word, that's what it said?"

"Yes, Sir."

"OK, thank you, Sergeant. Dismissed."

Squadron Leader Benjamin Viljoen was trying to remain detached, but it was difficult with his brother listed amongst the overdue.

He re-read the message chit, desperately seeking something that he knew was not there.

'Both pilots down... Crozier flying... Type XXI submarine probably sunk... heading due south... position roughly thirty miles north of mainland Ireland.'

Viljoen moved to the Operations Centre to organise the morning's rescue efforts. Confirmation that NS-X's had sunk the submarine was received right on 1700hrs, but did not lessen the anguish and pain he felt. Only seeing Dagga again would do that.

**2031 hrs, Wednesday, 7th November 1945. Kildare Street, Dublin, Éire.**

The room was full of tension, heightened by the low lighting, the crackle of an open fire, and the fug of pipe smoke.

67

The only occupants eyed each other adversarialy, testing each other's resolve, seeking out weakness and preparing to pounce on an unguarded moment.

The man in uniform leant forward, eyes boring into those of his companion as he made a small adjustment to the positions.

"Check."

As he let go of the piece, Colonel Dan Bryan knew that something was wrong, for the man opposite permitted a smug look to replace the previous stoic expression.

Richard Hayes, Director of the National Library of Ireland, in whose office the two men were enjoying their usual game of chess, shook his head slowly.

"Some people never learn, you know."

Bryan's eyes sought the truth on the chequered battlefield as Hayes almost caressed a Knight before removing the Colonel's checking Bishop.

"Check."

The Knight, its work done, sat almost taunting Bryan; exposed, unsupported, alone, and vulnerable, and yet, so invulnerable.

The move had revealed the Black Queen, which now lay in check on Bryan's King.

"Damn."

"Indeed, Dan."

Whilst not over yet, there was no way back for the Head of Irish Army Intelligence.

He capitulated in the time-honoured way.

Both men settled back into their chairs, sampling pipe and whisky in equal measure, the first part of their rituals complete.

The Library Director donned a professorial air as he examined a worn piece of paper.

"I believe that makes the tally sixty-three to twenty-one in my favour. A very precise ratio, Colonel."

"I do so hate smart asses, so I do."

Both men giggled comfortably, close friends who had enjoyed many such encounters.

Hayes leant forward and freshened Bryan's glass.

"So, any further news on our government's position?"

"No change, President de Valera has assured all parties of the neutrality of our country."

Both men understood that the real position was somewhat more complicated than that, as it had been in the previous war.

"My contacts with British Special Branch and the Allied intelligence and special forces continue as ever, although with new names and new targets."

Hayes sampled his whisky.

"And our own problem children? Are they still quiet?"

Throughout World War Two, Richard Hayes had assisted Irish G2 with cracking the codes used by German agents in their communications with the IRA, codes that still bore fruit for Irish Intelligence when the Republicans employed them.

"Well... you tell me, Richard. How did you get on with our problem?"

The problem in question was a number of messages crafted in a hitherto unknown code that defeated the best efforts of the Irish decoders.

Bryan has spent some time with another Hayes that very day, in an effort to pick at anything within the ex-IRA Chief of Staff's memory that could help unlock the new messages.

In 1941, Hayes had been tried and sentenced for treason by an IRA court, accusations and circumstantial evidence leading them to believe he was a spy for the Garda.

He escaped and handed himself in to the Garda, seeking protection.

Subsequently imprisoned for five years, Stephen Hayes received frequent visits from the authorities in an effort to pick his brain clean.

Hayes had been the main author of the notorious 'Plan Kathleen', the IRA's proposal to Germany for an invasion of Northern Ireland.

A large folder, containing all that G2 knew of the plan, sat on the generous sofa.

Richard Hayes cleared the chessboard away and, indicating the file, sought permission to examine it.

Bryan opened his palm in acquiescence.

The academic slid his glasses up his forehead and read steadily.

"The other decoded messages were simple, but of no substance. You concur?"

Hayes stopped reading.

"Yes, although there was some phraseology that intrigued."

The Colonel's interest piqued.

"I haven't seen them myself so enlighten me please."

"Two in particular, one of which was repeated in two of the messages."

Setting aside the folder, Stephen Hayes removed a hand written note from his jacket pocket.

"Yes, here we are. Two messages speak of site security, unusual in itself. This one gives a radio frequency but God above only knows what for. I assume your boys are on that already?"

The Colonel nodded, his monitoring department having yielded nothing from the discovery.

"Ah yes, this one. All Anger, whatever that may be, is a priority. Suggests itself as a codeword for an operation to me."

Something clicked somewhere, deep in the recesses of his brain and Colonel Bryan became uncomfortable, knowing that he knew something but not knowing what it was that he knew.

"May I use your phone, Richard?"

A simple nod from Hayes was all that was needed.

Bryan paused at the handset, placed it back in the receiver and backtracked to the door.

On opening it, he was confronted by a very eager looking young man, dressed in a well cut suit and smartly turned out.

"Mulranny, have the car ready in five minutes. We're going back to Kilmainham."

Kilmainham Jail was a large institution renowned for its harsh environment and regime. Closed in 1924 it had fallen into apparent disuse, which was exactly the way G2 liked it to be viewed.

Retrieving the phone, Bryan made the arrangements.

70

"Dr Fogarty? Bryan here. Something's come up and I need to chat with our friend again."

"No, that will not do, I'm afraid."

"Yes, tonight."

"Thank you Dr Fogarty."

Replacing the receiver, Bryan returned to the chess table and downed the rest of his whisky.

"I'm going to need that file, Richard. I'll have a copy sent to you first thing in the morning... but for now, I need it."

Reluctantly, the older man closed the folder and offered it up.

"I don't suppose you are going to share, are you?"

"If I knew what it was, I would. All I know is that the answer is in the Kathleen file and Stephen Hayes is going to tell me tonight."

"Can you get me that copy tonight?"

Bryan laughed.

"Keen aren't you? May I use your phone again?"

There was no opposition to that, so a copy was swiftly organised, to be delivered to the Academic's home within the hour.

"Right, I'll see what our canary has to say. You know how to get hold of me if you find anything."

The two friends shook hands and parted.

*I want no mercy... I'll have no mercy... I'll die as many thousands have died, for the sake of their beloved land and in defence of it. I'll die proudly and triumphantly, in defence of republican principals and the liberty of an oppressed people.*

*William Allen, Irish Republican.*

# Chapter 106 - THE COLONELS

### 0819 hrs, Thursday, 8th November 1945, airborne over the Western Approaches, approximately one mile north of the Irish mainland.

NS-D had spotted its stricken sister immediately, the familiar white shape standing out against the grey rock of the coastline.

The Mayo Republicans had dragged the damaged Sunderland north-eastwards and away from Glenlara, putting some two miles distance between the two before damaging the watertight hull and leaving the sea to do the rest.

However, the sea had contrary ideas and gently pushed NS-X into a modest bay three miles east of the IRA camp.

As had been agreed in the early morning briefing, in the event that the missing aircraft had been discovered, NS-D set herself down on the ocean and taxied as close as possible to the silent Sunderland, guns trained in case of trouble.

Each of the rescue aircraft had an extra dinghy aboard, so four of the crew made the short journey between aircraft.

NS-D's location report was received with mixed feelings back in Castle Archdale.

The open hatch invited the rescuers in, but all they found was a silence laden with death, for all aboard were beyond help.

Splitting up to search different areas, the Flying Officer in charge climbed the stairs to the palace, finding both pilots very obviously dead at their controls. Other bodies lay around the Flight Engineer's board at the rear of the space.

Elsewhere, other rescuers-turned-undertakers located the rest of the crew, each man pale and long dead.

The commander of NS-D instructed that the dead crew should be transferred to his aircraft, detailing two more men to go and assist, as well as to ensure that all secrets from equipment and charts were either recovered or destroyed.

After forty-five silent and nerve-wracking minutes, the job was complete.

Attaching a line to the silent aircraft, NS-D pulled her out into deeper water, where the rear gunner completed the work done by the IRA the night before, venting the hull with heavy calibre bullets.

NS-X sank quickly and silently. Her remaining depth bombs had been made safe to avoid announcing their presence to half of Ireland.

NS-D turned into the wind and drove herself airborne, heading back to their base with an awful cargo.

---

Hostile eyes watched their departure, as they had done from the moment the Sunderland had touched down.

As NS-D disappeared slowly from sight, Seamus Brown rose from his hiding place, gathered up his two colleagues and jogged off towards his base, hoping his report would calm the fears of the Russian officer.

## 0820 hrs, Thursday, 8th November 1945, Headquarters, G2 Irish Special Branch, Dublin.

The phone rang at his desk, causing the Colonel to jump, so engrossed was he in his work.

"Bryan."

The Colonel stretched as he listened to the brief information.

"Good. Ask him to come in please."

Replacing the receiver, Bryan walked to the side table and poured two cups of tea, one of which he held out to the newly arrived Richard Hayes.

Manoeuvring his visitor to a seat, Bryan resumed his former position.

"So then, what brings you to my office at this ungodly hour, Richard?"

"You know very well why I am here."

The two men enjoyed the fencing as a rule, but today there were other fish to fry.

"All Anger."

"All Anger indeed, Dan."

"Mr Hayes informs me it was an old codename, used back in the days before the Germans."

"So the codes wouldn't cover it at all. It's a double encryption?"

"Well, yes and no, Stephen. Fortunately, the IRA are not THAT bright. What we have is a simple code name that was encoded using old German message code. The name 'All Anger' means something to someone in its own right. It's not an encryption as such."

"Yes, I do understand that, you know!"

Bryan held his hands up in apology.

"Not teaching you to suck eggs, Stephen."

"When did this codename first come into being?"

Swiftly consulting his notes from the late evening session with the ex-IRA man, the Colonel spoke with authority.

"He says quiet adamantly it was 1933. He remembered because of Hitler."

"Didn't we discover something about that?"

The Colonel grinned.

"Yes... we did. They had a habit of using anagrams as simple codenames."

Such a statement posed a challenge the Academic could not resist.

Picking up a pencil, he begged a piece of paper and started to work.

*All Anger...*
*Angerall.*
*Enallgar.*
*Largelan.*
*Ellanrag.*

Within a minute, he sat back triumphantly.

"Glenlara."

"Impressive, Stephen, it took me a little longer."

That brought the slightest of scowls from Hayes.

"Forgive me. Now cast your mind back."

Hayes, his mind again tasked, slipped quickly from his annoyance into recall mode.

"Yes, I thought it was familiar... Glenlara, Cork. You had that trouble with the Garda ambush, the lads from Castleisland, just before the world went mad again, did you not?"

"Anything else?"

He racked his brain.

"The woods near there."

"Indeed, Stephen."

There had been two reports of strange lights in the woods between Glennamucklagh and Glenlara. The second report had resulted in the dispatch of a team and four Garda constables subsequently being shot to death in an ambush. One inexplicable issue of that ambush was the fact that their car and bodies were found at Barleyhill, the other side of the woods from the dead men's base at Castleisland.

Licking his lips free from sweet tea, Bryan asked the important question.

"Are there any messages that would tie in with that ambush and this codeword? My men can't find any at first look."

"I will check my own folders and see what I can find."

The G2 Commander nodded and then relaxed back into his chair.

"None the less, a number of my men and Special Branch officers, plus a company of the Army, are presently on their way to see what delights the woods contain."

**1100 hrs Thursday 8th November 1945, the Alpine Front.**

On the stroke of 11am, the artillery of Chuikov's and Yeremenko's forces commenced a barrage, hundreds of artillery pieces delivering thousands of shells in a storm that lasted thirty minutes precisely.

As the artillery ceased its activity, defending Allied units came up from their bunkers, moved up from secondary positions and prepared to face whatever it was that was coming at them through the heavy snow.

At 1140 hrs, Soviet artillery and previously silent rocket batteries fired as one, catching the deployed defenders by surprise and inflicting heavy casualties.

The plan required that the barrage would advance, commencing at 1210hrs and the plan was followed to the letter, shell shocked and battered Allied soldiers suddenly finding themselves overrun as Soviet infantry formations closed up and into their positions, hard on the edge of the advancing barrages. Chuikov's 1st Alpine Front committed itself in Eastern Austria, striking hard down upon the defenders of Northeast Italy, keeping his southern flank against the relative safety of the Yugoslav border, his right flank in touch with Yeremenko's 1st Southern European Front, the border between them agreed on as a small German village only recently made notorious; Berchtesgaden.

---

Konev's suggestion had been simple and well reasoned.

The logistics gleaned from the Yugoslavs were close at hand for the 1st Alpine and 1st Southern European. The units were fresh, whereas the enemy opposite them had been thinned out to reinforce the German front.

The Spanish had arrived and been inserted into frontline positions. Not quality troops by all accounts, certainly not up to the standard of the old Blau Division.

Other inferior units had been detected in Italy and Southern France, soldiers of limited worth, according to Soviet intelligence and Soviet prejudices. Negroes, Brazilians, French, Mexicans, Portuguese, and even small detachments from Cuba and Paraguay.

So, Konev had argued, with his plans for limited advances on the main front, combined with a rejuvenation programme and resupply schedule for the savaged Red Banner formations, now was the time to instigate the phase that brought Chuikov and Yeremenko into action.

The GKO had agreed and the dying started all over again.

Squadron Leader Benjamin Viljoen read the report in silence, detaching himself from the fact that he was reading about the death of his brother.

All secret map work, all radio code books, and all sensitive equipment had either been recovered or had been verified as destroyed within the aircraft. That ticked a lot of boxes on the RAF loss report he was filing.

All the bodies had been placed in the station morgue, awaiting proper ceremony at the Sacred Heart cemetery in Irvinestown.

Ten good men, not the least of which was his brother.

Larry Cox had been a good mate too.

The musing triggered something in his mind; an unease, a discomfort, a seed of something 'not right'.

Viljoen screwed his eyes up tight, trying to work through the smokescreen hiding the thought from full sight.

Again, he ran through Flight Lieutenant Edinburgh's report. Word for word, thinking each matter through.

He paused and re-read one section, and turned his attention to the transcript of messages from the ill-fated Sunderland.

The smokescreen cleared and the seed flourished in an instant.

He leant forward and picked up the phone.

"Corporal, ask Flight Sergeant Smith to report to my office. Immediately please. Thank you."

Viljoen held his peace for the eight minutes it took for Smith to present himself.

"I want to clarify something, Flight Sergeant. In your Flight's report he quite clearly states that you recovered the pilot's bodies from the cockpit. Is that correct?"

Smith relaxed, having expected a rocket over the wholesale destruction of No2 hut's electrical system, as undertaken by his pet Montague, since disappeared.

"Yes, Sir. Pettigrew and myself recovered the two of them."

"From the flight crew seats?"

"Yes Sir."

Viljoen cleared his throat very deliberately.

"Think hard about this, Flight Sergeant. Are you absolutely sure that both pilots were in the flight crew seats?"

The mental image that flashed up was immediately examined and confirmed his view, and was very quickly consigned back to the recesses of his mind, where all such awful memories should dwell.

"I'm absolutely positive, Sir."

The Squadron Leader nodded softly.

"Where was Arsey found?"

The darker dungeons of his mind surrendered up another pictorial horror.

"In the galley, Sir."

"Thank you for that, Smith. We'll speak about your bloody rat and the wiring another time."

Saluting smartly, Smith removed himself from the office and heard the occupant asking for the Base Intelligence officer as he closed the door.

As Smith set about the task of locating the errant rodent Montague, Flight Lieutenant Blackmore was gestured to a chair in his commander's office.

"Blackie, I'm afraid there's a problem with the report on NS-X."

"Oh? I thought the whole thing was well-written and covered everything Skipper?"

"Yes, and thank our Lord it did or we would have missed something. See here."

Viljoen passed the copy he had been reading, having circled the important part.

"Yes I see, very precise. Smith and Pettigrew recovered the pilot's bodies."

Viljoen held his peace, merely passing another report, similarly highlighted.

Blackmore read the short section, frown increasingly deeper with each word. He then held the two, one in each hand, his eyes flicking rapidly left and right, comparing facts in his mind.

"A mistake, Skipper?"

"I think not Blackie. Smith's a solid type and I've just pressed him on the matter. He sticks by that. Can't speak to Pettigrew until he's back obviously."

Pettigrew had been granted urgent leave to return to the mainland where his mother was dying.

"Error by the wireless op?"

"I don't see how that's possible Blackie, do you?"

It took but a few moments for Blackmore to deal with that one.

"The operator's message is very distinct, naming Crozier as flying the aircraft. He'd be able to see the flight deck from his position."

More silence as two sharp brains worked the possibilities.

Blackmore spoke aloud. More to ensure he was thinking matters through correctly.

"We've information, via the radio op, stating that Crozier was flying the aircraft. We've a report from Pettigrew, supported by Smith, stating categorically that the two pilots were removed from the flight deck seats."

His frown was as deep as could be, then his hairline jerked upwards as the muscles in his forehead took everything in the opposite direction.

"Clearly, someone's wrong. Obviously, there has to be a mistake."

Viljoen shook his head slowly, halting his Intelligence Officer.

"And what if they're both right, Blacky?"

"Both right, Skipper?"

The Squadron Leader nodded.

"Well, then I suppose," Blackmore spoke slowly, giving his brain time to unravel the simple possibility that Viljoen had dangled in front of him, "Someone in the crew was alive and put them back in their proper places out of respect?"

"Not quite what I was thinking, Blackie. Or?"

More mental unravelling took place.

"Or, someone else did so. Hang on a... pilots belong in the palace. Are you suggesting that someone else put the pilots on the flight deck, Skipper?"

"Of course not. That would be totally mad. Give me another alternative."

Blackmore missed the little edge in Viljoen's tone.

"I don't have one, Skip."

"Neither do I at the moment. So, is it possible that the aircraft put down near the submarine and they did it for some reason?"

Blackmore had started to shake his head before his CO had finished.

"The geography and timings don't work for that. The attack and sinking took place way up north. We're talking about right against the Irish coast here."

"Aren't we just, man," the South-African character suppressing the RAF Officer just for the shortest moment.

"Ok, Skipper. I'll see what I can rustle up with my contacts and I'll have a chat with the Doc after church parade tomorrow. I was just over at the OK Corral and he wasn't there. The orderly didn't know where he was. I'll search him out and get him to have another gander at the poor sods before we say our goodbyes. I'm off to the St Lucia this evening for a spot of lunch and the monthly intel exchange."

Viljoen had forgotten that.

"I'll have a chat with some chaps there and see if we can come up with something for you, Skipper."

"I'll be making arrangements with Sacred Heart for Wednesday, Blackie."

"We'll have something for you by then, I'm sure, Skipper."

### 1812 hrs, Saturday, 10th November 1945, RAF St Angelo, Northern Ireland.

The snow had not yet visited itself upon the Emerald Isle, but the weather was bad enough that it started to affect the comings and goings at RAF St Angelo.

Twenty-two minutes later than expected, a USAAF C-47 touched down at the County Fermanagh airbase and two American officers dismounted. After salutes and handshakes were exchanged with a British Army Captain, the American Colonel and his ADC were spirited away in one of two Austin staff cars set aside for those arriving. Their driver was a thin WAAF Sergeant with a face and disposition that only a mother could love.

80

Some forty-five minutes previously, an RAF Airspeed Oxford had landed more heavily, disgorging four shaken men. They received a similar service from the harridan and her fellow WAAF driver.

No sooner had the pair of Austins returned than the final visitors made their appearance.

A Lockheed Hudson in the livery of 54 Squadron RAF Coastal Command gently dropped to the tarmac and disgorged two shadowy figures that disappeared into an Austin at speed.

An experienced air force observer might have questioned that the aircraft was a Hudson Mark I, a type no longer flown by 54 Squadron. However, the subterfuge was, and always had been, sufficient to maintain the secrecy required by its users.

The Hudson had changed hands in 1942. It had once been a USAAF crewed aircraft that got into difficulty and landed on unfamiliar territory. That then changed its destiny. The crew were interned and the aircraft was taken into service by the new owners, Repainted in RAF markings, the maritime patrol aircraft was well suited to the clandestine purpose to which it was put.

An aircraft of the Irish Air Corps would attract too much attention and promote too many questions, whereas a version in RAF colours was very suited to the transporting of important people in secret.

### 1900 hrs Saturday 10th November 1945, Rossahilly House, Trory, Northern Ireland.

At 1900 hrs precisely, the nine men strolled through the exquisitely tiled hallway and sat down in the dining room of Rossahilly House, on the shores of Lough Erne, whose still waters, made almost magical by the reflecting moonlight, almost seemed to reach into the room through the large bay window.

The owner, the Right Honourable Percy Hollander, spent his evening in his opulent private study, his presence in Rossahilly considered necessary to lend cover to the comings and goings of the great men.

In less impressive surroundings elsewhere in the house, the assistants to the great men enjoyed the opportunity of relaxation and light conversation.

Outside the isolated residence, silent men kept watch, alert and with weapons ready.

Major General Colin Gubbins and Sir David Petrie had recovered from their heavy landing and were looking forward to their dinner.

Respectively, they were the heads of SOE and MI5. The two men had an uneasy truce, their working relationship often strained by apparent violations of their own imagined operational boundaries.

Colonel Valentine Vivian, Vice-chief of the SIS, and Major General Sir Kenneth Strong, SHAEF's G2 Intelligence Chief, had journeyed in by car from RAF Belfast, and had already discussed a number of matters of personal concern, having arrived an hour ahead of the main group.

Rear-Admiral Dalziel had also driven from Belfast, sharing a car with the two senior police officers who were heads of Special Branch in England and Northern Ireland, DCI Bertram Leonard and CI Michael Rafferty respectively.

The table was completed by Colonels Dan Bryan of the Irish Republic's G2 and Samuel Rossiter, head of the OSS.

Wine was poured and the fois-gras arrived, signalling both the start of the meal and the commencement of business.

---

Discussions had gone on into the small hours, so it had been agreed that breakfast would be served at ten.

It was the habit of these meetings that the morning's conversation was lighter in nature, although each man's remaining dilemmas often surfaced for group examination.

By prior arrangement, Percy Hollander, ex-Irish Guards and confidante of Sir David Petrie, took his breakfast separately, eagerly anticipating the few hours that he and Sir David would spend at the snooker table, once the bulk of visitors had departed.

Low voices alternated between praising the cuisine and discussing the minutiae of the Intelligence business.

Dalziel almost sat elsewhere, so put off was he by Gubbins' mound of fried kidneys. However, he decided to grin and bear it, if only to enquire further about SOE potential in Scandinavia.

Rossiter, a recent conversion to the decidedly British morning kidney ration, was also similarly interested and the conversation gained pace, dropping in volume, as interesting matters of mutual interest were uncovered.

It was the habit of these breakfasts, where relaxation and tiredness were key players, that good work was done between agencies that were often as suspicious of each other as they were of the enemy that they collectively fought.

Bryan, Bertram and Rafferty all enjoyed the more traditional fare of egg, sausage and bacon, all topped off with fried soda bread and white pudding.

The former lamented the failure of their operation at Glenlara, but amused his companions with the IRA's basic use of anagram codes.

Gubbins, Vivian, and Strong kicked the Polish issue around after the latter had taken a negative stance on the smell originating from the kippers being consumed before his eyes.

By twelve midday, all but one guest had departed, and that guest was well into a game winning break on Rossahilly House's snooker table.

**1712 hrs, Sunday, 11th November 1945, Base Commander's office, RAF Castle Archdale, Northern Ireland.**

The plan had been that Dalziel would be dropped off at the main gate of the RAF base and the two police officers would proceed on to their meeting with some local intelligence officers in Irvinestown.

The plan did not cater for the Sunbeam-Talbot Ten destroying a leaf spring in a pothole concealed by the overnight snowfall. Leaving the driver with the vehicle, the trio took the short walk to the camp's main entrance and sought assistance.

A party of fitters was sent and the Sunbeam was hauled into the base workshop for repair.

Squadron Leader Viljoen had organised drinks in his office and hoped to use the opportunity to glean more information as to the progress of the war.

More drawn to the other uniformed man, Viljoen and Dalziel discussed the situation at sea.

A knock on the door interrupted their conversation and the look on Blackmore's face told everyone that something worrying had happened.

"Skipper..."

Blackmore looked at the strangers in the room, deciding whether he should speak openly or get his CO alone.

Viljoen made the decision for him.

"Go on, Blackie. Speak freely, man. Get it off your chest."

Swallowing hard to gain some composure, Flight Lieutenant Blackmore dropped his bombshell.

"Skipper, Doc decided to have a gander at the crew's bodies this afternoon. He found something... I mean... Christ... something awful that simply doesn't fit. You need to see this straight away, Skipper."

"Awful? What is it, Blackie?"

"You have to see this, Skipper. Right now!"

"OK, deep breaths and give me a clue."

"They didn't die in the attack on the sub and didn't die because of a rough landing. They were shot."

"Fucking shot? By the sub then?"

"No, I mean executed, Skipper."

The policemen and the Intelligence officer had heard key words and their interest was piqued.

Viljoen rose quickly, started to apologise to his guests, and then thought better of it.

"Perhaps you would like to accompany me, gentlemen... Sir?"

The three men needed no second invitation.

---

"OK then, Doc, what have you got then, man?"

Holliday, the silver haired Medical Officer, source of the OK Corral nickname for the base hospital, delivered his verdict in simple words.

"Quite straightforward, Skipper. Aidan was killed by a bullet to the back of the neck, a wound that someone then tried to disguise by gouging the area, possibly with metal from the fuselage."

The elderly doctor had grabbed their undivided attention.

"My view is that Aidan Erasmus was killed first. I think they then realised their error and then chose a less obvious method of execution. The method used was one undoubtedly driven by hate."

That caused a number of eyes to narrow as imaginations started to work.

He moved to Magic's body and took his station on the opposite side of the trestle.

"In all my days, I have never seen anything like this. Never."

His five-man audience waited as he rolled the body on its side.

"When they first arrived, we gave them a cursory examination, nothing more. That's my fault, I'm afraid. Each of them was very obviously dead and the external injuries were in line with those we have seen before... crash trauma, explosive and shot wounds... et cetera."

Magic's corpse showed all the signs associated with a heavy landing and being thrown against something unforgiving.

"I'll perform a full autopsy but my initial examination of Flight Sergeant Malan would make me feel he was shot at least three times."

Viljoen took a step forward and sought out the evidence that Holliday had missed.

"You misunderstand me, Skipper. The wounds are internal."

Chief Inspector Michael Rafferty was the only one who immediately grasped the significance, his mind dragging back details of two 'assassinations' that he had been called to investigate.

"Jesus, Joseph, and Mary!"

Eyes turned to Rafferty, instinctively knowing that he understood something, as yet unrevealed.

Addressing Holliday, Rafferty spoke very deliberately.

"In '41, there were two executions of IRA members that we'd turned as King's agents. The bodies were badly beaten... but without external signs of the fatal injury."

There was no way he could lighten the blow.

"They had been executed with a pistol up the rectum."

Stunned silence.

Shocked silence.

Disbelieving silence.

The MO spoke first.

"That's what I have found. I think they killed Erasmus quickly and then realised their error. They then disposed of the others by... that method."

"He calls it the Silencer."

Dalziel broke from his thoughts.

"Who calls it the Silencer?"

The dark shadow on Rafferty's face was very obvious.

"Brown... Seamus Michael Brown. IRA executioner and second most wanted man in Ireland. And, interestingly, he's a Brit."

"What?"

"Conceived and delivered in Liverpool, Admiral. British born and bred."

DCI Leonard was in police mode immediately.

"Where and when was this, Squadron Leader?"

"North Coast of Éire, 5th December... Thank you, Doc. Full autopsy on each, reports as quick as possible."

The Squadron communications office was closer than his own sanctuary, so Viljoen led the group into the large room, grabbing at a map and setting it down on the table for all to see.

"We found her here," he indicated the precise spot from memory, "But she certainly would have drifted with the current, so didn't start there."

The five of them pored over the map.

"My God!"

Rafferty's outburst attracted their attention, his face draining of colour in an instant, as his mind raced to work out what he could say and, more importantly, what he couldn't say.

*'Oh fuck it!'*

He decided to say everything he knew.

"All Anger."

Leonard had been present during that conversation and immediately understood.

"Oh my eye, yes. All Anger."

The others did not understand.

"Our friends in the Republic have had the answer all along but just didn't realise it."

Leonard took the lead.

"They intercepted a message that spoke of 'All Anger', a simple code that they boiled down to a small hamlet in Limerick, one that had appeared suspicious for some time. An easy mistake to make."

Eyes turned back to Rafferty as he completed the story.

"G2 received intelligence about 'All Anger', a simple anagram code, employed when the IRA was less proficient in such matters. Our friends worked out that it meant 'Glenlara'."

He left out the part about the broken German code as a courtesy to G2.

"The Irish Intelligence put two and two together and went for Glenlara, Limerick, where there had been some trouble prior to, completely missing this Glenlara," he fingered the map, drawing attention to the coastal village that sat uncomfortably close to the location of the Sunderland Flying boat, "And I will bet that right here sits an IRA force... and more besides."

Dalziel got that message loud and clear.

Rafferty gave voice to his thoughts.

"Judas?"

"Bound to be, the bastards always stick together."

"Judas? I don't understand."

Blackmore spoke for the rest of the group but his mind was already awakening a memory from a distant briefing.

"Judas Reynolds. A real bad man. He and Brown are bosom pals and where one is... well, the other won't be far away. According to our intelligence, Judas is head of the IRA's Mayo Brigade."

They were all suddenly drawn to the map.

Dalziel was the only one who spoke.

"Glenlara, County Mayo."

Fig#74 - Éire and the Atlantic 1945 [Full copy]

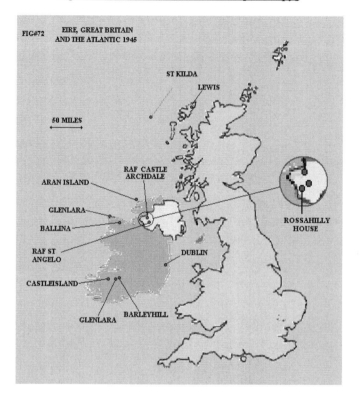

## 2142 hrs, Sunday 11th November, Glenlara, County Mayo, Éire.

There was a Mexican standoff, the Soviet Naval Marines with their superior firepower and training lined up in support of their officer, the more numerous IRA group murmuring and threatening their new allies.

Naval Captain-Lieutenant Ilya Nazarbayev stood before the bound and kneeling man, his Tokarev pistol pressed firmly against the sweating temple.

"By the authority of my command and under Soviet Naval Regulations, I find you guilty of murder and I pass a sentence of death, to be carried out immediately."

The growl rose again from IRA throats, one given more spine by the appearance of Judas Patrick Reynolds, striding purposefully through the snow, fresh from a successful visit to the nearby straipachs, although the young whore who serviced the sexual needs of the senior IRA man was declared strictly off-limits to anyone else and they would be at risk of losing their fleshier parts should they ignore Judas' warning.

"What the fuck do ya think ya're fucking doing, Ilya?"

Nazarbayev's eyes never strayed, did not blink, the barrel of his automatic pressed so hard against Brown's forehead as to sink into the flesh and leave a dent.

"This...this... whatever it is... has been found guilty of the murder of five English airmen. I am about to carry out the sentence."

"Oh no ya fucking ain't."

Reynolds' Tommy gun was suddenly levelled at the Marine officer and the danger mounted for all, as both sides tried to support their leader with more aggressive posturing and sounds of encouragement.

"Now, we've a situ-fucking-action here, Ilya. You isn't gonna kill my man; that's a fact now. You pull tha trigger and you'll die, as will yer men and many of ma boys. That means no base for yer Navy, no more subs... fuck all, ma son. So put the pistol down, boyo."

Judas Patrick was an animal, but he was no fool, and he saw resolve in the Marine officer's eyes.

He tried another tack.

"I will deal with him maself. He's not under your command... or your fucking regulations for that matter. He's my man. I'll deal with it."

The words found a chink and entered into Yuri's thoughts and the Tokarev withdrew from the petrified man's forehead.

"That's good, Ilya, that's real good, boyo."

Unusually for Judas, he made a difficult decision that proved a turning point.

"Ok ma Lads, knock it off now. Back to your beds. Show's over."

The IRA men reluctantly started to move away, each second bringing more relaxation to the watching Soviet naval infantry.

Nazarbayev withdrew his pistol completely.

"Stand down, men. Stand down."

A few men from both sides remained, either out of curiosity or to watch and protect their leader. There was no need. The tension had gone.

Hauling Brown to his feet, Nazarbayev pushed the bound man towards the IRA chief.

"Take him, but I will hold you to your word, Patrick. Punish him for his crime."

"My word on it, Ilya."

Nazarbayev left the scene quickly, turning into his quarters before the returning Soviet political officer, still adjusting his trousers after his own pleasures, could interfere with proceedings.

Judas slipped a knife into Brown's bonds and cut his number two free.

"Make yourself scarce for now, Seamus. Stay up at the Boyson's til I send for ya."

Brown rubbed his wrists and spat in the direction of Nazarbayev's billet.

"What about that bastard then, Patrick, I want 'im, I fucking want 'im bad."

Reynolds' eyes settled on the small hut and narrowed as his cunning mind searched for a resolution.

"All in good time, boyo, all in good fucking time."

### 1039 hrs, Tuesday 12th November 1945, Headquarters of the 11th Guards Army, the Böhmer Haus, Stadtsee, Sulingen, Germany.

Lieutenant General Kuzma Galitsky was less than delighted with the new operation that was to be entrusted to his already exhausted force.

A true follower of Zhukov, and never a great fan of Konev, he set aside his personal views and assessed the attack with a professional eye.

If it went well, then great rewards would be reaped. If it didn't...

*'Then there will be a price to pay.'*

An aide appeared at his side, a cough announcing his presence.

90

"Yes, Comrade Mayor?"

"The replacement officers are here, Comrade Leytenant General."

*'At last, some good news!'*

"Excellent! Show them into the dining room and make sure they are given food. I will be there shortly."

The Major trotted off to herd the gaggle of newly arrived officers into the school's dining room. He had anticipated his General's orders and the heavily panelled room was already laid out to provide refreshment to the dozen colonels arriving to fill dead men's shoes.

---

Galitsky, accompanied by his Chief of Staff, Lieutenant General Semenov, quietly observed the group and make swift judgements.

Ten men, Colonels and Lieutenant Colonels clad in immaculate uniforms, were clearly products of the search for qualified officers mounted across the length and breadth of the Motherland. Men from rear-echelon units, reserve units, or culled from some backwater on the Caspian Sea. Men whose chests bore the awards of service to the State in matters other than the business for which they were now assembled; combat.

Two more Colonels, stood apart from the others, were something completely different. Front line beasts, both of whom wore the Hero Award and more besides, marks of their prowess and, hopefully, competence.

There were vacancies across the range of Galtisky's formations, as the fighting had savaged his leadership groups.

With the new attack in mind and, in the knowledge of his own planning, he assigned the two smart but worn Colonels to the formation that would bear much of the strain.

On cue, Semenov announced their presence and the room sprang to attention.

Left to right, each man introduced himself as Galitsky welcomed them in turn, listening to a brief resume of each officer's service. Referring to a clipboard held out by Semenov, the 11th Guards' commander assigned each man to a vacant slot, once the newcomer's credentials had been established.

Galitsky turned to the last two Colonels, assessing each in turn and seeing firmness in each man, but also a weariness reserved for those who have spent more than their fair share of time playing with the devil's horsemen.

He nodded at the first man and returned his salute.

Each man introduced himself in turn.

"Comrade General, Polkovnik Deniken, formerly a battalion commander in 16th Guards Rifle Division of 36th Guards Rifle Corps."

"Ah yes, I've heard of you, Vladimir Vissarionavich. You have performed brilliantly throughout the war and your arrest was totally misplaced. I hope that you weren't ill-treated, Comrade?"

The truth would serve no purpose, so a lie slipped easily from his lips.

"My treatment was satisfactory, thank you, Comrade General."

Galitsky knew it for the lie it was.

He took a quick look at the clipboard just to confirm his memory.

"Well, Comrade Polkovnik, I'm afraid that I cannot spare you. Your assignment is not an easy one and you'll be taking your men in danger's path again. Competence attracts such tasks, of course."

Deniken's silence spoke volumes.

"You'll assume command of 1st Guards Rifle Division, within the 16th Guards Rifle Corps. I'm having as many of the men of your old unit transferred to you as I can find."

The sound of Semenov's pen scratching away on the list followed and Deniken received his written orders, the two officers exchanging salutes by way of terminating the exchange.

Galitsky turned to the last man.

He raised a hand, stopping the Colonel before he could even start.

"You, I know, Comrade Polkovnik. Your reputation precedes you. Again, your arrest was ill-conceived and I'm pleased that the authorities have seen sense."

He leant in towards the tank officer, lowering his voice and inviting the listener forward and into his confidence.

"From what I understand, we should have been awarding you another one of those stars, rather than holding you accountable for matters beyond your control."

Both men recovered their poise and Galitsky continued, introducing formality to cover his genuine respect for the man in front of him.

"You, Comrade Polkovnik Yarishlov, you are assigned to command 120th Special Tank Brigade, also part of 16th Guards Rifle Corps, where your undoubted skills will once more be tested in the service of the Motherland."

Semenov completed the form with a flourish, passed it to Yarishlov and stepped back.

"Now then, Comrades. Go and get settled in with your men. You'll have only a few days before the Rodina will call on you again. Use the hours wisely."

Salutes were offered and received and the two Colonels departed.

Galitsky and Semenov followed after a moment's pause and observed the two soldiers parting on the steps to the old school.

His shrewd eye took in every aspect of the scene.

"Those two are more than comrades, Ivan."

Semenov grunted.

"Those two are friends; we should use that to our advantage."

A second grunt.

"Let's have a look at the plan and see if we can't bring the 1st and 120th into closer cooperation eh?"

Semenov proffered the clipboard with a smile, the heavy markings clearly joining the two units together and annotated with a single word.

'Tovariches.'

"Just as well I know you're not after my job, Ivan!"

With a deadpan look, Semenov delivered the coup de grace.

"Not likely, Comrade General. I wouldn't get a Chief of Staff half as good as you've got, would I?"

---

Since August 1945, the 1st Guards Rifle Corps and 120th Tank Brigade had both suffered horrendous casualties and were now being pieced back together with a hotch potch of men and equipment.

In the case of the former, personnel from destroyed formations were combined with men who had once been incarcerated by the Nazi regime.

The latter was more fortunate, receiving a very high proportion of experienced men from the destroyed 2nd Guards Tank Corps.

No sooner had Yarishlov taken command of the120th Tanks than it ceased to be, by order of STAVKA, assuming the title of a formation immolated in the previous month's conflict.

Yarishlov found himself in command of the newly elevated 7th Guards Special Tank Brigade, its new elite status bought by the sacrifice of those no longer alive.

True to their gut feelings, Galitsky and Semenov restyled their planning to place the two units in mutual support.

On such whims are the fates of nations decided.

*It is absolutely true in war, were other things equal, that numbers, whether men, shells, bombs, etc, would be supreme. Yet it is also absolutely true that other things are never equal and can never be equal.*

*J. F. C. Fuller*

# Chapter 107 - THE ALPS

## 1057 hrs, Wednesday 13th November 1945, Headquarters of 1st Alpine Front, Schloss Maria Loretto, Klagenfurt, Austria.

Chuikov was delighted and yet, in the same breath, expressed disappointment.

The gains made by 1st Alpine were pretty much according to schedule, with the sole exception of Villach, where the British infantry and tanks had stopped his force bloodily, sending the lead formation reeling backwards.

His orders to the Corps Commander had been simple to understand.

'Attack again and take the position immediately.'

Chuikov was an uncomplicated general.

Unlike his peers in the European sector, he was prepared for the higher than normal expenditures in the necessaries of war, a preparation that had proved more than adequate as the nature and terrain reduced ammunition and fuel use. The additional toll on his men and animals in portering the heavy loads was not factored in.

A telephone discussion with Yeremenko, recently returned from a meeting with Marshal Konev, had proved timely and fruitful, the men finding their discussion revealed a potential issue at the join between their forces, one that was addressed by swift messages to the Army commanders, requiring a tightening up of the front before the Allies exploited the small void.

Yeremenko echoed Chuikov's experiences, in as much as 1st Southern European Front was seeing very little by way of Allied air activity.

Soviet air regiments, accepting the problems of operating in extreme conditions, seemed to be doing very well in support, although Yeremenko's Frontal Aviation Commander had reported higher levels of losses to weather and accident than normal.

None the less, both senior men accepted the ramped up losses in air units as an offset for the close support the Red Air Force was providing.

One coup had been the capture of two usable bridges over the Drau, the first at Patemion, the second totally undamaged at Feistritz an der Drau.

The Red Air Force had savaged a half-hearted RAF attempt to destroy the crossings and decimated a counter-attack aimed at recovering Feistritz. That four of the RAF aircraft had already crashed en route to the target had lessened the enthusiasm of the Allied flyers and the appearance of the Soviet LAGG's had easily dissuaded the Squadron commander from pressing home the attack.

For Chuikov, being able to put forces on the south-western bank of the Drau meant that his plan to capture Villach was greatly assisted. Its capture would trap a good size portion of the British Army against the Yugoslav border.

In a departure from his normal style, Chuikov had ensured that extremely specific orders had been issued and cascaded down to platoon level, stressing the importance of not violating the Yugoslavian boundaries, a brief he was given directly by Konev at each meeting and during each phone call. Yeremenko constantly received a similar instruction in regard to Swiss neutrality and its preservation.

However, Chuikov had additional and very secret orders that required him to orchestrate an attempt to bring the Yugoslavs into the war against the Allies. He was to promote circumstances where the British and Commonwealth units might be forced into some act that would drag Tito's soldiers into the fight. When he first received the order, his eyes were drawn to Villach and he cut his cloth accordingly. The capture of Villach was seen as an excellent opportunity to bring that about, by way of Allied units violating the borders of Yugoslavia in an attempt to escape being cut off, whilst the Red Army would be able to look innocent of the charge when the Yugoslavian leader started beating his chest.

The lead units of the 1st Alpine plunged south, taking advantage of their unexpectedly intact river crossings, forces either side of the river almost racing down the Drau valley, the important junction at Villach their goal.

**0027 hrs, Thursday 14th November 1945, Allied defensive positions at Töplitsch & Puch, Austria.**

Fig#75 - Allied forces defending and Puch, Austria, 14th November 1945.

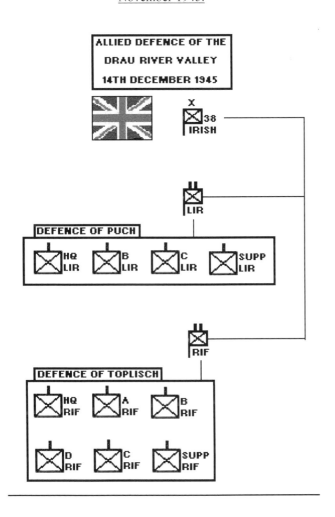

Fig#76 - Töplitsch and Puch, Austria, 0027 hrs, 14th November 1945.

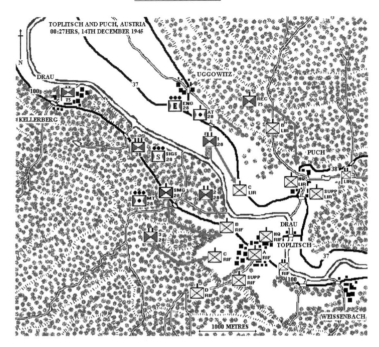

"It's so cold, Corp."

Kearney counted it off mentally.

*'That's the feckin dozenth time, boyo.'*

"That's cos it's fucking winter, Nipper."

"Wasn't ever this fierce at home, Corp, never."

Kearney's exasperation prompted him to mischief.

"Did yer hear that, Nipper?"

The new boy took a breath of the painful air before replying in a whisper.

"No, Corp, not a sausage, Corp."

The NCO raised an eyebrow in judgement, accompanying the gesture with a shake of the head.

"Blimey. Bloody deaf as well'a two left feet, ya eejit."

The boy had been with the platoon since June and seemed unable to grasp even the most basic of soldierly

98

qualities. However, Kearney was drawn to his honesty and gullibility in equal measure, hence them pairing up on one of the platoon's Bren guns.

"Listen harder now, boyo."

Private Walshe screwed up his eyes and strained his ears, concentrating on imagined shadows and sounds coming from the woods to his front. He failed to see the small motion of Corporal Kearney's left hand, flicking two stones to one side, one after the other.

"Feck me yes, Corp. Two noises, clear as day they were!"

His whispers sounded like shouts in the still night and Kearney wished he hadn't started the game, but only for a moment.

"That were the sound of ma balls dropping off, you stupid gobshite!"

The boy's clear confusion undermined Kearney's pleasure at the prank.

"Oh feckin hell, nipper! Just slagging ya. Jesus."

A third voice joined in.

"Shut yer fucking mouth, Kearney, yer fucking header. One more prank like that and I'll have the fucking stripes off yer... one more fucking time and that'll be an end to it, y'hear me?"

Not getting any reaction from the Corporal, Sergeant Reddan continued.

"Yer's just throwing shapes for the lad here, trying to impress. Now tend your front, Corporal and no more of this holy show!"

"Sergeant."

That was all Kearney managed.

Their small position, covering a modest junction on the Draubodenweg, was abruptly transformed from night into day as the first of a sextet of flares exploded and shed its light over the Inniskilling's positions and the No Man's land to their front, an area that was suddenly and very obviously occupied by moving figures, all closing rapidly.

"Jesus, Joseph, and Mary! Stand to! Stand to!"

With the light came bullets, lots of them, as the need for secrecy was gone. Soviet heavy machine guns started to bathe the British positions with lead.

Tracer bullets had more than one effect. In simple terms, the fiery tails permitted the gunner to adjust his aim more accurately, as he could see where the bullets were going.

An additional benefit was that the sight of deadly glowing lead tested the nerve of the most steadfast of men, and many a bullet that was missing by a yard had the effect of making a soldier duck or miss his shot.

Vickers and Brens started to compete with Maxims and DPs, and the ducking and missing spread to both sides.

Fighting also erupted north of the Drau River, where the much-depleted London Irish Battalion suddenly found itself in a similar predicament.

The whole valley became a whirlwind of flying bullets, mortar shells, and flares; add into the mix the shouts and screams of frightened, dying men, and the Drau had become a living nightmare.

Reddan had no choice. There was no-one he would rather be with less than Kearney, but the space between positions was too deadly to traverse for him to regain his own foxhole, so the ex-battalion boxing champion moved in beside the present encumbent who had knocked out three of his teeth in the process and brought his Enfield into play.

For each Russian that fell, it seemed another two rose to take his place.

The carrier platoon was a carrier platoon in name only, many of its vehicles having already succumbed to the needs of the European Front, subject of a low-key plan that had relocated some equipment to the active front, most of the remainder having become victims of the extreme cold.

However, the Bren guns remained, transforming the platoon's position into a hedgehog of light machine guns, one that possessed five times the firepower that the attacking Soviets were expecting.

The assault stalled.

**0937 hrs, Thursday 14th November 1945, Allied defensive positions at Töplitsch & Puch, Austria.**

Walshe remained rigidly at his post, the Bren gun seemingly just an extension of him.

100

Only the slightest of movements gave any indication that the young soldier was still alive, the barrel shifting imperceptibly as he checked clumps of enemy bodies for signs of life.

The last nine hours and ten minutes had witnessed a transformation during which the boy became a man, the inept fusilier became an adept soldier or, as the pain wracked Kearney thought, a pitiless killer.

The second attack had reached to within forty yards of the front foxholes and there it had withered in sprays of crimson, as the lead elements of the Soviet infantry were flayed to pieces.

An hour later, to the second, the third attack commenced and got within twenty yards. No flares rose until the wave of men was almost upon the Inniskillings but one Russian accidentally fired his weapon and that was warning enough for the Irishmen to rise up and stop the rush in its tracks.

A ragtag group of reinforcements had arrived in the dark of night. Clerks, drivers, and cooks, issued with a bundook and sent up to fill the gaps in the line.

The body of an elderly Pay Corps Private was now frozen solid across the brow of the firing position. He had been killed in the third attack and both Kearney and Reddan bundled the man into position for the extra cover and to hell with the niceties. After all, they didn't know the bloke.

The fourth attack came on the stroke of five o'clock and was made with less vigour than the others, for it was just the remnants of the infantry battalion that had been hammering away, lead forward by a wounded Major, a commander desperate for his unit's destruction not to have been in vain.

He died with most of his men, although the Ferryman exacted his price on the Inniskillings too.

Lieutenant Colonel Prescott, OC of the Battalion, fell to mortar fire in the first few seconds, having recently arrived at the crucial hot spot to make his own assessment of the situation.

At the last, the withdrawing Russians were covered by a few surviving Maxims, and it was one of these final bursts that put bullets into each of the three men in the Bren gun position.

The firing died away, leaving both sides to lick their considerable wounds.

Had some higher authority looked down into the small position then he may well have excused the three soldiers from further hardship.

No such relief came.

Only snow and an increasing coldness.

Walshe had felt nothing as a bullet passed through his upper chest, missing everything of note before it exited through his back strap.

Kearney took two in the neck and shoulder. The former was just a graze, painful and messy, but not incapacitating. The latter clipped his left shoulder joint and brought about excruciating pain that forced tears from his eyes.

Despite that, he managed to use his right hand to clip another magazine onto the Bren, as Walshe the 'Whirling Dervish', manifested himself.

Beside Kearney sat Reddan, his face wrapped in a crude bandage that was the best that Kearney could do in the circumstances, one that failed to mask the signs of fresh blood and hideous injury.

Hit in the side of the face, the Sergeant had certainly lost his lower jawbone completely. Through his tears, Kearney had quickly looked for the missing flesh, just in case stretcher-bearers made it through to take the silent man away. A second bullet had carried away Reddan's left eye and made a mess of the right one.

Not a sound escaped from the awfully wounded NCO, but his presence inspired the other two occupants of the position.

Three further attacks had been pressed hard, as a new unit replaced the one that the Inniskillings had gutted.

The 1st Alpine's second assault would have succeeded but for the timely arrival of more ammunition, permitting silent weapons to spring into life and reduce the assault formations to little more than wrecks of men.

A 3" mortar group arrived, quickly deployed nine weapons, and helped to put the attackers to flight, their barrage brief but perfectly placed amongst the second wave of soldiers. The tally of dead was miraculously low, but nearly a third of the Soviet soldiers lay wounded upon the frozen ground and many of their comrades took the offered opportunity to take an injured man to safer ground and, in the doing, quite happily removed themselves from danger.

The final infantry assault commenced at 0915 hrs and ground to a halt within fifteen minutes. This time the combination of infantry, mortars, and artillery proved far too much for troops whose nerves were already stretched to breaking point.

The 28th Rifle Regiment's third Battalion broke and ran from the battlefield, except for those who could not move under their own power, already felled by shrapnel or high explosives.

It was these that Walshe sought out with small bursts from the boiling hot Bren gun, killing anything that moved on the snowy field.

Merciless.

Cold.

Without an ounce of compassion.

"Stop it now, Nipper, will yer. They's had enough, boyo. Let 'em away now."

The sole reaction from Walshe was a gentle squeeze on the trigger and another four bullets were sent across the wintry field and into a Soviet soldier struggling with a shattered leg.

"Nipper! Jesus, Joseph, and Mary, will yer let 'em be now!"

The young man squeezed the trigger to no avail and immediately ripped off the empty magazine, holding out his hand for a replacement.

"Gimme."

Kearney shook his head and punctuated his decision with a dramatic flourish, flicking the ammo box lid shut.

"Stand down, Fusilier Walshe."

The boy's hand continued to hover in anticipation of receiving his needs, but Walshe's face was already changing as the imposed end to his tirade of violence brought about new and calmer thoughts.

He lit two cigarettes and, without a word, passed one to the wounded NCO.

The Bren was field stripped, cleaned, and reassembled before the medical team arrived and removed the wretched Reddan.

The Inniskillings' line had held.

## 1122 hrs, Thursday 14th November 1945, Divisional headquarters, 75th Rifle Division, Kellerberg am Drau, Austria.

"And that's your full report, PodPolkovnik?"

"Yes, Comrade Polkovnik. I cannot do this without tanks."

Colonel Ryzhov trusted the weary man stood before him and understood that he and his men had been through hell trying to push the Allied soldiers back from Töplitsch.

Gesturing at the dishevelled officer and inviting him to a seat where he could rest, Ryzhov leant on the table, rocking slowly on his knuckles as he contemplated the alternatives.

His 28th Regiment was badly beaten up but he had to preserve the unblooded 115th Regiment for the later assault at Villach, whilst the 34th Regiment was reorganising after its bitter fight at Feistritz an der Drau, ready for its leading role in the push south-east, a role it could only assume if the 28th Regiment did its job.

His eyes drank in every symbol on the map, its information not yet an hour old.

Part of him dismissed what he saw while another part shouted loudly for attention.

"Mayor Steppin, a word."

The harassed staff Major almost glided to his commander's side, his movement effortless despite the weight of papers and orders he was carrying.

"Are these bastards still held in reserve here, Steppin?"

He tapped the small township of Dobriach on the south-east end of the Millstatter See, some fourteen kilometres from where he now stood.

"Yes, Comrade Polkovnik, but I thought you said you didn't want them anywhere near us?"

Ryzhov pursed his lips.

104

"So I did, Comrade Mayor, so I did. However, the 28th needs tanks and needs them now, so we'll seek their release to us immediately. Understood?"

The commander of the 28th rose to his feet and moved forward.

Ryzhov acknowledged his presence with a slap on the shoulder.

"Mayor Steppin will contact Army and get these tanks released to my command... and you'll have your support, Comrade Kozlov."

Kozlov leant forward, examined the map, and immediately understood the senior man's reluctance.

Ryzhov put their feelings into words that lacked eloquence but did the job perfectly.

"To the Allied infantry, a tank's a tank, so the fucking Romanian turncoats'll have a chance to bleed along with the rest of us, eh?"

By the time that Kozlov had put forward a simple plan for employing their erstwhile allies, Steppin returned with confirmation that the 4th Romanian Armoured Group would be sent forward immediately.

Colonel Ryzhov had done all he could for the 28th Rifle Regiment, adding a short company from the 97th Engineer Sapper Battalion, a section of SPAA weapons and nearly half of the 124th Guards Artillery Regiment's guns to the assault.

Leading the attack was the rag-tag 4th RAG, its cosmopolitan contingent of armour having made the drive from Dobriach in excellent time, although some of its older vehicles were still lagging behind.

Leading the Romanian advance were three Panzer IV's, two model G's and one H, the most modern vehicles available to the 4th RAG.

They were flanked by four T34/m42's and two Sturmgeschutz III's.

Some way behind, a small group consisting of a Tacam R2, a Zrinyi Assault Gun, and a mechanically unsound Hetzer, struggled to close the action.

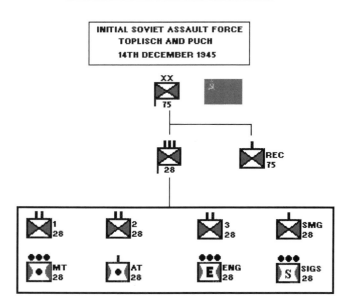

## 1500 hrs, Thursday 14th November 1945, Allied defensive positions at Töplitsch & Puch, Austria.

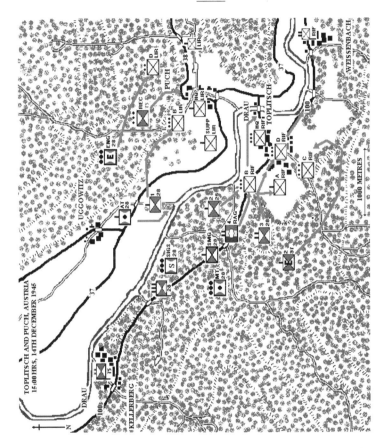

Kearney had declined to be evacuated, reasoning that Walshe would need a loader when, not if, the Russians attacked again.

He had accepted a dressing from the orderly who remained behind to tend the two men, occasionally wincing as the man worked to cover up the wound. The man was a conchie and, as such, had been ridiculed when he first joined the battalion. The contempt did not survive their first action, for the man, whose deeply held convictions prevented him from taking up arms, was no coward, and many a son of Ireland was plucked from peril by the slight effete orderly.

Walshe seemed not notice as the medic cut away at his greatcoat and battledress to get at the shoulder injury.

Satisfied with his work, Lance-Corporal Young RAMC moved off to find other employment.

As the pain of his wound mounted, Kearney started to regret his decision to stay put.

Within seconds of deciding to seek out a relief, his mind became focussed on the arrival of enemy artillery and mortar shells, undoubtedly a pre-cursor to another attack.

And something else.

*'Fuck! Tanks!'*

In a rough V shape, the enemy tanks moved slowly forward, their machine guns firing short bursts into anything that looked like it could house an anti-tank team, occasionally stopping to place larger ordnance on a suspicious mound or shadow in the snow.

Behind them, more waves of Soviet infantry moved purposefully forward, buoyed by the presence of the armoured support.

Kearney was woken from his thoughts by the stammer of the Bren gun as Walshe engaged the group nearest the Drau's southern bank.

"Nipper, have a go at that bastard there, now! He's got his turnip up, boyo!"

Walshe mechanically looked down the line of Kearney's good arm and saw the Panzer IV commander leaning out of the turret, engaged in animated conversation with a jogging infantry officer.

The Bren chattered three times, sending bullets into both men.

The tank officer slid inside his turret, his neck and facial wounds spraying blood over his shocked crew until there was little left to leak from his wounds and the man died.

Outside, the infantry Captain had taken five bullets in the groin and stomach, the heavy impacts throwing him against the side of the tank. Robbed of strength by his wounds, he was unable to avoid the fall onto the tank's bogies where, mercifully, he died instantly, his head crushed between track and roller.

Earth splattered the two defenders as the hull machine gunner attempted to avenge his officer, both Irishmen automatically dropping down behind the frozen corpse.

Kearney eased his wounded arm and risked a swift look over the top.

One of the T34s, attempting to engage the sole anti-tank gun supporting the Inniskillings, suddenly dropped into a rut disguised by a build-up of snow. The HE shell went wild and dropped well short. Unfortunately, for Kearney, it met resistance some ten yards in front of his position, its arrival coinciding with his risky attempt to see the field in front of him.

A flat pebble, the sort that water skimmers everywhere seek out for their best attempt, was forced out of the earth by the explosion and, at high speed, it struck Kearney on his right temple.

Suddenly Walshe found himself alone, and with a bloodied 'corpse' wrapped around his feet.

None the less, the young soldier continued to fire controlled bursts, picking off enemy soldiers with each attempt.

The artillery claimed a success; one of the T34s took a direct hit, smashing in the front of the vehicle and flipping the turret back onto the engine compartment. It was quickly wreathed in flames and debris was thrown in all directions as rounds cooked off and the intense fire melted the snow around it.

The sole six-pounder also added to the tally, striking a Panzer IV as it manoeuvred, putting its AP shell into the rear compartment. With the engine destroyed and a growing fire, the leaderless crew decided to evacuate, leaving the corpse of their young officer to be incinerated within his last command.

Soviet mortars cut short the celebrations and spread the crew and pieces of the gun across the snow.

Kozlov had to admit that the Romanians had done well and that the extra assets that Ryzhov had allocated had made a huge difference.

*'We have them this time!'*

Turning to his signals officer, he confidently gave him brief instructions.

"Inform Polkovnik Ryzhov that we are overrunning the line of resistance and that he should prepare phase seven immediately!"

Turning back to his observations, he was rewarded by the obvious signs of the British withdrawing, although the violent end of one of the Sturmgeschutz did not escape him.

---

Anton Emilian, Major of Tanks, commander of the Romanian armoured force, sat quietly watching as his crew struggled with the repair, the vital track having been severed by the strike of a PIAT round, just as the British infantry ran for their lives.

He carefully examined his dislocated middle finger, stroking it with his right hand, rehearsing the move that would bring it back into shape.

A group of dazed prisoners were herded past him and a small kerfuffle ensued.

An enemy soldier, wearing a Red Cross armband, had moved towards him and one of the Russians guards had 'tapped' him with his rifle butt.

The medical orderly held his hands out, palms up, placating the guard, slowly moving in Emilian's direction.

Young had spotted the Romanian officer's predicament and had moved only to offer his medical help.

Suddenly, both Emilian and the guard understood the orderly's purpose and both relaxed.

After a swift examination, Young's hand gestures overcame the language barrier and Emilian steeled himself for the pain.

It came and went quickly, not as much as he expected but more than he would have wished for.

He smiled and thanked the Englishman, but realised that his words were wasted.

Instead, he reached into his pocket and produced his recently acquired cigarette case, found when his unit stumbled across a hastily evacuated Allied headquarters position. Holding out the shiny object, Emilian indicated that it was a gift, one that Young accepted immediately, even though he was a non-smoker.

The guard chivvied his group back into some sort of order and Emilian was left to resume his critical assessment of the track repair work.

---

The cigarette case was plain and simple, all except for the prominent four-leaf clover that was mounted on its face.

As the group of prisoners made its way to the rear, the Romanian unit's Hetzer reached the field and promptly gave up the ghost.

Its commander, exasperated and in the foulest of moods, dismounted, and commenced a violent kicking attack on it until he realised that the inert object was not even offended by the assault, whereas his foot was now aching badly.

Belligerently, he stood his ground as the prisoners descended upon him, forcing the group to split and walk around him.

Hands on hips, he inspected each in turn until he caught sight of the cigarette case, its unique clover imprinting itself on his memory, suggesting that his Commander had perished and the body had been looted by the man holding it.

"Futui gura!"

The Soviet guard started to shout but the Steyr M1912 pistol was out in an instant.

Young's smile disappeared along with the top of his head as the enraged Romanian tank officer exacted revenge for Emilian's death.

Slipping the case into his pocket, Lieutenant Ionescu went in search of higher authority.

---

He was stunned to find Emilian sat with his crew, all tucking into bread and cheese, their track mended but lacking the fuel with which to move off the field.

"But I thought..."

"You thought what, Tudor?"

The Lieutenant was confused.

"I thought you were dead, Sir."

Emilian's eyes sparkled.

111

"Well, I admit my finger hurts," he waggled the damaged appendage with care, "But I think I'll manage to survive 'til the morning."

The crew appreciated the humour, but not enough to stop eating, so the rumble of amusement had no real form.

Ionescu fumbled in his pocket, produced the cigarette case and proffered it to a now puzzled Emilian.

"And where in the name of Saint Andrei did you find that?"

"An enemy soldier had it. I thought he'd killed you and looted it from you."

Emilian was no fool but he had to ask.

"So you took it back, eh? So, where's the man now, Tudor?"

"Dead. I shot him, Sir."

Accepting the cigarette case, he gestured that Ionescu should join them and the whole group fell into silence again.

As he chewed on the heavy bread, the Catholic in Emilian turned to God, the persistent dull ache in his finger sharpening his memory of prayers long gone by.

*'Oh Saints of our God, come to his aid. Come to meet him, angels of the Lord. Receive his soul and present him to God, the Most High. Amen.'*

And with that, Young became but a memory.

---

Walshe had managed to escape.

About a third of the Inniskillings managed to disengage themselves and fell back from Töplitsch to positions in Weißenbach, over one and a half kilometres further down the Drau River line.

Whilst Walshe and the others were integrated into the positions of the 1st Battalion, Royal Irish Fusiliers, those who had been slow to rise or wounded were herded up and marched away to begin a new life as prisoners of war. Eight-one men started the journey, sixty finished it, as wounds, the cold, and poor treatment took their toll.

Across the river, the London Irish had been displaced with heavy casualties and were staging a fighting withdrawal down Route 38.

At Spittal an der Drau, the prisoners of both battalions were loaded into small trucks, along with local Austrians of military age, despite the fact that no Kommando had been present.

Kearney the 'corpse', still dazed and with the mother of all headaches, was helped aboard and the doors locked into place by guards eager to find some relaxation indoors and away from the freezing temperatures.

As the 16th November gave way to the 17th, the small train bore over six hundred souls to a fate unknown.

### 0921 hrs, Friday 15th November 1945, 250 metres south-east of Barembach, Alsace.

Hunger had driven him to it; sheer desperation had forced decisions upon him, decisions that he would have baulked at in different times.

Hunger also played another part, in as much as the Soviet paratrooper was still out searching for food in daylight, so weakened was he by a lack of everything the body needs, save fresh water; something in abundance in the snow-covered Alsace.

Hunger produced a telling influence, drawing the man towards the soft sounds of contented chickens, temptingly originating in a small outhouse to the rear of the buildings on the junction of Rue de Juifs and the Rue Principale.

Hunger played its final card by making the man careless, its debilitating effects blocking the inner voices of the combat soldier, voices that shouted caution and were ignored.

The building was owned by a French family, presently encumbered with the billeting of a group of US war correspondents, all guarded by a small detail of military police.

One of the MPs, a Sergeant, was now covering the would-be thief with an M1 carbine.

The two men locked eyes and the Soviet paratrooper acknowledged the warning with a resigned look and fell exhausted against the building, knowing he had neither the wit nor strength to fly.

"Hey Boys!... Hey!... Boys!... Boys!... I've got me a chicken rustler!"

Three more MP's, in various stages of undress, turned out of the building, laughing at the pathetic unshaven man and his rags, closely followed by members of the Press Corps, some of whom carried cameras that immediately started to record the pitiful scene.

As was the agreement, no pictures were sent back for use until an intelligence officer had viewed and passed them as revealing nothing of use to the enemy.

It was fortunate for the Allies that the man with the photo duty that day was keen, efficient, and above all, very good at his job.

Something sparked a memory and he reached up to a shelf groaning under a ton of paperwork.

He searched a special folder for a comparison photograph, satisfied himself that he was right, and immediately rang his boss.

---

A phone rang on the desk of Georges De Walle, now permanently attached to French First Army.

He recognised the voice immediately, his counterpart in Dever's Army Group headquarters.

The man was all business, and his calls either fishing for or supplying information were always brief.

De Walle listened.

"Mon Dieu! Yes...thank you... yes, we are very interested... yes... I will... as soon as possible and with written orders signed by me... Yes, today. Thank you, Colonel."

Replacing the receiver, he made the calculations, grudgingly admiring the man in question.

*'Over three months.'*

He picked up the telephone again.

*'Makarenko... at last.'*

## 1100 hrs, Saturday 16th November 1945, Château de Fère, Fère-en-Tardenois, France.

To the second, the meeting was brought to order, the wood panelled banquet room providing a magnificent setting for the momentous event.

114

Eisenhower, prior to the start, had drifted around the room, noting, with no little astonishment, how the occupants seemed relaxed with each other, former enemies now united in a common cause, a cause in which they now saw a turn in fortune, despite the events in Italy.

The men sat patiently waiting to hear his words represented the leadership of those countries brought together to oppose the spread of the Red Army.

*'A goddamn who's goddamned who,'* as George Patton had put it when the meeting had first been suggested.

And now, here was the reality.

The Council of Germany and Austria was well represented, with Guderian, Speer, Donitz, and Von Vietinghoff all present. Ike noted that Guderian and Vietinghoff sat in their military groups, not with their national organisations, something that encouraged him greatly, for reasons he didn't quite understand.

The Generals were there in numbers, including every Army commander, save those presently embroiled in the nasty fighting in Northern Italy.

Spanish General Agustin Grandes sat silently, his animated conversation with the Cuban Brigade commander, General Genovevo Perez, now over.

The object of discussion, a prime Havana cigar, had, in the spirit of comradeship, been offered up willingly by Perez, and now sat gently smoking in Grandes' hand.

Its sister sat comfortably between the Cuban officer's lips.

The Commander of the newly arrived 1st Mountain Division of the Argentinian Army had cornered the senior officers of the Paraguayan, Uruguayan, and Portuguese forces regarding South American politics, the latter only because he was in conversation with Paraguay's senior officer in Europe when General Juan Peron had hijacked their private conversation. Peron was the most recent arrival in Europe, having flown in after his unit arrived, delayed by his 22nd October wedding.

Eisenhower had observed them all, men from the British Commonwealth and the United States mixing with a Colonel from Ethiopia through to the unusually tall Mexican General, all brought together for a common cause.

115

And now they sat waiting patiently for his delivery; a summation of events past, and a foretelling of events to come.

---

Eisenhower's summation of events up to the hour held little surprise for most.

In basic form, the Allied forces had taken big hits up and down the front line, a few disasters had happened and a few had been avoided.

In Italy, the new Soviet offensive was progressing, albeit slowly, aided by the poor weather and the accompanying restrictions on Allied air support.

Losses on both sides were generalised, the Allies having paid a high price in stopping the Red Army's forward momentum, the Red Army having paid a huge price in trying to maintain it.

Eisenhower finished his opening brief on a high note, showing how the major Soviet thrusts had run out of steam, and explaining the Soviet logistical problems that contributed to the obvious failures of the Soviet assault.

Ike didn't bother to ask for questions.

He introduced Bedell-Smith and took his seat, anxious to gauge the reaction of the commanders in the room, the men who would have to see through the plan to push the Communist forces back.

*'To the Polish Border and beyond.'*

The words seemed to haunt him at every turn.

Eisenhower particularly watched the Germans present, and was rewarded with looks of surprise when Bedell-Smith's aide uncovered the huge map, upon which was set the basics of the liberation of Occupied Europe.

*'Operation Spectrum.'*

Donitz's eyes widened and he acknowledged Eisenhower with a brief nod.

*'That's one to Vietinghoff for playing it straight.'*

Clearly, the German Liaison officer had abided by the secrecy directive, something that pleased Eisenhower immensely.

He did not see Von Vietinghoff's and Donitz's eyes meet briefly, otherwise he might have realised that Vietinghoff was a German first and an Allied liaison officer second.

The reaction in the room was satisfying; a mixture of stunned silence and softly spoken expletives.

Before the map had been uncovered, few in the room knew what it would reveal.

McCreery, Bradley, Devers, and De Lattre de Tassigny, appointed by De Gaulle to be his eyes and ears in the matter, all knew of the minutiae of Operation Spectrum. Bedell-Smith and close SHAEF staff, such as Colonel Hood, had worked tirelessly on the logistics of the plan, and on the integration of the numerous national groups, giving each a suitable role to play within the grand scheme.

One other man present knew everything.

He sat silently, almost smugly, acknowledging the looks that swept over him. Some eyed him envy, some in relief that the burden would fall to him, and some even in dislike for the man and matters past.

Whatever the reason they looked, George Patton relished the attention, for the map made clear that the initial responsibility for driving back the Red Army was his, with the vast, new, and extremely cosmopolitan US Third Army under his direct control.

Bedell-Smith allowed a few more moments for the map to consume everyone's attention.

All arrows pointed east, from those in Norway, Denmark and the North German plain, through Central Germany and to the Swiss border.

Eyes followed the arrows across Europe, inexorably moving eastwards, to the Polish border, and beyond.

Some officers, those with keener vision and eyes for some smaller details, now understood that the senior Naval officers were not there as window dressing, and that the USN and RN had a role to play.

Forty-seven folders were handed out, some already translated for the non-English speakers.

Bedell-Smith cleared his throat, took a sip of soda water and commenced laying out the master plan that was Operation Spectrum.

---

There was no pause for lunch and so one o'clock came and went as Bedell-Smith conceded the floor to the Army group commanders in turn, first Devers, then Bradley, and finally McCreery, whose 21st Army Group's area of responsibility had been adjusted to encompass Norway and the Baltic.

Tedder was ever present, introducing the Air support element that went with each senior officer's presentation.

Fig#79 - Operation Spectrum - December 1945.

Admirals King and Somerville worked in harness to outline the sub-operation 'Pantomime', projected for the Spring

118

and with the expectation of good weather, the Navy's big contribution to events. Whilst all could see the advantages, none failed to understand the risks of such an operation.

As Eisenhower waited his turn to sum up, he felt extremely pleased with the planning. They had been at great pains to ensure that all nations in the Alliance felt involved, but also careful to ensure that inexperienced troops were not left over burdened or exposed in what was to come.

Kenneth Strong, SHAEF's intelligence chief, completed his briefing, partially as an overview and partially detailing the shadier aspects of 'Pantomime' and ceded the floor to the Supreme Commander.

"So, Gentlemen, there you have it. Operation Spectrum is an all-encompassing general plan, outlining how we'll push the Red Army back into its own lands. We must expect difficulties along the way, so we must be flexible. The specific timings of each phase will be decided by this headquarters, and I intend to adopt a slow but sure approach, unless low-risk opportunity presents itself, in which case, we will judge it on its merits."

Patton had been a dissenter on that score, seeking, almost insisting on, being given his head, with no limits on what he could do except the fuel in his tanks and the food in the bellies of his men. Eisenhower had given him short shrift, drawing more than one look from the inner circle at his 'out of character' testiness.

"Your Army Group commanders will be holding separate sessions immediately after this briefing, and they will present your input to me tomorrow."

There were some disappointed looks amongst the ensemble, but it made good sense to reduce the group size into manageable chunks, as well as limiting the discussion to those involved with each aspect. None the less, each of the seniors knew that they would keep an ear open for anything that might be useful to pass on to another.

Hood caught Ike's eye, the slightest of signals confirming that the orderlies had luncheon ready.

"Gentlemen, I regret to say that the folders you possess may not leave this building and must be handed in at the document security station immediately you leave this room.

Your copy will be returned to you for this afternoon's briefings."

He let the few murmurs of dissent pass.

"To give our Armies enough time to stockpile resources, to go over the attack plans and for Allied Second Army Group to become 'fact', I have set the initial diversionary attack's time for 0300hrs on December 2nd. If the enemy responds as we anticipate, Operation Spectrum Blue, the initial main attack, will commence at 0800hrs on December 4th. We do not anticipate launching 'Pantomime' until early spring, probably part of Spectrum's phase Indigo. Good luck to you all."

The officers sprang to attention as Eisenhower turned and strode from the room, his exterior calmness beginning to crumble under the anxieties that ate at him, the responsibility weighing even more heavily than did his command of Overlord, some sixteen months previously.

Alone in his suite, it took three cigarettes and two coffees to restore any vestige of faith in himself and his ability to see the matter through to a successful end.

His mind tackled a niggling issue once more.

His men were tired, very tired, although replacements were arriving and some units were being rested in quieter areas.

The thought, as always, was balanced by the fact that the enemy had to be similarly tired and, by all intelligence reports, were not only greatly worn down numerically, but also hobbled by supply issues.

It was something that Von Vietinghoff had said that constantly troubled him.

Whilst the Generals present had all acknowledged the weariness of the Allied troops and balanced it against the state of their enemy, Vietinghoff's response had started with the assertion that the Soviet soldier was the most resilient fighting man on the planet.

*'A sip of water and a bite of bread will keep him fighting all day, Herr General.'*

Eisenhower shuddered involuntarily.

Not for the first time that week, he closed his eyes and prayed.

The Soviets, with their love of maskirovka, had been extremely impressed with the FUSAG operation during D-Day and subsequent weeks.

FUSAG, or First US Army Group, had been a phantom, a figment in the collective imaginations of the Overlord planners, and it had sold Hitler and his generals, hook, line, and sinker.

The German Army had continued to hold strong units in the Pas de Calais in response to the huge FUSAG strength waiting in England, an illusion perpetrated by double agents, inflatable tanks, false buildings and works, mock warships made of wood, and a complicated signals network serviced by a handful of men. The cream on the cake had been Patton, who led the false formation, although it must have grated on him to be deprived of his opportunity during the early days of Overlord.

It had worked once and, never being ones to set aside a good idea, SHAEF planners had decided to try it again, and so Allied Second Army Group was formed, although solely in the minds of men.

The wounded Montgomery was cited to command it, although the fact that the Field Marshall would never command men in the field again was known only to a handful in the highest echelons. His 'double' was already moving around the British countryside, trying hard to be noticed by someone with a link to Moscow.

The Soviets were no fools and the Allied planners intended to be careful to reduce the similarities to FUSAG as much as possible, even to the point of allocating real units, such as veteran units withdrawn for recuperation to volunteer units from across the world arriving in theatre to train and acclimatise; hence the designation 'Allied' rather than US or British.

In many ways, FUSAG started as an extra for which there were no great expectations. Events would later push it into a prime position in the new European War.

*Those that I fight, I do not hate; those that I guard, I do not love.*

*William Butler Yeats*

# Chapter 108 – THE DISCOVERIES

## 1201 hrs, Monday, 18th November 1945, Mikoyan Prototype Facility, Stakhanovo, USSR.

It had been an unauthorised flight, in as much as those in power at Mikoyan-Gurevich had not informed the People's Ministry of the Aircraft Industry, the Council of People's Commissars, Marshal Novikov of the Red Air Force, Malenkov of the GKO, who was the member with responsibility for aircraft production, or even Mikhail Gromov, Chief of the Flight Research Institute at Stakhanovo, whose facility was the location for the flight

The Mikoyan-9 was the Soviet Union's first attempt at a home produced turbojet aircraft and its maiden flight was a disaster.

Konstantin Djorov, temporarily detached from his assignment as OC 2nd Guards Special Fighter Regiment, had gently eased the aircraft into the sky and the problems had started almost immediately.

He tried to gain height and, even though the vibrations were decidedly worrying, he could not help but be impressed with the rate of climb and obvious presence of unbridled power in the MIG. Passing four thousand metres and still rising strongly, the vibrations grew worse and the experienced pilot decided to ease back on the throttles.

Whatever it was that happened next was unclear but its results were impressive to the observers on the ground; less so for the occupant of the test aircraft.

Djorov later explained that it seemed that his wings started to disintegrate, immediately followed by the loss of his rear stabilisers.

He could not explain what happened after that.

All he knew was that, one moment he had been wrestling with a dying aircraft, the next he was aware of a silence that was, to say the least, weird, and he realised that he was floating gently in the freezing cold snowy sky.

When he was brought back to the test base, one of Mikoyan's designers had asked him what he might suggest to help.

Djorov verbally exploded and got right in the face of the shrinking man, and at a range of about three centimetres let rip as only a man who has recently had a close acquaintance with impending death can do.

"You send me up in a fucking death trap and then ask me what I suggest? Fucking Idiot!"

Djorov stepped back, aware that it wasn't necessarily just the young engineer's fault.

He turned to escape the awkward moment, intent on cleaning up in the comfort of his billet.

Something caught his eye and he decided to make the most of the moment.

He pointed at the pair of aircraft sat outside the Mikoyan pilot's rest facility.

Moving back in closer to the engineer, but this time with a quieter approach, Djorov hissed his considered response.

"Design like that, Comrade Engineer, or build the Red Air Force some of them!"

The angry man left, leaving the design engineer both perplexed and thoughtful.

One of his older colleagues joined him and both watched the retreating pilot.

"Comrade Arushanian. Don't trouble yourself. The PodPolkovnik has just had a narrow escape and he's bound to be angry."

"Well, he is certainly that, Comrade Piadyshev."

Both men shared a modest laugh, as they both understood that they had contributed, in their own way, to Djorov's close shave.

"I asked him what he would suggest."

This time it was only the older man who laughed.

"Well, that would have done it for me too, you idiot! What were you thinking of?"

The sole answer was a shrug of defeat.

"I suppose his suggestion involved sticking something in a position within your back passage?"

"No, Comrade Piadyshev. He said we should give him some of those."

Filipp Piadyshev followed the direction of Arushanian's finger.

Almost mocking the designers and engineers of the Mikoyan Institute, two proven warriors of the sky, ex-German ME 262's jet fighters, sat in efficient silence,

## 1418 hrs, Wednesday, 20th November 1945, the heights, west of Muingcreena, near Glenlara, Mayo, Éire.

He was the third agent that Bryan had dispatched to the area. He also knew that he was the only one still alive, the other two having fallen victim to Judas Reynolds' stark policy on anyone 'out of place' found in the locale.

Thomas O'Farrell, and that was his real name, was clearly a career criminal with an arrest record as long as the longest arm, and he had spent a great deal of time in Éire's criminal institutions, mainly in solitary confinement..

In reality, Thomas Ryan O'Farrell, Sergeant in the Irish Army, was often detained, by prior arrangement, to permit him to take time to relax, his double life free from discovery, safe inside the protective custody of secure government facilities, as well as relaying whatever he had recently discovered about the Irish Republican Army.

His hurried deployment was not ideal, but Bryan had little choice in the matter, and so O'Farrell was dispatched with simple orders.

*'Confirm the existence of an IRA facility at Glenlara, establish numbers of personnel present and ascertain its purpose.'*

Bryan, always honest with his agents, informed O'Farrell of the previous attempts at approaching the site and their terminal outcomes.

Immediately that he had received the call from Rafferty, Bryan had contacted his local man and sent him off to observe the site.

His body had been found the following evening, ostensibly run over by a very apologetic farmer, a man with suspected republican tendencies. He had no idea the man had been sleeping in the long grass, but was very apologetic and offered to write a letter of condolence to the destroyed corpse's family, which offer was tactfully declined.

The second agent had been found drowned in one of the many ponds that littered the area.

That had been three days ago and the post-mortem, or at least the part that didn't lie as a matter of public record, indicated that the man had suffered a significant beating that did not tally with the suggested contact with the rescuing boat that the local police had put forward as a reason for the additional injuries.

But, as far as the local police and their republican friends were concerned, accidental death by drowning was the official cause of death.

At this moment, that was of no significance, as Thomas Ryan O'Farrell had just made a startling discovery.

A large Allied seaplane had just flown close by to seaward and the few civilians that had been in sight had disappeared.

As the drone of aero engines receded, he adjusted the thick waterproof on which he lay, noting that the snow had recommenced its efforts to freeze him to death.

He pulled the white blanket up over him and settled back into his over watch.

And almost missed the biggest prize of all.

"Fucking hell!"

He scolded himself for the outburst and focussed the binoculars on the face of Judas Reynolds, stretching in the open doorway, a roaring fire behind him.

*'You fucking Fenian bastard you, Judas, Bryan will be...'*

Another man came into view, not one O'Farrell recognised but one that made his heart miss a beat.

His mouth remained open but not a sound came. He didn't trust himself even to think.

The door shut as quickly as it opened, but the picture of a Soviet naval officer was deeply ingrained on his mind.

As he tried to order his thoughts, the approaching IRA security party drew his attention.

He started into his concealment routine, safe in the knowledge that the men never deviated from their patrol path, probably because of the deep snow but, O'Farrell thought with a professional contempt, *'they're just playing at the fucking soldier game.'*

It proved so again, and thirty minutes later he was back at the main road. A handset had been attached to the phone line that ran overhead and O'Farrell composed himself and his cryptic message as he pulled it from its hiding place.

Two hours later, acting on aa anonymous tip off, a police patrol caught a burglar in the act of stealing petrol from a shed in Aughalasheen and, in view of his attempts to resist arrest, as well as identifying him as a well-known criminal, transported the bleeding and insensible man to a holding cell at the Garda station in Walshe Street, Ballina.

The Inspector in charge of the patrol had been briefed on the need to get O'Farrell to the station and had initiated the beating to provide reason for the journey.

He would apologise that it got out of hand when the circumstances permitted but, none the less, he grudgingly respected the man, whoever he was, as did those others of his patrol that presently had their own appointments with the Police Doctor at Ballina, because of injuries sustained in the apprehension of Thomas O'Farrell.

The arrest, some might call it brawl, had been witnessed by one Noel Connolly, a young man for whom the pleasures of the straipach, the local whore, held no charm. He took his pleasures in the arms of an even younger farmhand in Aughalasheen.

On his return to Glenlara, Connolly mentioned the arrest, if only to boast how the unfortunate burglar had bested five beefy Garda before being felled by a blow from behind.

Brown, secretly back in the main camp for the evening, promised himself to find out what the Garda were doing in the area in the first place, and then went back to his quiet but animated discussion with Reynolds.

In the main, they turned a blind eye to Connelly's 'ungodly activities', rarely even acknowledging them.

However, this night, both men stared after the disappearing IRA man and then shared a conspirator's smile as cunning minds merged in a plan to dispose of a pressing problem.

Once the Garda had been attended to and, in the case of two of the bloodied men, had their wounds stitched, O'Farrell received the very best of attention himself, the police doctor's examination and treatment exceedingly thorough.

In line with his wishes, the examination of his lower regions was conducted in private, the doctor insisting on being alone, despite the protestations of the guarding constables.

The period by themselves permitted him to swiftly write out a report on the pad she produced from her medical bag. They didn't speak at all, except for matters that a doctor and burglar would converse about. However, the doctor was on the payroll of G2 and knew that she would meet another man later that night, a man who would want answers.

She memorised the note, pausing to confirm one word that stood out amongst the others, her mouth working without sound, his response a simple nod.

She lit both of them cigarettes, rechecked that she could fully recall the brief message and then consigned the note to a fiery end in the ashtray. After sufficient time had passed, the guards were summoned back and she went to report that the scallywag was fit enough to travel to Dublin. Interest had been aroused on the man's possible IRA leanings and the prisoner was to be taken there at first light.

Never one to miss an opportunity, Bryan had ramped up the 'legend' of O'Farrell, ensuring that any Garda with republican sympathies would put his agent's name in the spotlight, in the most advantageous sort of way.

---

The meeting was brief and took place in the quiet of her office within St Joseph's District Hospital, Ballina.

As the message made its way south, Dr Raymond made her way home to the Mount Falcon estate, where she and her family were staying, guests of the Aldridge family. It was a short-term agreement whilst they sought suitable property nearer to her work, an agreement that Bryan's department had made easy.

Her husband and children were already asleep and, as Dr Raymond had not yet returned, the butler was unable to help the police with their request. Replacing the receiver, he intended to inform her of the new call immediately she returned.

Anyway, it sounded like a nasty business and not one for a lady like Dr Raymond.

The police needed confirmation of death on a car driver; at least once the bits had been extracted from the car by the local fire brigade. The police officer had been quite happy to try to shock the old butler with the gruesome details of a wrecked car and a more wrecked body, hit head on by a lorry carrying hay bales, which skidded on ice.

It was not until the following morning that the Raymond family reported the doctor missing and the Ballina police realised the true horror of the situation.

---

The following day, news of Raymond's awful death reached Bryan's ears and caused consternation.

*'Accident?'*

*'Assassination?'*

The head of G2 decided that this was a complication that needed further investigation, so held back on telling his British contacts, at least until some more enquiries were carried out.

So the report from O'Farrell that he now possessed, which had preceded the awful news by only forty minutes, remained unspoken of and uncommunicated to his Allies.

His Allies had not yet passed on their own knowledge, for their own reasons,

Such were the games that the Intelligence services played.

### 2339 hrs Friday, 22nd November 1945, Glenlara, Mayo, Éire.

"Lieutenant Dudko!"

The lack of any response ensured a repeat of the hammering on the wooden door.

"Lieutenant Dudko!"

At last, sounds of movement betrayed the fact that the Political Officer had been wrenched from his land of dreams and back into the harsh realities of life, or at least the

128

reality that was about to be presented to him, courtesy of Judas' planning.

"Comrade Reynolds? What do you want? Is there a problem?"

"Yes there is, Major. I don't know where to start."

Dudko surveyed the falling snow and decided to deal with the matter indoors.

"Come in, come in, Tovarich."

"No, no, I can't do that. It's summat you've to see for yourself, boyo."

Reynolds played the part of perturbed and shocked man perfectly, his facial expression alone spiking Dudko's curiosity.

"One moment, Comrade, just one moment. Should we wake Lieutenant Masharin?"

"Our Comrade Masharin may not do what is right... what is needed here."

That intrigued Dudko, as well as massaged his ego.

"Explain, Comrade Reynolds."

The political officer swiftly slipped into his boots and pulled his greatcoat on before venturing outside.

"There's summat you've to see. Summat awful, Dmitri. I don't know what to do! You'll know for sure!"

Playing to Dudko's ego was a masterstroke and the naval officer was drawn further in.

The two were moving steadily towards a small building set apart from the rest, sometimes obscured by the flurries of snow, sometimes not, when the presence of three men nearby became obvious.

Brown and two IRA men stood shivering, ostensibly waiting to receive Reynolds and Dudko, whereas in fact they had been serving the more sinister purpose of ensuring that the occupants of the hut did not leave.

"Still there, Patrick. I don't know what to say, really I don't."

Reynolds put a 'comforting' hand on Brown's shoulder.

"Well, I've got Dmitri herenow. He'll know what to do, to be sure."

"What is so bad, Comrade Reynolds? You can tell me."

129

"I can't Dmitri, really I can't. We don't know what to do. You'll have to see for yourself."

So Dmitri Dudko, strings pulled by the hateful Reynolds, saw for himself.

Acting on orders, one occupant of the room, young Noel Connelly, had moved the curtain sufficiently for anyone outside to be able to see into the interior.

He had also ensured that the candle remained burning in order that, when Dudko looked through the gap, he would be able to see all that was required. Indeed, that proved to be the case and the Political Officer was in no doubt that the man penetrating the young Irishman was none other than the Soviet commander, Ilya Nazarbayev.

Reynolds and Brown had played their plan to perfection and now Dudko took centre stage.

"Mudaks!"

The Russian took a few moments to think through his course of action and then initiated a response.

"This is piggery, Comrades, total fucking piggery! Are your men armed, Comrade Brown?"

Both IRA soldiers pulled out pistols from beneath their heavy winter clothing.

"Follow me!"

His own Nagant pistol was out by the time he put his boot through the door of Nazarbayev's private quarters and interrupted the two homosexuals at their pleasure.

"Kapitan-Leytenant Nazarbayev, I relieve you of your command immediately and I arrest you for buggery and homosexuality."

Ilya Nazarbayev did not respond; there was nothing he could usefully say. His private life, previously secret, now lay exposed, his military career over and his future hold on life tenuous to say the least. All because of the needs and desires of the beautiful young Irishman who had been so insistent.

"Dress and go with Comrade Brown's men. I will decide what happens next at another time.

In two minutes, the Marine officer, flanked by the two IRA men, marched off to the small building that they used as a brig.

"Your man... I will leave to you, Comrade Reynolds."

"Thank you for that, Dmitri...and thank you for sorting this out."

The Political Officer nodded briefly, just now working out that command of the facility had fallen to him.

Dudko moved off quickly to organise his senior NCO's and inform them of the events that had elevated him to second in command by rank but, in reality, the de facto leader of Marine Special Action Force 27.

When he was out of earshot, both Brown and Reynolds started to chuckle.

They were joined by Connelly as he dressed.

"Oh now Noel, my little darlin'. Well done boyo, fucking well done."

Pausing only to sweep up a half-full bottle of something interesting, the three moved off towards the IRA quarters, high on the clear success of their revenge upon Captain-Lieutenant Ilya Nazarbayev.

### 1500 hrs Monday, 25th November 1945, two hundred and thirty miles west of the Isle of Lewis, the Atlantic.

Orders were orders and even the seemingly most stupid of them had to be obeyed.

Lieutenant Commander Mikhail Kalinin was now discharging his latest orders, ones that required him to take leave of his command and transfer aboard an unknown surface vessel.

At 1500 hrs precisely, B-29 broke the surface and the hatches popped to permit the deck watch to take post, as well as allowing the boat party to prepare themselves for the transfer.

Kalinin had been watching the strange vessel for some time, trying to work out what it was, and failing miserably.

Clearly, it wasn't anything specifically, although it closely resembled a number of vessels, and he rightly suspected that the 'Swedish' ship was not what it tried hard to be.

Aboard the 'Golden Quest', eyes took in the sleek lines of the underwater killer, more than one man nervous in case it was not the friend they expected.

Senior Chief Petty Officer Bjarte Sveinsvold had long since been released from the sick bay, his wounds mended, and he was a regular contributor to basic onboard tasks of the seafarer. His ability at splicing lines and welding was second to none, so he often found himself wielding a paintbrush. The nonsenses of military life were the same across the national divides.

He paused and took in the scene as an inflatable boat put out from the submarine and started the short journey across the roiling gap.

By the excited nature of the Soviet seamen and the uniformed presence of a guard of honour of eight Soviet Marines, the new arrival was something of a celebrity.

The man, clearly a senior naval officer, stepped aboard the 'Golden Quest' and exchanged salutes with the entourage of officers that had gathered to greet him.

As quick as he arrived, Kalinin disappeared in the direction of the Captain's cabin, pausing only to throw a magnificent salute in the direction of his former command.

A minute later, the vessel's number one emerged with orders.

Sveinsvold was to transfer aboard the submarine.

Three minutes later, his few possessions in a small linen bag, the USN Senior Chief was on his way to the B-29.

The submarine, boat crew recovered, began to sink below the waves and the surface vessel increased revolutions, both anxious to discharge their part in Kalinin's orders, both going in different directions, their paths never to cross again.

On B-29, Sveinsvold needed to be constantly on his guard, but his injuries saved him as he played on them and his 'loss' of memory, ensuring his brief voyage would be solely as a passenger.

---

Enjoying the finest tea he had tasted for a very long time, Mikhail Kalinin listened politely to the Captain's version of recent world events in general and, specifically, those involving the Red Army in Europe.

"So, Comrade Lipranski. What are your orders regarding me?"

"My apologies, tovarich. You do not know? I had assumed you would know. I'm to make landfall, when you will be met by an officer who will issue you with further instructions."

Lipranski wasn't being tedious, he simply didn't think, but Kalinin had no time for playing games as he had a date with a bunk and a full six hours sleep.

"Where, Comrade Lipranski?"

"Ah, again, my apologies. We'll dock in La Rochelle as soon as possible."

Kalinin hadn't even drawn breath before Captain Lipranski headed him off.

"There... ah... so I believe... the briefing officer was a little indiscrete but he knows me... you and a number of other naval personnel will be transferred to an Italian vessel, in which you'll complete your journey, Comrade Kalinin."

The submarine officer was deeply unimpressed but it was a done thing.

Despite close questioning, these was no further information to help work out why on earth Soviet Naval command had taken him from an operational command and set him on a course that would see him kicking his heels at sea for weeks on end.

Later, when Kalinin had safely transferred to the Italian flagged 'Grosseto', he was stunned to find out that the destination ahead was Dubrovnik.

His journey was not to stop there.

Over the coming weeks, he was to be smuggled through a still petulant Yugoslavia and into the more friendly Romania, where Kalinin and the others would be able to relax and travel more openly, moving on through the Ukraine, although their NKVD minders would still wish to conceal his identity.

And so, not that he yet knew it, weeks after leaving the B-29 in the Atlantic, Lieutenant Commander Kalinin would finally come to rest in a brand new and decidedly clandestine naval base at Beregovoy, on the shores of the Black Sea.

## Fig#80 - Gail River Valley, Austria, Overview.

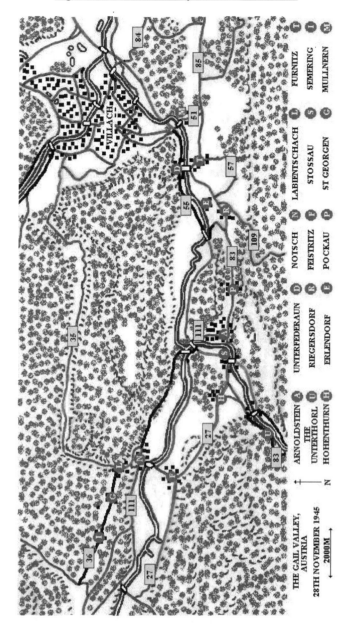

134

*He that fights and runs away,*
*May turn and fight another day.*
*But he that is in battle slain,*
*Will never rise to fight again.*

*Tacitus*

# Chapter 109 - THE LANCERS

## 0930 hrs, Thursday, 28th November 1945, Arnoldstein, Austria.

The 6th Armoured Division had suffered badly in the few days of the Italian War, much of its sacrifice going unrecognised, as the situation demanded that a part here and a part there was sent to act as a fire brigade in desperate defence.

Units attached to other formations withered and died, their passing lost in the mourning for the larger formation.

However, the totality of it all meant that 6th Armoured had been badly savaged.

The force that had assembled in defence of the vital junction at Arnoldstein was an excellent example of a tactical formation in disarray.

The 26th Armoured Brigade, on paper at least, consisted of three cavalry regiments and a rifle battalion.

The 2nd Lothian and Border Horse was remarkably intact, but miles from Arnoldstein, committed into the front line, south of Innsbruck.

Between them and Arnoldstein lay bits and pieces of the two Lancer regiments, split apart from their parent formation by the necessities of war.

The fighting to the east had been protracted and bitter, the Allied defenders stubbornly clinging to ground soaked in the blood of both sides. What had expected to be captured within days was now a week, sometimes more, behind schedule and the Red Army commanders were in a blue funk.

Soviet casualties had been heavy but the relatively successful defence had, with few exceptions, crippled the Allied divisions defending.

As a result, ad hoc units sprang up everywhere, bits and pieces thrown together in an attempt to form something cohesive with which to resist the enemy's renewed advances.

Ambrose Force, named for the Brigadier that led it, pulled together bits and pieces of units that had already suffered badly, and combined them to make up an all-arms defensive formation charged with holding Arnoldstein at all costs.

Originally, the relatively sleepy hollow that was Arnoldstein had been occupied solely by a small unit of Churchill tanks, five Mk VII vehicles that had been left behind with an engineering section and their crews some weeks ago, ordered to follow on once repairs had been affected. The men, tankers and mechanics alike, chose to misinterpret their orders, enjoying a safer life behind the lines in relative peace and comfort.

Their peace was shattered by the arrival of Ambrose Force.

Fig#81 - Ambrose Force, Gail River Valley, 28th November 1945.

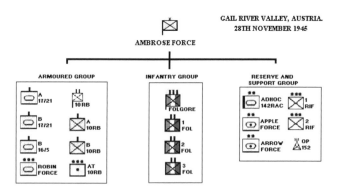

The 17th/21st Lancers, equipped with Sherman tanks, and also two Challengers that had appeared from '*Only God knew where*', represented the smaller contribution to the armoured element. The 16th/5th Lancers, the senior cavalry unit in the brigade, made up the bulk, their twenty-four

Shermans of all shapes and sizes more numerous by exactly two to one.

Infantry from the 10th Rifle Brigade, anti-tank guns, including some of the deadly Archer SP vehicles, and artillery from 152nd Field Regiment provided support.

Other units were en route to make up the numbers, not the least of which was an Italian infantry battalion that had formed from men not willing to cede their country to the Communists.

It was, on paper, a formidable force and it had formed a strong defensive position across the Gail River valley, the expected prime route into Northern Italy for the Red Army forces of 1st Alpine Front.

Peaks up to fourteen hundred metres formed the southern side of the Gail valley, those to the north achieved two thousand metres in places, confining the combatants to the valley floor.

Unfortunately, some would say inexcusably, there were few maps available to the defenders, and some were even forced to use local tourist maps from before the 1939 war, or even school geography books.

That, combined with the fact that the Brigadier commanding refused to acknowledge that he was suffering from concussion, brought together all the ingredients for a disaster in the making.

All eyes faced eastwards, when only one pair firmly fixed upon on the west might have saved countless lives.

---

The tankers were surly, that was for sure.

Stood at attention, or at least what counted for attention in this wayward group from 142nd RAC, they all remained staring ahead, declining to answer the question put to them by a very angry Lancer officer.

The 17th/21st Captain, in receipt of a complaint and damming information from angry locals, had discovered the totality of the local church's altar display secreted in one of the RAC's service vehicles, something that exercised him greatly.

As far as Ambrose Force was concerned, the men of the 142nd were already top of everyone's shit list, as it was pretty obvious they had intended to sit out the war until their peace was interrupted by the arrival of the lead Lancer units.

Looting the church was inexcusable in any case, but the general mood meant that the 142nd troopers were in big trouble.

Captain Charles Stokes-Herbst was gathering momentum, his eyes taking in the shoddy state of the nearest of the five Churchills parked nearby.

That it belonged to the RAC's Sergeant and highest ranker was just too much.

"You, Sergeant, your vehicle's a bloody disgrace, man!"

"Sah."

The unit insignia, bridge weight indicator, and all other markings were either faded by the weather or covered with muck. The rough tarpaulin shelters that the RAC troops had thrown up prevented snow from adding to the problem, but also ensured that the issue was noticeable, unlike Stokes-Herbst's tanks, whose pristine markings were concealed beneath a thick white layer from the previous night's downfall.

No one failed to recognise the sound of incoming rounds and the arrival of Soviet high-explosive shells released the RAC troopers from the Lancers' wrath.

"Get them mounted up, Sergeant. We'll sort this out later."

No sooner had his backside hit the passenger seat than his driver had the jeep leaping forward, anxious to get himself inside thick steel protection as soon as possible.

Elsewhere, the dying had already started.

---

The screams were awful, but they reflected the suffering of the poor man whose entrails had been flung far from his body as shrapnel disembowelled him in an instant.

A shocked medic from the Rifle Brigade did not even know where to start so, unusually for the experienced man, he didn't, his mind constantly rejecting a course of action, which caused him to remain static.

Others tried but the man, the Major commanding 17th/21st, died a painful death as a few hardy souls tried to

138

gather up the pieces in the hope that medical science could make him whole.

Other lancers were down, mercifully killed instantly by the large calibre shell. A Corporal lay in soft repose, almost unmarked, save for a bloody eye cavity, marking where a modest piece of metal had entered and taken his life. Next to him, laid precisely parallel, was the corpse of the WO1, the senior soldier in the 17th/21st, who had first picked up a lance before the end of the Great War and whose extended career had been the very model example for any NCO.

Other shells were falling, the first arrival having been a premature discharge, for which the gun commander was already receiving a roasting. That the shell had arrived in the centre of an orders group was unknown to the Russians, but it had robbed the two Lancer units of much of their 'leadership talent' in one bitter blow.

Captain Haines found himself upside down against a stone wall. He rolled, mentally checking the continued presence of his limbs and vital organs, dragged himself upright, and shook his head to try to clear the ringing. Like everyone who had been stood in the circle, he had not heard the shell, either on its way or even the explosion.

All the same, his ears seemed to be the only parts that bothered to inform him that they were suffering.

Groggily, he rose to his feet and surveyed the scene. He saw mouths moving and saw activity but all that assailed him was the constant ringing.

"Bollocks!"

Leastways, that is what he thought he said.

He spotted the dead 17th/21st Major and, fighting back the natural revulsion, realised that he had just become the senior man and, by default, the armoured commander of Ambrose Force.

*'Oh bloody hell!'*

### 1020 hrs, Thursday, 28th November 1945, the Gail River valley, Austria.

"Driver... advance!"

The idling engine took on a deeper note and the tank lurched forward into whatever the whiteness held in store.

Major Emilian's objections had been brushed aside and the Armoured Group's commander, keen to impress his Soviet peers with the communist zeal and commitment of his force, insisted that the attack went ahead as scheduled, virtually nil visibility being seen as an equal factor for attackers and defenders.

Which, in some ways, it was, although being in a tank advancing into a roiling white wall of snow, knowing that the unseen battlefield ahead holds men with guns who do not have your best interests at heart was, and will always be, a daunting prospect.

Fig#82 - Soviet 40th Army lead units, Gail River Valley, 28th November 1945.

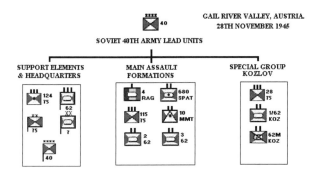

Emilian's force was not the only armour in the attack. Nine heavy ISU-152's from 680th AT Artillery Regiment were moving behind the Romanian vehicles, ready to focus their energies on swatting aside any resistance.

Enemy artillery had started to respond but, as expected, could not be properly directed and clearly resorted to falling on pre-determined locations, places that the hasty Soviet attack plan had deliberately avoided. As a result, few men fell and the wave of tanks and infantry closed on the Allied positions virtually unhindered.

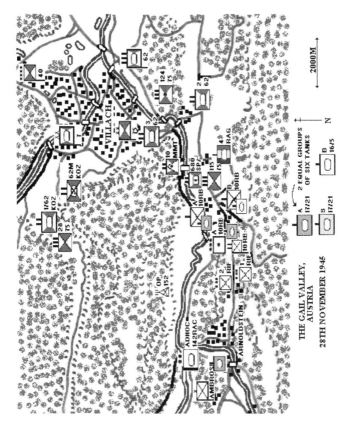

The Lancers were drawn up behind the first infantry positions, just to the east of Erlendorf and Riegersdorf.

The concept had been simple at the time, as the hull down positions they occupied provided reasonable fields of fire.

The snow reduced vision so much that the first Romanian tank was virtually on top of the infantry's trenches before it was spotted.

The enemy tank, a Panzer IV, the Lancer gunner noted automatically, took a hit on the turret without harm, its own machine guns lashing the positions in which the Rifle

Brigade stood, causing casualties amongst the men who waited to beat back the accompanying infantry.

Then, all hell broke loose.

"Fire!"

---

"Hit the bastard again, Nellie!"

"He's disappeared, Boss. Can't see the bastard... hang on... ON!"

"FIRE!"

The 76mm cracked and sent a high-velocity shell across the battlefield, intended for a target some three hundred yards away.

The snow eddied round with the wind and made a concerted effort to obscure the Panzer IV. Had the shell missed it might have succeeded, but it struck home, and the ex-German tank blossomed into a fireball instantly.

"Good job, Nellie!"

Haines, understanding the problems posed by the heavier snowfall, changed tactics and pushed his units closer to the infantry. His own tank swept up to the forward positions in the nick of time and was the first to successfully engage.

Corporal Oliphant was already seeking out a fresh victim as Haines popped his head out of the turret for a better look.

The Rifle Brigade's positions exploded, partially from a volley from the defenders and partially from a well-timed shoot from the enemy mortar battalion assigned for the closer support work.

Haines grimaced in horror as men and pieces of men flew skywards, the infantry positions bathed in high explosive and shrapnel.

The Soviet infantry let out a loud 'Urrah!' and surged forward ahead of their tanks, eager to get in close.

Haines surveyed the scene, aware that he had more responsibilities than just fighting his own unit and tank.

Assessing the battle, he quickly realised that the present positions were untenable.

The Lancer captain had first strapped on a tank in 1938, firing his first angry shot during the German Invasion of the Low Countries.

He was considered an exceptionally competent officer by those above and below him and, what was more important to his men, he was lucky.

Only once had the war touched him directly and the deep scar on his cheek and missing segment of his ear were visible reminders as to how lucky he could be.

On 22nd February 1943, an Italian mortar shell had exploded on the engine compartment of his Crusader III tank during a fight with the Centauro Tank Division, as 6th Armoured tried to relieve the pressure on the beleaguered US troops at Kasserine.

Pieces of the shell sliced through his right ear and across his right cheek, severing one of the headset wires. More pieces sliced through the headset earpiece just above his left ear, and yet another piece cut through the slack cord at throat level. One of his epaulettes was torn off and his watch face was shattered by another piece of metal.

He remained in the line, despite his injuries and, since that day, had ridden his luck, probably far too often.

Today he felt that all that was going to change.

Keying the mike as he reassessed his decision, he heard Oliphant yell a warning.

"Fuck me! Target, tank to front. ON!"

Haines could do no more than give the order.

"FIRE!"

He released the mike as his eyes went in search of whatever it was that Oliphant had killed, at least judging by the sounds of celebration in his ears.

He found it easily.

"What the bloody hell is that, Nellie?"

The huge vehicle was belching black smoke and the crew were already on the ground and running, pursued by bullets from some of the infantry.

"Fuck knows, Boss, but it's a big soddin' thing and it's dead."

Whatever it was, it was certainly bad news for Ambrose Force, as it was not alone.

"Nellie, fire at will for now. I gotta speak to the pongos."

Keying the mike once more, he sought out the officer commanding the hard-pressed Rifle Brigade. After the initial exchange of call signs, Haines gave his orders.

"Sahara 6 from Cassino 6, I will cover your withdrawal to Baker line. Keep the swine off you until the arty comes in, then toss smoke and move immediately. Clear, over?"

"Cassino 6 from Sahara 6, it may be too late already, old bean. We've over a dozen tanks to our front. Can't you engage them, over?"

Fig#84 - Allied defensive lines in the Gail River Valley, 28th November 1945.

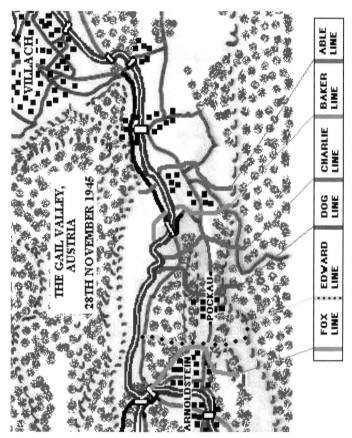

144

Sparing a moment for a look, Haines could see nothing except the impressive white storm.

"Sahara 6 from Cassino 6, negative. Can't engage... no visual... not a bleeding thing. Arty on way soon. Stay on the air, over."

He assessed the position of the enemy advance as best he could and made a small notation on the edge of the tourist map before dialling into the artillery.

The tank leapt violently as Oliphant engaged something and, judging by the whoops, engaged it successfully again.

Passing coordinates based upon some hastily jotted down figures he had been given earlier, Haines waited as the gunners of the 152nd RA prepared their Sexton SPs.

A single shell arrived, its explosion barely noticeable in the flurries, but sufficient to mark a miscalculation on Haines' part.

Cursing inwardly, he adjusted the fire, dropping two hundred and waited once more.

The hull machine gun on his tank starting sending small bursts of fire into the whiteness, as the gunner managed to recognise darker patches moving rapidly forward.

The second ranging shot arrived.

*'Close enough.'*

"Fire for effect until further. Cassino 6 out."

Switching to the Lancer's radio net, he briefed his commanders on the plan before ensuring that Acting Captain Robinson took command of the 16th/5th.

Haines, as the overall armoured commander, could not afford to be drawn in and lose the big picture.

"Anything to front, Nellie?"

"Not a sausage, Boss."

"Roger. Stumpy, back her up and get us into cover back there. We're on our way to HQ."

The Sherman moved smoothly backwards, lumps of snow falling away as the rough ground caused 'Biffo's Bus' to stagger and shudder.

Haines took some time to survey the scene, feeling a sense of satisfaction as the artillery smashed down just in front of the infantry positions, or at least the positions they had occupied, the retreating men clearly visible now.

*'Clear... I can see the buggers...'*

Puzzled, he looked upwards and realised that the snow had almost stopped falling on his position.

*'Bollocks!'*

"Cassino 6, all Cassino elements. Rally on Baker, rally on Baker, immediate. Snow is stopping. Engage immediately.

Driver Clair, known as Stumpy for reasons that were all too obvious when he raised himself to his full height, such as it was, heard the radio call and anticipated the next command, swinging the rear of the Sherman in behind a solid stone wall that marked part of the second position, created on the edge of Erlendorf and Riegersdorf.

Oliphant took advantage of the lack of movement.

"Vehilce to front... target on... shit and bollocks... Misfire!"

Haines initiated the procedure.

A second attempt failed, as did the next attempt. After that, the breech needed to be opened and the dodgy shell removed and launched as far away from the tank as possible.

That task fell to the loader, Trooper Powell, as inoffensive looking a man as it was possible to meet, so clearly entitled to his nickname 'Killer'.

"Opening breech!"

The noticeable tremble in the loader's voice betrayed the nervousness of the moment.

Powell immediately saw the indentations of the firing pin and his concern increased.

At the moment his fingers touched the round, the Sherman rocked, the turret resounding like a bell. No-one needed telling they had been hit.

Haines wanted to shout at the loader but decided better of it, not wishing to break his concentration.

Oliphant was not so shy.

"Those big bastards have seen us now, Killer, so speed your fucking self up or I'll come back and fucking haunt you!"

The shell was out now and Powell pushed himself and the shell up through the hatch.

Seconds later, he dropped back inside, his cheeks blowing out as he finished battling with his fear.

146

"Good work, Killer."

Whilst the loader had been outside, both Haines and Nellie had checked the firing mechanism and quickly came to the conclusion that the fault lay with the shell, not the gun.

"OK lads, drama over for now. Load up HVAP and be quick about it."

The high-velocity armour-piercing shell was the best available to the Sherman crew when it came to killing other tanks.

"Target Sp to front... on!"

Nellie had decided that the big ones would go first.

"Fire!"

The Sherman rocked and another Soviet vehicle was hit.

"Over to you now, Nellie."

Haines returned to his planning, surveying the positions taken by his Lancers and finding himself generally satisfied.

One tank seemed more forward than the others and certainly more exposed, its machine-guns hammering out in an effort to protect the retreating infantry.

A quick look through his binoculars confirmed which vehicle call sign it was.

*'Banshee.'*

Switching to the squadron net, he keyed the mike.

The sudden huge fireball stopped him in his tracks, his mouth wide open, as the Sherman was literally torn apart by something huge and unforgiving.

A 152mm shell had simply demolished the vehicle.

His own tank jerked again, as Nellie replied in kind.

The target, another of the huge ISU-152s, stopped immediately and exhibited no signs of life. No hatches were opened followed, no urgent scramble for survival apparent. No fire or smoke came from it. The leviathan was knocked out, its crew not dead, but all badly wounded, and definitely out of the fight.

Soviet supporting mortar fire was being adjusted expertly and shells started to drop amongst the British infantry as they neared their second line positions.

Binoculars again pressed to his eyes, Haines swept the advancing enemy for some sign of the controllers. As the snow continued to peter out, spotting the enemy vehicle proved to be easier than he had expected.

"Nellie, see that halftrack with the antennas... two o'clock... tucked in behind that bush. HE and take it out."

"Still got aitch-vap in, Biffo. Next shot."

Haines let it go.

Biffo was a nickname he had acquired because of his legendary capacity to get into scraps, normally with Allied contingents, and normally managing to drag his mates into matters against their will. Despite the frequent use of his fists to settle disputes over matters of signal insignificance between parties generally too 'oiled' to remember what started the fight, Haines' combat and leadership qualities secured him promotion from the ranks and eventual command of a troop in, and then leadership of, B Squadron, 16th/5th Royal Lancers.

Oliphant decided to aim the shell rather than just get rid of it.

A small enemy SP had come onto view behind the halftrack and he put his shell into the superstructure, causing the vehicle to manoeuvre erratically, whilst seeking cover behind a farm building.

Killer slotted an HE shell home and it was quickly on its way for a fatal rendezvous with the observer vehicle from the Soviet 10th Mountain Mortar Regiment.

The British infantry still lost men to the mortars but they remained unadjusted for some time, enough to ensure that the Rifle Brigade could get organised for phase two.

A Sherman disappeared in a huge fireball as another of the ISU's made a hit.

"Cassino 6, all Cassino elements. Concentrate on the big SP's. Take 'em out of the fight now."

Four had already been savaged, two by Oliphant, much to the gunner's merriment.

The Lancers focussed their main guns on the ISU's and the heavy SP's suffered badly, the two surviving commanders finding excellent reasons to withdraw to positions out of direct sight.

---

Lt Ionescu was crying and screaming.

He was the only casualty in the Hetzer, the small SP that Haines' tank had put a shell into a few minutes beforehand.

With the damaged vehicle now safely tucked away behind an old storage building, his crew were trying hard to get the wounded officer out of the vehicle and away for medical treatment as soon as possible.

Any movement they tried, and each breath he took, tortured Ionescu's shattered body, producing extremes of pain.

One moment he had been encouraging his men to advance, the next the whole vehicle smelt of burnt metal and flesh. Lieutenant Tudor Ionescu had been ripped open, exposing both lungs and liver to the appalled gaze of his crew.

The 25pdrs of the British Sextons rocked the small SP, the pitter-patter as shrapnel struck the metal sides began to unnerve the men, as did the screams of their officer.

The senior man, a Corporal and the vehicle's gunner, took a lump shrapnel in the back, killing him instantly.

The remaining two crew members lost their nerve and ran, leaving Ionescu in the snow to die alone.

---

Major Emilian was crying and screaming, his command in tatters and half his crew dead around him.

Although untouched himself, the Rumanian was covered with blood, the products of his gunner and loader, both killed by the inexorable passage of an armour-piercing shell on its way through the turret.

The radio was silent, despite him screaming orders at his men; silent for two reasons.

Firstly, there was no one left to hear his calls, the only vehicle undamaged being the Zrynyi II, its engine having given up the battle shortly after the advance through Müllnern, five kilometres to the east.

Secondly, his radio had been destroyed by the same shell that had claimed his turret crew.

Another shell struck the front of the tank and Emilian found himself sprayed with the detritus of the driver, whose body lay directly in the path of another AP shell.

Almost dreaming, Emilian slowly wiped the bits and pieces from his face, and hands, and arms, and chest, and...

Seven seconds after the last impact, Major Anton Emilian mind collapsed and he suffered a total psychological breakdown.

He shouted loudly into his microphone, cursing Hitler, Antonescu, Stalin and King Michael equally, commanding his officers to press home the attack, squealed at anything he could see for stealing his mother's apples and, finally, screaming an order for coffee as he imagined himself in his favourite watering hole in Constanta.

His screaming turned to maniacal laughter as he noticed the severed handset. He threw it at the dead gun crew, cursing them for their silence and pushed himself up out of the turret with the flags that were on hand to replace the radio.

He made patterns with the two flags, none of which would have been recognised as proper orders by anyone, even if he had been seen.

---

Actually, he was seen, but not by his own side.

"Look at 'im, the stupid bugger!"

The hull machine gun fired a short burst, knocking the man off the tank turret and onto the snow below.

"Jesus Christ but he's still going!"

Haines took time to focus on the single man who was behaving so erratically.

Clearly, some bullets had hit the man as he now only waved the one flag, his right arm dangling uncontrolled at his side.

None the less, he continued to make his signals in the direction of anyone and anything that he could spot.

"Let him be, lads. He's had enough."

Emilian had dropped to the ground, exhausted by his exertions, drained of energy, and weakened by his blood loss.

The flag still jerked feebly as the dying man kept up his efforts.

Sparing his enemy a final look, Haines turned back to managing his defence.

"Let him be."

A moment beforehand, some miles behind the lines, a Sexton had fired a shell that would prove less forgiving.

150

It arrived about two feet to the left of the Romanian officer and transformed him into pieces no larger than a matchbox.

## 1135 hrs, Thursday, 28th November 1945, Headquarters of Force Ambrose, Hohenthurn, Gail River valley, Austria.

The Soviet attack had been driven off at a cost. The infantry losses were more than made up for by the arrival of an Italian Battalion, with two more en route.

However, the 16th/5th Lancers needed to pull in the tanks of the 17th/21st to make up their own numbers; exactly half of their starting vehicles were either knocked out or so badly damaged as to be of no further use. Part of the reserve B Sqdn moved up, taking up the middle of the line, in between the two ravaged lancer units.

Haines and Stokes-Herbst had consulted on the position, given their head by the strangely disinterested Brigadier Ambrose. The senior officer had even given them his only decent map before returning to dictating orders to his staff regarding the required shaving routine in cold weather.

The two Lancer officers were too tied up in their own concerns to really understand that Ambrose was not fit to command. The staff of Force Ambrose was, for the most part, too inexperienced to challenge a senior officer of proven credentials, and with such an immaculate record of accomplishment.

Outside, the two Captains broke out their cigarettes and spread the map on a dodgy trestle table. One look at it told Haines that the defence was vulnerable, possibly much more than that.

"Bollocks. We've got nothing here, Charlie. Didn't even know this road was here."

The failure in the maps was starkly revealed by the one decent bit of cartography in the unit,

Each man produced his own map, the one each had worked from until now.

Neither showed what was obviously a reasonably sized route circumventing the Arnoldstein position, starting in Villach and ending in Nötsch, just over two miles west of the highly important position.

Stokes-Herbst hissed in disgust.

"Christ, we may already be outflanked, even surrounded! We best fall back, you'd say?"

Haines scratched his cheek.

"Not down to me, is it? I'd say not though. Let's go and put it to the Brig and see what he has already planned."

Spreading the map out before Ambrose, who set aside his irritation at having his dictation interrupted, Haines pointed out the possibilities, expecting the man to have made provisions and to have placed men there.

He had not, and the Lancer Captain now realised that the Brigadier was not fit to serve.

"In which case, Sir, I suggest we move the RAC boys west... to sit in Nötsch... support them with a battalion of the Italians and reposition the Archer reserve... in case all hell breaks loose up the Gail Valley."

Haines reasoned that if he could get agreement to the reorganisation, he would set things in motion and tackle the Brigadier's ability to command afterwards.

He had not allowed for what actually happened.

"Right ho, Captain. Now, you get it all organised. I'm off for a lie down before tiffin, brief me if the Germans look like being troublesome."

Ambrose disappeared, heading off to his tent for a sleep, leaving the two Lancers and the Force staff shocked and silent.

Haines suddenly realised that everyone was looking at him.

It is said that nature abhors a vacuum. The same applies to the military.

*'Oh bollocks!'*

"Right, you heard the plan. Get them moving now and get them moving fast. Charlie," he turned to the 17th/21st man, "With a battalion of Eyeties and the Rifle Brigade, you'll have more infantry than you had before, by a country mile. Free me up three of your tanks from the Stossau reserve, the best mechanically, to act as a mobile group. Get them positioned here." He tapped the map, indicating a track running from the main road just west of Pöckau.

"Call sign... call sign will be...," his mind went blank.

Stokes-Herbst ventured a suggestion.

"Robin?"

"That'll do, Charlie. Robin it is. Make sure you're topped off and ammo'ed up. Have a chat with the munitions officer before you leave, but get my mobile group in position as soon as poss, ok?"

The radios in the command centre had already contacted the 142nd RAC and the Italian unit, both units acknowledging the new orders without question.

The Archer unit remained worrying uncontactable.

Whilst the staff might have been young and inexperienced, they were nothing if not efficient, and the Archers received written orders as soon as was practicable, orders directing them to new positions at Stossau.

Haines took one of the staff officers to one side, giving him a delicate task that would require a certain sensitivity.

The commander of the Folgore Regiment, the Italian Infantry unit, was soon on the radio, confirming his orders and the dispatch of his second battalion to Nötsch, with a mortar platoon in support.

The Folgore's battalions were not full sized, but were undoubtedly big enough to make a difference.

The third battalion was drawn up in Arnoldstein, where it started firming up the defences.

Again, the efficient Italian Colonel was on the radio, reporting to the British 'Brigadier' on a successful deployment. Haines had seen no reason to inform the Folgore commander of the change of leadership.

The 142nd were noticeable by their silence.

Captain Biffo Haines, aware of the facts of Stokes-Herbst's encounter with the RAC troopers, took it upon himself to make sure that the Churchill tanks were moving.

The Churchills had not moved; neither were they started up, nor had the light shelters been moved away.

'Biffo's Bus' drew up on the road outside of the farm yard that the 142nd had selected as their home.

Haines ducked his head into the turret and exchanged a few words with his crew before climbing out and dropping into the snow.

Fig#85 – The problem at Notsch, Gail River Valley, 28th
November 1945.

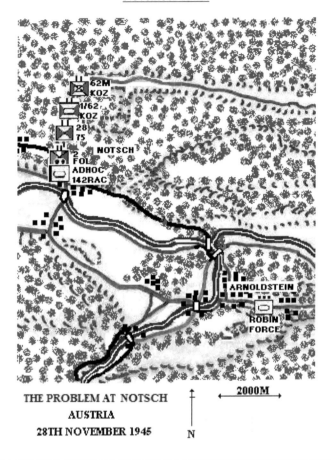

THE PROBLEM AT NOTSCH
AUSTRIA
28TH NOVEMBER 1945

2000M

N

"Sergeant."

The man saluted.

"Name?"

"Massala, Sir, Sergeant, 142nd RAC."

He didn't wait for a reply from the Lancer officer,
swinging into his prepared statement and pointing to a few
men, either lying on wooden benches or sat around gripping
their stomachs.

154

"Sir, some of the lads've got a right case of the trots. At least two from each tank. We can't move without 'em, Sir."

The story was backed up by sounds of moaning from one or two of the 'affected' men, made more dramatic by more clutching and rolling of bodies.

Saying nothing, the Lancer officer moved forward, looking over the sorry bunch, who all managed to avoid eye contact, which, in itself, told him a great deal.

"Two things, Sergeant. Firstly, if you and your bunch of no-hopers are going to feign the shits, at least have the sense to smell of shit or look like you are shitting."

The Sergeant looked uncomfortable for all the wrong reasons.

"Secondly," he took his beret off and indicted his tank, "If you and your lousy bunch of knob jockeys don't get your fucking arses in your tanks and down the road pretty pronto, then my gunner will start with your vehicle and won't stop until they are all in flames... leaving you wankers free to join the poor bloody infantry. Are we clear, Sergeant?"

"Sir, the lads have..."

Haines grew in stature and in volume.

"Are we clear, Sergeant?"

The RAC Sergeant set his jaw.

"We ain't doing it. We simply ain't bloody doing it. We've been through it all too many fucking times... far too much to die now... all of us."

The man's voice grew in pitch as the words came tumbling out, his 'incapacitated' men realising that their subterfuge had failed and another tack was needed.

"My men here...all of us...we've done our bit, god knows... and fucking more besides... more than you high and mighty soddin' regulars and that's that, so..."

Had the NCO but realised it, the Lancer officer Captain Haines had disappeared and had been replaced by something called Biffo, a creature with a short fuse and little capacity for compromise.

One straight right put the Sergeant on his backside in the muddy snow of the courtyard.

The Lancer extended his hand, the Sergeant so confused that he accepted the help without question.

Biffo posed a simple question.

"What was that you were saying, Sergeant?"

The NCO regained his senses and spat some blood away, barely missing Haines's tank overalls.

"Sir, you gotta understand. We've been through hell, in this one and the last. Me and the boys are done... really we are. There's no fight left in us."

A murmur from the rest of the RAC troopers supported the assertion.

Biffo and Haines silently wrestled for supremacy and unusually, especially given the circumstances, Haines won through.

"So, you think you've done your bit and now you intend to sit this out, eh?... EH? Leave your mates to fight... whilst you sit back and press wild flowers? Is that it?"

The sarcasm stung a little and the Sergeant stood a little taller.

"Yes, Captain, we've done our bit and more... and our mates have been killed by the dozen...and for what, eh? For fucking what?"

He turned to his men, almost preaching to them, rather than reasoning with Haines.

"For what? Get rid of one fucking Hitler and another comes along straight away. A few yards here, a few yards there... and all the time we bury our chums."

Biffo was back in the ascendency again and the Sergeant had an extreme close-up of the angry lancer's face.

"Listen to me, you sorry excuse for a fucking soldier. You and your men'll do as you're ordered for a number of reasons. One, because you're soldiers and you obey orders. Two, because if you don't, all of your mates will have died in vain."

The Lancer officer focussed his attention purely on Massala.

"And three... 'cause if you don't, I'll stretch the lot of you wankers in the snow... starting with you, sunshine. Fucking comprendez... Sergeant?""

The delay in stating the man's rank supplemented the contemptuous tone, stinging the Armoured Corps NCO as it was meant to do whilst, behind Biffo's back, the fourth reason had traversed its gun and was pointing at the nearest Churchill,

156

with Stumpy and Killer, equipped with sten guns, covering the group from the driver's and loader's hatches respectively.

"So... you and your sorry bunch get your tanks moving... and we'll say no more about this. Clear?"

The Sergeant exchanged looks with some of his men, the little shrugs and head movements telling the watchers that the Lancer officer had won the day.

"Clear as crystal, Sir."

"OK then. Stay on the net... and if you see anything, anything at all, I need to know straight away. If you and the Eyeties can't handle it, I have Archers and a ready troop of Shermans that can get up to you. Call signs Apple and Robin. Released on my orders only, clear?"

For the benefit of the surly group that was starting to sort itself out, Haines increased his volume.

"You're not alone in this fight, lads, just as you're not alone in losing mates, We've all done our bit... and I wish we could all just go home... but we can't, not while the sodding Russians keep this nonsense up. We've to stay here... and we've to do the job, otherwise it'll be your sons," he selected one of the older troopers for some serious eye contact, "Or your grandsons who'll have to do the business for us... and then what would we think of ourselves, eh? EH?"

The grumbling continued, but they moved smartly enough to their vehicles.

"Sergeant, a word."

Taking the RAC man aside, Haines laid it out clear and simple.

"If you and your men do this right, we will say nothing more about any of it, Sergeant."

The man nodded.

"However, Sergeant, if you or your men let me down in any way, I'll visit myself upon the lot of you and you'll pray for the sodding Redcaps to take you away. Are we clear?"

"Clear as crystal, Sir."

The NCO's nose trickled blood again.

"Good luck to you and your men, Sergeant."

A brief salute was exchanged and both men quickly to their tanks.

Nellie made a great play of following each vehicle with the gun barrel until his commander put an end to the game.

With 'Biffo' safely back in his cage, Haines waited until all the Churchills were on the road before moving back to the headquarters position.

## 1214 hrs, Thursday, 28th November 1945, Headquarters of Force Ambrose, Hohenthurn, Gail River valley, Austria.

By the time Haines returned to the headquarters, Brigadier Ambrose was on his way to the rear. The medical officer, a man scrounged up from one of the Eighth Army's rear echelon units, decided that Ambrose needed to be evacuated and that he was the only one who could go with him.

Haines sought out the staff officer he had entrusted with the task and nodded his acknowledgement.

The Italian Colonel had arrived to report to the Brigadier, only to find that he was now the senior officer on the Allied side.

To be fair to him, the man had the common sense to understand that he was not equipped to lead the tanks, so he was openly relieved when Haines returned.

Colonnello Dante Pappalardo was perplexed by his sudden elevation to leadership but took it in his stride, unaware that he had already taken orders from the Lancer officer he now commanded.

The basic position seemed sound enough, or as sound as it could be, especially as Haines' provision for Nötsch was soon to be in place.

Another Soviet attack had fallen before the Rifle Brigade and Italian infantry force, but again, had cost valuable British tanks.

Stokes-Herbst reported two more 16th/5th losses and four from 17th/21st.

"The bridges, Capitano? They are ready?"

"No, Sir, they are not. Brigadier Ambrose had requested some engineers to prepare them, but none have arrived."

One of the Lieutenants passed Haines a message chit.

158

"Here we are. Demolition squad requested at 1312hrs on 26th November. Acknowledged and action was promised, Colonnello."

"Merda! So where is our next line of defence?"

The staff placed a hastily prepared overlay on the map the Colonel had supplied, an Italian army map of superior quality.

The next position lay between Riegersdorf and Pöckau, then just outside of Pöckau itself.

After that, one further line obstructed the approaches to Arnoldstein before the defensive positions were set in Arnoldstein itself.

"So, we have some time, at least. Tenente, repeat that request for demolition team please."

The Lieutenant moved off to the radio immediately.

"Your thoughts, Capitano?"

"Sir, these positions," he ran his fingers over the ones between Arnoldstein and Riegersdorf, "Are less than satisfactory for the tanks. No field of fire for us really."

The snow had gone and visibility was now excellent.

"We need to hold this line as long as possible... that way I can guarantee the best support for your infantry forces, as well as the artillery observers having the best possible opportunities to do good work."

Pappalardo could understand that.

"So why not bring all of your tanks up to this line, Capitano?"

*'Good question, Colonel.'*

"The enemy's artillery is very effective, so we can't bunch up, Colonel."

Haines thought that the rate of tank losses would ensure that all his assets were up front soon enough, but kept the thought to himself.

"These tanks at Stossau, Capitano. Why not move them up closer?"

Pappalardo had spotted the six tanks from A-17/21, set back as a reserve.

"Nötsch is the short answer, Colonel."

For the first time, Haines realised that the major issue was even clearer on the Italian Army map.

159

"Our maps were inferior, so we initially missed this possibility," his finger described the road that bypassed the front line and led straight from Villach to Nötsch.

"Ah, this is why your Generale di Brigata needed my battalion. And your tanks too?"

Haines kept a straight face.

"Yes, Colonnello, we've sent a group of five heavy tanks from the Royal Armoured Corps to back up your men."

He took a quick look at his watch and smiled.

"They should be arriving any time now, Sir."

*'If they know what's sodding good for them!'*

"Excellente, Capitano, excellente."

The Italian screwed up his eyes, examining a notation more closely.

"What is Inniskilling?"

"Irishmen, Colonel. Survivors from a battle up north. Enough escaped to form two platoons, which are sat there as a reserve. Of limited use, I'm afraid. The men are knackered, Sir, totally knackered."

"Nakered?"

"Tired, exhausted and fought out, Colonel."

"Ah, I understand. Then we will leave them alone for now, Captain."

The Inniskillings that had escaped Puch were taken out of the 1st Royal Irish where they had taken refuge and sent back to the rear, where reinforcements were intended to marry up and make the unit an effective fighting force once more.

However, the requirements of war overtook the idea in short order.

The Colonel cast his cap to one side and selected a thin cigarette from his case, lit it and pored over the details of his force.

"Now, what can we do to annoy our red friends?"

"You mean attack them, Colonel?"

"Yes, of course. I have spent too long running alongside the Germans not to know the value of a good counter-attack when it is least expected."

*'Now you're my sort of fucking Colonel.'*

Much as the Italian really did want to have a go, there was simply not enough information to make any informed judgement on a possible counter-attack, so he reluctantly let the idea slide... if only for a moment.

One of the other staff members suggested that the bridge at Furnitz might need some attention and Colonel Pappalardo jumped at the possibility.

"Do we have the ammunition for such fire? Without affecting our defence?"

Without needing to check, the staff Lieutenant spoke with certainty.

"Most certainly, Sir. There's absolutely no problem with our ammunition supply for artillery. The RA boys are sat on top of an ammo depot."

"Then let us send the Communists at the bridge a few shells, Lieutenant. As soon as possible."

Pappalardo was a belligerent man who had learnt much of his soldiering in Russia with the Alpini Division 'Guilia'

The artillery, resting after its efforts in halting the previous attack, did not welcome another call to arms so soon but set about the task and soon dropped their shells on the bridge and environs.

The Allied commander had no idea whether the shells did good work, but it was enough for him to know that he was hitting back for now.

As the shells passed overhead, Pappalardo and Haines set about planning a more pro-active defence.

Their efforts were to prove in vain as two events made all the difference and condemned Ambrose Force to destruction.

### 1434 hrs, Thursday, 28th November 1945, Gail River bridge, Unterfederaun, Austria.

Pappalardo, ever aggressive, got a little creative with his artillery and mortars and, seeing that there was no shortage of ammunition, it seemed wholly reasonable.

The Sextons switched their fire randomly between the different bridges and areas that he and Haines had identified.

At 1434 hrs, after a ten-minute breather, the 25 pounder Sextons started up again and dropped on the crossing point at Unterfederaun.

After two salvoes, they quickly swapped to the Furnitz road junction, hoping to catch the Soviets unawares.

The second shell to arrive at Unterfederaun took the life of the commander of 115th Rifle Regiment, the assault formation of the 75th Rifle Division. It also took the legs of the divisional commander, Colonel Ryzhov.

Two lorry loads of nurses were passing by and they stopped to attend to the wounded and dying.

The last but one shell of the final salvo struck the raised stone block on the north end of the bridge, transforming it into a thousand pieces of life-taking natural shrapnel.

Some of the nurses were literally torn apart by the deluge. All twenty-seven were hit and none were spared awful injury. Fourteen were killed outright.

Ryzhov had sustained one further hit. A piece of rock the size of an egg destroyed most of his neck, leaving his partially severed head dangling by a crimson thread.

The screams of the wounded women penetrated even the most resilient of minds and Soviet infantry from the 115th Regiment moved quickly to help. Sometimes they found someone who could be saved; more often, they just helped to ease suffering or ensured that some young girl did not die alone.

The 75th had spent most of its war in Iran, so such horrors were new to them.

Their thirst for a reckoning would have a profound effect upon the battle to come.

**1439 hrs, Thursday, 28th November 1945, hasty defensive position 300 metres south-east of Labientschach, Austria.**

The 142nd RAC had moved their tanks into rough cover, facing north-west, with Notsch immediately at their backs. In front of them, some three hundred metres, was the first defensive line of the Italian battalion. In between the two forces, but nearer the tanks, the mortars positioned themselves to the flanks and out of the line of fire.

The Italian infantry found themselves covered in mortar shells, arriving unexpectedly from no one knew where.

The tankers of the 142nd RAC tensed ready, their guns loaded, eyes glued to episcopes and periscopes, seeking out the enemy force that would inevitably emerge into view.

On the orders of the Italian battalion commander, the mortar unit started throwing its own shells in the direction of the pass situated between Notsch and St Georgen, the previously unsuspected and unprotected route through the Alps and into Northern Italy.

The pass carried Route 35 from Villach to join with the 27 at Feistritz an der Gail or, in terms of this battle, offered a superb access route for a sizeable all-arms Soviet force to move into a position behind the main Allied defensive line.

For the want of decent maps, many men would die.

---

The lead recon element of the Soviet force had been tremendously unlucky.

It had tucked itself away to observe, taking up a position away from anything that could be credibly targeted by the enemy, only to fall foul of the happenstance of war, as the first Italian mortar salvo went off target and neatly dropped on and amongst the four vehicles, causing enough death and destruction to knock the unit out of the fight for some time to come.

The lead Soviet battalion commander suddenly lost his 'eyes', but felt he had received enough information to order his men into the assault.

His leading two infantry companies, equipped with lend-lease universal carries, swept into Labientschach and found it undefended.

Covered by this forward force, a small group of SP's and infantry made a turn to the north-west with the intention of taking St Georgen and creating a defensive block, should any Allied threat appear from the direction of Semering or beyond.

As this force manoeuvred, Lieutenant Colonel Kozlov, eponymous commander of Special group that had been sent down the pass, committed part of his armour and two further motorised infantry companies, fairly reasoning that surprise was on his side and he should press Nötsch as soon as possible.

### 1455 hrs, Thursday, 28th November 1945, the Gail River valley, Austria.

Zhumachenko, the commander of 40th Army, had a schedule to stick to and he was already behind.

He had been forcefully reminded of that by his superior officer, Chuikov, a commander incapable of subtlety in word or deed.

Indeed, the commander of the 1st Alpine Front had previously sent extra units to the 40th, just to ensure the breakthrough went smoothly and it was one of those units, the 7th Tank Corps, which was now amassed against the depleted Ambrose force, spread along approximately eight miles of the Gail River valley.

Zhumachenko had already reinforced the depleted 28th Rifle Regiment, creating a combat group, adding tanks and motorised infantry to Kozlov's command and dispatching it through the mountains, intent on falling upon the Allies positions in and around Nötsch.

It was this force that had recently engaged at Labientschach. Even though most of the formation belonged to the fresh 7th Tanks, command lay with the 75th Division's regimental commander, Lieutenant Colonel Novak Kozlov.

Under Chuikov's direct instructions, Zhumachenko had committed the majority of the 7th Tanks to the initial and subsequent assault phases, expressly to break through and open up routes into Northern Italy.

With Chuikov's 'encouragement', he had added the entire 62nd Tank Brigade to the renewed assault, with the promise of more support from Front reserves if he was quickly successful.

Zhumachenko was a professional officer who had started as a private, He fully understood the value of the common soldier's life, hence his attempt to outflank the enemy position with Kozlov's force.

His finesse might have worked in its own right, but for the direct intervention of Chuikov, for whom time was more important than extra names on a casualty list.

Therefore, as news of Kozlov's attack reached the leadership of Ambrose Force, the commander of 40th Army unleashed his own version of a tidal wave.

### 1501 hrs, Thursday, 28th November 1945, Allied western defences, the Gail River valley, Austria.

Katyusha and artillery rounds arrived on target, sweeping the Baker defensive line with death-bringing high explosive and shrapnel.

The tanks were, for the most part, unscathed, although most sported new silver weals where metal had struck metal.

The Tommies of the 10th Rifle Brigade suffered badly as dozens of men were virtually obliterated.

Charles Stokes-Herbst watched in horrified fascination as one man was tossed skywards by an explosion and, before he could fall to earth, another burst seized him and threw him towards the clouds again. Four times the body came down, only to be sent back up again, each time less than it had been before.

The fifth descent finally permitted the shattered remains to come to rest, unrecognisable and awful, dropping on top of the rear hull of the nearest Lancer Sherman.

The 17th/21st Officer vomited down the side of his turret.

Wiping the residue from his mouth, he dragged his eyes from the vision and back to his front, comprehending the enormity of the assault at the same time as his tank commanders scared voices filled the airwaves with reports.

"Oh my fucking god!"

As far as Stokes-Herbst could see there were tanks. To the Lancer it seemed that the T34's of an entire Soviet tank regiment were bearing down on his position.

It would not have been of any comfort for him to know that behind them were more armoured beasts, and that it was actually an entire tank brigade shoehorned into the narrow pass, sixty-two tanks intent on reaching ground well behind his present location.

Over him or through him, it made no difference to them.

He thumbed his mike.

The 17th/21st's leader's voice was cut short and those tank commanders exposed in their turrets were startled by the huge explosion that sent pieces of Stokes-Herbst's Sherman flying in all directions.

An undetected ISU152 had put a shell into the tank and hit everything it needed in order to bring about a catastrophic end to Stokes-Herbst and his crew.

The squadron net was filled with voices, some demanding orders, some suggesting options, all decidedly unnerved by events and the presence of so much enemy materiel.

Moving up from the headquarters, Haines understood that command needed to be re-established quickly so he cut across the airwaves, his voice alone helping to steady the nerves of most of the listeners.

Not yet in a position to issue definitive orders, he soaked up the information that his tank commanders relayed, building up a mental picture of a disaster in the making.

Standing in the cupola, the Lancer officer should have seen the approaching problem, but was too intent on listening to the radio.

Clair shouted a warning as he flung the Sherman to the right, noticing just in time the huge shell hole in the road to their front.

Nellie Oliphant squealed as his head connected with the breech, causing him to recoil automatically.

His head, shooting backwards at speed, perfectly connected with Haines' groin, incapacitating him in an instant. The tank commander dropped into the tank, clutching his genitals as Oliphant struggled to regain his senses and work out what the red stuff in his eyes was.

Powell took one look and acted.

"Stumpy, pull her into cover now. Biffo's hurt and Nellie's pissing claret all over the fucking place."

A gruff acknowledgement and the tank shifted into a lower gear. The light through the hatch all but disappeared as the Sherman was taken into the safety of some nearby trees.

"Need a hand, Killer?"

The gunner had already worked out what had happened.

"Nah. Nellie nutted the gun again. I'll check it for damage obviously."

"That's funny, no really."

Nellie didn't mean it of course.

*'Prat!'*

"Biffo took Nellie's head in the goolies. Someone else can check them for damage later. I ain't touching them for all the tea in China."

There was no need for a headset to hear the guffaws from the two men in the hull.

Stumpy, grinning from ear to ear, took the initiative.

"Right ho then. If you're fine with the mental case and the eunuch, Sparkle and I'll stick some more juice in the bus, quick like."

The driver and hull gunner swiftly slipped out of the tank to drain down the fuel drum lashed on the back of the tank.

Powell got the bandages out of the kit and started to work on Nellie.

"Just a small thing, mate. Less'n half inch, I swear. Just a lot of blood. Not even a lump."

Killer cast an eye at the incapacitated Haines every now and again, feeling the man's pain but, without a doubt, seeing the funny side. He stayed silent in that regard, with no intention of testing matters, as he suspected that a heavy blow in the bollocks would have given the punchy officer a sense of humour failure.

As he cut the bandage lengthways, so as to make a pair of ties, a slightly more coherent groan announced the return to life of the tank commander.

"Urghh. Fucking hell! What hit me?"

Winning the battle of 'keeping a straight face', Powell finished his work on the person responsible.

"'Ardest substance known to man, boss. Our Nellie's noggin. Took you in the meat 'n two veg... right and proper."

Haines, the pain still incredibly intense, realised he had been lost to the battle at a crucial time.

Straightening himself as quickly as he could, which was anything but quick, he took up the headset that had been wrenched from his head as he fell.

There was no traffic on the net.

He switched to command frequency to forewarn Colonello Pappalardo.

Nothing.

The set was dead.

He moved the frequencies.

The set remained stubbornly rooted in silence and that silence was heavy with meaning.

---

The waves of infantry and tanks had washed over the Baker line.

Some infantry and tank commanders had decided that, in the absence of any orders, a prudent withdrawal was called for, and what defence there could have been was swiftly undermined by the appearance of holes as a Sherman here, a section of infantry there, pulled back.

Isolated pockets of the Rifle Brigade resisted and, under specific orders, the attackers ignored them and swept on, eager to pursue and push forward.

The Folgore infantry, supported by the four 6pdr anti-tank guns of the Rifle Brigade, exacted a price from both T34's and infantrymen, but their rally was brief.

Acting Captain Robinson was long dead and the leadership spine in the 16th/5th was presently a CSM. His tank stood like a rock, attracting knots of infantry to it, the already bypassed defensive position building in strength by the second.

It could no longer be ignored and the third battalion of the 62nd Tanks, committed forward from reserve, focussed all their energies upon it, high explosive and solid shot raining down upon the concentration of British soldiery.

The Sherman stopped firing, not destroyed but out of the fight, its crew almost catatonic with shock and horror at the sight of the CSM's headless body collapsed in the well of the tank.

Soldiers of the 115th Rifle Regiment moved forward in a focussed assault, their minds still full of the hideous events at the Unterfederaun Bridge.

British riflemen and tank crew surrendered, hands in the air, most with the blank faces and distant eyes of men who had been through hell.

A tanker fell, shot dead in revenge by a young Soviet Corporal who had cradled a dying nurse.

Another followed, this time a Rifle Brigade officer, selected for no other reason than he tried to protest about what was to come.

The sixty-two prisoners were herded into a hollow behind the CSM's tank and ordered to strip. Eleven accompanying NKVD troopers gathered up the uniforms and dog tags before the Chekist Captain nodded to his infantry counterpart, satisfied that he had obeyed his orders to the letter.

He watched, dispassionately, as the men of the 115th worked out their angst, replacing their grief at the deaths of those at Unterfederaun with a bloodbath, engorged by their frenzied bayonet practice on men who could do no more than raise a fist in their own defence.

Tanks and infantry moved on once more, leaving no witnesses to the events in the hollow.

The sixty-two uniforms, most with pockets containing papers and personal artefacts, plus the dog tags, started their journey to their destination, the temporary camp of an NKVD penal unit...

In a concealed position...

In the Wurzen Pass...

On the Yugoslavian border.

## 1607 hrs, Thursday, 28th November 1945, Headquarters of Force Ambrose, Hohenthurn, Gail River valley, Austria.

During the Second World War, the Italian Army had gained a reputation as slackers, lacking in soldierly skills, and being poorly led.

Erwin Rommel had once said 'Good soldiers, bad officers', which more accurately reflected the worth of the better formations of the Italian Army.

However, the Folgore Regiment had landed on its feet with Pappalardo, and it was thanks to his efforts that some Allied units escaped the debacle.

The reserve Sherman troop, call sign Robin, had been committed to stiffen the western defences, especially when the 142nd RAC disappeared from the airwaves and the Italian infantry commander reported his desperate position.

Reforming a reserve, the Italian Colonel put together two groups of Archers, Apple and Arrow, each supported by a group of his infantry, complete with armoured transport.

---

'Biffo's Bus' had been swept along in the tide of retreat, Haines acknowledging that he could no nothing to stop the withdrawal for the moment.

His chance came and went at the 'Charlie' line. There were no forces posted there, nothing to identify 'Charlie' as a firm defensive position, so there was no encouragement for those fleeing to stand firm and fight back,

At the 'Dog' line, he seized the opportunity and broadcast his orders, halting the few survivors from the 16th/5th and 17th/21st, turning the tanks around to support the men of the Folgore who had established themselves once more.

Getting some semblance of organisation took Haines some time, but he was soon able to report to Pappalardo.

"Firensay Dicky, Firensay Dicky, Cassino Six over."

The Italian Colonel himself answered.

"Cassino Six, Firenze Dieci receiving over."

"Colonel, Able, Baker, and Charlie lines are down. Repeat, Able, Baker, Charlie are down. I'm organising on Dog but need back up. Request release of Robin, Cassino Six over."

Haines was more than annoyed to find out that 'Robin' had already been sent to the eastern defences.

However, Pappalardo sweetened the disappointment.

"I have a group of six guns and infantry which I'll send right no...," the Italian Colonel was cut short as a number of heavy calibre rounds fell around the headquarters, "Fanculo! Cassino Six receiving over?"

"Firensay Dicky, Cassino Six receiving over."

"Cassino Six, we were just hit hard. Wait..."

Pappalardo unkeyed the mike and took a moment to survey the surroundings. At first glance, it appeared that the HQ had been lucky.

170

His second in command had already started to organise another headquarters move.

"Cassino Six, Firenze Dieci, we have to move. Will send the guns and infantry immediately. Call signs Apple and Arrow. I may be offline for a while. Over and out."

Haines started at the silent radio for a moment.

Switching channels, he got through to the TD's at the first attempt, sending the SP's to the important height that dominated Pöckau and the Dog defensive line.

On his own initiative, the Italian infantry commander deployed his men to the north slope to screen the Archers, something Haines wholly approved of when the situation reports started to come in.

Organising those soldiers and tanks that had escaped the overrun Baker line, Haines created a bastion on and north of Route 83.

They had no chance to rest.

## 1629 hrs, Thursday, 28th November 1945, Headquarters of Force Ambrose, Kartner Strasse, Maglern, Gail River valley, Austria.

The headquarters was hastily set up, in as much as the radios were placed on the rear of a wooden cart, tables and chairs were rounded up and the security platoon dispersed around the farmyard.

Pappalardo watched as Haines' information on the latest assault was mapped. The Lancer officer was clearly under pressure but still coping and leading the defences well.

Prioritising his problems, the Italian officer turned his attention to the west, where contact had been lost with his infantry force commander.

Last reports had a large all-arms Soviet unit pushing that battalion hard.

Combined with the recent communication from the 'Robin' group, the whole thing stank of disaster.

Two of the three Shermans had been incapacitated, one by a simple track breakage, the other by a more serious engine problem. The third tank, that of the section's commander, decided to remain in close attendance.

Aircraft of both nations arrived over the battlefield, expanding the options available to both sides.

Thunderbolts and Mustangs fell upon the Soviet ground forces, whilst Shturmoviks and PE-2's similarly attacked the Allied defensive positions, both sides with remarkably little success, considering the amount of ordnance they expended.

Other aircraft started to arrive, some with stars, some with roundels, all with the intent on blowing up the ground trrops or shooting down the enemy's machines. A full-blown air battle developed, even as the winter's evening started to draw in.

402 Squadron RCAF had been disbanded in July 1945 and was one of those recently reformed and sent to Italy, training to prepare for their New Year move to the German Front.

Four of their Spitfire Mk XIV-Es arrived over the battlefield, carefully shepherding another four Spitfires, Mark IXs, each with a 500lb bomb aboard.

The ground controller, until recently decidedly redundant, was trying hard to control the air battle and losing the struggle, as more assets arrived hand in hand with more cries for help from the defenders.

"Firenze Dieci, Firenze Dieci, Robin Six over."

Something in the man's voice made the radio operator answer his call as a priority.

It also drew the attention of the GC and Pappalardo.

His report was a blow to the defenders.

"Firenze Dieci, tanks and infantry in company strength on Route 111, heading east," the Robin commander paused as he checked his map and made his best guess, "Approximately one thousand yards east of Nötsch and advancing, Robin Six over."

Again, the lack of decent maps did not help the defenders.

The RAF officer scanned the paperwork he was struggling with and offered up the Mark IX's.

Pappalardo gave the operator an order and the harassed man keyed the mike.

"Robin Six, Robin Six, Firenze Dieci. Can you identify force on Route 111 as enemy, over."

The silence suggested that the harassed Sherman commander was attempting to do just that.

"Firenze Dieci, Robin Six, negative at this time... but they're not being fired on from Nötsch and have just been overflown by enemy aircraft... without being attacked, over."

That could mean only one thing to Pappalardo so he gave the order, even then advising caution and proper identification.

The RAF controller vectored the Spitfires in on the reported position, using the main map for accuracy and passing on the need for proper recognition of any target before attacking.

The Folgore Commander switched his attention to the battle growing on the Dog line.

---

The flight leader recognised the type instantly, as did the rest of his pilots.

"Skipper, Blue Two, ain't they ours?"

Flight-Lieutenant Pearce had a brother-in-law in the British Guards, and he had heard of the letter that the badly wounded man had written home.

"Blue Two from lead. Lend-lease... the Red's have a bundle of them that they used at the start of this shite. Don't be fooled, Doc."

None the less, Pearce strained for the best possible view, but was interrupted by a call from the cover section.

"Blue leader, enemy fighters, ten plus, three o'clock high, break left under us... break ...break."

Blue section's pilots were all experienced men and the four Mark IX's reacted like the thoroughbreds they were.

The cover section drove in hard, knocking two LAGG's from the sky in one frenzied burst of activity.

However, there were more.

"Red Leader from Blue, attacking now."

The Red commander's acknowledgement was brief, his own problems paramount, as three LAGGs singled him out.

"Blue section, line astern, follow me."

Pearce took them away from the battle, slowly turning so that he could in over Nötsch and see what was happening there.

Even under pressure, it was obviously full of Soviet soldiers and hardware, a fact reinforced by the numerous tracers that rose from the burning town.

*'That settles that.'*

"Blue section attacking... armour to front... maintain intervals... acknowledge."

Each pilot in turn reported in, making the adjustments to ensure that they were far enough behind the aircraft in front to avoid the blast of its bomb.

Red section, now ahead of them, lost an aircraft and the screams of the pilot as he nosedived into the ground unsettled everyone, even those who flicked the radio switch before the end.

Pearce selected the lead tank and drove in hard, releasing his bomb when it was impossible to miss.

*'I don't see any plods.'*

The thought was of little import as all of Pearce's resources were concentrated on flying.

Blue Two took the second, Blue Three attacked the fourth, leaving Blue Four to take the rearmost vehicle, and only he failed to destroy his target, the five hundred pounder stubbornly refusing to release.

The Mark IX's now became fighters, although Blue Four was greatly hindered by the unwanted load.

Blue section rose up into the melee just as a flight of US Mustangs attacked from above, ending the dogfight almost instantly, the combination of the growing evening, lack of fuel, and mounting losses forcing the Red fighters off the battlefield.

### 1635 hrs, Thursday, 28th November 1945, Route 111, one mile southeast of Nötsch, Austria.

Pearce's brother-in-law had seen combat on the first day of the new hostilities, a day when the Red Army employed many of its lend-lease vehicles to fool the defenders.

Whilst his Guards unit had dealt harshly with the Soviet-manned Churchill IV's, the effect of the subterfuge was considerable, and the now dead Guards officer had written of it in his letters home.

142nd RAC was equipped with Churchill VIIs, although the difference, at the height and speed that Blue

174

section was travelling at, would not have been easily noticeable, least of all to a man with a reason to want to kill them.

A combination of circumstances brought about the attack.

In the first instance, the cowardly withdrawal of the tanks, leaving the Folgore behind to fight and die. The RAC Sergeant had withdrawn his tanks as soon as the first shells started to fall on Nötsch, with no thought for those he was supposed to support.

Secondly, the Robin's report of tanks and infantry on Route 111, heading east, although there were no 'plods', as Pearce put it.

Thirdly, there was no fire from Nötsch aimed at the moving armoured force, brought about by continued resistance from the Folgore infantry, a combination of low ammunition levels, and confusion between the tank unit commander and Kozlov.

Fourthly, the sudden arrival of a another Soviet fighter unit, which placed extra pressure on Pearce and his men.

Fate contrived to bring about the circumstances that meant that three of the five RAC tanks were destroyed; destroyed in the complete way that a direct hit from a 500 pound bomb achieves, without fail.

The remaining two tanks ran into a horrified 'Robin' troop, where they were halted and set to face the enemy in Nötsch.

Whilst the surviving RAC troopers were almost immobilised by shock, Sergeant Massala suffered from no such concerns over the tragic loss of his comrades. Openly, he set his face to the enemy. Inside, he set his mind to devising an escape.

---

Red section had lost two, including the leader. Blue left one burning lump of shattered metal and bone on the west bank of Gailitz, adjacent to the bridge that carried Route 111.

Six Soviet machines had fallen and others, some smoking, were still being pursued by the eager Mustangs.

As 402 Squadron returned to their base at Belluno, the unpalatable news of the friendly fire incident was received in Pappalardo's headquarters.

Buoyed by the recent arrival of some engineers, already set to work to destroy the Gail bridges, the news of the self-inflicted injury deflated the entire force.

There would be no recriminations against Pearce. Not that day; not any day.

Pilots, tired, stressed, returning from their third mission of the day, made an error of judgement on the approach to the Belluno airbase. Perhaps it was the bomb that gave the aircraft different characteristics on the approach.

Perhaps it was fatigue on both their parts.

Whatever the cause, the two thoroughbred aircraft started to occupy the same piece of Italian sky. Blue Four's propeller shredded the tail of Pearce's Spitfire, causing it to flip into a brief spin that offered no chance to escape the aircraft.

Blue Four performed a brief fiery cartwheel across the Italian fields, punctuated by the detonation of its bomb.

The two surviving pilots landed their planes, eyes heavy with silent tears.

Back on the Gail River, the situation was dire.

### 1735 hrs, Thursday, 28th November 1945, Defensive line Edward, one kilometre east of Arnoldstein, Austria.

Dog line had been overwhelmed, but Haines had withdrawn his force in good order and now occupied Edward, the last tenable position before Arnoldstein.

The Italians had taken heavy casualties on the heights but, or so it seemed anyway, had stopped the Soviet infantry's outflanking move in its tracks.

The aircraft of both sides had quit the battlefield, banished by the darkness that fell so swiftly.

Ambrose Force's dwindling supply of flares was being carefully husbanded, the defenders more reliant on the flashes of explosions for advance warning of any more enemy attacks.

Pappalardo finished up a brief radio exchange with Haines, during which both men agreed that the Russians would come again, and come soon.

Poring over the map, the Italian officer found himself faced with an unpalatable decision.

Sliding a cheroot into his ivory holder, he weighed the situation carefully.

His concentration was disturbed by a noisy exchange between two officers and then by one of them, his aide, striding purposefully to his side.

"Colonnello, the engineers are ready now."

The Major consulted his notepad and placed his finger on the relevant locations; the Route 111 bridge at Kraftoolstraβe, the Route 83 bridge at Kartnerstraβe, and the temporary structure at Greuth.

"One, two, three. The Primo Capitano asks for ten minutes to get back to his position. Then he can fire one and two on command, Colonnello. Three is a separate matter, for when we have all fallen back, of course."

Pappalardo nodded and drew his cheroot down heavily, filling his lungs with the comforting smoke, making the tip glowing red enough to add more illumination to the map.

"Anything from 2nd Battalion and Maggiore Lastanza?"

"Nothing, Sir, although the nearest troops report that a fight's still going in Nötsch."

"Keep trying to get through to them. Let me know immediately."

The Aide moved off to the radio, leaving Pappalardo to make a crucial decision.

*'Withdraw now?'*

With the arrival of the Soviet force at Nötsch, Route 111 was compromised, the defence was compromised, as 111 was one of the key requirements of the Arnoldstein defence.

The defences at Tarvisio were not yet ready but were, at least, partially occupied by fresh forces.

*'What good will we do here?'*

The sound of a renewed enemy artillery barrage broke the relative silence of the early evening.

*'If I pull back now and they attack at the same time?'*

If that happened and the Soviets caught his inferior force on the move, the result would be massacre.

It was a difficult decision.

One that Pappalardo was about to make until everything changed.

The staff Major interrupted his Colonel's thoughts.

"Colonnello, we've got through to Lastanza... he's falling back, still in heavy contact. Primo Capitano 'Aines reports enemy tanks and infantry attacking his position in regimental strength."

Pappalardo smiled a smile that held no humour.

He spoke, more to himself than the waiting officer.

"So, it is decided then."

"Colonnello?"

"Tell Lastanza to pull back, with all possible speed, over the bridge... here," he indicated the one wired for demolition at Kraftoolstraße, "Pull the rest of the covering force back over it now and," he confirmed the details his memory had summoned up, "Get them to form a barrier, facing west... on Route 27 here... to the other side of Hohenthurn."

The Major made the necessary note, understanding that his commander was concerned about a Soviet advance from Nötsch through Feistritz.

Pappalardo took a deep breath.

"Order Capitano Haines to hold and not, repeat, not disengage until the enemy's beaten back. Then he must withdraw immediately over the Kartnerstraße Bridge, which will then be blown."

*'Just in case.'*

"Maggiore, I'll write these orders up quickly. I intend to do a fighting withdrawal down Route 55 onto the Tarvisio position. Clear?"

The Aide saluted and left Pappalardo to his thoughts once more.

The enemy artillery was dropping in intensity, partially because of orders limiting speculative fire and partially because an Allied night fighter had called in an artillery strike that caught part of the 124th Guards Artillery Regiment redeploying.

He strode to the radio in time to hear Haines' acknowledgement.

"Are you done, Maggiore?"

"Yes, Sir, as you directed."

"Good. Now, prepare to relocate."

"Hold? Fucking hold?"

Haines felt like punching the radio.

"ON!"

"FIRE! We'll be fucking lucky to survive this shit!"

The Sherman rocked back as the 76mm removed another tank from the enemy's order of battle.

"Nellie, you're on your own at the mo, ok?"

"Roger that, boss."

The turret smoothly traversed as Oliphant went about his trade efficiently, no after effects of his head wound apparent.

Haines, his testicles reminding him of their ordeal with every little movement, stuck his head out of the turret to take in the battlefield.

The Edward line was alive with tracers and explosions. Whilst he could see little detail, the line seemed to be holding.

And then, it wasn't.

In the light of a big explosion, the Lancer officer spotted a large group of Soviet infantry pushing through on the left of his tank.

"Enemy infantry left, one-fifty yards. I'm on the fifty."

He spoke into the radio first, seeking out his small infantry reserve and calling them in to block the gap.

Two platoons of the Royal Inniskilling Fusiliers moved forward quickly.

Haines grabbed the large .50 calibre machine-gun mounted on his turret and rotated the cupola to his left, bringing the weapon to bear.

The M2 Browning was equipped with API ammo, with an APIT tracer every fifth round for targeting.

The heavy bullets started to chew away at the enemy soldiers, who went to ground as one. Not lacking in courage, a number of the infantrymen began to take shots back at the Sherman, and more than one twanged off the turret or hull side of 'Biffo's Bus'.

Although Haines had only hit six or seven men, he distracted the force sufficiently for the first Irish platoon to rush forward and engulf the Russians in a storm of hand grenades.

The Royal Inniskillings' second platoon moved around the fighting and sealed the breach in the lines, immediately pushing back a larger group of enemy intent on following their comrades through the hole.

The tank officer was impressed, having had lesser expectations of the exhausted Irishmen.

Haines ceased fire as the rampant Fusiliers mopped up the Soviet incursion.

He half considered intervening as flashes from exploding shells illuminated bayonets working on helpless wounded Russians.

A whoosh focussed his mind on other matters as an enemy solid shot missed the Sherman by a matter of feet.

Dropping back into the turret, Haines got reacquainted with his own vehicle's situation.

"ON!"

The breech recoiled and the gun spat another HVAP shell across the snow.

"Bugger it!"

The shell had missed by a country mile.

"Up!"

"ON!"

Again, the gun boomed.

"Hit!"

Haines looked and saw the aftermath of the strike.

"It's not dead, Nellie. I'm back now, ok?"

Clair put another one up the spout.

"Up!"

"ON!"

"FIRE!"

A miss.

"For fuck's sake, Nellie!"

Haines snatched a look at his gunner and noticed the yellow fluid seeping from Oliphant's left ear.

"Up!"

"ON!"

"FIRE!"

Almost at the same instant that the 76mm was fired, an 85mm shell arrived and thumped into the hull machine gun position.

---

Over in the positions now occupied by the Royal Inniskilling Fusilier's first platoon, the desperate plight of the Sherman was spotted, and two men ran to the stricken tank to help.

Patrick Walshe was first up on the rear deck of the smoking Sherman, where he was confronted with the head of an obviously unconscious man emerging from the hatch.

The loader's hatch opened and a blackened tanker slipped out and started to pull up on the insensible body as another pushed from below.

Walshe weighed in and the two men easily extracted the badly wounded Oliphant, so much so that Haines, the man beneath, overbalanced and fell onto the turret floor.

Shaking his head to clear his vision, the Lancer Captain took in the interior of the Sherman, the only illumination coming from something indescribable that was burning slowly in the machine gunner's position.

Stumpy Clair was still in the driver's seat, struggling to push himself out, his broken right leg and arm hindering his efforts.

Haines took one look at Sparkle and gagged, the burning corpse destroyed by the impact of the Soviet tank shell.

That it had not exploded had granted the rest of the crew another life.

"No time for ceremony, Stumpy. Here we go."

He grabbed the injured driver, ignoring the curses and screaming, repeating the exercise of holding the man up to the hatch.

Again, strong hands took hold of the tanker and he was pulled up and out of the turret.

Pausing only to grab the Thompson submachine gun from its position, Haines exited the Sherman and helped bring Stumpy down to ground behind the smoking M4.

The other Fusilier and Oliphant were stretched out side by side.

"They've both copped it, boss."

Killer's words cut him like a knife.

Nellie's ears were leaking blood as well as synovial fluid. His already fractured skull had taken another pounding when the tank was hit; fatally so.

Pulling himself together quickly, Haines watched as Walshe splinted Stumpy's leg, inflicting pain as he moved swiftly.

"How you doing, short stuff?"

Clair gritted his teeth as the young Irishman pulled tight on the bandaging.

"Ballet lessons are off, Boss."

That drew a weary smile.

"Well, I think walking's off for a while, Stumps."

Leaving Walshe to look after his driver, Haines raised himself up to get a look at the battlefield.

There was next to no firing now; what there was seemed most likely to be an Italian, Irish, or British soldier firing a final shot after some retreating Russian suddenly highlighted by an explosion or a muzzle burst.

"Bloody hell! We've only sodding held 'em again!"

Jubilation was quickly displaced by duty and Haines swung himself up onto the tank, leaning into the turret to make an assessment.

"Killer, grab an extinguisher and put this fire out. It's going nowhere."

There were things left unsaid in that order.

Fiddling with the radio, Haines got through to the headquarters first try.

"Firenze Dieci from Cassino Six, enemy attack halted. They have withdrawn. Your orders, over."

Pappalardo did not hestitate.

"Move now, Cassino Six, move now. I will alert yje artillery," he accompanied the words with a finger pointed straight at the Artillery Liaison officer, already briefed as to the task for his guns, "Get your command over the bridge and reform your line, over."

The Sexton artillery crews, almost out on their feet, redoubled their efforts and put down an accurate and constant barrage, turning the No Man's land in front of 'Edward' into an area in which life could not thrive.

Haines completed sending his orders to the force clinging to 'Edward', and then paid attention to his own survival.

It was Stumpy who pointed out that the tank had only stalled and was probably mechanically sound.

The possibility could not be ignored, although either Haines or Killer would have to point the Sherman.

Biffo slid into the driver's seat, patently ignoring the awfulness to his right, still smoking, although no longer lazily burning.

The 'Bus' started first time and he slid the reverse gear in, slowly dropping the tank back into a depression.

He then exchanged places with Killer, leaving the loader to do the best with the controls whilst he and Walshe manned the turret.

Stumpy was tied in place on the engine grilles and anaesthetised with copious amounts of Korn.

Haines quickly showed the Irish infantryman how to poke a shell into the gun, all the time hoping it would not be necessary. In any case, one of their last remaining HVAP shells lay sealed in the breech.

'Biffo's Bus' was the last Allied vehicle to quit the 'Edward' defensive line.

### 1833 hrs, Thursday, 28th November 1945, Route 83, west of Arnoldstein, Austria.

The withdrawal of Haines' defence force had been completed swiftly and without drama, save some spectacular strike by the Sextons, the huge fireball illuminating the white countryside for kilometres in all directions.

For the former defenders of Nötsch, things were different.

Again, Massala and his surviving men had quit their positions, reversing away, leaving behind the 2nd Battalion of Folgore and the remnants of 'Robin' to stem the flow from the west.

By the time that Lastanza had got his unit back to the bridge, the tanks of 'Robin' had been destroyed or overrun, the Archer SP's had been destroyed, and all he had to his name were a few mortar men and a comparative handful of his battalion.

Pappalardo had directed that Lastanza should wheel his force back westwards and block the approach from Nötsch.

Even had the savaged battalion been able to get there, they would have been swept aside by advancing Soviet units as Kozlov pushed his main force along the southern side of the river, in an attempt to catch the rear of the Allied position.

He succeeded.

Pappalardo, his headquarters now relocated to the junction of Pessendellach and Oberthörl, found his command group in the way of the Soviet advance.

The remnants of Lastanza's and Haines' forces pushed as hard as they could, anxious to make the Italian border.

The radio crackled, informing the survivors of Ambrose Force of the assault on the headquarters.

One company of Folgore's 3rd Battalion thrashed its vehicles to get there in time.

The surviving Challenger, damaged, yet still defiant, decided to follow on too.

The Sexton barrage was falling away for no other reason than the total exhaustion of the crews, but they persevered and, in their superhuman efforts, aided in the destruction of the survivors of Ambrose Force. The evening was illuminated by the HE bursts and Kozlov's force, more specifically, the Artillery Officer attached to the assault force, could easily see the surviving vehicles of the Lancers and their infantry support falling back.

The reduced Soviet artillery and mortar units brought a concentrated fire down, killing many men and knocking out much of the surviving equipment.

---

The Headquarters had been overrun before the Folgore relief company could arrive.

Pappalardo tried to ease his body slightly, but only succeeded in increasing the pain over his tolerance threshold.

One grenade had virtually taken his left arm off at the elbow, the bloodied limb occasionally tweaked as the stump moved and the remaining sinew moved with it, much like a worm on a fishing line.

A piece of stone had been thrown up and that was proudly protruding from his chin, embedded in the flesh and bone.

The blast had thrown him some distance and he had landed on a typewriter with such force that it ruptured his liver and broke three ribs. He had bounced and come to rest in a perfect sitting position, propped by a stand of four ammo boxes.

Strangely, he had not lost consciousness, although he wished he had. He watched on as his men, both British and Italian, were all killed or wounded around him.

His aide, the Major, took a bullet in the throat and dropped to the earth clutching the fatal wound. He was dispatched with a savage kick to the same area by a Soviet soldier young enough to be the Major's son.

The British Artillery officer was hammered to the ground and beaten mercilessly. Pappalardo could only watch the man suffer as his face and upper body swelled up and blood leaked from a dozen wounds.

One of the blows had exposed part of the man's brain, obviously causing serious damage.

For the few minutes the Englishman clung to life, his cries that of an infant scared by a shadow and needing his mother.

Pappalardo wished him quickly dead.

One of the headquarters NCO's, a corporal, had obviously killed at least one of the attackers and he was given special treatment, a sharpened spade ending his life, its recovery from his skull taking the strength of two men and causing more ignominy to the corpse.

The last British Challenger had success, its 17pdr gun knocked out two T34's in short order.

The Soviet infantry swept over it quickly. Two grenades down the open hatch were followed by a full magazine from a PPSh, filling the interior with a host of angry insects, many of which found homes in already dead flesh.

The relief company, caught on the move, suffered badly at first, but found a position to defend and screamed for help. Artillery would have helped but the sole link with the Sextons was mewling his last seconds away, his radio equipment shattered, along with his skull.

185

Fig#86 – Death from the West, Gail River Valley, 28th November 1945.

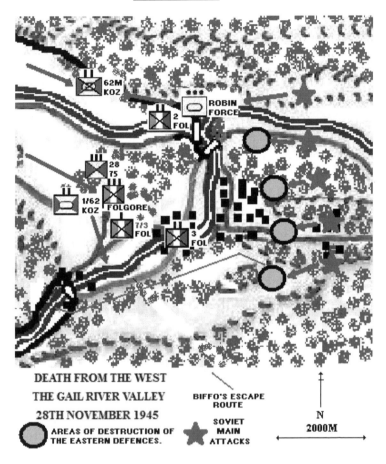

**DEATH FROM THE WEST**

**THE GAIL RIVER VALLEY**

**28TH NOVEMBER 1945**

AREAS OF DESTRUCTION OF THE EASTERN DEFENCES.

BIFFO'S ESCAPE ROUTE

SOVIET MAIN ATTACKS

N

2000M

Arnoldstein was lost and its defenders desperately scrabbled for the safety offered by the Italian border.

Kozlov again switched the focus of his assault, directing a tank company of the 62nd, with squads of his own infantry hanging on for dear life, down a side route with orders to reach the river.

To the north, the Soviet main force, hampered by a lack of bridging equipment, had halted at the river. Encouraged by their seniors, units resorted to swimming across the river, leaving heavy weapons and much of their kit behind them.

It was a gamble, but it paid off, as the Red Army soldiers maintained the pressure on the retreating units.

They herded Ambrose force, driving them onto the waiting tanks of the 62nd Tank Brigade and soldiers of the 28th Rifle Regiment.

A single Churchill VII rattled southwards, intent on escape at all costs and without regard for its comrades.

A full-blown collision with a Folgore motorcyclist caused consternation amongst the struggling soldiers, the 741cc Bianchi disappearing under the offside track, along with the leg of the unfortunate rider.

However, the Churchill did not stop, rattling at its top speed down the Unterthörl on its way to safety.

Seven tank shells struck the vehicle within half a second of each other, those that hit the front were repulsed by 152mm of armour, those that targeted the side sliced through weaker metal to explode inside the tank.

The Sergeant in the cupola was expelled by the force of the internal explosion, his burning body describing some kind of perverse rainbow in the sky as it fell to ground next to the railway line.

Furious Italian infantrymen, until that moment chasing the tank, fell in a storm of bullets as the Soviet blocking force announced its presence.

Demoralised, Ambrose Force tried to gather itself for an attack, but the attempt to break through was half-hearted and surrender became more of the norm as hopelessness and a wish to survive replaced duty and the mirage of safety across the border.

Some die-hards made alternative decisions, often those who had already had experience of life in as a prisoner of war. Such displays of resistance were dealt with quickly and harshly as the Soviet infantry rushed forward to take prisoners and, of course, remove anything of value from their enemies.

---

Pappalardo was indignant.

Silently indignant, as he could do nothing, his wounds too severe and his strength long departed.

He used his eyes, as best he could, to transfer his contempt to the Soviet soldier who was ripping off his medals and rifling his pockets.

The Russian's eyes fell upon the fine leather holster and he knocked Pappalardo's protective arm aside to get at its contents.

Proudly brandishing a well-worn Beretta M1934, the infantryman was satisfied that he had taken all there was to take.

Pappalardo watched on in silence as his beloved Beretta disappeared into the man's bread bag, along with his other possessions.

He tried to move, to remonstrate, to prevent, but the act brought on excruciating pain, the like of which he had never known before and he finally dropped into merciful unconsciousness.

### 1959 hrs, Thursday, 28th November 1945, on the bank of the Gailitz River, 500 metres from the Italian border, Austria.

Not for the first time that day, Haines was livid.

'Biffo's bus' had been drawn up in a concealed position so that he could dismount and make a plan.

His binoculars betrayed the full extent of the tragedy of Ambrose Force. The white sub-light of the snow was aided by a modest moon, and both were bolstered by buildings and vehicles burning steadily.

What struck Haines most was the silence that had now descended, only broken by the occasional shot or explosion of a vehicle surrendering to the flames.

There was nothing he could do but look after himself and the few men that had gravitated towards one of the few running Allied tanks.

Whilst he was deciding on how to proceed, the Sherman made its own decision and broke down

A moment of throaty metal graunching was quickly followed by more terminal sounds as the engine seized, its life-giving oil eventually having leaked away unnoticed.

188

<u>Fig#87 - The end, Gail River Valley, 28th November 1945.</u>

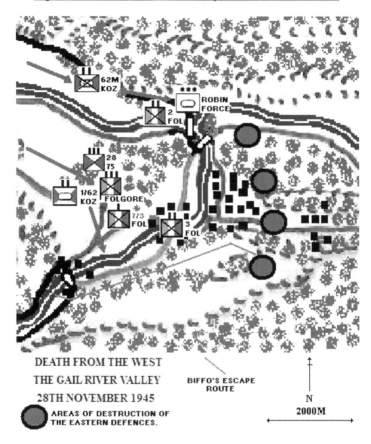

**DEATH FROM THE WEST**
**THE GAIL RIVER VALLEY**
**28TH NOVEMBER 1945**

⬤ **AREAS OF DESTRUCTION OF THE EASTERN DEFENCES.**

BIFFO'S ESCAPE ROUTE

↑ N

**2000M**
←——————————→

.

    Killer emerged from the driver's hatch and announced his verdict.

    "She's fucked, Biffo. Won't even turn over now. Engine's seized."

    "Great."

    Which, clearly, it wasn't.

    With some sadness, Haines cast his eye at the tank that had been their home and had seen them safely through half of the Italian campaign and the start of this latest abomination, but his eye was caught by an Italian soldier waving to his comrades.

He followed the man's gestures all the way to the riverbank.

*'A boat!'*

Haines took a moment, turning back to survey the ongoing surrender, weighing his alternatives and making a decision.

Sliding back down the slope, he gestured at the new-found hope.

Grabbing the young Lance Corporal's shoulder, he issued a quick instruction.

"Walshy, nip down to that boat and gimme the nod if it's watertight."

He spared a look around at the rest of his motley crew.

"Make sure the eyeties don't do a runner with it, ok?"

"Sir."

Something in the young soldier's eyes made Haines add a note of warning.

"Don't shoot any of them, ok? Just make sure they don't do a runner with the bugger."

"Sir."

Haines looked at the back of the departing Inniskilling and understood.

*'Boy to killer, courtesy of the bloody school of war.'*

He returned to the immediate needs of his men and a simple hand gesture brought the Italian Lieutenant to his side.

"If that boat's up to the job, we're all getting in it and heading up river... quietly and with no fuss. I need you to find things we can use as oars, anything that'll shift water, ok? Understand?"

The Italian officer did not bother to tell Haines that he had studied at Cambridge so understood him perfectly, he just acknowledged and got on with the job.

Killer sidled up to his commander and sought silent permission to light a cigarette.

"Makes you wonder, dun it boss."

Haines knew exactly what his loader was on about.

"The Eyeties've done well today. Some bloody hard fightin' men there, eh? Why didn't they do it up the blue, eh?"

"Beats me, Killer... but thank fuck they were up to it today... or we'd all be dead... and that's a fact."

His statement was accompanied by a smile as the young Irish Fusilier gave him the thumbs up from the river bank.

"Ok, Killer, we're leaving. Organise Stumpy and get him in the middle of the boat. I'm going to make sure the bus won't be of any use to the bastards."

Killer remonstrated immediately.

"Hang on boss. You can't do that. It'll bring the Reds down on us like a ton of bricks."

Haines slapped the loader's shoulder, part in annoyance that his man should think him that stupid.

"Give me some sodding credit, Killer! Now, get Stumpy away."

With the help of three of the Italians, Stumpy was carried gently to the boat, a fully intact and larger than it looked rowing boat.

Haines slipped inside the turret, having first placed a can of petrol on the top.

Opening the breech, he slipped the unfired HVAP round out and placed it on the floor, replacing it with an HE round that he only partially inserted into the weapon. He then added a few more HE rounds to the pile on the floor and slipped a pair of primed grenades into the pile.

Killer returned and stuck his head in through the turret hatch.

"We're ready to go boss. The Eyeties are very keen. You ready?"

"Soon. How we off for rowing stuff?"

"There's four oars and the infantry have scared up some planks."

"Take my Thompson, grab the shovel off the bus, and get that boat moving. I'll be quick as I can and I'll swim out to you... but what I'm doing probably won't buy us too much time."

"Ok, boss. Just hurry up."

Alone again, Haines paused to pay one last moment of respect to the remains of Sparkle before he exited the tank.

He dipped the ties he had salvaged in the petrol can, tying them together to make something long enough to hang inside to the floor and have enough left to tie to the MG pintel.

Fishing in his pocket, he extracted three Woodbines from his pack and pushed them together, making one long cigarette.

The contents of the fuel can were then added to the interior, although the Lancer was very careful not to disturb the lethal pile in the middle of the floor.

His final act was to slip one end of the 'cigarette' under the knotted section of the ties and light the other end.

The boat was already moving southwards, the men working up a sweat in the cold night, moving against the flow of the river.

Haines plunged into the icy water and his testicles immediately protested at the new indignation, albeit only for a moment, as the chilled water provided an anaesthetic effect for his aches and pains, and the cold in general provided the greater distraction for the exhausted officer.

---

The burning head of the super cigarette came close enough to the petrol soaked tie that the heat it brought to the process was sufficient to start combustion.

The tie burned, slowly for a moment but then, almost as if fanned into life, flared and made the journey to the end of the edge of the cupola in two seconds.

It did not need to go further.

The interior of the tank was rich with fuel vapours, actually too rich to burn, but the hatch area provided the perfect area for the vapours to ignite.

Orange flames danced eagerly, burning up the fuel greedily, dropping lower into the turret until the perfect point of air-fuel mix was present.

Half a kilometre away, Lieutenant Colonel Kozlov was on the radio, receiving the accolades offered freely by his army commander, Zhumachenko.

His immediate promotion to command of the 75th Rifle Division was announced, part of his mind controlled his mouth and delivered the expected thanks, the other part directed his thoughts to consider how much of the division was left to command.

He watched absent-mindedly, as the orange glow transformed the distant area in quite an entertaining fashion, flames shooting skywards as if confined by a cylinder fifty feet high.

Then it exploded.

Haines, dripping and shivering, watched as 'Biffo's Bus' came apart, unsure of which of the possible mechanisms had claimed her.

The flames died down almost as quickly as they started and the night was returned to relative darkness, a safe darkness that swallowed the boat and its seventeen souls headed south in search of safety.

### 1048 hrs, Saturday, 30th November 1945, Natzwiller-Struthof prison camp and hospital facility, the Vosges, Alsace.

Makarenko had made an excellent recovery, especially as he was in the hands of Stefka Kolybareva, her own hideous injuries healing well and permitting her to do light duties to help ease her mental anguish.

Two beds down from Makarenko lay Rispan, the valiant Major's injuries more severe than first thought.

Today was the General's first time out of bed, and he was revelling in the freedom that the stiff backed chair offered.

A number of men from the Zilant attack force had survived to be nurtured in the hospital facilities of the former concentration camp, now prison camp, to be passed into the detention area when medical science had put them back together.

Next to Makarenko was Egon Nakhimov, still recovering from his ordeal and one of the last of the survivors to surrender to the recorded announcements from Makarenko, pleading with his men to turn themselves in, and guaranteeing them fair treatment.

Only one man from Makarenko's last command remained out in the forests.

Thus far, Nikitin had not surrendered.

Intelligence officers had swept down upon the Soviet General, keen to extract as much information from him as possible, seeking him out at all hours and without the niceties of medical permission, most being unceremoniously ejected by the hospital staff, who feared for their patient's life.

Over time, they relented, permitting short sessions, which were sufficient for a picture of the Zilant operation to be completed, adding new detail to their own existing knowledge.

Makarenko's own views and attitudes initially made the margins of debriefing reports but, as they seemed to become stronger and more personal, interviewers started to record a tantalising possibility, one that was eventually discussed by men with higher responsibility.

De Walle, one of those who took control of the exploratory operation, selected his man very carefully.

The hospital ward, in fact, most of the camp, was bugged, and listeners had reported back that Makarenko had been fully apprised of the massacre of his wounded men, good treatment of the prisoners, and subsequent events.

Colonel Albrecht Haefali, temporarily transferred from his infantry command at De Walle's request, was greeted like a hero by both Rispan and Kolybareva, who introduced the Legion officer to Makarenko.

Although he could not understand a word of what the two said, Haefali knew he should be embarrassed.

Makarenko extended his hand.

"Thank you for the lives of my officers... and friends, Colonel. Thank you."

Releasing his grip and wearily dropping back into the chair, Makarenko accepted the drinking cup from Kolybareva's hand.

"So, how may I help you, Colonel Haefali? As a soldier, I have said all that I can say already."

Looking at the other wounded Russians and at the Doctor, Haefali gestured at the audience.

"You may say whatever you have to say in front of these soldiers. I trust them with my life, Colonel."

With a smile, the Legion officer nodded in understanding.

Haefali remembered what he had been told to say, briefed at length by Allied intelligence officers. Immediately, he rejected it all and went his own way.

"Sir, I believe that I am here because your officers would introduce me to you in a positive fashion and, with that, you might look upon what I have to say without some of the normal reservations."

Those wearing headsets in the nearby monitoring shed started voicing their anger, fearing the legionnaire had blown the mission at the first moment. De Walle cut them short immediately, despite his own similar concerns.

"Shut up and listen!"

The three men settled back down, two writing in shorthand, recording the conversation, one each in English and French.

"Very open of you, Colonel. Why do you tell me this?"

"General Makarenko, I'm doing this openly so that you can understand that I'm doing what I believe to be right, not at the bidding of some... shadow with no name."

He waited whilst Kolybareva offered up another cup of water.

"I have been given information to present to you and I will do so... but I will do so because I think you should know, not because of it being part of some grand intelligence trick."

"Colonel, please go on."

Three hundred metres away, in a warm monitoring hut, De Walle smiled.

*'Nicely done, Albrecht. Very nicely done.'*

Haefali was undoubtedly a man of honour, but he was an Allied officer first and foremost, so more than happy to use his situation for the cause.

De Walle's joy increased as the Legion Officer delivered the information received from the Soviet contact, covering the way that the Soviet leadership had misrepresented so much to sway the Military through to the damming suggestion that an informer's report on a less than complimentary exchange regarding the Soviet leader, between Makarenko and Erasov, had directly contributed to the massacre of Makarenko's men. Personal revenge against the paratrooper General, as well as hubris, played a part in the fool's errands that were the Zilant missions.

The suggestion that the accident to his friend might have been more by design than happenstance and that the liquidation of Colonel Erasov's entire family had taken place as Makarenko was in the air, returning from the funeral, brought noises of horror from all those present.

In the monitoring shed, a hand picked up a phone and a voice commanded an immediate connection.

"Sir...De Walle here... Yes, it went well, very well. We mustn't rush it, but I think we can consider the next phases likely and plan accordingly, Sir."

The grin was permanently stuck to the Deux officer's face.

"Thank you, Sir. Haefali was superb, of course," unashamedly pointing out that the man he had chosen had done the job, "And if this goes as we hope... well, we know what could happen."

Replacing the silent receiver, De Walle took his leave and went to meet up with Haefali in the old SS camp commander's house nearby.

*Alas, regardless of their doom, the little victims play! No sense have they of ills to come, nor care beyond today.*

*Thomas Gray*

# Chapter 110 - THE WARNINGS

### 0902 hrs, Sunday, 1st December 1945, Glenlara, Éire.

Twenty minutes beforehand, Submarine B-29 had dropped beneath the agitated surface of the Atlantic, ready to spend the daylight hours on the bottom, resting in silence.

She had arrived the previous night, her patrol cut short by a close encounter with the growing anti-submarine forces that the Allies were deploying.

Twenty-two hours after her rendezvous with the 'Golden Quest', a patrolling B24 Liberator spotted the schnorkel, and that began an intense hunt, with the B-29 as the prey.

Whilst relatively undamaged, the bashing that the vessel had taken whilst evading the depth charges and hedgehogs of the hounding anti-submarine group, over a period of nearly thirty-six hours, had reduced her crew to virtual wrecks, and nine men to actual ones.

Those nine were now being cared for in the small but reasonably well equipped facility in the Glenlara base, their broken bones set and wounds stitched. Those men that could be spared from the crew were recuperating in a barracks set aside for the sub crews, finding the sound of the growing wind unsettling but, once sleep came, nothing else mattered and they could enjoy the safety of their dreams.

Seamus Brown had overseen the extra security sweeps that were always mounted when a sub was due, or at the base, and was now involved in a much more pleasurable duty.

Normally, such a duty would be beneath him but, in this instance, he was making an exception.

The Soviet marine stepped back and rattled the keys in the lock, opened the door, and checked that it was safe for Brown to enter.

"Top of the morning to you, Comrade Nazarbayev. I hope the accommodation's up to standard for you."

For the next few minutes, the Marine sentry heard sounds from within, sounds that he easily imagined were fists on flesh. As his former commander was firmly bound, he understood that the beating was a one-way affair.

---

Whilst Brown was taking further revenge on Nazarbayev, Dudko was doing the rounds of the sickbay, ensuring that the new arrivals were comfortable as well as checking on their Soviet resolve, or at least the resolve of those who were conscious.

One of the latter was suffering from concussion, the inevitable result of a high-speed impact between a watertight door and the human head.

Snoring loudly, the sleeping man drew Dudko's attention.

Casting his eyes over the bruised face, one eye obscured by the bandage that held dressings in place on two nasty wounds, he was suddenly drawn to a modest tattoo on the man's upper right arm.

Alarm bells started ringing in his head, bells that made him fumble with his holster and produce his Nagant pistol.

He pointed it at the casualty's head.

A quiet descended on the hospital, as the recognition of danger spread from man to man like a forest fire.

Dudko shook the man's shoulder gently.

"Hey, Yank. How ya feeling now, pal?"

He shook the shoulder again, harder this time and repeated his question.

The figure started to wake up.

"Hey, Yank. How ya feeling pal?"

"Don't shout for fuck's sake. I hear you."

Sveinsvold opened his eyes and looked straight into the muzzle of a large pistol, held approximately two foot from his face.

Evidently, the Swede's look encouraged an explanation from Dudko and he tapped the tattoo.

"S.Q.P.A.C. 1837."

Sveinsvold said nothing, but the Political Officer explained aloud for the benefit of the onlookers.

"Si quaeris peninsulam amoenam circumspice. It's a Latin inscription. It means 'if you seek a pleasant peninsula, look about you'... and it's the motto of the American state of Michigan."

He leant closer to Sveinsvold, giving him the full benefit of the end of the announcement, "And has no place on the arm of a Soviet submariner."

Dudko summoned a guard and, in spite of the protestations of the Irish and Soviet doctors, the barely conscious Sveinsvold joined Nazarbayev in the simple jail.

### 0100 hrs, Monday, 2nd December 1945, Headquarters of SHAEF, Trianon Place Hotel, Versailles, France.

Bedell-Smith and Bradley were poring over some of the finer details with Von Vietinghoff, a tableau of normality set against a backdrop of excitement and worry, as the Allied Armies prepared to take their first steps on the long road back to Poland.

Eisenhower crushed the pack as he extracted and lit the last cigarette, all of his nervousness directed at the packet, and he used all his strength to extinguish its existence, squeezing as if it were the very neck of his opposite number.

He had just finished a phone call with General De Lattre de Tassigny and was buoyed by the confidence that the dapper Frenchman exuded.

George Patton strode in, similarly confident, although his part in the grand scheme did not commence for many hours yet.

### 0103 hrs, Monday, 2nd December 1945, GRU Commander's office, Western Europe Headquarters, the Mühlberg, Germany.

Whilst, unknown to the newly crowned head of GRU Europe, her son languished in an IRA jail, Nazarbayeva was woken from her slumber by an extremely agitated Poboshkin.

"Comrade General!"

199

"What... what?"

She snapped into what represented consciousness at the second attempt.

"Comrade General, apologies, but you must see this report immediately."

He continued to knock until the bleary-eyed woman opened the door. Her crumpled officer's shirt and skirt betraying the fact that she had simply taken off her uniform jacket and dropped onto the office cot bed to sleep.

"Come in."

"Apologies, Comrade General, but this won't wait."

Tatiana poured a glass of water and cast an eye at the piece of paper in question.

"Where does this come from, Comrade?"

"From Amethyst."

"Refresh my mind please, Comrade Poboshkin."

In truth, Tatiana was certain she knew who Amethyst was, but needed a little extra time to gather her wits.

"We tried to get Amethyst planted in the German forces. It would appear that we've succeeded, Comrade General."

He held out the message, a simple but worrying warning that had travelled through a number of agents before being transmitted by a Colonel Lowe at Baden-Baden, an error that the Deuxieme Bureau, who were supposed to be watching his activities closely, would repent at leisure.

Bad news has a habit of focussing the mind and Nazarbayeva was suddenly very much alert.

"0300hrs? This morning? And we've just got this now? Mudaks!"

Nazarbayeva re-read the message to make sure that she fully understood its contents.

*'Blyad!'*

The decisions started to flow.

"Get me Marshal Konev on the phone right now, and then wake up the staff. Move."

Poboshkin moved.

She slammed the door and struggled into more presentable attire, emerging to take the receiver held out by Poboshkin.

The words tumbled out, her speed of delivery driven solely by the lack of time left for the Red Army to respond.

"Comrade Marshal, my apologies for waking you but there's a serious matter that has just been discovered and it can't wait."

She picked up the message and quoted it word for word.

Poboshkin could hear Konev's reply as if he were stood in the room with him.

"What? You tell me this now, Comrade General? Now? This is a fucking shitty joke. We've no reports of activity... no indications that the swine are even in that area, and yet you want me to alert the whole fucking 3rd just on a single report?"

Konev had been present in Stalin's office when the Dictator and Beria discussed the questions of Nazarbayeva's loyalty and he had been short in his dealings with the upstart woman ever since.

Nazarbayeva took a deep breath.

"Comrade Marshal Konev. This news has come to us late. But we must believe it and act upon it or..."

"Don't you dare... don't you dare fucking tell me what the Army must do! There are no indicators for this. None at all! Comrade Beria assured me that any assault would come further north, where we've identified many of their prime formations."

Nazarbayeva pushed harder.

"Comrade Marshal, this attack is centred around a prime formation, one that's already hurt 3rd Red Banner deeply. The Allies may well be intent on an attack further north but, for now, they're coming further south and Marshal Yeremenko needs to be warned."

Konev was caught between this new, but unsubstantiated information, and Beria's glib assurances that the enemy would strike to relieve the pressure on the Ruhr later in the month.

There was also the matter of his view of the woman giving him this latest intelligence.

Beria's assurances won the day.

"I'll speak with Marshall Rokossovsky as soon as is practicable."

Nazarbayeva found herself holding a phone that gently buzzed, as the commander of the Red Banner Forces of Soviet Europe abruptly ended the conversation.

Whilst she had been talking, a number of her staff had filtered in, ready for whatever she needed of them, some even dressed for it.

"Get me Marshall Rokossovsky."

---

Marshal Rokossovsky was indisposed, but she spoke with the competent Lieutenant General Petrovich, the deputy commander of the 3rd Red Banner.

Kuzma Petrovich had none of Konev's reservations about Nazarbayeva's credentials and started sending the necessary warnings and moving key units, such as artillery, whose positions were likely to have been noted and the first to receive any Allied bombardment.

Marshal Rokossovsky arrived, endorsed Petrovich's moves and suggestions, and continued the good work, as well as making a bold decision to redeploy some forces into their second positions prior to the attack, relinquishing those further forward in exchange for reduced casualties.

Whilst the 3rd Red Banner Central European Front was coming to full readiness, Nazarbayeva had taken the plunge, hanging her career, and possibly more, on another phone call.

"Comrade Nazarbayeva. Do you frontline soldiers never sleep?"

"My apologies, Comrade General Secretary."

The call lasted two minutes, which was also close to the time that Stalin spent on the telephone with Konev immediately after finishing his call with the GRU general.

Finally, the bald commander of the Red Army in Europe relented and called Rokossovsky with the warning.

The wily Polish Marshal gave no hint that his forces were already on the alert, content to claim the glory should the intelligence prove true and, if not, he now had Konev's orders to fall back on.

## 0153 hrs, Monday, 2nd December 1945, Headquarters of SHAEF, Trianon Place Hotel, Versailles, France.

Major Foster approached clutching some new paperwork, presenting it for her commander's attention and signature.

"Nervous, Anne Marie?"

"Yessir."

Eisenhower grunted.

"Well, so you should be. This isn't going to be a walk in the park; just the first step on a long trail to victory."

He stopped short, realising he had just quoted from a speech he was working on.

"Sorry. I didn't mean to lecture. But..."

His voice tailed off.

Tedder's aide was moving quickly through the throng of officers, one man in a sea of men, but one that stood out as having purpose in his movements and, to Ike's eye, a purpose that was not going to bring positive news to his attention.

For once, Eisenhower's memory failed him and he could not recall the man's name.

"Squadron-Leader. You look like a man on a mission."

"Sir, Marshal Tedder thinks you should see this immediately."

Eisenhower read the report and the colour drained from his face.

"Walt... Brad... George... gentlemen."

He held up the report, almost as a lure, bringing his senior advisors into a huddle.

"Arthur sends us news that his night assets have detected large scale movements by Soviet units in the area of our diversionary attack." The report made its way to Bradley, then Bedell-Smith, doing the rounds as each man used the time to arrange his thoughts.

"Ok, Gentlemen. This would seem to indicate that the enemy knows we're going to attack. They may not know the timings, of course, but this is not regular activity as I see it."

203

He turned to the RAF officer who shook his head in support of Ike's belief.

"So, do we halt the attack? Do we let it go on in? Do we have any other alternatives?"

Both Patton and Bradley went to speak and, unusually for George Patton, he permitted Bradley to continue without interruption.

"Sir, this is a diversionary attack. Its success is based around providing a diversion and drawing some of the enemy's assets down."

Ike consulted the report again and continued, quoting directly.

"Evidence of redeployment by many Soviet units in the area of Rainbow Black's deployment and beyond. Movement considered likely repositioning of forces to alternate positions."

He tapped the paper with the back of his fingers.

"Here...this bit. Sizeable forces seem to be moving south from the Cologne area. The hounds are going to fall upon them."

He gently placed the paper on the small table and took up a new cigarette.

Patton took his chance.

"Ike, we gotta let 'em go on in. As Brad says, it's a diversion, and it seems it sure as hell got the bastards' attention already."

His finger poked the report.

"They're shifting their assets in case we take them out with pre-planned barrages. Hell, we might even get some hard intel from the air boys as to where they've relocated. Either how, we gotta let 'em go, Ike."

It made sense, although there was not a man there that didn't understand that the price had just gone up and that many more would die.

His mind made up, Eisenhower called the Comms Officer.

"Get me General Devers on the phone, then General De Lattre please."

Von Vietinghoff clicked his heels, coming to the attention.

"Herr General, if you please. May I speak with the ground commander myself?"

Not a man there failed to understand why that request had been made.

"Certainly, General. And please give them my best wishes and my sincere apologies that I cannot relieve them of this onerous duty."

Von Vietinghoff saluted and went to place his own call as Eisenhower took the phone's handset and started to brief General Devers as to what his command was about to walk into.

### 0217 hrs, Monday, 2nd December 1945, Forward headquarters, Assault units for Operation Rainbow Black, Pfalzburg, France.

The main headquarters was safely placed out of harm's way at Sarrebourg, but those who would directly control affairs were somewhat closer to the action, five kilometres behind the jump off point, north of Saverne.

In the town hall of Pfalzburg, or Phalsbourg, depending on which nation had prepared the map that day, a number of officers were gathered, taking and issuing final orders.

When the phone had rung, it had not seemed out of the ordinary, submersed in a sea of such phone calls and the general hubbub of a military headquarters preparing for combat. Its content had announced itself as important by the look of thunder that it brought to the face of the Legion General. As he listened to the words of a German General, many miles away in Versailles, a quiet descended on the room, as more and more noticed the genuine pain that spread across Lavalle's face.

"I see. Thank you for letting us know, Herr General."

The silence was complete as Lavalle finished the call.

"Yes, I'll give them your best wishes. Thank you, Herr General."

A number of minds were already working overtime, piecing together the little information they had.

*'A German General... is ringing us direct... best wishes.'*

Lavalle had the floor.

"That was General Von Vietinghoff, ringing from SHAEF main headquarters."

Ernst-August Knocke pre-empted the moment with a few simple words.

"They know we're coming, don't they?"

Eyes that had sprung to the black clad Legion Officer slowly returned to their commander, Lavalle, who could only agree.

"Yes, they know."

St. Clair, who had been about to leave for his forward post, asked the question foremost in the thoughts of all.

"And they still want us to go, Mon General?"

"Our orders stand."

"Scheisse verdamnt!"

"Agreed, Derbo. Now, legionnaires, let's use the time left to do what we can."

In truth, that was very little, except to let their men know that the enemy was not going to be asleep, but wide-awake and ready for their attack.

---

Lavalle took Molyneux's phone call, only half-listening to the man's exhortations and revellings in the glorious opportunities presented by war.

He excused himself and cut the call short, terminating Molyneux in mid-rant about the value of the bayonet.

Knocke looked at him enquiringly.

"I believe our leader feels we should bayonet charge them and put them to flight before marching on Berlin."

The smile was genuine, as was the calm that the legend exuded.

There was no one else in earshot, so Knocke spoke as they normally did in private.

"To be frank, Christophe, I'm glad that Plummer is there to keep a rein on the man. It saves me disobeying orders. Anyway..."

206

As he spoke, he sketched a new fire plan on the spare map he had just unfolded.

Lavalle examined it and could only agree.

"That would fit in with the projections you made on secondary positions. Shame we can't get anything more from headquarters, but I see no sense in wasting our ammo on empty trenches. We'll go with that, Ernst."

Knocke made to move away but Lavalle intercepted him, taking hold of the map.

"I'll speak to the Arty. You get yourself to your HQ now. Look after yourself, Ernst. Good luck."

"And good luck to you, my friend."

They shook hands as friends and saluted as comrades in arms before Knocke left the building.

As the jeep bounced down the road, Ernst Knocke found himself thinking about the trials ahead and his normal confidence surfaced.

Confidence in the abilities of his men was a given.

Confidence in the abilities of Legion officers like Lavalle and St.Clair had been well earned.

Confidence in the abilities of those who stood in overall command...

'Scheisse!'

### 0240 hrs, Monday, 2nd December 1945, Headquarters of 3rd Red Banner Central European Front, Hotel Stephanie, Baden-Baden, Germany.

Rokossovsky and Trubnikov walked outside and took in the chilled air.

The senior man drew in a bracing lungful and surveyed his surroundings.

"No more snow arriving, tovarich. What's here won't melt but, if we're to believe the cloud readers, it won't snow for another two days at least."

The Marshal breathed more deeply, as if sampling the air would supply him with insight on the matter.

"Are you sure you don't want pre-emptive artillery, Comrade Marshal."

Rokossovsky shook his head.

"I don't think so, tovarich. Let them settle in where they are now. There will be plenty of time for them to get rid of their ammunition when the enemy starts up."

The ammunition issue was a constant thorn in their side now.

"Besides, it might pay us to let the enemy think they have us on the hop, eh?"

Trubnikov wasn't sure about that, but his boss was, so that was good enough for him.

Rokossovsky took in the night sky, clear and crisp, the stars giving a remarkable display.

"Air thinks we'll have good numbers up over the battlefield at first light. If they come."

Trubnikov nodded and fished in his tunic pocket, producing an ornate crystal and silver flask.

Flicking the top, he offered it to Rokossovsky who took a deep draught and handed it back before the effects hit him.

He coughed his way through the traditional toast.

"Na zd...zdoro...vie."

"Na zdorovie!"

The Deputy Front Commander acknowledged the toast with a raised flask and took his own deep pull on the contents.

Trubnikov's throat expressed its own objections immediately.

Rokossovsky raised an eyebrow.

"Savage stuff, Comrade Trubnikov. What exactly is it that's burning my insides out?"

After another cough, a reply was forthcoming.

"Apparently, Starshina Fillitov has access to an unlimited supply of it, which was supposedly liberated from an enemy headquarters store. He said it's Napoleon brandy, but my vote goes for turpentine."

The two shared a laugh, despite the tensions of the hour.

"Another, Comrade Marshall?"

"I think not, tovarich. We'll need a clear head if General Nazarbayeva is to be believed."

It was 0258 hrs.

# Fig#88 - La Legion Corps D'Assault, Spectrum-Black, 2nd December 1945.

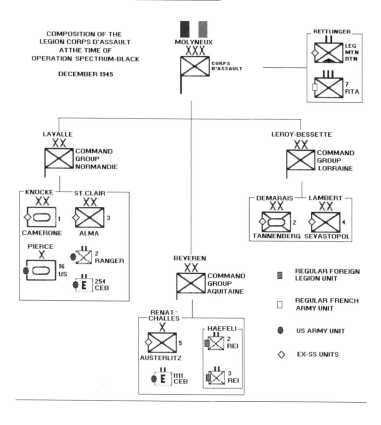

*I knew that, if the feat was accomplished, it must be at a most fearful sacrifice of as brave and gallant soldiers as ever engaged in battle.*

*General John Bell Hood CSA*

# Chapter 111 - THE WARCRIMES

## 0310 hrs, Monday, 2nd December 1945, Assault force, Monswiller, Alsace.

The Legion artillery, plus that of the 16th US Armored Brigade, as well as numerous extra batteries attached for the operation, opened fire at 0300hrs precisely, lashing the designated enemy positions with high explosives and deadly pieces of metal moving at high speed.

Some batteries continued to fire upon the old locations, the change of orders not having arrived in time.

Others, better informed, dropped their ordnance amongst the occupied positions of the suspected second line, or those areas where artillery and support units might have displaced to.

Generally, the warning to Rokossovsky's units had been successful, and few men were killed in the torrent of shells.

Soviet artillery and mortars opened up in reply, shooting blind, but knowing that the enemy had to come certain ways.

The Soviet fire had some success, but the Allied radar troops were in position, and the counter-battery units, silent until fed the right ingredients, served up death to many of the Red Army artillery and mortar crews.

At 0310 hrs, the order was given, sometimes in German, sometimes in French, occasionally in English.

"Vorwärts!"

"En avant!"

"Advance!"

DerBo's Gebirgsjager Battalion immediately pushed forward on Routes 133 and 178, their mission being the occupation of Dossenheim-sur-Zinsel, Neuwiller-lès-Saverne, and La Petite Pierre, for the purpose of securing the northern flank of the attack.

If all went to plan, the Mountain troopers would hardly be involved.

Part of Pierce's 16th was in direct support, with the rest of the 16th a few kilometres to the south, tasked with gaining ground as far as Pfaffenhoffen in the first instance, and also to act as a secure northern buffer to cover the main Legion thrust that intended to go to, and through, Hagenau.

The plan was also to threaten the isolation of Strasbourg, an area that had drawn large Soviet reinforcements since Operation Thermopylae had virtually annihilated the Soviet 19th Army. That the remnants of that army, hastily assembled into a Special Combat Brigade, had been slotted into the line on the focal point of the Legion assault was considered a wonderful bonus, for they would remember the Legionnaires, and that would be to the Allies' advantage.

In addition, the Legion Corps was tasked with threatening Karlsruhe, something that the Allied leadership felt would not be ignored by Soviet command.

Some large Red Army formations lay to the north, formations that SHAEF planners wanted to see moved away before Spectrum Blue was initiated.

Eisenhower had already discussed the possibility of delaying Patton's attack for twenty-four, perhaps even forty-eight hours, agreeing that the decision did not yet need to be made. He decided against consulting Patton on the matter, knowing only too well what the man would say.

### 0403 hrs, Monday, 2nd December 1945, Mobile Command Group, 16th US Armored Brigade, two kilometres south-west of Hattmatt, Alsace.

Brigadier-General John L. Pierce was unhappy, and he let his staff know it.

The prongs of his advance had made quick progress, the 16th pushing ahead on a frontage of just under four kilometres.

It was not wasted on him, nor on those who received the same reports, that positions expected to be manned seemed

211

to have been hurriedly vacated, with only a few hastily laid booby-traps left behind by their former owners.

Fig#89 - Operation Spectrum Black, Alsace, 2nd December 1945.

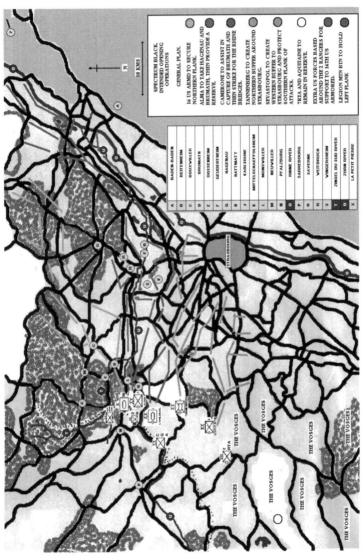

The main southern push had moved over the small watercourse, La Zinsel du Sud, making the junction of Routes 716 and 116 on schedule.

Moreover, at very little cost.

Pierce was not to know that his southern prong should have met resistance on the small river, but an error on the part of one Soviet Colonel, withdrawing past his allotted stop line, meant that the way was left clear.

Not so for the northern force, where the lead infantry and recon elements ran straight into a determined enemy with a lot of firepower. It had stalled at the La Zinsel, but this time the same frozen dribble of water had cost him a whole bunch of his doughs, as well as the 18th's Armored-Infantry's battalion commander.

Pierce's vehicle, an M9A1 half-track stuffed with the paraphernalia of command, was pulled over under snow-laden trees. The breeze was strong enough to stir the branches and occasionally dislodge a white deposit to fall on the cameo below like a one-sided snowball fight.

The 16th's senior officer had his normal set-up erected; a trestle table surrounded by a canvas screen, with a camouflaged sheet roof strung from the half-track to a pair of poles, all of which provided sufficient shelter and area for him and two others to work.

Consulting the situation map, a solution presented itself immediately.

"Here's what we do. 18th will keep up the pressure, but keep it low key. No hero stuff. We shift one of their companies north and cross here... at the end of this track. It's frozen good enough for foot infantry to cross. They can pick up their tracks later."

His CoS was furiously making notations.

"They then turn south and come into the top end of the defences."

Pierce checked his map in the half-light.

"The Rangers can send a company, no, two companies to the south. In fact, send the whole unit. Tell Lieutenant Colonel Williams to cross the Zinsel eight hundred metres to the south of Hattmatt and form a block oriented to the east and south-east. He's then to strike northwards, in support of a further infantry attack by the 18th. Tie in with

Hetherington on timing, but the pair of them must get this sorted a-sap. Clear, Edwin?"

Colonel Greiner understood the orders and moved into the halftrack to get the signallers ready, once he had formulated the orders in a proper military fashion.

Pierce moved on to other matters, knowing that his boys would get the job done.

---

Williams, the Ranger's commander, unfolded his map and beckoned his officers in closer.

"And that's that, boys. Leave Charlie at point, but push Dog and Easy in close behind."

The responsible officers nodded their understanding.

"Move and move fast. Get over the water straight away and give me breathing space, say... all the way up to Route 116 here."

He indicated the most junior man present, now in charge of Fox Company whilst the normal commanding Captain was treated for a dislocated knee.

"Gesualdo's Fox boys will move straight over and push north to this road here, securing me a start line."

The map rustled as Williams repositioned it.

"You two, you got the lead here, Barney, will push Able and Baker through Fox, and drive hard into the flank here."

Barney Meade, no-one but no-one called him Barnett, acknowledged without a word, his gruff, silent approach to matters hiding the dynamic go-getting combat officer that he was.

He shared a look with the commander of Baker Company and nodded.

Williams continued.

"Timings and comms have gotta be tight here. Watch for the 18th's boys coming in from the west, as well as some more driving down from the north. I want no foul-ups. Clear?"

It most certainly was.

"General Pierce wants this done quick, so he can pass his armor on and get at Bouxwiller before the schedule goes to pot."

214

He folded the map with an air of finality.

"It sure as shit ain't gonna be us that lets him down, so get your boys moving... watch yourselves... hit 'em hard... and let's get it done. Any questions?"

There were four.

Two confirmations of orders, one regarding call signs, and another on what would happen next. All were swiftly dealt with and the leadership of the 2nd Ranger Battalion went on their way.

### 0515 hrs, Monday, 2nd December 1945, Hattmatt, Alsace.

Major Din was suffering.

His both ears were bleeding, Shockwaves from impacts adjacent to his command position had caused damage to the delicate organs. US 155mm guns had swept his location, a mixture of ground and air burst causing severe casualties amongst the 424th's survivors, old soldiers that he had managed to extricate from the debacle that had spelt the end of the 19th Army in Alsace.

The Soviet forward command position was in what was left of a modest wood, just west of the Rue des Acacias, north of Hattmatt.

Din had instinctively moved out of his better-appointed headquarters, partially to get closer to the action for better control, and partially in case the enemy had done their reconnaissance properly.

His instinct proved correct, as the command point was destroyed by artillery in the first strikes.

424th Regiment had represented the largest surviving formation in 132nd Rifle Corps, and the Corps was quickly disbanded and its bits and pieces used to bolster other savaged units.

For want of anywhere better to put it, the 424th was taken under the mantle of the Special Combat Brigade, but then quickly attached directly to the 3rd Guards Cavalry Corps, another unit that had suffered badly in the preceding weeks.

The weight of Spectrum Black fell upon units 'resting' in a supposedly quieter zone of the front line, and Din's men found themselves the focus of attention in and around Hattmatt.

Fig#90 - The assault on Hattmatt, 2nd December 1945.

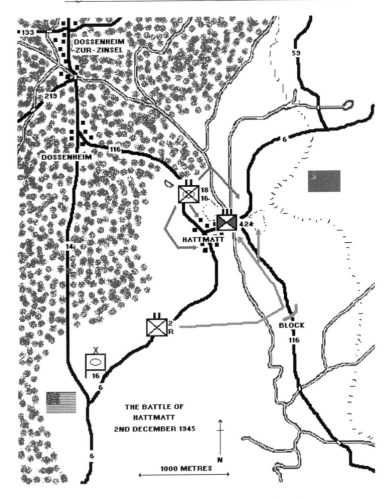

THE BATTLE OF
HATTMATT
2ND DECEMBER 1945

1000 METRES

N

The 424th was under pressure from three sides as
Pierce's plan squeezed Hattmatt hard.

The sound of a Maxim opening up nearby barely
registered on Din.

The white ground was profusely marked with
patches of brown, black, and occasionally, red, where the
artillery had turned over the snow and transformed the
landscape and the men clinging to it.

216

Everywhere Din looked, he could see his men up and firing at an enemy whose numbers seemed to be growing every second.

*'This is hopeless. I can't hold here.'*

"Oleg, report into command. Request permission, on my authority, to withdraw to position three. Bystro! Dawai!"

The signals officer worked the radio and got through quickly.

Colonel Pugachev, commander of what was left of the 22nd Guards Cavalry Regiment, listened sympathetically, still mourning the decimation of his unit near Wolfegg.

He seized the radio from the startled Cossack operator.

"Can you hold for another hour, Comrade Din, over?"

Oleg Stavins turned to his commander for a response but the message had gone unheard.

"Comrade Mayor!"

The injured eardrums prevented his commander from hearing, so Stavins tapped Din on the arm.

He turned, the modest touch breaking his concentration.

More 155mm artillery arrived, clearly moving forwards like a rolling barrage, and away from the advancing American infantrymen.

The ground shook, and the noise of the nearest shells penetrated even Din's damaged ears.

"What?"

"The Polkovnik wants to know if you can hold another hour, Comrade Mayor."

Din took another quick sweep around the positions he could see, sensing the pressure on his men, feeling their resolve start to crack, knowing the answer instinctively.

"Tell Polkovnik Pugachev that we'll be lucky to hold for another ten minutes."

Din turned again, his attention caught by a different type of motion, as one group of his men rose and fled, leaving a vital hole in their defence of the main road, Route 116.

His arm shot out and he shouted.

"Starshina, sort that out!"

The senior NCO, waiting nearby with a group of picked men, was ready for just such an occurrence and led his men forward to plug the gap.

Turning back to the communications officer, Din saw, rather than heard, the explosion.

As the 155mm shell exploded on the edge of the headquarters position, the Major somehow remained intact and untouched, the wierd selectiveness of high explosives ensuring that the artillery shell did not claim him that day.

In fact, he barely felt the blast, the vagaries of explosives leaving him untouched and upright, although he nearly suffered injury as Stavins' head, almost surgically removed from his shoulders, sailed past his own body with inches to spare. It was accompanied by parts of the radios, tables, weapons, and men that had been placed against that side of the position.

Back in the enemy artillery positions, gun layers added extra range again, moving the barrage on another fifty yards, and so Din was not troubled further by their shells.

The only survivor of the 424th's Regimental Headquarters took up his PPD and, now totally deaf, went out to lead his men in their last fight.

### 0545 hrs, Monday, 2nd December 1945, north of the Zinzig River, Hattmatt, Alsace.

Barney Meade was screaming louder and louder as his death approached. He had not received a scratch in all the combat he had particpated in during WW2, or in any of the actions he had led in the latest bloody affair.

It was a unit joke that he would make it home without the obligatory Purple Heart.

A Soviet mortar shell, one of the few that the enemy unit had got off before Baker Company overran them, had exploded virtually at his feet.

One leg was missing, with next to nothing left for the medic to get a tourniquet on. His testicles and penis were severed, the same shrapnel having penetrated deeper, shredding his bladder and lower abdomen.

More pieces of metal had punctured his upper body and arms, the one piece that hit his head having opened up the right orbit, from whence his mutilated eye hung.

Fig#91 - Forces involved in the Battle of Hattmatt, 2nd December 1945.

**OPPOSING FORCES**

**THE BATTLE OF HATTMATT**

**2ND DECEMBER 1945**

**SOVIET DEFENCE**

**ALLIED ASSAULT**

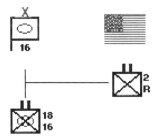

The medic had already put morphine into the grievously wounded Ranger officer, but it hadn't touched the pain. He selected another ampoule and plunged it into the surviving thigh, exposed when the blast had torn off Meade's trousers. This brought almost instant relief to the tortured body, or at least, quiet to the tortured ears of the command group gathered around their dying leader.

The radio crackled.

"Angel 6, this is Washington 6, report, over."

The radio remained silent as no-one moved to answer.

"Angel 6, this is Washington 6, report, over."

The unit's senior non-com held his hand out for the handset.

"Washington 6, this is Angel one-three. Angel 6 is down... hard. We're continuing the attack, over."

There was a moment's pause whilst those bland words were consumed by the Ranger CO in the battalion CP..

"Roger, Angel. Keep up the pressure, Reports are they're cracking. Good luck. Out"

Williams wanted to ask much more, but now was not the time.

*'In any case, Barney Meade's goddamn indestructible.'*

By the time that Lieutenant Colonel Williams had that thought, Barney Meade was dead.

---

Part of Baker Company was in prime position, unexpectedly so, and its senior officer on the ground called in the good news to a troubled Williams.

Having overrun the mortar position, two platoons of 'Baker' had pushed on along the edge of a rise and found a perfect spot that looked over Hattmatt, as well as providing a position from which they could flay anyone withdrawing from the Alsatian village.

1st Lieutenant Barkmann, the senior rank in the two platoons, did not yet know that he was the senior rank still standing in the company but, for now, he had other problems.

A sudden surge of enemy caught his eye and he readied his men for combat.

Flares rose, illuminating an almost surreal landscape.

One of Baker's .30cal Brownings started lashing out, an unnoticed group of Russian infantry having approached almost to grenade range. A number of the enemy fell, the rest melting back to safer ground to consider their options.

Which options were the same as for the rest of Din's unit.

Stand and die, or run and live... maybe.

Most chose the latter course of action, and Barkmann's two platoons had a field day as they lashed the flank of the retreating forces.

Much of the Zinsel's ice had been broken by artillery, and most of the retreating Russians focussed on the bridge, perhaps not realising that the water was shallow enough to wade, probably dissuaded by the prospect of being soaked in chilled flowing water.

The bridge was being swept clean by the Rangers of Baker Company, more and more men arriving to reinforce Barkmann's original force, all immediately bringing their Garands, BARs, and Brownings into action, dissuading any real efforts to cross.

Din arrived with a gaggle of his men in tow.

"What's happening, Leytenant?"

"Comrade Mayor, the fucking bastards have the bridge covered. They're up on that small rise in numbers. I've no Maxims to cover us, but I've sent two DPs to the top floor to suppress the swine. My Serzhant is gathering men behind the bushes there," he pointed across the road, "Ready for when I give the command. We've found some old ladders and stuff to throw across the water so we can get at them."

Din slapped the man's shoulder.

"Good work, Comrade!"

The younger man stiffened.

"Do you wish to take command of the attack, Comrade Mayor?"

Just for a moment, Din considered the officer, question, and his response to it.

*'Is Burastov looking for a way out?'*

**'No. Not Nikanor Burastov. He's a fighter, remember?''**

*'Is he just doing what he thinks is right in offering?'*

**'Probably.'**

*'If I say no, will I look like I'm backing out?'*

**'Who cares?'**

"No, Comrade Burastov. You continue in charge. I'll organise the rear party. Send up two reds when you're over and have pushed them off. Clear?"

"Yes, Comrade Mayor. Thank you."

Burastov slammed a fresh magazine into his Tokarev pistol.

*'Good. I was right.'*

The two officers checked their watches and agreed on a time designed to allow the Burastov and the Serzhant to be fully prepared, and for Din to get the rearguard ready.

### 0601 hrs, Monday, 2nd December 1945, Hattmatt, Alsace.

Din didn't hear the whistle, the agreed signal, but didn't need to, as the feeble sound was swiftly submersed in a sea of violent noise, as a sudden increase in firing marked the start of the attack.

To his front and right flank, the Amerikanski were pushing hard, and he knew that the road behind him had to be cleared; otherwise, his command would become just a memory.

He risked a look over his shoulder and managed to recognise that his men were closing with the enemy, although he also took in the many still shapes that marked the expensive progress of the assault force.

One of his men shook his shoulder, bringing his focus back to his own immediate problems.

To his front, a surge by a sizeable group of American infantry had gained a foothold, and the two forces were exchanging grenades at close range.

Flares shot skywards, illuminating the scene, offering better conditions for the professional killing to come.

The sharp explosions of grenades, and the subsequent vision of newly wounded guardsmen focussed him, his concentration clearly affected by the nearness of the artillery round that had wiped out his staff.

Bringing his mind back to structured thought once more, Din saw a greater peril as a group of six M5A1 halftracks bore down on his northern flank. The 18th Armored Infantry force decided to bring their tracks to te battle as the conditions permitted it.

Coordinating with the attack to Din's front, the armoured vehicles .50 calibre machine guns spouted bullets in all directions, few of which came anywhere near their intended targets as the tracks bounced forward.

The 424th had a few anti-tank rifles, and some of these cracked out their 14.5mm armour piercing bullets, claiming hits on the attacking tracks.

Two fell out of the attack, one immediately after the other, as heavy bullets struck home.

The infantry component bailed out of the rearmost track whilst the machine-gunner remained to use the gun in support of the attack. The other crew member, the driver, was screaming in shock and horror as he tried to clean the bits of a 2nd Lieutenant from his face and body, the effects of two hits from PTRD bullets having had a catastrophic effect on the dead man's upper body.

The foremost halftrack spilled part of its human contents, many of whom were bloodied by the passage of the armour-piercing bullets through their vehicle. Six men remained inside the smoking wreck.

None the less, Din could see that his flank would be lost in short order.

Again, his eyes moved to the other side of the Zinsel, desperate to find the glow of red flares, but finding only the mix of white snow and grey smoke.

In desperation, he gave voice to his thoughts.

"Come on, Burastov! For all our fucking sakes, come on!"

---

On the small height above the Zinsel, all was bloody chaos as death and horror strode the hasty positions of the Rangers' Baker Company.

1st Lieutenant Barkmann was in a world of his own.

No sound, save a gentle buzzing in his ears, his stunned senses even managing to partially mask the vibrations of nearby explosions, so disoriented was he by the glancing blow from a Soviet rifle butt.

His attacker had perished to another Ranger, who in turn had died to a bayonet thrust from behind.

Barkmann's eyes took everything in as his brain struggled to comprehend the images, whilst it also tried to regain a modicum of control over the stunned officer's arms and legs.

It failed on all counts.

However, the concussion did not prevent Barkmann from seeing the horrors in front of him and, occasionally, feel a glimmer of recognition of a face.

Corporal Thomas Ward presented such a horror, rolling around with a Soviet soldier, both men intent on strangling each other, hands and arms bent for the sole purpose of throttling the life from the other man.

A moment of recognition flared in Barkmann's mind as Ward's face bulged and changed colour, the Russian's greater strength proving vital in the struggle.

The smallest part of Barkmann's brain screamed at him to do something, encouraging an extraordinary effort to save Ward, but it remained unheard amidst the greater mists of his injury.

Ward died.

Another man, a new arrival in the Ranger Battalion, fell to his knees in front of Barkmann, his chest ravaged by a burst from a submachine gun.

The man looked almost offended and affronted that he had been shot.

The corpse toppled forward, falling so that the head smashed face first into Barkmann's left foot, causing his recent sprain to announce its presence once more.

A Soviet officer appeared on the edge of the position, waving his pistol and encouraging his men forward.

Barkmann watched in befuddled fascination, almost in slow motion, as red weals sprang up on the man's body, the impacts throwing the wounded man back from where he came.

Drawing on everything he could muster, Barkmann started trying to get his mind back on track, trying to ease himself into a more upright position.

His efforts were thwarted by a heavy impact on his right side, two struggling men smashing into him as each tried to gain the upper hand.

They fell to the ground, one on top of the other, the Ranger underneath coming off far worse. The Russian drove his elbow into the American's solar plexus as they fell, the combination of the impact with the ground and the weight of the Soviet soldier causing internal damage and driving the breath from the Ranger.

Holding the disabled American in place with one hand, the Soviet soldier brought out his knife and stabbed the helpless man repeatedly in the chest and throat, continuing long after life had left the farm boy from Indiana.

Barkmann felt the start of some sort of functional control returning, and he tested his belief with an act of great concentration, willing his body to try to sit up.

The effort failed, but his limbs started to move in some resemblance of the orders they were being sent.

In front of him, an enemy soldier screamed, a bullet thumping into his lower abdomen, doubling the man over in pain.

The screams continued, burning further into Barkmann's recovering senses and, surprisingly, not hindering but helping the process of his mental return.

He sat up and started to take in the bigger picture.

There were wounded men from both sides, in and around the position.

The cries of more wounded and dying men made themselves known as the recovery of his senses accelerated.

Those same senses announced that he could now hear, but that they also believed that they were now less assaulted with the noises of battle.

Which was true.

The firing had stopped.

## 0642 hrs, Monday, 2nd December 1945, Mobile command post, five hundred metres west of Hattmatt, Alsace.

Brigadier-General Pierce was still not happy.

The position at Dahlem had been taken, but the schedule was all to cock. The resistance had not been so easily swept aside as had been anticipated, the main reasons being the larger number of Soviet troops than had been expected, and the fact that they fought like mad dogs.

Another factor contributing to his unhappiness were the casualty figures that were filtering through.

18th Armored Infantry had taken relatively light hits, except, for some reason, the hierarchy was ravaged.

By all accounts, the brief tenure of the latest commander of the armored infantry was terminated when he was relieved by the Battalion Intelligence Officer. The Captain in question was presently on his way to the rear in a straightjacket, having suffered a mental collapse.

The Rangers had taken some heavy blows and over a company were either on their way to hospital or awaiting the ministrations of the graves registration units. Again, a lot of the leadership talent had suffered, although not the high level of dead that had ravaged the 18th.

Offset his own numbers against what was near to a full Red Army battalion removed from the communist's order of battle, and Pierce should have been happy.

Pierce and Greiner worked the map and savoured the fresh coffee, perked up with a nip of something that one of the men had produced to ward off the increasingly chill.

"We can't afford to hang around here, Ed. We've lost time. Should be here?"

He indicated a position on the map, seeking confirmation of his interpretation of the timetable.

"Yes, Sir. We can press on immediately. The arty's already moving up, ready to support."

Pierce drained the last dregs of the warming concoction.

"Excellent. Now, contact 18th and tell 'em to swiftly manage the prisoners. Get our MP's moving up a-sap to take 'em off their hands. But tell the 18th that I want them moving forward on their route of advance within ten minutes and no later."

Greiner made the usual notes.

"The Rangers took the bigger hit, so tell Williams to shake out and expand his ground the other side of the Zinsel, up to Route 59... right flank on the Wullbach... here... left to the 6... here... but not to get involved in anything at Imbsheim yet. Reform his hurt units into something he can use and sort out his prisoners a-sap. We're not hanging around."

The pencil waggled, recording the orders.

Greiner posed the question.

"The armor's nearly up, Sir. You gonna give 'em their head now?"

Smiling as his mug was being refilled, Pierce considered the idea.

"No, I think not. Keep their fuel topped off and let the 18th close Imbsheim. If they ain't needed there, then we cut them loose. I wanna hold them as long as possible, keep them organised, on line, and raring to go, Ed. Kapische?"

"Jawohl, Herr General."

Pierce spluttered as the involuntary laugh clashed with the process of swallowing the hot liquid.

"Goddamnit Ed! What've I told you about trying to be funny in my presence!"

"I can't immediately recall, Sir. Now, I'll attend to these orders."

---

Barkmann was still groggy, but back on his feet, nodding to a man here and there, slapping a shoulder, or inspecting a small wound as he went from man to man.

Baker Company had been knocked about but was still in fighting shape.

Able had been hurt the most.

Williams, in receipt of Greiner's orders, quickly organised some lightly wounded Rangers to look after the prisoners, shoehorning a number of Able survivors into Baker Company, and finally creating an extra reserve force for the battalion headquarters.

The Ranger commander had selected the small hill as a convenient place to hold an orders group, and as he waited for the officers to arrive, he sorted out the tactical orders from Brigade into orders that he could pass to his men.

Nearby, a pair of medics loaded a bloodied Russian officer onto a stretcher and headed off towards a small hut near the river, where the enemy wounded were being collected.

The man was crying.

Not tears of pain, but tears of frustration. Burastov had failed in his mission, and the 424th had been cornered and destroyed.

Williams did not spare the wounded Russian a second thought, concentrating on his planning.

Acknowledging Barkmann's presence, Williams spoke quietly with the young officer now commanding Baker Company and drew him into the next stage of the Ranger's war. Running his pencil over the map work, Williams was pleased to see that Barkmann seemed up to the task ahead. Sending the Ranger to grab some coffee, Williams moved to his table, a pile of ammo boxes, and starting making notes on the margins, before his concentration was interrupted by firing from the village.

## 0651 hrs, Monday, 2nd December 1945, the waste ground, Rue Principale, Hattmatt, Alsace.

In Hattmatt, the survivors of the 424th, both wounded and unwounded, were herded onto a piece of ground to the south of the Rue Principale.

Din constantly spat blood as he assisted a wounded comrade into the holding area.

He had been felled in the close quarter fight; an enemy soldier had rushed him and slammed his helmeted head into his face at speed.

The resultant broken nose was painful and his eyes resembled those of a Panda as the bruising spread across his face. His lips were shredded by the impact and he had no front teeth worth a damn.

Din found a small mound and carefully propped the wounded soldier against it, leaving him to the care of others as he moved amongst his men, acknowledging their efforts, and encouraging them to hold their heads high.

He did not immediately notice the demeanour of the US troops, but when he did, he understood completely.

He pushed his way to the edge of the mass of men, directly opposite what was clearly the man in charge.

Hindered by his facial injuries, Din tried to remonstrate, but his English was insufficient for the task, as was the understanding of the American Captain; not that his understanding of Din's entreaties would have made the slightest difference. After all, he had orders from the General himself.

The Soviet soldiers began, one by one, to understand what their officer was shouting about and their agitation grew.

Most stood and faced what was about to happen, resolved to their fate.

Some saw matters differently.

Din gave the American officer a look of total hatred and watched as the man's attention was drawn elsewhere, a surge by a few prisoners trying to give themselves some chance of survival.

Shouts were followed by shots as the Armored Infantry shot the rushers down, the volume of fire growing as they turned their attention to the mass of prisoners on the waste ground.

Din screamed, holding up his hands, first to the firing Americans, then turning and trying to calm his men.

A heavy machine gun joined the slaughter, then another, and then there were four such weapons, pouring bullets into the helpless men.

A single bullet clipped Din's thigh, its passage and the resultant pain bringing a strange moment of peace to the condemned man.

He turned for the final time, facing his enemy, hawking and spitting a huge gobbet of bloody phlegm at the criminals who were killing his men, particularly at the man who commanded the slaughter.

Din launched himself forward, intent on killing the bastard with his bare hands.

---

"What the fuck is that?"

No one could supply Williams with the answer or, at least, no one could state for sure what it was, although most suspected the origins of and reasons for the firing.

"Lukas, get a squad down there pronto and find out what the fuck's goin' on."

Barkmann sent his Senior NCO and a squad from Baker Company off to investigate.

On their return, First Sergeant Ford gave a short but sober report on events near the Rue Principale.

The orders group concluded, Williams dismissed his officers and found himself alone.

He gazed off towards Hattmatt, towards an imagined spot containing nearly two hundred slaughtered Red Army soldiers, and he prayed.

*'Eternal rest grant unto them, O Lord, and let perpetual light shine upon them. May the souls of the faithful departed, through the mercy of god, rest in peace. Amen.'*

## 2nd December 1945, Hattmatt; the aftermath.

Rumours of the massacre spread through the 16th like wildfire, subsequently making their way through the Legion Corps, and all the way to the ears of De Lattre himself.

Pierce ordered the arrest of the officer responsible for the shootings, but the 18th's Captain was quickly released.

Greiner's orders came under close scrutiny.

To Williams and the Rangers, the orders had been simple enough to understand.

To the 18th's Captain Pallister, catapulted into command by the loss of a number of higher ranks, and clearly suffering from the pressure that was bound to build upon a relatively inexperienced man under those circumstances, they were also simple to understand.

His interpretation of the order to swiftly manage the prisoners within a ten minute time scale meant only one thing.

In the end, the whole matter was glossed over and ignored, even omitted from some of the biographies that appeared post-war, although Greiner's orders were subsequently criticised for being imprecise and open to interpretation.

Whatever the cause, whatever the reason, wherever blame was to be laid, Hattmatt is accepted as the first of a chain of events that has now entered into history as one of the most unsavoury and brutal episodes in the chronicles of warfare.

*If we are ever in doubt about what to do, it is a good rule to ask ourselves what we shall wish on the morrow that we had done.*

*John Lubbock*

# Chapter 112 - THE KILLINGS

### 1127 hrs, Wednesday, 4th December 1945, outside of the Mairie, Rue Principale, Mittelschaeffolsheim, Alsace.

The advance of the Legion Corps had, so far, been slow and bloody. Alma had suffered a reverse at Wingersheim, when a Soviet counter-attack caused a temporary withdrawal. It had been a difficult call for St.Clair, but Lavalle saw an opportunity in the manoeuvre and approved the decision.

The Soviets, eager to show the hated SS their metal, over-extended themselves, and Alma turned on them in terminal fashion.

Knocke reoriented the Normandie Group just in time to stop a drive into his northern flank, with part of Uhlmann's tank unit arriving perfectly on the flank of the advancing Soviet units, and putting the survivors to flight.

There was a time implication for the Allied attack, but the destruction of a whole Soviet brigade was a bonus, especially when the whole point of the plan was to draw down Red Army reserve units, pulling them away from the main thrust to the north.

The slow advance of the Legion had already persuaded Eisenhower to check the main attack and, back in Versailles, the SHAEF commander watched the developments in Alsace, waiting and judging his moment.

The Legion advance continued and, for the second time, units of Camerone entered Mittelschaeffolsheim.

---

Braun surveyed the scene.

He and his running mate, another Panther, had dropped into position on the junction of Routes 30 and 228,

Braun covering north-eastwards, and the other tank watching the south-east approaches.

Legionnaires from the 1st RDM were pushing up through the wrecked buildings, steadily ensuring each building was clear before progressing onwards.

The retaking of Mittelscaeffolsheim had been a brief affair, but not without cost.

The first attack had cost the tank unit two precious vehicles, both Panzer IV's. In the second sortie, one of the Panthers had spectacularly succumbed to a direct artillery strike, and with it, another group of Kameraden from the old days had perished in the blink of an eye.

The 1st RDM put in a ferocious assault and the Russians defences melted away.

Braun, leading the tank's point unit, had seen no reason to believe that all the enemy had gone and, until Speer got his act organised, Corps standing orders were that Panthers were far too precious to be risked up front in town fighting, unless an extraordinary situation existed.

The barrel of Braun's Panther moved gently from side to side, the gunner following each surge of infantry, moving from cover to cover.

There was no firing, no resistance.

Nothing.

The 1st's legionnaires started to move more quickly, and a feeling of relaxation spread throughout the assault force.

After briefing his crew, Braun emerged from the Panther's turret, dropping to the ground at the front of the tank. He quickly moved off to the left to consult with the 2nd Company commander, Capitaine Durand.

After his excellent conduct in the assault on the 'Leningrad' position, during the relief of Stuttgart, Durand had been fully accepted by the ex-Waffen-SS soldiers, and he had done nothing but reinforce their high opinion of him since.

He greeted Braun with a smile and the offer of a cigarette.

"Danke, Capitaine. I take it we are clear? Your men seem to think so."

He gestured up the road at what had been a relaxed scene.

It was now anything but.

A group of men had gathered outside a large building, and they were clearly extremely agitated.

The radio crackled into life and Durand took a report in total silence, the words spoken by the officer up the road burning into the hearts of everyone present in an instant.

"I'm coming up. Out."

In a controlled fashion, Durand placed the handset down on the low brick wall.

He braced himself against the brickwork, screwing his eyes tight in an effort to compose himself.

Durand turned to Braun, his voice failing to disguise both the horror and the anger that had started to burn his insides.

"You don't have to come, Major..." somehow, the RSM rank did not seem appropriate in the circumstances. He placed a hand on the tanker's shoulder.

"Johannes, don't come."

"But I must."

Signalling for his tank to move up the road behind them, Braun and Durand took the short walk to the place where an old comrade and friend had met his end.

---

Most of the men who were stood around the awful apparition had seen service on the Eastern Front, and should have been used to the excesses that often marked that awful campaign.

Despite that, more than one was in tears, and more than one had spilled the contents of his stomach.

All had approached and exceeded the normal extremes of anger.

The small body had experienced the very highest levels of pain and suffering; that was wholly obvious to the eye. The pieces that had been removed lay around the site of what could only be described as a place of sadistic torture.

Cyrille Jaoa da Silva Vernais, Legion RSM, veteran of countless battles, and credited by Knocke with much of the responsibility for the successful integration of Legionnaires and ex-SS, was very messily dead.

Even the inexperienced eye could detect that he had died in the extremes of pain, his face still holding an expression

233

of a man fighting back his surrender to the awfulness that had been visited upon him.

His tunic had been ripped open and his chest and stomach skin had been cut off, as had his fingers.

His ears and his nose had also been taken and they were pinned or nailed to the wood around his head, as in some macabre joke.

Braun, his eyes full of tears, could detect that nails had been driven through legs and arms, pinning Vernais to the wooden door of the Mairie, which, in themselves, must have caused the most excruciating pain.

The senior NCO's trousers had been removed and his manhood had suffered a few thrusts from a knife or bayonet but was, perhaps surprisingly, still attached.

Beneath his feet, a small fire still smouldered. It had probably not amounted to much at its peak, but had been more than sufficient to roast the Legionnaire past the ankles.

A piece of paper was sticking from Vernais' mouth but the onlookers had not removed it. One of the German legionnaires sought silent permission from Durand and removed it with reverence.

"It's in German... well... sort of."

He looked at it, and then passed it on to the next man.

The note finally reached Durand, who shared the text with Braun.

*'Your friend die crying like a baby. So will die all you SS bastards!'*

Braun looked back at the corpse of the man he considered a good friend, and wished that the old NCO had stayed behind in camp. Vernais had returned from Sassy only a week beforehand, bringing new men with him. He had sought out a return to Camerone, and to the 1st RDM, and they had welcomed him with open arms.

Clearly, he had somehow got detached when the withdrawal had happened.

The rest was evident.

Durand took a deep breath and spoke softly, and with genuine affection.

"My Legionnaires... now... let's get our old comrade down eh?"

234

One of Vernais' old soldiers from Syria produced a groundsheet and everyone worked silently and with the great estrespect, slowly removing their old comrade from the door, moving the tortured body to the sheet and wrapping it, hiding the horrors from further examination.

Canteens containing non-regulation liquids appeared and the men consumed freely, both drinking the health of the dead Vernais and seeking to find the solace that only alcohol can offer.

Durand and Braun moved quickly amongst the men, restrainin their consumption, reminding them of the fights to come and the need to remain alert.

Braun retained his focus and spoke the men.

"Kameraden, there'll be time for us to mourn, but it is not now."

The angry rumblings were not directed at Braun, but the men needed something to focus on and, for the moment, he was it.

"We must go on and do our jobs... and you know that he wouldn't have it any other way, eh?"

That drew more than a few positive responses.

"So... let's honour him by being the best that we can be and, I promise you, when we can, we'll all come together and drink to his memory!"

He pointed up the road, Route 30, which led to Brumath.

"Now... let's remember we're legionnaires and honour his memory by doing what legionnaires do."

Braun's voice increased in volume and his anger bubbled over.

"The enemy... the shitty bastards that did this," he pointed at the wrapped form, "They're that fucking way," his finger moved back to the road, stabbing violently in the direction of the front line, "And you and I have a urgent fucking appointment with the swine!"

---

Durand had sent a written message, one that he spent some time writing. Such things should not be spoken of over the airwaves.

The note made its way into the hands of Ernst-August Knocke, and then further up the chain of command to Lavalle.

The knowledge of what had been discovered in Mittelschaeffolsheim spread through Camerone at lightning speed, seeping out into Alma and the 16th Armored. It was not long before most of the Legion Corps D'Assault was aware that they had lost one of their best in extraordinarily awful circumstances.

Fig#92 - Legion Forces committed to Brumath, 4th December 1945.

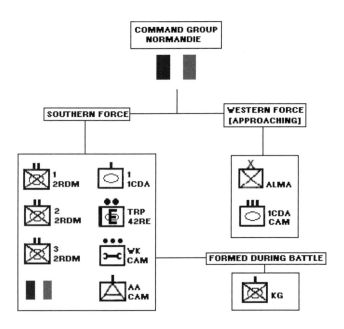

The story, by the nature of matters spread by word of mouth, grew and grew, until those at the end of the chain were utterly shocked at the loss of a full platoon beheaded and the beloved Vernais emasculated and ripped apart.

Truth or not, motivated professional soldiers suddenly had another reason to close with the enemy, and less of a reason to conduct themselves within the rules of war.

## 1507 hrs, Wednesday, 4th December 1945, outside of Brumath, Alsace.

Soviet resistance on Routes 30 and 226 had been overcome, the legionnaires of the 1st RDM sweeping all before them.

Olwsheim had proven a tough little nut, but thirty minutes of close-quarter fighting had reaped a good crop of prisoners, and driven the remaining enemy out in full retreat, giving the Legion control of both Route 60 and Route 226.

The advances continued, two of the three columns coming back together at the junction of Routes 30 and 60

Until they came to Brumath, where the attack floundered in a hail of machine-gun bullets and anti-tank shells.

Braun's Panther had taken five hits, and he had quickly reversed under the cover of smoke grenades. Hastily deployed mortars from the RDM added their own smoke to cover the withdrawal.

---

"We can wait for Alma to come into position, probably for hours yet... and certainly in the dark, or we can attack again... now."

Durand listened to his Battalion commander think aloud, the harassed man's eyes straying between the commanders present.

"If we're going to go again today, we've to go soon. The light."

Braun need say no more than that.

The low cloud that was keeping the air forces at home brought with it the strangest of lights, an almost perpetual dusk that would undoubtedly accelerate the end of daylight, such as it was.

"Durand?"

Commandant Emmercy sought an opinion from a fellow Frenchman.

Fig#93 - Brumath, 4th December 1945.

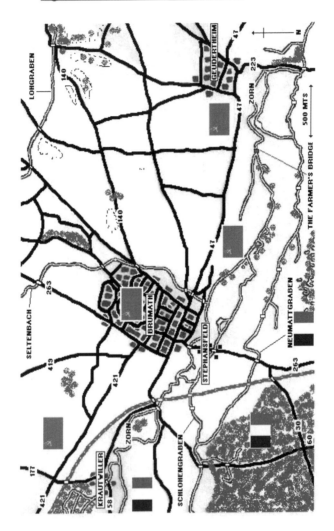

"I'm not the one to ask, Commandant. My men can do it, of course, but not without tanks in close support... that's a question for Braun to answer."

Despite the fact that he was the only non-officer in the orders group, Braun now had everyone waiting on his words.

"We'll go, but it won't be without cost. The enemy seems more oriented to the south edge of Brumath... probably to protect the '47' and keep their supply route open."

He pointed at, and then drew an imaginary line, east from Stephansfeld.

"If we move to the right here... and then drive at speed straight north, we should be able overcome them before they reorient. "

Emmercy looked round his leadership, noting their grasp of the plan.

"The Neumatt and Schlonen are not obstacles to my tanks. In any case, this small farmer's bridge is still standing, as are most of concern to us... and our English panzer-pionieres can put one of their wonders over the Zorn... here."

He fingered a point on the small river.

The recently arrived British tank officer recorded the location in his notebook. The 2nd Lieutenant was part of a small group from the 79th Armoured Division, whose units had been spread throughout Germany at the beginning of the new war.

At first, the British 'funnies', a troop of the 42nd Assault Regiment RE that had been doing demonstrations for French general officers, had been the subject of much derision, but those German soldiers who had experienced their capabilities in Normandy soon silenced the doubters.

Braun had decided that the Churchill bridge layer would earn its corn by spanning the Zorn River.

"Hauptmann Durand's men can accompany us in their halftracks... but we'd need a distraction attack down the same axis we've just tried."

That made sense to all.

Emmercy pondered the suggestion.

"Yes, ok. I'll get some artillery down on the south-western edge... here and here. You take 1st Company," he nodded at Durand, "And drive hard to here. They'll turn for sure ,and then I'll push the rest of the force hard up the road and Brumath will be ours."

# Fig#94 - The Battle of Brumath, Legion assault, 4th December 1945.

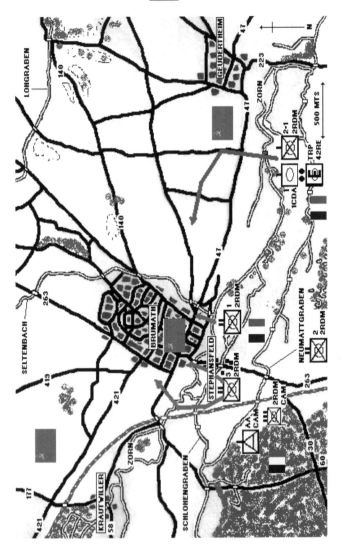

There was no time to lose, so the command group synchronised watches and sped off to their respective units to get ready.

"What the fuck?"

Braun looked, but did not believe his eyes.

Again he spoke, this time directing his words at his men.

"What the fuck?"

His crew didn't answer.

In truth, they hadn't been inclined to resist when the idea had been put to them by ex-Hauptscharfuhrer Stepanski and, now that the reality of it was now in front of them, the events of Mittelschaeffolsheim had priority over the observing niceties of war.

1st Company boasted a strength of eight Panthers and three Panzer IVs, and each had its own pitiful cargo of Russian prisoners, all from the group taken when Olwusheim had been overrun.

Most had been butchered at the time of surrender, but a few, very few out of the two hundred or so that had raised their hands, had been taken alive.

Between four and six Russians were 'sitting' on each tank, mostly bound in place; those that weren't were kept in position by the threatening muzzles of weapons held by the grenadiers positioned on the rear of the tank.

Braun's gunner finally spoke, the issue now resolved in his mind.

"Human shield, Johan. Old Stepanski's idea. Make the bastards think twice about firing at us, eh?"

The Senior NCO's mind processed the sight, but the vision of Vernais appeared, stronger than the appalling images before his eyes.

"Fuck 'em."

He waved his hand above his head, the circular motion bringing his tank commanders to him.

The quick briefing commenced without giving the POW's a second thought.

Durand's company arrived, halftracks racing into position, ready to support Braun's tanks.

The plight of the Soviet prisoners drew every eye, but not one word was spoken in protest.

The men of the 1st RDM cared little for the swine who had tortured their talisman.

Most of the halftracks now sported a large white 'V' on each side, which stood for Vernais or Vengeance, depending on which legionnaire was asked.

Behind Braun's back, the sound of falling artillery signalled the commencement of Emmercy's distraction, giving only ten minutes for the preparations to be completed.

The Churchill bridge layer arrived, accompanied by two Churchill AVRE's carrying fascines, the 2nd Lieutenant's own little touch to the attack.

His joy at being able to add to the plans of the veteran soldiers he was supporting evaporated in a microsecond. He had seen the Legion tanks.

"What the deuce?"

The Churchill halted and the young officer dismounted, deciphering the numbers on the Panthers as he worked out which tank belonged to Braun.

He spotted the NCO scaling the rear of his tank, avoiding the reluctant passengers at the front of the tank.

"I say, Sergeant Major. We can't do this, we simply can't."

Braun looked at the British tanker and back at the Russians.

"It's done, Now, we attack, and you... you put your bridge in the right place. Let's move it, Herr... err... Lieutenant."

Lieutenant Johnson wanted to say more, understanding that he had the rank, but didn't say another word, understanding that he possessed no authority in the eyes of these men.

He re-entered his tank, mind in turmoil, his sensibilities and morals under assault before a shot had been fired.

"Sir?"

Johnson looked at his gunner, his face white.

"You ok, Sir?"

The laugh that came from Johnson's mouth was bordering on hysterical.

"No, Godfrey, I'm bloody well not, ok. See what they've done? Bloody Nazis."

Corporal Godfrey and the rest of the crew had noted the prisoner's plight whilst Johnson was out of the tank.

"Who could do such a thing, Godfrey? It's awful and, what's more, it's against the Convention."

"Never mind, Sir."

Johnson looked at his gunner as if he was a beast from another world, which in many respects he was, for Godfrey had seen combat enough for two men.

"Never mind? Never mind? What sort of bloody swine would do that?"

He pointed through the wall of the turret at the rough position of the German tanks.

Godfrey looked at him.

"We did it on the Scheldt at Westkapelle."

Johnson was horrified.

"What?"

"I said that we did it on the Scheldt... Sir. The bastards had killed Windy Miller... and done in Don Humphries too, all in the space of two hours. Surrendering as a fucking distraction, whilst one of their mates snuck round with a 'faust and popped his tank in the jacksy."

The young officer had could not speak, his mouth hung open as his concept of the British fighting an honourable war was stripped away with a few words.

"We had no problem with it... and it stopped the bastards from firing for sure, all except one, who musta been a fanatic. He hit our Winnie but didn't penetrate."

The chuckle that came next wasn't forced in any way.

"Made a right bloody mess of his chums though."

"But... but... it's just not on... it's..."

"What? Not fucking cricket? Not according to the rules of war eh? ... or the fucking convention eh?"

Johnson recoiled again, as the sneer of contempt from Godfrey undermined yet another of his prized understandings of the way war was conducted. The assault on his sensibilities and understanding of the niceties of the rank structure was only just beginning.

"Lieutenant, for crying out loud, pull yourself together! You ain't playing rugger or cricket at fucking Eton now. Them over the other side... they ain't cads or boundahs...

they're bastards... bastards who'll kill you without a moment's thought or hesitation. This is war, and you can't fight war with rules. There's no fucking umpires to call no ball, no referee to whistle up for a foul, offside, or forward pass. Kill... or be fucking killed... that's what it's about, and if all those red bastards die in saving one of our boys, I'll not shed fucking tears for 'em."

The radio crackled with the order to advance, breaking the tension, and, despite the lack of orders from a shocked Johnson, the Churchill pushed forward, flanked by the AVRE's.

### 1600 hrs, Wednesday, 4th December 1945, Brumath, Alsace.

Fig#95 - Soviet Forces committed to Brumath, 4th December 1945.

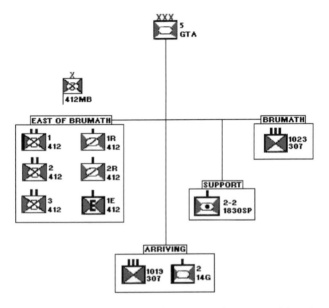

The Churchill was slow, very slow, something that Braun had not factored into his timing.

However, the farmer's bridge was still there, and his lead armour was close to it, the Panzer IV's placed on the right flank, away from whatever the defenders of Brumath could hurl at them.

A contact report crackled in his ear and he immediately acknowledged it, checking his episcopes.

Dissatisfied with the vision, he pushed himself upwards and raised his eyes above the edge of the cupola.

"Schiesse! Tank at eleven...hull down behind the small rise...see it?"

Braun's gunner mumbled a positive response.

"On."

"FIRE!"

The 75mm belched its shell and Braun stayed in place to watch the results.

A mass of earth and bushes suddenly rose up in his field of vision.

*'Short, dammit!'*

"Up seventy-five."

"Target tank. On."

"FIRE!"

Another miss, but it was almost directly on target.

Something in his brain was trying to get Braun's attention, but he was blocking it as he fought his tank.

"Target tank. On!"

"FIRE!"

A flurry of sparks indicated a hit but the white streak soaring high into the sky told them that it had not penetrated.

The nagging continued and broke through.

*'They're not firing at us!'*

Switching to the command net, Braun gave his orders.

"All stations Dora, all stations Dora, press in now, and do it quickly. They're not firing at us. Repeat, press in close now."

Switching to Durand's channel, he requested that the RDM stayed tight to his tanks.

---

The Churchill VII bridge layer was shifting as fast as she could, but it was still pitifully slow. On a good day, and with a decent tail wind, the bridge layer could do fifteen miles per hour on a road, compared with the Panther's noteworthy thirty. Across country, the Panther was even more superior.

This meant that Braun's tanks were at the small river before Johnson brought the bridging tank up.

"Dora Zero One to Dora. Find cover and continue to engage. Out."

Still not a single shot had been aimed at the Panthers, although Durand's halftracks had experienced the spectacular destruction of one vehicle, struck by something very large and unforgiving.

Braun's Panther slewed sideways into a small depression, the turret half masked by a hedgerow.

"No target."

The gunner was the absolute master of the deadpan unflustered voice, something that greatly endeared him to Braun.

He found the man another one and it was probably whatever had killed the RDM's halftrack.

"Two hundred metres behind the same hillock we just shot at. See the building there. Wall to the right."

The turret shifted, and the gunner found his prey.

"You sneaky bastard. Target, gun. On."

"Fire. Load HE."

The Panther fired a solid shot at what both Braun and the gunner had identified as a large field gun. HE would have been a better shell with which to kill the 152mm artillery piece, but it wasn't needed. The AP shell struck the front of the right side trunnion and sent the barrel whirling from its mount. The heavy lump of metal acted like a scythe through corn when it mowed through the crew tending it. The barrel smashed through a small outbuilding, and finished its journey in the ammo lorry that had been hiding behind the flimsy structure, with spectacular results, also bringing about the loss of the Soviet artillery battery's radio links.

---

The diversionary attack had done its job, up to a point, but the delay getting over the Zorn was a huge problem, and no amount of screaming down the radio could make the Churchill move faster.

The light was failing, the snow had started again in earnest, and everything seemed to be going wrong.

Braun and Durand had their forces exposed, although part of the RDM had angled towards the bridge, ready to follow the Panzer IV's that now broached the crossing point. A huge flash preceded the bang, and many eyes watched as the farmer's bridge and lead Panzer went skywards.

*'Fuck it!'*

"Dora Zero One to Dora. Take cover. The panzer brücke will be here soon, and then we can cross. Hang on, Kameraden."

Durand decided to send his infantry forward on foot, and Braun could not oppose the idea.

Looking for another target, Braun noted the legionnaires dismounting and charging the river.

Tracers leapt out of the failing light and men dropped into the snow, adding scarlet to the white blanket.

The Churchill rattled by, heading to a point where a small track terminated on the opposite bank.

The two AVRE's followed suit, the three tanks creating a spear point, an armoured triangle, inexorably advancing to conquer the Zorn.

The bridge layer halted on the riverbank and quickly set its bridge in place.

Then it was hit.

The whole front of the Churchill disappeared in a deadly whiteness as a huge HE shell struck the vertical glacis, its 152mm armour plate sufficient to resist penetration, but not to deny the concussive effect of such a large explosion.

The driver and hull gunner were reduced to jelly, bones shattered by the huge blow. Both died within seconds.

In the turret, the loader was blown against the turret wall, fracturing his skull and smashing his right shoulder.

Godfrey was temporarily blinded as his sights shattered, the shock wave also dashing his head on unyielding metal, which nearly knocked him out.

Johnson broke his left wrist, and nearly trepanned himself on the inside of the cupola, peeling part of his forehead back as the metal edge did its work.

Braun slammed his fist against the wall of the Panther's turret.

The Churchill had to move or the bridge was useless to them.

Another shell struck the wounded beast, but it was of a smaller calibre, and did not damage the tank.

The two AVRE's pushed in on the right of the bridge and, one after the other, efficiently put their fascines into the water.

"Dora Zero One to Dora. Use the bundles to the right of the bridge. Move up now and straight over... fan out once across. One-five, watch to the north-east. Over."

One-five, Stepanski's tank, let two others roll over the fascines before he decided to cross.

---

Inside the bridge layer, Johnson struggled to decipher the messages from his brain.

He could smell explosives, fire, blood, faeces, urine, vomit and fuel, all of which told him that he needed to be elsewhere immediately.

He squealed as his broken wrist announced itself, denying him the leverage to push up through the hatch at the first attempt.

Again he tried, this time successfully, and he welcomed the fresh cold air that greeted him.

Braun spotted the movement and tried to contact the British tank, but the radio had lost the uneven struggle against the large calibre HE round, something he had suspected the moment the shell hit the Churchill.

He willed the young officer to do something.

*'Move the tank, Englander... move the fucking tank!'*

There was no point in shouting, it was too far, and the noise of battle was growing as the Panthers on the other side of the bridge started to work the battlefield.

On the Churchill's roof, Johnson cleared his head and peered back inside at is crew.

Godfrey was coming round, and the loader was also showing signs of life.

"Corporal Godfrey! Godfrey! Shape up, man! Get yourself sorted. Get ready to evacuate on my order."

Not waiting for a reply, Johnson rolled off the turret, unaware of the unwanted attention he was now getting. The twang of bullets striking the tank's armoured plates did not penetrate into his consciousness, so focussed was he on the task he had set himself.

Through the open hatch, he could see that his driver was beyond help. He grabbed at the corpse with his one good arm and, thankful that the man had been nigh on a starved dwarf, Johnson exerted his strength and managed to get the body partially out of the seat, and slid the body in the general direction of the hull gunner.

A bullet nicked his calf, the sting making him work harder.

Sliding down through the narrow opening, Johnson worked to push the driver out of the way.

Another huge shell landed near to the tank, rocking the Churchill, causing Johnson to bang his head. A steady stream of blood emerged from the small but deep wound caused by the prominent corner of an electrical junction box above the driver's position.

Having made enough room for himself, he restarted the tank, praying that the engine would catch.

It did, but the plume of black smoke informed the defenders that the Churchill was once again a target.

Dropping the tank into reverse gear, Johnson grabbed the tiller bar with his good arm and started to move the vehicle away from the bridge.

'Well done, Englander!'

"Dora Zero One to Dora. Bridge is clear, I say again, bridge is clear."

Speaking on the intercom, he gave the order to push forward, all the time watching the Churchill.

To its right, a Panther followed closely on the heels of one of the AVRE's, both British tanks now across the water.

Braun smiled, but his eyes took in something on the periphery.

He snatched up the radio and tried to get through, even though he knew it was useless.

"Nein, nein, get out, Johnson, the bank's giving way, get out now!"

The last heavy shell had affected the integrity of the river bank, and it seemed that only Braun could see it as plain as day.

No one would ever know if Johnson had felt it start to go, or even if he heard Braun's cry over the radio.

The bank slowly gave way and forty plus tons of Churchill slithered, left side first, into the water.

A man started to emerge from the turret hatch.

Something acted as a stop; possibly a submerged rock. Momentum and gravity took over and the heavy tank rolled over, coming to rest upside down in the freezing River Zorn.

---

The water flooded into the tank.

Godfrey, half in, half out of the turret, was mashed and virtually cut in half as the vehicle rolled into the water. He was dead before he had a chance to drown.

The loader died without regaining consciousness.

The interior light by the driver's position stayed illuminated, even when both it and Johnson were immersed by the inrushing waters.

Abject terror seized the young tank officer, but his screams were silenced by the water that flooded into his mouth.

As the water closed over him, the light stayed bright in the icy waters, illuminating his desperate efforts to hold his breath, and then to drink the river dry.

The bulb flickered and died.

---

Braun's Panther moved carefully over the engineer bridge, which was now attracting a lot of attention from Soviet artillery and mortars.

The unfortunate men strapped to the Legion vehicles had worked, up to a point, until someone in the Soviet command made a difficult decision. The change was marked by the unexpectedly spectacular end of one of Braun's Panthers.

A large calibre shell hit the Panther on the hull glacis, transforming three of the POW's into jam in the blink of an eye. It was followed by two more hits, this time from something smaller, but just as deadly.

The tank, its crew, the surviving prisoners, and the Legion grenadiers riding on the back, all disappeared in a huge orange and red rose, obvious pieces of all four parts of the whole travelling large distances in the explosion.

Only the running gear remained to identify where the German tank had once stood.

## 1620 hrs, Wednesday, 4th December 1945, Laager positions of the 1st Battalion, 412th Mechanised Brigade, one kilometre east of Brumath, Alsace.

On paper, the brand new 412th Mechanised Brigade was a reasonable formation, certainly hampered logistically by being equipped with numerous tank types, but helped by the veteran tankers and infantry that made up over 70% of its personnel.

On paper.

In reality, it was under equipped in numbers, under supplied with the basics of war, the morale of veteran and recruit alike shot to pieces and, generally, in no fit state to confront a competent enemy.

None the less, Colonel Blagoslavov received his call to arms, and started to get his ragtag unit organised for battle.

When Operation Thermopylae had finished, the remnants of a number of Soviet units were banded together and efforts began to make them fit for purpose once more.

The old 38th Guards Tank Brigade had been struck from the army list and its personnel and some of its surviving armour had ended up under Blagoslavov's orders as a new formation.

As part of the process of recovery, Blagoslavov's command was temporarily attached to the 3rd Guards Cavalry Corps, which unit had also suffered grievously in the battles of November 1945.

Each of the three mechanised battalions in the 412th was under strength, but it was difficult to find any Soviet armoured unit with a full TOE in December 1945.

His 1st Battalion was where Blagoslavov concentrated the main armoured firepower and offensive strength of his fledgling command, the new restyled mechanised brigades being both a response to the Allies' own organisation and an implementation of lessons hard-learned on the battlefield.

Eight IS-II's, one IS-III, and five T34/85's, supported by two full battalions of infantry, plus support units, gave the 1st presence and hitting power.

The 2nd Battalion was mainly based around six SU-100's, supported by six T34m43's, armed with the 76mm gun. A new infantry battalion, fresh from training, provided the manpower, supplemented by engineer and mortar companies. Short in numbers, the green soldiers made up for the lower establishment with their apparent enthusiasm.

3rd Battalion was a patchwork of anything else that came to hand, mostly Soviet armour that had seen better days, the occasional enemy vehicle, and even a brand-new Pershing tank that had been captured during the US retreat in Southern Germany.

The real strength of the 3rd lay in its infantry element. Dismounted Cossacks and Guards infantry from the slaughtered 3rd Guards Tank Corps, a total of five full companies, all high quality troops, plus good mortar and anti-tank gun support units.

The 412th also had two recon units, each of four T-70 light tanks supported by more guardsmen from the old 3rd, carried into battle in recently seized US halftracks.

An engineer company and artillery battery completed the strength of the 412th.

On paper.

Blagoslavov knew better than to believe pieces of paper.

2nd Battalion was presently virtually useless to him, half of its vehicles non-runners left behind in a field east of Hagenau, awaiting spares for both the SU-100's and the worn out T34s.

The 2nd's infantry component was closer to hand and, with the commencement of firing nearby, he had ordered it to halt its training and make the short journey from Weitbruch to the south.

The 1st Battalion was settled in north of the Selterbach, but not of any great use, its armour affected by mechanical problems, shortages of everything from lubricants to ammunition. A recent check with the commander probably meant that it could put three of its IS-II's into the field, supported by a similar number of T34's, if they scrounged ammo from the non-runners and the mechanics toiled like hero workers, which, of course, they would,.

The 3rd Battalion, with its diverse tanks and experienced infantry, was concealed in a modest gully just off Route 140, roughly one thousand five hundred metres north of Geudertheim.

On the flank of Durant's assault force.

---

A line of vehicles and men came out of the growing darkness, moving slowly, but with purpose.

Stepanski was looking elsewhere on the battlefield and the call from his gunner startled him.

He looked to his front, his binoculars seeking out any details with which to identify these new targets.

He did so, at least with a few of them, but decided not to complicate his message with that sort of detail just now.

"Dora One-five, all Dora. Enemy tanks, minimum ten vehicles, and infantry in battalion strength approaching from north of Geuderheim, range seven hundred metres. Engaging!"

In the command halftrack, Durand checked his map.

In Braun's Panther, another map received urgent attention.

Both men decided that this was trouble with a big T.

Braun acted first.

"Dora-zero-one to Dora One. All Dora one, reorient to face northeast... assume defensive positions."

He checked the map once more before he directed instructions to the Panzer IV unit.

"Dora-zero-one to Dora Two. All Dora two, take position on river line, facing north. Engage new enemy force."

Happy that his HQ vehicles would stay on station to support Durand's infantry, Braun switched to the command net and briefed his superior.

His report was met with some consternation, the presence of this new force undetected and, probably much worse, unsuspected.

Fig#96 - The Soviet surprise, Brumath, 4th December 1945.

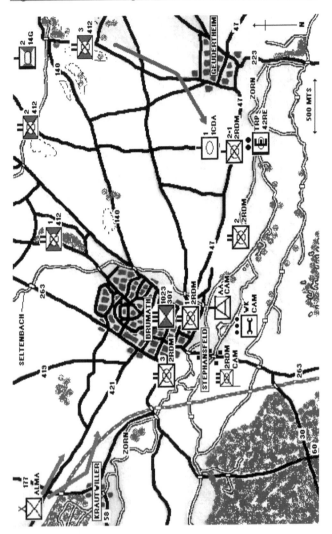

Allied intelligence had missed the 412th completely, and the Legion was about to pay the cost. A small mathematical error on the part of a young navigator from Alberta was not detected by either his squadron intel officer or RAF photo interpreters. That resulted in some six square miles of Alsace remaining unphotographed; the six square miles containing the 412th Mechanised Brigade.

---

"Dora-one-five to Dora-zero-one, over."

"Go ahead, Dora-zero-one, over."

"One-five, the enemy armour is a mixed type force. At least one American M26 and two Shermans. I see a Panther for certain. Total fourteen armoured vehicles identified at this time, over."

Remembering to unkey the mike, Stepanski howled with delight, as his gunner sent one of the Shermans into the next world.

"Zero-one, roger. You must hold. Zero is pushing on with plan. Help's on its way, over.

Stepanski reply was never sent, his radio disabled as a 90mm shell from the M26 wiped the side of his turret, removing one of the Soviet POWs in the process.

It had been a mighty blow, and the smell of damaged electrics filled the turret space.

Smoke then arrived from somewhere. There was no clue to its cause or whereabouts.

Stepanski switched to the intercom.

"Gunner, fire on your own authority. Crew, check for damage. There's burning somewhere."

The extractors were working at full pelt, but failing to make gains on the sickly smoke, the taste of which brought back horrible memories for men who had seen their friends die in burning tanks.

The loader complained that he couldn't open the rear hatch so the spent 75mm shell case went out the cupola, closely followed by Stepanski.

"Commander out."

Stepanski levered himself out of the turret and found the cause.

A dead grenadiere was hanging on the side of the turret, blocking the ejection hatch. The body was burning steadily.

To Stepanski's first sight, it seemed that a phosphorous grenade had been detonated whilst still attached to the unfortunate soldier, and it was the products of the burning uniform and flesh that had been drawn inside the Panther.

Noting the live grenade still attached and already warming in the fire, Stepanski gave the corpse a shove with his boot, sending it to the ground alongside the tank.

He rapped his knuckles on the ejection hatch and immediately heard the sounds of metal clips being opened. He was nearly struck as a hot shell case sailed out in short order.

The 75mm cracked again, the recoil nearly breaking his grip on the cupola as he dropped inside the Panther again.

---

The 90mm M3 was a very powerful gun, more than capable of dealing with most tanks on the battlefield.

The high-velocity round struck the barrel of Stepanski's Panther, gouged a two-foot long indentation in it, and then deflected onto the curved mantlet. It struck the gunner's sight in millimetre perfect fashion, driving the quality optical device into the brain and then out the rear of the man's skull, as the shell expended its energy burrowing into the armour.

It did not explode.

The end of the round stood proud of the inside of the tank by some three inches, finally held in place by the mantlet.

Its presence was noted and both men waited for death to come.

It still did not explode.

Both Stepanski and his loader were covered with the blood of the dead gunner, and both found themselves unable to speak, the shock disabling both men, albeit temporarily.

Stepanski recovered first.

"Schiesse!"

He spoke quickly on the intercom.

The gunner was obviously dead.

"Gun's fucked. Klaus is dead. I'm going to take over one of the other tanks. As soon as I'm gone," he looked at the loader, "You take command and get the tank back to the werkstatt. Alles klar?"

The replies were standard and expected.

"Good luck, Kameraden."

Stepanski propelled himself upwards.

Stepanski's Panther reversed back to the river ,and he yelled both encouragement and warning, neither heard, as he watched the vehicle move away, the occasional solid shot sweeping past the moving tank.

He dragged himself into cover, his damaged knee leaving a trail of blood in the snow.

Where the bullet had come from, he didn't know. It hadn't been meant for him, of that he was sure; just a rogue touring the battlefield, having missed its original mark.

But it still hurt like hell.

At the river, the Panther swung swiftly and the tank accelerated forward, rattling the engineer bridge as it bounded over the water.

The trouble with using the bridge, something about which they had no choice, was that a canny gunner could anticipate where a tank would be at a given moment and no skill on the part of the driver could overcome that.

The Pershing gunner, selected for the captured tank because of his capabilities, was such a gunner, and he timed his shot to perfection.

The 90mm shell struck the rear plate, right on the bottom edge, slamming straight down into the bridge, through it and into the river below.

The impact knocked the drive train offline and the tank came to a halt after a few metres.

The gunner of a battered old SU-85, selected for the post solely because he had put himself forward as a gunner, although he was normally a loader, fired his first shot in anger.

The Panther's shell ejection hatch had been pulled shut but the strike by the 90mm had sprung it open. Not fully, in fact, only slightly, but sufficiently for a solid 85mm shot to pass millimetre perfect through the gap.

It took the loader in the head, killing him instantly, and ricocheted off the inside of the turret, smashing into the floor ammo panniers.

The resultant explosion killed the remaining members of the crew.

The surviving two POW's, still lashed to the outside of the Panther, experienced all the horrors of being slowly burnt to death as the interior fire consumed the German tank.

Stepanski screamed in horror as his men died before his eyes.

---

Braun and Durand were in big trouble.

The Soviet mechanised force was perfectly placed on their flank, and looked like being strong enough to overrun them.

What had seemed like a good idea, utilising the bridge and fascines to flank the enemy defences, had turned sour on them, opening them up to a disaster, unless they could hold long enough for friends to arrive.

The main attack on Brumath had petered out in the face of stiff resistance, as well as the knowledge that the original plan had failed.

The plight of the attacking force was known to the Legion's higher command, and the airwaves were full of urgent orders, all designed to save the day.

Alma redoubled its efforts and pressed hard from the north-west and, although still some distance away, the impending presence of the Legion unit alone caused a shift in Brumath's defences.

Knocke, decidedly further forward than he should have been, organised and sent forward a small Kampfgruppe, mainly Camerone, partly Alma and even a few vehicles from Tannenberg, ordered to move up from the forward maintenance facility.

Aware that Uhlmann's main tank force was some time away, Knocke committed the scratch armoured company to supporting the endangered units at Brumath.

He also committed himself.

### 1729 hrs, Wednesday, 4th December 1945, the Zorn River, east of Brumath, Alsace.

Fighting with tanks at night was undesirable, to say the least, but on this night there was no choice.

258

Whilst the light from destroyed vehicles, burning vegetation, weapon flashes, and flares, provided some illumination, it was an untrustworthy light, and one that often deceived the eye.

Braun's Panthers still clung to the north bank, hanging tight to a semi-circle of land two hundred metres either side of the crossing point.

Soviet artillery sought them out and one valuable tank had been knocked out by a direct hit.

Durand's men had pushed in front of the Panthers, providing a screen to keep the Soviet anti-tank hunters at bay.

They were extremely effective, so much so that the Soviets had stopped trying to get men close to the tanks.

Red Army and Legion gunners exchanged shots across a surreal battlefield, the white snow-covered landscape illuminated by the yellows, reds, and oranges of battle, all set against the back drop of a night sky that had once again grown clear and starry, the driving snow now but a memory.

Even the two British AVRE Churchills were in action, braving fire from tanks they could not kill, their Petard mortars throwing large explosive charges at the enemy infantry.

A familiar and inspiring voice crackled in Braun's earpiece and that of a number of listeners on the Camerone radio net.

"Anton One to all Anton units. Maintain your positions." Knocke waited whilst the acknowledgements occupied the airwaves, taking the opportunity to clear his throat and rehearse the message for the ad hoc group, "Anton to Valkyrie, execute plan two, execute plan two. Anton One, out."

There were only two plans, and a swift look at the battle situation through his binoculars had told him all he needed to know.

Plan One called for crossing the river and continuing the attack.

Plan Two was a plan to withdraw the assault force back to the relative safety of the southern bank and hold the river gainst all comers.

"Anton One to London, move up. Anton One out."

A Churchill IV, another of the 79th Armoured's engineering tanks, pushed on towards the river, seeking out a suitable spot to lay its bridge.

The relief force fanned out as Knocke briefed both Durand and Braun on the plan.

Unknown to Knocke and his crew, the command Panther stood out like a sore thumb.

One of the Sturmgeschutz that had been taken from the repair facility had broken down directly behind the Beobachtungspanzer Panther, catching fire as a fuel pipe spilt its contents inside the engine compartment.

The growing blaze illuminated the command tank, a distinct black shape against a fan of yellow drawing many eyes from across the river.

No sooner had the briefing finished than the command Panther shuddered as a large round hit the ground beside it.

Knocke's tank had no main gun, the extra room providing more radio space. Excellent for control, but no good when heavy metal was being exchanged in a stand up fight. In his normal command tank, a Befehlspanzer with the standard 75mm, he could hold his own on the battlefield, but this replacement vehicle, normally used as a mobile artillery OP, had been selected solely because it was suitable for the extra room it provided, but it was not fit to go in harm's way with a turret armament of just an MG34, mounted in a ball mount. That fact alone normally meant that Beobachtungs vehicles tended to tread lightly on the battlefield, relying on hiding, rather than confrontation.

Before anyone could react, a second shell struck the Panther on the left sprocket, causing catastrophic damage to the drive train and track.

Knocke could see two more white streaks on their way across the battlefield and, although they both missed, he knew the Panther's luck was out.

"Driver, can we move?"

"No sir. It's totally fucked."

"Crew, bale out."

The radio operator and Knocke gathered up the sensitive documents and exited the vehicle.

Dropping off the rear of the disabled command tank, the burning Stug almost taunted him, declaring its part in the loss of his vehicle.

'*Schiesse.*'

He pointed at one of the American scout cars and issued orders to the tank crew.

"Once the fire's out, get Zeppelin up here to fix my tank," Zeppelin was Camerone's Werkstatt unit, "But stay away from it 'til it's not silhouetted by the fire. That's how the Reds saw us."

The tankers looked at where their leader was pointing, more than one curse illustrating their understanding of the bad luck that could have ended their lives.

"I have to be in there," he pointed at the growing battle at the river, "So, I'll exercise my rank and kick someone out of their cosy vehicle. I'll send them to you, so keep your eyes open. Alles klar?"

The four men nodded, suddenly aware that their talisman was leaving them.

"Take care, Kameraden. Turnips down 'til I get back. Now, raus."

The tank Knocke had set his sights on moved position, labouring by the sound of its engine, and dropped in behind a small but thick stand of trees.

Selecting his moment, he pushed himself out from behind the disabled command tank and started on the three hundred metre journey, hugging a low line of hedgerow.

---

Knocke had heard correctly. The tank had mechanical problems and two of its crew were already on the repair.

"So, can you fix it or fucking not?"

The flashlight moved around the V12 engine compartment, indicating concentration.

"Only if you shut the fuck up and let me get on with it."

The two men were head down in the engine bay, having pulled up two of the gratings.

"Fucking oil everywhere. Have we still got any with us?"

The junior man, the tank's driver and mechanic, hummed a response and then managed a single word.

"Bin."

The senior man, his American tanker's tunic sporting the odd combination of Legion eagle, Tannenberg armband, German Cross in silver, Iron Cross First and Second class, Black wound badge, and a much newer Croix de Guerre, moved to the back of the turret to check in the crew bin.

Finding three five-litre containers, he dropped back down behind the cover offered by the turret and lit a cigarette.

"Fifteen litres s'all we've got, Klaus."

"That's all I could lift from the spanner grenadieres."

Taking a deep draw on his cigarette, Sergeant Köster, formerly known as SS-Scharfuhrer Köster of the 503rd SS Schwere Panzer Abteilung, spoke to the turret crew, making sure he and his glowing cigarette end stayed firmly behind cover.

"How's his shitty hand?"

The gunner popped his head out of the hatch.

"Broken two fingers at least, Rudi. Nasty tear. Dislocated the other two, possibly even sprained his wrist. He's not loading the fucking gun any time soon, that's for sure!"

"Great," which it obviously wasn't, "Get it bandaged up and I'll decide what we're going to do."

The gunner dropped back inside to finish bandaging the loader's mangled hand.

When the tank had dropped into a gully obscured by snowfall, the loader had put his hand out to steady himself and inadvertently slipped it into the locking mechanism of the rear hatch.

Momentum did the rest, as his weight ripped the webbing between middle and fourth finger, the two smaller fingers snapping with gunshot sounds that even Meier the driver had heard.

Working the problem, Köster noted the approaching figure, and found himself sniggering at the man's strange crouching run.

Amusement turned into curiosity.

Curiosity turned to concern, and he pulled out his Browning Hi-Power 640b.

He would have no hesitation in letting the strange man have all thirteen rounds if he had to.

Concern turned into relief as the uniform identified the man as a friend.

Relief turned into disbelief, and quickly turned into incredulity as the indistinct figure materialised into 'The Legend'.

He dismounted and shot to attention.

"Zu befehl, Oberfuhrer. One tank, five men present, one wounded. Vehicle is presently disabled by a mechanical problem. My driver is assessing the issue now, Sir."

Knocke had no time to reply as another voice stole the opportunity from him.

"Oh do shut the fuck up, Rudi. This is no time for your fucking games, you idiot! Now, get me the tool kit. I need a fucking wrench. Something not right here."

Knocke nodded, and Köster disappeared to get the tools.

When he returned, he found his General head down in the engine compartment and in conversation with the driver.

"I went from Panzer IV's to Panthers, so this beast is a mystery to me. But surely that much oil didn't come from just **that** loose joint?"

Meier considered his reply.

"We had a sudden loss of oil pressure. A big near miss... must have shook the shitty thing loose... enough pressure to bollock it out, kamerad. But... maybe you're right. Hang on."

He slid further down.

"Fuck it. Here, hang on to that and point it down here."

The oily torch was thrust into Knocke's left hand.

Köster considered the moment, feeling a growing despair, and then offered up the wrench to his commander's free hand.

Knocke took it, the light of battle sufficient for his wink to be noticed.

"Here, Klaus, the wrench."

A dirty hand reached up and took the tool, managing to transfer a considerable amount of the sticky black fluid onto his unknown helper.

Knocke's mind clicked, recalling a document he had seen over two years before.

"Bolts, Klaus? I remember there was often an issue with them. Bolts de-threading under pressure, sub-standard workmanship caused by the Allied bombing as I recall. De-threaded by your near miss possibly?"

From below came the sounds of a man thinking aloud.

"Hmm. Come to think of it... hang on."

The wrench worked away, metal tapping on metal as the handle moved within the comfines of the compartment.

"Yes indeed, Kamerad. Nice spot. You'll go far in this man's army with a brain like that."

The wrench attacked bolt after bolt, the exertions starting to tell on the tank driver.

"Seen much action, kamer... can't...keep...calling... you... kamerad... " each individual effort on the wrench gave him a natural pause in his speech.

"What's your name, son?"

Köster almost passed out on the spot.

"Call me Ernst... for now."

Knocke played the game, mainly because he wanted the man to complete his work, not suddenly come apart because his commander was present, but the humour of the situation wasn't wasted on him and he was perfectly prepared to momentarily become the prankster he had once been known as.

"Rudi?"

"Yes, Caporal-Chef Meier?"

Köster went formal to try and focus his driver on the present 'unusual' situation.

The effort was wasted.

"Can we keep our kamerad Ernst here? He seems to know his business, unlike you. Maybe he... can... go... in... charge. Right, that's it."

The laugh was genuine.

Meier emerged and started using a piece of waste linen to clean up, failing to notice much about the man next to him.

264

"I've done the fucking best I can for now. Suggest we keep the revs down 'til I can get new bolts. Five are stripped badly, well fucked. Precious little thread to tighten on."

"Good knowledge there, Ernst," he turned to his helper, his mouth automatically speaking the words he intended before he realised that Köster was not being the playful arse he had thought earlier, "Can I trade you in for this useless piece of... oh scheisse!"

His mouth fell open, but his automatic reactions took over.

Springing to attention, an oily hand marked his forehead in a salute.

"Zu befehl, Oberfuhrer. Temporary repair has been completed. Tank will be ready for combat once the oil level has been restored, Sir."

As Knocke received his report, his thoughts grabbed at the memories of what he had said in the last few minutes and whether a firing squad was out of the question.

Knocke slapped Meier on the shoulder.

"Then get it done, kamerad, and let's start killing some Russians."

Meier, anxious to avoid Knocke's further attention, swung into immediate action.

Knocke found himself staring at the man, searching his memory for information but his excellent memory presently deserted him, failing to recall anything of note. He would speak to Köster later. Very few drivers or corporals were so honoured, so there had to be a good story behind why the dirty man with the grubby ripped panzer overall sported the Knight's Cross at his neck.

Addressing Köster, the commander of Camerone was more formal.

"I need your radio and your tank, in that order, Sergeant."

Köster dropped inside the tank and brought out the headset.

He waited for Knocke to establish contact with Braun and Durand before informing his commander of the full nature of the crew problem.

"You can load then, Köster. Get your man back to the aid post. My crew are up by my disabled command tank,

Send him up there and they will sort him out. Now, if our driver has finished, let's go and rescue our Kameraden."

---

The loader slipped off the tank and made his way towards the disabled command vehicle. He paused to watch the Tiger I move out from behind the stand of trees, take position behind a wall, and start to work the battlefield.

For a moment, he wished he was safely tucked up inside the huge metal box but a shell clanging off the turret mantlet told him he was safer where he was going, so he set off, reversing the route Knocke had used.

He was never seen again.

### 1809 hrs, Wednesday, 4th December 1945, east of Brumath, Alsace.

The fight had halted for a moment, the Soviets drawing back, leaving a number of their vehicles and men on the field.

The legionnaires north of the river had been savaged, but had clung on.

Braun had four Panthers and one Panzer IV still intact, whilst Durand had lost forty good men keeping the Soviet infantry away from the tanks.

Both AVREs had succumbed, as had 'London', the Churchill IV, but not before its bridge was properly in place.

Knocke judged that the moment was right to withdraw the trapped force but paused, sensing an alternative.

He swept the battlefield with his binoculars.

What was it?

*'Something is happening here.'*

"Switch channels. Command please."

Once on the main command channel, Knocke got a surprise.

His previous attempt to get hold of Alma had failed, his communications confined to other members of the relief force, and those across the water.

His ears deciphered the messages of the lead Alma units and Uhlmann's tanks organising themselves for the assault on the north-western edge of Brumath.

266

*'I knew it.'*

He waited for a gap in transmissions, drinking in the details of what Alma and Uhlmann intended.

"Anton One, Anton One to all units on this channel. Proceed as you have just stated. I'll move in support. Watch for friendlies to your front advancing from the river line. Do not move out of objective zweiundzwanzig. Acknowledge. Anton One over."

He moved on to brief his small force, Braun and Durand, realising that fate had placed an opportunity in front of him.

Plan Two had become Plan One.

He transmitted a brief message.

"Anton One to all units. Initiate Plan One, Initiate Plan One. Vorwärts."

## 1815 hrs, Wednesday, 4th December 1945, Brumath, Alsace.

Alma, supported by Uhlmann's armour, threw themselves upon Brumath.

Braun's force was suddenly relieved of pressure as his opposition became aware of the greater threat posed by Alma.

Accepting the casualties of a swift attack, the main Legion assault smashed into the Alsatian town, and overran the enemy defensive line, scattering units in all directions.

Some withdrew down Route 47, immediately coming into contact with vehicles from the 412th Mechanised units that had been split off and sent to bolster Brumath.

The traffic jam became a bloodbath as Uhlmann, then Knocke, ordered an artillery attack on the disorganised Soviets.

The Legionnaires of Alma pressed close, so close that a handful of casualties were caused by friendly fire, but the net result was the Brumath fell in less than half an hour.

Consulting the map, Knocke ordered Alma to take Route 140 to the north-east, aimed at Weitbruch, but always watching for an opportunity to fall upon the force that had given Braun such a hard time.

Knocke's own force was ordered to advance and hold position on Braun's units, although Knocke expected that he would move his men on quickly.

As per plan, one platoon of tanks and two of infantry moved to the south of the river, acting as a covering force.

The Allied artillery was called off, its work of butchery near complete, and Alma pushed forward again.

---

Senior Sergeant Ivan Balyan could not believe his bad luck.

This was not his fight. He'd just taken the opportunity offered by his recent wounding to travel south to visit his brother, Igor.

His own unit, 1st Guards [Motorised] Sapper Brigade, was part of 1st Red Banner and had seen extensive action in recent weeks.

Wounded during an air raid near the Hunte River, Balyan was patched up and took advantage of eight days leave to visit his younger brother's anti-tank unit in Alsace.

The Legion's whirlwind attack, and the frenzied defensive efforts of the Soviet commanders, saw him temporarily assigned to the AT company salvaged from 3rd Guards Tank Corps and absorbed by the Cavalry Corps until, as the NKVD Lieutenant had shouted as he waved his pistol in all directions, Balyan was otherwise ordered.

Sat to the left of the deadly anti-tank gun, Balyan operated a covering DP machine-gun, his job to ensure that enemy infantry did not overrun the gun and crew. It also provided him with an excellent view of his brother, who would act as one of the loaders on the BS-3.

A few had been salvaged from the destruction of the Corps; others had been acquired from units similarly savaged.

The 100mm BS-3 had been acquired by accident, the weapon, prime mover, and ammo carrier, all found in perfect condition at Dingsheim, north-west of Strasbourg.

Igor Balyan's 'new' officer had no hesitation in acquiring the killer weapon and, as one of his best men, the younger Balyan found himself assigned to its crew.

Fig#97 - The Battle of Brumath, Third assault and Soviet counter-attack, 4th December 1945.

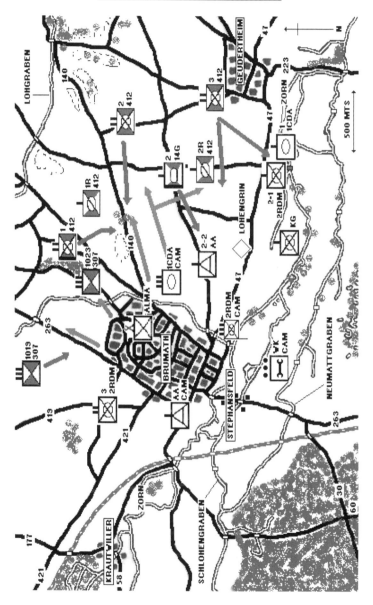

269

3rd Guards Tank Corps had gone into combat with 76.2mm Zis-3s, and most of them lay smashed or abandoned in Alsace.

The Soviet anti-tank gunners, as always masters of camouflage, waited patiently as target after target emerged from Brumath.

The order was given and, as the sky was filled with the white light of flares, the one and a half companies opened fire.

The 100mm's gunner knew his craft and targeted a Panther tank moving behind the first wave, clearly faster than the rest, but also quite clearly being skilfully manoeuvred from cover to cover by a man who knew his business. The extra aerials the vehicle sported helped in his decision making.

The shell had taken the Legion tank in the lower hull side, immediately under the turret.

The tank lazily coasted to a halt, and flames could be seen quite clearly through the round hole that marked the penetration point of the solid shot.

Men, uniforms smoking, or worse, emerged from the stricken tank to be met by fire from infantry weapons and, although none were killed, two of the men clearly staggered away wounded.

The Soviet artillery added to the defence, engulfing the advance of Alma with Katyusha rockets, and shells from a 203mm Howitzer company.

One such huge shell descended on a Legion halftrack and left little of the vehicle and its twelve-man crew behind.

The effect upon the Legion soldiers was almost tangible, the veteran Red Army soldiers sensing immediately that a blow had been dealt, which immediately caused them to redouble their efforts.

The Legionnaires still attacked, but with less focus than before.

The artillery of both sides repositioned, removing that element from the battle temporarily, but the anti-tank guns, a pair of SU-100's, and the repositioned Pershing continued to flay the Alma soldiers.

More Soviet tanks resisted Knocke's flanking move, and that too came to a halt.

Knocke understood that the seesaw battle had, once again, tipped in favour of the enemy, and sought a way to snatch the initiative back.

"Berta-One, Berta-One, Anton-One, over."

Knocke repeated the message, although he suspected he would do so in vain.

There would be no reply, for the Balyan's BS-3 had killed Uhlmann's tank with its first shot.

He closed his eyes in a brief plea to higher authority and spoke to the next in line.

"Caesar-Zero-On..."

The 122mm struck the Tiger's gun mantlet, shaking everything from radio to man, but not penetrating, although the hot glow of its strike made it through the armour to the left of the gunner's sight.

"Crew, report in."

"Driver ok, engine fine, Sir."

"Loader ok and ready, Herr Oberfuhrer!"

"Gunner, weapon up and ready, S-S-Sir."

The last report betrayed the fright the man had just received.

Meier reported in again.

"Willi's dead. He's just dead."

Eyes dropped to take a look and the man was clearly that, eyes open and distantly fixed, head lolling back beyond the point of comfort.

"Driver, reverse and left, gunner sweep centre to right."

The Tiger moved immediately, the white-hot trail of another 122m shell punching the air where Knocke's tank had been a moment before.

"Target tank, Stalin type, nine hundred metres. Halt!"

"ON!"

"FIRE!"

Nothing.

"Again."

Still nothing.

"Driver, reverse and left again. Gunner, fix it now."

Immediately the gunner spotted the problem and repaired the linkage issue caused by the direct hit.

271

He waited until the tank stopped moving again.

"Target tank, Stalin type, nine fifty metres."

"Fire!"

The 88mm recoiled as it spat its deadly shell in the direction of the enemy vehicle.

The target was concealed by a shower of white-hot sparks as shell met armour plate.

"HIT!"

"Well done, gunner. Again."

Knocke observed as the Tiger's gunner put an 88mm right on the money, the IS-III again erupting in a cascade of tortured metal.

The monster shrugged off the hit, and put its own shell in the air.

Knocke smiled as the enemy shell tore high and wide.

"Again."

Knocke watched as another shell struck the Stalin tank, the tracks disintegrating. Even at that distance, and in the weird light of a night battle, Knocke could observe two of the heavy track links scythe through a group of supporting infantry, metal tearing flesh in an unforgiving fashion.

"Again. Between the tracks."

The IS-III, hit whilst attempting to move, had exposed its wounded side sufficiently for 'Lohengrin's' gunner to make a telling hit but the light suddenly went and he baulked sending a shot into darkness.

"Lost target!"

Knocke rejected the flare pistol, knowing he would illuminate himself more than the target.

One of Alma's mortar crews did the work, tossing illumination almost perfectly, so perfectly that the other tanks adjacent to the IS-III became immediately apparent.

"Got the schwein. ON!"

"Fire!"

Knocke ignored the break in procedure.

The 88mm took the heavy tank just above the nearside front road wheel.

Deflected upwards by the bulk of the floor plate, it entered the fighting compartment, moving through the driver's seat and striking the turret ring. Again deflected, the armour-piercing shell passed through the commander's body before striking the back wall of the turret and exploding.

"Well done, gunner. New target, left eight, range nine forty."

The IS-III was clearly dead, and now provided excellent illumination of the surrounding area, revealing a cluster of four adjacent tanks to the Tiger's gun.

Knocke went through the motions of tank commander automatically, aware that the crew around him were a special group of men, a team, welded together in adversity.

The gunner drew his critical eye and he took in the man's decorations, including the shiny new Croix de Guerre.

Something clicked in his mind, and he spoke his thoughts.

"Ah, Lohengrin."

Köster smiled.

"You remembered, Oberfuhrer."

"Target tank, nine hundred."

"Fire! Indeed. Général St.Clair spoke of little else for some time... Sergeant Köster?"

Posed as a question, the acting loader could only grin and nod as he ejected the smoking shell case and slotted another home.

"Target tank, left six, nine hundred. I'll give you your Tiger back as soon as possible, but for now, you're stuck with me."

A shell dropped next to the Tiger, the clatter of metal fragments sounding like a rain shower on the vehicle's side.

"Target tank, eight seventy."

"Fire! Driver, relocate, forward and left."

*'They're moving forward!'*

---

Burning tanks and vehicles littered the ground east of Brumath.

A line of tanks and half-tracks indicated the high-water mark of the Alma advance, to the east of them numerous fires betrayed the price the Soviet defenders had paid to stop them.

Fire illuminated the battlefield, outdoing the efforts of the moon and stars, whilst producing smoke that tried hard to smother the battlefield.

The night was sometimes clear, the next moment the men on the ground could see no more than a few feet in front of them and, often, found themselves choking in thick acrid smoke.

The artillery and mortars of both sides, now in new positions, added to the creation of a living nightmare.

Knocke was correct in assessing that the Soviet force was advancing again, but could neither assess its strength nor objective, although he could take a guess at the latter.

After a radio exchange with the Alma's commander, St.Clair, he understood that things were out of control. The units of 'Normandie' were all stretched beyond their normal limits, and finding well organised and aggressive defence turned into counter-attacks, almost in the old SS style.

Radio messages from hard-pressed units brought more and more contact reports, building a picture of a growing Soviet presence on the field; certainly one well in excess of the intelligence reports.

Again, leaving the crew of 'Lohengrin' to fight the enemy to his front, Knocke concentrated on the bigger picture, pencilling marks on his map and rattling out an order here and there.

The tank moved unbidden, forward and left, angling itself behind a ramshackle wall.

The 88m roared; the crew celebrated another kill.

Knocke heard all and gathered everything in the background of his mind as he concentrated on the radio messages; one message in particular, that spoke of a disaster in the making.

*'Schiesse verdamnt!'*

One of his units was in dire need and Knocke acted immediately.

"Gun, cease fire. Driver, reverse back to the track and then swing north-west. Best speed, Meier, best speed."

Köster took up his seat, blowing out his cheeks and rubbing his aching arms, sparing the Legend a quizzical look.

The Tiger surged forward up the track, Meier coaxing the very best out of the Maybach engines that propelled the fifty-six ton tank according to his will.

"Part of Martha's about to be overrun, and we're all that can stop it, Sergeant. Ammo?"

"Mostly HE now, Oberfuhrer. Nine AP shells only... and we don't have a logistics train with us."

Tannenberg was away to the south, and neither Camerone nor Alma had any Tigers on their strength.

Knocke, in a way that only Knocke could carry off to perfection, spoke with conviction.

"Nine will do the job nicely."

'Lohengrin' did not let them down.

"Martha-Two-Two, Anton-One, nearly with you. Hold on. Over."

One of Camerone's flak units had moved up with the Alma, and it was their cry for help that Knocke had heard.

"Driver, turn right fifty metres. See that clump? In behind that, left side."

The Tiger took the turn, and Meier skilfully dropped Lohengrin in on the left side of the clump of trees.

*'Not a moment too soon!'*

"Numerous enemy to front. Gunner, target tank, left eight, four hundred."

The electrics whirred, bringing the 88m online and filling the gunner's sight with the green metal side of an IS-II.

"Target tank, four hundred."

"Fire!"

The solid shot struck home fatally.

"Gunner, target tank, right three, four hundred."

"Target tank, four hundred."

"Fire!"

Like automatons they worked, smashing the IS-II's in turn. The fifth shot was a total miss, and two targets needed a second AP shell to ensure the kill.

The solid shot came and went, and then HE was used, with no chance of penetration, not that the Soviet tankers knew that.

Having lost six of their number to the single enemy tank, the tank unit lost heart and started to fall back, hastened along by the spectacular impacts of 88mm high-explosive shells.

Blagoslavov's command had been reinforced and Knocke had fallen upon the flank of a heavy tank company, just in time to save his Flak unit.

"Well done, Kameraden, damned well done."

The crew of Lohengrin had added another chapter to the tale of their exploits, and it would spread and grow, the more so because the commander of Camerone had fought the tank for most of the battle.

"Eighteen HE shells left, Oberfuhrer."

"Then I'll ask no more of you and your men today, Sergeant."

Knocke had spotted an infantry command vehicle behind a barn two hundred metres away.

"Your tank, Sergeant Köster... and thank you."

Making sure the crew could all hear him, he continued.

"Gentlemen, it's been a privilege. Get yourselves back and sorted. When this is over, we'll speak again."

"Now," Knocke braced himself on the cupola to address Köster and prepared to pull himself out, "Get your tank fit for action and your men rested."

"Zu befehl, Oberfuhrer."

---

Knocke found himself at the command vehicle of the 2nd Battalion, 1st RDM, being briefed on the unfolding disaster by a wounded Commandant Emmercy.

Clearly, there were more Soviet formations, tank heavy ones at that, than they had expected.

The Red Army had counter-attacked in strength from the north, and Alma was being forced out of Brumath, electing to withdraw through choice, and with control, rather than risk being driven out in a disorganised fashion.

Knocke, presented with a full size map properly annotated, acted immediately, issuing orders to get his command out of the growing disaster around Brumath.

The Legion would retreat in a controlled fashion, and regroup south and southwest of Brumath, shortening the line.

Braun's force had already moved back over the river while it could, orienting defensively to halt any attempt to cross, as well as protect the approach from Hœrdt.

Elsewhere, the Legion assaults had been blunted in a bloody and expensive fashion, the cost in men and materiel high on both sides.

However, it was at Brumath, and to the east, that the greatest sacrifices had been made.

The 412nd Mechanised Brigade lost all but seven of its tanks, and a quarter of its infantry lay dead upon the field.

One in ten of the Alma lay dead, other units that had been in support equally savaged.

Losses in Legion equipment were huge, worst in tanks and SP guns.

And Uhlmann was missing.

---

It had been an extremely difficult night.

Rest did not come for many at the French First Army Headquarters.

Throughout the night, the Legionnaires and GIs of the Corps D'Assault laboured against growing odds, mostly without gain, and always at cost.

Each and every assault had been stopped in its tracks, although the Soviet strength grew as that of the Corps D'Assault declined, the hospitals and dressing station full to overflowing with the injured legionnaires and GIs of the US supporting forces.

Command Group Normandie had taken the brunt of the serious fighting and remained the heaviest engaged of the three groups. The 16th US Armored Brigade was in reasonably good shape, despite the fact that it had tangled with some very serious Red Army tank formations. Alma was mauled, as was Camerone.

Command Group Lorraine had fared much better. Tannenberg was relatively intact, but was spread thin in an effort to relieve the pressure on its comrades from Normandie.

Sevastopol was moving to take over some of Tannenberg's ground, so her sister unit could close up again.

Command Group Aquitaine had the lightest load, and it was presently being manoeuvred into positions where it

277

could take over from Camerone's decimated units, supported by the arrival of the 7th Regiment Tirailleurs Algerie from Corps reserve.

Général d'Armée De Lattre received an extremely difficult phone call, the more so as despised the man who had made it.

*'Molyneux.'*

Reports from Plummer had suggested that the man was actually acquiring some competence. A private conversation with De Walle had revealed the contents of yet another such exchange, when Lavalle had expressed his surprise at the contribution Molyneux had made in the planning of Spectrum Black.

*'Perhaps we are all wrong about him?'*

De Lattre snorted openly.

*'Perhaps not!'*

The man had been virtually on the verge of tears as he presented the bad news.

The notes De Lattre had made were for his use only. The results of Spectrum Black would already have been translated onto the situation map downstairs.

Picking up the phone again, he directed the operator to place his secure call.

278

*The whole art of war consists of guessing at what is on the other side of the hill.*

*Arthur Wellesley, subsequently The Duke of Wellington.*

## Chapter 113 - THE DECISIONS

### 1606 hrs, Thursday, 5th December 1945, Headquarters of SHAEF, Trianon Place Hotel, Versailles, France.

"A good evening to you, General."

Eisenhower was in the planning room, poring over maps with most of the command group for Spectrum; Smith, Tedder, Bradley, Patton, Dönitz, Guderian, Somerville, and McCreery.

Von Vietinghoff was absent on a visit to Alexander in Italy. Devers was busy with his own problems, and he had easily accepted De Lattre's request to speak directly to Eisenhower.

Also present were two men from the darker professions, remaining aloof and silent until their time to contribute came.

None of the officers present had yet benefitted from the latest reports from French First Army, so focussed had they been on their own part of the plan.

Ike covered the mouthpiece and mouthed the name of the caller. Everyone stopped for the moment, waiting for the Supreme Commander to get the good news.

The look on Eisenhower's face sent out warnings long before he started to repeat what he was hearing.

"Spectrum Black has been stopped."

Guderian and Patton exchanged looks, wondering if all the planning was about to go out of the window. The two had established a professional working relationship, based on mutual admiration for the qualities of the other, stirred with the obvious personality differences, and tempered with the distrust that clearly remained from their time as adversaries.

"I'm sorry to hear that, General, really I am. Can you hold what you have?"

Eisenhower scribbled as De Lattre spoke.

279

*'Legion Corps decimated. Spectrum Black advances approximately half of intended distance.'*

Eisenhower nodded at the telephone, at a man who was so many miles away.

"Yes indeed. That was noted by our reconnaissance. At least six corps equivalents. That represents two of their army formations at the very least, General."

Part of Spectrum Black had been aimed at moving some of the Soviet units southwards, and it had achieved that aim rather too well for the Legion Corps.

Clearly, De Lattre was concerned over the ratio of forces.

Again, Eisenhower nodded out of habit.

"I will authorise that immediately, General. Give me an hour and I'll send you something else too."

Ike grimaced, feeling the man's pain.

"Please thank your unit commanders, General. They've done all they could."

The Commander gripped the phone demonstrably tighter, his voice adopting the reluctant tone that was always present when Eisenhower asked men to do the impossible.

"Can you continue to bring them down on you, General? Agitate? Local attacks? Keep their moving units on the march south?"

Ike closed his eyes, initially to pray for the right answer, and then in thanks that the man immediately supplied it.

"Thank you, General."

De Lattre came to the end of his call.

"Yes. Thank you, General. We will not waste the opportunity your brave men have granted us. Good night to you, General."

Replacing the telephone in its cradle, Eisenhower remained staring at the inert object.

"Sir?"

It was Bedell-Smith who had spoken first.

Eisenhower recovered his poise.

"Sorry. Gentlemen, the French have been stopped."

His hand shot up immediately he saw that Patton's body started to twitch.

280

"No! Not now, not the hell now, George. They did what we asked of 'em, and they brought down a world of hurt upon themselves so that your boys can have an easier ride... so not now... not ever."

Eisenhower's voice climbed steadily as he spoke, his final five words almost spat directly at Patton.

The men in the room almost recoiled, for such passionate displays were extremely unusual for their leader.

George's pathological disregard for his French allies and their capacity for fighting was not well known, except to the men in the room.

His disdain for the ex-SS units had not been hidden from the moment they came into being.

Eisenhower, clearly affected by the conversation with de Lattre, had fallen on him heavily.

Out of the others in the room, only Bedell-Smith did not show the slightest traces of a smile at the cowing of the buoyant commander of Spectrum's main assault phase.

George Patton was heavily disliked by Bradley, as the two had history that went way back. The Germans, grudging admirers of the man's record driving through France, felt the American's brashness hid away limitations that would surface if things did not go to plan. The British, at least those present, tolerated him, but did not enjoy his presence, which was as much as a result of his ability to get under people's skin as his blind faith in his own invincibility.

Eisenhower brought them back to him as he lit his cigarette.

"Gentlemen... Spectrum Black's now effectively ended. De Lattre will try and make further distractions, but his units have been hammered, so no great progress is now possible."

Letting them digest that for a few seconds, Ike cast a quick look at the map.

"They have been successful bringing down these units, away from where they can harm the main attack."

Others joined him in his examination of the plethora of coloured arrows and markings that designated the plan for Spectrum.

"Before that call we were agreed that they'd already done enough. I'm sending some extra troops to bolster them...

I'll sort that with you shortly, Walter... so what we've to examine is any change caused by the losses to the French. Brad?"

Eisenhower deliberately called in his senior field commander to make the first contribution.

"Sir, we've very little time before we go in."

Bradley paused between each point.

"The Commies've moved considerable assets out of our line of advance, and we were happy to go on that basis, before the call, that is."

He looked at Patton and Guderian, the two men most burdened with direct responsibility for the main assault.

Neither spoke so the commander of the US Twelfth Army Group continued.

"We'd like more assets to move away, but I assume that'll risk causing us trouble down in Alsace there?"

There were enough nods for him to understand he would get no argument on that point.

"Unless the Navy and Air Force can show me otherwise, I think we gotta go in the morning, as planned."

It was not as originally planned, but delay had been forced upon the Allies by unforeseen circumstances.

"Good point, Brad. Admiral?"

Cunningham looked at Donitz, who gave a firm nod of the head.

"The naval aspects of Spectrum are ready to go on schedule, Sir. Unless Admiral Donitz can say otherwise, I would absolutely recommend that we go on Friday. We cannot risk 'Red' being discovered beforehand and, if we delay, I'll have to keep my fleet circling out here," he stabbed the North Sea, "And that will do nothing for those aboard the ships."

Dönitz did not wait for an invitation.

Golding, ever-present to interpret, had not even started before the diminutive German Admiral had concluded.

"Sir, Admiral Dönitz states his belief that Spectrum Blue should go on Friday as planned, Sir."

Eisenhower looked the German in the eye.

"Thank you, Admiral. Arthur?"

Tedder, Ike's second in command and highest-ranking Air Force officer in SHAEF was similarly straightforward.

"Sir, we've the weather we need across the areas of concern, guaranteed as best can be until Monday. If we delay, I grant you, I'll have my assets get stronger, but I may not be able to bring them to bear if the weather falls away. 'Green' is unaffected by the French's problems. I say go."

Eisenhower nodded to his deputy, sliding his matches to the RAF man who was clearly in search of ignition for his pipe.

His gaze turned to the two men responsible for the sharp end of the ground attack.

"So, gentlemen?"

Patton, still annoyed by Eisenhower's relative harsh handling, remained unusually silent.

Guderian slowly turned away from the curtained window he had been looking at, his gaze trying to burn through the heavy hangings and into the night sky beyond.

Clearly, he did not trust his English for the statement, so Goldstein was called into action again.

"Sir, General Guderian states that much depends on the weather so, if it is as Herr Stagg says, then we must go as planned. Delay risks discovery of all parts of Spectrum."

Eisenhower nodded his head and turned to Patton, looking him directly in the eye, not challenging the man, but firmly letting George know that the previous matter was closed.

Patton's haughtiness returned in an instant and, with hands on his hips and chest thrust out, George S Patton, commander of the US Third Army, shared his thoughts.

"Just say the goddamned word, Ike, and we'll march all the way to Moscow, starting ten o'clock Friday morning."

No one had expected any different.

### 1607 hrs, Thursday, 5th December 1945, GRU Western Europe Headquarters, the Mühlberg, Germany.

"What?"

"The NKVD are convinced that this assault near Strasbourg is a feint; a maskirovka. They have reports that the Allies will move elsewhere, as a main attack, within the next seventy-two hours, possibly as soon as tomorrow, Comrade General."

"Where? Do they know where?"

Nazarbayeva was normally softer in her dealings with her staff, especially Poboshkin, but the nature of the report had unsettled her.

"Not for certain, but there are German ground formations involved. That places it on or either side of the Ruhr area. The NKVD have discounted Italy, I'm assuming because of the source of their information."

She took a drink from her glass, the cool water bringing the moment's pause she needed to gather her thoughts.

"We'll deal with how we've missed this later. For now, re-examine every report we've had for the last two weeks... and reassess on the basis of what we now know, or what our comrades of the NKVD believe we now know. Find me something, Andrey. My flight's at 1725 hrs, and I want everything we can put together to brief the General Secretary."

---

Alone in her office, Nazarbayeva's mind went through everything she could remember, occasionally picking up a piece of paper, or making a note of her own on a pad.

After nearly an hour, she was no closer to making any meaningful discovery.

The knock on the door both broke her concentration and intrigued her, for it carried with it a sense of urgency that, in present conditions, could only mean progress.

Her aide almost ran to the desk, the Captain that followed behind slower and more wary of the new commander.

"Comrade General. This is Kapitan Ivashutin. He has been monitoring information regarding our field agents, with my permission, of course."

From that, Nazarbayeva clearly understood that Ivashutin had been freelancing something in his department, undoubtedly outside of his normal duties, but that Lieutenant Colonel Poboshkin intended to stand by the man, in spite of the serious indiscretion.

That told her much before another word was spoken.

"Kapitan."

At Poboshkin's invitation, the nervous man laid a handmade map on the desk.

The annotations were meaningless to the uncoached eye, which in this case was everyone but Ivashutin.

Clearing his throat, he repeated what he had told Poboshkin ten minutes beforehand.

"Comrade General, this is something that I was doing in my own time as a monitoring exercise. This map records matters between the 1st and 31st of October."

He tapped the hand written legend, meaningless words and numbers that clearly meant something to him.

"Sir, you'll note that I took security seriously and encrypted my results."

"Comrade Kapitan, please. PodPolkovnik Poboshkin's already vouched for you and further discussion on your... personal project will take place under his authority. Just give it to me straight and to hell with the ass covering!"

"As you command, Comrade General. Each of these marks is a message that originates from one of our field agents as best as can be interpreted on the basis of tasking and known operating base..."

Ivashutin's voice trailed away and he coughed deeply. Nazarbayeva gestured towards the carafe and Poboshkin filled three glasses quickly, setting one on the desk for each of them.

"Thank you, Sir."

Ivashutin's glass emptied and his dry throat was refreshed.

"Excuse me, Comrade General."

He produced a second map and laid it next to the first so that the two were easily compared. Tapping the legend, he continued.

"This covers the same group of agents from 1st to 30th November.

Nazarbayeva could not help but be shocked.

"Go on, Comrade Kapitan."

As she spoke, she shared a look with Poboshkin who aired his thoughts.

"He's sold me, Comrade General."

Picking up in confidence, Ivashutin tallied off the reasons why normal procedures did not reveal the issue. He was stating the obvious, but Nazarbayeva let him have his moment.

"Agents in the field cannot always contact us on a given schedule, and we are used to them dropping out for weeks at a time without problems. Because of recent events, the volume of work has been maintained as some agents have become prolific in their reporting. Because of the way we assign control of our agents, the lack of central monitoring has counted against us this time, Comrade General."

Normally, criticism of the system was not acceptable, but he had a point.

"So, Comrade Kapitan, translate this for me."

"Comrade General, what you see here is an area, from Venlo down to Luxembourg, where agent reports have greatly reduced, compared to October."

He sought eye contact with Poboshkin, and was rewarded with silent encouragement.

"Comrade General, in October we had thirteen agents, possibly as many as sixteen, at work within this area."

Checking the pad in front of him, he dropped his bombshell.

"For certain, twelve, possibly fourteen of those have made no reports in November, whereas here...and here," he indicated the military zones above and below the virginal white paper, "The reports are flowing thickly."

Her eye examined the two maps, acknowledging the void created south of the Ruhr, through the Hürtgenwald, and into the Ardennes.

"And your opinion and interpretation, Comrade Kapitan?"

Ivashutin was momentarily confused. The number of times that a general officer had sought his view on anything could be counted on the fingers of a hand with no fingers.

Nazarbayeva decided to put him at his ease as best she could.

"Speak freely, Comrade Ivashutin."

"Sir... Comrade General... I believe that this area has been created by the Allies counter-intelligence forces removing or displacing our agents as they have built up a large assault force. I have no proof, but PodPolkovnik Poboshkin has ordered a review of agent's reports from November, which might help us understand better, especially if we look at them in the context of this suspicion... Comrade General....Sir..."

The quiet unnerved Ivashutin, both senior officers fixed upon and absorbed by his map work.

"What is your job, Comrade Kapitan?"

"Comrade General, I head the logging section. All reports come through us for logging and filing."

"Not any more. You'll be allocated four men and a second officer to create a new section specifically to officially undertake," she spared a wry look for her aide, "The task that Comrade PodPolkovnik Poboshkin wisely asked you to commence... in October?"

Again, Ivashutin looked uncomfortable

"Err, September, Comrade General."

"September?"

"Yes, Comrade General."

The man had been wrong to do what he did but his efforts, ones that could easily earn him a place in a Gulag, had highlighted a problem long before it would have been found.

Her mind was made up.

"PodPolkovnik Poboshkin will sort out your new personnel and a suitable place of work. You will keep him informed at all times, understand?"

One nod was enough.

"Thank you for taking the risk and bringing this information to us, Comrade Ivashutin. You could easily have said nothing."

Nazarbayeva picked up an official letterhead and wrote a formal note, which she passed, to her aide.

Sharing his smile, she concluded the session.

"Now, go with Comrade Poboshkin and report back to me once you have settled into your new office. 1900 hrs on Saturday should give us both sufficient time. Make sure he's properly dressed please, Comrade Poboshkin. Dismissed."

The two officers saluted formally, one knowing everything, the other knowing nothing, at least until he was shown Nazarbayeva's written order promoting Ivashutin to Major, effective immediately.

Tatiana looked at the closed door, her mind working hard on how she would present the information and conclusion to the General Secretary.

But first, a warning to Konev.

She picked up the phone.

Konev was listening to the latest planning direct from Marshal Kirill Meretskov, the man who replaced him as commander of the 2nd Red Banner.

Transferred in from Manchuria, where his services in the scaled down Far East force were not required, Meretskov had spent a lifetime soldiering, making Marshal despite having been arrested in the early days of the Patriotic War.

Quietly briefing his commander, Meretskov was interrupted by Petrov, still in place as CoS for the 2nd Red Banner.

"Comrade Marshal, GRU General Nazarbayeva for you. She states it is extremely urgent."

Konev snorted.

"I've heard of this Nazarbayeva, Comrade. Efficient woman, by the rumours."

"Well, you've heard wrong, Comrade Meretskov. She's a meddling cow who seems to have attracted the sponsorship of the General Secretary. I don't know why, especially as she was close to that fool Pekunin."

The bald Marshal leant forward and whispered.

"Maybe he's sticking it up her arse, eh?"

Konev laughed loudly, failing to notice that Meretskov did not join in.

"I heard from Georgy Zhukov that she's efficient, honest, and without side."

"Well there you have it then! Support from Zhukov is to be trusted as much as a shed full of sex-starved Cossacks!"

The phone rang.

"Meretskov... yes, good day to you Comrade General... yes, he is."

The receiver was held out to Konev.

---

Nazarbayeva screamed in anger.

"Idiot! Fucking useless idiot! Prick of a man!"

The door burst open and Nazarbayeva was temporarily alarmed as Poboshkin materialised behind the Tokarev that had been the first thing to make an appearance.

"I'm sorry, Comrade General. I though you... err... sorry."

"Come in and shut the door, Comrade PodPolkovnik."

When the two were alone, Tatiana again gave vent to her anger."

"That man's an idiot!"

Poboshkin could attach that label to a number of people so ventured the question.

"Who, Comrade General?"

"Konev. He tells me that air reconnaissance has reported nothing in that area for weeks, patrols have taken prisoners from second-rate units, and that I am panicking unnecessarily. Prick!"

Poboshkin, Nazarbayeva's confidante, decided to remain silent.

Regaining her composure, Tatiana moved on.

"I must go shortly. Do you have the files ready for me?"

"Yes, Comrade General. The last copies of agent's reports are being made. I must point out these two particularly."

He passed a piece of paper bearing the notations that marked it as coming from a highly placed agent and requiring sensitive handling.

"I remember this report well. Our man in their Air Ministry. Central European mainland on Wednesday at 1000, so he believed. Yet another opportunity for GRU to look bad, sending out warnings for non-events. The man's normally so reliable too!"

"Yes, Comrade General. Now this one."

The second report had only arrived an hour ago, so was new to the GRU commander.

"Wheat? Who is Wheat? Remind me, Andrey."

"Wheat is a Portuguese officer in their London Embassy, Comrade General."

In her right hand, a report from a low-level source relayed very firm rumours of a forty-eight hour delay to a large Allied operation.

In her left hand, a report from a high-level source stating that an Allied attack would commence on Wednesday at 1000.

"Tomorrow, at 10 then."

"It would seem so, Comrade General."

"I'm sure the Comrade General Secretary will agree."

### 2328 hrs, Thursday, 5th December 1945, the Kremlin, Moscow.

Her own aircraft had made a precarious landing at Vnukovo. Despite the best efforts of clearing crews, the snow and ice combined to make her aircraft slide dangerously off the runway and onto a grassy area.

As she stood waiting for her car to pick her up from the point that the aircraft had come to rest, she was a full witness to the tragedy that befell the next aircraft to land.

A Yak-6 of Soviet Naval Aviation bounced heavily and veered offline, clipping one of the fire tenders that had rushed to the aid of Nazarbayeva's Li2.

The Yak, its two crew and three naval officer passengers had died as the light aircraft cartwheeled across the snow, the wood and fabric coming apart too easily to provide any possibility that life might survive the experience.

The distraction of finishing her presentation to the GKO was welcome as her car sped to the Kremlin.

Now, stood before the powerful, she waited as her bombshell was assessed.

"Comrade Marshal Beria?"

The NKVD chief was, unusually, in his uniform, and it didn't suit him.

"Comrades, I cannot refute this information. Indeed, some of it ties in with what my own reports have indicated."

Prior to the GRU briefing, Beria had been at great pains to emphasise the latest NKVD intelligence assessments, and the new information dovetailed with his submission perfectly.

"Comrade General, what did Marshal Konev say to this news?"

"I directed my aide to present the evidence to Marshal Konev personally. I'm not aware as to how it has been received, Comrade Marshal."

Beria, of course, was aware of how the woman's telephone call to Konev had been received earlier that day.

As was Stalin.

Not bothering to go through the motions of gathering consensus, the General Secretary acted immediately.

"I will ring Comrade Konev now and advise him that this intelligence is to be heeded. We will also release more assets to his command."

Nazarbayeva was gestured towards an ornate gilt chair, one of a number that had occupied the room for years, possibly even back to the time of Catherine the Great. Folklore had it that the burn marks on Stalin's favourite were as a result of Napoleon's 1812 attempt to destroy the Kremlin, whereas the reality had more to do with the leader's lack of control over his smoking materials.

Stalin's conversation with Konev took less than five minutes.

---

The rest of the GRU briefing had gone like clockwork, absent of the normal fencing with Beria.

Whilst Nazarbayeva was pleasantly surprised, she sensed that the NKVD Marshal was keeping his powder dry.

As if by prior arrangement, the majority of the GKO took their leave.

As the door clicked shut, Stalin spoke one word.

"Pekunin?"

"Comrade General Secretary, my investigations are thorough, but still incomplete. However..."

Opening a separate compartment in her briefcase, Tatiana extracted two copies of her interim report, passing one to each of her seniors.

Stalin started to thumb through it immediately, but Beria did not even pick it up, preferring to observe the woman in her delivery.

The General Secretary put the folder down and reached for his tea.

"Give me a précis please, Comrade General."

"Comrade Pekunin's personal agent Leopard supplied the information on the SS Legion attacks on the 19th Army, which was communicated in good time, indicating no wish to undermine the success of the Rodina's operations."

She moved on from Leopard, for now.

Dangerous ground lay ahead, and she had rehearsed her dance across it.

"I have found sufficient evidence of motivation of a personal nature, aimed directly at yourselves, Comrade General Secretary."

Stalin gently tapped out his pipe, his eyes keenly assessing the woman in front of him, seeking out and satisfying himself that the honesty he always found in her presentations was still in attendance.

However, Beria froze, part in concern for what was to come, and partly as a snake prepares itself before striking.

Lighting a cigarette, Stalin spoke softly and without threat.

"Such a statement requires clarification, Comrade Nazarbayeva. Please continue."

"I have personally examined some papers left by Comrade Pekunin. No-one else in my office knows of their existence, let alone their contents, Comrades."

That was a risk in itself, for it meant that only one mouth would need permanent shutting, if the two men so decided, but Tatiana had elected to take that risk as it suggested confidentiality to the two powerful men in front of her, and could reap benefits for the future.

It also protected her soldiers.

"His papers suggested that his son and family were executed on the orders of Marshall Beria, for reasons other than the production problems at the son's manufacturing facility."

Stalin's raised hand stopped Beria's denial in its tracks.

"Go on, Comrade General."

"The papers went on to suggest that Marshall Beria had a personal issue with senior staff within GRU, and that he illustrated that point with an example, stating that Marshal

Beria showed some measure of joy when informing him of the death of Paratroop-Lieutenant Vladimir Yurievich Nazarbayev. He also implicated Marshall Beria in the betrayal of a special operation in Spain that resulted in the death of a number of our agents, one of which was Lieutenant Oleg Yurievich Nazarbayev."

Again, Stalin's hand, this time raised more forcefully, stopped Beria's outburst.

A cigarette had replaced the pipe, and it was placed very carefully into the ashtray.

Stalin clasped his hands together, and spoke in a measured tone.

"I'm aware of that operation and yes... it was handed to the Spanish on a plate... as a necessity for the good of the Rodina."

His eyes bored into those of the woman, and the mother.

"Had I known that your son was directly involved, I wouldn't have made a different decision, Comrade Nazarbayeva. It may be hard for you and your husband, but the Rodina and the Party must always come first."

Such candour from Stalin was unbelievable and, this time, it was Beria that was lost for words, even to his inner self.

Tatiana, her face devoid of any emotion, summoned up the right words whilst something stuck fast, echoing constantly in her ear.

*'The Party and the Rodina must always come first.'*

"Comrades... my sons, my husband, and I... we all understood the demands of our service and the sacrifices we might be asked to make. I do not question your decision. I'm relaying my knowledge of Pekunin's motivation without hiding anything from you, Comrade General Secretary."

Beria, aware that Nazarbayeva's words had struck home on his boss, changed his tack and sought permission to speak.

Stalin nodded.

"Comrade Nazarbayeva. You and I have had our differences, but I can assure you that the Spanish decision was necessary. I can also assure you that I would not hold any joy in the death of one of the Soviet Union's sons. How Pekunin could have made that assumption... well... perhaps his intent was to cause friction between us."

Drawing down on the last of his cigarette, Stalin gently exhaled the smoke.

"Proceed, Comrade."

"There was a list refuting a number of the reasons that the GKO cited for going to war, reasons which Comrade Pekunin stated persuaded the Army leadership to fall fully behind the venture, Comrade General Secretary."

"Such as?"

"By example, the Churchill plan, 'Unthinkable'. According to the GRU file it was an exercise in strategic thinking that not even Churchill took seriously, and no different to some operational planning that we ourselves undertook in May and June this year, Comrade General Secretary. Pekunin states that we, the intelligence services and the GKO, knew this to be the case, and deliberately presented a jaundiced view to our military."

"And what do you think?"

Beria polished his glasses furiously, something noticed by both of the others.

"The NKVD file clearly states it differently. I cannot argue with the contents of that file and, I assume, it was that which gave the GKO its view, Comrade Marshal."

"Quite so, Comrade Nazarbayeva, quite so."

"There is more, but I found no evidence to support his assertions, Comrade General Secretary."

Nazarbayeva hesitated noticeably, drawing comment from Stalin.

"Comrade General, so far your report has been full and frank. Please continue."

"Comrade General Secretary, I discovered that General Pekunin had directly approached Comrade Molotov. I believe in an effort to secure his support in some sort of move for power."

For once, Tatiana was surprised, as there was no visible reaction from either man.

"I hasten to add that it was recorded that Comrade Molotov rejected the advance, Comrade General Secretary."

Beria and Stalin exchanged looks, the Molotov point being one that had figured centrally in their assessment of Nazarbayeva's loyalty.

Puzzled by the silent exchange in front of her eyes, Nazarbayeva had no idea that she had just passed a test.

Stalin gave silent assent for Beria to explain.

"I can tell you that Comrade Molotov approached me regarding Pekunin's overtures, and the Minister greatly contributed to the General's treachery being uncovered, which finally culminated in your order to arrest him, and the subsequent shooting of the traitor and his supporter, Kochet..."

Beria was not used to being interrupted and his displeasure was written across his face had Tatiana but noticed it.

"Comrades, I have found no evidence of any treachery on the part of Comrade Leytenant General Kochetov."

"He tried to shoot you, woman! What more evidence do you need, eh?"

Suppressing Beria with an icy look, Stalin turned, his visage becoming instantly warmer, encouraging the GRU officer.

"Carry on, Comrade General, carry on... tell us what you have discovered."

"Comrade General Secretary, I have discovered nothing, absolutely nothing at all, that would lead me to even suspect that Comrade Kochetov had any involvement in any of Pekunin's apparent betrayal."

She could not go the full hog and denounce her mentor, but Tatiana certainly intended that the innocent Kochetov's family should not suffer.

"Then we shall take you at your word, Comrade General. There will be no further action against the Kochetov family. Proceed please, Comrade."

Stalin was clever at using words when he needed to be, drawing a smile from Beria.

Unbeknown to Nazarbayeva, three generations of Kochetovs had already perished at the vengeful hands of the NKVD. No further action was available, unless they could be pursued into the afterlife.

"I have examined some of the exchanges between Comrade Pekunin and his agents. Particularly, I found some irregularities in his dealings with Agent Leopard, the operative who supplied information regarding the French SS units, information that, in the light of events, now seems somewhat suspect."

Beria had no idea of this issue and remained silent, concentrating on every word.

"I came across information that led me to believe that Comrade Pekunin clandestinely met with Agent Leopard on 22nd October in Böblingen, Germany. I also know that Marshal Rokossovsky was present at that meeting."

Both senior men leant forward, somehow resembling vultures preparing to feast on a corpse.

"The Marshal was very open about that meeting. He informed me that the agent had delivered information on the enemy dispositions, information that encouraged the advance into Alsace and subsequently brought about the destruction of at least one of our armies in that region. That information was wholly vouched for by Polkovnik General Pekunin."

Both vultures could see a clear image of the corpse of Rokossovsky at their feet.

"Comrade General Secretary, if you will permit me, I will state quite categorically that Marshal Rokossovsky had and has no part in any matter that is contrary to the interests of the State."

The image melted away.

"Noted, Comrade Nazarbayeva. Continue."

"My understanding of Agent Leopard is that he's in the guise of a Polish Army Major, attached to the French Army as a liaison officer and..."

A violent cough stopped her in mid-flow, causing Stalin to make a simple gesture, directing his henchman towards a carafe of water on a tasteful gilded table near the door.

Unhappy at being a serving boy, Beria performed the act of providing Nazarbayeva with a drink with as little grace as he could get away with.

"Sorry. Agent Leopard was used to control the enemy senior officer Knocke. You will remember that we held his wife as a hostage, and that she apparently died in circumstances that were possibly dubious."

Beria had more direct knowledge than Stalin did, but this was the first time that he had heard of any doubts about the Primorsk matter.

Nazarbayeva surged forward.

"GRU and NKVD investigations apparently revealed that an errant SS unit had attacked the NKVD troops in Primorsk, during which attack the Knocke family were killed..."

"Apparently, Comrade?"

"Comrade Marshal, I raised my concerns at the time. I felt it far-fetched that an SS unit would have remained silent for so long, and would have selected such a target as its first action."

Clearing her throat, she took the opportunity to drink a little more water.

"Comrade Pekunin did not agree with me, so the report was ratified and accepted, despite my views on that and other issues."

"It's a hasty man that doesn't listen to your words, Comrade Nazarbayeva," Stalin chuckled his way through the statement, ignoring Beria's demonstrable surprise at the unexpected and, in the circumstance, decidedly out of character humour.

"Thank you, Comrade General Secretary. I must say that I've kept an eye on the region, and there have been no further attacks attributed to a roving group of SS soldiers."

"Nothing?"

"Yes, Comrade Marshal, there have been attacks, but they are all verified as being opportunist elements seeking rations, or ex-military groups trying to disrupt our forces. Nothing at all SS."

"I understand your suspicions, Comrade Nazarbayeva. Is there more?"

"Comrade General Secretary, I have always had concerns over the identification of the bodies of Knocke's family. They were all burnt, a fate that befell few of the occupants of Primorsk, and something that was very convenient in making identification difficult. According to the GRU report, the bodies of the two girls were found together in their house, which, circumstantially, was seen as sufficient proof of identity for the investigators."

Another sip of water relieved the growing dryness.

"The wife's body was exhumed and identified by jewellery found on the corpse. Such items are easily placed on a body. In short, I find the evidence unsatisfactory and, looking at the actions of the legion units that were supposed to be controlled by Knocke's blackmail, there seems little evidence of any positive influence exercised by our agent at all, Comrade General Secretary."

She drained the rest of the glass.

"Comrade General Secretary, my investigations continue, but I have yet to find conclusive evidence that Comrade Pekunin acted in betrayal of the state, although there is some doubt over the effectiveness of some of his agents. Certainly, I find myself questioning some of the decision making, but that may just be hindsight."

Stalin's affability and tolerance seemed to disappear in one noticeable breath and he, very deliberately to both watchers, extracted another cigarette and went through the motions of tapping it down and lighting it before speaking.

"Comrade General. Your investigations must continue. Your efforts to keep secret these matters is noted... and the State thanks you."

Beria seemed to want to say something, but lost his chance.

"Two of your sons are dead, and that is a personal tragedy. There is nothing I can do to change that. Both have died for the Rodina, and the Party, one as a soldier hero, the other in a way that is wholly regrettable... but it **was** necessary, Comrade."

Stalin stood and pulled his tunic into place, the cigarette dangling from the corner of his mouth, reflecting his peasant roots.

"Comrade Nazarbayeva, I wish I had a thousand like you, soldiers who do their duty without question and without fear for their own position. Continue your investigation, and send me your final written report when it's complete. Dismissed."

*Remember that upon the conduct of each depends the fate of all.*

*Alexander the Great*

# Chapter 114 - THE FRIDAY

### 0055 hrs, Friday 6th December 1945, Soviet Temporary Detention Camp 130, Baranovichi, USSR.

"Hold the light steady, man!"

Desperation and tiredness made the surgeon shout at his helper.

"Damn it! Clamp."

"We have no more clamps, Sir."

"The pegs, give me a peg."

Needs must, so the wooden peg was quickly inserted into the inner thigh of the Sikh Corporal who lay dying on the crates that counted as a surgical table in Camp 130.

Imprisoned in six houses on the southern outskirts of the town, formerly the old Jewish Ghetto, seven hundred and eight Allied prisoners were miserable, cold, and badly treated. Most worked for fourteen hours a day, reconstructing the large airfield, as well as creating new military and industrial areas around the Red Air Force site.

They had been nearly a thousand when the work had started, but the harshness of the regime and the climate took their toll. The work was now complete, but for a few minor matters that the POW's strung out as best they could, purely on the basis of 'better the devil you know'.

Seven hundred and eight became seven hundred and seven, as blood loss and shock claimed the Indian soldier, victim of heavy kicks from a rogue horse.

The Sergeant orderly relinquished his hold on the man and stepped back, allowing the mean light to illuminate unblinking eyes.

"He's gone, Sir."

Dryden cursed.

"All for the fucking want of the right kit. Another fucking life lost. For God's sake!"

299

His helper, Hany Hamouda, an Egyptian 2nd Lieutenant, started to remove the equipment from the huge thigh wounds, incisions made by Miles Dryden in an attempt to patch up the arteries that had been torn by the shattered bones of both femurs.

As he did so, he spoke the inventory aloud, a routine agreed by the medical staff to avoid leaving valuable equipment in a casualty.

"Three clamps."

"Check."

"One stainless steel retractor."

"Check."

"Four wound hooks."

"Check."

Handmade from deer antler, they hooked into the flesh of the casualty and held open wounds for Dryden to work.

Simple but effective.

"Scalpel."

The officer removed it from Dryden's hand, the naval surgeon seemingly reluctant to give up the blade; it had been a huge concession by the camp's commander.

"Wound frame."

The frame was a simple folding square that served the same purpose as the hooks, holding open an area for the scalpel to work.

"Four needles."

"Check."

"Horse hair thread, one bob."

And so the list continued, not one that would have graced a proper surgical facility, but the prisoners had done well to acquire the few bits that offered Dryden and Hamouda even the smallest opportunity to save lives.

"Soldering iron."

"Candle."

"Six body straps."

"Check...check...check..."

"List complete, Sir."

It did not take long to inventory the medical equipment in Camp 130.

"Ask the senior Sikh NCO to come and see me immediately please, Hany."

"Sir?"

"They have their own ways with their dead. I would not wish to cause offence."

As a Muslim, Hamouda could understand fully, and was surprised at himself for not thinking of it.

"Sir."

The Lieutenant left, to be replaced by the hospital dogsbody.

"Tea, Sir, milk, and two sugars, as normal."

A mug of something steaming made its way into Dryden's hand; it wasn't really tea, just a concoction flavoured by some of the local flora. Milk and sugar were nothing but distant memories to all the prisoners in 130.

Drinking the warming brew, Miles Dryden watched the nimble Egyptian pick his way across the snowy landscape before entering the hut set aside for the Sikhs and Gurkha soldiers.

The Egyptian Officer had no place on the battlefields of Europe; his presence in 130 was a pure freak of happenstance.

He had become a prisoner of the Germans during the first Battle of Alamein, and endured a long captivity, only to be freed by British forces in April 1945. For some reason, known only to Hamouda, he avoided returning to his homeland, and somehow attached himself to the 15th Scottish Division's medical services in Lubeck, post-war.

He was captured by the Red Army on the second day of the new war, when his small hospital was overrun.

Dryden's own path to Camp 130 had been less fraught, as his naval detachment in Murmansk was bloodlessly taken into captivity on the 6th August.

The two shared the medical responsibilities for their charges, although the naval man did the majority of the surgery, Hamouda's broken glasses hindering him too much for the delicate work.

The senior Sikh arrived with a bearer party shortly afterwards, and they took their kinsman away.

His ward round completed, Lieutenant Commander waited for the card school to form, the 'hospital' being the only place where light in the dark of night would not draw unwelcome attention from the guards.

301

The players arrived together as usual, and the pack of cards, dirty and damaged, was dealt out four ways.

To Dryden's left was Acting Major Kevin Roberts, a Canadian, wounded and taken prisoner at Tostedtland on 13th August.

"Pass."

The next to act was Albert Barrington, a Canadian Lieutenant taken prisoner in the same battle.

"One heart."

The next in line made a great play of examining his cards.

"Aye, I'll pass."

RSM Robertson looked at the naval man, challenging him silently, which challenge Dryden met with a deadpan face.

"One spade."

"Pass."

His partner could not resist a dig.

"Any chance of ye playing the game, Major, Sah?"

Roberts grinned.

"No speech play, RSM. You know the rules."

The grins were universal.

"Two diamonds," Barrington announced with considerable gusto.

"Ah'll double ye, Sah."

Dryden laughed the sort of laugh that could easily be imagined to originate from a vulture circling a dying beast.

"Three spades."

Robertson was fit to burst, and his partner's pass did nothing to assuage his concern.

Barrington milked the moment.

"Four spades."

"Get ye the fuck, Lieutenant, Sah!"

Dryden leant forward.

"I'm unclear about that terminology. Is that a pass, Sergeant Major?"

Robertson looked down his nose in mock anger.

"Aye, that it is, damn your black hearts!"

"Good. Pass."

Roberts accepted the NCO's scathing glare for his final pass.

The hand was never played.

Within moments, the doors of the hospital flew open and in charged members of the security detail, shouting, screaming, sometimes lashing out.

"Collect up everything now, Doctor."

"What?" Dryden sat there in the midst of chaos, still clutching his hand of cards, staring at the Soviet officer.

"You're leaving tonight, Doctor, so get everything you need ready... in ten minutes. These men will help. Dawai"

---

Before dawn started to spread its light across the land, the four bridge players, Hamouda, the two orderlies, and four guards were onboard a small freight wagon, heading southeast.

Behind them, the seven hundred prisoners of Camp 130 were efficiently liquidated.

### 0947 hrs, Friday 6th December 1945, Headquarters of SHAEF, Trianon Place Hotel, Versailles, France.

"A routine probing attack... nothing more, Walter."

"Are you sure, Brad?"

Bedell-Smith spoke into the receiver again, questioning the General on the other end more closely.

From the nods, the rest of the officers assumed that the answers he received were positive.

"Thank you, Brad. If anything changes, let me know immediately."

"General Bradley says that Simpson states it's normal stuff, Sir. Every day of late, somewhere along his line, the Reds probe early in the morning. Nothing too dramatic, probably just enough for their infantry commanders to report stiff resistance, and then curl back up in the warm for the rest of the day."

With the exception of the morning skirmishes, whole sections of the front had become relatively quiet. The temperature outside recognised no uniforms or causes above any other, and was equally harsh on the soldiers of both sides. Most of the frontline had become an area of stalemate, where no attempt to advance was made.

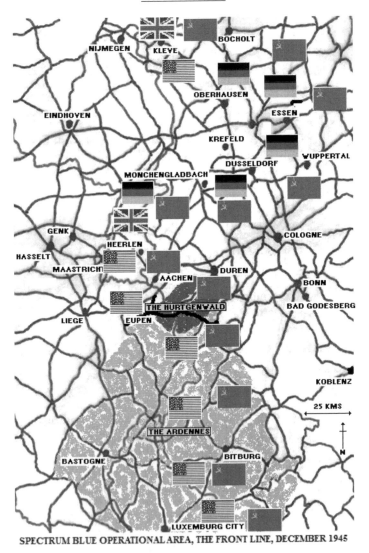

SPECTRUM BLUE OPERATIONAL AREA, THE FRONT LINE, DECEMBER 1945

That was particularly true of the Hürtgenwald, scene
of intense fighting during the German War, where the boot was

now on the other foot, with US divisions in defence on favourable terrain.

Everything seemed right; was right.

Eisenhower lit another smoke from the dying cigarette he had started at the sound of the telephone ringing and Bradley's first words.

He went through his checklist yet again.

*'The plan is good, and we've been over it time and time again...check.'*

*'Weather...good as it can be for us...check.'*

*'Enemy responses...none as yet...check.'*

*'All assets in place...all in place...check.'*

*'Supplies...we're well provisioned and want for nothing...check.'*

*'Morale...spoiling for a fight, so George says anyways...mind you, so does Guderian...in his way...check.'*

The cigarette leapt to and from his lips with every thought.

Suddenly, the filter stopped a few millimetres from Ike's lips.

*'Feel worse than D-Day, don't you, bud? So what's wrong then, eh?'*

The answer would be supplied before midday.

### 0955 hrs, Friday, 6th December 1945, Headquarters, 2nd Red Banner Central European Front, Schloss Rauischholzhausen, Ebsdorfergrund, Germany.

"This is worse than fucking Kursk."

Petrov couldn't argue, as he hadn't been present at the great defeat of the German invaders.

Not that it mattered, as he knew what his commander, Marshal Kirill Meretskov, Konev's replacement as OC 2nd Red Banner, meant.

Anyway, the Marshal hadn't been there either.

They had done the best they could in the time they had been given, the hours since the warning spent adjusting, preparing, reinforcing, replenishing, and waiting.

Above all... waiting.

Petrov knocked back the small vodka the two men had permitted themselves, placing his empty glass alongside that of his boss.

Meretskov finished reading the letter from his protégé, the young Stelmakh, folded it, and put it back in the envelope, his mind suddenly filled with thoughts of his old comrade, Georgii Stelmakh, killed by the Luftwaffe in 1942.

He waived the envelope at Petrov.

"The boy's doing well, Tovarich. Just like his old man it seems."

Permitting himself a smile at the memory of his old friend, Meretskov stretched, and watched as the clock ticked its way to 10 o'clock.

"It is begun, Ivan."

As if to emphasise the moment, a phone rang, its trill sounding more urgent than normal to the ears of men whose wait was now over.

## 1000 hrs, Friday 6th December 1945, the Ardennes, Europe.

Hitler had done it in 1940, and again in 1944.

It had seemed more than reasonable to the Allied planners that their forces could do it going the other way in 1945. Better supplied, better equipped, and with air superiority over the battlefield.

One thing that was not really appreciated was the difference in opposition.

In 1940, it had been an unprepared and poltically demoralised French Army.

Four years later, in the main, it had been US Army units that received the onslaught, many new to war, some more experienced but so tired and battle weary; all unprepared.

The element of surprise had been key on both occasions.

The lack of it was to be key to many a young man on this occasion.

Allied planning for the opening of Spectrum Blue, the opening ground attack of the Spectrum Operations, required fighter-bomber strikes throughout the rear areas of the Soviet front, particularly to deal the legendary Soviet artillery a deathly blow.

Heavy bombers were targeted against the crossing points on the Rhine and other watercourses, both hamstringing any movement of reserves and munitions, as well as denying an escape route for the frontline formations.

On the ground, three main thrusts pushed out from the Allied lines.

From Nuess and Wersten came the German 101st Korps, pushing down the Rhine on either bank, its sights set firmly on Cologne.

To the south, US 17th Corps, part of US Third Army under George Patton, was tasked with making the running through the Ardennes to meet the German Korps at Cologne, trapping 6th Guards Tank Army and 5th Guards Army in a pincer movement.

Additionally, US 3rd Corps was to assault towards Koblenz, and the junction of the Mosel and Rhine.

Whilst the land was white, there was no falling snow, and visibility was excellent across the battlefield, permitting ground-attack aircraft to successfully engage, bombers to hit their intended targets, and artillery spotters to bring their enemy under close scrutiny.

The Allies advanced relatively unopposed.

### 1209 hrs, Friday, 6th December 1945, Dahlem, Germany.

Up to two minutes ago, the advance had been a relative breeze, with only the occasional resistance from a seemingly broken Red Army.

Signs of hasty flight were everywhere, although not all Soviet soldiers had managed to escape.

Only at Reuth had it been a problem for the 90th US Infantry, and Captain Towers had lost half a dozen men in a few minutes of frenzied activity.

Love Company of the 359th Infantry Regiment had moved off the main route to check out the small village.

The welcome of the local populace was cut short by the stammering of a DP 20.

Four GI's and twice as many civilians had been put down in the first burst. Two more of his men died during the

307

storming of the Chapel, along with four of the Soviet soldiers who had been left behind.

Two others found themselves in the hands of the enraged townsfolk, and were beaten to death before Towers could intercede.

Had he been so inclined.

Love Company had radioed in a contact report and was immediately rewarded by being ordered to take point as the slated unit, King Company, had a mine problem at Stadtkyll.

One platoon of K had attempted to manouveure around the deadly mined ground, and found itself in L Company's area, so was swiftly attached to Towers' command.

So, with orders for swift movement still ringing in his ears, Towers pushed his men forward, trading a little caution for speed of advance, right up to the point that mines became the least of his problems.

Fig#99 - US forces committed to the assault on Dahlem, 6th December 1945.

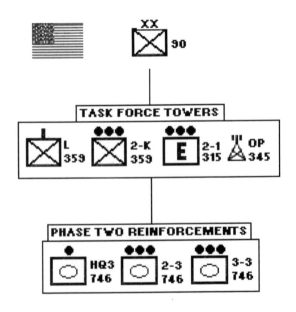

Five halftracks were knocked out, some burning, some just resembling Swiss cheese, some of the enemy heavy machine-guns equipped with ammunition capable of penetrating the armour plate. The 12.7mm DShKs claimed victims amongst the men packed in each vehicle.

One vehicle disgorged its crew, the men heading for the cover of a gully that proved to be a deadly nest of anti-personnel mines.

The explosions continued long after the squad of men had been ripped to pieces by unforgiving metal.

Mortar shells were arriving all over the area around the stranded advance party.

Handset to his ear, Towers shouted and waved his fully functioning arm at his men.

"Get back into cover, goddamnit! Baines! Baines! Back there...move back there!"

Fig#100 - Soviet forces committed to the defence of Dahlem, 6th December 1945.

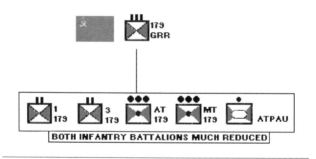

Baines, the NCO in command of the nearest track, missed the message, but knew his trade well enough to order his M5 into some excellent cover, mainly provided by a thick stone wall.

The woods swallowed up the rest of the men and machines, as Love Company pulled back.

There was a sudden silence in Towers' ear, as the insistent voice stopped demanding situation reports, offering him a chance to reply.

309

Towers shouted back into the radio, blood flying from his lips, split open when he collided with the back of the driver's seat.

"Jupiter Six, I've five tracks down, including my air co-op... probably twenty of my boys outta the fight. Can't advance without armor, Sir. The commies have got heavy MG's cited everywhere to my front, some to my flanks. Mortars coming in all over, accurate too. Ground's open and all white. No cover at all. I've a hatful of men down... I need air... and more men and tanks...above all tanks. Over."

Fig#101 - Battle of Dahlem, first attack, 6th December 1945.

A mortar shell sent snow and pieces of undergrowth flying over the frozen pond he was sheltering beside.

"Jupiter Six, yessir, that'll be great. I'll wait for them to arrive..."

Apparently, that was not the Colonel's plan.

"Say again, Jupiter Six."

Towers found himself hugging the snow as the angry zips of passing bullets seemed to grow in intensity and volume.

"Jupiter Six, I know that, Sir, but suicide's still suicide, and that's just what you're ordering me to do."

Removing the handset from his ear, the exasperated infantryman calmly handed it back to the radio operator and then exploded

"Goddamned son of a fucking bitch!"

A figure tumbled in beside Towers, sending up a flurry of snow.

"Goddammit, soldier!"

Wiping the snow from his face, Towers checked out his panting 2IC.

"You're hit, Harold."

"Just a scratch, Cap'n."

Henderson played with the material, demonstrating the passage of a bullet.

"Get that arm looked as at soon as you can, Harold."

"It can wait, Cap'n."

Towers held out his map, ending the exchange.

"We're here. They're here, here and... I guess... here."

"Definitely seen fire coming from the road ahead. Nothing from those trees yet though, Cap'n."

"Forget air. It's all gone sour... Colonel Bell, bless him, wants us to push on a-sap... straight up the goddamned road. Barrel through, he says."

Henderson wrinkled his nose up in disgust.

"Well, that ain't happ'nin is it?"

"No way. Neither am I going into the woods to the right there. That stinks to me."

The two pored over the map, subconsciously registering the decrease in enemy fire.

"Here, Harold, just here. That's where I'm going. I'll leave you some of the boys, plus the heavy weapons... and the arty boys. All you gotta do is make enough noise to keep them occupied. I'm going to hook up here, moving left, almost to Baasem... and then come hard up these roads, parallel with Route 110."

It was a plan, better than the frontal assault ordered, but the area was restrictive, as was the timescale placed upon the 90th Division, pressure that had cascaded down to find a place firmly on the shoulders of Captain William Speke Towers, commanding Love Company, 359th Infantry.

Both men risked a look over the edge of their cover.

Towers gesticulated right then left.

"Over there, see? Looks perfect, don't it? Bet yer ass they've sown it all up ready. On the left flank here it's more open in many ways, but I reckon we can deploy out of sight, and use those tracks and the hedges to get close enough."

Henderson could see the reasoning behind the call, but still felt that the left was too exposed, and said so.

"I hear you, Harold. But we're behind the goddamned eight-ball. Can't stay here, and we can't go straight up the road, so it's the best I can do."

A mortar shell arrived nearby, making both men duck. The screams that followed drew their gaze, and the cries of 'medic' told them all they needed to know.

"Goddamnit! I'm moving off at 1230. Get your heavy weps online to support me."

He consulted the map once more.

"I think the airfield, up on the left flank here, may be necessary, once we've taken the village, but have your boys ready to switch fire to this area here," Towers circled a patch of trees and open ground around Route 110 as it wended its way northwest, past the old Luftwaffe Dahlemer airfield.

"If any surprises come, I want the heavy weps ready to put down some fire on it, ok? I'll dial Travers in on that location too."

He checked the air, almost as a dog does when sensing change.

"Best shift the boys some. Betcha this is all vectored too. Keep a good eye on the right flank there, just in case, Harold. I don't trust those woods. And if the tanks turn up,

312

make sure they come to me first, but hang on to enough to make noise up the main road, ok?"

"Gotcha, Cap'n. Good luck, sir."

"And to you, Lieutenant."

Towers checked first and leapt up, running for all he was worth towards the halftrack he had shouted at earlier. He arrived, breathless and aching, his backside reminding him of its recent brush with Soviet metal.

The radioman barrelled into him, helped by the nearby explosion of something larger than a mortar.

The wood that Towers had declined to occupy disappeared in a volley of Katyusha rockets, fired by a unit missed by the ground attack squadrons.

---

Towers got his men into position, and found enough time for a face to face with the Artillery support officer.

2nd Lieutenant Travers had upped his game since the mistakes on the Argen River, and the 359th had managed to keep him close, getting him transferred into the 345th Field Artillery.

Sergeant Baines welcomed the arrival of his CO with a wave, his own facial injury preventing effective communication for the moment.

A piece of mortar shell had removed four of his teeth and opened his cheek from ear to lips.

It hurt, and bled like hell.

Back on the radio, Towers briefed in the platoons he was taking with him and then checked his watch.

*'Time to get moving.'*

"OK Driver. Move over to the left there. Nice and steady."

He grabbed at the .30 cal side mount as the halftrack surged backwards.

Placing a reassuring hand on the young driver's shoulder, Towers tried to calm the frightened boy.

"Easy, son, easy. Try not to shake the old man around too much, eh?"

Again, the halftrack surged, causing him to grab at the mount again, this time moving forward and to the left, but with more control this time.

Dropping his mouth down to ear level, Towers gave the driver directions.

The halftrack stopped behind a wooden barn, adjacent to another vehicle, this one undoubtedly belonging to First Sergeant Micco.

Most of Love Companies tracks sported a .50cal as main armament, with two .30cal on either side.

Micco's track benefitted from some serious scrounging; the .30's had been replaced with .50's, the pulpit .50 removed and the position field modified to take a 20mm Oerlikon.

It gave the unit an extra bit of firepower, and Micco was Micco, so even Towers let it go.

Acknowledging the wave from Micco, Towers spoke into the radio.

"Tombstone Four-Six to all stations Tombstone Four-Two, Tombstone Four-Three, move 'em out."

Two platoons of Tower's company pushed forward out into the fields to the west of Route 110, seeking out the tracks that would take them closer to Dahlem, willing the halftracks to shrink beneath the level of the vegetation that covered the approach route.

Travers had some of his 105mm guns set ready to bring down smoke to permit the tracks to close; the others maintained a steady fire on the outskirts of the German town.

The smoke shells started up on cue, restricting Artem'yev's vision almost immediately.

He spoke in grudging respect.

"This one knows his business, Comrade."

The Major next to him grunted, examining the advance, as best he could, through his own binoculars.

Artem'yev placed his own prized German set on the brick wall, his arms suddenly weary, the impending combat already weighing heavily upon him.

Bailianov looked at his commander and smiled.

"Yes, he knows his business, but so do we, Comrade Polkovnik."

"That we do, Boris Ivanovich... although Comrade Karamyshev might offer a different opinion."

General Karamyshev had attempted to relieve Artem'yev prior to the final assault on Sittard. Both Artem'yev and his second in command had refused to accept suicidal orders, and used their experience to achieve the same results in a different way, albeit at the cost of the latter's life.

The General received promotion and a new command as a result, preventing him from following through with his threats.

None the less, in a private meeting, Karamyshev had made sure that the Colonel understood he was permanently on the shit list.

Fig#102- Battle of Dahlem, second attack, 6th December 1945.

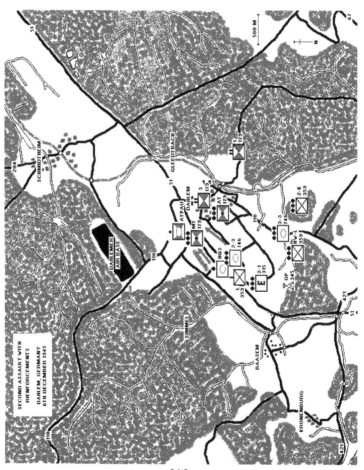

Bailianov checked to make sure that the Communications officer was poised ready, before returning to survey the battlefield; the static enemy force was still sat astride the main road, and the new force, only occasionally visible through the smoke, moving up on the right flank, behind the hedges and trees heavily laden with snow.

Artem'yev waited.

Bailianov waited.

The Communications officer waited.

Seconds seemed like minutes.

Artem'yev nodded.

Bailianov slapped the Communications officer on the arm.

The Communications officer spoke one word.

"Fire!"

### 1238 hrs, Friday, 6th December 1945, Dahlem, Germany.

Even with the cover of hedgerows and small copses, Towers' men had taken casualties when the Soviet gunners opened up.

76.2mm and 85mm guns engaged the half-tracks direct, and heavy DSHK machine guns lashed out at the soldiers abandoning knocked out or damaged vehicles.

Travers got the divisional artillery responding and at least two of the defensive AT guns were knocked out.

Henderson had the Heavy Weapons platoon working hard on supporting the attack.

A dozen Sherman tanks from the 746th Tank Battalion had arrived, sent forward by Colonel Bell in response to Towers' plea. Bell was a competent commander and, contrary to Towers' belief, fully understood the predicament that Love Company now found itself in. He even added some combat engineers for good measure.

Henderson retained one Sherman platoon, and directed the remaining seven tanks to follow in Towers' wake, up the left flank.

---

The infantry Captain threw the handset away in disgust.

On the back of the Sherman was an EE8A telephone system, put there as a means to communicate with the tank commander. In this instance, the means simply refused to communicate.

Climbing on the back of the tank exposed him to enemy fire, but he needed to talk to the man in charge.

He rapped on the hatch three times and shouted his name, rank, and unit.

The hatch moved upwards cautiously, revealing a white face and the muzzle of an M1911A.

"Say again, pal."

"Towers, William S. 359th Infantry."

The grip on the pistol visibly relaxed, and the hatch opened a few more inches.

"Ayres, 746th."

"Your squawk box is bust, Captain."

It was not an admonishment, just a statement of fact.

"Noted."

Captain Ayres spoke rapidly into his microphone before giving Towers his full attention.

"What's the buzz then, Captain? Whatta we got ahead here?"

"Bunch of anti-tank guns for certain, spread along the front in front of Dahlem there. We got reasonable cover all the way, but the bastards've still picked off a few of my tracks. Arty's slackened off some; probably counter fire has knocked 'em back"

Ayres lit two cigarettes and passed one to Towers.

"Thanks. We gotta pick up the pace again. Dahlem's an important piece of real estate, and we'll get chewed out if we don't get it soon. So, here's the deal."

Towers quickly moved his finger around the map, indicating a couple of tracks, central to the advance of the Shermans.

Ayres ventured a small alteration and the plan, such as it was, became set in stone.

Looking at his watch, Towers worked out the time he would need to brief in his leadership and get the company online for another surge.

Taking a deep draw, he savoured the unfamiliar taste of the British Players cigarette.

"I might have to take up with these. Easy to come by?"

"Easy enough when you have lots of shit that the Limeys wanna trade for."

Flicking the butt to one side, Towers returned to business.

"I've got 1254. You?"

"Same as. How long do you need? I can be done in three."

"Longer... 1310... say... 1315."

Towers nodded in confirmation of his calculation.

"OK...1315 we kick off straight down the tracks. I'll get my men to your tanks in good time. The rest of my outfit'll be in the tracks. Good luck, tanks."

"Break a leg, infantry."

## 1315 hrs, Friday, 6th December 1945, Dahlem, Germany.

Colonel Bell had scared up as much artillery support as was humanly possible in the short period of time available.

Shells from 75mm to 8" fell upon the Soviet positions in and around Dahlem.

Towers ordered the assault in, and the lead tanks slowly moved forward, each with a knot of infantry in its wake.

Behind them came the remaining halftracks, ready to surge forward once the tanks had beaten a gap in the defences.

Last of all came the combat engineers, acting as a reserve, mixed in with two ambulance tracks and Towers' newly commandeered command halftrack.

As the assault force moved forward, it almost seemed like parts of the German town were rising hundreds of feet into the air before returning to ground level, only to be propelled skyward again by some new explosion.

The supporting US artillery was right on the money, and the Soviet defenders were taking casualties.

Henderson's heavy weapons group was silent at the moment; their own mortars would do little to add to the shock and destruction of the main barrage, and Towers' concerns about the airfield had increased.

A shell emerged from the wreckage of Dahlem, streaking past the lead Sherman by a comfortable distance.

The sole noticeable response was a small increase in speed from its intended victim, but the men inside the tank were sweeping the ground to their front, seeking out the danger.

Soviet mortar rounds started to drop around the two lead elements, causing the infantry groups to stoop more, their crouching advance would have seemed almost like a comedy act if it wasn't being played out on such a deadly stage.

Casualties were remarkably light as only three men were plucked from the groups, none of which was hit fatally.

But there was a problem.

*'Slow...too goddamned slow!'*

Towers was conscious of the fact that the Katyushas had already been used, and it was part of his plan to get as tight to the enemy as possible whilst they reloaded, where the notoriously inaccurate rockets could not be fired.

"Healthy-two-six, Healthy-two-six from Tombstone-four-six over."

He had to repeat the message before Ayres acknowledged.

"Healthy-two-six, you gotta push ahead a bit quicker. My boys'll keep up, but you gotta get tighter, Healthy."

"Roger, Tombstone."

Within seconds, the Shermans had all accelerated and the accompanying infantry groups had raised themselves from jog to run to stay with their mobile shields.

One of the supporting halftracks, easily recognisable as Micco's, fired off every weapon aboard as concealed Soviets soldiers rose from cover to engage the tanks at close quarters.

"Shit! They've got tank hunters in the hedges!"

*'FUBAR!'*

Towers already had the radio in his hand.

"All Tombstone and Healthy call signs. Be aware, enemy infantry concealed in the hedges, Tombstone-four-six over."

Even as Towers formulated the second part of his message, he noted his doughs rushing past the lead tank, putting in an assault on an unseen group of Russians.

Other groups pushed forward, moving ahead of the tanks, some charging into unoccupied clumps of hedge and trees, others assaulting a position that suddenly erupted violently.

One Sherman was smoking badly, a panzerschreck in Russian hands having struck it fatally.

---

The report that Starshina Kon and his vehicle had reached Dahlem did nothing to calm Artem'yev's rising foreboding.

"Where are my rockets, Comrade Bailianov?"

"We can't get through, Comrade Polkovnik."

Artem'yev gripped the binoculars tightly, working off a little tension in the doing.

"There are reports of heavy air activity across our rear, Sir. Maybe..."

"I don't need maybes, I need my rockets, and I need them now, before they get closer," emphasising his point, Artem'yev waved one hand across the battlefield to his front, "The enemy's bunched. I need them now, Comrade Major!"

"I've sent a vehicle back, Comrade Polkovnik, but I fear..."

Two shells bracketed the headquarters position, shaking men and equipment, but causing no real damage, except to strained nerves.

"Boris Ivanovitch... get me my rockets."

Turning away, the Soviet commander brought the glasses back up to his eyes and focussed on a small bend in the southern track.

---

Behind Artem'yev's line, the Katyushas had received a beating.

One unit had been detected by radar and received a thorough going over from 8" artillery, taking it out of the fight for some time to come.

Another had been discovered by returning ground attack aircraft, most of which still possessed enough munitions to make a complete mess of the ammunition and headquarters vehicles.

Only one battalion remained fully functional, but it was presently in transit to an alternative position, the commander using the excuse of the artillery and air strikes to move his unit closer to Moscow, or at least that was how the subsequent courts-martial would probably interpret the withdrawal.

There would be no further rocket support for Artem'yev's force.

---

A squad of US Infantry rushed forward to secure the hedges around the bend that was the subject of ARtem'yev's attention, and found no resistance, although fire from Soviet forces nearer Dahlem wounded the young 2nd Lieutenant leading the force.

The second in command waved the supporting tank forward, and organised the eveacuation of his former leader.

Artem'yev had left the firing of the charge to one of his platoon commanders, and the man chose the perfect moment to order detonation.

An electrical pulse, sent down a thin wire, initiated a three hundred kilogramme explosive charge that had been dug into one of the small grassy banks and then concealed with snow.

Some of his soldiers, assigned to help the engineers who laid the charge, had packed gravel and stone around the bomb, despite the engineers' assurances that it would not be of any advantage, as three hundred kilos of explosives would be enough to clear the area by itself.

The engineers had left for another assignment, but their legacy was impressive.

The explosion was tremendous, and those soldiers that had cleared the hedges to the south of the bend were swatted away in an instant.

The Sherman tank was eight metres from the blast.

Towers had his binoculars focussed on the spot, and his eyes baulked at the brightness of the light.

None the less, as he jerked his head away, part of his brain detected the sight of many tons of tank propelled sideways at high-speed.

From his position, Artem'yev had anticipated the explosion, so was not affected as Towers was.

He observed, seemingly in slow motion, as the thirty-three ton lump of metal wiped through half a dozen men on the north side of the bend, completing the suffering of the supporting infantry group.

Fascinated, Artem'yev observed the tank rolling some distance, sending track links and externally stowed equipment flying in all directions, until coming to rest on its naked wheels.

The crew had died horribly, churned like butter in their steel coffin.

Towers hammered his fist on the halftrack, knowing he had just lost a lot of men.

Artem'yev hammered his fist on the sandbags, knowing he had just struck a huge blow.

The former grabbed the radio, and organised his reserves forward to cover the hole, whilst the latter listened angrily to the report on the fate of the Katyusha support.

On the northern track, advancing GI's and tanks paid more respect to the ground over which they advanced, seeking out detonation wires, and looking for signs engineer activity.

A young soldier from Oklahoma saw something that scared him, and used his bayonet to cut through a wire three seconds before a Soviet Leytenant ordered the second charge's detonation.

Anti-tank guns engaged the northern force again but were quickly silenced by a combination of direct tank fire and mortars from the Heavy Weapons, brought to bear by Towers' direct command.

"Tombstone-four-six, Healthy-two-six, Route two looks open all the way, suggest plan three, over."

Ayres, leaving the engagement of the AT guns to his gunner, had searched the track and ground ahead, seeing nothing but an invitation to move forward at speed.

Plan Three was a joint surge by the tracks and tanks on one axis, and Towers went with it immediately.

Artem'yev saw the movement, and understood the danger.

"Blyad! The other charge is a dud. The Amerikanski are attacking there, on our right, surging with their tanks and halftracks. Tell Kon to engage the right flank, now! Now!"

Bailianov gave the order, and the radio operator sent Starshina Kon his instructions.

---

Starshina Kon, twice Hero of the Soviet Union, was a very experienced soldier. Once a Colonel of Artillery, Stalin's purges had brought him to the very bottom of his existence, before fate took a hand and he was freed, once more to became a soldier, although he always declined to become an officer when promotions were offered.

Once bitten, twice shy.

With a reputation second to none, he was transferred into the Army Tank Prototype Assessment Unit, in order to bring his expertise to bear in ensuring that Red Army's new vehicles would be the best that they could be.

The ATPAU had sent one group to the west, to serve within the Red Banner forces.

Part of the group was at Dahlem.

One tank, one tank crew, one maintenance section, and a group of civilian engineers and designers, the latter very keen to see their hard work in action on the field of battle.

Kon had brought the tank in question to the field, and it was Artem'yev's ace in the hole.

---

"Fucking hell! Something's got Hettie!"

Hettie, an M4A3E8 Sherman, was already roaring away like a cooker, her crew incinerated in an instant.

Ayres had no idea where the shot had come from, but he was sure it was something new.

"Joe, move left to that clump... get us out of sight pronto."

The driver shifted down easily and the tank surged towards safety, just in time to get out of the way of a silver streak, as a Soviet shell missed the turret by less than a metre.

The pungent smell of urine filled the inside of the tank as more than one bladder emptied itself in fright.

Ayres had spotted the flash and looked at his map.

He radioed Travers, requesting some artillery.

Satisfied that his own tank, 'Hawkeye', was in cover, he jumped out and moved up through the snowy undergrowth, the tank's Thompson submachine gun cradled in his arms, just in case.

The arrival of Travers' salvo coincided with him spotting the all-white enemy vehicle as it moved away from the artillery strike zone.

*'Shit, the bastard bugged out.'*

Kon was too wily a soldier to spend too long in one spot, and he had been well away from the strike that accurately fell on his former position.

Ayres also knew his trade, and had been pushing vehicle recognition with his unit since day one of the new war. However, this one wasn't in the book.

*'What the fuck is that?'*

It was a question that none of the Soviet soldiers would have been able to answer either, so new was the prototype tank that Kon had brought to the day's combat.

At just over thirty-nine tons, the T54, known until recently as Obiekt137, was equipped with excellent armour, a 100mm main gun, fender mounted defensive machine guns, and had an increased combat range.

All in all, it promised much.

However...

The list of faults was long, as Kon and his crew found issue after issue with the design. Today, it would have its christening on the hardest test facility known to man; the modern battlefield.

The strange Russian tank disappeared behind some burning buildings before Ayres' gunner could get a shot.

The radio was suddenly alive with warnings about something new and nasty in the Soviet inventory.

---

"Well, at least the gun works, Comrades."

Starshina Kon joked for the benefit of his crew, as the driver nursed the tank into cover, its engine temperature rising dramatically with a suspected coolant leak.

*'Make that yet another fucking coolant leak,'* Kon thought to himself, as his crew were already quite jittery.

He pulled out a dirty notebook and made some additional entries, announcing his solution to each in turn.

"Right. Oleg, get that traverse fixed. Check the fuse box first. Maybe it's the same as last time."

"Leonid, coolant... and tighten every hose before you top it up this time."

The driver had already been ribbed to death over his previous efforts.

"David, stand security. I'll be back soon, Comrades."

Kon dismounted and left his crew to overcome the latest difficulties his tank had thrown at them, both of which were serious enough for him to seek a safe refuge to repair. The enemy artillery was dropping close, but seemed disinterested in the area the T54 was presently sat in, having already worked it over heavily.

As the tank commander moved through the destruction wrought by the American artillery, he saw the products of the high-speed union of metal and flesh scattered in all directions, the infantry company positioned here at the start of the battle having paid a heavy price.

Twenty could easily have been forty corpses, as pieces lay close to other pieces, but did not necessarily originate from the same son of Russia.

A Junior Lieutenant lay wrapped in a blanket, ready to be evacuated although, to Kon, he looked like he had already made his final journey.

An infantry Captain sat smoking, staring at an imagined object a thousand miles away, clearly in shock, and not functioning.

His men protected him, failing to report his breakdown, so the whole company, or what was left of it, was commanded by a dirty and bloodied Senior Sergeant from the attached mortar unit.

"Comrade Starshy Serzhant. Looks like you've had a shit time, Comrade. How are your soldiers? Can you hold?"

Had it not been for the two HSU's on Kon's chest, the answer might have been very different, but the NCO realised that the tanker was a serious soldier.

"Comrade Starshina, I've sixty-one still standing, thirty-six've been evacuated to the aid station," the Starshy Serzhant gesticulated at a slightly grander house, apart from the main group that formed Dahlem's western environs, "And fifty-one unaccounted for or dead."

*'Fifty-one? Fuck!'*

As an ex-artillery officer, Kon could appreciate the work done by that arm of service.

*'Poor bastards.'*

He paused long enough for the NCO to know that he appreciated their plight before doing what he had come to do.

"I've got problems with my tank, and my crew must have time to fix it... Comrade...?"

"Ponichenkarova. Dina Ponichenkarova, Comrade Starshina... and yes, we will hold."

The woman slipped the magazine from her PPD and checked its contents simply by weighing the metal in her hands.

Sliding the magazine back in place, Ponichenkarova took a swig from her water bottle and proferred it to Kon, who was extremely surprised to find it contained water.

"Thank you, tovarich."

He reciprocated by sharing his cigarettes as the female NCO explained the defensive position to him, pointing out where the surviving mortars were concealed, something that was wholly necessary as, even when told they were there, Kon could still not see them.

The position contained two 76.2mm Zis-3 guns, three DSHK heavy machine-guns, and three of the increasingly rare Panzerfaust.

The tank commander could not help but be impressed by the woman's calm approach and manner.

However, he was more impressed by three mugs of something hot that arrived in the hands of an extremely attractive young Junior Sergeant.

Renata Astafieva handed the scalding coffee to both NCO's, and started on her own after accepting a cigarette from Kon.

"How is the ammo, Renata?"

"Twelve per weapon at the moment, Comrade Ponichenkarova, but I have sent Tania and her tribe back to pick up more. That was ten minutes ago."

Kon choked as the hot liquid hit is throat, announcing the presence of something more serious than coffee.

Astafieva smiled disarmingly.

"Special brew, Comrade Starshina."

"Nice, very nice. Thank you, Comrade Mladshy-Serzhant."

The landing of a mortar shell interrupted the calm scene, and all three were back to business immediately.

More shells followed, betraying increased American interest in their position.

"I'm afraid that may be because of me, Comrades. Tanks do attract such attention."

Ponichenkarova knocked back the last of her drink, drawing an incredulous look from the tanker.

"Well then, Comrade Kon, perhaps you should be back there, spurring your men to higher efforts in their repair work."

Kon searched for humour in the statement but found none. Ponichenkarova was just business, and her business was keeping her troops alive, so getting the lame duck moved was a priority for her.

Ignoring the burning pain, he finished his own drink and handed the cup back to the pretty young soldier.

"Spassiba, Comrades. Best of luck."

When he got back to the T54, the news was encouraging.

## 1334 hrs, Friday, 6th December 1945, Dahlem, Germany.

"Fire!"

Ponichenkarova punctuated her command by slapping the back of the DSHK gunner.

The machine-gun hammered out 12.7mm bullets, and strikes were obvious on the front of the approaching half-track.

The Zis-3 to her immediate left was already dead, its front shield distorted and displaced by an HE shell. The crew had been swept aside by the same burst.

The Sherman it had fired at was similarly shattered, although its crew had managed to abandon before the wreck was engulfed in fire.

All along the defensive positions, weapons fired at the attacking Americans, but less than before.

The attackers were much nearer already and few seemed to be stopped by the defensive fire.

Screams drew Ponichenkarova's attention, and her eyes caught something tossed high as an enemy mortar round found something prepared to explode in turn.

Immediately, the hardened NCO understood that the ammo party had been hit as it returned.

The 179th's mortars would be without ammunition for the foreseeable future, a fact that Astafieva breathlessly arrived to confirm.

"Shit, fuck and abhorrence! Right, get your mortar crew prepared as my reserve, Renata. Grab all the auto weapons you can find and have them set... there."

She pointed at a hollow bordered by low bushes.

"Any breach in the line... any hole... you go at it immediately. Don't wait for me to tell you to attack... and don't give the bastards time to settle, ok?"

Again, an enemy shell punctuated the exchange, wiping out the other DSHK machine-gun with a direct strike.

"Once you've pushed the Amerikanski out, reform your unit. Now move, Renata, move!"

The lithe blonde sprang away from the position, returning to the mortars and organising the crews as Ponichenkarova's fire brigade.

---

"Roger, Healthy, wilco."

The Shermans had poured fire into the enemy position and the dividends were apparent for Ayres to see, so he had informed Towers.

"Tombstone-four-six to all Tombstone-four call signs, push now, push now, straight down the track and into 'em!"

His senses, as well as Ayres' report, told him that the enemy was ready to come apart.

328

The last enemy anti-tank gun had been destroyed and now decorated the battlefield like some macabre flower, its barrel representing the stem, the trails forming the open bud. The body hanging from the breech played no part, except to add a small patch of scarlet to the scene.

The men of the 90th closed in as the enemy fire fell in volume.

Here and there, a GI dropped to the snow, screaming or silent, alive or dead.

Towers watched as the leading soldiers washed over the Soviet line, taking surrenders in the main but, occasionally, finding resistance.

A group of infantrymen, supported by two Shermans, rushed forward, heading towards an earthwork fringed with sandbags and crates; obviously a defensive position of importance.

Opposite and to the left, Towers watched a group of Russians rise up and smash into the doughboys, shooting down a number as they moved forward.

Colt met Tokarev.

Garand met Mosin.

Bayonet met bayonet.

The American infantry were driven off, and the small group of Soviet soldiers went to ground in and around the bunker.

A smoke trail reached out from a burning house, narrowly missing the intended target; Ayres' M4A3E8.

Head out the turret, Ayres spotted the source, and lashed the spot with.50cal from the turret-mounted weapon.

"God, but that was fucking close, Preacher."

"Amen to that, my Capitano. He watches over us... and don't blaspheme in my presence, y'hear me now."

The chuckle that accompanied the statement was suddenly strangled, and changed to a simple spoken statement as 'Preacher' Stevens saw the Grim Reaper coiled and ready to strike like a rattlesnake.

The T54.

"We're gonna die."

The blast sent Ayres flying from the turret. Those watching swore that he was blown at least thirty yards high and thirty yards wide, coming to ground in a thick snowdrift that cushioned his fall, leaving only a severed right hand and modest burns to concern him.

Corporal Stevens, lay preacher and gunner, plus the rest of Ayres' crew, died instantly, as the 100mm shell, delivered by Kon's main gun, ripped into the tank and exploded.

Two shells streaked across the battlefield, both striking the turret of the T54 in spectacular fashion, and both seemed to fail to cause any apparent damage.

Inside, Serzhant Kolesnikov let everyone know what had happened.

"Fucking power traverse is fucked again, Comrades."

Kon made an instant decision.

"Leonid, back up now, back to where we were. Make smoke."

The T54 was equipped with a prototype smoke device that was operated simply by diesel being over-injected into the engine.

As the tank retraced its steps, a further two shells whipped through the gathering smoke, missing by some distance, but close enough to illustrate the wiseness of Kon's relocation.

A dull clang signalled something striking the tank, but nothing that overrode the concern that arose as a smell of burning reached four sets of nostrils at the same time.

Kolesnikov spotted the problem immediately.

"Fuse box is smoking again."

Quality control on the prototype was not brilliant, to say the least, and such events were commonplace, something that would have to be addressed before the Red Army took the T54 into battle in numbers.

Leonid Kartsev added to their woes.

"The engine's gone funny on me, power dropping off."

Again, Kon reacted quickly.

"Stop smoke, Leonid."

The order made sense, as the smoke system might well be affecting the performance of the engine.

"Done."

The engine note did not change for the better, and they could all sense the growing labour of the V12 diesel.

"Not happening, Roman, it's something else."

The smell of burning was stronger now, definitely more than just the fuse box, and eyes flicked around the vehicle interior seeking the source.

"Temperature climbing! Shit! I need to close it down, Comrade!"

Kon flipped the hatch and discovered the source of the burning smell immediately. The dull clang had been part of a large bough dropping on the tank. It was burning steadily and giving off plenty of smoke, some of which was being drawn back inside.

Ducking his head back into the turret, he checked his intercom, noting that it had just surrendered to 'unforeseen technical difficulty' once more.

*'Fucking shit kit!'*

"Leonid, back up another twenty metres, then knock it off."

"Yes."

When the tank came to rest. Kon and Kartsev took less than minutes to discover the problem.

A water hose had blown, a weak spot giving way under the pressure.

"I have a spare, Comrade. Five minutes. But we need more water."

The crew were experienced enough to know that the snow would provide all the water they needed.

Leaving Kolesnikov to work on his traverse again, Kon and Morozov dragged the burning wood off the tank and used it to good advantage, melting snow in the metal buckets that the crew possessed for a myriad of purposes.

"When Leonid is done, we're fucking off. The tank is falling apart around our fucking ears, and I can't risk it being left to the capitalists."

They were given extra speed by the sudden sounds of intense fighting nearby, immediately understanding that the infantry were being heavily pressed.

Ponichenkarova's mortar crew reserve had been swallowed up quickly and was no longer effective; in reality, no longer existed.

The handful of survivors were embroiled in the heaviest fighting, with no hope of recovery.

Astafieva was losing consciousness, the thick fingers around her neck constricting both her airway and the blood flow to her racing brain.

She struck out, connecting with the large American, her efforts in vain as the man continued to throttle the life out of her.

Warm liquid splashed across her face, once, then again, as a bayonet exited the man's shoulder, and then his chest.

The animal sound that came from him penetrated her cloudy mind, but still he clung on, determined to take her with him.

Astafieva saw the blur as a rifle butt, swung with desperate force, smashed into the left side of the dying man's head, propelling him to the right and breaking his hold.

The gurgling stopped as she regained her senses, the unconscious GI asphyxiated by a combination of snow and blood.

Her saviour, Ponichenkarova, dropped to her knees, the exertions of the kill making her breathless.

"Renata...are you... alright... thought... the bastard had... killed you."

Astafieva gingerly felt her neck, grimacing with the pain of the severe bruises that were declaring themselves.

Words did not, actually, could not come, so she just nodded.

To show her willingness, she took up her Mosin rifle and dragged herself up to the edge of the position.

Ponichenkarova's SVT had no ammunition left, so she discarded it in favour of the American's Garand.

Rummaging around in the dead man's webbing, she pulled out some spare chargers and tried to work out how to load the weapon.

Astafieva's rifle cracked, startling her in her moment of concentration.

A croaky voice revealed that the younger woman was feeling very vengeful over her brush with death.

"Got you, you bastard."

The rifle clacked as the bolt was worked, followed by another shot, and a repeat of the triumphant croaking.

Ponichenkarova thought she had the American weapon worked out so raised the rifle and picked a target.

*'An officer. Good!'*

---

Towers was flung to the snow by the force of the blow on his right hip, the pain of the strike immediately cutting through the anger he was experiencing as his men were being killed and wounded all around him.

Ponichenkarova had hit her target but, in another sense, hadn't.

The bullet had actually struck the main body of Towers' Colt automatic, wrecking the weapon. However, it failed to penetrate the skin and left only a heavy bruise, although it would be a little time before the shocked officer realised that he hadn't been fatally wounded. His misery was complete when blood started to flow from his old wound, opened when he hit the ground and impacted with a rock beneath the snow.

---

"Good gun."

She was impressed with the capitalist weapon, slotting in the first charger, having fired the three rounds she inherited with the rifle, hitting everything she aimed at.

Astafieva slapped her arm and pointed.

"There, Serzhant... they're getting round us!"

A group of American soldiers had overcome one position, and were using a hedgerow to get behind the main defensive line.

Both rifles aimed at the group and let fly.

Neither hit their targets, but the men dropped instantly into cover.

Two small explosions quickly followed, and chemical smoke started to drift over their position.

"Move! Quickly!"

Ponichenkarova grabbed Astafieva and rolled them both out of the position.

Both of them heard the thuds and braced themselves.

Two grenades exploded simultaneously.

Dina Ponichenkarova squealed as a piece of metal cut across the back of her left calf as, simultaneously, another destroyed her left ankle.

None the less, she again grabbed her companion and dropped back into the position, bringing the Garand up as dark forms took shape in the smoke.

Astafieva fired the first shot, and was rewarded with an animal like scream as one of the attackers was struck in the belly.

The leading shape transformed itself into a crouching runner, an M3 submachine gun spraying bullets as he charged.

Two of them struck Ponichenkarova, one in her shoulder, missing everything of importance and passing through into the snow beyond.

The other struck her left arm, shattering the humerus just above the elbow joint.

Astafieva, having just put down another of the grey shapes, transferred her aim to the closer target, ignoring the tug as one of his rounds carried away her epaulette.

She shot him in the neck, and the dead body dropped to the snow like a rag doll.

Turning back to the other attackers, Renata Astafieva was swatted to one side by an exploding grenade.

The pain was intense as her right chest and side were peppered with fragments. The force of the explosion ripped part of her clothing away, exposing soft pink flesh lavishly decorated with fresh blood.

An American rose above the position and shot the screaming Ponichenkarova in the chest, silencing her noise in an instant.

He dropped in beside the wounded Astafieva and looked around, seeking further targets and threats.

Finding none, he examined the wounded girl, paying particular attention to the curved breast exposed by the explosion, the erect nipple leaking a steady stream of blood where the minutest sliver of metal had slashed the aureole.

He squeezed the soft female flesh hard, not caring about the pain he inflicted, causing the blood to run more freely from the nipple and a previously unnoticed wound on the underside of the perfectly rounded form.

He looked around again and made a decision.

He ruffled up Renata's skirt, exposing her thighs, and quickly worked to expose much more.

Astafieva struggled,but a single short punch knocked the fight out of her for long enough to allow the soldier to roll on top of her, unbutton his fly and release himself.

A loud crack brought Astafieva out of the cocoon the blow had sent her to, as did as the sight of the would-be rapist's head exploding, as a Garand round punched through bone and brain.

Remarkably, the man was still alive, or at least breathing by some automatic response, his ability to understand, talk, speak, and remember,forever destroyed by the passage of the bullet.

Ponichenkarova let the rifle slip as her strength failed, the extraordinary effort of raising the Garand hastening her end.

Astafieva rolled over to the dying woman.

Even in death, Ponichenkarova had something to say, and she tried as best as her destroyed lung and blood loss allowed.

"I've always loved you."

Ponichenkarova had never let on, but Astafieva had always felt that the older NCO treated her differently.

"I know, Dina," she lied, "And I love you too, Lapochka," which wasn't a lie.

For the few seconds they had left to share together, both knew they would never have what could have been.

Dina Ponichenkarova coughed, and a huge stream of blood fell from her mouth and nose.

"Lapoc..."

'Sweethea...'

The old NCO died, her staring glassy eyes providing a warning that Renata Astafieva saw too late, the movement reflected in them translating itself into a stunning blow to the back of her head.

"You fucking bitches, YOU FUCKING BITCHES!"

The incensed GI shot Ponichenkarova's corpse in the face three times, destroying it utterly. He turned the Garand on Astafieva.

The uncovered breast, the skirt pulled up exposing shapely thighs, the surrender in the girl's eyes, one, or all of them, gave him a moment's pause, and the rifle lowered as more basic thoughts replaced revenge.

Checking around quickly, he propped the rifle against the snow bank and dropped into the position and on top of the wounded Russian.

A hand worked hastily on his trousers and Woods was quickly ready. He entered her and drove himself as deep as he could, the pain of the experience focussing Astafieva's stunned mind, but not giving her the tools to prevent the violation.

The grunts commenced as the rape neared its conclusion, the frequency and depth of his thrusts indicating that he would soon expend himself.

The American let out a moan as he shot his semen inside her, shuddering in ecstasy, and forgetting where he was for the briefest of wonderful moments.

His memory was refreshed by a hand that grabbed his webbing and pulled him off Astafieva.

The terrified girl froze at the face of the man that held a Thompson submachine gun hard against the nose of the rapist.

The voice chilled her further for, although she failed to understand a word, the threat it carried was very clear indeed; but the anger was not directed at her.

"Woods... so help me God... I should shoot you now... you bastard... you fucking bastard..."

He pressed the terrified man into the snow with the weapon, his other seeking to comfort the petrified woman.

Towers composed himself, tenderly pulling Astafieva's clothes up over her as he made his decision.

"Private First Class Woods, Robert H, I am arresting you for rape and murder under the authority granted to me by the Articles of War."

He grabbed the prisoner's Garand and tossed it to one of his waiting men.

There was much more that he wanted to say, but Towers had a battle to fight.

Eyes fixed on the wretched Woods, he spoke to the man who had caught the rifle.

"Corporal, take this man back to the rear and keep him secure until I return. Any trouble... any trouble at all," his eyes burned into Woods', stifling any building petulance, "Anything he does, if he gets outta line, deal with it. Break what ever you have to to shut the bastard up, but don't be shooting him. He's gonna dangle. Clear, Corporal?"

"Yessir."

With a less than gentle prod of his own rifle, the newly appointed gaoler encouraged the prisoner to move off.

Towers moved aside, and let the medic do his work on the Russian girl, allowing his mind to switch back to the battle.

---

The US assault had taken the enemy line, and the combat engineers were pushing on, backed up by the remaining tanks.

The breakthrough attracted extra assets from higher authority, and the rest of the 746th Tank Battalion was focussed on the spot, leading the point elements of the 4th US Armored Division, unleashed by a certain pistol-toting general who was champing at the bit to get at the enemy.

90th Division had sustained some heavy casualties but had, in the main, done the job.

Love Company had had the fight knocked out of it, and was holed up on the northern and southern edges of town, steering clear of central and eastern Dahlem, for fear of enemy artillery.

A modest counter-attack was put in, seemingly without much conviction, for it was easily driven off by Micco's super-equipped halftrack.

The Soviet forces then melted from the field.

Light artillery fire bothered the new defenders for some moments, enough to cause yet more casualties amongst the exhausted GI's.

The incoming fire came and went in minutes, the Soviet unit responsible receiving a thorough working over from USAAF Thunderbolts, causing it to concentrate more on survival than supporting their weakened front lines.

### 1503 hrs, Friday, 6th December 1945, US Army Forward medical post, Dahlem, Germany.

Towers gritted his teeth as the unsympathetic orderly fished around for more wooden splinters.

One of the final shells tossed into Dahlem had struck an old hay cart, sending small slivers of aged wood in all directions, depositing at least thirty small, but excruciatingly painful pieces, in Towers' back and rear portions.

The orderly had started with a wicked piece, some three inches long, carefully removing it from the Captain's neck ,and then continued the journey south, removing pieces of wood on every visit to the swollen bleeding flesh.

"Hey, Cap'n. Didn't you get it in the arse down south?"

There was a moment of silence.

The young medic, fresh from medical school in California, delivered to the 90th just after the war kicked off again, failed to spot the signs.

"Never forget a face, and this one looks familiar."

The high-pitched laugh completed the job of pissing the officer off.

Towers rolled over as, as best he could, and engaged his victim in soft fatherly tones.

"Son, I swear to you, one more fucking word outta place and I'll transfer you to the graves registration unit... where you'll dig the holes with a spoon. Kapische?"

The smile held no humour.

"Uh yeah...Cap'n. I got it... sorry."

The arrival of a badly wounded Henderson did nothing to improve Towers' mood, neither did the sight of Baines' mangled hand, an horrendous injury the Sergeant had sustained when dismounting a halftrack late in the day's fighting.

Landing heavily, he had overbalanced into the offside assembly and the hand was crushed between track and roller as he tried to check his fall.

Shortly afterwards, the surgeons removed the hand at the wrist, and Baines' fighting days were over.

---

Across the front, Soviet forces had repositioned in response to the warnings, reducing their casualties from air strike and bombardment, trading ground for lives saved. As the US and German forces advanced, resistance stiffened, and the experience of Dahlem was repeated in a score of small German villages from the Ruhr to the Ardennes.

Patton threw his men forward, pushing his commanders hard. Guderian, commanding the German pincer forces, understood that the situation was not as had been envisaged, and requested Eisenhower to discontinue the attacks.

"Spectrum Blue will continue as planned, Field Marshal. Make every effort to keep to the timetable."

Eisenhower had said a number of other things, comments designed to soothe and to cosset the angry German, who had succinctly responded, with a phrase that wasn't readily interpreted into English, but that suggested that the timetable was already to hell in a handcart.

--- Earlier in the day ---

### 1230 hrs, Friday, 6th December 1945, Route 109, the Wurzenpass, Yugoslavia.

The plan was not without risk, but the benefits would be huge if it went well.

And it started very well indeed.

Men and women, soldiers who had lived on their wits for years, fell easily, as white-clad special troops invested the defensive position, killing quickly, killing efficiently and, above all, killing quietly.

Their victims were Slovenian partisans, who had joined together in the new Yugoslav Army under Tito, forming the 31st Slovenian Division 'Triglav'. Their victims stood no chance, and succumbed within minutes.

The second phase of the deception commenced on cue, vehicles and tanks sweeping down the Wurzenpass, spitting flame in all directions, engaging the Yugoslav main line.

Here and there, a soft-skinned vehicle flitted from cover to cover, depositing some of the dressing necessary to complete the NKVD plan to draw Yugoslavia in the new war.

The tanks, the half-tracks, the weapons, and the uniforms, were all British Army, as were the corpses that were being spread about the battlefield.

Only the living men, firing the tank guns or using Bren guns to flay the Yugoslav defensive positions, were not British, although the casual observer would see only British uniforms and insignia.

The sixty-two 'British' soldiers, actually Soviet penal soldiers, were there for a single purpose; to die and die well, ensuring that their families would be favourably looked on by a grateful state.

The defending soldiers started to fight back, calling down artillery, and even attracting a passing pair of venerable Yugoslavian crewed ME-109's, previously removed from German control.

The attacking force started to take casualties, and the senior NKVD officer commenced withdrawing his men, making sure that the two who had fallen were carried away by comrades, and that any wounded had their lives extinguished.

A nearby Sherman exploded, victim of a direct hit from a Soviet-made 76.2mm field gun, visibly melting the snow around it as the fire quickly grew in intensity.

The first Messerschmitt made a mess of its approach and banked for another attempt. Distracted by zipping tracers, the pilot misjudged the turn and a wing tip clipped the top of a boulder, sending the aircraft cartwheeling through the trees.

The second aircraft dropped to the attack and killed a number of men and vehicles with a mixture of bombs and bullets.

Low on fuel, the ME109 departed for its base, the pilot shouting into his radio, informing the world that the Allies had attacked Yugoslav soldiers.

### 1230 hrs, Friday, 6th December 1945, Trieste, Italy.

Checking his watch, the Yugoslav Captain felt the tension grow.

'Blyad! They're late...the fucking things are..."

The negative thoughts disappeared as a storm of light and sound engulfed the positions of the 2nd New Zealand Division opposite.

'Yes! Now...come on...'

A second wave of explosions added to the mayhem that descended on the border between the Yugoslav and Allied forces in Trieste, these designed to cause casualties, amongst the curious and brave who would respond to the first bombs.

The NKVD agent had been ordered to bring the two factions into conflict, and the time bombs had been the first part.

Bringing the stock of the rifle to rest on his cheek, he lined the scope with a suitable target and pulled the trigger.

Up the road, a New Zealand Major died instantly as the bullet transited his head.

A second shot killed the Sergeant who ran to his aid.

The agent lined up the third victim, reasoning that the Allied soldiers would be particularly angry at this kill, as he stroked the trigger and shot the nurse through her neck.

He could hear the desperate, frightened squealing she managed to produce, in spite of her gaping wound. Part of him was appalled as he moved to other targets. Firing more hastily now, his accuracy dropped and only one more kill was confirmed, although each target fell bloodily to the road.

Discarding the rifle, he descended the stairs in time to rally his men, and bring the enemy under a steady fire, noting with satisfaction that few of his soldiers had died when his charges exploded.

Yelling oaths and screaming for vengeance, the NKVD agent exhorted his troops to attack and they responded to the calls from their favourite Captain.

Machine-guns and rifles sent bullets flying up and down the road on which the two units sat, claiming casualties in both uniforms.

The final straw for the Yugoslavs was the messy death of their beloved officer, his upper chest destroyed by a burst of Vickers .303.

They charged and closed, with no mercy in their hearts.

---

The ME109 had taken some solid hits from ground fire, and the engine was protesting as oil escaped and temperatures grew.

None the less, the pilot calculated that he would be on the ground at his base in Kranj before the situation grew critical.

His calculations became meaningless as a short burst from some Hispano cannons wrecked the meandering aircraft.

The pilot had no time to react before the Messerschmitt literally came apart around him, and he fell a thousand feet to his death.

Military personnel on the ground cursed the enemy aircraft and did their best to knock one of the three RAF Spitfires from the sky.

The three aircraft turned and headed westwards, their mission accomplished far more easily than had been anticipated.

Diving for the ground, the three lend-lease aircraft dropped out of sight before turning northwards and crossing into Soviet-occupied Austria, from whence they had come.

### 1805 hrs, Friday, 6th December 1945, GRU Commander's office, Western Europe Headquarters, the Mühlberg, Germany.

"So, we have a dilemma, Comrade Poboshkin."

"Yes, Comrade General."

The analysis of the destruction of Soviet 19th Army in the Alsace had been inconclusive, in as much as, it had concluded different possibilities.

342

As was the habit with Soviet thinking, criticism of the system was less favoured than criticism of an individual. Therefore, the report had led with the prime finding that Agent Leopard had been turned in some way, and had been a willing partner in the disinformation that led to the 19th's annihilation.

Close behind that came the possibility that Pekunin contrived the Leopard report himself.

The third suggestion was that Allied intelligence services had discovered the plan, and spread their own maskirovka, fooling Agent Leopard into submitting the misleading report.

Nazarbayeva herself had some doubts over the deaths of Knocke's family, and these surfaced in her reasoning as she started to favour the third on the list.

Poboshkin had a different view.

"If he is our agent, why did he not warn us of the French attack, Comrade General? Such an operation could not have been planned without his knowledge. 'Amethyst' managed it, so why not 'Leopard'? The lack of a report has to indicate that he's, at best, inept... and, at worst, a turned man."

Often Tatiana had observed hard decisions being made by her former boss, but now she was the one who had to decide.

Poboshkin pressed further.

"Comrade General, remember we have the records of one personal meeting between Pekunin and 'Leopard'. Again, that implicates the agent surely?"

Nazarbayeva did not add to that part of the conversation.

Instead, she moved to decision making.

"Whatever is the truth here doesn't matter, Comrade Poboshkin. His reports are not trusted, and the agent is now a liability. If he is turned, he can betray his network. The decision is easy, as we must protect our assets in place."

As she spoke, Nazarbayeva wrote out the formal order. It was the first time she wrote a document tantamount to a death warrant, and she hoped above hope it would be her last.

*In war, there are no unwounded soldiers.*

*Jose Narosky*

# Chapter 115 - THE TEARS

## 0507 hrs, Saturday, 7th December 1945, La Petite Pierre, Alsace.

They had come in their hundreds, possibly thousands, and come quietly bringing death and revenge in their hearts.

415th Rifle Division, the sole remaining functioning unit of the disbanded 89th Rifle Corps, had been absorbed into the brand new 1st Motorised Army and found its tried and trusted skills required, as a fresh fall of snow blanketed the battlefields of Alsace.

Only two regiments, the 1323rd and 1326th, remained, one each targeted on opening the way for the motorised divisions recently released from Stavka reserve, and now tasked with crushing the French attacks.

Spectrum Black had attracted not only the new motorised troops, but also the 6th Guards Cavalry Corps from 2nd Red Banner reserve, as well as the entire 25th Tank Corps, temporarily assigned from 3rd Guards Army.

The Siberians of the 415th moved through the dark of night, and fell upon the positions of the Legion's Mountain Battalion.

Those ex-SS legionnaires at Neuwiller-lès-Saverne were quickly overrun, along with some of Pierce's rear echelon, some three hundred men dying or falling prisoner in a dozen minutes of frantic activity, silent at first, until the attackers were spotted by those who lived long enough to raise the alarm.

At La Petite Pierre, the larger part of the Mountain Battalion force had a stroke of luck, as the alarm was raised before the silent killing had progressed too far.

Rettlinger was startled from his snooze by firing near at hand, certainly within his perimeter.

Whilst his body, still recovering from its wounds, was normally stiff and took some while to get organised, the adrenalin flushed into his system and permitted rapid action.

Derbo strode to the door and took a look outside, and was immediately presented with the awful vision of a desperate close-quarter fight rolling around one of his anti-tank gun positions.

He turned back to his staff.

"Get a warning out that we are being overrun by enemy troops... Norbert at Neuwiller first... then Corps... no... General Pierce's headquarters. You," he pointed at three of his young officers, "Follow me!"

The situation at the 75mm PAK position was clearly being resolved in the Legion's favour, but another pressing issue presented itself.

Two of his Legionnaires were shot down as they ran from a house on the edge of the position, the windows of the building suddenly alive with muzzles spitting bullets.

Derbo dropped down beside a pair of soldiers operating an MG42, set up to defend the headquarters.

"Ackerman... that building there... keep it under fire."

The gunner followed Rettlinger's arm motion and pulled the weapon over in a small arc.

Quickly making a decision, Derbo continued.

"Watch for our counter-attack... from the left there."

The snow-covered barn seemed perfect cover to concentrate an attack force. The blown snow had also formed a white wall high enough for the Legionnaires to get close at the run, and without having to crouch.

"Understood, Sturmbannfuhrer."

The ex-SS soldiers always seemed to slip back into their former rank structure during moments of stress.

---

The 415th had spent a few hours in the company of survivors from the 412th Mechanised Brigade, from whom they had heard of the brutal actions of their opponents, excessive even for the hated SS. Their anger grew and grew with every new story.

They brought it all to the Battle of La Petite Pierre.

In the two-storey house that Rettlinger had selected, fighting was still in progress on the upper floor, where six of his soldiers valiantly resisted all attempts to force the landing, which open space was littered with dead and dying Siberian infantry.

Incensed, they scaled the exterior as best they could, and stormed into the occupied spaces, overrunning the defence.

The two men who survived the assault were hacked to pieces with knives and spades in a frenzy of revenge.

Meanwhile, Rettlinger assembled a scratch force to counter-attack.

---

The MG42 did its work magnificently, slashing at any movement in the windows, and keeping the defenders cooped up.

Rettlinger had gathered a dozen men to him. His three officers, eight of his Legionnaires, and a French war correspondent who had attached himself to the Legion Battalion.

His protestations ended when Derbo removed his camera and replaced it with an American grease gun.

"There's no fucking civilians today, newspaper man. It's kill or be fucking killed. Stick with us, and remember who's side your on!"

He quickly sketched out a plan, and the small group attacked, intent on implementing a swift and violent assault.

---

Before they set off on Spectrum Black, one of Derbo's NCOs had 'acquired' a case of British No 77 grenades from a Spanish infantry unit's supply dump. Each man in the group, not including the reporter, had two.

Four were used to create a smoke screen, greyish-white smoke mixing with the snow to create an almost continuous vista of nothingness.

Avoiding the centre of the developing smoke, the group rushed forward, each window receiving at least one of the white phosphorus smoke grenades, whose other ability was to encourage fire.

With four of his men acting as a security force, Derbo oversaw the slaughter, as Soviet infantrymen tumbled out of doors and windows, driven out by the unforgiving smoke and growing flames.

Each was shot down without mercy, even the Correspondent relishing his turn in the killing.

The security force established themselves in a small position to the front of the burning house, as Rettlinger led his reduced group towards the anti-tank position.

Checking that the gun was still capable of being used, and that the enemy had been driven off, he took his group back to his headquarters.

### 0522 hrs, Saturday, 7th December 1945, Forward headquarters, Assault units for Operation Rainbow Black, Pfalzburg, France.

Lavalle, until recently stretched out on a pile of cushions salvaged from the wrecked lounge furniture, wiped the sleep from his eyes, and tried to get into the operations area without bashing into too many sharp edges.

Summoned by one of his Lieutenants, he arrived in the midst of organised panic, as Derbo's message had been followed by others, all indicating a major Soviet counter-attack in progress.

A coffee was pressed into his hand, the orderly so intent on moving on quickly that he knocked the steaming mug, causing a surge of brown liquid to splash up his commander's shirt, scalding the skin underneath.

Lavalle did not notice, his attention fully focussed on the situation map that was in a state of flux, his staff correcting and adding information with each new report.

The same Lieutenant who had so rudely awakened him presented him with a written message.

It was from Molyneux and he expected it to be about as much use as a chocolate fireguard.

He was right.

*'Resolve the situation immediately... Counter-attack... Push back the enemy...la la la... You're a fucking idiot, mon General.'*

347

The message found its way into the round metal 'filing cabinet' that the clerks emptied every couple of hours or so.

"Get me General Pierce."

## 0528 hrs, Saturday, 7th December 1945, Mobile Headquarters, 16th US Armored Brigade, Ringendorf, Alsace.

"Right, listen in, people!"

Pierce's voice brought an instant quiet to the chaos.

"General Lavalle's ordered us to hold in place pretty much everywhere, create a mobile reserve force in case the enemy needs his fat ass moving outta our positions, and hang on tight to Camerone and Alma on our southern border there."

He pointed at the map and eyes automatically followed his gesture.

"We also got us another mission. Some of our Legion friends have gotten into a whole heap of trouble at Dossenheim, Petite Pierre, and Neuwiller. You can see that we can't let that stand."

Moving closer to the main map, he tapped each location in turn.

"If the commies overrun those points then we are in deep shit... and I do mean deep shit."

He looked at Greiner, just back from the radios. He raised an eyebrow of enquiry and was greeted with a shake of the head.

*'Godfuckingdamnit!'*

"We've no contact with Dossenheim, so we gotta assume that we'll have to push the Reds out of it. That's where we'll focus our main force."

He listed many of the small units that had been held in reserve, a tank platoon here, a mechanised infantry platoon there.

"Get them formed up and on the road a-sap. We should have air today, which will help for sure. Now, the boss is sending a full RCT from the 2nd Indian Head to bust through to Petit Pierre from the north."

He turned back to the map to consider Neuwiller and La Petite Pierre.

348

"Ok, so maybe they will get there in time, but seems to me they've some hard yards there, and the enemy ain't getting any sweeter."

Pierce leant over the map again.

"So, I believe it will fall to us to do both the deeds, and we need to scare up some assets."

He grimaced as he recognised two notations in prime position.

*'Shit.'*

"George."

Lieutenant Colonel George S Williams, commander of the 2nd Ranger Battalion, had already worked it out and knew what was coming.

"Yes, Sir."

His voice betrayed him.

"You got Neuwiller and Petite Pierre, George. Just get in there and keep them ours. The Legion boys are having one hell of a time."

Pierce wished it could be otherwise, but the 2nd Rangers was it. He still tried to sweeten the pill.

"I'll shake you out some armored support... and some artillery too, George."

"Yes, Sir."

"Your orders are to move to Petite Pierre, through Neuwiller, as quickly as possible. You'll defend both villages in harness with the Legion Mountain Battalion in situ... and you will not, repeat not, relinquish your hold on them. When the 2nd Division arrives, then give 'em Pierre, and focus on Neuwiller. Are we clear, George?"

"Yes, Sir."

The 2nd Rangers had been to hell and back over the last few days, and had been placed in a rear position to recuperate. The Soviet counter-attack changed that but they, as well as their commander, were tired and washed out.

Pierce knew this, but difficult decisions are always the privilege of rank.

"Good luck, George. Get your boys moving. I'll send the support to... Griesbach... to rendezvous with you."

Williams saluted and turned on his heel, followed by the other Ranger officer. Both men had arrived the evening beforehand to plead in person for some reinforcements and time out of the line, and now left with a half-cocked mission that would cost more Ranger lives.

As he watched their backs, Pierce felt a spreading chill of belief that he was sending them into the fires of hell.

*'Goddamnit!'*

---

Daring to venture outside once more, Rettlinger rolled across the small gap and crawled up behind the MG position.

He came to rest face down in the crotch of the loader.

The former SS-Gebirgsjager was quite dead, a small trickle of blood from the corner of his mouth being the only indicator of his passing.

"Just happened, Sturmbannfuhrer. Fucking mortar round."

To his front, the building was burning fiercely, adding to the illumination from other fires that were gradually claiming Petite Pierre from end to end.

Cradling the ammo belt in his left hand, Ackerman pulled the weapon's trigger, sending round after round into a group of enemy soldiers forming for a rush.

"Could    do    with    some    more    ammo, Sturmbannfuhrer."

Casting his eye around, Rettlinger could only see the one belt, and that was around the fresh corpse.

Pulling the man up, the cause of death became apparent as the head lolled to one side, and a huge hole was revealed in the rear of the soldier's skull and neck.

Derbo clipped the fifty round belt to the end of the one already inserted into the deadly machine-gun.

"I'll get more to you as soon as I can."

Rettlinger didn't wait for a response and threw himself back across the gap and into the doorway of the headquarters.

Scrambling further inside, he grunted in pain, his wounded arm announcing its displeasure at a thumping impact with the doorframe.

"Sanders! Grab as many of those as you can carry and act as loader on the '42 outside."

The Sergeant, once an Oberscharfuhrer in the 24th SS Gebirgs Division "Karstjager", moved swiftly to obey, snatching up four boxes of ammunition and disappearing from sight.

"What news, menschen?"

"General Pierce's coming from the east; he's moving his forces now, Commandant. Nothing from the western force, but we are assured they are on their way."

The French officer was clearly rattled but still doing his job, not prepared to let his country down in the face of the Germans.

"Good. And us?"

Milke, the Battalions Operations officer, produced a hand drawn map.

"Sturmbannfuhrer. This is our perimeter. We may still be able to breakout to the south-west... if you order it."

The short Captain waited for a moment to let Derbo think on that.

"Do we have orders to withdraw, Hauptsturmfuhrer?"

"No, Sir. General Lavalle's orders are to remain in place for as long as possible. This is an important junction, and it protects the Amerikan Panzers rear."

"Then we move on to matters of defence."

"Sturmbannfuhrer, the untermensch penetrated our lines here, here, here, here, and here. We have counter-attacked successfully here and here. They still hold these other positions. For now, the enemy attacks have stopped."

"Reserves?"

"Us."

That drew laughs from the veterans present, which bemused the French reporter, whose German language skills were insufficient to share the joke.

The camera now shared the shoulder quite comfortably with the grease gun, the thrill of killing a new and wondrous thing to him.

Rettlinger consider the sketchy map.

"Well, we must have some bodies. Take them from here, where we have not yet been pressed. One in three... and here also... but make it one in five only. That should give us," he made the quick calculation. "Thirty-two men."

Milke made it less, but he would manage to find the extra bodies to make his commander's maths a reality.

"Right, that's one twenty man storm group. Who to command?"

All but the reporter stepped forward.

"Koch. Plug any hole, retake any position. Reform your men once the situation is restored. Klar?"

"Zu befehl, Sturmbannfuhrer."

"The remainder will be positioned here under my command. Any questions?"

The Mountain Battalion made its preparations for the next bloodletting.

### 0602 hrs, Saturday, 7th December 1945, Mobile Headquarters, Task Force James, 2nd US Infantry Division, south of Rimsdorf, Alsace.

"Hell yes! We're going to war, Major. We're goddamned going to war!"

Major Carter had already seen enough of what war had to offer, unlike his new Regimental commander, a recent arrival, sent to replace the one recently promoted to be Cheif of Staff for an infantry division just arrived in theatre..

Colonel Albert Mortimer James Jnr was a stereotypical pompous asshole, portraying himself as a 'Southern gentlemen', but who was, in reality, a man who existed without many of the redeeming features of those he so badly caricatured.

His Regiment had been banded together with some extra support elements, rebranded as Task Force James, and hastily sent to the support of the French Foreign Legion forces now floundering in the face of the increased Soviet military presence.

He saw himself as Custer-like figure, leading his men to the rescue, and had said so a number of times.

Carter, a student of American History, glibly reminded him of Custer's fate, which reasonable observation earned him a fifteen minute tirade.

James apart, the leadership of the Task Force were all combat veterans, so the tanks and infantry were soon rolling towards their rendezvous with the Legion at Neuwiller.

## 0700 hrs, Saturday, 7th December 1945, Mobile Headquarters, Task Force James, 2nd US Infantry Division, Ottwiller, Alsace.

The column of smoke and the noise of the explosions announced the problem before the radio crackled into life.

Colonel James was relieving himself outside the command track, so it fell to Carter to receive the report of contact from the lead elements at Petersbach, three kilometres up Route 9.

The point, part of the 2nd Recon Troop, had taken solid hits on the outskirts of Petersbach, losing two vehicles to enemy fire.

The unit's commander was calm enough to identify T34 tanks as responsible for the ambush.

Carter's mind was already addressing the problem. For a moment, he considered not calling James, but relented, sending the clerk to fetch the Colonel.

Drawing heavily on his pipe, James stumbled into the halftrack.

"What gives, Major? I see the smoke up there."

"Sir, the enemy has ambushed our point outside of Petersbach. T34 tanks are reported, as well as infantry and mortars. I've prepped the tank-destroyers to move up to back-stop the lead elements on your order, Si..."

"You've what?"

"I've prepped them for a move up to form a defensive line here, Sir."

Carter indicated a point of higher ground, just south of the junction of Route 9 and 107.

"Well, we won't be doing that, I can goddamn tell you, Major!"

Carter looked at the Colonel in a neutral way.

"We are attacking. Our orders are clear, Major. Order the lead elements to coordinate and push the enemy out of that village."

Carter looked at the Colonel in disbelief.

"Sir, we have T34 tanks identified in that position, supported by infantry and mortars. Our intelligence report tells us that Petersbach is in our possession. Clearly it isn't, so it

353

would seem that the Soviets are attacking. To send our boys forward into that is..."

He stopped and deselected the word that would have put him way out of line.

"Is what, Major Carter? Bold? Carrying the fight to the enemy? Carrying out our orders? What?"

Carter looked at the Colonel in a neutral way.

"Sir, we don't know what we face. If we are savaged, we'll not be able to discharge our orders, and those Legion boys'll pay the cost of our failure."

James looked at the Major with contempt.

"If I didn't know that you'd been decorated for bravery on a number of occasions, I'd think that you're a fucking coward, Major Carter."

Every head in the halftrack had been studiously avoiding looking at the pair, but such words drew them all to gaze at the two officers.

Colonel James saw the silent reactions of his men.

"As you were, soldiers!"

The men snapped round to focus on their own posts once more.

"Major Carter, you will order the lead elements to form for a frontal attack on Petersbach, straight down the '9, using speed and superior fighting ability to overcome the defences."

Carter considered his response carefully, but had only started preparing it before the radio crackled into life and the world changed.

He held eye contact with James, both men silent, listening to the reports from the point column as they were assaulted by a large wave of T34's, probably a regiment's worth, with infantry support.

Keeping his eye contact with Carter, Colonel James spoke rapidly.

"Tell the lead elements to hold and await reinforcements. Radio the TD's and have them move up as previously discussed."

James paused as 105mm shells streaked overhead, artillery support fire brought down to halt the Soviet thrust.

"Is all of Second Battalion closed up?"

Carter suddenly realised that the words were directed at him.

"Yes Sir. When contact was made, the battalion spread out either side of Route 107, on that higher ground, north-east of Lohr."

James looked down at the map and made some decisions, bringing Carter in closer.

"Get First Battalion positioned at this stream here," he ran his finger along a small watercourse on the outskirts of Lohr.

"Third can move up the Route here," he tapped Route 13, that joined the '9 just west of its junction with Route 107.

"Get 'em up to the junction and then we'll see what gives. Send a company of the 741st boys with them."

Task Force James had two companies of the 741st Tank Battalion in its inventory.

"Yes, Sir."

Carter translated the Colonel's words into orders that could be transmitted and, within moments, the soldiers of Task Force James were tasked and organised.

James relit his pipe, making no effort to hide his annoyance, staring at his Major without a hint of comradeship.

Carter reported back that all had been done as ordered.

"Thank you, Major Carter. Troops, listen in!"

The surprise was tangible, but more was to come.

"You heard the exchange between Major Carter and me. I withdraw my comments, and apologise to him without reservation. He was right. I was wrong. I'll do better next time. Now... as you were."

James brought his lighter to his pipe bowl and puffed away madly, his eyes fixed upon Carter, the faintest hint of a smile mainly concealed by the flurry of smoke.

Carter nodded gently, understanding that James had just demonstrated a quality scarce amongst men, let alone leaders of men.

'Son of a bitch.'

Task Force James had run into an advancing element of the 25th Tank Corps, detached from 3rd Guards Army, tasked with threatening the northern flank of the Legion incursion.

The 2nd Division's soldiers would advance no further that day, or the days to come.

The Legion would get no help from that quarter.

### 0728 hrs, Saturday, 7th December 1945, Mobile Headquarters, 16th US Armored Brigade, Ringendorf, Alsace.

Pierce received the two reports without emotion, or at least, any external display of note.

Inside, he part screamed and part bled.

The parts that screamed understood that the 2nd Infantry had been halted by a Soviet combined armored and infantry force at Petersbach, and that the Rangers push had all but withered in the woods, west of Griesbach.

The part that bled had listened impassively to the news that Williams, the Ranger commander, had been carried from the field, felled by an enemy mortar round.

"Jeez, Ed. Tell me there's some good news. Neuwiller? Dossenheim?"

"They've had no contact from Dossenheim yet. Our advance is slow, but we are still moving forward. Nothing from Neuwiller, Sir."

"Nothing?"

"Nothing since the last report, made when the Legion boys occupied it."

Pierce took a deep breath and a big decision.

"Hold the Rangers in place, Ed."

Pierce waited as Greinert issued the orders in clipped tones.

When his number two had finished, he continued, albeit briefly.

"Let's get 'em some more muscle before we ask 'em to move forward again. Talk to me."

"There's a unit of the 712th at Imbesheim. It was missed off the maps initially, as the majority of the battalion had moved on."

The much-reduced 712th Tank Battalion had been added to the 16th's inventory late in the day, but proved a welcome addition with its mix of late model and very special Sherman tanks.

"Two platoons of Sherman Calliopes. They were left behind because of supply issues. These have been resolved, Sir."

"What's that... two miles?"

"Yes, Sir."

"Then get 'em up there right now, Ed."

The orders were sent.

"Now, what else can we send the Ranger boys?"

## 0810 hrs, Saturday, 7th December 1945, five hundred metres north-west of Griesbach le Bastberg, Alsace.

"Roger that, out."

Lukas James Barkmann took a moment to compose himself. His ankle continued to remind him of its condition, even though he had been off it for some time now, hidden away in the roadside ditch that represented his command post.

The initial advance from Greisbach had been stopped dead, enemy tanks and guns forcing the Rangers to ground virtually as soon as they moved off.

Two of his supporting Shermans were burning on the field, joined by at least six transports, victims of the intense defensive fire.

Lieutenant Colonel Williams had been in the nearest one, the upside down jeep smoking, but not alight, oil cooking on the hot engine.

The Rangers' commander had suffered no wound that could be seen, but was insensible and could not be roused, having been thrown from the jeep by the force of the explosion. He came to rest in a snow drift that received him far more gently than a stout tree accepted the Colonel's driver. The dead man remained wrapped around it in an embrace of death, his bones shattered by the unforgiving immoveable trunk, his ankles almost touching the top of his head.

Barkmann shifted his eyes from the sight and concentrated on the job in hand.

"Ok fellahs, we've got some more armor now. Rocket-equipped Shermans. They can get close enough to put down a world of hurt on the Commies in the tree line."

The Sherman concealed nearby fired at something distant and, even through the sound of the steady enemy barrage, the officer group heard whoops of joy celebrating that something with a Red Star on it died.

The tank's commander, the senior man of B Company, 5th Tank Battalion, celebrated with a smile and a joke.

"Seems like the boys are doing ok without me!"

Barkmann spread his map on the pile of snow that counted as a table.

"Captain, the 712th boys wanna go in just behind you. They need to get closer."

"Makes sense," Captain Ewing conceded, "They've only got the 75, so they're under gunned for this party."

Barkmann nodded and accepted a cigarette with a snort of derision.

"Still smoking these goddamned corks, Al?"

Gesualdo pretended offence.

"Only Herbert Tareyton's for me, Lukas. My body's a temple."

Barkmann took a deep draw and feigned disgust before continuing.

"We're going to go on 0830."

He looked around the other Ranger officers, the weariness evident on each dirty and bloody face.

"Those Legion boys need us. Reports are that they are close to being overrun in Pierre. There's nothin' from Neuwiller at all. The northern relief force has run into a whole bunch of trouble. It's stuck and going nowhere fast.

"So, it's the normal shitty deal, but it seems that it's all up to us."

"So, we lead the way again, eh?"

"Very poetic, Al. I'll remember that."

Gesualdo had referred to a statement made by General Cota, in Normandy, which later became the basis of the Ranger motto.

"The attack will focus on the flanks... here and here," Barkmann pointed out the tracks that ran parallel to, and north and south of, the main road, Route 233.

"We'll push hard both sides, and then close around their positions like a jaw. Once we've done that, we'll re-evaluate but old man Pierce wants our asses in Neuwiller pronto. We have the promise of some air, but not yet. Arty is available as before. The 712th will plaster the wood line as soon as they're in range, but remember, the goddamn things fly everywhere, so keep tight and don't push up too far until they've pulled their show. 'Kay?"

Murmurs of understanding were enough for him to proceed further.

"I have 0820...on my mark... three... two... one... mark."

Watches were synchronised.

"Right. Keep your heads down, but push hard. Those Legion boys are counting on us. Questions?"

"Yep. Your boys riding or walking?"

Inside, Barkmann scolded himself. His Rangers would know automatically, but not the tank officer.

"Shit. Apologies. Tight in behind, I think, No sense in creating targets for their MG's."

Ewing nodded.

"Right, anything else?"

The silence told him all he needed to know.

"0830 it is. Good luck."

The group broke up, leaving Gesualdo and Barkmann finishing up their cigarettes.

"Task Force Barkmann, eh?"

"So Pierce now calls us, Al."

"I'm honoured to fight alongside such a famous warrior."

"Fuck off."

Both men sniggered, then fell into silence again.

"Something occurred to me before the briefing, Al. Weird."

"I figured. You think too goddamned much."

The smile betrayed Gesualdo despite the deadpan delivery.

"Legion Etrangere."

359

"Yes, the Foreign Legion. Top of the class, Lukas."

"No, you pea brain. Look."

Barkmann wrote it out in his notebook and showed it to his friend.

"Ah, I see... well I'm damned. A sign... or a divine message perhaps?"

They chuckled, and finished their cigarettes.

Barkmann took one last look at the pad before putting it away.

Shaking hands with Gesualdo, they went their separate ways.

As Gesualdo dropped down beside his own NCO's, he could still recall the message that Barkmann had penned.

'l e g i o n   e t R A N G E R e.'

*'Son of a bitch.'*

## 0836 hrs, Sunday 7th December 1945, Route 233, the Greisbach - Neuwiller road, Alsace.

Ewing's Shermans were doing great work, burning and smoking enemy vehicles and guns were littered throughout the Soviet positions, marking success after success. Not without cost. Four of the 5th Battalion's Shermans had been knocked out of the fight in as many minutes.

Ranger casualties had been very light, even to those groups whose metal shields had been knocked out.

However, some unheard command changed all that, as the edge of the woods came alive with spitting fire, a veritable hail of bullets searching the battlefield for soft flesh.

Barkmann's soldiers started to die.

He dropped into a small gully, his own tank cover left behind, engulfed in flames where some large shell had stopped it dead.

Raising his binoculars, he felt a frustration that the Calliopes had not yet done their job.

Sweeping either side of his position, his company was moving up the slower central route, one damaged tank caught his eye.

"Goddamnit!"

"Sir?"

"One of the 712th has been disabled already, and they still haven't fired."

First Sergeant Ford was an old hand, and had an alternate explanation for the one that was foremost in his officer's mind.

"It'd be easy for them boys to loose off their whizz-bangs and bug out, wouldn't it? They're just doing it proper and getting in range, Lootenant."

To Barkmann, the army consisted of the 2nd Rangers, and then some other units. He considered Ford's words.

"Fair comment."

He dropped his binoculars to his chest, and prepared to advance. The 712th then showed what they could do.

"What the fuck?"

The remaining six T34 Calliope tanks started to unload their 4.2" rockets, sixty each, the tube sets aimed simply by adjusting the main gun on each tank.

It was an awesome sight, but more so when the rockets arrived on target.

Whilst the rockets were relatively inaccurate, there were a hell of a lot of them, and the 712th transformed the Alsatian landscape into a montage from the Great War.

Grabbing the radio from his operator, Barkmann spoke rapidly.

"Boxer-Six, Boxer-Six to all units, all units. Press in hard and fast, roll over them whilst they're still reeling. Out"

The responses came back as he passed the handset on and sprang forward, followed by the rest of his company, green Ranger uniforms contrasted by the snow.

Across the battlefield, infantry and tanks pressed forward, although the tanks sensibly kept close to their infantry protectors.

The 712th pushed in tight, wisely as it proved, for the Soviet artillery started to hammer the ground in front of the ravaged defensive position. Most shells fell uselessly on unoccupied ground.

A bullet tugged at Barkmann's trousers, the hot metal sliding across the side of his calf painfully. Perversely, it also cut through the euphoria caused by the Calliope strike, and brought his ankle problem to the fore.

He started to limp, but still maintained the pace.

A movement to his front made him shoulder his Garand and fire off three quick rounds. He ran over the spot, but there was nothing.

A grunt nearby drew his attention, and he turned as one of his Rangers slowly dropped to the ground. Another movement to the man's left drew the remaining five rounds in his rifle. A spray of red indicated that at least one bullet had struck home.

Two Rangers leapt into the position, and a burst of Thompson finished off the wounded Russians.

Smoke burned his throat and lungs; the very earth seemed to be alight around him.

Nearby, a Soviet tank, he didn't recognise the type, burned steadily, the acrid rubber smoke the source of his own discomfort.

Barkmann paused to recharge his Garand, noticing how so much of the snow had been melted away, either in the blasts, or by the subsequent fires.

Ford leapfrogged his position, dropped into a shell hole, and found himself in a horror show.

Not one body was intact.

Even the old hard-bitten NCO exceeded his tolerance, spilling the contents of his stomach at the sight.

He had jumped into a charnel house of pieces, entrails and gore spread evenly across the sides of the hole, with pieces of body here and there, some even recognisable for what they might once have been.

An arm.

A leg.

A... head?

A... something.

*'Oh, you poor bastards!'*

Recovering as best he could, Ford picked himself up, both physically and mentally, crawling out of the hole, presenting his Rangers with a bloody sight straight from the darkest of nightmares.

Barkmann dropped beside him.

"Fucking hell, Sarge. You ok?"

Reasonably, the Ranger officer thought his NCO had been wounded.

"Lotta dead bodies in there, Lootenant. Just messy... so fucking messy."

Barkmann risked a look over the edge of the hole and immediately wished he hadn't.

"Oh my."

A bullet zipped his way, throwing up a little earth as it hit the edge of the hole.

It served to focus both men and take their thoughts away from the horrors in front of them.

"There's one at the base of the tree there. See him?"

Barkmann pointed, but it was unnecessary, as Ford's rifle spat a single bullet that sped across the no man's land and shattered a skull.

All around the two men, other Rangers were pushing forward as resistance slackened even further.

A group of three Soviet soldiers sat cross-legged on the bottom of their position, eyes staring at something a thousand miles away, no more aware of their surroundings and predicament than the dead they shared their emplacement with.

None of the three men had dropped their weapons; they remained clutched tight to their chests, as a scared child holds his favourite teddy bear for protection from evil.

A Corporal practised his Russian on the group, but to no avail.

More Rangers screamed and shouted at the Soviet soldiers, who continued to look at something beyond comprehension.

A Ranger BAR gunner shot them at close range.

On the flanks of the attack, the Rangers and tankers pushed in hard, clearing the few occupied positions with grenades or HE shells.

Some Soviet soldiers surrendered, those that were still capable of thinking rationally anyway.

Others, like the group of three, sat shocked and stunned and, like the three, some died because they could neither hear nor understand their executioners.

Very few of the defenders were capable of fighting, but those that were did so to the best of their ability.

A few more Rangers were wounded or killed before the positions were taken, and the firing stopped.

Two of the Russian tanks contained dead men, although the vehicles were operational.

"Concussion and blast, Lootenant."

The mess hanging from one of the turrets was awful.

"That's his lungs, Lootenant."

The blast had driven the Soviet tank officer's lungs out of his body, to hang from his mouth like pink and red petals.

For men, such as Barkmann and Ford, who thought they had seen everything that combat had to offer, the fight for the Griesbach-Neuwiller road took them to extremes they never wanted to visit again.

Gesualdo limped up, his right thigh gripped tight by a fresh bandage.

"OK, Al?"

"Friendly fire, can you believe it? Goddamned friendly fire!"

Barkmann could not help but grin at his friend.

"Later then... over one of your shit cigarettes. Now, we gotta get moving.

"I hear that. My boys are in good shape. Want me to take the lead?"

"'Kay. Tie in with Ewing for some close support. I shall pull the 633rd TD boys up now. Let's go."

They shook hands.

"Al."

"Lukas."

Gesualdo limped off again.

"Sergeant Ford, get the doggies up and moving. We've a war to win."

---

As the American force prepared to move off again, welcome assistance made itself available, in the form of A-26B's from the 416th Bombardment Group.

Much of the USAAF unit had been stateside when hostilities had commenced again and, for various reasons, had not come back together until mid-November.

Their A26 Invaders carried a world of hurt, both internally and externally.

Sixteen .50cal machine guns and a 6000lbs load of ordnance.

Twelve aircraft were airborne and, as yet, had not been engaged, so they were able to focus all their power on the Red Army units sat between the Rangers and the position at Neuwiller.

Avoiding the road, two groups of three aircraft swept north-west, screaming over the top of the Rangers, commencing their attack from the red smoke that marked the limits of the Ranger advance.

Each dropped half of their load of bombs, ravaging a large area either side of Route 233.

The next two groups of three repeated the procedure, dropping their ordnance further on.

Both groups then swept back over the area, sweeping the ravaged ground with .50cal rounds.

For the Rangers, it was seriously impressive and professional work, and Barkmann was determined to make the most of the opportunity.

He pushed his men harder, upping the pace of the advance, spreading groups out to the edge of the swept area, in case any defenders rallied on the flanks of the beaten zone.

Careful to protect his men from his own Air Force, he ordered more red smoke put down as they advanced.

Six aircraft swept overhead, the 416th circling with impunity, no ground fire of note to concern them, and definitely no enemy aircraft to challenge their mastery of the airspace over the battlefield. They repeated the attacks, moving the bomb line forward by seven hundred yards

This time the secondary explosions were obvious.

Reports from the Squadron Commander indicated major damage to a Soviet tank unit that had been concealed, but not well enough to avoid the attentions of the Invaders.

Barkmann knew that Ewing would be listening, but he also remembered that assumption was the mother of all fuck-ups, so he confirmed that the tanker had heard the report.

"Roger that. We're on it, Boxer Six."

Ewing was a career soldier, and understood that the Ranger officer was a competent man who was just playing it by the numbers.

Amidst the burning Russian tanks to his front, one still exhibited life, its turret turning from side to side.

Inside, a soviet tank commander, fresh to the battlefield, condemned his men with his exhibition. Urine and faeces dripped down his legs, creating a smell they could recognise, but it was his inability to make a decision that brought their premature end.

Ewing had no such problems but, in truth, he hadn't just been bracketed by 500lbs bombs.

The commander of the 5th Battalion's tanks got a shot away; a high-velocity armor piercing that did just what it was supposed to do.

The young Soviet tank officer was the sole survivor as firstly the shell and then the vehicle innards it displaced, scythed through the four men, two in the hull and two in the turret.

## 0931 hrs, Saturday, 7th December 1945, in and around, La Petite Pierre, Alsace.

"Sturmbannfuhrer?"

Derbo looked at the orderly bandaging his leg and nodded at the enquiry.

"Feels fine, Willi... thank you."

He stood up and tested the leg, wincing at the initial pain, but soon getting himself under control.

He patted the old medical orderly on the shoulder.

"I owe you a drink, Kamerad. Are you free later, say, eight o'clock in the promenade bar?"

More than one of the weary Mountain troopers managed a laugh, and more than one was too exhausted to hear.

Rettlinger's perimeter had shrunk as the Soviet attackers redoubled their efforts, and no one there was under any illusions as to what would happen next.

He was still clinging to the two road junctions, having pulled all his men into the five hundred metre long oval that covered Route 9's junctions with the 135 and 7.

Actually, he had pulled back nearly all his men, for a small group had become isolated in the village cemetery, on the northeast edge of St Petite Pierre; they were still fighting.

It seemed that the heaviest combat of all rolled through the monuments and headstones, the screams of the frightened and the dying often louder than the sounds of the weapons doing the Grim Reaper's work.

The fighting had started to lessen, but it had taken nearly an hour for silence to descend on the positions.

Eight men filtered back from the bloodbath in the cemetary

The Castle Lützelstein had already been abandoned, its defence pointless, a few white flags left to shield the handful of wounded that had remained, unable to be moved. They retained their weapons, just in case, and each man had a grenade, should something more unpalatable than death threaten them.

Some seven hundred metres from where the ex-SS officer moved amongst his men, another commander was exhorting his troops to one final huge effort.

"Listen to that, Comrades, listen."

The sounds of exploding artillery, and the crack of tank cannons were timely.

"That's the enemy trying to get through to this bunch that we've bottled up."

Astafiev favoured his right leg, a growing bruise on his thigh indicating where he had contacted the tree stump that lay hidden beneath a layer of snow.

"We'll make one last effort, a final attack. We will overrun them," the emphasis on 'will' made a number of faces swivel his way, "And then prepare this position against the forces that are coming to relieve the SS swine."

The former identity of the defenders had become known some time beforehand. That information quickly passed from mouth to mouth, bringing an increased savagery to the Siberian's attacks.

"Comrade Mayor Toralov."

He looked at the once-immaculate figure, now black from head to toe, and carrying a dozen wounds.

"Comrade, I need one last effort from you."

Toralov stiffened by way of reply, his broken jaw not permitting anything above a grunt here and there.

"You'll command the wounded, who'll all be assembled at this point here."

Astafiev indicated a pair of houses that had yet to burn, although they had not escaped unscathed.

"On my command, you'll open up upon the Germanski and keep firing until you see us on their position."

The Major nodded and eased the PPD on his shoulder, looking around at a few of the men who would share the duty with him.

"The rest of 2nd Battalion will hold behind this position, ready to come forward to prepare the defence, once 1st Battalion has overrun the last defenders."

The sound of aircraft gave him pause, and the Soviet Colonel looked up as a number of twin-engine aircraft swept over La Petite Pierre without engaging which, for the 415th Rifles, was good, as they bore the white star of the USA.

---

"Air support, Kameraden. Air support at last. Help is not far away now, so we must stand firm. They'll come again, and it will be all-out so be aware. We must hold out, not long now, but we must hold out. If we fall, our Amerikan allies will have a hard time of it."

Such was the perimeter that the Mountain Battalion now occupied, that Rettlinger could see every pile of bricks or scrape in the snow that was held by his men.

The last enemy assault had overrun the new battalion medical post and Koch's platoon had been unable to take it back.

Koch himself had not returned from the effort and his fate was unclear, with some of his comrades believing him killed as he ran forward, whilst others thought they saw him gain the canvas and wood position.

Either way, an experienced officer had been lost.

Milke was now in command of the emergency unit, reduced to nineteen men, including those who had been retained by Derbo.

"You know what you have to do, Bernhard."

It wasn't a question. Ex-Hauptsturmfuhrer Milke was an old and trusted soldier.

"Remember, Kameraden. They are coming for us. You know it; you can hear them coming. Hold on... hold on just a little while longer... and I'll buy everyone a drink, not just Willi!"

The first laugh was drowned by the arrival of Soviet mortar shells, falling all over the position, no more than 300 metres across at its widest point.

"Hals und Beinbruch, Kameraden!"

Dropping into a low crouch, or as low as such a mountain of a man can get, Rettlinger moved off quickly to his chosen point of defence; the part of his position nearest the enemy.

Heavy firing started behind him, quickly accompanied by the sounds of distress from men recently wounded.

He dropped into his position, struggling for breath, and rubbed his aching thigh, trying to prepare for what he knew came next.

---

Astafiev had decided to lead his men from the front, and the point he had chosen to attack was the obvious one. The shortest distance between his positions and that of the hated enemy.

He moved amongst his assault force, slapping a shoulder here, or shaking a hand there.

Some distance away, Toralov's small force had started laying it on thickly as the mortars expended their last few rounds of smoke and HE before dedicating themselves to finding more ammunition to the rear.

Asatafiev risked a look over a broken brick wall, and was greeted with a gift from the gods.

The nearest building was now bathed in smoke from two mortar rounds, the adjacent structure adding more smoke to the situation as fire took hold.

Holding his Tokarev pistol firmly, he stood and yelled at the men of the 1st Battalion."

"Comrades! To Victory! Urrah!"

The cry grew in three hundred and forty throats as his men rose up with him and plunged across the small but deadly piece of No man's land, where fire from unsighted enemies plucked the life from man after man.

The momentum was unstoppable and, firing as they ran, the Siberian infantry smashed into the Mountain troopers positions.

At first, submachine guns, grenades and pistols ruled.

One Siberian soldier stumbled through a walkway in a snowdrift and found himself behind a group of three Legion troopers, who themselves were throwing grenades and firing into a struggling section of soldiers caught between some barbed wire and a larger snowdrift.

Even as the grenades exploded and claimed many lives and limbs, the single Siberian killed all three Legionnaires with a prolonged burst at close range, which turned the snow crimson, and decorated it with small pieces of their bodies, blasted away by the sustained fire from the PPSh.

It was kill or be killed.

It was also kill and be killed.

The PPSh gunner never felt the bullet that entered the back of his neck and added his own fatal contribution to the crimson montage in the snow.

Rettlinger stepped over the corpse and organised a small group of men to fill the latest hole in his line.

Through the snow gap came more Siberians, and Rettlinger charged, screaming and firing at the same time, the ST44 dropping each of the three men with none of them able to return a shot.

Drawing hard on the cold air. Derbo dropped to his knee at the entrance to the snowy walkway and fired off the rest of his magazine as two more Soviets sprung forward.

Two men of the initial rush were only wounded and their cries started to sound stronger and stronger, especially when Rettlinger stepped on one's face.

One of Derbo's men rushed up to assist his leader, pausing only to shoot both men in the head.

The Russian Front had taught harsh lessons and often harsh actions were the only answer, many a man had been lost when leaving a wounded enemy behind him, and the young Mountain trooper had no intention of allowing himself or his commander to be shot in the back.

Rettlinger changed out his magazine, conscious that it was his last one, and that it was already light by five rounds.

A grenade dropped perfectly in the entrance of the snowy walkway, causing both men to dive for cover.

The wait was awful.

*'Dud?'*

Derbo posed the question to himself, even as he rolled away. He risked a look up at the entrance.

He yelled a warning, but the Siberian soldier there got off a shot with his rifle.

The Mosin bullet passed through the young Trooper's pelvis, clipping the hip socket on its way through.

Howling with pain, he shot his opponent four times, the Gewehr 43 falling silent only because it was empty.

Gritting his teeth, the Mountain soldier rolled away and grabbed for another magazine.

He neither heard nor saw the grenade that killed him.

It had been poorly thrown, but its explosion propelled a deadly piece of metal through the left ear and into the German's skull.

Rettlinger missed the death; he was quickly looking around, knowing he was losingthe fight, as more of his positions were becoming overrun with enemies.

He screamed and cursed as he watched the reduced reserve group rush forward, his eyes firmly fixed on Milke as the man's body received multiple hits from an enemy DP weapon. His old comrade was thrown back into the advancing troopers, dead before he ever touched the ground.

"Bastards! Fucking bastards!"

Another grenade exploded in the snowy entrance, but only served to announce to Rettlinger that the enemy were coming again.

He shot the first man through, only wounding him, as the ST44 jammed.

Derbo struggled with the weapon until he was knocked aside by a heavy blow.

One of his men charged past him, firing an MG42 from the hip.

"Sorry Sturmbannfuhrer... but he was going to have you!"

Ackerman had deliberately knocked Derbo over to save him.

There was no time for further exchanges as Ackerman dropped to the snow and poured fire through the entrance and into Siberian soldiers still moving across No Man's Land.

Rettlinger turned, guided by some sixth sense, his Walther in his hand.

The bullet struck the Soviet NCO in the chest, throwing him backwards, even as he drove the SVT40 bayonet into the side of the Legion officer.

Rettlinger roared like a wounded bull and shot the dead man again.

A Legion bullet came from nowhere and slammed into Rettlinger's shoulder, passing millimetre perfect through the gaps in the bones.

A hazy shape appeared in the smoke nearby, the rifle and long bayonet betraying the shadow's allegiance.

The Walther barked twice and Rettlinger was rewarded with screaming, then silence.

Rettlinger coughed and blood rose in his throat.

Ackerman dropped by his side.

"Sturmbannfuhrer, I'm out of ammo. There's hundreds of the red bastards and I can't stop them now. Too exposed here. C'mon."

He quickly tossed a grenade at the entranceway and helped Rettlinger to his feet, the officer's uncomplicated flesh wound spilling huge quantities of blood down the greying-browny-white snowsuit.

The two staggered the thirty yards to the nearest friendly position, only to find one side of it alive with soldiers from both sides, rolling around in close combat.

Ackerman placed Rettlinger in a comfortable position, finding a Thompson and two clips for the weakening officer, before charging forward.

Blood-loss now started to tell, as the battle became less distinct and hazy to his eye. Rettlinger felt detached, almost a neutral observer of the events that unfolded.

Whilst part of his mind was still a soldier and tried to command his hands to pick up the Thompson, it lacked the energy and power to overcome the lethargy that was overpowering him.

So he watched as Sanders was pinned to the ground and stabbed repeatedly with bayonets.

He could barely manage a twitch when the grenade landed nearby, although part of his brain was alert enough to know he was about to die and then understand that he had been saved by someone leaping on the charge.

The brave soldier was lifted by a flash and bang, gutted and disembowelled by the force of the charge.

He had saved a number of his Kameraden by his selfless act, but it served no purpose in the end.

Rettlinger focussed on the soldier.

*'Fleischmann?'*

The piece of flesh left steaming in the snow and blood had indeed once been called Willi-Jon Fleischmann.

The soldier-part of Derbo's brain rallied and overcame adversity, commanding the Thompson to rise in his hands, but the flesh was weak; it was too heavy.

His right hand found the Walther he had tucked in his belt and an extraordinary effort brought it out and up.

Through the mist, Rettlinger sought a target but was unable to identify friend or foe for certain, until a man, shouting in a language he first heard five years beforehand, stood separate from the rest.

He fired the last two rounds and, even though the act exhausted him, he noticed that the shape had gone.

---

Astafiev tried to stop his men, shouting at them, grabbing at those in reach as they started killing men who had been wounded or bludgeoned into unconsciousness.

None of the Mountain troopers surrendered, and few were captured, save those cowed by their injuries.

Some of the Siberian soldiers heeded Astafiev's entreaties, but others paid no attention.

He jumped on a raised area and shouted at his men.

The first Walther bullet passed through his lower stomach, nicking a kidney on its way out of his back.

The second bullet demolished his right knee.

The sight of their commanding officer falling to the snow simply encouraged the Siberians to greater excesses.

---

Astafiev moaned in pain, his stomach on fire, his right knee presenting him with the most excruciating pain.

Some of his men searched the enemy dead for medical supplies, desperate to find pain relief for their Commander, but there was none to be had, so they listened to him suffer.

Some men cried, not just for Astafiev, but also for the many old comrades and friends that lay still in the snow or gathered in the makeshift hospital area.

Other cried because they were mentally shattered, the savagery, and awfulness of the fight way beyond their previous experiences.

Others acted, determined that the greater suffering would be visited upon the legionnaires, the Germanski, recalling the recent horror stories of the mechanised infantrymen who had fought these German-legionnaires before.

Second Battalion had swept up into the positions and immediately set to work restoring as much of the defences as possible, in case an enemy relief force arrived to stake its claim to this blood-soaked piece of Alsace.

Two platoons from Second Battalion entered the Castle. Upset that they had not had their opportunity for vengeance, they were delighted to be presented with a final opportunity.

The Legion wounded were massacred but not without Siberian losses, which only egged them on to further excess.

Grenades set the old structure's contents alight and the few Legionnaires that were dragged from the old castle were summarily shot or bayoneted in short order.

Soviet soldiers smashed up the wooden garden furniture and creating a cleared area in front of a dilapidated bistro bar on the junction of the 9 and 135.

Others ripped the wooden shutters from the ground floor windows to declare their support for what was to come.

Another group of First Battalion survivors collected dead enemy soldiers, creating a mound in the small grassy area that had served as the bar's beer garden.

374

Nineteen Mountain troopers were still alive, most taken from the final Legion casualty station, which had been brutally liquidated with knives, up close and personal.

Each of the eighteen men were bound to the corpse of a legionnaire and placed around the base of the mound.

The nineteenth legionnaire, *'the bastard that shot Astafiev'*, was given special treatment, and placed, like a fairy on a Christmas tree, atop the mound.

It took but a moment for the petrol to be shaken over the living and the dead alike, immediately drawing screams of fear from those who were mentally alert enough to know their approaching fate.

Men vied for the privilege of initiating the revenge, and a fight broke out until a Senior Sergeant stepped in, suggesting that those who wanted to participate could do so together and 'if the three of you fucking idiots don't stop fighting each other, I'll have your fucking balls off!'

Matches were struck and, on a signal, dropped onto the fuel soaked men.

---

Astafiev later claimed that the sound of screaming broke through into his unconsciousness state and that, lying on what counted for stretcher in the shattered Petite Pierre, the minutes that he endured the awful screams and squeals of those being immolated were the worst of his life.

In the centre of the village, the lust for revenge rapidly drained from the Siberians, as they watched their prisoners writhe in agony as they were burned alive.

Atop the pile was Rettlinger, his mind and vision greatly cleared by what was about to come.

He rose as best he could, debilitated by injury and blood loss, encumbered by wrists tied behind his back. Standing upright, he debated throwing himself forward in the hope that someone would shoot and grant him a quick death.

His leg gave way, and the possibility was gone before the decision had been made.

Rettlinger looked at as many of the enemy as he could, despite being petrified, his eyes showing his hatred for all present, and also carrying his determination to die as well as he could.

Flames licked around him and the pain doubled and redoubled.

He stayed silent, a silence that was now only broken by the roaring of flames as all others had now succumbed to the ordeal.

And then, he broke.

The sound.

Unreal.

Awful.

*'Holy Mother!'*

Some looked away in disgust at, both at themselves and those who helped create the abomination. Others remained fixed on the writhing man, almost as if to look away would dishonour him.

*'Let him die quickly!'*

Some looked at each other, seeking guidance, needing only a nod or a shrug to shoot the enemy officer to relieve his agony.

But no one fired, so Bruno Rettlinger died the most horrible of deaths, exactly seventeen miles from where he was born.

## 1226 hrs, Saturday, 7th December 1945, La Petite Pierre, Alsace.

The assault of Neuwiller had arrived unexpectedly, at least for the Soviet Major in charge of the remains of 1326th Rifle Regiment.

Based on his intelligence reports, he had concentrated the larger force to oppose the attempted relief effort from the southern Allied force heading up from Dossenheim, and successfuly so, as the allied push ran out of steam..

His earlier reports had not included news from the defence forces allocated to the southeast and Route 233, and so the arrival of Task Force Barkmann was both a surprise and a disaster for the Siberian soldiers.

The few Soviet tanks left in support were rapidly overwhelmed by a combination of 76mm shells from Shermans and M18 Hellcats of the 633rd, leaving the American tanks free to harvest the infantry left after the air and artillery strikes.

An incursion by two Shturmoviks claimed one of the M18 tank destroyers, but the two aircraft were driven away from the battlefield as three Mustangs arrived, bringing their own modest ordnance to the party and planting it perfectly on the battalion command post in between a cluster of buildings two hundred metres south-east of the main village.

In truth, the aircraft had been aiming at a grand house nearby, not a nondescript clump of trees.

Not that it made any difference to the command structure of the 1326th Regiment. Most of them were assembled for an orders group, and all of them died in the explosions, the first of the one thousand pound bombs alone would have been enough as it penetrated the roof of the hastily constructed bunker, wiping through the second in command before detonating at the feet of the harassed Major.

The Rangers and Engineers swept forward and through the first line of defence with relative ease, destroying pockets of resistance with well-directed tank fire, followed by close infantry assault.

Neuwiller was overrun quickly, and the Ranger combined force, leaving 254 US Combat Engineer Battalion in place with a little armor stiffening, rolled up Route 134, heading for La Petite Pierre.

They pushed on hard and were lucky. No organised resistance was encountered until nearly on the southern edge of La Petite Pierre.

In fact, the advance had moved forward so quickly that both Gesualdo and Barkmann, encumbered by leg injuries, had trouble keeping up the pace.

Gesualdo was, in some ways, more fortunate, as his lead unit ran into a group of Siberians who were determined to stay put, giving him a chance to join up with his men.

Quickly organising some close support, Gesualdo led his Rangers into the smoking ruins of the house that the tenacious enemy had occupied, now converted to a pile of bricks by the ministrations of two Shermans.

As he picked his way over the rubble, his leg gave way and he fell.

Instinctively, his arm shot out, finding the perfect hole down which to slide, before his not inconsiderable frame hit the bricks and the weight of his body in motion strained the bone past its point of tolerance.

Through the diminishing sounds of battle, the snap of his left arm was heard for many yards in all directions, causing more than one soldier to duck in self-preservation.

Gesualdo passed out with the pain, and it fell to his radioman to scream out for a medic, his eyes focussed in horror on the arm, bent at right angles with bones protruding from broken skin.

The Rangers pushed on, encouraged by their NCOs and the few surviving officers, the Soviet forces almost melting away before their advance.

Barkmann heard of Gesualdo's injury and felt relief that his friend had survived the fight with only a broken arm.

He pressed on, starting to gain on his forward troops, warning them to be aware of Legion defenders ahead.

They now found no resistance; no die-hard soldies selling their lives for a few yards of Alsace. The enemy was not to be found.

If it was at all possible in a world ripping itself apart, something in the Alsatian air brought a moment's pause across the battlefield. Those who were more pragmatic argued that it was the obvious product of burning flesh that every nostril detected.

Others believed they sensed a revulsion in the very ground they trod on.

Men migrated to the horrors on display in front of the bistro.

Rangers, engineers, and tankers, stopped and took in the sight. Many an appalled mind refused to acknowledge what they saw there, and many a stomach rejected its contents.

Barkmann hobbled up, sensing what he was about to find.

*'Goddamnit Al, I need you now.'*

First Sergeant Ford stood waiting for his commander, face set; hardened, impassive, but betrayed by his eyes.

Barkmann stood with his hands by his side, watching the decreasing fire continue to charr flesh and burn uniforms away, but not enough to hide the identity of the bodies.

"Oh Jesus, Walter."

Ford was too engrossed in his own mental battle to acknowledge the use of his first name.

"Ne'er seen anthin' like it in all my days, Cap'n, no sir."

Some civilians appeared, clearly shocked and stunned by what had gone on in their home village.

A monk, his face bloodied by some unknown injury, stood before the terrible bonfire and made the signs of his faith repeatedly, calling for forgiveness on those who had brought about the terrible event, and seeking to bring mercy to those that had suffered so badly.

A burst of firing made everyone dive for cover, all except the old monk, who continued his entreaties.

Up the road, one of the Rangers had just executed a badly wounded enemy NCO, the same one who had ruled on the squabble over lighting the pyre.

"NO! Stop firing!"

Barkmann strode forward, pointing at the young Ranger who had just dispensed justice as he saw it.

"There will be no more! No more, you hear me?"

He took a deep breath, and raised his voice.

"Men... this is the worst thing I've ever seen in my soldiering. Far and away... and you all know we've been through some deep shit together."

He pointed at the pile.

"These men were our Allies..."

He swallowed hard and composed himself.

"We were not in time to save them... but that's not our fault. We couldn't have done more. You all know that. YOU ALL KNOW THAT!"

He started to move amongst his men, placing a calming hand on a shoulder or patting an arm as he went.

"You ALL know that we couldn't have done more for these boys."

Turning back to the smouldering heap, he spoke, almost as if addressing the fallen.

"This... this is awful... but we cannot... we must not... and we will not... let it make us into the same as those that did it."

He reached the two dismounted armored officers, Watkins and Ewing, the commanders of the 712th and 5th Tanks respectively.

"We cannot become the same as the swine that did this."

Ewing looked away, but Watkins held his gaze, the anger spilling from every pore in his body.

"You," Barkmann pointed at an experienced Corporal,

"You," a young 2nd Lieutenant.

"You," a Sergeant from Gesualdo's company.

"Me."

He drew a few more looks and waved an expansive hand over the group.

"Us."

He created a moment of silence to emphasise his point.

"All of us were at Hattmatt where... a mistake was made... a mistake that cost many Russians their lives."

He nodded as a thought occurred to him.

"Perhaps that is why, eh? Maybe that's why this... this abhorrence happened?"

He saw that some of the men could see his point.

"Perhaps we can help turn this off now... by not becoming like those who did this and... I don't know... maybe starting to make up for Hattmatt?"

Barkmann had failed to spot the enemy soldier at the feet of one of his Rangers, cowed and bruised.

The American pulled the Siberian rifleman to his feet, both suddenly the centre of attention.

The Ranger shoved the prisoner towards Ford.

"One prisoner, Sergeant."

Ford looked around him.

Directly opposite the bistro was a modest house, relatively undamaged by the battle that had raged around it.

The wooden hatches that protected the entrance to the basement stood invitingly open.

Two Rangers stood nearby, and Ford called to one.

"Rigby, you been in there?"

"Yep, Sarge.

"Secure is it?"

"One way in, one way out, Sarge."

Turning back to the Ranger with the prisoner, the First Sergeant jerked his thumb at the basement entrance.

"Stick him in there."

The fortunate Siberian received another shove, sending him on his way.

Barkmann continued.

"Now boys, let's get this place secured pronto, and get ready for defence, just in case. Move!"

The crowd immediately dispersed to their duties.

Watkins shook out a Chesterfield for himself, and then offered the pack to Barkmann and Ewing.

"Lukas, right?"

"Yep. You?"

"Jeff, Jeff Watkins."

All three men drew deeply on the cigarettes and turned to face the pile of corpses.

"You gonna call this in, Lukas?"

"'Spose I gotta. I mean... Jesus, Jeff. Whatever makes people do that?"

"Hate," stated Ewing, matter of factly, without thought that his view would be challenged.

"Simple as that?"

"Yep, I reckon. Look fellahs, most of us don't hate most of them, do we? I ain't got no beef with the Russkies, save they're shooting at me and mine. Never had a beef with the Krauts either, for that matter, but," Ewing took another draw on his cigarette, "But the Japs. I fucking hate 'em, every last man jack of 'em. My bro died in the Bataan March."

No further explanation was needed.

"I'll get on the horn straight-away. Told the General we got the place already. But he does need to know about this."

---

Before he got to the radio, Barkmann was waylaid by one of his men and the monk. The French-speaking Pfc translated the old man's version of events, giving the Ranger officer the whole horrible picture.

He was cut short when reporting to Pierce, the general terminating the radio exchange with the briefest of statements.

"Hold in position and await my arrival. Out."

## 1403 hrs, Saturday, 7th December 1945, La Petite Pierre, Alsace.

General Pierce stood in silence, hands upon hips, sucking his lips quietly as he took in the sights that La Petite Pierre had to offer.

Acting Captain Barkmann had briefed him fully, on both the military situation, and the story behind the grizzly sight now served up to the two officers.

"Goddamnit, Barkmann, but it's a hell of a thing."

Pierce grabbed the Ranger by the shoulders and talked as a father to his boy.

"C'mon now. Don't you go thinking you or your men are to blame for this, son."

By the reaction, Pierce knew that the young officer was plagued with nagging doubts.

"Son, I travelled up that road aways. I saw what you and your boys went through to get here. I don't see how you coulda got here any sooner, really I don't. Everyone did their best by these poor boys," he looked over at the smouldering pile, "But it just simply wasn't enough, just not enough...," somewhere in his words he seemed to turn from speaking to Barkmann to addressing himself, "Especially when faced with men who could do that... what sort of men do that?"

He snapped out of the moment as quickly as it arrived.

"You understand me, son?"

"Yes, sir."

"You make sure your Rangers know that... and make sure they know it from me... hell... I'll tell 'em myself... get the..."

Pierce halted as the apparition came into view. A stretcher being carried by four Soviet prisoners under the supervision of a Ranger First Sergeant.

He looked at Barkmann quizzically.

"No idea, Sir."

The stretcher was laid at the feet of the US General and one of the prisoners knelt by the side of the badly wounded man it held.

The Soviet officer laboured his words, and the stretcher-bearer had to lean further forward to understand.

382

Nodding at his commanding officer, he stood and saluted both Americans.

"My Colonel asked is he is speaking at the American commander please?"

Pierce gave Barkmann the stage and stepped back a short distance.

"I'm the commander of the force that retook this village."

Translating Barkmann's words, the Siberian rifleman listened as Astafiev spoke softly.

"My Colonel wanting to say thank you and to apologise for what is happen here."

More words flowed from Astafiev's mouth, even though his first tranche had yet to be fully delivered.

"He try to stop it, but he is shooted. He say that his men seed him bloody and lost mind. He also say that all have hear of Red Army soldier being shooted in other battles near here."

Dropping to a knee, he took more input from Astafiev, his voice softer as his wounds made their presence felt.

"My Colonel wanting to thank you for not shooted his prisoner men. He know it would have been most easy."

"Someone had to turn it off... someone had to stop the killing. What we do to each other as soldiers should not be like this."

He pointed at the pyre.

The Siberian soldier translated back Barkmann's words and those present could see the wounded Colonel's acceptance, his head nodding as he looked at the pile of dead.

Astafiev raised himself up on the stretcher as best he could, given assistance by the translator.

He spoke a few words in his native tongue, words that brooked no argument.

Two more Siberian soldiers helped him to his feet.

Practising his words in his mind, he made himself as at attention as his damaged body permitted, leaning on the interpreter, but still in immense pain.

"Thank you, Leytenant."

The salute was pretty good for a badly wounded man and Barkmann responded in kind, as did Pierce.

The effort proved too much, and Astafiev was helped back onto the stretcher and quickly carried away.

Pierce broke the moment carefully.

"Ok then, Lieutenant. As you're it, and seeing on what you've done so far today, it seems reasonable that you make Captain permanently."

Fig#103 - Forces involved in the Battle of La Petite Pierre and the Allied relief attempts, 7th December 1945.

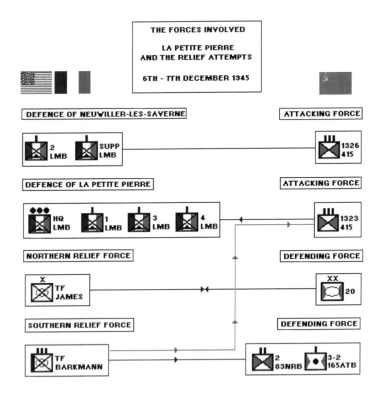

He shook hand and continued.

"Now, get your boys reformed, just in case. The 2nd Infantry boys should be here soon, and you'll hand the position over to them... and then get yourself the hell outta Dodge. I want you and your boys in Phalsbourg and resting. Clear, Captain?"

"Yessir."

"Leave the Legion bodies to the 2nd. They can do the deed."

"Sir, no Sir. Me and my boys'll do that. We owe it to them, Sir."

Pierce understood well enough.

"Son, you don't owe those poor boys anything... but I understand why you'd want to do it. Carry on and good luck, Captain. I'll be seeing you soon."

Pierce took one last look and moved to his jeep, on his way to report to General Lavalle, deciding that his speech for the Rangers was unnecessary.

### 1509 hrs, Saturday, 7th December 1945, Forward headquarters, Assault units for Operation Rainbow Black, Pfalzburg, France.

They had gathered for an orders meeting, and now they sat in stunned silence.

Lavalle.

Bittrich.

Knocke.

De Walle.

De Valois.

St.Clair.

The fact that the Mountain Battalion had been overrun was not news.

That there were no survivors was a horror that they had not anticipated.

That the survivors had been killed in such a fashion went beyond every line of moral decency and honour that any of them had ever drawn.

More than one eye was moist in grief and anger.

"Rettlinger?"

Strangely, it was Anne-Marie de Valois that posed the question. She had always liked the roguish man, and recognised the hurt inside him.

"Mademoiselle," Pierce bought himself a moment to think, "He died in the defence."

Anne- Marie knew a lie when she heard one and, in her own fashion, let Pierce know that he was transparent.

Lavalle joined in.

"Tell us please, John."

Reluctantly, Pierce relayed the full information, seeing the pain in all their eyes as he described how Derbo had been singled out for special treatment.

St.Clair rose to his feet angrily.

"And your man let these bastards live? Eh? EH? How could he do that, mon Général, eh?"

Knocke saved Pierce the struggle for words.

Knocke stood and, as was his habit, pulled his tunic down and into proper order.

"The Ranger commander was quite right, Benoit."

St.Clair looked at Knocke in astonishment as the German continued.

"Since Spectrum Black commenced, we have seen combat in its rawest and most vile state, all enhanced by atrocities," he looked at the commanders around him, "For which none of us is innocent, no matter what the provocation."

Nodding to Pierce, Knocke spoke in soft and reasonable tones.

"We should thank your man, General Pierce. He will have saved a great deal of suffering over the weeks and months ahead. He was quite right, although I doubt that I would have exercised the same judgement had I been there, although, for me it would have been more personal."

"Thank you, General Knocke."

And that drew a line under the matter, for now.

The group then continued on to deal with the fact that the Legion was stalled and coming under increased pressure. Their eyes turned to the north... and to Patton.

*In war, whilst everything is simple, even the simplest thing is difficult. Difficulties accumulate and produce frictions that no one can comprehend who has not seen war.*

Carl Philip Gottfried Von Clausewitz

# Chapter 116 - THE FOLDER

### 1758 hrs, Sunday, 8th December 1945, Headquarters of 'Camerone', Gougenheim, Alsace.

As he had waited for his driver to return, Polish Army Major Kowalski had engaged the Legion officers in conversation, never turning away an opportunity to scrounge up information, even though he was now a double agent.

Two Majors started arguing over the map work, inviting another officer in to clarify matters.

Placing his own load of paper on the cabinet, the Capitaine attempted to lay out the aspects of the plan that were contested.

The top file caught Kowalski's attention and he acted on impulse, encouraged by the heavy marks of secrecy emblazoned on its cover.

He swept the file into his own handful of reports and newspapers.

Next, he smashed his shoulder into the cabinet, sending paper flying in all directions as he seemingly tried to control a coughing fit.

Excusing himself, he moved towards the stairs, only to walk into his driver, fresh from parking the jeep.

Side by side, the two mounted the stairs in silence, he for the second floor rooms that were used for officer's quarters, she for the attic rooms where the female staff were domiciled.

He opened the door of his room and stepped back, permitting Gisela Jourdan to step smartly in before anyone had a chance to see her in the out of bounds area.

He closed the door and turned around.

Jourdan pushed him gently back against the door and knelt in front of him, liberating his manhood from his trousers in one easy and practised movement.

Her mouth closed around him and she commenced a brief but intense demonstration of her skills as a fellatrix.

His approaching orgasm overtook him and the contents of his hands fell to the floor, her head replacing them in his grasp as he worked her on him, gaining more impetus with each pull of her soft mouth onto him.

Jourdan kept her mouth around him as he moaned, shuddered and expended himself.

Even though she stayed firmly fixed to him as he came back down to earth, her eyes nearly burst open when she spotted the 'Top Secret' stamp on the file mixed with the Polish Liaison reports, the Polish-language newspaper, and the Stars and Stripes.

She instantly memorised the few things she could see, even as her Polish lover expended the last drops of his lust inside her.

Gisela knew what she had to do.

---

Having left Kowalski snoring, victim of post-orgasmic torpor, Jourdan sorted out her uniform and stepped smartly out into the corridor, wishing to appear unconcerned should she be spotted.

She wasn't so much spotted as nearly knocked over, as a Legion Captain barrelled into her in his haste.

"My apologies Fraulein...err... Sergent."

She regained her composure.

"Accepted, Capitaine."

The Legion officer did not ask her what she was doing there; neither did he seem to want to prolong the contact, so Gisela quickly saluted, leaving both of them free to move on.

At the signals section, she begged a telephone so that she could call her lover.

"Hello Max? So sorry to leave it so late, but can you tell Captain Logan that I won't be able to honour our date tonight and ask him to ring me at my quarters as soon as possible?"

That told the OSS agent on the other end of the line that the call was extremely urgent.

"OK, will do Gisela. Two minutes."

Smiling at the ex-SS NCO, she pointed at a small office presently unoccupied.

"I will get a call shortly. Can I take it in there, please?"

The Signals Sergent-Chef nodded and pointed her to the seat, taking in her fabulous legs all the way from his desk to the leather chair some yards away.

The phone rang and one of the staff answered. Under the direction of the 'peeping tom' NCO, the call was passed through to Gisela, who ensured that the German Legionnaire's attention was fully on her legs and thighs, and not on whatever she was going to say.

The voice on the other end was all business.

"This better be good."

"My man is in possession of a folder marked top secret. Code-named Spectrum, sub-named as black, blue and possibly red. I couldn't see any more. It had 'Normandie' and 'Camerone' clerking receipt marks. Instructions required."

Colonel Sam Rossiter knew exactly what the folder contained, and he also instantly knew that he could not risk the information in any way.

Gisela smiled at the leering NCO, almost popping his eyes out of his head as she ran a hand over the suspender that was now the focus of his attention.

"Keep him occupied. Do whatever you have to do, but don't let him out of your sight. No way, no how. And that goddamn file is your priority. Nothing matters more. Nothing. Clear?"

"Very clear, Captain Logan."

"I'll have a team with you...within two hours. We will do this discreetly if we can, but that file is too valuable to risk."

Jourdan giggled as if sharing a smutty joke with a familiar lover, further enticing the German signaller with the promise of more thigh and a wicked sexy smile.

"I understand my instructions."

"That file is your priority. Clear?"

For the benefit of the drooling watchers, Jourdan finished the conversation in a louder and more playful fashion.

"But of course, Darling. You may have whatever you want later. Au'voir Cherie."

Straightening her skirt, Gisela strolled from the room.

389

"Thank you so very much, Sergent-Chef. I shall remember how kind you have been. Perhaps you are off-duty tomorrow evening."

She actually knew that he wasn't.

"Another time then. Thank you again."

Three minutes later, she was back in Kowalski's room.

The file was nowhere to be seen.

### 1823 hrs, Sunday, 8th December 1945, Headquarters of 'Camerone', Gougenheim, Alsace.

The rules had been broken but, as 'Amethyst' finished deciphering the message, he understood why.

The old man who had bumped into him as he entered the billet spoke a keyword, as well as an apology, so that he would know that he had been passed something of importance.

'Amethyst' read the message again, drinking in every syllable, and confirming his interpretation.

*'Tonight.'*

It wasn't just a random thought based around the urgency stipulated in the three-sentence communication.

The man named was four rooms down the corridor from where the Soviet agent had his temporary sleeping quarters.

He rubbed his left arm, somehow bruised when he had bashed into that woman driver, the thought that she no longer occupied the 'Polish' bastard's bed an advantage he knew he should take advantage of.

"Tonight."

*'No! Now!'*

### 1851 hrs, Sunday, 8th December 1945, Headquarters of 'Camerone', Gougenheim, Alsace.

'Amethyst' changed into an old uniform, one not out of place in the headquarters, but certainly one that could go missing without problems. He removed his Walther P38 and holster, both of which had been his companions in the field since he had first fought the Allies in Normandy.

390

Fishing about on top of the wardrobe, he grabbed the old nail and slid the bed to one side.

Inserting the nail in the gap between the boards, he turned it and pulled up, the bent end providing just enough purchase to bring the old board out of its place.

Inside, wrapped in an old piece of cloth, were a few pieces of important paper, all forgeries of course, and another cloth package.

This he opened carefully, exposing a British-made Welrod silenced pistol, an item he had clandestinely purchased whilst training at Sassy some weeks beforehand. It had been offered for sale by an ageing French Maquisard, and the old resistance fighter had died silently when the pistol was tested.

'Amethyst' had not been in the first wave of ex-SS Legionnaires to go into action, joining up with Camerone only recently.

Even though he knew that the magazine was full and the weapon ready for use, he still went through the checks, inspecting the .32ACP rounds and testing the bolt action.

He quickly rolled an old map and slid the twelve inch long barrel inside it, concealing the magazine and trigger in his hand.

He took a deep breath, and opened the door.

### 1854 hrs, Sunday, 8th December 1945, Headquarters of 'Camerone', Gougenheim, Alsace.

Jourdan had spotted the file without too much effort. Kowalski had awoken and remembered his acquisition, hiding it in plain sight in a small pile of paperwork, whilst concealing the 'Top Secret' markings. The red colour attracted her eye none the less.

Seizing the moment, he had leapt on Gisela as she removed her clothing and taken her roughly and hard, quickly expending himself and falling back onto the bed once more.

Gisela Jourdan had neared orgasm herself, but he had finished too quickly for her liking.

She slipped from the bed to where a washstand was concealed behind a screen.

Splashing some cool water over herself, the combination of the surprisingly warm quarters and her recent

391

exertions having brought on a good sweat, she debated waiting for her lover to recover ,or whether to take matters into her own hands.

Her mind registered the smallest of sounds and tried to identify it, ending up with a choice between door and cupboard.

The second sound was much less open to interpretation, accompanied, as it was, by a spray of crimson over the headboard and wall.

She scrambled for her jacket, desperately feeling for the Walther PPK in the secret inside pocket, the same lump of metal that had caused Amethyst's unexpected bruise.

She made too much sound and the wooden screen opened up in the centre, riven by the passage of a .32.

The subsonic round clipped her thigh.

Jourdan dropped to the ground, but failed to see anything worth shooting at.

Rolling out, she found herself staring into the barrel of an all too familiar Welrod.

"Gently, Fraulein, gently."

The situation was bordering on surreal.

The Legion officer, clad in an ex-SS camouflage uniform with French markings, the OSS agent naked from head to toe, both holding pistols capable of killing the other.

However, only Amethyst had a gun pointed at a target.

Jourdan thought fast.

*'If he was going to kill me, he'd have done it.'*

Even though the thought process was flawed, it enabled her to relax and place the Walther on the floor.

'Up and onto the bed, if you please... quiet... no nonsense, Fraulein."

He permitted himself to enjoy the superb body as Gisela Jourdan raised herself up and onto the bed next to the dead Kowalski, ignoring the detritus that had been blasted from his skull as the Welrod's bullet took his life.

Her eyes flicked towards the pile of papers containing the file, and instantly she knew it was an error.

The Legionnaire moved backwards and ran a hand over the same pile, uncovering the words that betrayed its importance.

The German Legionnaire had clearly been after the Polish officer and, equally clearly in Jourdan's opinion, was now deciding how to proceed.

She tried her normal tactic.

"Want to fuck me then, eh?"

Amethyst, his mind busy resolving the unexpected situation, allowed part of his mind to assess the pleasures he was going to miss sampling.

Jourdan saw the eye movement and misinterpreted it, opening her legs wide to expose herself to more intimate examination, as well as creating a distraction of her own.

Kowalski had been a man of habit and one habit, so he had said, was because he was a Pole, and always felt unsafe. He slept with a gun as well as a woman.

As part of Amethyst's mind examined the body of the woman he was about to kill, another part saw the small movement.

Jourdan's hand found the cold metal and slipped around the Beretta M1935 that Kowalski always kept under his pillow.

It was out and moving, even as the German reacted.

He was quickest.

The Welrod chugged and the bullet hit Jourdan in the throat.

Quickly, Amethyst picked up his spent cartridge cases, slipped them into his pocket, and then dragged Kowalski's corpse off the bed, changing the dynamics of the room sufficiently, in his own mind at least, to confuse any investigation.

Slipping the folder into his trousers, Amethyst took a last look at the woman struggling for breath, her eyes widened both by the shock of the wound, and in indignation at her approaching premature death.

He listened at the door and, deciding that the landing was clear outside, opened it and slipped out into the corridor.

The last lifeblood spilled from Jourdan's wound, even as she found the strength to pull the trigger.

The .32 Beretta round caught Amethyst in the left upper arm, passing through flesh and muscle.

Stifling a yelp of pain, the Legionnaire moved quickly along and into his room, aware of the sound of a pistol dropping onto the floor, and easily imagined the Beretta slipping from lifeless fingers.

Hässelbach, the first man to arrive at the open door, found a room full of blood and two naked bodies, one still utterly compelling despite the obvious neck wound.

Everything was placed in the hands of the Legion Military Police.

Or it was, until forty-nine minutes later, when an OSS detachment, complete with De Walle, arrived with a set purpose; they found that the situation was very different to that they had anticipated.

Whilst the loss of Agent Jourdan was regrettable, she was way down the priority list for the OSS team searching the room.

They left her corpse stiffening on the bed in a pool of congealing blood, only disturbing her when it became necessary to check the bed itself.

The file already nestled under the floorboards four rooms away, in the care of a man biting hard on a wad of cloth as he fished inside his arm for a .32 bullet.

De Walle had a brief meeting with Knocke to explain the full situation.

The search was widened and Amethyst, his arm wound bandaged and concealed under long sleeves, found his room being searched by a man in American uniform and a French legionnaire military police corporal.

He sat and watched proceedings as he moved swiftly with a needle and thread.

He was comfortable that the hiding place would not be found, even when he had to get off the bed in order to let the American move the bed frame.

He was comfortable that the uniform holed by Jourdan's bullet and marked with his blood would not be discovered. Quick work with scissors and a razor had transformed the hole into a tear such as blemished many of the uniforms worn by members of Camerone and, in any case, he was studiously working on its repair even as the search continued.

What made him uncomfortable was the silent presence of Knocke, stood on the threshold, sometimes watching those in the room, sometimes checking other activities out of Amethyst's sight.

The search completed, the Legion Captain found himself alone, save for the presence at the doorway.

"You look tired, Hauptsturmfuhrer. White as a sheet, in fact. Get some rest. Start at 0900hrs at the earliest. Alles klar?"

"Alles klar, Brigadefuhrer. Danke."

"And make sure you do, Weiss. You know I'll know."

"Zu befehl, Brigadefuhrer."

The door closed and Amethyst, also known as Ulrich Heinz Weiss, formerly of the 12th SS Panzer Division, smiled to himself, safe in the knowledge that there was a very great deal that Herr Knocke did not know.

### 1237 hrs, Monday, 9th December 1945, US Seventeenth Corps Headquarters, Prum, Belgium.

Patton slammed the telephone down so hard that it shattered the cradle, leaving him still holding the damaged Bakelite handset as his staff sought cover from the shrapnel generated by his anger.

"Goddamned weather. No air until further notice."

Taking up from where he had left off before the telephone interrupted, Patton dropped his voice and continued calmly, ignoring the signaller who started to replace the broken telephone.

"So, they chewed the Fourth Armored up real bad at Blankenheim this morning. Bruce Clarke'll get 'em back on line for sure, but it's messed up the timetable again!"

Charles H. Travers, the Major General commanding US Seventeen Corps scowled.

"Yes he will, General, but the boys are dog-tired and the equipment's breaking down. Clarke's report shows that one assault failed purely 'cause of the icy conditions and engine failures. We gotta give the tankers some maintenance time."

"No... hell no! We're pushing the Commie bastards back and we will not stop! Give 'em some help, Ben. Whatcha got to give them some impetus?"

A quick look at the map suggested something.

"The 808th is tucked in behind and close, General. It's been knocked about some, but they can be on the road immediately."

Patton couldn't remember what the 808th TD rode into battle, so asked the question.

"M36's, Sir."

"Get 'em rolling, Ben. I'll leave you to put a burr under Clarke's arse. But I want your Corps in command of this area, and particularly the junction of Routes 51 and 477 today. No excuses, Ben."

"Sir."

Like a whirlwind, Patton swept out of Travers' headquarters as swiftly as he arrived, leaving only shattered Bakelite to mark that he had ever been there.

His Dodge WC57 car was already hammering across country for his next call to 'encourage' Ernie Harmon's Twenty-second Corps to greater efforts.

---

"OK you sleeping beauties! Rack 'em up and move 'em out!"

Christensen, Master Sergeant of the HQ Company, 808th Tank Destroyer Battalion, strode amongst the snoozing men, clapping his hands and shouting, occasionally taking a kick at a reluctant body.

The 808th had been on a maintenance run all morning and had stopped for lunch. It seemed to the tired men that it was only two minutes since the order to rest had been given.

Gear was made up and stowed as the roar of V8 engines filled the air.

A jeep containing the commander of the 808th, Lieutenant Colonel McDonald, swept up the road, to join the head of the column.

This move was all about speed.

The M36 Jacksons started to move off as the entire battalion took to Route 51, heading towards Blankenheim.

---

'Spectrum' was already coming apart at the seams, its timetable in tatters as stiff Soviet resistance and Mother

Nature combined to make things very difficult for the Allied forces.

There were five schedules in the Spectrum plan.

'Black' had actually been too successful and brought down the hounds of hell upon the Legion Corps, inflicting huge casualties on one of the Allies' prime formations. Whilst that smoothed the way for the US Third Army, the concern now was that the large Soviet forces drawn to Alsace might find other employment, possibly looking westwards once more. The dilemma facing the Allied Generals was that the enemy needed to be kept in place in Alsace, not permitted to return to the north, where George Patton had plans for a change of ownership.

However, the Red Army units left opposing Patton's advance fought like mad dogs, extracting a heavy price from the attacking US units.

To the north, the German thrust towards Cologne went well at first, not quite the Blitzkrieg, but close enough to make one or two of the German veterans recall happier days.

However, the attack of 101st Korps ran into stiff resistance from the 3rd Guards Tank Army and elements of 5th Guards Army, before being fought to a bloody standstill at Leverkusen and Wipperfürth.

'Green', the overall air plan, was proving successful without being dramatically victorious, probably because of the unreliable weather conditions, causing many abandoned missions. Overall, close-support missions were reasonably successful, but losses across the range of the Allied air inventory were more than expected, and the heavy bombers much less successful than hoped.

'Red' was still ongoing and due to come to fruition soon, although those in command doubted that it would now contribute to the main attacks in Central Germany as had been hoped. None the less, it was vital to proceed in order to test the viability of Spectrum Indigo, or whatever it would be called when it commenced, scheduled for 1946.

'White', the FUSAG style subterfuge based around a fictitious Allied Second Army Group, seemed to be keeping the Soviet 1st Baltic Front in Northern Germany in place and not interfering with the northern side of the Ruhr, which had been a fear of the Allied planners.

397

Eisenhower teetered on the edge of calling the whole Spectrum Operation off.

His political master, President Harry Truman, had called that very morning to encourage his commander to press home the attack. Almost as if orchestrated, Churchill had contacted Eisenhower to enquire as to the progress of Spectrum.

As always, Ike turned to his closest advisors for guidance.

George Patton had been against aborting Spectrum, as had McCreery and Bedell-Smith.

Devers, understandably, had supported the possibility, if only to free up some assets to make sure he could deal with any Soviet counter threat.

Bradley had sat on the fence, laying out his views on both actions and leaving the decision to Ike.

Tedder had argued the case for a partial halt to Spectrum, permitting the naval and deception plans to proceed whilst curtailing the other parts, perhaps because the RAF and USAAF had spent weeks moving assets in secret for the culmination of Spectrum Red.

In the end, Eisenhower let the whole thing run, turning to Spectrum Red to provide some stimulus to the main assault, albeit by an indirect route.

---

The tension in SHAEF headquarters was tangible.

It often was before big operations but, somehow, this time it felt different.

'Spectrum' was in trouble; certainly as far as the land war was concerned.

Eisenhower, Bedell-Smith, and Bradley sat engaged in small talk, occasionally interrupted by a new report, or a question from one of the staff.

One report concerned Italy and the destruction of a Red Army drive adjacent to the Swiss border. In general, the Italian front had descended quickly into stalemate, more because of the increasingly awful conditions than for reasons of stalwart defence.

Reports from Alexander suggested supply issues for the enemy forces, as did most reports across the board, but the weather across the Alpine region was diabolical, and it seemed that even the winter-hardened Soviet army was having difficulty.

Either way, it was welcome good news.

The coffee kept coming.

Eisenhower smoked and smoked, betraying his nervousness.

If Spectrum Red went according to plan, the Soviets would be chasing shadows for hours, if not days, during which they would lose considerable numbers of their air and naval assets. The opportunity to demonstrate Polish loyalty would prove a winner for later, should the expected opportunity present itself. If the operation ran long enough, then there was even a chance that assets could be drawn northwards, and away from Central Germany, making Patton's job easier.

If...

It was Bradley who noticed the increase in volume first, a sure indicator that something was amiss.

He nudged Bedell-Smith and pointed at two Colonels and a Brigadier General in animated conversation.

"Something's put a burr under their collective asses, Walter."

John Cunningham, the Brigadier General in question, recently returned from his spell in hospital post Frankfurt air raid, took the two reports, and moved towards the three senior men.

Eisenhower had also noted the agitated nature of the staff discussion.

"John, what gives?"

"Sir, we have received two reports from Italy."

Perhaps understandably, all three men relaxed, so focussed were they on the cold waters of the Baltic.

"Go on, John."

"Sir, the initial report was from Field Marshal Alexander, indicating an angry communication from the Yugoslavian leadership regarding our armed incursion into their territory, and the deaths of nearly one hundred of their soldiers."

The three mouths spoke as one.

"What?"

399

Cunningham was about to confirm what he had just said, but was interrupted.

"And the second report?"

Eisenhower cut to the chase.

"Sir, it's from General Freyberg reporting a Yugoslavian infiltration and attack in progress at Trieste."

Things started happening thick and fast from that point, and within thirty seconds, Eisenhower was passed a telephone by a Staff Captain.

"Sir, Field Marshal Alexander for you. Urgent, sir."

"Harry, I've just heard. Tell me what you know."

As Monday slipped quietly into Tuesday, Harold Alexander revealed what he knew about the supposed British Army provocation that precipitated the Yugoslavian attack.

Which, of course, was precisely zero.

He had more information on the Trieste situation and elsewhere along a suddenly active thirty-mile front in North-east Italy.

A front recently seen as relatively quiet had abruptly become the most volatile place in Europe.

Within fifteen minutes, General Grandes, the Spanish liaison officer, immaculately dressed, despite his rude awakening, was being consulted on the movement of Spanish forces in Italy.

Meanwhile, to the north, Allied sailors commenced Spectrum Red.

*Hearts of oak are our ships, hearts of oak are our men.*

*David Garrick.*

*Traditional Naval toast for a Tuesday-*
*'To our men!'*

# Chapter 117 - THE ILLUSION

### 0017 hrs, Tuesday, 10th December 1945, the Kattegat.

"We're in position Lechlade now, Number One."

"Thank you, Nav. Skipper, we're in position Lechlade."

"Expose port, Number One."

The orders flowed around the decks of HMS Charity and the port searchlight exposed, shaded in red, sending a reduced beam of scarlet light towards the eastern shoreline.

Charity was a modern C Class destroyer, commissioned on the 19th November 1945.

She was the flagship of Force V, the Royal Naval contribution to the Spectrum plan.

All the officers on her narrow bridge had their binoculars focussed on the shore, its illuminated signs of civilization betraying that it was not a land at war.

"There it is, Number One."

Everyone saw it as clear as day.

A single green light.

The Swedes were good to their word.

The Charity's Captain looked at the muffled figure set aside on the bridge wing, and received a nod.

"Number One, Signal all ships, Proceed as planned, Godspeed."

The First Lieutenant made off to the yeoman waiting at the signalling lamp, and supervised the procedure.

"Sparks, send to the Admiralty. Lechlade Green, Send our position and time of contact."

"Aye aye, Skipper."

Commander Hamilton Ffoulkes, Captain of HMS Charity, accepted the scalding hot mug of Kai from the rating who always seemed to magically appear at the right moment.

A second mug went to the shadowy figure, who acknowledged its presence with a grunt, his mind consumed by the task his flotilla was about to undertake, and the risk that it could all go so horribly wrong.

He sighed audibly, attracting comment from Ffoulkes.

"Sir? The Kai not to your liking?"

"Come to mention it, Commander Ffoulkes, it's a smidgen light on the chocolate, wouldn't you say?"

As it was anything but light on chocolate, Ffoulkes was at a loss on how to respond.

"Possibly light on condensed milk, Admiral, but the chocolate level seems fine to me."

"The perfect mug of Kai evades us all, Commander."

Rear-Admiral Jacques stepped forward, the low light on the bridge illuminating a smiling face.

"Now, the Swedes are doing their bit. So, it's down to us to give the Russians a fright and stir their little ant's nest up."

"Indeed, Admiral. Twenty minutes to Oxford I suggest."

The points of signalling were named after places on the Thames, starting with Lechlade at the source of the great river, all the way to London, which marked the place where they would either convince the enemy that a mighty fleet was on its way into the Baltic, or they would provide light target practice for whatever ships and aircraft the Soviets could muster.

Spectrum Red was a sham; a Trojan horse, designed to fool the Soviet forces into moving some ground forces but, above all, drawing their air and naval forces into the attack, and a trap of monumental proportions.

Oxford Green.

Pangbourne Green.

Reading Green.

The points came and went, each muffled red display bringing a reply indicating that all was well.

Ahead of the destroyer and flagship were two minesweepers, HMS Jason and HMS Rye, plying their trade in silence. The Navy was taking every precaution with Spectrum Red.

Behind HMS Charity came the many smaller vessels; Vosper, Thornycroft, and White MTB's, even two ex-US Navy Elco boats, each of the twenty-eight lesser vessels towing four to six even smaller vessels, each of which had been specially prepared for the huge part they had to play in Spectrum Red.

There had been more when they had first gathered in Findhorn Bay, near Forres, in Scotland, but the waters of the North Sea were rarely benign, and sixteen, plus one each of a White and an Elco, had been claimed by the unfriendly waters. The White had caught fire and burnt out in record time; the Elco had simply floundered and dragged down her five charges.

The area of Findhorn Bay had been constantly overflown by aircraft from the 19th Operational Training Unit, based at nearby RAF Kinloss. The OTU continued to watch over the special convoy of MTBs and smaller ships until Coastal Command units based in Denmark took over the responsibility, and overwatched Force V into the entrance to the Baltic, where they joined with another force of boats from Harwich, each towing three additional vessels.

A handful more had floundered before they passed Helsingborg, also known as Reading Green, before the order came and the lights came on.

Aboard each towing vessel, a range of switches were engaged, causing lights on small masts to illuminate. A few presented failed circuits, but enough worked to do what was needed.

Close at hand, they looked like exactly what they were but, from distance, in the dark, they could possibly be interpreted as an armada about to enter the home waters of the Baltic, the backyard of the Soviet Navy and Soviet Naval Aviation, a matter that the planners at SHAEF knew would not go unchallenged. In fact, they were counting on it.

---

It had been Tørget's idea.

There was no way that the Allies would have dared suggest it, of course, but the Swedish leadership were more on side than previously, following the revelations involving the GRU spy, Admiral Søderling. The head of Military Intelligence now had plenty of allies in his own government, all of whom were prepared to do anything to upset the Soviet balance, short of declaring for one side, or the other.

The mission served two purposes.

Firstly, it enabled the Swedes to officially state that they did not permit the Allied intrusion, and actually made efforts to resist against it, although the anti-aircraft batteries that fired skywards had a number of MI officers on site, each aware of special unwritten orders that outlined the general expectation of the Swedish High Command that no shell should come within a thousand feet of any of the attacking aircraft.

As is the habit of these things, not all went to plan, and one Lancaster was fatally struck, crashing on a sliver of Soviet-held Denmark.

The destroyed aircraft and dead crew would later add weight to the information that started to flood into the intelligence and command headquarters of the USSR, evidencing Sweden's assertion that they had not been complicit and stood firm against the incursions.

The second reason the mission went 'noisy' was to ensure that a small group of Russians was wide-awake as Force V passed them.

In the opening moves of the new conflict, a small group of Soviet Naval specialists had been landed on the southern end of Saltholm Island.

They had been tasked with monitoring naval activity in the Øresund, and they had been very successful.

Bletchley Park had been the first to detect them and their signals were monitored closely. Their reports mirrored Swedish naval activity, or the few small scale naval excursions undertaken by the Royal Navy and her allies. It was decided to leave them alone, for now.

The Danes were compliant allies and did not disturb the Soviet observers, although they mounted patrols from their fort, on the northern edge of Saltholm Island, studiously failing to note anything untoward.

The RAF's contribution to Spectrum Red swung into action.

Two flights of aircraft from 617 Squadron RAF, selected for their ability to metaphorically 'drop a pebble down a chimney', flew into Swedish air space, their purpose to attack Göteborg, or at least, to look like they had.

The first group planted their bombs on and around Gota airbase. Everything of worth had been moved into the rock shelters, created in the cliff face during 1942. Old J8 fighters were exposed to the falling bombs, and a dozen were destroyed. The obsolete aircraft, known as Gladiators when in RAF service, served no great purpose, and besides, modern replacements had already been purchased from Britain two months beforehand, or at least the paperwork would reflect that, before the delivery of the twenty Spitfires took place.

617's second group made an excellent job of destroying a few acres of woodland in the suburb of Delsjo, particularly chosen because it would ensure that the nearby Soviet Consulate was wide awake, and talking urgently to Moscow.

Two Mosquitoes from 105 Squadron RAF were tasked with bringing the war even closer to the consulate and the first pass destroyed the second largest building in the compound, a building identified by Tørget as staffed purely by NKVD personnel.

Goteborg's power was cut by a senior power company official, who had been briefed on his personal responsibilities to his country beforehand, but the Consulate had its own generator.

Just prior to the loss of power across the city, the second Mosquito had reduced the generator building and the nearby garage to a smoking ruin, thus ensuring that the Consulate's desperate calls to the Motherland were cut short.

The Light Night Striking Force of 105, 139, and 692 Squadrons RAF, flying Mosquito bombers, carefully 'attacked' Swedish coastal emplacements, as would have been done, had a Naval force been forcing a passage into the Baltic.

Using skill to drop their HE far from the Swedish guns, or putting the occasional deliberate dud on target, and generally bathing the positions with light, the LNSF contributed greatly to the illusion that SHAEF was trying to create.

The planning took account of the position of the Saltholm observers ,and was timed to the second to ensure that Force V was, at no time, directly illuminated by the RAF strikes.

Part of the Swedish contribution was to ensure that the coastal illuminations disappeared, as would clearly be prudent for a country suddenly finding itself under attack, also ensuring that the naval forces could move past Saltholm without a revealing backdrop of light.

---

On Saltholm, the Red Navy observer group had become accustomed to quiet and boring nights.

This one transformed for them as aircraft clearly attacked the Swedish shore installations, some ten kilometres away.

Whilst their mission was to report on seaborne activity, the Captain in charge felt that he needed to call this one in, and so the radio lit up with his report.

The activity was noted by a dedicated team in Bletchley Park.

Twenty-one minutes later, they noted further activity, and the cipher team was passed a message that they, disappointingly, took nearly sixteen minutes to decode.

Sir Roger Marais Dalziel picked up the receiver, waiting as a secure connection was made.

"Sam, good morning. Report from the boathouse. The canoes have been spotted heading to the canal, and are safe and sound."

Dalziel smiled at the reply.

"Soon enough, Sam. Good night."

---

Eisenhower took a sip of his coffee as Rossiter, grinning from ear to ear, replaced the receiver with a flourish.

"Sir. They've been spotted and reported as a large, but unidentified, enemy naval force, possibly over one hundred vessels, sailing south-east into the Baltic."

Ike checked his watch.

"Thank you, Sam. I think we'd better get Arthur up and ready, so that his boys can do their thing."

406

Eisenhower had ordered Arthur Tedder to rest, prior to the implementation of Spectrum Red and, it was noted, he hadn't argued much.

Turning to Somerville and the recently arrived Dönitz, Ike could see that they had both understood the latest development.

"So, Sir James. When's 'lights out'?"

He quickly consulted with the small German Admiral, nodding as Donitz pointed at a figure from a column of figures that detailed the timings of Spectrum Red.

"0405 hrs, Sir."

### 0401 hrs, Tuesday, 10th December 1945, Ten miles south-south-west of Trelleborg, Sweden.

The sound had attracted her at first.

Delicately caressing her sonar gear at first, the sound of turning screws of all shapes and sizes had grown and enticed her forward.

The 'Lembit' and her companion, L3 'Frunzenets', were on a mission to re-mine the waterway south of Øresund, and were running straight in towards Force V.

Lembit's apparatus had detected the approaching sounds, and her crew had gone to battle stations, followed a minute later by L3.

Lembit was an ex-Estonian Navy submarine that had begun life in a British shipyard, being launched in 1936. She was labelled a mine-laying submarine, with eight torpedoes and twenty-four mines to strike out with.

L3 was an older submarine that first tasted the cold water of the Baltic in 1931. She also carried mines, twenty of them, as well as twelve torpedoes.

The two Soviet captains made very different decisions, once they had spotted the wave of barely distinguishable lights about to ride over them.

The Lembit's commander, an old and wise sea dog with a penchant for survival, dropped his submarine to its full safe depth and turned southwards, intent on finding somewhere that he could safely surface and contact his superiors, once his radio had been repaired of course.

L3's Captain, Peep Korjus, a young and ambitious Estonian Senior Lieutenant, saw only glory, and a chance to save the Motherland from further hurt.

L3 commenced its attack, increasing revolutions to bring the vessel around for a flank attack on the approaching fleet.

---

"Fuck me sideways, Bert. There's a fucking sub underneath us! Number One! Number One!"

HMS Charity had pulled clear of Force V, or as the Admiral put it, 'The blasted Blackpool Illuminations', and killed her engines, floating peacefully on the soft Baltic waters, the two minesweepers doing the same on two different stations, further south.

The First Lieutenant had only just left the Sonar room when Miller, the untried operator, heard the sounds of electric engines coming up to speed.

Petty Officer Albert Coots cuffed the young operator.

"Proper reports, you idjit boy."

The First Lieutenant plunged back into the sonar cabinet in response to the shouted calls.

"What gives, Coots?"

"Sub, right underneath us, Number One. Heading three-two-five degrees, speed coming up to eight knots."

"Right underneath us?"

"Aye sir."

"Sound action stations!"

The bells rang throughout the ship and ratings either closed up or rolled out of their pits.

"What the blazes, Number one!"

Ffoulkes trusted his man, but the effect of the bells and a sudden conversion from total quiet to noisy confusion caught him off guard.

"Sub, Sir, Right underneath us."

He repeated the updated details of the sonar contact, all on the bridge accepting that it was an enemy, as there were no 'friendlies' within a hundred miles.

HMS Charity was swinging in the light breeze.

"She is moving ahead of our bow."

The Admiral burst onto the bridge, his call of nature caught short in the excitement.

Experienced enough to let the captain do whatever needed to be done, he held his peace, and waited to discover what was happening.

"Range ahead now, Number One?"

A moment's pause as the officer ducked his head into the cabinet.

"Two-five-zero yards, Captain."

Ffoulkes eyes burned bright with instant decision.

"Hedgehog. Fire!"

The Midshipman keyed the switch, alerting the forward crew manning the multi-warhead Hedgehog and, within three seconds, two dozen sixty-five pounds charges started to leap from their rails.

---

The sounds of the surface vessel coming to life above them had given everyone on L3 a real fright, so unexpected was it.

L3's commander shouted his orders, bringing his men back to focus on their duties, and ordered the engines to the fullest possible speed as he tried to manoeuvre.

The multiple splashes were heard by the Soviet crew, as was the first explosion.

The spigot charges dropped through the cool water, relying on a direct hit to explode.

A charge detonated against the engine room main hatch, destroying its integrity in the blink of an eye. A second charge struck four foot further towards the bow, accelerating the flooding in the huge space.

The engine room crew died without reporting their impending deaths.

None the less, Korjus knew his ship was finished, the sudden up angle informing him, and the more experienced members of the crew, that their end was nigh.

Three more charges struck home, and the control room was breached.

L3 sank to the bottom of the Baltic, the forward torpedo crew condemned to some more tortured hours of absolute terror, before they resorted to detonating one of their charges to end their suffering.

Four of her mines floated free, and headed towards the cloudy winter night sky.

### 0405 hrs, Tuesday, 10th December 1945, Thirteen miles south-south-west of Trelleborg, Sweden.

"Now, Ffoulkes."

"Yes, Sir. Sparks, send it."

HMS Charity's radio officer clapped his hand on the signaller's shoulder and nodded.

The key tapped out the simple words that initiated the last but one phase of Spectrum Red.

By the time the radio officer was happy that the message was out, the signs of its recognition and implementation were converting darkness into light as, across Force V, the towed vessel's second electrical circuit was energized.

The small ships contained mixtures of high-explosive and ingenious contraptions designed by naval minds trying to outdo each other.

The minesweepers and MTB's fired off depth charges and main weapons, adding deep rumbles and tracers to the growing confusion.

For those aboard the Lembit, it seemed like the hounds of hell had been unleashed, all baying for their blood, and totally determined to hunt them down. The venerable submarine went deeper, but could not avoid the storm of noise that was being generated on the surface.

Above, back in the fresh air, the towed vessels were becoming less and less numerous, as explosions and fire claimed them one by one, which was the idea.

Much of Force V started to disappear below the waters of the Baltic, the towing vessels extinguishing their own lights, and immediately running northwards, through Øresund, past Saltholm.

The Soviet party on the small island now had other problems, the continued disturbances seemingly having attracted a strong force of Danish Marines, who were all over

410

their secret position, forcing them to keep well hidden, and therefore unable to spot anything passing to the north.

Meanwhile, across Soviet-occupied territory, telephones started to ring.

*Never interrupt your enemy when he is making a mistake.*

*Napoleon Bonaparte*

# Chapter 118 – THE TRAP

## 0441 hrs, Tuesday, 10th December 1945, GRU Commander's office, Western European Headquarters, the Mühlberg, Germany.

"Comrade Nazarbayeva. Why is there an Allied naval force in the Baltic, seemingly in large numbers, which none of my intelligence services know anything about?"

Woken from a deep sleep, Tatiana sat upright in the camp bed, set in her office as usual, her mind starting to clear rapidly as doubts and fear entered her mind, an effect only too common for those woken early by a call from the General Secretary.

"What has apparently happened, Comrade General Secretary?"

Poboshkin averted his eyes as his commander stood and moved to her desk, picking up a pad and pencil, not the blouse and trousers that would have caused her aide a lot less embarrassment.

She started to record his words, listing reports from various arms of service in and around the Baltic, all of which combined seemed to indicate that a large-scale Allied operation was in progress.

"Comrade General Secretary, there has been nothing regarding any large enemy naval force in the area. Not from ourselves or from the NKVD. I find it difficult to imagine that any large force could have assembled and moved in undetected, but I will look at that again."

Even Poboshkin could hear the anger in the replying voice.

"No, Comrade General Secretary, that is not what I'm saying. Clearly, these reports have some basis in fact, but what they represent may not be what they say they represent."

The situation was getting unbearable for Poboshkin, so he gallantly held out Nazarbayeva's tunic, in an attempt to draw her attention to the fact that a bra and knickers were

412

insufficient to protect her modesty, and moved him closer to seeing his commander naked than he wanted to get.

She ignored the item, placing her hand over the telephone.

"You've seen a woman before. Now, get me the file on their Allied Second Army Group immediately, and order up any naval reports we've received on unusual assemblies and groupings of enemy vessels over the last month, now."

Returning to the receiver, she spoke in a controlled fashion, buying time for Poboshkin to return.

"Comrade General Secretary. The only ground force of note that would be available is the new Allied Second Army Group, a formation that has raised suspicion in both GRU and NKVD circles."

Stalin understood this, and also understood his 'protégé' was stalling. His reply focussed her on his needs.

"Yes, Comrade General Secretary. I will review everything we have that can have a possible bearing on these reports and contact you immediate... as you say, Comrade General Secretary."

Poboshkin placed the folder in front of her and she flicked to the page she had summoned from memory.

"There was a brief rise in activity, immediately followed by a modest reduction in radio traffic three days ago, Comrade General Secretary. Our view was that it was an exercise, given the lack of naval activity."

Nazarbayeva winced, and the phone moved away from her ear.

"That may well be the case, Comrade General Secretary. But the only reports of any substance are the usual convoys from America."

She summoned something from memory.

"One of our agents reported a large force of their motor boats flotilla leaving Harwich some while ago. That was passed to Navy for review."

She didn't mean it to sound like passing the buck, but the man on the other end of the phone was an expert in the field,and interpreted it as such.

"No, Comrade General Secretary. As you say, it was not considered important at the time. They are small vessels of little worth. However, we have recently seen a concentration of larger Allied naval assets in the southern end of the Adriatic. Again, w..."

Stalin had no interest in the Adriatic, and swung into a tirade.

Nazarbayeva took the opportunity to slip into her shirt and jacket.

"Yes, Comr... ye... As you order, Comrade Ge..."

She took the receiver from her ear, and gently handed it to Poboshkin.

Considering her words carefully, she slipped into and adjusted her skirt.

"There will be no more sleep tonight, Andrey. Get everyone at their desk within fifteen minutes."

"Yes, Comrade General. What are we looking for, Comrade General?"

"According to reports from the Baltic Fleet, diplomatic sources, agents, and Red Army ground forces, the Allies are presently entering the Baltic with a large naval force."

As he turned to go, Poboshkin realised there was more.

He looked back.

"The GKO is concerned that it may be an invasion force on its way to Northern Germany... or Poland."

Poboshkin nodded and went about his business with speed, leaving his commander to check over the Second Allied Army Group file once more.

She found nothing.

There was nothing to find.

### 0559 hrs, Tuesday, 10th December 1945, headquarters of the Polish Home Front, the Fenger Palace, Torun, Poland.

"All units in position, Comrade General."

Colonel General Vasily Sokolovsky was impressed.

NKVD Major General Oleg Piersky was impressed.

For different reasons of course.

Sokolovsky was commander of the Polish Home Front, the large group of Polish units banded together, and placed solely in the defence of their homeland.

The general distrust in their will to fight the Allied nations had condemned them to a static life, and the gradual decline of their combat power, as units in Germany benefitted from the equipment that was steadily stripped away from them.

None the less, the two Polish Armies still represented a very considerable force, and one that was now fully arraigned along the North coast of their home country.

Admittedly, they had practised and practised, and part of the units were already in position, following an exercise the First Army commander had staged without notice, or request to higher authority.

Previously, Sokolovsky would have visited the man to tear a strip off him but, General Zygmunt Berling, the officer in question, seemed to have changed his mood of late. No longer bordering on uncooperative, he was now knuckling down and no longer afflicted by the surly nature that had marked the last few months.

In fact, the unannounced exercise, which would have earned Berling a sanction of some sort, could now only be seen as a stroke of good luck.

NKVD officer Oleg Piersky was there, poised ready for the slightest indication of disloyalty, backed up by a large number of NKVD divisions, all strategically placed to be able to swoop on any Polish headquarters that looked suspect.

His subsequent report to Moscow was heavy in praise for the readiness and commitment of the Free Polish Forces, and did much to restore a little faith in their will to fight.

Spectrum Red was wholly successful in that regard.

For now, two armies of Polish soldiers crewed guns and tanks on the beaches of the Southern Baltic, ready to repel the imminent allied invasion.

"Shall we displace, Comrade General?"

Sokolovsky considered the suggestion, mentally working his way through the checklist of command, before responding.

He nodded at the NKVD officer's suggestion before speaking with in a commanding voice.

"Gentlemen, we shall move to the secondary command centre immediately. Execute the Alpha Plan."

Activity commenced in every corner of the Fenger Palace, as those tasked for the Alpha plan took up the necessaries of their jobs, ready for the move to the alternate command point, set in the forest between Torun and Bydgoszcz.

Within five minutes, the advance guard of the Polish Home Front's headquarters was on its way to a set of inconspicuous wooden lodges, concealed in the tall trees that surrounded Cierpice.

---

Reports started to come in to 1st Baltic Front, the headquarters for all units in occupied Denmark.

Hazy at first, but soon firming up into definite actions at the airfields and anti-aircraft bases throughout the islands.

Casualties were not known, but the reports suggested high losses in equipment, particularly aircraft.

### 0600 hrs, Tuesday, 10th December 1945, Kluczewo Airfield, Poland.

"Attention!"

The aircrew sprang to their feet as their regimental Commander strode in, his faithful hound, as always, at his heels.

"Comrades, be seated."

As always, the eyes of the youthful were drawn towards the shining gold star, signifying a Hero of the Soviet Union.

Major Sacha Istomin had come a long way since the award of his medal following the 14th September raid on Birkenfeld.

If nothing else, he had aged a thousand years; life in the Red Air Force tended to be exciting and brief for most; those that survived carried many unseen burdens.

Istomin had risen to command the 21st Guards Bomber Air Regiment, and had led the unit in fierce combat that, in the end, brought about its total destruction during the air battles of October.

416

With his surviving nine air crew, he was sent to establish a new formation, the 911th Bomber Regiment, and today was to be its baptism of fire.

"Comrades, today we are called to arms in defence of the Motherland. The situation is serious and perilous, but I know you will do all that the Rodina asks of you."

The base intelligence Officer rolled back a screen, revealing a map that was mainly blue.

"The Allies navies have broken through into the Baltic, and sunk some of our submarines. Our command believes it could be a force designed to attack into either Northern Germany here," he made everyone jump as he slapped a pointer to the map, "Or here, the northern coast of Poland."

He replaced the pointer on the lectern.

"Information is limited, but there are reports of possibly more than one hundred vessels, types unknown, passing Saltholm Island during the night.

"We have been tasked to respond to any reports of enemy activity in the area off the Polish Coast. We will have full bomb load, and we take off at 0700hrs. Any questions?"

There were a few.

*What type of enemy vessels? Warships? Merchantmen?*

*What air cover do they have?*

*Where exactly are they?*

Istomin could only shrug his shoulders.

"I don't know, Comrades. We;ve been taken by surprise, and must do what we can today. Now, make sure you've maps for all areas... from Denmark to Leningrad. The 911th Regiment will not be found wanting on this day. Good luck, Comrades."

The salutes were formal and smart.

Istomin strode from the room, no longer the joker, but a man for whom life had become very serious. Now he was a commander who cared for his men, and recognised a bad mission when he saw one.

Across Northern Germany, airfields mirrored the activity at Kluczewo, as Soviet aircraft of all shapes and styles prepared to rise and defeat the enemy armada.

417

Across Northern Germany, Norway, and Denmark, and also on the decks of aircraft carriers at sea, Allied aircraft were being made ready to rise up and meet them, and to destroy the greater part of Soviet air and naval power in the Baltic.

Rainbow Red was a trap.

---

As dawn spread across the sky, aircraft started to come into contact with those that they sought.

In truth, only the Allied aircraft found their targets, as the Soviet ships and aircraft had nothing to find.

Hundreds of Soviet aircraft, and scores of naval vessels were on their way to the affected area, and clashes started before the sun was clear of the horizon.

Swedish Air Force aircraft made a great play of policing their own air space against all comers, but it was unimportant, as the Allies had no need to overfly Sweden anymore, and the Red Air Force had other things on their mind than gaining a new and powerful enemy.

---

The Lembit was an early victim.

An absence of the noises of pursuit had brought her to the surface, anxious to breathe some fresh air, and get off a radio report to Baltic Fleet Headquarters.

She had failed to detect her killer as she rose to the surface, and was slow to detect the approach of high speed screws.

The radio worked and started into the report, informing command of a large naval force and the loss of their comrade.

It was cut short permanently.

Two torpedoes struck her at either end of her starboard side, and she went to the bottom in seconds.

HNoMS Utsira, once a British V Class submarine, had been as lucky as the Lembit had been unlucky.

At the Baltic Naval headquarters, the incomplete message was interpreted correctly, and Lembit was considered lost, although not in vain, as the radio message gave them a rough area of where the enemy fleet was now.

418

The Norwegian submarine, having recently deposited some serious looking men on Mon Island, slipped away towards her assigned station in the Hjelm Bugt, south of Mon.

---

Istomin's regiment was one of those pulled from their own search area and sent towards the Island of Mon, just a few kilometres west of where Lembit had been sunk.

The latest reports on the commando raids all over Soviet-held Denmark were limited, and often garbled, but were enough to make them believe their own deductions and commit to them.

Contact between the air forces were expected, and no-one saw anything out of the ordinary in the reports of clashes.

The Soviet pilots were ordered to bore in on the enemy ships, regardless of loss, the considered naval advice convincing everyone that the destruction of any troop carriers and supply ships was of maximum importance.

So, being brave men for the most part, that is exactly what they did, accepting the casualties as they drove in hard, all the time searching for their prime targets.

Aircraft after aircraft splashed into the Baltic, the majority bearing the Red Star.

---

Istomin's Tupolev-2 led the mainly inexperienced men of the 911th Bomber Air Regiment, some of whom felt the pressure for no other reason than they were flying over water for the first time.

All could hear the reports of combat from an area ahead. None were of contact with the enemy fleet; all described contact with the allied protective aircraft screen.

Istomin had taken his regiment through the gap between Sweden and Rønne. They looked down, noting a number of the Baltic Fleet's vessels carving white trenches in the blue water, as they raced towards the growing battle.

One, he thought it had been a destroyer, exploded and was gone beneath the water, as quick as it took to focus the eye.

The water betrayed three white lines, the wakes of small vessels, certainly not Soviet, now heading at a very high speed towards the west, and the entrance to the Øresund.

The Regimental commander's radio operator called in the details, as the rest of the unit snatched looks at the small but vicious battle that was developing off the shore of Sweden.

Istomin swept the sky to his front, and saw them high and to his left.

"Attention! Unknown aircraft, high, bearing 260 degrees. Come right 10 degrees. Increase speed on me."

The 911th responded like veterans.

Casualties amongst the Soviet bomber crews had been extremely heavy since the first day in August, and less than a half of the original aircrew were still flying; the rest were either lying between clean sheets in hospitals or beneath freshly turned soil.

Those that were left lived by their nerves, senses, and skills.

Istomin's senses told him they were in trouble.

His aircraft recognition skills confirmed it.

*'Mosquitoes.'*

Fortunately for the 911th, the Mosquitoes Mk VIs in question, 22 Squadron RAF, were already vectored in on a low-flying group of Tu2s, naval aviation versions equipped with torpedoes.

Each RAF aircraft sported four Hispano cannons and four .303 Brownings.

Their firepower was tremendous, and the torpedo bombers suffered badly, five of their number falling in the first pass.

Istomin focussed his young fliers on their own survival, calling them away from the sight of the fighting that now seemed to be spreading all around them.

Another Soviet vessel was blazing below them, but only two white wakes were speeding around, indicating that the enemy had been hurt too.

Excited shouts drew his eyes back to the torpedo bombers, and he saw two Mosquitoes wrapped together, steadily whirling into the sea below.

He also saw a tell-tale flash.

"Attention! Unknown aircraft, high, bearing 280 degrees..."

His mouth stopped working. These aircraft he knew too.

*'Germanski bastards!'*

And closing fast.

"Attention, gain height left, gain height left, stay together, stay tight. Attacking aircraft are Germanski!"

The distinct FW-190s, D9 versions, were not so efficient at altitude, which the commander of the 911th knew, so he made the decision to gain height.

3rd Jagdstaffel was a mixed unit, and the FW190s were more than happy for their enemy to go higher, where their other aircraft were waiting.

The eight Focke-Wulfs drove in hard and managed to pick off two of the Tupolevs with cannon and machine-gun fire, although the flight leader felt his performance drop off as one Soviet gunner put some rounds on target. The FW190 side-slipped away, the Hauptmann watching his gauges with increasing concern.

3rd Jagdstaffel tore into Istomin's Regiment from above and below, and ripped it apart.

---

"He's dead, Comrade Mayor. The weapon's fine."

"Stay there and use it, Fyodor. There's two coming in on your right now. Rolling left."

Fyodor Taw pulled the remains of his friend away from the Berezin machine-gun, and took up position, just in time to get off a burst at something he had never seen the like of before.

It was one of six Dornier 335 Pfiels in the 3rd's inventory.

The Pfiel, or 'Arrow' as it was better known, was a push-pull aircraft with an engine on each end, capable of speeds in excess of four hundred and fifty miles per hour.

Two swept past Istomin's right side, having overshot.

They found other prey, and employed the lessons of their first attack, the two inexperienced pilots throttling back to ensure that they put much of their cannon fire on target as possible.

The Tupolev came apart as 30mm and 20mm shells literally destroyed its structure, allowing the wind and forward momentum to do the rest.

Istomin spared the dying aircraft a quick look, recognising that it belonged to his one surviving crews from the old days.

"Two more on our tail, Comrade. Ready to roll right... now!"

The Tupolev responded like the thoroughbred it was, but the pilot still heard and felt impacts.

The defensive machine-guns hammered out, and immediately squeals and shouts of joy filled his ears.

An orange shape almost caressed the cockpit as it shot past, the Dornier streaming fire from its wounds. 12.7mm shells had wreaked havoc on the nose area. The German pilot battled with his aircraft, even as the front engine started to tear itself from its mountings. Fuel lines continued to deposit product throughout the area, and the flier realised that his craft was doomed.

Not soon enough, as the nose came apart, and the engine parted company with the fuselage before coming back into contact with it, the propeller chopping into the right wing and causing it to fail.

The Dornier, now as aerodynamic as a cardboard box , started to freefall in a gentle spin.

The pilot could do nothing but sit in his doomed aircraft, and ride it into the Baltic, as the centrifugal forces kept him pressed into his seat and unable to bail out.

Istomin did not see the Arrow's end, his own concerns more pressing, as his control column started to shake uncontrollably and the Tupolev inexplicably lost height.

He checked his instruments.

*'Running hot?'*

A quick look confirmed damage on the starboard engine cowling. Closer examination revealed a leak of something vital, possibly coolant, plus extensive damage to the right aileron hinges.

"Just you and me now, Comrade Mayor. They're both dead."

The Ta-152 version of the Focke-Wulf was designed for high-altitude interception; sleek, deadly, and the ultimate killer in the Focke-Wulf series. Its performance at lower altitude was not so good, but it was more than adequate for the task of chopping down an injured Tupolev.

Unterfeldwebel Feinsterman drifted in behind the wounded Soviet bomber and lined up the shot.

A stream of tracer from the upper machine gun position angered him, and he shifted his aim, destroying the area with his cannons.

It was not until he tried to press his pedals that he realised that his right thigh had taken a bullet, and that not all was well with the Focke-Wulf.

The smell of burning reached his nostrils at the same time as the iron smell of his own blood.

The smoke came next, and he overshot his target as he struggled to establish what was happening to his aircraft.

Istomin, following the path of the 152 carefully, decided to manoeuvre upwards in a rapid rise, not realising that the enemy pilot had his mind on other things.

The tip of his port propeller clipped the rear of the German aircraft, adding to Feinsterman's misery.

As he wrestled with the virtually unresponsive aircraft, Istomin also had his own problems, as the rise had unseated part of the starboard aileron. The port propeller also remonstrated against its rough treatment, and started to spin off centre, providing an equally interesting and terrifying problem for a pilot already struggling to keep his aeroplane in the sky.

A second 152 made an attack, producing many hits and making Istomin's decision easy.

He reached for his parachute, but the aircraft bucked without his hands on the controls. He grabbed them again, and slipped into the harness as best he could one handed. Changing hands, he reached around and noticed the third 152 making a beam attack.

The stream of cannon shells virtually tore the canopy from the Soviet aircraft and Istomin found himself in an icy stream of air, as the front of the aircraft started to disintegrate.

Snapping the harness lock, he took the opportunity provided, launched himself towards the growing hole, but found the air pressure defeated his attempt.

Bizarrely, the Tupolev flew more steadily since the major damage, although the loss in height was faster now.

Istomin felt the jerk as the aircraft pulled up, rising sharply as one part or another of the control surfaces was destroyed by the next attack.

The Tupolev stalled and provided a moment of suspension; no forward momentum, nothing except a second of calm. That enabled the Soviet pilot to propel himself through the gaping hole, and into free air.

Once his canopy had opened, he watched in fascination as the bomber slowly fell away into the sea.

Looking around, he saw the remains of his regiment attempting to flee. The German fighters took them down one by one.

The last surviving Tupolev simply fire-balled and described an incredibly bright orange arc across the sky, before extinguishing itself in the cold Baltic below.

The air battle moved away, leaving Istomin to ponder his swimming abilities, and wonder about the enemy pilot dangling from the parachute three hundred metres below him.

---

Spectrum Red was more successful than the planners could have hoped.

The massed Allied fighters, over five hundred in total, consisting of training squadrons, reforming squadrons and just hastily thrown together air units, ripped through the Naval and Air force regiments, greatly assisted by the Soviet orders to press home the attack on a non-existent surface fleet.

Torpedo boats and submarines enjoyed great success against the little ships of the Baltic fleet, although not without sustaining losses of their own.

The MTBs, secreted in small bays and coves, dashed out to plant their torpedoes in the innards of passing destroyers and minesweepers, sending eight to the bottom in as many hours, as Spectrum Red continued. There seemed no end to thet supply of fresh fodder thrown at them by desperate men in the higher echelons of the Baltic Naval command.

USAAF bombers carried out an unhindered attack on the Polish defenders of the First Army, hammering part of their northern shoreline.

Amazingly, they pulverized a position that General Berling had ordered evacuated only an hour beforehand, and few Polish casualties were sustained. The Polish AA gunners put up a spirited defence, but failed to hit any of the American aircraft.

A second US group destroyed an NKVD divisional camp just outside of Kolobrzeg, where the reverse was true. The bodies were too numerous to count and, in any case, those who would have counted them lay amongst the dead.

Yet more USAAF squadrons struck targets across the Northern European coastline, hammering Soviet defensive positions that could oppose a forced landing.

German infantry of the 264th Division launched an attack on Møn and Falster Islands, linking up with small groups of the SAS and SBS, who had been landed by submarines, tasked to wreak havoc on the Soviet air and AA defences.

The advance was halted on both islands, short of Allied expectations, mainly because of fanatical resistance by the 40th Guards Rifle Corps.

The five hundred plus Allied aircraft lost thirty-nine of their number, mainly to other aircraft. They inflicted at least three hundred casualties on the Soviet air forces, as well as sinking numerous vessels of the Baltic Fleet.

The Naval contingent inflicted its own significant losses on the Soviets, claiming another eight enemy aircraft destroyed, along with fourteen destroyers, eleven minesweepers, and numerous smaller craft.

One old MTB had been sacrificed to subterfuge, carefully beached and wrecked by a small crew, who 'fell' into the hands of Swedish Military Intelligence officers, and were subsequently paraded as aggressors by a Sweden anxious to portray a rigorously enforced neutrality.

Two smaller Soviet vessels had actually been destroyed by the Swedish defences, so the destroyed MTB was seen as support for the notion that the Swedes did not take sides.

HMS Rye, one of the minesweepers that had accompanied Force V, was caught by three Ilyushin-4 torpedo bombers and sunk, two torpedoes cutting the old ship in half

HMS Sabre, an S Class submarine, failed to return home, and it was subsequently discovered that Soviet bombers had sunk her off the Island of Fehmarn.

As the day turned its back on the sun, the last acts of the tragedy were played out.

---

Istomin had tied his life raft to that of the German pilot, producing something that supported both their legs, or at least his, and what was left of his enemy's.

Feinsterman's right thigh was a mess. Five bullets had struck home, mangling the flesh, but missing artery and bone by some lucky chance.

Another bullet had shattered his ankle and destroyed the nerve endings, which was why Feinsterman had not felt the fire start to consume his toes.

The cold water continued with its anaesthetising effect, but the German was still in a lot of pain and moaned constantly.

It had taken Istomin a little while to realise that the enemy pilot had also broken his arm when he hit the water, and so he took over the duty of passing the man water from his supply.

Extracting a cigarette from his waterproof container, Istomin lit it and slid it between the lips of his recent adversary.

The man's eyes responded in thanks.

The extreme cold played its part, and soon the German was dead, leaving Istomin to try and survive.

He pulled the jacket from the corpse, wrung it out as best he could, and wrapped himself in it to keep the growing wind away from him.

The cold gnawed at him, reducing him to a shadow ,and eventually he fell in unconsciousness.

He did not feel the hands that grabbed hold of him, and lifted him the short distance into the rowing boat.

The lifeboat, a cutter, the sole boat launched from the stricken destroyer Gremyashchy, contained the sixteen survivors of the dive-bombing attack that had sunk their ship.

Three men had succumbed to their injuries, and Istomin was laid on their bodies and covered a tarpaulin as the oarsmen took up the stroke once more.

The commanding officer, an engine room Lieutenant, leant over the side and stabbed the life rafts four times each, releasing the air, and letting Feinsterman's body slip below the waters.

---

To the southwest, HNoMS Utsira had moved to the mouth of the Øresund, ordered to watch for any Soviet naval penetration northwards, in pursuit of the retiring Force V.

Whilst running silently, her crew celebrated the sinking of the Soviet submarine with a bottle of Pils each, specially laid up by the Captain for such an occasion.

Even as the First officer and the Navigator clinked their bottles together, a low metallic sound rang through the hull.

Some knew what it was and prayed.

Others knew what it was and drank their beer.

The rest died in ignorance.

L3, or rather one of her mines, claimed the last victim of the day, a day that had destroyed Soviet Naval Aviation in the Baltic, destroyed many Air Force bomber Regiments and, as Vice-Admiral Tributs candidly said shortly afterwards, left the Baltic Fleet just about capable of policing a children's swimming pool.

Had it not been for Trieste and the Yugoslavians, Eisenhower and his staff would have been elated.

### 0937 hrs, Wednesday, 11th December 1945, Karup, Denmark.

The USAAF Colonel sat comfortably, sharing a coffee and pastries with the Danish Air Force officer.

"Well, as you said, Oberst Lauridson. The Germans have done much of our work but, that being said, my birds have some very special requirements. Shall we?"

He wiped his fingers on a napkin and pulled out a large blueprint, unrolling it on the Danish Colonel's desk.

"These are the works that'll need to be completed before the base is considered ready, but they sure don't amount to a hill of beans, and won't take more than a month tops, depending on the weather."

Quickly considering the sketch work, Lauridson shrugged.

"Sooner, Colonel. Two weeks at the most... depending on the weather"

"No Sir. Most can be done in two weeks, yes, but not these."

He pointed out two pit-like structures to be installed on the south side of the base.

"These need to be very robust, and are of special construction, Colonel. Four weeks for them. I've built some before, so I know what I'm talking about."

Finishing his coffee, curiosity overcame Lauridson.

"Whereabouts, Colonel."

The USAAF officer's eyes hardened for the briefest of moments before he realised he could speak openly.

"Somewhere much warmer, Colonel Lauridson. Little place called Tinian. Now, shall we get our engineering people fired up?"

*If we lose the war in the air, we lose the war, and we lose it quickly.*

*Bernard Law Montgomery*

# Chapter 119 - THE CONFUSION

It was a bad day.

The orders had gone out to the Air regiments, and those that were left had risen into the morning sun and, yet again, found no armada, save for one that was airborne.

Casualties were not as heavy as the day before, mainly because fewer aircraft had been available to attack.

Allied heavy bombing attacks along the Baltic coast, all the way to Leningrad, were relatively unopposed, although the claims from the anti-aircraft units were impressive.

The simple fact was that the enemy fleet could not be found, over a third of Soviet Denmark was lost to ground attack, and that Soviet blood had been spilled at an alarming rate, even for men used to heavy losses in the cause of victory.

The hierarchy of the Red Navy was in a state of shock, so bad were the figures that had arrived from airfields and naval bases surrounding the Baltic.

The destroyer force simply wasn't any more. Those at sea who engaged in the fight had been slaughtered. Those in port had received close attention from Allied heavy bombers, and many would need raising from where they had sunk at their moorings, and most of the rest would need months of repair.

The venerable battleship, 'Oktyabrskaya Revolyutsiya', sunk by the Germans in September 1941 and subsequently raised, was sunk permanently by Lancasters operating in daylight with Tallboy bombs, the RAF planners understanding that her significance was more in the hearts of the Soviet people than in her effectiveness in combat.

The cruisers Gorky and Kirov were damaged, the former by a German mine left over from the previous war, the

429

Captain falling foul of the minefield as he attempted to drive his charge out of Kronstadt.

Kirov had been bombed in place, and the fires were still raging.

The Baltic submarine force had taken a beating, but was the nearest thing to a force that could be considered relatively effective.

Almost as if a higher authority conspired to heap woe on woe, the overdue elektroboote B-29 was now considered lost, which, when combined with the sinking of the Golden Quest the previous day, eliminated the Soviet naval presence in the Atlantic.

The Air Force leaders was almost in a daze as reports of whole bomber regiments lost filtered through. Escorting fighters had experienced heavy losses too, and the efforts to restore some sort of reasonable air power in Northern Germany and Poland were consuming them, as they worked hard to pull in replacement units from all over the USSR.

The arguments flowed back and forth.

"We cannot attack that which we cannot find!"

A fair statement, particularly when the Soviet air reconnaissance force was a shadow of its former self.

"There have been no landings on any shore."

*'Does that mean they are still sailing?'*

More than one wondered it, but Vice-Admiral Tributs assured everyone that the Gulf of Bothnia was enemy free.

Nazarbayeva's report had been taken over the phone whilst Stalin enjoyed early morning tea.

It dovetailed with that of the NKVD, increasing the mystery. Both agencies had now identified a large enemy carrier force in the North Sea, not that Soviet aviation or the navy could now interfere with it. In any case, that snippet of information supplied some answers as to where the huge numbers of Allied fighters had come from. Only one land asset had been identified as possibly being part of an invasion force, a German formation embarked in the southern Norwegian ports.

In short, there was nothing to support the report from Saltholm regarding a hundred ships.

So, the big question was clear. What was the possibility of a large invasion fleet, or any large force of ships for that matter, at sea in the Baltic?

The answer to the question also now seemed clear.

It did not mean that there definitely wasn't, but it did raise the spectre that there were was Allied maskirovka at work, and that the whole thing had been a giant trap.

Unusually for Stalin, he had not ordered changes at the top, with the accompanying grave consequences for the former incumbents, although the reason for this might have been that he was distracted by other matters.

The Allied attacks in central Germany were still progressing, albeit slowly, in the face of some stubborn defensive work by 2nd Red Banner.

The Italian Front had been seen as causing greater problems for the Allies and yet, so it seemed, the Capitalists were coping remarkably well. Indeed, the logistic issues seemed to be posing more of a problem for his forces than the enemy.

*'Yugoslavia.'*

The possibility of Tito's hordes joining the fight would once have excited him but now, in the face of his logistical nightmares, it did little to promote positive thought.

*'So...'*

He listened as the men around him argued more and more, watching more their attitude than taking in what they were saying. It was easier to understand what was in a man's heart by watching, rather than listening. Lies were easy enough, as he well knew.

*'So...'*

He rapped his pipe stem on the table, the clacking sound eventually calling everyone to a respectful and silent order.

"So... we have been dealt a defeat."

He raised his hand to prevent the normal patriotic outpourings from the sycophants, cutting off their protests in an instant.

"We've had setbacks before, and we will have them again, Comrades. What is of great importance to me... and to the people... is how we now deal with this."

He cued Beria in with a simple glance.

"Comrade General Secretary, I have Marshal Konev's report. He recommends renewing the offensive on all fronts, keeping the pressure on the Allies."

"Which we must expect from Konev. He's a bull... but is it realistic, Comrades?"

Stalin already understood that it wasn't, the logistical issues alone preventing it.

Molotov chipped in knowingly.

"Surely our logistical problems prevent that from being a possibility, Comrade General Secretary?"

"Indeed they do, Comrade, but Marshal Konev is thinking too aggressively and, perhaps, not seeing the full picture. We must ensure that our decision is what is right for the Motherland."

More than one in the room looked at the Leader, faces expressionless, but surprised by the unusually restrained rhetoric, and the absence of shouting and threats.

Bulganin cut to the chase.

"So what is it that you propose, Comrade General Secretary?"

Stalin paused to relight his pipe, taking in the heavy smoke, his answer already prepared, as was the question he had given to Bulganin before the start of the meeting.

"I propose that we cease our attacks..."

He stopped, not because he wanted to but because the hubbub that sprung up prevented him from being heard.

There had been times, in the German War, when such talk would have earned a trip to Siberia for many, a neck shot for others. To think in such a way had been defeatist and yet, here, now, the General Secretary was making the suggestion himself.

The noise subsided and he continued.

"We can press on, as Konev suggests... and we will win victories because of the valiant efforts of our soldiers but we will waste our resources piecemeal, as we do not have the logistics to back up our men's efforts properly."

He placed the pipe on the table.

"Mistakes have been made," Beria winced, "Our security forces have redoubled their efforts in securing our lines of communication, and the partisan attacks have dropped significantly."

Novikov, the Chief of the Air Force, knew what was coming next.

"Our Air Force has tried to stem the enemy bomber attacks, but has failed. Not due to lack of effort," the Air Marshal was no less astounded at Stalin's conciliatory tone than the rest of the room, except Beria, Molotov and Bulganin, who knew what was to come.

"He stood up slowly and leant forward, taking his weight on his knuckles.

"No, not due to lack of effort, but because we have not given them the tools with which to fight the Fascists!"

He slammed his hand on the heavy wooden table, causing more than one man to jump. None mentioned that it was the Capitalists who were the enemy now. Perhaps he meant the few Germans in the equation?

"Our soldiers have performed courageously, and they have carried most of Germany before them. In a few months of fighting, against the best that the Allies can offer, they sit on the shores of the North Sea, and our Cossacks can water their horses in the Rhine."

The nods were universal.

"We must accept that we do not have the initiative now, as we must accept that we will only get it back if we here give our soldiers, sailors and airmen the weapons to do the job."

He stood and leant on his knuckles, a position he adopted only when he had serious points to put over.

"We must redouble our efforts in production, in transportation, in training," as he stated each point he selected the face of the responsible person, his eyes giving no quarter in their intensity, "In leadership, and in planning."

He sat down again, so quickly that some missed the move.

"Our men need more of everything... and better of everything... and we shall provide it, and provide it quickly."

He lit a cigarette.

"We have new and improved types tanks, aircraft, and submarines. They must be of good quality, and we must give them to our troops in numbers."

Stalin gestured to an NKVD Major stood by the huge double doors.

433

The man disappeared immediately.

"Comrades, I have asked someone to attend us, and give his opinion on matters. Despite some recent difficulties, he has rarely failed us, and his opinion will be useful here."

The door clanged shut and all eyes swivelled to see who it was.

"Reporting as ordered, Comrade General Secretary."

Georgy Zhukov looked bright and alert.

"Thank you, Comrade Zhukov."

The Marshal moved forward, placing his notes on the table, but knowing he would not need them.

"Comrades, I have been asked to review the present situation, and make military-based suggestions as to how best to continue with the defeat of the Capitalists."

More than one smiled at the tactful and face-saving statement.

"I see no option but to discontinue the main attacks at this time. Logistically, we cannot support them, neither in Germany, nor in Italy. Our Yugoslavian Allies have finally stirred, but the same situation exists for them, and we simply do not have the assets to keep them supplied too."

"We are producing weapons and materiels at excellent rates, but there are serious issues with quality control, issues that Marshal Beria is addressing with vigour."

Everyone knew what that meant.

"Much of what is produced never gets to our rear echelons, let alone the front line. For example, some types of large calibre artillery shells are in short supply. We produce 120% of the stated requirement each month. In November, 57% arrived with the Army in Europe. Over half went where? Partisans, low standards, accidents, all claimed a portion."

"We have trained replacement pilots and shaved time off the programmes, apparently without reducing standards," he acknowledged Novikov with a small gesture of his head, "And yet the casualties amongst these new airmen is considerably higher than it ever was in the German War. There may be other reasons for that, and I know Marshal Novikov is hard at work to find a solution."

"Our Navy has performed miracles in the Atlantic, way beyond what was hoped, and they are to be congratulated. But that is now over, and we will struggle to even maintain our control over the Baltic, unless we give them something more to work with."

More than one present wondered if they had any sort of control over the Baltic after the previous day's events.

"Our soldiers have performed magnificently, driving back the Capitalists to the Western borders of Germany itself, and sometimes beyond. But they are at the limit of their advance, their capabilities and, in some cases, their endurance."

He took the plunge, not sure if the guarantees he had been given would hold good, or whether he was about to become a sacrificial scapegoat on the altar of Stalin's plans.

"If we hold now and permit our forces to recover and rearm, build up our resources, gather more intelligence, and plan thoroughly, then our victory is assured."

Stalin looked around to see if there were any doubters. One or two hard-liners stood out, but he rapidly convinced himself that there would be no issues.

"It is my recommendation, based upon my directknowledge of the situation and recent reports, that the main attacks are called off until we can improve the supply situation and provide replacement men and equipment to all our forces in the field. That does not mean that we should not continue to probe and keep the Capitalists off-balance, but we must give our soldiers time to train, re-arm and recover."

"Thank you, Comrade Marshal."

"If I may, Comrade General Secretary. I was handed this report in error as I waited to be admitted. The contents have a bearing on this meeting."

The handed the report to Stalin who read it and, in turn, passed it to Beria.

The piece of paper, bearing the signature of the Chief Meteorological Officer of the Red Army, was unequivocal.

The discussion went on for some time after Zhukov had left, but was never in doubt. Not that it had been in doubt from the moment Stalin had decided upon the course of action some hours previously, but he had wished to avoid the normal blood-letting and banishments that went with such matters.

The vote was taken and there were no dissenters. A quick discussion followed on another matter, and ended in similar agreement.

435

An hour later, Konev received his orders and the news that Marshal Zhukov was now placed above him as the new Commander of Soviet Ground Forces.

---

As for Yugoslavia, Tito was furious that some of his commanders had launched an unauthorised attack on the Allies, and would have sanctioned those responsible. However, the support he needed for such an action would not have been forthcoming, so he chose the path of Janus.

On one hand, he permitted the forming of a volunteer army, which he would send to fight with the Russians in due course, having finally halted the attacks on Trieste, and in the other places that had seen flare-ups.

On the other hand, he sent trusted emissaries to the Allies, with conciliatory messages, citing the British attack as a cause, explaining that he would keep Yugoslavia out of the war, but that he could not prevent a volunteer unit from being formed to fight with the Russians. He deliberately did not mention how big the force would be.

To Tito, that kept him in play with both sides and, importantly, maintained the borders of his new country.

### 1107 hrs, Wednesday, 11th December 1945, Headquarters of SHAEF, Trianon Place Hotel, Versailles, France.

"Preliminary reports indicate that we've given their air force another good going-over this morning. They keep on coming, but less of 'em, Sir."

"Good news, Walter."

He had poured a coffee whilst his CoS spoke and pushed the mug across to Bedell-Smith.

"Thank you, Sir. Navy says that the torpedo boats got in amongst them again last night ,but it got a bit messy. We lost quite a few boats. Cunningham's pulled them back for now."

Both men sampled their drink in silence, Bedell-Smith understanding that Eisenhower was now doing some quality thinking.

Three officers arrived together, and were silently motioned to chairs. They also knew the routine.

"So, Spectrum Red has been a success, in as much as we have inflicted heavy casualties on Soviet naval and aviation forces. Our losses have been incredibly light, thank the lord."

He motioned Von Vietinghoff towards the coffee service.

"The Poles will profit from it in time as well," he spared Rossiter a nod in acknowledgement for his contribution to that side of the planning.

"On the ground, we are coming to a halt, despite what George says. Will we make Cologne and encircle them?"

The shaking head betrayed his thoughts on the matter.

"Do we call the rest of Spectrum off?"

"No, I don't think so, Sir."

McCreery spoke with an unusual forcefulness.

"Sir, we've just pulled off a magnificent coup against their northern forces, but that cannot cloud our judgement."

Eisenhower looked at British General and invited further comments.

"Sir, I think we must try and complete the opening phase of Spectrum Blue whilst the assets are in place and the men still have the capacity. It's going to get colder, so my people tell me, and we may get to the point where Mother Nature may dictate to us. I spoke with General Bradley this morning and he shares the same view."

He added a quick afterthought.

"If we stop Blue now, all those French boys will have died for nothing too."

McCreery was getting no negativity from his audience and Bradley's agreement counted for a lot with Ike.

"The air force can continue their mission regardless, in fact, they must, or months of good work will be lost as the enemy rearms and restocks."

He acknowledged the arrival of a coffee poured by Von Vietinghoff.

"White has been successful, and laid the groundwork down for the rest of Spectrum in the spring. We can't abandon that, Sir."

Eisenhower waited for Von Vietinghoff to finish drinking before addressing him direct.

"And your view, General?"

The German wasted no time whatsoever.

"I agree with Generals McCreery and Bradley. Finish up Blue, and then postpone until we are properly ready."

Eisenhower nodded at the unequivocal statement.

"Walter?"

"Sir, the way I see it, we can stop Blue now, without prejudicing the greater aims of Spectrum. Blue will be finished, of course, but we can develop some of the other alternatives we discussed, and maybe get an improvement overall."

Ike nodded at his CoS's words, wondering if Bedell-Smith was just playing Devil's Advocate.

"Well, one thing's for certain. A decision is needed soon. George is pushing hard and about to cut loose some more of his force on a flanking move, and Field-Marshal Guderian has pushed a tank division up front, ready for a full push on eastern Cologne."

That was only news to Rossiter, who, as he put it, did not normally concern himself with the trivia of frontline battles.

The sound of footsteps interrupted everyone's train of thought, and Eisenhower raised his eyes to find Group Captain James Stagg clutching paperwork as if his very life depended on it.

Stagg had obviously moved swiftly, a bead of sweat on his forehead despite the coolness of the room.

"Jimmy, what's got you so fired up?"

"The weather's changing, General, and not for the better."

Everyone, even Rossiter, was suddenly wholly attentive.

"All our data reports indicate the temperature will drop dramatically, starting next week, probably Tuesday."

"Yes, you briefed us on that last week, Jimmy. Has that changed?"

"Yes, Sir. I now believe that we will see low temperatures of a record nature."

"What's record mean exactly?"

438

Bedell-Smith couldn't help himself, and held up his hand by way of apology to his boss.

None the less, the question stood.

"Sir, the lowest recorded temperature in Germany was nearly -38°. That was 1929. In 1940, Belgium experienced -30°, Austria, up in the Alps, dropped to -52° in 1932."

Eisenhower was shaken.

"You mean we are heading for those sorts of temperatures, Jimmy?"

"No, Sir, not exactly. We've looked at all the predictions and historical data."

Stagg took the plunge.

"I believe it will be worse, the worst ever recorded, with the very worst reserved for Scandinavia, Denmark, Holland, Western Germany, all through the Alps and into Northern Italy."

He selected a chart that showed where the Meteorology analysts thought things would go.

Eisenhower exploded.

"Minus 45°? The Rhine Valley... Cologne... minus 45°? Can this be an error?"

The remark stung Stagg and Eisenhower knew it, but he had to ask.

"Sir, there is always room for error, but this data has been checked, checked, and rechecked. I will guarantee this to 5° either way."

*'So it could be 5° colder!'*

Rossiter put their thoughts into words.

"Jeez but that's fucking cold!"

"Guaranteed?"

Eisenhower sought indecision in his Meteorological supremo and found none.

"Guaranteed, Sir."

"Thank you, Jimmy"

Stagg departed and Ike nodded to himself as he rapidly digested the latest information.

"That's the decision made then."

Ike stood up, suddenly aware that he had been deprived of tobacco for an unusually long period of time, picking a new pack from the side table, and getting a cigarette lit in record time.

439

"Walter. Tell George and the Field Marshal that they have until Sunday to get Cologne. After that, it's a no-go. Tell them what Stagg just told us."

He continued speaking, including the rest of the room.

"We've discussed this scenario, but it seems it's gonna be much worse than we anticipated. I want our provisions for cold weather checked, and any problems highlighted immediately. Arthur's going to love this, I don't think!"

The sniggers were genuine, despite the circumstances, as the low temperature could prove to be a big problem for the Allied air forces.

The more so when some talented tenor started singing Christmas songs as he strolled the grounds on sentry duty.

The room cleared, all except Rossiter, who had another story to tell, leaving the two of them with a newly-arrived fresh coffee pot.

Both men laughed as some noisy NCO started ripping a strip off the tenor, his colourful language and intense humour bringing some light to Eisenhower's dark morning.

"So, Sam, what brings you here?"

"You asked to be kept in the loop over the Soviet agents, Sir."

"Indeed, Sam."

"The one that was with the French, supposedly a Polish officer. He was killed on Sunday, supposedly by the woman he slept with. But it wasn't her."

"Sounds like a detective novel. Why not her?"

"She was one of ours. She's dead too."

"Sorry to hear that, Sam. So what does it mean?"

"It means the French still have a problem."

### 1131 hrs, Wednesday, 11th December 1945, Route 51, North of Eicherscheid, Germany.

"Pull over, man, goddamnit!"

The big WC51 Dodge staff car pulled into a rough area, allowing the front passenger to stand.

His hands caressed the .50cal that was mounted there, betraying his agitation.

"Say that again, Walter."

Patton listened to the same words, repeated at a slower pace, as a teacher might do to a pupil that doesn't quite grasp the lesson.

"Sunday! You kidding?"

Clearly, Bedell-Smith wasn't kidding.

"I understand my orders, General Smith. Yes, I will."

As the exchange ended, Patton threw the handset skywards in anger. The item returned to ground, pulled back by the cable, dropping undamaged into the snow.

The signaller pulled on the wire and recovered his instrument.

Meanwhile, Patton continued to rant and rave as he extracted a map from his case.

Calm overtook him finally, and he flopped back into the seat.

Slapping the driver on the shoulder, he spoke slowly and deliberately.

"Now, son. You make this thing sing, and I don't care what gets in your way. Drive over it if you have to, but just get me to the 4th's forward command post quickly."

"Yessir!"

The powerful Dodge leapt forward and Patton almost considered an admonishment, but decided he had asked for it. Besides, the staff car was virtually flying down the road towards the headquarters of the 4th US Armored's command group.

He consulted the map, starting to plan his new push on Cologne, something he found difficult as the Dodge bounced on every rut the road had to offer.

He had achieved little but a few tentative thoughts before his four star flags arrived at Iversheim, the headquarters of the 4th US Armored Division.

Normally the centre of attention, Patton was surprised to find that he was not the focus of the headquarters staff.

The commander of the 4th was holding centre stage as he bawled out the CCA commander, Johnson Greenwood, summoned for a face to face exchange.

"Force the road, goddamnit. We don't have time to go around, not now. The Krauts are gonna hit Cologne again, and we gotta be there to help. You're pussy-footing around too much. Push the boys on now!"

Both officers noticed the figure of their commanding General and saluted immediately.

"Bruce, JP," Patton acknowledged each in turn, "Someone wanna tell me what's going on here?"

Clarke, regretting being so openly hard on Greenwood, ceded the floor to the Brigadier General.

"Sir, my boys took Euskirchen about an hour ago. Swisttal a short time later. CCB are moving on past Zulpich, and into the rear of the Hürtgenwald. CCR are hung up at Meckenheim, where the commies have launched a counter-attack."

The facts of the situation reported, Greenwood moved on to less steady ground.

"Sir, my boys have taken some bad knocks, and I just want time to pull them back together. Besides, the situation at Meckenheim is unclear; I don't wanna hang my ass out and get fucked by some Soviet column coming from that direction."

Bruce Cooper Clarke shifted uncomfortably.

"No, JP, no. You get your boys on the road now. I know they're tired, but so's the goddamned commies. Weather's our problem. Real cold weather coming on in. Be with us next week, early. So no let up now. Push hard and keep pushing. Drive these red bastards back. You understand, JP?"

"Yes, Sir. My supplies've just caught up, but I'll go as soon as we're topped off."

Patton's hand slapped his breeches hard, the sound like a gun shot.

"No, the fuck you will, JP! Keep pressing hard, all the time, all the way. Supply'll get to you in the field if necessary, but you gotta keep pressing. Don't let the commie bastards get set."

Greenwood understood that his General was a charger, a man who pushed his men to the limits to get the job

442

done. He also knew that his men had been fighting for months now, some without the benefit of the short breaks they had been able to occasionally organise, and that some were close to breaking point.

Fig#104 - Combat Command 'A', 4th US Armored Division, Euskirchen to Weilerswist, Germany, 11th December 1945.

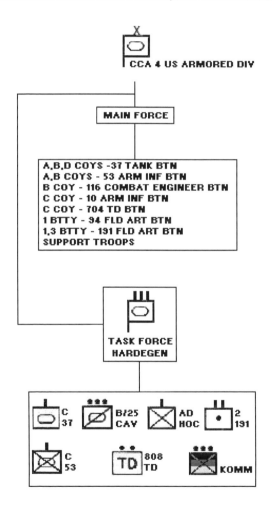

"Sir, my command will be moving within thirty minutes."

"Attaboy, JP. You know if we keep moving the casualties'll be lower. Now, I'll leave you to it. Bruce?"

Patton extended an arm and swept Clarke outside the tent.

"General, I was on the verge of relieving him."

Unlike his reputation suggested, Patton rarely relieved his officers, and was surprised that the genial Clarke had reached that critical point with one of the best officers in his command.

Clarke saw the question in his commander's eyes and decided straight talk was needed.

"I think he's nearly done, General. He's been at the front now...what... since Normandy? A lot of officers have come and gone, but not JP... Old Reliable."

Patton nodded in understanding.

"Well, I'll tell you straight, Sir. I think he's cracking up... lost sight of things some... almost like... like what he says is the state of his boys is actually a reflection of him... like he's telling me that he's burned out and exhausted, which I think he is."

"He looked just fine to me, Bruce. His unit's done good from France to here... and he ain't failed yet, has he?"

Clarke persisted.

"I know, General, and I wasn't going to let him fail now. I think he needs to be away from here."

Patton rubbed his chin, turning to examine the busy Brigadier General through the open tent flap, seeing a man hard at work, acquiring intelligence from the divisional staff, updating his own information before moving off to put his command back on the road to Cologne.

"Alternatives?"

"Go with him up to CCA and give him my support, but he'd know what I was doing for sure."

"Uh-huh."

"I could leave Bill Bridges with him," Clarke thumbed in the direction of Colonel Bridges, one of his aides, and a soldier of no little repute, "And he can step in if there's trouble."

"I like that one better, Bruce."

444

Never one to waste much time, Patton strolled back into the tent and pulled Greenwood to one side where they could not be overheard.

"JP, we've given you the ball for some hard yards here. Wish I could lighten your load, but we've got a job to do."

Making sure he wasn't overheard, Patton adopted his softest tone for one of his old warhorses.

"I've asked General Clarke to give you some assistance here. Colonel Bridges'll be temporarily assigned under your command. Use him to lighten your load, ok?"

"Yes, Sir, General. Thank you."

Those simple words of thanks told Patton that Clarke was probably right, and that JP was near the end of his tether, for such intrusions would normally not be welcome, and seen as a lack of trust, but he was now committed.

He left again, passing Bridges on the way in.

Clarke was waiting beside his halftrack.

"Sir, Bridges is briefed, and I've told him to take over if things go bad."

"Shit, Bruce. He'll do just fine. Now, I think CCR would benefit from our presence, don't you?"

In seconds, the two vehicles were hammering down the road to Wormersdorf, where CCRs commander was trying to sort out a growing mess.

*Some say the world will end in fire, some say in ice.*

*Robert Frost*

# Chapter 120 - THE COLD

### 1300 hrs, Wednesday 11th December 1945, Route 194, near Grossbüllesheim, Germany.

Fig#105- Soviet 38th Army, Euskirchen to Weilerswist, Germany, 11th December 1945.

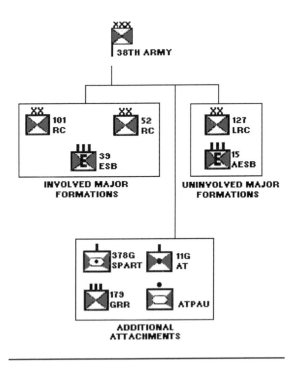

Fig#106 - Dispositions, Euskirchen to Weilerwist, Germany, 11th December 1945.

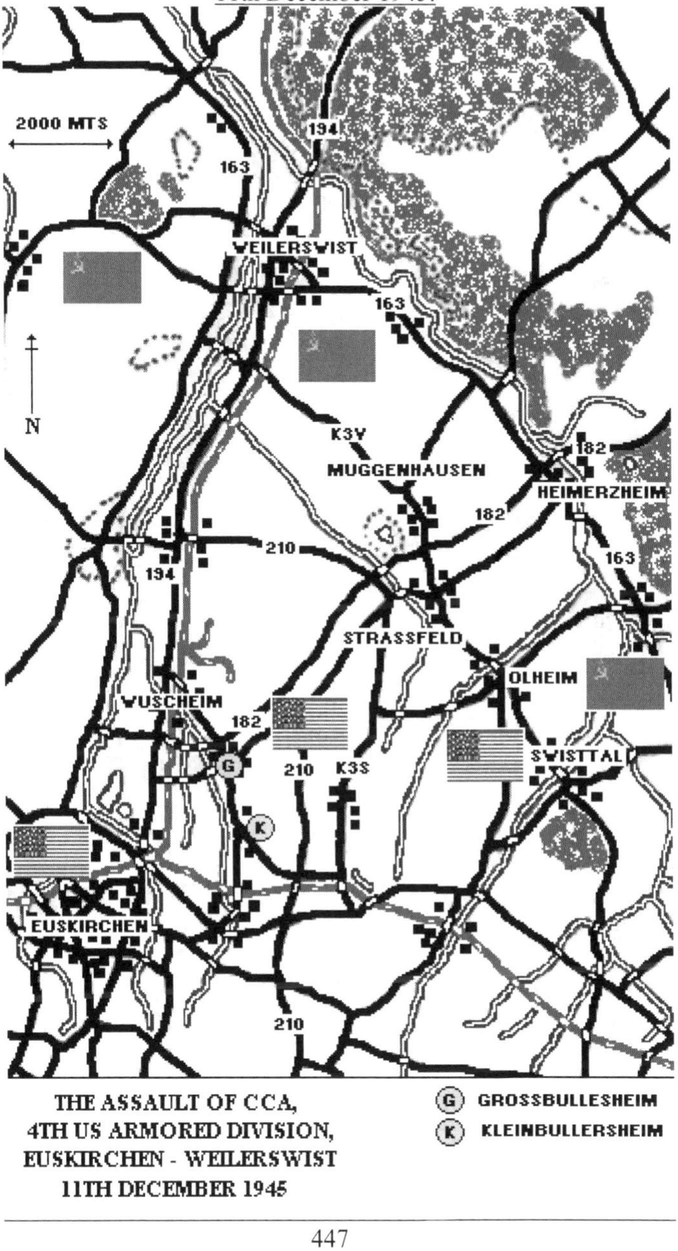

**THE ASSAULT OF CCA,
4TH US ARMORED DIVISION,
EUSKIRCHEN - WEILERSWIST
11TH DECEMBER 1945**

(G) GROSSBULLESHEIM
(K) KLEINBULLERSHEIM

The point unit of CCA had been stopped cold, just north of Wuschheim, on Route 194, precisely coinciding with a snowfall that was constant and heavy.

Even as Brigadier General Greenwood was making new command decisions, the air was rent with the sound of vehicles exploding, and the screams of wounded men.

"Here, we push here instead. Get Hardegen's outfit online and moving straight away. Get'em to take the 182 and outflank these motherfuckers."

His staff rushed to put the new plan into action.

The compact mixed force, led by Major John Hardegen, was waiting in Kleinbüllesheim, ready to exploit the success of the main advance, but was now tasked with finding an alternate route forward and round the blocking force holding up the main body on the 194.

It was, in essence, a smaller version of CCA, with tank, armored infantry, cavalry, and artillery components.

Greenwood had already sent some of the mechanized cavalry to reconnoitre down Route 182, and the reports had been favourable.

That they had also been favourable for Route 194 did not occur to him at this time, so consumed was he with pushing his command forward.

All the smaller watercourses were frozen solid, something that increased the options for his forces, but he knew how much the Red Army loved breaking up ice with explosives once troops were on it, or over it, so prudence still played a part.

His HQ vehicles were already covered in a thick layer of snow, and the battlefield's visibility was greatly reduced, the large flakes falling even more thickly than before.

Reasonably, he and his officers considered that was the same for both sides.

Alas, the Gods of War are rarely reasonable in their dealings with man, as Task Force Hardegen was about to find out.

# Fig#107 - Initial assault of Combat Command A, 4th US Armored Division, Route 194, Germany, 11th December 1945.

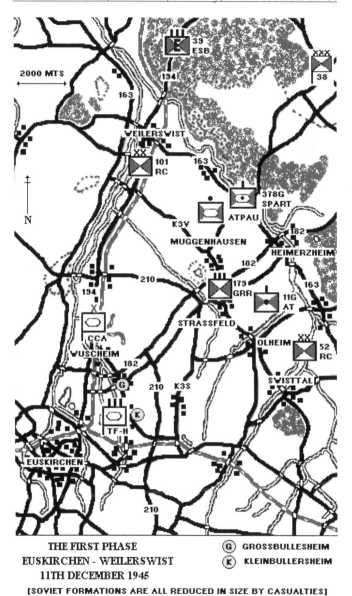

THE FIRST PHASE
EUSKIRCHEN - WEILERSWIST
11TH DECEMBER 1945

G  GROSSBULLESHEIM
K  KLEINBULLERSHEIM

[SOVIET FORMATIONS ARE ALL REDUCED IN SIZE BY CASUALTIES]

The cavalry's Greyhound armoured car literally came apart as Hardegen scrutinized its careful advance, something of inordinate power just destroying it in an instant, and ending the lives of all four crew.

Whatever it was, it was to be avoided, and Hardegen screamed into his radio immediately.

"All Mohawk elements, get off the road, get off the road. Dragonfly, get some smoke down either side of the 182, on the bridges and river line, over."

"Dragonfly, Mohawk-six, roger."

Dragonfly, the call-sign for the 191st's artillery officer, contacted the waiting 155mm howitzers.

Zinc chloride smoke shells soon began to burst all around the river and road ahead, drifting back towards the task force and masking the flames of the destroyed M24.

No further shots came from the defenders, wherever they were.

Hardegen was on the radio.

"Mohawk-three-one, push your element down the track to Strassfeld. Push on one mile, and then turn north. Come in on the flank. Be careful, Chris. Mohawk-six, over."

"Roger Mohawk Six. You too, boss."

The seven medium tanks selected, one tank platoon enlarged by two stragglers, bolstered by a platoon of M5 Stuarts from D Company, pushed off to the right, followed by their supporting infantry element from the 53rd Armored-Infantry, plus two M36 Jacksons, last remnants of one of the 808th TD's platoons, recently adopted by the infantry.

CCA was in it up to its neck, but didn't yet know how deep.

The main thrust up the 194 had run straight into a prepared defensive position, manned by determined infantry from the 101st Rifle Corps, backed up with anti-tank guns, mines, artillery, and a few tanks.

Hardegen's force, sent on its flanking mission, had hit the join between the 52nd and 101st Rifle Corps, filled with a composite force of exhausted units.

450

Artem'yev's guardsmen, pulled back for a rest, were once again pitch-forked into a cauldron of fire.

However, they were not unsupported.

The gun that had claimed the lead M20 was a 152mm, mounted on a tank chassis, in the form of an ISU-152 of the 378th Guards Heavy SP Gun Regiment. It had seven of its friends on the field.

There was also one other vehicle assigned to Artem'yev's command.

Fig#108 - TF Hardegen's assault on Müggenhausen & Strassfeld, 11th December 1945.

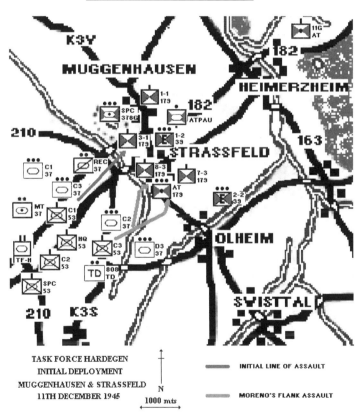

TASK FORCE HARDEGEN
INITIAL DEPLOYMENT
MUGGENHAUSEN & STRASSFELD
11TH DECEMBER 1945

N

1000 mts

INITIAL LINE OF ASSAULT

MORENO'S FLANK ASSAULT

Captain Christian Moreno was experienced enough to understand the task ahead, and he pushed his element hard towards the track he had selected.

Strassfeld was the first objective. He studied the map closely and decided to change the approach.

"Mohawk-three-three, Mohawk-three-one, over."

The reply from 1st Lieutenant Garcia was tinny and light, the effect of the radio, not the man himself.

"Mohawk-three-three, Take D/3rd and your group south onto the Strassfelderweg. I'll send a platoon of the armored infantry and some change to back you up. Push up, do not enter the village. Leave D/3rd to cover, shift right, and then envelop, understood, over?"

"Mohawk-three-one, Mohawk-three-three, roger and understood. Sixty-one on my right flank. I'll need one of those platoons to cover my right flank and rear, over"

"Mohawk-three-three, Mohawk-three-one, the Stonewalls will come with the doughs. They are for the flank and rear cover. Now move 'em out. Over and out."

The Stonewalls were the M36 Jackson tank-destroyers, the civil war reference having been too hard to ignore.

Hardegen checked with his binoculars, watching in satisfaction as the well-trained men of his command implemented his orders.

"Driver, move up."

His own Sherman surged forward towards Strassfeld.

### 1344 hrs, Wednesday, 11th December 1945, Strassfeld, Germany.

Artillery started to drop in and around Strassfeld. Large calibre rounds of all varieties, all with the potential for death and injury in common.

Artem'yev could simply not believe it.

After all they had been through, yet again, he and his men found themselves in the hottest of places.

He shouldn't have been there by rights, having been summoned to a 1400hrs meeting with the Army Commander, but the weather had cancelled the trip, so he found himself in command of three hundred and forty-seven exhausted men and women, sat on a piece of German real estate that the Allies very much wanted.

Again.

He turned to his officers.

"Once more then, Comrades. It seems once more before we can escape this hellhole!"

On the wall of the old carpenter's shop, a hand-drawn map of their positions had been carefully created, positioned next to a German army map that held the more precise details of the position.

Because the hand-drawn map was in larger scale, Artem'yev briefed from it.

"The Amerikanski are advancing cautiously, and our men will slow them down for a while. It won't last, and they will be here soon enough."

He circled the village with his hand.

"Our anti-tank guns will do what they can, but it won't be much, I think, so we'll pull them out early on, clear?"

The young anti-tank Lieutenant commanding the last handful of AT guns from the 179th didn't actually understand, but was grateful for the reprieve he had just been given, having resigned himself to dying at Strassfeld, alongside his three gun crews.

"The timing of that... well... that's your call, Leytenant. Hurt the Amerikanski for sure, but I want you out and redeployed here, with as much as you can salvage," he pointed out a small raised area of no more than fifteen hundred square metres, sat just north of the junction of Routes 182 and 210.

"Your job then is to stick fast to the hill, come what may. Cover the road... and Müggenhausen to the north, and watch our flank to the south here."

The AT officer didn't bother to remind the Colonel that there was only one lorry and that the other two Zis-3s would have to be pushed by hand. Artem'yev wasn't that sort of Colonel.

"I've asked for a couple of the SP's from the 378th, and anything else that can be spared. Comrades, for what it's worth, I think they'll swing their whole advance through here if we don't hold."

Weary men suddenly felt wearier at the thought of more heavy fighting.

"This will be the last time. When this one is over, I'll march you to the rear myself, Comrades. With or without orders!"

He lifted them enough with his words. None the less, none of them were under any illusions.

"We will not resist at distance, not until we get tank support, otherwise the Amerikanski tanks will just swat our men away with their shells. Entice them closer, where we can fight their infantry up close, and their tanks cannot fire for fear of killing their own, clear?"

The nods were controlled, but they knew why Artem'yev was choosing this path.

"We're better in close, so their numbers won't count. Getting them in close'll also switch off their artillery."

Artem'yev held up a hand, silencing two of those present before they started to complain.

"I know, Comrades, but, at the moment there isn't any, and that's the way it is. Our units have taken heavy losses at the hands of their air attack regiments, and we may not get any artillery or rocket support at all."

He needed to lift them again.

"Commander 11th Guards Anti-tank is going to release some of his 76mm's to form an artillery unit for this area. If we hear a unit called Murmansk on the system, that's them, and we get them working straight away."

"Back to the village, Comrades. Keep their tanks out and make them go around. Once they move round the flanks, then the big boys can pick them off."

That was easily understood.

"No retreat, Comrades, Not one centimetre beyond the plan. It cannot be allowed, or the Capitalists will split open the two Rifle Corps, and there'll be hell to pay."

Artem'yev knew, just as they knew, what that order meant.

"Here is important."

He pointed to the area east of Strassfeld.

"We must not let them past us and round there or we will be cut off. The 52nd Corps will be moving units into Heimerzheim, but that will take time. We must expect no help from that quarter for now. When we pull back from Strassfeld, these positions, north of Olsheim… we hold them, come what may."

He emphasized the position.

"There are two AT guns already in the defences, plus some of the engineers. We will hold there."

A partial company of engineers had taken a wrong turn, and found themselves unable to refuse Artem'yev's 'suggestion' to remain, so now formed part of his force, part in Strassfeld, part in the secondary defences.

The plan was relatively simple and without frills, not that there were the resources or time for either them.

Artem'yev addressed the interloper, a highly decorated tank commander, who had arrived without warning.

"Starshina, you've already chosen your ground and it suits our purpose. I know you have special orders but, for all our mother's sakes, just let me know if you have to move back."

Kon nodded his understanding, also acknowledging that the infantry Colonel understood the value of his vehicle.

"I hope it won't come to that, Comrade Polkovnik."

"Remember, Comrades. Listen for Murmansk and no retreat. Good luck now."

The orders group broke up as the enemy artillery increased in its fury, a sure sign that an assault was about to begin.

### 1349 hrs, Wednesday, 11th December 1945, outside of Strassfeld, Germany.

"Roger, Mohawk-three-three, out."

Moreno ordered his units to advance, despite Garcia's contact report.

After all, it was just a handful of mud bandits, and they had been dispersed.

The anti-tank fire had stopped abruptly, the sole victim, a halftrack, lay smoking just off the track ahead. The track's .50cal was working the building line ahead, the gunner desperate to avenge the two buddies that lay unequivocally dead in the front seats.

455

The unrecognizable bodies had taken the full force of an anti-tank round striking the engine, and passing through to the dashboard before exploding.

It was a miracle that anyone had survived, not that the gunner would see it until the tears and anger subsided.

Other infantry had dismounted and run forward, encouraged by the relative absence of fire from their target.

The lead Sherman, a 105mm howitzer equipped M4A3, seconded from the gun platoon, put one of its large shells into the nearest building with unusual results.

Fire spurted from every window as it exploded, but the structure itself seemed to hold, until something gave and it folded in on itself like a house of cards.

The snow reduced visibility and thus affected all ranges of fire, helped further by the smoke and dust from the German village.

The 105mm closed a little more, encouraged by its destruction of the large house.

Alongside, Garcia's Sherman moved level, ready to provide support as the howitzer tank did its job.

From a hole to one side rose its killer, clutching a grenade. Taking rapid aim, the Soviet guardsman threw his RPG-6. He was an experienced tank hunter, and the RPG-6 was a much improved anti-tank weapon.

He had dropped back down into the hole before the American tank crew could raise a shout, and the grenade detonated before they could scream.

When the grenade exploded, its HEAT charge focussed its power and punched through the side of the turret.

Apart from a modest hole, no external damage was evident.

Inside, the story was different.

The loader and gunner had been transformed by the explosive blast. Garcia had lost both feet from the knees down, as he was pushing himself up and out the hatch at the time of impact.

His upper body strength came to his rescue and he propelled himself out into the cold, rolling onto the engine cover and off the back of the vehicle. He screamed as his shattered left leg hit the ground first; the second scream that followed immediately afterwards was louder than the first. The right leg came down, still with a partial foot attached, the swinging lump of boney flesh welting his left stump above the separation point.

Mercifully, Garcia dropped into unconsciousness.

His driver, shocked and stunned, reversed the tank.

The hull gunner sprayed bullets in all directions, hoping to stave off a repeat from any nearby grenade thrower.

It was not until the Sherman had reversed back some forty yards that the driver noticed the flattened body of his commander.

The machine gunner was too busy to notice, seeing only the shapes of the enemy in every shadow and swirl of snow He only stopped firing when he realised that the driver was vomiting into his lap.

They both abandoned the damaged tank and ran for their lives.

The infantry went to ground, and took the grenade thrower's positions under fire.

Two more RPG-6's hit the 105mm Sherman, but the throwers were less skilful.

Neither exploded and both bounced off the tank, which slowly continued on its advance, seemingly unaware of either the grenade attack, or the loss of their cover.

One of the watchful infantry put two Garand rounds through the chest of a grenade thrower, dropping him back into his snowy hole.

A special group from the 39th Engineer Sapper Brigade watched closely, assessing the position of the enemy tank, preparing to fire the explosives buried in the road.

The turret traversed and the gunner selected a building at random. In the blink of an eye, a 105mm shell blotted the group out. The Sherman crawled forward, rolling over one hundred kilos of Soviet explosives that would now not be detonated.

Inside the tank, the realization that they were alone suddenly hit the commander, and he ordered a halt.

The tank lashed out at all the surrounding buildings, leveling them one by one, as the hull machine gun sought out targets, or just expended ammunition to calm the crew's growing nerves.

When Garcia's tank had been knocked out, Moreno had pushed more of his force forward, and two Sherman 'Easy Eight's' moved on either side of the howitzer tank.

Two Soviet soldiers rose up with RPG-6s, but both were cut down before they could release their grenades.

Despite the lack of fire from the village ahead, all three Shermans lashed the rubble.

The armored infantry pushed up again, their halftracks supporting with .50cal fire. They rushed past their armored comrades, achieving the edge of the village without loss.

Pushing his own element forward, Moreno took the lead and broached the edge of the village, seeing only friendly GI's moving ahead of him.

As per his plan, the remainder of his armor switched to the right, intent on enveloping the village.

He had started to key the mike, having mentally rehearsed his message about the impending fall of Strassfeld, when he realized that such a message would be premature, as the uniforms moving to his right were not those of his own men.

The group of Soviet soldiers charged into the armored infantrymen, PPShs and PPDs lashing the position with a hail of bullets, dropping many of the men before they had a chance to respond.

Moreno could offer no support, but screamed into his radio, summoning more of the 53rd's infantry forward.

The position was reoccupied by triumphant enemy soldiers. Not one GI escaped, and Moreno watched helplessly as four men were dragged away.

In his peripheral vision, he now noticed that the assault he had watched was being repeated in a number of other places and, all except in the rubblised gasthaus nearest his tank, repeated with exactly the same bloody result.

Hardegen was in his ear, desperate for information.

Moreno called it as he saw it and, in many ways, he was right. As he suggested, the lack of resistance on the run in had been to draw the force forwards, and into a close encounter with the Soviet infantry.

"Mohawk-six, Mohawk-three-three. I urgently need more infantry. The place is full of commie foot soldiers and we can't progress, over."

"Roger, Mohawk-three-three. Use your reserve for now. Pot's dry 'til I get reinforcements, over."

Moreno had hoped to get his own extra resources but, as that wasn't going to happen, using the combat reserve seemed reasonable.

"Mohawk-six, Mohawk-three-three, roger. We are moving around the objective, but we won't be able to help you for some time, over."

Hardegen had figured that one out for himself, knowing now that his flanking manoeuvre had bogged down, and had simply resulted in him losing part of his own resources in Strassfeld, resources that would not be able to support him at Müggenhausen, hence his own plea to his commander, Greenwood.

Next to no assistance was forthcoming from that quarter, as the rest of CCA had its own problems on Route 194.

Greenwood grudgingly released another refugee from the 808th, only recently arrived and on the strength of CCA, plus a short company of men formed from the supporting services, and a platoon of German kommandos from Euskirchen, who had come out of hiding and presented themselves when the US attack rolled the Russians back.

The new troops came at a price, as Brigadier General Greenwood ordered Hardegen's force to push through Müggenhausen, and on into Weilerswist, without delay, which in Greenwood language meant 'at all costs'.

Hardegen remonstrated, to no avail, and Greenwood's radio fell silent as the fighting on Route 194 grew in intensity.

### 1414 hrs, Wednesday, 11th December 1945, Route 182, west of Strassfeld, Germany.

"Fuck, fuck, and double fuck!"
"Santa Maria, Major! It's that good, is it?"
Hardegen grinned uncomfortably at his gunner.

"Well, Giuseppe, you could say that. The old man has his own problems... leastways, so it seems. Apart from a few bits of extra change, we're on our own."

'Bismarck', Hardegen's M4A3E8 Sherman, accelerated smoothly as the force moved into the attack.

Soviet artillery was light and ineffective and, as was the case with Strassfeld, little or no resistance was offered on the run in.

All save whatever it was that fired at the lead Sherman, missing by, as Hardegen's driver quaintly put it, 'a gnat's cock', before burrowing into a snow drift and exploding against a tree trunk.

Hardegen, having ordered his tank to move towards cover, searched hard and found what he was looking for.

"Gunner, target at ten o'clock, four hundred and fifty. Load HVAP. C'mon DeMarco, move it."

The turret swung past the position and Hardegen was about to override before the gunner corrected.

The words almost blended together.

"On!"

"Fire!"

Hardegen watched through his sight as the 76mm shell struck the ISU-152 on the right-hand side of the barrel, appreciating, almost in slow-motion, the impressive display of white hot sparks as the HVAP deflected and moved on into the housing, where it burrowed through the armor and struck the trunnion of the huge weapon as the 152mm was starting into recoil, its own shell flying harmlessly over the top of Hardegen's vehicle.

The displaced gun wrought havoc inside the Soviet SP, taking it out of the fight.

In the absence of any orders from his commander, the ISU driver made a judgement call and quit the field at the highest possible speed.

"All Mohawk elements, Mohawk Six, orient left and manoeuvre towards that high ground."

In so doing, he took a calculated risk by exposing his right flank to Strassfeld but, based on Moreno's report, he felt it was a risk worth taking, especially as part of the other force was moving around to the east of Strassfeld.

"Dragonfly, Mohawk-six, over."

"Mohawk-six, Dragonfly, over."

"Dragonfly, put some arty on the height ahead, then advance north in stages," he consulted his map as the Sherman started to rock from side to side as it pushed forward over uneven ground, "Up to five hundred yards. Make sure you steer clear of the junction on the K3... err... Vernicher Strasse, clear? Over."

"Mohawk-six, Dragonfly, Clear, Out."

The 191st Artillery again showed what it could do under the guidance of a competent observer and, within two minutes, the position around where the ISU had fired from was carpeted with HE rounds.

Hardegen drove his force forward, urging his commanders to push their drivers, the command cascading down, as the commanders ordered their drivers to get everything possible out of their tanks.

The lead Sherman disappeared in smoke, its right track paying out, eventually flopping uselessly off the rear bogies, the left track driving the tank in an arc before the vehicle came to a halt, facing precisely north-east.

Inside the Sherman, the driver was screaming in agony, the shock wave from the anti-tank mine having shattered both his ankles.

The hull gunner was unconscious, his wounds more severe, his right side damaged by the force of the explosion, his thigh already expanding as the internal blood loss mounted.

Hardegen went for his radio, ready to cater for any new threat, but chose to stay silent for the moment, leaving that situation to one of his officers whilst he took in the bigger picture, and listened to the frantic reports from his other force, east of Strassfeld.

### 1438 hrs, Wednesday, 11th December 1945, Route 61, east of Strassfeld, Germany.

Moreno had already had the hard experience of seeing his best friend die, and in a way outside that considered 'acceptable' to the combat soldier.

Now, hell was being visited upon him, and he wrenched the earphones off his head, refusing to listen to the screams of dying men any longer.

In any case, they had now stopped, them and the radio beyond repair as the flames consumed everything in the stricken tank.

He cast a baleful eye at the Sherman ahead and to the right, the fire rising in a straight line from the open hatches, wherein five men, one of them his senior NCO and rock since day one, were being incinerated in their knocked out tank.

Another Soviet shell crossed the no man's land, seeking to inflict more death.

The sound of it striking metal was intense, and the deep clang rang across the snow covered ground.

The target, another Easy Eight, shrugged off the shell and it careened skywards, disappearing from sight somewhere behind Moreno's field of vision.

Two halftracks darted right, keen to be out of the field of fire of whatever it was, heading for some hedgerows.

The lead vehicle hardly lost any speed as a solid shot punched through the rear compartment, easily penetrating the metal on both sides, and hardly noticing the two armored infantrymen that it dissected on its travel.

The driver lost control on an icy match of road and the M3 fishtailed before coming to rest, nose down in a ditch adjacent to the road.

Half the remaining crew had enough wits to throw themselves out of the vehicle.

Starshina Kon ensured that the next round was an HE round, and it was right on target, destroying the halftrack and its remaining contents.

The T54 shifted position again, quickly dropping back and left into a wooden redoubt, complete with an earth and board roof.

The delay in moving brought Moreno's tanks closer.

"There, that small mound dead ahead. Something just moved!"

There was no time to tear the hull gunner a new asshole for his procedure, but Moreno filed it for when they got out of the battle.

*'If we get outta the goddamned fucking battle!'*

The gunner was clearly losing it, his voice reflecting his fright."

"On-n."

"Fire!"

The 76mm spat a shell at whatever it was in the small bunker, and was rewarded with the clues of a metal on metal strike.

"Lay it on the fucker again, Smitty!"

---

"Calm down! Calm... down! It didn't penetrate! Find the tank that hit us."

The ATPAU's experimental T54 had only just moved into the position when the shell had struck the front of the turret, sending sparks everywhere, and firing up into the earth and wood roof, sending the result of three hours work by some helpful infantrymen sky-high in less than a second.

"Target. On!"

"Fire!"

The T54 bucked as it put a shell into the air. The movement hadn't ceased before a squeal of delight rose from Kolesnikov's mouth, the impressive end of another enemy tank marked by the turret, still tumbling through the air.

---

Moreno wilted as the tank immediately to his right was blotted out, the turret turning end over end as it flew through the air, before coming to rest on the edge of the small frozen lake. The hot metal melted much of the ice surrounding it and it sank slightly into the earth, coming to rest in an upright position, resembling a dug-in tank waiting in ambush.

The gunner had already put another shell into the position ahead, but without the same rewards offered by his last effort.

"Driver, jink, goddamnit it, the turret's turning on us."

He had only just realized what it was he was looking at, and now understood that their enemy was definitely a tank, and it had selected them for its undivided attention.

The Soviet 100mm shell struck the corner of his glacis and deflected away into the snow.

"Again, Smitty, again!"

"On!"

"Fire!"

The movement of the Sherman prevented a decent shot, and the shell went wildly wide.

The enemy tank also missed.

Moreno's Sherman closed the gap.

---

"Calmly does it, Oleg. You can do this. Fire when you're ready."

Every essence of Kon's being wanted to shout at the man and reverse his tank away, but his training told him otherwise, and he calmly encouraged the gunner to do his job.

The 100mm recoiled as another shell was sent on its way, striking the very top of the Sherman's mantlet before travelling a few feet further, removing the .50cal at the pintel mount.

The enemy shells continued to miss as the Sherman bounced around but, by way of return, the distance was closing, and the Sherman was nearly in the relative safety of the same small copse that had hidden Kon's tank.

Except for one small difference.

---

"C'mon! C'mon! Pedal to the metal, Marty! C'mon!"

No sooner had Moreno shouted the encouragement than the tank slewed, one track with firm grip, the other losing it in a slushy, muddy hole that deprived the tank of traction

The tank slowed considerably, and continued to lose forward momentum as the left track sought purchase on something about as resistant as water.

Perversely, the sudden arrest of their forward movement spared them, and the 100mm shell streaked past without contact.

Although it came at the cost of being an easier target, the Sherman was now a better gun platform and Smith put the sight on the enemy tank. Part of him acknowledged the unspoken suggestion that it was not one he'd seen before, whilst the other part required silence as it concentrated on killing it, whatever it was.

An HVAP flew from one tank to the other in less than a second, with spectacular results.

The T54 had just started to reverse away, relocating to yet another position, when the 76mm shell struck its front left bogie, stripping it, and the track it held, from the tank.

Inexorably, the shell moved on, removing idlers and lodging in the rear drive, jamming it solid.

The 100mm had fired virtually at the same moment and the shell struck the centre of the glacis plate of the Easy Eight, deflecting against the hull side, through the hull gunner before exiting into the floor area, and wreaking unknown damage under the revolving turret floor.

The smell of tortured metal, blood and smoke overrode their every sense and the hatches quickly flew open, propelled by desperate men.

Moreno grabbed his gunner.

"The fucker's still alive, Smitty. Let's give her one more now. One more, mano."

Smith was scared out of his wits, but responded automatically to the voice of his commander, dropping back down into his seat. The loader was long gone, so Moreno pushed home another HVAP.

"On."

"Fire!"

Nothing happened.

"Shit! Misfire!"

Smitty started the procedure automatically.

Firing the gun a further three times, one for luck, Smith gave the order to his loader and the breech was opened. With the utmost of care, Moreno extracted the shell and nestled it carefully in his arms.

It was still there when a 100mm shell punched through the hull front and exploded against the rear of the crew compartment, roughly one and a half foot from Moreno.

Two explosions combined.

---

"Nice shooting, Oleg. He blew up rather nicely."

"When the fucking thing works, this is a great gun."

That was true, and Kon had found himself wishing he had been able to take it into battle against the German Panzers at Kursk, during Bagration, or at the Seelow Heights.

Another Sherman was filling his sight.

"Target front, four degrees left."

"On!"

"Fire!"

The tank caught fire and the crew bailed out.

---

Moreno's driver, witness to the destruction of his tank and his friends, dashed away and threw himself into a depression in the ground.

From there, he stood witness to the destruction of yet another of Moreno's force.

He turned when the sound of heavy breathing reached him, expecting to find a fellow tanker seeking refuge.

The Siberian Kandra ripped into his chest, and he fell bleeding into the snow.

The other Soviet soldier crawled past his gasping comrade, avoided the dying American, and slipped up to the edge of the hole. He calmly flipped up the sights of the last but one Panzerfaust his company possessed, and waited for his moment.

---

"Mohawk-six, Stonewall-one, over."

Hardegen had heard some of what had gone on, and feared the worst. It fell to the commander of one of the 808th's Jacksons to fill him in on the gory details.

Master Sergeant Christensen told the story without emotion, and in as few words as possible.

He was interrupted by the arrival of a large caliber shell.

The 100mm transited the turret from front left, brushing the breech without causing damage before striking the corner of the open turret and down through the back of the turret, carrying on to clip the rear body and burying itself in the snow a few yards from the Jackson.

No one was so much as scratched by the transit of the large shell.

"Motherfucker! Find the bastard, find him now!"

That proved a lot easier than expected, as the T54 was again producing smoke, thick oily smoke that announced its position to the world.

"Crew, bale out!"

Kolesnikov looked at his commander.

"I can try mending it. He's still alive, Comrade!"

"As are we, Oleg, but not for long if we don't get out. The gun's fucked so that's that. Now, bale out!"

He went, leaving Kon alone.

Picking out his notebook, he quickly studied the list.

Leaning forward, he grabbed the technical manual and inserted flares in it and its accompanying additional notes. He placed a shell in the breech and left it half out. A few more shells were added to the floor.

He opened a small fuel cock and fuel oil began to flow into the fighting compartment.

An enemy shell struck his tank, rocking it hard and dislodging the shell in the breech.

Kon lunged forward, and stopped the casing from dropping to the floor.

Quickly he re-inserted it and performed the final act.

He opened a small box in his position and pressed two buttons simultaneously.

Sticking his head out to check the battle situation, he was nearly decapitated by a 90mm shell screaming past the turret. As it was, the heat hurt his eyes, and he swore he could smell singed hair.

The Jackson had missed, and so he lunged for safety as the demolition charge burned away.

The results were spectacular for both the T54, and the remaining portions of the bunker position it was in.

Christensen was claiming the kill when a panzerfaust struck the glacis of his tank, wounding both men in the hull.

He grabbed the 'grease gun' and threw himself off the SP, intent on hosing down the bastard who had hit his tank.

Firing as he ran, his mind barely registered the shape of another panzerfaust emerging from the position.

He snatched for a grenade before realizing that he had none, his eyes widening as the enemy anti-tank soldier took careful aim.

Screaming like a banshee, he hurled the empty grease gun at the enemy soldier, and redoubled his efforts to close the man down before he fired.

He failed.

---

"Job tvoyu mat... but that was fucking disgusting!"

Kon couldn't agree more.

Both he and Morozov had been looking straight at the small battlefield cameo, unable to interfere, but none the less concentrating intently on who would win the small race for life or death.

Neither had expected to watch the enemy soldier transformed into a fog of liquid and small pieces by the direct strike of a panzerfaust warhead on his chest.

The firer seemed little better off, lying in the snow on the edge of his position, face down and motionless. The soldier who had been behind him seemed in a state of shock, the whole area round the vaporised American soldier transformed into one giant flower head comprising various shades of red.

The Jackson crew was too busy trying to get themselves to a position of safety to realize that their commander had given his life for them.

Checking the T54, and being satisfied that its secrets were destroyed, as per orders, Kon called his men together and they started off at the run, keen to put as much distance between them and the advancing enemy force.

### 1503 hrs, Wednesday, 11th December 1945, Strassfeld, Germany.

The advance had been stopped dead, Moreno's force gutted by the T54, some anti-tank and anti-personnel grenades, a few hand-picked anti-tank infantry, and a whole lot of good luck.

The surviving doughboys had migrated westwards, dropping into the edge of Strassfeld, where they found themselves under close assault by Artem'yev's Guardsmen.

Artem'yev's wound was painful, but did not persuade him to leave the battlefield.

He had been flung against a brick wall when an engineer charge exploded, and his arm had snapped with a sound that exceeded that of the fierce fighting taking place for every brick and stick that was once Strassfeld.

"There, we will attack there!"

His left arm tucked in his tunic and supported by bandages, he wielded his pistol, using it to inform his assault group where he intended to attack next.

"Urrah!"

The twelve man group shouted as they sprang forwards yet again, the bodies of ten of their comrades left behind in other hotly contested places.

The man running next to Artem'yev screamed and fell, rolling over a few times before coming to a silent halt.

Another took his place.

Artem'yev tried not to notice that his men migrated to positions around him, in an effort to prolong his life and preserve him from harm.

An American soldier appeared in front of him, raising his head to take a look at the attacking Russians.

Artem'yev blew the man's brains all over the wall behind him, immediately leaping in through the window the dead man had once occupied.

He overbalanced on landing, his broken arm unable to offer assistance, falling awkwardly, and smashing the broken limb into the chair the American had been resting on.

Artem'yev screamed in agony.

Another US soldier clattered round the corner into the area and put two rounds into the next Guardsman as he climbed through the window.

The Carbine shells didn't kill him, and he went down, holding his shattered crotch.

One bullet did for the next man, catching him on the bridge of the nose and scrambling the brains beyond, dropping the corpse half in, half out of the window..

Recovering himself, Artem'yev put four shots into the American, throwing him back against the door frame.

More men arrived from both sides, and the small area became a seething mass of humanity, as men battled to stay alive whilst exhibiting no humanity whatsoever.

It was truly awful, but reflected Artem'yev's plans to bring the enemy close, and was exactly the same in many other positions throughout the ruins of Strassfeld.

A man fell heavily against Artem'yev as he struggled to raise himself up, dislodging the pistol from his grasp. A second blow occurred, and the Soviet Colonel found himself face down on the floor with one man's full weight on him, plus the majority of another man's, as two soldiers strove to throttle the life out of each other.

Again, the agony of his broken arm overcame him, and he noisily vented the pain.

The weight lessened as another American soldier took an interest and joined in.

He pulled back the Soviet soldier's head and ran his knife from ear to ear, bathing both his comrade and Artem'yev in blood.

"Thank... thanks... Walter..."

The rescued man coughed and gasped his way through his thanks and stood as best he could, unwittingly allowing Artem'yev to recover his Tokarev.

Two rounds smashed into the lower back of the rescued GI, three more destroyed the chest of Walter, his saviour.

Artem'yev's intervention changed the balance in the fight, and the last armored infantryman was shot down by a burst of PPSh, leaving two survivors moaning on the floor.

An experienced corporal shot them both.

Artem'yev, deftly sliding a full magazine into his Tokarev one-handed, slapped a few shoulders and led his men on.

A grenade landed at his feet and he kicked out, making a heavy contact, and sending the deadly object back through a doorway.

It exploded, sending a shower of dust and plaster in all directions.

Some sixth sense warned Artem'yev.

"Out!"

His men threw themselves out of the windows and doors, their departure marked by the arrival of at least four more grenades.

Reduced to five men, the others had exited on the other side of the building, Artem'yev waited for the grenades to explode and then led a charge along the outside of the old stable block, turning through a damaged doorway into where he assessed the enemy grenadiers had secreted themselves.

He was spot on, and his rush found four backs turned towards him.

He shot one man between the shoulder blades, one of his men almost cutting the others in half with his PPSh.

Firing in the adjacent room caused the group to drop to the floor, using the bodies, both dead and alive, as cover.

The unmistakable sound of a PPSh announced the presence of the rest of his assault squad, and he warned his men not to be too hasty should figures appear in the entrance.

He was right, and two more of his men arrived. Eight, including himself, now mustered in what had obviously once been a tack room.

Posting two men, he permitted a moment to have a drink from canteens, but there was no time to smoke or eat.

Artem'yev could sense that the Americans were breaking.

The next position that he and his men swept into was empty, or at least occupied by men who had long since ceased to care.

US soldiers were seen scurrying between piles of rubble across the street, and a couple of Artem'yev's men contributed a few bullets to help them on their way.

Moving outside, the small assault group ran headlong into a body of armored infantrymen intent on 'repositioning' to the rear.

The lead Guardsman brought up his PPSh but was beaten to the draw by his counterpart, whose grease gun wrecked the man, and splattered the hideously wounded soldier's comrades with blood and gore.

The falling body brought Artem'yev down, and the soldier behind him followed, falling on top of his commander, winding the both of them.

The only man in the Soviet group possessing a bolt-action rifle took cool aim, and dropped the enemy soldier with a single shot, his screams loud, but brief.

Two soldiers were rolling around on the floor, each trying to gouge the eyes out of the other.

The small courtyard was suddenly too densely packed to provide room for anything of submachine gun size or above, so the two groups resorted to knives, pistol and hands to overcome their enemy.

Artem'yev, struggling to his feet, received a punch on his broken arm. The pain was extreme, and he bellowed as he crouched to protect it from more harm.

Struggling for breath he moved back, narrowly avoiding a kick aimed at sending his head into orbit.

The US soldier was off-balance, and he fell against two more soldiers struggling for supremacy. A knife quickly flashed and another GI was out of the fight, victim of one of his own and the mists of close combat.

Artem'yev struggled to wipe the tears from his eyes with his one good hand, all the time retaining a grip on the pistol in it.

His rifleman had an American soldier on the floor, his full weight pressing down on the Mosin that was placed across the man's throat.

The American was turning purple and the defending hands were weakening in their effort to push the weapon away.

An small American NCO raised his knife, intent on plunging the blade into the Guardsman's back, his face suddenly betraying shock as his strength left him in an instant, one of Artem'yev's bullets ripping through the man's chest.

He fell to the floor, dead before he had covered half the distance.

At the courtyard doorway, out of which the US troopers had charged, Artem'yev saw an enemy.

The young GI stood holding a .30cal by the triggers and barrel, pointing it into the courtyard, undecided, or just too plain scared to make a decision.

The area was rapidly emptying of American resistance, and soon the decision to fire would be more easily made.

Artem'yev put a bullet through the boy's stomach, dropping him to the ground in agony.

The last two GI's were overwhelmed and killed quickly, one earning numerous kicks for slashing the throat of the rifle soldier.

A grenade bounced off one wall and exploded.

One of Artem'yev's men squealed in pain as three fragments took him in the chest and stomach; another silently absorbed the agony of hot fragments in his thigh and arm.

Artem'yev fell against the wall and slid down it, leaving a red trail as he went.

One fragment went straight through him at the joint of neck and body, the bleeding instant and profuse.

Another slashed open his broken arm, just below the elbow.

With his injuries, the assault group lost its impetus, and the few survivors did what they could for their comrades, but advanced no more.

Elsewhere, the remainder of his Guardsmen drove back the surviving armored infantry, forcing the surviving US tanks to fall back and, by ten minutes to four, Strassfeld was wholly in the hands of the Red Army.

The snow fell thickly, covering many of the horrors.

## 1550 hrs, Wednesday, 11th December 1945, Müggenhausen, Germany.

Whilst the battle had raged in Strassfeld, Hardegen had pushed his men and tanks hard against Müggenhausen.

The promised Soviet artillery support had arrived, and was hurting the Task Force badly.

Sometime during the attack, he was unsure as to when the defining moment had occurred, Hardegen realized that his force was being beaten, and that to preserve what was left he needed to get in closer and cling to the enemy infantry for all he was worth.

As he rushed his troops forward, orders to the mortars called for the rapidest of rapid fire, and US bombs starting doing grisly work amongst the enemy infantry.

473

Only 'Bismarck' and one other Easy-Eight had made it to the edge of the village, the ISU152's proving to be awesome adversaries.

The attrition in vehicles had been extreme, and the arrival of six T34's from the 12th Guards Heavy Tank Regiment* had threatened to turn the tide.

The newly arrived Jackson had earned its keep, dispatching four of the tanks in as many minutes, proving the worth of its 90mm gun.

Fig#109 - TF Hardegen's second assault on Müggenhausen, 11th December 1945.

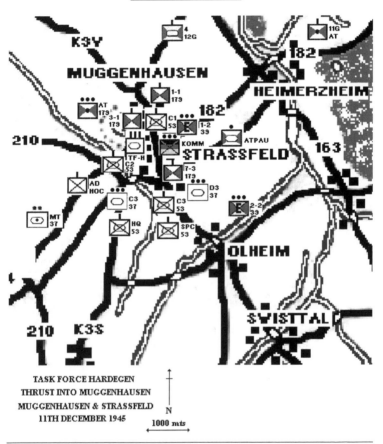

TASK FORCE HARDEGEN
THRUST INTO MUGGENHAUSEN
MUGGENHAUSEN & STRASSFELD
11TH DECEMBER 1945

N
1000 mts

One of the ISU's put a heavy shell on target, and the M36 tank-destroyer was transformed into pieces of flying scrap within a micro-second.

Hardegen's tank killed it with its second attempt, bringing his total kills in the brief combat to five.

The mixed infantry group had charged recklessly into Müggenhausen, and immediately encountered the same problems as the nightmare endured by the armored infantry in Strassberg.

The clerks and cooks tried, and no-one could have asked more of them, but they were not proper combat soldiers, and the casualties they took reflected their weaknesses, as well as the strengths of the guardsmen who fought with them.

The German unit had been there before, many of the men were veterans of the Russian front.

If it was at all possible, the close combat between the Kommando and Guards infantry was even more bestial than that elsewhere across the frontage of CCA's defeat.

The sight of hated uniforms spurred Artem'yev's men to superhuman effort; the vision of the old enemy drove the Kommandoes to incredible effort. The two combined left little room for decency and humanity, both of which took a back seat to the imperatives of survival and revenge.

Soviet artillery continued to sweep the field, and Hardegen had decided to press forward and stay in support of his infantry, rather than leave them without armor and face annihilation.

The two Shermans stood as a redoubt, and provided a rallying point for the US soldiers in Müggenhausen, standing proud around the junction of Rheinbacher and Rochus Strasses.

The 191st Artillery was keeping Hardegen's force alive, the excellence of their craft combined with the skill of the observer, Lieutenant Higgins.

An enemy rush manifested itself, and both Shermans opened up, lacing the snow and rubble with tracers, each of which was accompanied by three equally damaging but invisible friends.

The rush died in an instant, almost as if the men had immediately been recalled.

Hardegen narrowed his eyes, expecting some sort of trick.

His ears warned him first, their unspoken warning reinforced by red smoke rising from the enemy positions.

His eyes searched the snowy sky and found his nemesis immediately.

Two enemy aircraft were already lined up for an attack.

Rising up out of the turret hatch, he sensed rather than felt the zip of bullets around him, as the Soviet infantry force saw his intent and tried to put him down.

He fired the .50cal, knowing he was out of range, but using the device to warn those around him.

The two Shturmoviks, IL-2's of some age, recently recommissioned to try and make up the shortfall in Soviet striking power, drove in side by side and opened fire, each of them field modified to take improvised mounts for RS132 rockets.

They carried sixteen each, putting thirty-two in the air, targeted on an area some three hundred by four hundred yards.

Hardegen gritted his teeth and kept the .50cal going, walking his tracer stream into the left-hand aircraft without noticeable effect.

The rockets started to arrive amongst the American force.

Higgins' halftrack took a direct hit, killing the valiant artillery officer instantly.

One rocket seemed intent on coming down the barrel of his machine-gun, and Hardegen felt panic rise.

He controlled it and watched as the thing flew past and exploded behind his tank.

Swiveling the gun, he saw his bullets strike home behind the cockpit of the foremost Shturmovik.

Other rockets exploded, obscuring his view of the enemy aircraft, but he knew he had wounded it badly.

Something flew across his line of vision, this time from right to left, his imagination suggesting that more enemy aircraft had arrived, until the sight of a mangled body skidding across the snow told him otherwise.

The rockets had knocked the stuffing out of the defenders, and caused many casualties in the tight packed ruins and gardens.

The two Illyushins turned lazily and commenced a bomb run.

Each carried four hundred kilos of bombs, the leader four one hundred kilo general-purpose weapons; the second aircraft bore eight, each fifty kilos fragmentation bombs.

It was immediately obvious that the leading aircraft was using 'Bismarck' as an aiming point.

"Toss red smoke," Hardegen shouted to anyone in range; some even heard him and complied.

Blue smoke rose from the Soviet positions, showing that the man in charge there knew his job.

Another pannier of ammo had been passed up and Hardegen slapped the top of the .50cal down hard, having slipped the new belt home.

"Get out now! Quickly, boys! Move!"

His crew needed no second invitation and quickly evacuated the tank, seeking safety as far away as possible.

The Browning machine-gun started flinging lead into the air but, whether it was the increasing volume of snow in the air, nerves on the part of Hardegen, or good flying by the enemy pilot, no hits were apparent.

Two bombs dropped from the mounts, followed by two more a second later.

A bullet clipped his right arm, the enemy infantry bringing him under fire. They were champing at the bit to get at the Americans, once the aircraft had done their work.

The first bomb struck the road and deflected into the ruined artillery halftrack.

The second bomb hit dead centre of 'Bismarck's' glacis plate.

Neither exploded.

Neither did the third or the fourth, although the final bomb did kill three GI's as it wiped through their snowy redoubt like it wasn't there.

The inexperienced ground crew had failed to remove the safeties from the weapons, and the pilot, the Regimental Commander, a Colonel with a fearsome reputation, promised retribution for the risks he had faced; all for no reward. That he should have checked too did not occur to him.

He banked away hard, avoiding the tracers rising from the American position, the snow obscuring critical data for the briefest of moments, but sufficiently long enough for his misjudgement, brought on by his anger, to condemn him.

A wing tip clipped the treetops on the hill and the Illyushin wobbled, dropping lower still.

The next tree top proved more of an obstacle and the impact knocked the aircraft into a nose dive, the Shturmovik instantly burying itself in the snow.

There would be no retribution for the ground staff back at his base. Neither would there be any aircraft for them to work on this day, as four Mustangs arrived and smashed the surviving Soviet aircraft from the sky, but only after he had added his own bomb load to the mess below.

The fragmentation bombs wreaked havoc amongst the armored infantry, but completely missed the ad hoc infantry force to the west.

The Soviet infantry charged forward.

"Urrah! Urrah!"

They were met with stiff fire, but it was much reduced, and the casualties they took did not deflect them from their purpose.

Close quarter fighting ensued and crept ever closer to 'Bismarck'.

Hardegen did what he could with the MG, but the ammunition was soon gone.

Pausing only to slap his tank's side as a farewell, he strode towards the position to his front.

DeMarco lay in the ruined entranceway, shivering in the cold, part of his stomach deposited on the ground beside him, the thin sheet a medic had thrown over the desperately wounded man already moved aside by the growing breeze.

Morphine coursed through his veins, more than was necessary for pain relief, the medic deciding that he could but ease the gunner's suffering on his journey into the next life.

Shouting drew Hardegen's gaze from the dying man, and he tried to focus his eyes on the men running at him.

*'Jesus!'*

He brought up the Colt 1911A and put the leading Soviet engineer down hard. The second man had a flamethrower.

Hardegen's second and third shots spun him round as he fired, and two of his comrades took the full force of the flames.

The screams were awful as three of the Soviet engineers were consumed by fire.

A burst of submachine gun fire, originating from the Soviet side, dropped all three to the snow and ended their suffering.

Hardegen saw friendlies off to his right and moved towards them, firing off another two rounds at indistinct movement near the burning corpses.

He dropped into a position and lay on the icy floorboards, gasping for breath,

The men around him, all armored infantrymen, except for an old German in a Pickelhaube, poured fire in all directions, as the isolated post fell under determined attack.

Whilst the old German cut a comical figure in a white fur coat and with the stereotypical pointed German helmet atop his head, he clearly had seen action before, and kept his rifle firing steadily.

At least one other flamethrower was closing in, the hiss as its flame melted snow bringing fear to those who could hear its malevolent approach.

The position's commander slapped a Sergeant's shoulder, directing the man's attention to the threat.

The shot was clearly successful and the Captain moved away.

In a calculated fashion, the Sergeant took two more shots, the last of which sent a fireball through the attacking enemy engineers as it exploded the dead man's flame thrower tanks.

Hardegen was noticed and the Captain moved quickly over to his side.

"You ok, Major?"

His minor wounds had transformed his tanker's uniform into a mass of red spots, misleading the Captain into thinking that Hardegen was badly wounded.

"Fine, Captain. Are we secure here?"

"No Sir. They're all over us like a nasty fucking rash. I have a man checking out a route so as we can bug out. 'Til then, we gotta hold, Major."

479

"Ok. I could use another weapon. Whatcha got for me?"

"Plenty, Sir. They're lying around everywhere here. Help yourself. I recommend their wooden submachine gun with the round mag. Fucking lethal thing."

"OK, Captain. My tank's still running if we can get back to it. I can drive and we can ride rather than walk."

"Sounds like a plan, Major. But the commies may have their own ideas."

The officer rolled away and then scrabbled to his feet, moving off towards the farthest part of his defence.

Hardegen returned the nod from the Sergeant as he went in search of weapons.

He found them in the adjacent space; US weapons stacked on one side, Soviet weapons the other.

He took the Garand instead of the recommended PPSh, and selected ammo for both the familiar rifle and his Colt.

Against his wishes, he forced himself to pick up a bayonet and clipped it to the Garand.

Returning to the first room, he found the sergeant lying flat on his back in a pool of blood and the position now occupied solely by the comical German.

The Sergeant had no face, and the bloody mess on display grinned with bared teeth exposed where the soft tissue had been stripped away by the impact of something very solid.

The bubbles of blood showed that the horribly wounded man still lived.

Shouting something in German, the old man gestured at Hardegen, bringing him into the adjacent firing position.

Grinning as he selected a target amongst the attacking Soviet soldiers, Hardegen spoke in the old man's language.

"Ja, ich kann es ertrangen, alten Manne!"

The old soldier laughed.

He had ribbed the American officer in German, asking him if he could bear it as he brought him up into a firing position.

"Yes, I can bear it, old man," had been Hardegen's response.

The two stood side by side and shot down enemy after enemy, despite a close bullet dislodging the ridiculous Pickelhaube from the veteran's head.

The German language conversation continued, almost isolating the two from the events around them.

"Where'd you learn your soldiering then, Grandad?"

"Tannenberg, boy. My first battle. Now those Russians could fight. Then the British. Hard men, they were too. This lot are easy."

As if to mark his words, the Mauser spat another bullet into the body of a crawling Russian.

"Mind you, boy, there are a fucking lot of them!"

And then he was dead.

Neither of them had seen or heard the grenade that exploded behind them, leaving one man untouched, except for ringing in his ears, the other peppered with death-dealing shrapnel.

Seeing the explosion, a group of previously unnoticed engineers rose up and charged.

The Garand contributed one bullet before the charger leapt out, the metallic sound spelling doom for Hardegen.

He had no time to reload.

Ducking down, he avoided a burst of SMG fire by rolling to his left, over the dead body of the old man.

The first engineer lost his footing as he launched himself over the wall and dropped heavily onto the brickwork.

Hardegen lunged and the bayonet slipped into the soft flesh easily, but refused to slide out.

The bayoneted soldier provided a barrier to those following, at least long enough for the Colt to come to hand.

The next two faces that appeared got a round each, dead centre.

Another grenade was dropped over the wall, rolling alongside the corpse of the old German.

The explosion defiled his corpse but did not harm the tank officer.

A movement up high betrayed an attacker, and the Colt pumped out bullets as a shape flew through the air.

The soldier had climbed up onto the porch and thrown herself down on the American below.

Her dead weight struck him and knocked him to the floor.

The Colt was empty and there was no time for a new magazine. The old man's Mauser rifle was too far away so Hardegen grabbed what he could and defended himself.

A rifle butt slammed into his upper right chest and knocked the wind from him momentarily, but not enough to stop him flailing with the sharpened spade he had taken from the dead woman.

It cleaved the man's face to the bone and stuck in his neck for the briefest of moments.

Hardegen was becoming frenzied.

The spade came away and he lashed out at the engineer, whose weapon strap had become entangled in the ruins, depriving him of its use.

The soldier ducked and moved left, receiving a slash across the shoulder blade.

He went down as two bullets hammered into him.

The Captain had arrived with a hard-faced corporal and they shot down the remaining attackers.

Hardegen dropped to his knees, gasping, his exhaled breath almost like a cloud of steam.

The Captain unravelled the PPSh's strap from a protruding metal stanchion and handed it to Hardegen.

"Try that for size, Major."

Unable to talk, he accepted it with a nod.

The spare ammo pouch came next, after the Captain had finished off the wounded engineer.

"Bad news, Major. We're fucking surrounded. We ain't inclined to surrender either. We've seen what these bastards do to prisoners."

He moved his head, checking the enemy positions to his front and saw nothing of note.

"Less'n you got any objections, we're planning to keep this place for a'whiles longer, then bug out after dark. We've got a route planned ready for the time we can slip away."

"Fine by me, Captain."

[*12th GHTR were well-known scroungers of running tanks and are documented as having up to nine T34's on their strength at any one time, in addition to their full compliment of IS-II's]

---

That the night would bring opportunities for escape was not wasted on the Soviet force, and they quickly determined not to permit the opportunity, redoubling their efforts.

A concerted assault overran the ad hoc group of bakers and clerks, the men surrendering once the horrors of close combat started to reveal themselves.

Two brave men stalked the surviving Sherman and destroyed it with satchel charges, its destruction signaling the start of the final attack.

True to the Captain's word, the armored infantry held fast, and the whole gutter fight of blade and blood was repeated, the last few survivors of the Soviet attack either cut down or bludgeoned to the floor as day gave way to night.

Elsewhere, the news was disastrous, as the US Third Army was battered to a total halt by the Red Army's exhausted formations, and the superhuman efforts of its Air Force.

That both Soviet ground and air units paid heavily for their efforts was of no consolation to George Patton, and he was stunned to find that his normal 'get up and go at 'em' attitude failed to win the day.

At first he railed, then ranted, then tried to threaten those he visited or radioed.

Only as the day developed did Patton realize that he had lost a very major portion of his command, that his men were exhausted by their efforts, and that, in a very real sense, he had experienced a defeat.

The call he made to Bradley was the most difficult call he ever had to make, his personal feelings rising again as he spoke to his former inferior and admitted that the attack had run out of steam.

"Well, you made some ground, George. Can you hold it?"

Patton considered the reasonable question, although it felt like a slap in the face.

"Yes, Brad, we can hold, especially if the weather's gonna be as we've been told. Gonna need reinforcements though. I've lost a lot of my best boys in these hours."

Bradley gave a respectful pause, not yet appreciating how many Allied soldiers had fallen in Spectrum Blue.

"Hold what you've taken then, George. We will get you some extra men and supplies as soon as possible."

Bradley couldn't believe his ears.

"Get me them straight away and I'll push forward again before the worst of the weather sets in.

"NO! It's over, George."

"It sure as shit ain't over, Brad. I've lost a lot of boys out there and I'm gonna have some goddamned payback!"

"It's too late now, George. The weather will be on us and that will be that. Just concentrate on holding for now. That's an order."

Words guaranteed to put Patton's hackles up.

The silence was deafening.

"You know, George. Guderian lost a lot of his boys too. This one just didn't go our way, ok?"

"Yes, Sir."

"Good night, George."

"Good night... Sir."

---

CCA, 4th US Armored Division had been virtually destroyed, along with major lumps of the rest of the division... and the 17th Corps... and the Third Army.

Greenwood and his command group were, in the main, dead. The few survivors already walking through the night snow towards an uncertain fate.

Elsewhere, US 3rd Corps attack had run into trouble, as units tasked with stopping the Legion units to the south, turned north and vented their anger upon the flank of the 14th US Armored Division.

Whilst the 14th had rallied and fought off elements of both the 6th Guards Cavalry Corps and 25th Tank Corps, the opportunity to advance did not exist, and the unit slipped into defence.

To the north of Cologne, the advance of Guderian's forces had been painfully slow and costly beyond measure, the recently formed Panzer-Grenadier Division Deutschland virtually destroyed as it threw itself on the Soviet defences.

Other German Republican forces had suffered badly, and the German attack had also come to a halt in front of Burscheid and Leverkusen.

The weather played its part, snow reducing visibility and proving a leveler, reducing the effectiveness of the Allied formations.

In the air, the situation was less clear, with both sides having successes and failures, although the claims of the Allied pilots would indicate a three to one ratio of kills on the day.

### 2120 hrs, Wednesday, 11th December 1945, Müggenhausen, Germany.

His mind started to clear, first recognizing the coldness of the air that entered his lungs.

His body came alive slowly, the aches and pains of wounds and bruises making themselves known as his mind sorted through the signals one by one.

He groaned, an immense headache coming out on top of his internal cataloging of his problems.

He raised his hand to his head, or rather tried, instead finding that he couldn't because he was under something heavy.

His eyes opened reluctantly, but he found things were fine, the soft light of a burning building ample to see by but not enough to make the headache worse.

The weight was a body.

Extricating an arm, he tried rolling the corpse down his body, but found it impossible.

Using both arms, he got a purchase and eased the cadaver enough to be able to bring his body into play.

His arms protested, as did his back, and his legs, but he extricated himself and fell against the damaged wall, panting with the exertion of it all.

The light of the fire illuminated the face of the armored infantry Captain, frozen in horror and incredulity, as a burst from a submachine gun had ripped him from crotch to neck.

Fig#110 - The end at Müggenhausen, 11th December 1945.

TASK FORCE HARDEGEN
MUGGENHAUSEN - THE END
MUGGENHAUSEN & STRASSFELD
11TH DECEMBER 1945

N
1000 mts

TASK FORCE HARDEGEN WAS
VIRTUALLY DESTROYED ON 11TH
DECEMBER 1945. ITS SURVIVING
UNITS WERE ABSORBED INTO
OTHERS IN 4TH US ARMORED DIV

ADDITIONAL SOVIET
UNIT THAT TOOK PART
IN THE BATTLE.

ADDITIONAL SOVIET UNIT THAT
ARRIVED TO LATE FOR THE
BATTLE.

There were more bodies, all of them in olive drab, and bearing the insignia of the 4th US Armored on their upper sleeves.

Hardegen looked around and found his Colt with ease, spending much more time looking for the spare clip.

There were no Soviet bodies, the victors having taken them away for proper respects to be paid.

The tank officer tried to remember what had happened, but only flashes of memory suggested themselves to him, not enough to recall how the full details of those last few minutes, but enough to suggest to him that his lack of memory was an advantage.

Now, out from under the protection of the body, the cold started to affect him and he sought extra layers as the temperature dropped dramatically.

He scrabbled on all fours, moving into other areas, finding little of value, every US body having been stripped down to the shirts and trousers, every item of winter gear removed by the victors.

He found a helmet comforter and sliced it open, slipping it over his head and around his throat, to act as a scarf.

One of the armored infantrymen was quite large and his trousers offered a warming second layer for his legs but, stiff with frozen blood and urine, they proved impossible to remove from the corpse.

A canteen missed by the Russians offered hope and its contents burned his throat. Whatever it was, it tasted good, and gave him the impetus to move on.

The old man lay there, his corpse violated even in death. The German uniform had proven too much of a provocation and they had beaten the old body, urinated and defecated on it in their memory of the years that the Motherland was subjected to death and hardships by the hands of the German Invaders.

Whilst the thought was abhorrent to Hardegen, he understood that he had to have it to survive, so he eased the ripped and bloodied white fur coat off the stinking corpse, tidied it up as best he could, and then slipped it on, immediately feeling the benefits.

Hope rose in him and he searched around for a weapon. The Soviet PPSh had disappeared, as had any of the Soviet equipment. The Garand was proving very popular with the Soviet soldier, and they had also been taken away.

The Mauser rifle lay where it had been dropped.

Before he picked it up, he checked that the metallic weight in the coat pocket was ammunition for the venerable rifle.

It was, and so he felt properly armed again.

Hardegen moved quietly through the ruins, the soft sounds of singing and soldiers relaxing penetrating the relative silence that night had brought to the battlefield.

He froze as two sentries walked slowly through the rubble towards him.

Thinking quickly, he hid in plain sight, lying down next to some more dead GI's, the white coat concealing most of him in the reduced light, although the tiredness of the two soldiers played its part as well.

The sentries moved on.

Hardegen came to the place where his gunner had been wounded, but the body was gone.

For a moment, his hopes rose, but his mind brought him back down to earth, throwing up images of the wounded DeMarco that suggested the man was long dead.

As he moved towards 'Bismarck' something in the sky above exploded, the flash being enough to betray the face of a sentry posted on the tank.

Whilst every essence of his being told him to move on, he decided to do what he could and prevent 'Bismarck' falling into enemy hands.

The first part was easy, the soft snores betraying the sentry's lack of alertness, and condemning him to death.

Normally, Hardegen did his killing at distance from within an impersonal metal box, but this day had brought forth new horrors for him to experience.

He looked at the man from cover.

Small.

Older, certainly a father, probably a grandfather.

*'You or me, Tovarich.'*

He had learned his lessons well and the sentry's throat was quickly opened to the elements, the hot blood steaming in the sub-zero night air. Hardegen held the man tight as the engineer struggled against the inevitability of his approaching death.

He moved quietly and slipped inside the tank, using his knife to saw through cables and prise gauges from their mounts.

Knowing he needed to put distance between himself and Müggenhausen, Hardegen decided to concoct a plausible scene.

The small body was easily moved, although not without blood spilling down his already soiled fur coat. The dead Russian was dropped inside the tank.

The blood was everywhere in any case, but the freshness of the recent kill betrayed itself, so Hardegen spent a few moments grinding it into the snow and making it look more like the product of the afternoon's fighting.

In the rear box, he found the twine he sought and slipped it into his pocket.

Once in the turret, he used his torch to see what he was doing.

The vehicle had not been looted and contained a lot of what he would need to survive.

He would give up the Mauser when he had made it to a safer distance, but the Thompson was to be his preferred weapon and he placed it on the turret roof, along with the spare clips.

Chocolate bars and cigarettes were harvested from all sorts of nooks and crannies, even ration packs were found, and soon he needed a bag in which to carry his 'fortune'.

The grenades, there were two, were tied together and then wired to the floor of the turret. Four HE shells were added to the pile, as well as all the grease and oil containers he could find.

Tying the twine to end pin of the grenades, he took a last look at the 'Bismarck' before slipping out of the Sherman. He emptied a can of petrol into the compartment and then policed up his items and moved away.

The twine was only forty-three metres long, but he found a good position and made ready.

Sensibly, he decided to check the route he intended to use and quickly satisfied himself that it was clear.

He pulled hard on the twine.

It separated in front of his gaze, a weak point giving way some few feet in front of him.

Slipping back out into the snow, he tied a knot and joined the two ends firmly.

He pulled again, once back in cover.

The sound of one explosion was clearly heard and was certainly enough to bring investigation.

An occasional tongue of yellow betrayed a fire within the tank, satisfying Hardegen that he had achieved the destruction of 'Bismarck'.

He pushed the Mauser into the snow and pulled more over the top, hiding the weapon from casual inspection.

Picking up his bag, and the thompson, he turned to leave.

The bayonet doubled him over as it was rammed into his stomach.

Hardegen dropped to the knees, but was held upright by the wicked blade and rifle.

The Soviet Guardsman gently turned the rifle and with it, the steel inside Hardegen, twisting the wound in such a way as to make the American scream in pain.

A second bayonet slammed into him, adjacent to the first, both infantrymen determined to make the Amerikanski suffer for the deaths of their comrades.

The long blades were pulled out simultaneously, permitting Hardegen to slump to the ground.

The first soldier prodded him in the shoulder, hard enough to draw blood, but not sufficient to penetrate deeply.

The second man chose the thigh for his next thrust, glancing off the femur, and bringing louder screams from the American.

The Soviet rifleman laughed, for all of two seconds, until his comrade's head exploded, destroyed by a point blank shot from Hardegen's Colt.

The Mosin exploded in his hands, the finger automatically triggering off a round. Hardegen's femur did not survive the passage of the 7.62mm round.

Hardegen's next three shots blew out his spine, and the man was thrown across the space and into the snow.

The destruction of the Sherman had started a response, and the additional sounds of screams and firing had ensured that the entire Soviet force stood to.

Through the extremes of pain, Hardegen heard running feet and prepared the pistol, although he couldn't seem to manage to hold it up now.

His eyes were growing misty.

A shape came into view, silhouetted against the growing fire in 'Bismarck', followed by another, then more.

The weight of the Colt was too much and it stubbornly refused to rise from the snow.

His vision cleared, albeit for just a moment, allowing him to watch his tank explode internally.

Hardegen smiled.

The Soviet officer brought up his PPD and emptied it into Hardegen at point-blank range.

Bailianov replaced the magazine and spat on the riddled corpse, directing his men to retrieve the bodies of their comrades.

The snow redoubled its efforts and fell thickly to ground, covering the bodies of two thousand men and women who had fallen in a single battle.

Tomorrow would be another day.

*All skill is in vain when an angel pees in the touchhole of your musket.*

*German proverb.*

# Chapter 121 - DER SCHWALBE

### 1239 hrs, Friday, 13th December 1945, approaching Baltiysk Airfield, USSR.

Djorov had recovered his sense of humour, his November near-miss slowly becoming more distant in the memory.

The problems with the Yakolev-9 meant that he asked for, and was given, permission to rejoin his command, whilst the engineers fixed the problems with the revolutionary plane.

The 2nd Guards Fighter Regiment was Djorov's pride and joy. Its pilots were veterans, all skilled in the arts and intricacies of flying combat aircraft and, most importantly, staying alive.

2nd Guards had been spared from the blood-letting over the Baltic, set aside as a reserve by Red Air force Command, just in case of some allied lunge at the Motherland.

2nd Guards was also very different to other Soviet fighter units, in that it flew all conceivable types of aircraft, testing, in battle conditions, the limitations and capabilities of each.

Which brought Djorov and his men to the task in hand, conducting take-offs and landings from reduced length runways.

Higher authority had decided that the results of using a full length runway, painted to set out a shorter length, would be unreliable, as there would be less pressure on the pilot to get the landing right.

As is the way of such things across the armies of the world, Djorov and his men were not consulted on this decision, just given their orders, which permitted them to curse the leadership for their stupidity. However, secretly, some thought that it might be a reasonable point.

Today, a flight of aircraft from the 2nd Guards was practicing on the runway at Baltiysk, having flown the short distance from their home base at Lugovoye, until recently the Luftwaffe airfield of Gutenfeld, set adjacent to Königsberg, some forty kilometres to the east.

The Yaks, LaGGs, and MiGs had all landed safely, although that wasn't always the case.

The previous day had seen two old campaigners die.

The first, a Hero of the Soviet Union, had crashed on landing when his Focke-Wulf Ta152 lost part of its landing gear.

Half an hour later, another experienced pilot died when he failed to recover from an accidental spin.

It was a hard double blow to a unit that had suffered very little in the new war.

Those pilots that had already landed gathered to watch their commander perform the most difficult task of the first session.

In the control tower, landing clearance was given, and the betting concluded.

---

"Blyad!"

Djorov knew he had messed it up again and hit the throttles.

The twin Jumo turbojets roared in response to the call for additional power, and the ME 262 sprang back into the sky once more.

In the control tower, a greasy hand swept up the handful of roubles, the winner permitting himself a throaty laugh before he considered the new proposition from the radio operator.

"Deal."

More roubles were placed out and the tower crew turned back to see where the ex-German fighter was now.

Djorov knew that he needed to clear his mind. Three failures in a row was too much, so he exercised his command decision-making powers and altered the schedule.

"Svetlana, Svetlana, Swallow-One, discontinuing landing cycle... now on performance testing. Will return to landing cycle in two-zero minutes, over."

'Svetlana' responded, eyeing the roubles on the top of his radio cabinet.

"Swallow-One, Svetlana, Received. Out."

The radio operator eyed the old Sergeant suspiciously.

"Leave it there 'til he gets back then eh? It'll keep, boy."

He nodded, leaning back to stare up into the bright snowless sky, hearing the ME 262, but not seeing it.

---

With plenty of fuel onboard, Djorov had decided that an altitude test would help relax him before he tried the landing again.

The problem was that the ME 262 needed at least one thousand two hundred metres to land on, whereas he was trying to put the aircraft down on one thousand and a bit.

He had joked that the bit could be all important.

As the Allies knocked out more and more airfields, the Red Air Force had turned to using roads and autobahns, just as the Luftwaffe had done in 1945.

Those pieces of road that were of an appropriate length had also started to receive attention from enemy bombers, so the 2nd was ordered to find procedures to shave take-off and landing distances from all types of aircraft.

As a number of ME 262s had fallen into Soviet hands, it was considered important to get them into combat as soon as possible. Pilots were in training for the task, and Djorov was expected to present his written report on new procedures before the end of December, hence the additional pressure he felt.

For now, that pressure was lifted by the sheer joy of uninhibited high speed flight.

Enjoying the sunlight, not totally believing the reports that most of Europe lay under a blanket of snow and afflicted by record lows, he drove his aircraft upwards, gaining height easily as the big turbojets consumed fuel, further lightening the aircraft.

The ceiling for the ME 262 Schwalbe was supposed to be eleven and a half thousand metres, but issues with the quality of fuel had kept the three birds that 2nd Guards operated to well below eleven thousand.

The latest fuel issue had promised much, the recently discovered ex-Luftwaffe stock instantly set aside purely for the jet fighters.

And so it proved, Djorov's delight at soaring past eleven thousand growing as the Schwalbe exhibited no signs of slowing.

It was a beautiful day to be a fighter pilot.

---

On the ground at Karup, the mission had seemed more than reasonable.

Now, literally in the cold light of day, the bomber crew felt less than happy.

Captain Barnes pushed the aircraft as high as he could, but it was probably still within the capabilities of most Soviet aircraft.

Of some comfort was the full squadron of Mustangs that flew beneath the single aircraft, and the two groups that were sweeping ahead.

One of his crew had already witnessed a fireball a few thousand feet below, where a single Soviet interceptor had met a premature end at the hands of the escort.

Enemy activity was light, in fact, they had been told to expect none of note.

The true bonus for the men of the misleadingly named '63rd Reconnaissance Training Section' was that Spectrum Red had hammered most of the Soviet units that could have sprung to the defence of their 'target'

The mission could have been run over friendly territory, with different parameters, without the fanfares that had accompanied the briefing; most certainly without the two scientists onboard.

However, the hierarchy had decided to conduct the dry run over enemy air space, a decision on which Barnes and the rest of his crew had not been consulted.

Never a man to take things for granted, Barnes was on the case of his gunners, making sure that no one would sneak up on his pride and joy, 'Jenni Lee'.

Since he and his crew had landed at Maaldrift in Holland, the brand new silver-plate B-29 had been secreted away on the edge of the large air base, shrouded in secrecy, permitting a small work team to work on further converting the already modified bomb bay.

On the 3rd of December, 'Jenni Lee' had made the short trip from Maaldrift, landing in total secrecy at Karup Airfield, Denmark.

Today, the B-29 was tasked with making a high altitude precision run against the city of Königsberg, not releasing, but testing the procedures for release for a city attack.

Once the attack practice run was complete, the weapon would be released on a small Soviet airbase at Baltiysk, where its six thousand, three hundred pounds of Composition B explosive filler was expected to do good work.

It was a pumpkin bomb, a device that resembled the real thing in every dimension and detail. Whilst the Pumpkin was a deadly device in its own right, the weapon it mimicked was far more lethal.

The bomb bay contained a substitute for an Atomic bomb.

"Navigator to Pilot. Standby for course change. Come right to 102° on my mark."

The mission, when it came, would require pinpoint navigation, so it was practiced constantly.

"Navigator to Pilot, course 102°. On my mark... five... four... three... two... one... mark."

The B-29 dropped its right wing as Barnes moved the 'Jenni Lee' onto a course of 102°, and a rendezvous with the city of Königsberg.

---

The rate of climb had slowed dramatically and Djorov levelled his Schwalbe out.

*'One-one-six-seven-five metres? Not bad at all!'*

The new fuel had obviously done wonders.

It was the best he had achieved to date.

Perhaps the ground crew's efforts at polishing the fuselage and lightening the load had also not been in vain.

His mouth split so wide in its grin that the smile might have been seen from the ground had it not been immediately terminated as a flash told Djorov that he was not alone.

---

The bombardier, Capt Philip Bradford, was one of the best in the business, which you had to be to get a foothold on one of the 63rd's aircraft.

His Medal of Honor had helped, well earned during the horrendous second raid on Schweinfurt.

But his skill in the black art of dropping bombs was legendary, and the 63rd had come looking for him when it was first put together.

His cat like vision now came into play, and he saw the threat.

"Pilot, bomb aimer. Aircraft at 12 o'clock high. Type unknown, but he's coming straight at us. Jeepers but he's fast."

The plan had been that any threat would result in a mission abort, and the thing that was closing, seemingly at the speed of light, was undoubtedly a threat.

"Radio, call the escort. Tell 'em we got company and get 'em up here fast."

Barnes gripped the controls firmly, assessing the approaching aircraft, realising that it was growing unexpectedly larger with each passing second.

*'Jeez but he's fast!'*

"Gunners, pilot. We'll pass him down our port side. Stay alert, cos he's going like mustang that sat on a cactus!"

The words were hardly out of his mouth before the enemy aircraft had gone past.

Not a gun was fired.

"Port waist to Pilot. What the fuck is that thing?"

Port waist had spent his war fighting the Japanese, so had only heard tales about the Schwalbe.

The tail gunner had spent his time over Europe so was confident in his reply.

"Port waist, Tail. I confirm that as a Messerschmitt two-six-two turbojet fighter. Aircraft recognition needed lessons for you, Arnie!"

"Pilot to all positions, Keep it tight. What's he doing, tail?"

"Coming round, big arc... round to our starboard side. He's too fast. Reckon he's a new boy, skipper."

---

*'Incredible!'*

Djorov had been flying the ME 262 Schwalbe for some time now, but never in combat, and the stresses, strains, and nuances, were very different.

He had made a hash of his direct attack and now, repeated the error in his efforts to attack the rear of the huge bomber.

As he struggled to sort out his manoeuvring issues, he went through the mental list he had recently read regarding the leviathan.

*'B-29 Superfortress, four engines... eleven crew... pressurized crew compartments for high altitude work... radar bombing sight... top speed three-fifty... something... errr...doesn't matter... twelve to fourteen machine guns... up to ten thousand kilos of bombs... suka!'*

His eyes caught movement and he concentrated on it, discovering four Mustangs rising up to meet him.

Still, he decided he had time for an attack, provided he could sort himself out.

---

"Tail, Pilot. He ain't read the notes for sure. He can't seem to get into an attack position."

Barnes had seen the ME 262 streak past, heading back towards where it had come. Still not one shot had been fired by either side, but he was experienced enough to suspect that wouldn't last.

"Crew, Pilot. I'm going to drop height and turn towards our fighter escort. No sense in staying up here now... and we are turning for home."

The navigator had already fired off a position for the radio operator to report back, and now passed on the course needed to take them back to Karup.

'Jenni Lee' turned lazily and bled off height.

---

The Schwalbe flicked around to port. Djorov, conscious of the rising fighters, suddenly realized that the lumbering heavy bomber was in the perfect line before him.

Reacting quickly, Djorov decided to lose speed, something normally abhorrent to any fighter pilot.

The momentum took the Schwalbe forward, but the lessening of the throttle gave him a precious extra second of time to line up for a perfect shot.

The German aircraft was equipped with four Mk108 cannons, especially designed to knock American bombers out of the air.

Normally, only four hits out of its sixty six round capacity had been required to knock a B-17 from the sky.

The payback was that the range needed to be short and, for a fast mover like the 262, that brought other issues for the pilot.

Djorov thumbed the triggers, and the maschinen-kanone spat out a mix of 30mm HE and AP shells.

But only for a moment… and in that moment Djorov realized where his crew had made some extra weight savings.

Each kanone had only ten shells, and all of them were either in the air or buried inside the Superfortress.

He ignored the metallic thuds, reacted like a cobra, and tweaked his wing position so as not to collide with the tail plane of the huge bomber.

He streaked away, suddenly aware that the thuds had done something of note to his aircraft, the gauges for the right-hand turbojet all recording dramatic events within the cowling.

---

"Got the motherfucker! That's one to the Arnoldman!"

In his joy, Sergeant Carnegie had failed to realize that his position was equally precarious.

'Jenni Lee' was on borrowed time.

Barnes was emitting low animal-like moans, his hands gripping the controls as best he could whilst his eyes swept the gauges, narrowed against the chilled air that flooded in through the shattered Perspex.

Both his feet had all but gone, and he touched protruding bone to the bits of pedals that were left.

He passed out, and the Superfortress started a last roll to the right.

Bradford checked his body for missing portions and surprised himself by finding everything present. Considering the state of what was left of the nose cone, he was lucky to be alive.

Moving back into the aircraft, he felt the roll to the right before he realized the cause.

Barnes had regained consciousness, but was fading fast.

Bradford had been in this situation before.

He grabbed the half of the co-pilot that still occupied the seat and slid it away, climbed in, ignoring the wet and sticky residue.

"I got her, Skipper. Give her to me now."

Major Barnes held firm.

"Bomb-aimer to crew. I need someone on the flight deck now."

There was only silence.

---

The ME 262 was also dying.

Djorov, more by luck than judgement, regained a vestige control of his aircraft and dived away from the Mustangs, who moved to the stricken bomber rather than pursue him.

Joy turned to fear as he realized there were others rising up towards him, and he battled with the tactical problems as well as tackling the issues presented by an aircraft trailing flame and smoke from one of its engines.

He tried his radio again, but it was still dead.

He knew it was there, he had used it, but it didn't stop him wondering if the crew had removed that as well.

The thought amused him, but only until the right engine started to come apart, streaming pieces of metal behind him.

The streamlined aircraft was now flying like a house brick, but at least he was pointing in the right direction.

Keeping an eye on the vengeful Mustangs, he drove the Schwalbe as hard as he dared towards Baltiysk.

In the rear of the American aircraft, three gunners and the radar operator had no idea what was going on up front but, whatever it was, they knew it was bad.

The starboard waist gunner, Pops, had simply appeared to give up and die. There was not a mark on him, but he had gone to meet his maker none the less.

The cannon shells that struck 'Jenni Lee' had severed the communication system between front and back, as well as killed or wounded everyone of the air crew in the front section, save Bradford.

Both port engines were now stopped and feathered, the fire suppression system having done its job well.

Bradford surveyed the instrumentation and read 'Jenni Lee's' doom in the ones that worked.

A hand touched his arm, making him jump.

"Are we gonna die?"

He snatched a look and saw the terrified face of one of the scientists, the man's clothing covered with the blood of another.

"Not if I can fucking help it, Mister. Who's left back there?"

The civilian was so far beyond his comfort zone that he couldn't find the words.

He just shook his head.

"Ok, Mr Scientist. You get the aid kit and look after my pilot. Get them legs bandaged up, and get him laid down behind us here."

The aircraft lurched, giving the petrified man impetus.

Bradford felt the pressure and applied more left stick to try and keep the aircraft level. Things were starting to deteriorate, and he knew they wouldn't get back to Karup.

"Shit!"

The altitude had disappeared and he hadn't really noticed. The water was so much closer and distinct, each wave top easily picked out.

Both starboard engines were giving up full power but 'Jenni Lee' was still dropping. Both starboard engines were also running very, very hot.

Bradford his decision.

501

"Mister Scientist, I'm gonna have to put her down in the wet while I've got some engine power left."

"He's dead."

His head jerked around, taking in the wide staring eyes of the man who had been his best friend.

He concentrated on the aircraft again, using the moment to deal with the pain of his loss.

Ahead, through the tears, he saw something that offered hope.

"Mister, you better tie yourself into that seat, 'cause God just offered us some hope."

He nodded at the pilot's seat, and watched as the scientist made a right hash of the buckles.

Once the man was secured, Bradford briefed him on what he intended to do.

"Look ahead there... see... an island. I'm gonna try and beach the 'Jenni Lee', or ditch her as close as possible, so we got a chance to swim or wade ashore, ok?"

The civilian's terror knew no limits, and he started to rock uncontrollably.

"You'll be alright, Mister. Now, sit back... and enjoy the ride!"

'Jenni Lee' descended until she was almost kissing the Baltic.

### 1304 hrs, Friday, 13th December 1945, approaching Baltiysk Airfield, USSR.

A dozen Yak-9's had happened on the scene and an air battle ensued, the result of which, quite surprisingly, was in the balance. Four from each side had been knocked out of the sky, leaving the Soviet Fighter regiment with a two aircraft numerical advantage.

It also meant that the US fighter squadron had no inclination to chase Djorov further, so his approach to Baltiysk was unhindered, except for the fact that the Schwalbe was failing fast.

"I can't get through, Comrade Polkovnik."

Unsurprising, not that they knew it, for Djorov's radio pack looked like Norwegian Jarlsberg.

The base commander was now in the control tower, the excitement and anticipation having filtered through to his office and broken into his traditional afternoon nap.

He had eyed the pile of roubles with suspicion at first, but allowed them to remain there, conscious that life for the tower crew had little excitement.

Or at least hadn't had until today.

The small smudge on the horizon had started to grow, and it could only be Djorov returning.

"Get the fire tender moving."

The Sergeant moved swiftly, conscious of the fact that the money had been spotted, and keen to keep the base commander happy.

The ancient fire truck moved off within a minute, its bell ringing for all its worth, the old men who comprised its crew trying desperately to remember which end of the hose was which. Baltiysk was a very quiet backwater, and their skills, such as they were, were rarely needed. In fact, never needed, until today.

The ME 262 was closer now, and clearly in a great deal of trouble.

Down by the runway, the officers and men of the 2nd Guards gathered to witness their leader's return.

---

"Job tvoyu mat!"

The undercarriage refused his reasonable order to lower and engage. The hydraulics had been another victim to the heavy .50cal rounds that had ravaged his aircraft.

The balance between bleeding off speed, and not falling from the sky like a lead balloon, was consuming his attention, and Baltiysk was approaching fast.

There would be no chance of a second effort.

Djorov held the stick firmly, sensing the aircraft through its vibrations, adjusting as his instincts came more into play.

The Schwalbe dropped lower, and he applied a little more engine power.

The port turbofan changed tone dramatically, protesting at some unseen problem.

*'Blyad.'*

However, the extra knots he had coaxed from it did the job, and the aircraft steadied for sufficient time.

He started humming something faintly musical. Nothing he had heard before, just a few mixed notes suggested by a mind more occupied with deep concentration.

*'The runway's closing fast.'*

He adjusted throttle.

*'The Schwalbe's going too fast.'*

The angle of the stick altered slightly in response.

*'The runway is nearly underneath me.'*

More stick.

*'The Schwalbe is going too fucking fast!'*

Less throttle…watch stall.

*'The runway is…'*

He cut the power and placed the engine pods on the concrete surface as a tender lover places his hand on the shoulder of his woman.

Gently, softly, like a caress.

*'Yes!'*

The sound was excruciating. The light cowlings disintegrated, bringing both engines into contact with the runway.

Both engines came apart bit by bit.

Suddenly, the Schwalbe angled and the tail bit into the concrete, ripping off a sizeable portion instantly.

The port engine started to bite harder and the ME 262 swung to that side, feinting towards the trees before the starboard engine dug in and the port engine broke away with half the wing, the spectacular ignition of aviation spirit causing more than one of the old firefighters to consider immediate desertion.

The veteran fire tender labored towards the oncoming aircraft, careful to avoid any possible clash.

Djorov clung to the stick, leaning one way then the other, moving the controls from side to side in a useless attempt to steer his blazing aircraft.

Before he knew it, the sound of tortured metal had gone and the Schwalbe was stationary.

He pushed on the canopy and felt the full heat of the fuel fire on his left cheek.

Rolling out to the right, he fell onto the concrete, the hand he put out to steady his fall doing nothing more than striking the runway first, dislocating his little finger before the rest of his body hit hard.

Two puffing firefighters dashed in and dragged the aching pilot clear, whilst the others, surprisingly swift in their work, applied foam to the spreading fire.

Djorov dragged himself to his feet and brushed himself down, the dislocated little finger suddenly announcing its presence when he caught it in his lifejacket.

Examining the destroyed aircraft, he marveled at the number of holes he could see.

The Superfortress gunners had hit him hard, and he knew he was lucky to be alive.

Members of his regiment started to arrive and more than one offered up a cigarette or a canteen of fiery liquid.

Questions about the enemy contact were greeted with confirmation of damaging the enemy leviathan so severely that Djorov doubted it would make it home.

The spirits lifted, and many a swig of something non-regulation was taken in celebration.

Now that he had seen that his commander and friend was uninjured, Djorov's second in command strolled around the peripheries, making a great play of looking at the runway, up and down, grabbing his chin and looking thoughtful.

Captain Oligrevin was not only the second in command of 2nd Guards; he was also a notorious clown.

Djorov moved over, a gaggle of his men moving in his wake, keen to listen in.

"So, Comrade Oligrevin, are you not happy to see me safe and sound?"

The Major look at Djorov as if it was the first time he had noticed him.

"Of course, I'm delighted by your survival, Comrade PodPolkovnik, truly I am."

Djorov, his hands trembling a little as the shock started to work on his system, understood the false mocking tone for what it was.

"Come on, man, spit it out. Did you see promotion and command as I came fluttering by, eh?"

"Well, Comrade, you know me. Always the man for the mission."

Behind Djorov, men lifted by their commander's survival started to grin.

"You are a model second in command, Comrade Mayor."

"I know, Sir. So may I be the first to congratulate you on completing your mission."

Djorov suddenly got it, as did a few of the others. He decided not to spoil Oligrevin's moment.

"Comrade PodPolkovnik, I believe you achieved the allocated task in approximately... eight hundred metres."

The roars were genuine, as was the heavy slap that Djorov.

Djorov actually found himself checking the distance.

"Not quite what the Rodina expected of you, Comrade PodPolkovnik, but I'm sure your report will do your efforts justice."

"I'm also sure it will, Comrade Mayor. And to honour your efforts, you get to drive the other Swallow tomorrow."

All pretence gone, the two men hugged and kissed as only Russian men who have shared great dangers could do.

## 1304 hrs, Friday, 13th December 1945, approaching Østerkær Island, Sweden.

The Superfortress skimmed the ice-cold water with her left wing but Bradford exerted all his strength and recovered just in time.

Straightening the wounded beast, he assessed the distance to the shoreline and decided that now was the time.

"Brace yourself, Mister."

He angled the fuselage, and immediately the rear end started to bump on the water.

In the rear, the rest of the crew, unaware of Bradford's plans, panicked.

The shoreline approached as the friction started to rob the 'Jenni Lee' of momentum.

One last effort on the stick kept the aircraft 'airborne' for a few more seconds, before the fuselage dropped and started to skim, all the while the propellers on the starboard side turning, lashing the water, bending and starting to destroy themselves.

The feathered port props created drag themselves.

There was no control now, and Bradford could only watch, almost in slow motion, as the nose hit the water and a virtual tidal wave was scooped up and thrown at the two men in the pilot's seats.

He couldn't see and couldn't breathe, his mask ripped off and the weight of water pushing him into the seat.

He used his other senses, and realized the aircraft was slowing considerably now.

In his mind he had the picture of where he was, and what he hoped would happen.

Medal of Honor holder or not, he was scared of water, and had tried to ensure that 'Jenni Lee' would slide onto the low beach and he would walk off as dry as a bone.

Dry he certainly wasn't, but the thump and then scream of tortured metal told him the Superfortress had reached the beach, and he felt relief beyond measure.

The beach was quite flat, slightly angled up from the water's edge, with only two obstructions, large rocks, to possibly impede the progress of the 'Jenni Lee'.

The shattered nose hit the larger of the two rocks and folded, the impact slowing the forward rush until there was nothing but the sound of water dripping and gurgling within the cockpit area.

The civilian engineer retrieved himself from the fantasy world in which he had cocooned himself to avoid the terrors of his approaching death.

He checked himself out, first mentally, and then physically, his hands finding everything where it should be and no damage of note.

The gurgling sound that he had heard actually wasn't water at all.

It was Bradford.

In the final impact, a piece of aluminium strut had been pushed forward like a lance, and caught him in the lower throat, raising him up out of the seat by two feet and holding him firmly in place.

The blood dripped down the metal, combining with the fuel and water mixture that started to drain out of the holes and gaps that the fight and crash had created.

From outside, the red streaks could be seen running freely from holes, as blood drained from a number of bodies, those in the back of the Superfortress having all died in the crash.

The gurgling stopped, which left only the civilian and the seagulls to survive the cold night to come.

*If you kill enough of them, they stop fighting.*

*Curtis Lemay*

# Chapter 122 - THE CHARGE

In the north of China, the cold weather was having a negative effect upon the military plan, but only slowing it, not bringing it to a halt. That was partially because the Red Army and Japanese soldiers were performing brilliantly, and partially because the Chinese Nationalist enemy was greatly weakened.

Central China was relatively inactive now, most main objectives taken, and the enemy being held in place without any difficulty, although further advances were on hold, pending the resolution of the difficulties in the south.

Marshall Vassilevsky was in pensive mood.

The central and southern areas were solely staffed by Japanese forces and, whilst their military ability was unquestioned, their technical capability and logistic issues were causing major problems, even to the point where Chinese and American counter-attacks were starting to show successes.

His paratrooper operations, previously cancelled, were converted into a major relocation of Soviet airborne forces, landing infantry units, lock, stock and barrel, in the southern force zone, where they could add to the Japanese efforts and, hopefully, restart the advance.

The heavier weapons, tank, artillery and vehicles, would come by train.

A new force, the Third Red Banner Army, was created around four key units; 31st Rifle Corps, 1st NKVD Parachute Brigade, 4th Tank Corps, and 2nd Guards Rocket Barrage Division. Other smaller support units would be attached and sent south as transport capacity became available.

His CoS, Colonel-General Lomov, was already having issues with the transport plan. The senior Japanese Liaison officer, Major General Yamaoka, was screaming down the phone to some unfortunate officer whose job was to sort out the difficulties at Nanjing, where two trains, containing tanks from the 4th Tank Corps, had come off the rails, paralysing the network, and requiring following units to redirect through other, longer routes.

That would have been enough to exercise all three men as it was, without the newly arrived report from Jingjiang, where US naval aviators had taken down the road and rail bridges over the Yangtze, further complicating the logistics of the Soviet move.

US warships sailed virtually unchallenged off the coast. The Japanese air assets were held back by the Imperial Command to support the new assaults and to protect vital assets.

Without an element of humour, Vassilevsky had quite reasonably stated to Yamaoka that a rail bridge over the Yangtze could quite reasonably be seen to be vital.

"Nikolai Andreevich, make a note. Ask our esteemed comrades in Pacific Fleet Command... and our esteemed allies of the Imperial Navy and Air Force," Lomov swallowed noisily, betraying his anger with the situation, "And ask nicely," Vassilevsky knew his CoS could be quite abrupt at times, "Tell them we need them to do something about the enemy carrier force in the East China Sea. Matter of importance and urgency et cetera, et cetera. Explain the reasons. Send it from me."

Vassilevsky, waiting on a new batch of fresh coffee, caught the eye of his CoS and raised an eyebrow in warning. Colonel-General Lomov accepted the admonishment with a shrug.

"Now, gentlemen, we need to make sure that Okamura knows of the delays and acts accordingly. General Yamaoka?"

"At once, Marshal Vassilevsky."

The Japanese officer strode from the room, intent on phoning Yasuji Okamura direct.

In the absence of a decent drink, Vassilevsky fell back on his trusty pipe.

"So, the NKVD brigade is there... and it's complete?"

"Yes, Comrade."

"One full division of the 31st Rifle Corps, without heavy weapons."

"Yes, Comrade Marshal?"

"And nine tanks from the 4th?"

"Err, no, Comrade Marshal. The reports were in error. Six of our tanks arrived. The other three are the last German vehicles we had retained. They were shipped separately, but arrived at the same time, destined for use by our friends."

"Three months was all we expected, so I suppose we can't complain."

"No, Comrade. I admit... I'm impressed by their achievements."

A secret Soviet study, not for general circulation, and definitely not for the sight of any Japanese officer, had predicted that the captured German vehicles would have an operational life of three months at the maximum. It had reasonably suggested that a lack of spares, combined with an anticipated decline in the numbers of qualified mechanics, would add to losses sustained in combat, and that the areas in which the vehicles might operate were not wholly suitable, also contributing to losses.

The Japanese forces had done extremely well, although the numbers of vehicles had declined across the range of units. Even so, advance elements of the Japanese 63rd Special Army were now only sixty kilometres from Nanning.

Coffee arrived and the Marshal set aside his pipe in favour of a large mug of the steaming hot liquid.

"Sort out this logistical shit storm and we should be fine."

Lomov wondered whether that was for his benefit, or whether the Marshal was trying to convince himself.

Vassilevsky, mug in one hand, ran his finger steadily down the map, following the run of Route 487, all the way to Nanning.

### 1229 hrs Sunday, 15th December 1945, 3rd Imperial Special Obligation Brigade 'Rainbow', Route 487, Luoliao, China.

Captain Nomori Hamuda was praying in the 'Way of the Gods', as Shintoism was sometimes translated.

The war had taken its toll on 'Rainbow' and left scars on all of its soldiers, be they physical or mental.

One of their running mates, the 2nd 'Moon' Brigade, had been erased from the order of battle in three days of heavy fighting, the handful of unwounded soldiers transferred to the 1st 'Sun' Brigade to fill in the huge gaps there.

Hamuda finished his devotions and arched his back, his aching body the victim of relentless miles in a hard steel shell.

Fig#111 - Imperial Japanese Army forces, advance down Route 487, China, 15th December 1945.

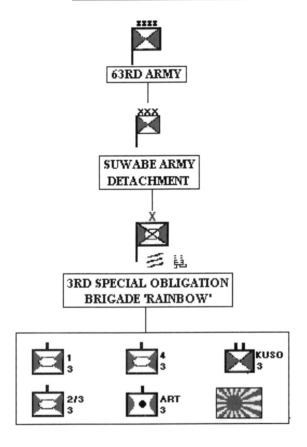

Panther Masami, the 'Elegant Beauty', had lost nine of her sisters, a further one also now absent, being repaired with pieces scrounged from the wrecks of her running mates.

As it was Hirohata's tank, and the fiery young officer was overseeing the mixed German-Japanese workshop personnel, Hamuda knew it would be back in line as soon as was humanly possible.

The last four running Panthers were now behind the leading units, resting and doing maintenance whilst the 2nd Group, a composite of 2nd and 3rd Companies joined together because of casualties, drove hard south, pushing the Chinese forces before them.

Kagamutsu had become the unit's leading tank ace, his score boosted by two days of close combat with the 5th Chinese Tank Battalion, twenty-nine rings proudly displayed on his gun barrel, eight more than his closest rival, Hirohata.

Hamuda was lagging behind now, being ten adrift of Sergeant Sakita, the third highest scoring tank commander. Tank encounters had become rarer as the US-Chinese tank forces started to avoid direct contact with the deadly special tank units of the Imperial Army.

Or at least they had done, until the Pershings started to arrive. It was one of the big American tanks that had left its indelible marks on Masami, three silver gouges silently recording how close he and his men had come to death.

The last white ring on Masami's barrel represented that Pershing tank, left to rust on the banks of the Malai River, where Hamuda's Panther tank had finally killed it.

All of the Rainbow's Panthers looked shabby and much the worse for wear, the marks of combat evident everywhere the eye fell.

To combat the hollow charge shells of the bazookas, sheets of metal had been placed on struts, much as like the Schürzen used on Panzer IV tanks, although the Japanese attempt was less successful, only one of the Panthers maintaining a full set, that being the irrepressible Hirohata's mount.

The fuel bowsers had finished topping off his tanks, so Hamuda's mind turned to food.

## Fig#112 - Chinese Nationalist and US forces deployed in Luxuzhen, China, 15th December 1945.

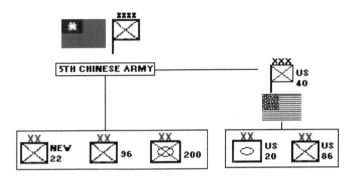

The pleasurable thought was no sooner nicely nestled in his anticipation than his brain shelved the idea in favour of recognising the sharp sounds that started to assail his ears.

He focussed his mind, and realised that it was firing, large calibre firing by the heavy reports.

The familiar sounds of Rainbow in action, the 88mm guns on the two Tigers joined with the 75mm's of the Panthers, almost overriding the lower voices of the 47 and 57 millimetre peashooters on the Shinhoto and Chi-Ha tanks.

It was the unfamiliar sounds that concerned him most; whatever those were, they weren't Japanese, or German for that matter.

He wiped an imaginary speck of dust from his watch.

*'12:37.'*

Kagamutsu's Panther was sliding into a forward defensive position already, the Sergeant-Major alive to the possibilities to their front.

Hamuda waved at an enquiring face and the message was received. Sakita's Panther slid across to the left of the road, slipping behind a mud wall that could have been made for the purpose of secreting a tank behind it.

Masami was purring gently by the time he got to her, where he found the infantry commander waiting.

He took a report from his loader, who had been trying to raise the 2nd on the radio, without success.

To save mounting the tank, Hamuda accepted the offer of the infantryman's map.

"Have to find out what's going on first. 2nd are off air at the moment. I'm going to move my tanks up carefully. I'll want a platoon of your men riding with each group of my tanks. Be prepared to move the rest up the flanks here; half and half ok?"

The Captain was experienced in infantry-tank coopertion, so needed little futher information.

Fig#113 - The battlefield, Route 487, Luxuzhen, China, 15th December 1945.

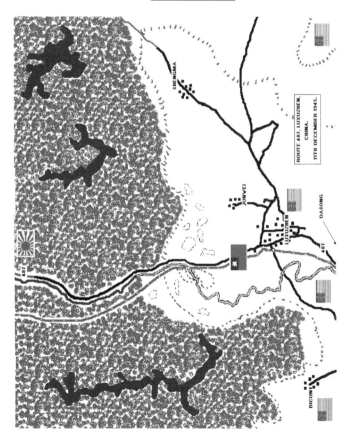

515

"Hopefully 2nd Group and your Major can cope by themselves, but I can hear something I don't like up there."

Captain Yamagiri snorted his amusement, his eyes concealed behind the sunglasses that his wounds required he constantly wear.

The Infantry group commander, Major Kusoa, was, as Hirohata had so delictaely put it, *'Nothing but a stiff-assed chikushou kuso Samurai desk warrior with more bark than ability'*. That lack of soldierly skill had already translated into higher casualty rates than any other infantry battalion in the Special Obligation units, with the possible exception of the 'Moon' unit. Survivors from that were still turning up, even now.

A louder nose distracted both men, the cause arriving in a wave of muddy water. Hirohata's Panther slid to a halt adjacent to his commander's tank.

His arrival again saved Hamuda the climb to the command tank's radio.

"Commander, 2nd has been ambushed. Badly hurt too. I've been talking to the artillery Lieutenant. He's panicking to be honest. Can't raise Major Kuso; can't raise any 2nd Group tanks at all. Your orders, Commander? "

"Is that all you know? "

"Yes. Commander. Except the evidence of our own ears. "

Hamuda looked at the map again and made a decision.

"Across country. We'll all go across country. Straight up the road to the wood line, then we split off the road. Take seven and ten with you, push up on the right side, keeping two hundred metres inside the lake line. Hold here..." Hamuda pointed to a position level with the southern edge of the body of water.

"Observe and report... we'll make a plan once we're both in position. I'll take Kagamutsu and go up the left, target the edge of the ground above Shengma. We'll take one platoon of infantry each, one pushed up the 487 to backstop the 2nd. The rest make defences here. Captain Yamagiri, you get hold of reinforcements and secure this road junction. Clear? "

Both men understood the easy orders.

"Five minutes. "

Yamagiri was already shouting orders to his men.

## 1237 hrs, Sunday, 15th December 1945, Route 487, North of Luxuzhen, China.

"Driver, advance!"

The Sergeant in command of the lead armoured car made the decision to press on and took the lead himself.

"Sunflower-seven. Way ahead looks clear. Moving up to next location."

In his turret, as well as in that of his commander, pencils made notations and marked the vehicle as moving towards the next terraced hillock.

The vehicle was a Marmon-Herrington Armoured car, once owned by the British Army in Malaya, taken from its former owners at the fall of Singapore.

Three had found their way into the 63rd Army, and the surviving pair were leapfrogging their way forward in advance of the fighting force built around Rainbow's Second/Third Company combined unit.

The South African-made vehicle pulled over, making use of a bamboo thicket and the terracing to gain good cover and concealment.

Sergeant Haro slipped to the ground, his Nambu pistol in hand, and easily mounted the simple steps that edged the nearest piece of terrace, permitting him to gain some height.

His gunner kept a close eye on the NCO, all the time retaining a purposeful grip on the MG34 that had recently been installed in place of the Bren gun that had been with the armoured car since it was captured.

He watched as Haro scanned the ground, the binoculars sweeping in regular patterns, making sure that there was nothing of note on the next bound forward.

Satisfied, Haro gave the hand signal and the gunner radioed the all-clear.

Both men only realised how quiet it was when the distinct roar of a Ford petrol engine broke the silence.

Two minutes passed as the commander's Marmon-Herrington pushed on fifty metres and continued to edge away from the second terraced hill.

Behind Haro's vehicle, the roar of heavy engines grew as the two Tigers and solitary Panther Tank moved up, flanked by the last surviving Panzer IV and a gaggle of Chi-Ha's.

A small herd of goats scattered ahead of the lead armoured car, displeased at being disturbed at their luncheon.

One brutish looking beast pulled at a tasty looking hedge.

It fell forward, not as natural vegetation, but as one very obviously made-made piece of camouflage.

"By my ancestors! Ambush!"

Fig#114 - The Battle of Luxuzhen, 15th December 1945.

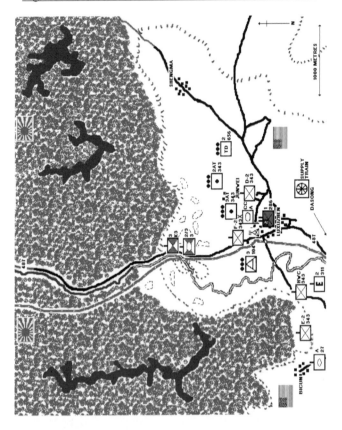

Haro was up in a moment, bounding down the steps to his waiting vehicle.

"Ambush! Ambush!"

The gunner sent the radio message loud and clear, coinciding with the first volley of shots from the hidden anti-tank guns that surrounded Route 487.

But for the goat, the 2nd Group would have been further forward, and in bigger trouble, if it was possible to be in bigger trouble.

The first volley destroyed the Panzer IV, the lead Tiger, and sent three Chi-ha's to the scrap yard.

The second Tiger lost both tracks but momentum took it the short distance to a patch of boggy ground where it sank deep into the mud, providing it with an excellent hull-down position.

Haro turned back to see what his unit commander was doing, only to see a shattered piece of metal and rubber burning fiercely where the Marmon-Herrington had stood a moment before.

Something that resembled a man was crawling across the muddy road, leaving a trail of smoke behind it.

The gunner questioned Haro without words and accepted the nod. He pulled the trigger, sending a few merciful bullets into their unknown comrade.

Haro slid into the vehicle, ordering a reverse into cover as the MG34 burst brought unwelcome attention.

A shell exploded on the terracing, rocking the vehicle violently.

The Sergeant was halfway through a report to the tank unit commander when he realised his words were going nowhere and the radio was dead.

Risking a look out of the turret, he found that the aerial had been carried away by something, most likely the anti-tank round that had struck the terracing.

Haro gave the driver reversing instructions, and the armoured car chopped down a number of small trees, coming to a halt in a depression behind the terraced hill.

"New aerial."

With little more than that, Haro was out of the vehicle and straight into the repair.

He worked quickly, all to a backdrop of death and destruction, as the ambushing anti-tank guns worked their way through the 2nd/3rd Company tank force.

Machine guns now also added their load of life-taking metal to the valley, as enemy heavy calibre weapons punched out bullets at the infantry force trying to deploy for an assault.

By the time Hamuda and Yamagiri had questioned the competence of the infantry Major Kuso, the man was already spectacularly dead, caught simultaneously by three bursts of .50cal shells.

## 1240 hrs, Sunday, 15th December 1945, Route 487, North of Luxuzhen, China.

Japanese battlefield intelligence was never brilliant and, as the Pacific War had come closer to the home islands, and Japan was more and more isolated, its intelligence services could only search for crumbs with which to feed the machine of war.

Ships had been seen at Fangcheng and Zhenzhu Harbours, yet more at Beihei, ships that spewed forth men and equipment in large numbers.

A few men and women survived close encounters with vigilant Chinese secret police, at least long enough to get a message down the line.

None made it through, the last messenger, a ten year old girl delivering a letter for her 'uncle', had a confession beaten out of her and was then left to drown in a shallow gully alongside the Suixi–Zhanjiang road.

So, the 2nd/3rd Group of the Rainbow Brigade walked right into a prepared defensive position manned by some very serious men with big guns.

Colonel Edgar J. Painter, commander of the 20th US Armored's Combat Command A, and senior man on the field that day, had no choice but to let the guns loose ahead of time.

*'Damn that goddamned fucking goat!'*

He found some small satisfaction that the beast that had blown his ambush was already with its maker; he would ensure the carcass would serve as a square meal for his headquarters that evening.

*'A goddamned fucking goat of all things!'*

CCA had brought very little of its firepower forward, logistics proving difficult in a country firmly rooted in the 18th Century, but it brought some extra force to the field, in the shape of part of the 343rd RCT, quickly sent up to make up for the absence of infantry in CCA, its own regular armored-infantry battalion diverted away from the Southern Chinese ports by submarine warnings.

Both the 20th and 343rd had some action in Europe at the end of the German War, but both came to it late, and their experiences were relatively untraumatic, pushing against a beaten enemy, and so the men were unusually eager to get to grips with the enemy.

Both partial units were augmented by a special tank-destroyer group with three distinct elements. The first two consisted of two platoons of 3" AT guns and one extended platoon of 90mm AA guns respectively, the latter the modified version capable of engaging ground targets. The third element, slated to be part of the 86th Infantry Division's order of battle, was a Headquarters and 1st platoon from the 656th Tank-Destroyer Battalion, sporting four M36 Jacksons, and an equal number of M20 utility cars.

It was one of the 90mm AA guns that had destroyed the lead Tiger with its first shot.

The M36's sat on the right flank of the Chinese-American force, waiting their moment.

To complete the firepower available to Painter, the 413rd Armored Field Artillery Battalion was already lobbing its 105mm high-explosive shells to the rear of the 2nd Group, equally interfering with either reinforcement or retreat.

The 413rd was one of the few units in the US Army that had been converted to the M37 HMC, and this was their first time using it in action.

Painter nodded in satisfaction at their work, the shells constantly arriving on the money, denying the enemy the road and everything for two hundred yards west and east of it.

"George. "

Immediately, Colonel Bloomquist of the 343rd Infantry moved closer.

"George, I think we need to push your boys up on the left there, through the woods. Don't think they've got tanks in there, so push them up hard and get 'em flanking the sons of bitches. "

The planning had anticipated an infantry advance up the left flank, using the relative safety of the trees. There were huge gaps between some of the trunks, some wide enough to drive two vehicles side by side through, but it seemed the entire Imperial Army armoured group was on or near the road. None the less, George Bloomquist had made sure his lead formation sported extra bazookas, just in case.

"I'm gonna commit my tanks with your boys. Tuck 'em in behind until they can cut loose into the flank of these sons of bitches. Clear, George?"

"Sure thing, Colonel. "

Even though they were both the same rank, it was Painter that held command.

Bloomquist moved off to his portion of the headquarters bunker, calling his CoS to him to issue the orders.

Major Norris, Painter's equivalent, took the opportunity presented and spoke softly to his commander.

"Sir, should we move the TD's across into the flank now. Maybe push up some infantry as a screen to the right flank?"

Edgar Painter was the sort of officer who encouraged free expression amongst his officers, so such a suggestion was of no surprise to him.

"I think not, Willie. Leave the doughs where they are for now. They've prepared positions and we still don't know the strength of this lot. Get... err... Crowther's tanks moving up the left, acting in support of the infantry. He knows the plan."

The man's name had nearly escaped him.

Had the six Shermans arrived earlier then he would have pushed them up to make a firmer left side to his position.

But they hadn't.

He gestured at the rapidly declining enemy force spread across the gap at the exit from the forest,

The pain on his face was very real as he witnessed an enemy shell wipe out one of his 3" guns, complete with its crew.

Swift retribution did not ease his pain at the loss of his men, the disintegrating Chi-Ha barely registering as he looked for survivors amongst his men, his knuckles white as he gripped the binoculars.

Some of the enemy tanks, and most of their infantry, had now disappeared from sight, taking cover in the small folds in the ground, or behind the unusual terrain features, oddly shaped areas of higher ground, that marred what would otherwise have been a perfect ambush site.

Still, he had a plan.

"Major Norris, order Butter to commence preset fire, commencing with Alpha."

Norris confirmed the order and was quickly at the radio, overseeing the transfer of the instruction to call sign 'Butter', the commander of the 413rd Artillery's three batteries.

The plan required one battery to continue discouraging retreat or reinforcement, whilst the other two put their ordnance down on pre-ranged locations behind cover.

Alpha, selected in haste earlier when Painter and a security detail quickly traversed the battlefield, was a very obvious place for an ambushed column to seek cover, and so was quickly brought under fire.

Whilst the results were not known, the observing officers were content that the Japanese were having a hard time of it.

He considered using his artillery to engage the hull down Tiger, but resisted, instead ordering the 90mms to concentrate solely upon the heavier vehicle until it was destroyed.

---

Even inside the noisy tank, the sound of tank cannons and machine guns could be heard quite clearly.

The artillery barrage seemed to have slackened off, for a reason Hamuda could only guess at.

His guesses came down to low ammunition, or a lack of targets.

As the edge of the forest started to declare itself ahead, Hamuda halted his two tanks in cover and gestured to Kagamutsu, who understood his commander's needs precisely.

Armed with an MP40, the Sergeant-Major dismounted his tank and moved quickly after his officer.

The two dropped and crawled the last twenty yards to the edge of the woods.

Without his binoculars, Hamuda could see enough. With them, the problem grew fourfold, although the opportunity that was presented also tantalised him.

His mind quickly worked the issue and came up with a resolution.

"Sergeant-Major, if I call it in, we'll strike to this point and break off towards those vehicles there, having stopped to make sure we kill them."

Kagamutsu understood his officer's concerns; the enemy vehicles looked dangerous, the size of their guns evident even to the naked eye.

He pointed out the infantry positions.

"Keep your distance from those... and we'll just cut straight across the enemy position. Clear?"

"Hai."

The doubt originated from a lack of knowledge on Hirohata's status.

A flurry of fire from the woods a mile away to their right.

Hamuda's decision changed instantly.

"Right. The Marquis has run into enemy. If nothing else, that's a distraction. We move now. Go!"

The two ran back to their waiting tanks, quickly briefing the infantry before they mounted up and the Panthers leapt forward.

---

It was Sakita's Panther that had opened up the battle in the woods, swatting away a group of astonished GI's.

The 20th may not have seen much fighting in Germany, but there were few in the unit's ranks that couldn't recognise a Panther tank, even in the colours of the Imperial Army.

Hull and turret machine guns lashed the short undergrowth, putting down a number of soldiers permanently.

Angling his tank, the driver evacuated his bowels as the trail of a bazooka shell rose towards his face.

The rocket clipped the driver's episcope, diverted, and nicked the top of the mantlet, neither contact sufficient to cause it to explode.

The bazooka shell detonated against the bough of a tree, some thirty yards behind the Panther.

There was no chance for the crew to reload, as the driver took revenge for his embarrassment by running the pair down.

The two other Panthers shook out behind Sakita, with Hirohata in the centre.

The infantry component stayed level with the tanks, selecting anti-tank threats for special attention, leaving the armoured vehicles to enjoy the harvest.

The lead platoons of Bloomquist's Charlie company fell back in disarray, moving back past the advancing Shermans from the 27th Tank Battalion's A Company.

The tanks were a mixture of four M4 easy eights and two M4A3E2 Jumbos, both with 75mm guns.

War can be peverse sometimes, and a wood would never be considered as tank fighting country, but the first tank versus tank engagement of the newly-arrived US Army in Southern China occurred in the woods, west of Route 487.

---

Sakita growled at his gunner, talking the man onto the target that was steadily moving forwards.

"Driver. As soon as we fire, move on up to that big tree head and angle left."

The gun roared and the Panther surged forward instantly.

"Baka! You missed!"

The accusation could not be refuted, as the chunky looking tank started to weave towards a clump of bamboo near another large tree.

Its gun belched flame and a solid shot struck the side of the Panther without penetrating.

A tree trunk prevented the Japanese tank from turning its long barrel, buying the American crew the opportunity for a second shot.

The 75mm struck the Panther's mantlet and flew skywards.

Onboard the Sherman Jumbo, and not for the first time, voices condemned the lack of penetrative power of the 75mm gun. The commander screamed at his idiot gunner for firing at the thickest armour on the enemy tank.

The Panther edged forward, permitting its gun to bear and placed such thoughts beyond the American tankers. They died as the AP shell slammed into the Jumbo, the extra armour of the Sherman easily defeated by the close range of the battle.

Hirohata engaged an Easy-Eight to his front, and watched as his shell punched its way through the driver's front plate.

Hatches were thrown open, and a wisp of smoke followed the bodies abandoning the damaged tank, the commander slower than the rest, his severed left leg lying in the well of the turret.

"Again."

A second shell helped the American on his way, the explosion lifting him up and throwing him into some bushes, the thick growth offering a soft landing pad from which he crawled away, as best his wound permitted.

The third Panther, on the left end of the line, destroyed another Easy Eight with its second shot, the crew abandoning the Sherman as it transformed into a fireball.

At ranges of no more than two hundred yards, the tanks stalked each other in the undergrowth.

---

"What the goddamned hell? George!"

Bloomquist shouted back.

"I'm on it, Colonel."

Edgar Painter could guess, but wanted proper information before he committed himself.

The infantry commander moved across the headquarters.

"Colonel, they ran into tanks and infantry. Your boys have already lost three and my lead platoons have fallen back."

Painter leant past Bloomquist, enquiring about the tank unit.

The signals officer had bad news.

"Nothing, Sir. Nothing at all. Can't raise them and there's no command net traffic from Crowther."

The CCA commander understood what that meant.

*'Crowther... one of the new boys... the skinny one?'*

He summoned up a mental picture of the man he now considered dead, and dismissed it just as quickly.

"Right. Any more on the enemy, George?"

"Three tanks, plus at least a company of infantry."

"Types? What sort of tanks, George."

"No info as yet, Colonel. I'll get my boys to hold, but they'll need some support."

Painter looked at the tactical map.

"The Combat Engineers. We will swing them up behind you."

The map taunted him in a couple of places, mines indicated in areas where the enemy now would not go, courtesy of a four legged discovery.

"Hell, they can put some mines down in front of your positions. No need to dig them in, just get them lined up and stop the bastards. I'll pull two of the TDs too, George. Backstop for now, but maybe we can move 'em up later eh?"

---

The Jacksons received two messages, one shortly before the other, and from very different sources.

Firstly, from the RCT commander, ordering two of the powerful SP guns across the valley and up in support of the hard-pressed left flank.

Two of the Jacksons pulled out and moved off to the west.

The second message was unequivocal, and without need of words.

A high-velocity 75mm shell took the rearmost tank destroyer in the engine compartment, wrecking it completely.

A second shell sought out the other Jackson and penetrated the thin turret rear, exiting the nearside front armour, just to the left of the mantlet, having passed through the gunner and loader on its inexorable advance.

The TD commander came apart mentally and started to scream, the awful sight of his gun crew immediately flipping his mind.

Driver and radio man needed no second invitation to quit the damaged vehicle, jumping out and heading for cover, even as a second shell arrived and put an end to both the vehicle and the screaming.

Finally reacting, the two remaining tank-destroyers turned their barrels and prepared to engage the pair of Panthers that had emerged from the woods.

Within the space of two seconds all four vehicles had fired and the high velocity shells passed each other on the battlefield.

All missed their target.

Fig#115 - The Battle of Luxuzhen, Hamuda's counter attack, 15th December 1945.

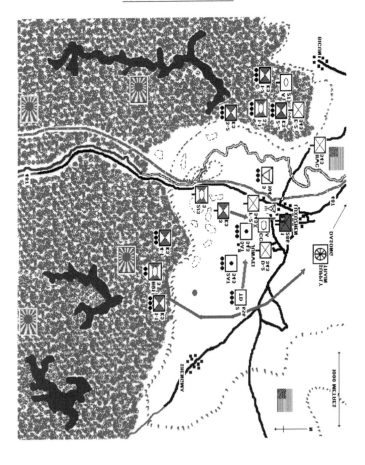

"Standby, driver. As soon as they fire their next shot, we'll halt. Gunner, make it count."

"Hai."

The reply came in unison and both men steeled themselves.

A shell streaked across their front.

"Stop!"

The Panther came to a halt and the gunner waited briefly as the suspension recovered.

The 75mm spat its shell.

"Move!"

Slowly pulling away, the driver watched as a white blob crossed the divide, seemingly intent on hitting him.

The clang was incredible, the solid AP shot deflecting off the corner of the glacis immediately to the left of his head.

Hamuda shouted over the intercom, but he might just as well not have bothered.

The driver's hearing was temporarily shot by the stunning impact, and all attempts to get the tank to halt fell on unreceptive ears.

The radio op's machine gun started to rattle, as American soldiers started to fire or run, depending on how they coped with the approach of the deadly Panther.

Hamuda ducked into the interior and slapped the driver's shoulder, using hand gestures to pass on his orders. The driver immediately steered the tank to the left of the infantry positions ahead.

Clicking to the tactical frequency, he made a call, completely ignoring the procedures, noting one of the remaining enemy TDs now burning brightly

"Ashita from Masami. Enemy infantry dug-in in strength ahead. Turn left...," Hamuda quickly checked the map before continuing, "Move around south of Luxuzhen and rejoin the others. Over."

"Ashita. Understood."

In truth, Sergeant Major Kagamutsu didn't wholly understand, but recognised that his commander had just committed them both to a very dangerous course of action indeed.

The two Panthers, bouncing along at the best possible speed, moved to the left of the infantry position and into an environment filled with unexpected opportunities.

Ahead was the logistical train of the American force.

## 1301 hrs, Sunday, 15th December 1945, Three hundred metres south-east of Luxuzhen, China.

Kagamutsu was pleasantly surprised, the progress of the two tanks virtually unmolested, save for some hastily fired mortar shells that arrived where they had been nearly a minute beforehand.

Occasionally a hard target presented itself; jeeps, carts and lorries mainly.

One of the TD unit's M20 armoured cars had attempted to draw the two tanks away from a gaggle of lorries.

Both Hamuda and his senior NCO were impressed with the bravery of the crew in making such a worthless sacrifice.

Once the armoured car was destroyed, the two Panthers turned their attention to the supply unit, and wiped it out in less than two minutes.

Beyond that, a group of mule carts containing everything that a Chinese infantry battalion needed for war were the next victims.

Despite being an animal lover, Hamuda felt he had no choice. Using the machine guns sparingly, the two Panthers fell into column formation and drove down the road, crushing everything in their path.

A Sherman sporting a 105mm Howitzer tried its hand, planting a shell in the ground only six feet in front of Hamuda's tank.

The driver, hearing slowly recovering, was suddenly afflicted by a lack of vision, as a large portion of China was thrown over the front of the tank, blocking episcopes and vision blocks.

The gunner and radio operator shouted.

"I'm blind!"

"Can't see!"

Neither could Hamuda, a huge lump of soil and bamboo strewn over the top of his cupola.

Going from a snatch of memory, he shouted an order.

"Steer right!"

They were saved by Kagamutsu.

The Sergeant Major stopped his tank, making sure that his shell went home.

The Sherman withdrew, the howitzer now at an odd angle, set in a mantlet distorted by a direct strike.

Looking at his leader's tank, it was obvious what their problem was.

"Masami from Ashita. Enemy tank down. You may halt quickly. Over."

"Received."

He watched as Masami came to a halt. Small figures emerged to push at the earth and vegetation that had covered the Panther.

Within thirty seconds, Masami was moving again, sights firmly set on a group of vehicles that were desperately manoeuvring to escape over a small bridge ahead.

Beyond the chaos at the crossing point, Hamuda could clearly see American tanks reversing out of the woods, firing as they went.

'Midori Takushi' was too much of a mouthful, so Hamuda cut it down.

"Takushi from Masami, over."

The classical voice of the Marquis Hirohata returned, bringing a smile to Hamuda's face.

"Takushi from Masami. We are to your south-east, advancing to the river and on the flank of your enemy tank force. Over."

"Masami from Takushi, received. I see you. Suggest you take the tanks in the flank and then we join up at the bridge. Over."

"Takushi from Masami. Agreed. Out."

"Ashita from Masami, over."

Kagamutsu acknowledged.

"Ashita from Masami. Orient to the north. Watch our flank. Out."

"Received."

The two Panthers went about their separate tasks.

### 1311 hrs, Sunday, 15th December 1945, headquarters, CCA, 20th US Armored Division, Luxuzhen, China.

"Goddamnit! George, have some of your men reposition to the south-east. The bastards are going round behind us!"

Bloomquist was on it in a moment, repositioning some of his assets to face the threat of the Panthers moving to the south of Luxuzhen.

Colonel Painter was doing the same job with some of his own troopers, moving anti-tank guns to cover to the south-west.

A bazooka-heavy platoon took to its vehicles and pushed south

The enemy force to his front was cowed, but not yet beaten, the damn Tiger tank proving invulnerable, despite several definite hits on the turret.

He decided, quite rightly, that the main threat now lay with the tanks to his rear and in the western woods.

The 413rd's guns were redirected to the woods, as close as humanly possible to the retreating Shermans and infantry.

Hamuda had also contacted his artillery, and a steady fire fell amongst the traffic jam at the river bridge.

Before his eyes, the resolve of the American and Chinese troops broke as the final straw of the Panther's arrival finished off the work started by the artillery.

That the Panther was not engaging them, but the US tanks to their west, was missed by the panicky soldiers.

A rout commenced, as men left vehicles still running and threw themselves into water that offered an illusion of safety. So confused were the soldiers of the CCA's supply train that they failed to comprehend the arrival of more enemy tanks on the other bank.

The combined US tank-infantry force was now outgunned and outmanoeuvred, Hamuda's gunner claiming a third kill in as many shots.

The surviving Shermans and half-tracks made off to the south-east as fast as they could, leaving Hirohata to turn part of his force in towards the river bridge.

The slaughter of the logistical train stepped up a gear.

Whilst the bloodletting behind him grew, Kagamutsu spotted the anti-tank guns moving to new positions.

"Gunner, target, vehicle, right five, eight hundred metres."

The electric traverse moved the heavy turret the small distance required.

"On."

"Fire."

The gunner had slowly traversed back, leading the M5 tractor and was confident of a hit. The shell missed the fully tracked prime mover and ploughed into the 3" anti-tank gun it was towing.

Kagamutsu slapped the gunner's shoulder.

"You lucky bastard."

"The ancestors smiled upon me, Sergeant Major."

"They can do it again then. Zero, eight fifty metres."

Another shell sped across the battlefield, missing its intended target by some distance.

"Again."

The jittery gun crew were bailing out of their vehicle when the HE hit the front plate. The tractor was destroyed and one of the crew was stripped of every appendage and hurled onto the roof of a small hut. He died before a medic could reach him.

Hirohata's force had also split, the Marquis himself standing back, overwatching his tanks and infantry as the remaining two Panthers drove hard into the few units that had crossed the bridge unharmed.

Gradually, the slaughter abated as the three Panthers started to run out of viable targets, the main guns falling silent, leaving the machine guns to pick up off a morsel here and there.

Perversely, it was Kagamutsu who spotted the new danger.

"Ashita to all units. Enemy tanks coming out of Dasong. Type unknown. Over."

Every tank commander looked south but, with the extra height of his position, it was Hirohata that could see best.

"Masumi from Takushi. Four enemy tanks on the railway line, coming north. Pershing type, over."

Hamuda, always aggressive and equipped with a tank that supported his idea of modern combat, debated quickly.

The temptation to stay and slug it out with the monster enemy tanks was clear, and very tempting.

But, where there were four, there could be more, and all of his tanks had taken punishment already.

His head won the day.

"Takushi from Masami, over."

Hirohata obviously expected the order, which momentarily reassured Hamuda that it was the right one.

He polished up the finer details.

"Takushi, stay in the woods but keep an eye on us as we move up through 2nd. Over."

Clear on his orders, Lieutenant, the Marquis Ito Hirohata, ordered his two lead Panthers back into cover and melted away before the Pershings could engage.

---

The last but one shell had landed inch perfect.

The Japanese guns had been relocated to the river bridge but some shells were already on their way when the order came.

Colonel Bloomquist, 343rd Infantry, had left two minutes beforehand, intent on rallying the men and guns to the south.

The decision spared his life.

Those of the 343rd's staff that had remained behind were less fortunate, although none of them suffered.

The blast had ripped through the headquarters position, and few men escaped without some injury.

Three of CCA's personnel were dead, with another five badly wounded, including the Chinese Battalion commander.

The radios were smashed, and the whole headquarters was a shambles.

Edgar Painter had sustained a most unusual injury. Not one that overly incapacitated him, but it was painful for sure.

Halfway between his wrist and elbow, a pair of scissors protruded from his flash. The blast had picked them up from one of the field desks and sent them flying like a knife, striking the Colonel in the right arm.

It didn't reduce his movement, but every change in posture brought a stab of excruciating pain, and he had no grip worth a damn.

Through the fire of his wound, a sound broke through, one new to his experience, but one that registered with him because of stories he had heard from men who had been on the receiving end.

"Banzai! Banzai! Banzai!"

In relocating some of his force, Painter had thinned out the men in between him and 2nd Group. Two Chinese platoons had run away as soon as the opportunity presented itself, leaving AT positions, and precious little else, between the CP and the enemy.

The shell, in destroying his radios, had deprived him of the means to plug the gap.

Infantry from the 2nd/3rd rose up and charged forward, closing upon a brace of 3" AT weapons and their infantry support.

"Banzai!"

Painter had to admit that it was frightening.

One of the 343rd's piss-ant 37mm guns, weapons that had been universally mocked when discussed in conjunction with the possibility of enemy Panther and Tiger tanks, spat out a hail of shot, its canister round proving extremely effective at wiping away groups of charging Japanese soldiers.

"Banzai!"

A .30cal crew worked feverishly to unjam a weapon that had fired but a single bullet before falling silent; the approaching screaming, the glistening bayonets, the growing covering fire from enemy guns, all combining to reduce their calmness to a nothingness of fear. The gun would not fire again this day.

"Banzai!"

The 37mm coughed once more and a dozen enemy soldiers were thrown over in disarray. The screams of the charging men mingled with the screams of the hideously wounded.

The AT gunners started throwing grenades, and looking to their small arms as the 'medieval horde' grew closer.

"Banzai!"

The Japanese commander, waving his pistol and sword in encouragement, ran straight onto an exploding grenade, which gave him more forward momentum, but robbed him of his life in an instant.

Another canister round was fired and more men were wiped away by the stream of steel balls.

An armoured car dashed forward on the flank and its German machine-gun lashed the 37mm's servers, silencing the weapon.

"Banzai!"

The headquarters officers and soldiers had come into action, picking off men here and there, careful to avoid hitting their own.

A running Japanese threw aside his rifle and slammed his hand against his helmet, immediately throwing himself into the first anti-tank gun position.

More experienced soldiers would have realised that the man was arming a grenade by striking the primer on the metal protecting his head.

The grenade went off, killing or incapacitating the whole gun crew.

The next three Japanese soldiers into the position used their rifles and bayonets to finish the job.

"Banzai!"

The surviving Japanese officer, 2nd Lieutenant Tanji, leapt the shallow trench and dropped beside the two men at the .30cal; both were paralysed with fear.

Their hands were half raised but the officer's sword was unforgiving and he swept the blade into them, two blows each.

Behind Tanji, the rest of his unit was either on or over the defensive line.

"Banzai!"

A knot of enemy formed behind some small rocks and started to pick off his soldiers.

Before he could organise an attack, the friendly armoured car rolled around behind them and removed the threat.

The other anti-tank gun position was taken and the gunners slaughtered to a man.

However, the doughboys of the 343rd were proving a sterner test, and Japanese victory was not yet assured.

He called a small group around him and swept down the trench line from east to west, bringing an advantage to every little fight as the small force moved along the position.

The Marmon-Herrington was suddenly lashed with machine gun bullets, two M20's charging out of the town to do battle.

Tanji spared a moment to take in the unusual sight of warring armoured cars, as his men completed the rout of the defending infantry, a few GIs running back as fast as they could.

His own men celebrated.

"Banzai!"

Tanji realised what the next enemy position was.

"One more effort! The Emperor demands it of us! There is the enemy commander! There! Follow me!"

The surviving forty-two soldiers rose up as one and charged.

"Banzai!"

---

Haro and his crew were having a bad time of it with the six-wheeled enemy cars, who were not only faster, but also packed a bigger punch with their .50cal machine guns.

The MG34 equipped Marmon-Herrington was decidedly outgunned, even before men appeared in the open-topped structures of the M20s, each armoured car introducing a bazooka to the fight.

The MG34 fell silent as the belt ran out.

"Reload, you moron!"

This was no time to lose firepower.

Both enemy vehicles slowed to give their weapons a better chance to hit, providing Haro with an unexpected opportunity.

"Right, pull right now and head to the river. Weave, but push quickly."

The driver responded instantly and the South African built vehicle bounded, its acceleration making all the difference as two rockets cut through the air near where it had been a moment before hand.

The MG34 chattered briefly, the slowed M20 nearest presenting a better target than previously.

Haro noted the pieces fly off the machine gunner. He was also sure that the reloading bazooka man had taken a good hit in the head.

"Good shooting. Maybe not such a moron after all."

The exchange was good-humoured; the gunner had been with Haro for years.

.50cal bullets struck the rear of the vehicle and more than one passed through the crew compartment. Haro felt the loss of power immediately, which was quite strange as the engine was in the front. The engine picked up again quickly, but the bigger armoured car was gaining.

However, Haro's manoeuvre had not really been about making it to the river. He had brought the pursuing M20 into a place where it could clash with an all together different proposition.

---

"What's that fish breath doing?"

"I nearly killed him, Commander."

"Hmm."

The Marmon-Herrington had just bounded out of cover, racing at top speed for the river, surprising everyone on Masami.

Behind it, and following the same path, the M20 emerged, seemingly oblivious to the Panther's presence.

"Gunner engage."

It was a difficult shot as the enemy vehicle was moving fast. The gunner followed the vehicle, the traverse just about keeping up before settling in because of the decreasing angle change.

The driver of the M20 made a mistake.

Turning left to round an obstacle, he presented a moment of advantage to Masami, one the gunner took full benefit of.

Even then, he only just clipped the armoured car, but its armour offered no resistance and the nearside front was destroyed in an instant.

"Fakku! Load high explosive!"

The M20 was a sitting duck and the 75mm HE shell completed the work done by an ordinary armour piercing round.

The American armoured car died spectacularly.

Hamuda ordered the Panther forward again and returned the wave from the commander of the strange armoured car, who had obviously deliberately risked himself to draw the enemy vehicle across Masami's bows.

*'The man has courage.'*

---

## 1350 hrs, Sunday, 15th December 1945, headquarters, CCA, 20th US Armored Division, Luxuzhen, China.

The headquarters personnel stood their ground and fired everything they had at the screaming horde.

To no avail for, although they knocked a number of men down, more than enough made it to the bunker to ensure the Japanese victory.

"Banzai!"

Colonel Edgar Painter calmly fired his Colt left-handed, selecting a different target with each shot and, to his surprise, hitting with most.

His officers and men went down under the surge of bodies, and the screams of dying men invaded every part of his consciousness.

The 1911A hung open on an empty magazine, and he quickly tried to put another magazine in, his right hand unable to contribute to the process.

One Japanese soldier saw him and plunged forward, screaming loudly, intent on skewering the American officer.

Painter side-stepped and the bayonet sailed past his side, ramming into the sandbags.

The automatic pistol struck the soldier twice across the nose, and the insensible man dropped to the earth, out of the fight.

Trembling with the shock and the enormity of what was happening, Painter was again unable to slide the new magazine home before he was seen by another enemy rifleman.

This man fired and the bullet punched into Painter's abdomen, throwing the American commander against the bag that was spilling its sand from the bayonet tear.

Painter bellowed in pain, as much for the new wound as the sandbag's impact with the scissors still lodged in his right arm.

The magazine was in the slot, but not home, so he slapped the butt against his thigh and thumbed the slide into place.

The rifleman was already down, put to death with a triple shot from a Garand.

Lieutenant Tanji, fresh from ramming his sword into the stomach of a young corporal, kicked the dead man off his blade and turned towards Painter.

The Colt fired and the .45 bullet smashed Tanji's left arm just above the elbow joint, almost severing the limb. His pistol fell from useless fingers, but he gave no cry of pain. Only one single word escaped his lips.

"Banzai!"

Tanji steadied himself and walked purposefully towards Painter, who shot twice.

The Japanese officer, knocked backwards by the energy of the bullet clipping his left shoulder, smashed face and chest first into an old tree trunk, used to hold the camo netting roof over the bunker.

His nose and mouth erupted in streams of blood.

Inside his body, the savage impact of a protruding piece of tree caused a rupture of some blood vessels in his lungs, and small quantities of red fluid started to enter the damaged lung.

Shaking his head to clear the mist, Tanji pulled himself up onto his knees, and then struggled to stand up, the obvious spread of blood on his stomach indicating another area of damage, above the right hip.

Again the pistol barked, but this time the American officer missed, the growing presence of the vengeful swordsman affecting Painter's aim.

Tanji had moved forward nearly ten feet before the next two rounds hit him. Actually, only one, the first shot struck his binocular case, deflecting off the metal and narrowly missing his neck as it went on its journey.

Spun slightly by the initial impact, the second round slid across the Japanese officer's chest, gouging the skin and leaving a long and bloody trench in the soft tissue as it passed through.

Tanji fell to his knees, the pain overcoming him momentarily. Again, he stood up, coughing and spitting blood as more of the bloody broth worked its way from his damaged chest and face into his lungs.

Painter could see his death approaching, and he tried hard to steady his nerves and make the telling shot.

*'The head, the fucking head, go for the fucking head!'*

It was not the best decision, as such shots require better judgement and a cooler head.

He fired and missed.

"Banzai!"

Painter screamed.

"Nooo!"

Tanji's sword stabbed brutally as he summoned his last reserve of strength.

He drove the katana point first into Painter's windpipe, penetrating the spinal cord beyond.

Death was instantaneous, whereas Lieutenant Tanji, totally spent by his final effort, took a few more minutes to travel to his ancestors.

The few survivors were quickly bound, except for the two wounded Chinese officers, who were bayoneted to death. The senior NCO made the decision to fall back after the tanks and armoured car, leaving only the dead behind.

The soldiers of Rainbow faded away into the woods, where they dug in and waited for further orders.

Whilst the mish-mash of the 20th Armored and 343rd Infantry Regiment had completed its mission and halted the Japanese advance, the price it paid was far in excess of what it could afford.

Had they known it, perhaps it would have been of some solace to the survivors that they had badly damaged the Rainbow Brigade, and whilst the American war machine could guarantee to bring replacement men and vehicles to the fight, few such opportunities were available to the Japanese.

*For they have sown the wind, and they shall reap the*
*whirlwind.*

*Hosea, Ch8, V7.*

# Chapter 123 - THE DACHA

Happy birthday to you,
Happy birthday to you,
Happy birthday, dear Comrade General Secretary,
Happy birthday to you.

### 1006 hrs, Wednesday, 18th December 1945, the Dacha complex, Kuntsevo, USSR.

*[Some content of a sexual nature]*

The first one had been built to order for Stalin, and was designed by the architect Merzhanov.

During World War Two, Stalin and his entourage had done much of the planning for the victory of the Fascists within its wooden walls.

An additional storey was added in 1943, and a lift installed for additional access.

The rest of the hierarchy of the Communist state quickly realized that having their own dacha at Kuntsevo would provide them with opportunities of access unavailable anywhere else, and so other buildings sprang up, carefully designed to afford the full creature comforts, but not to eclipse that of the leader.

It would have been difficult in any case, as Stalin's dacha was set inside a double fence system, protected by an array of anti-aircraft guns, and topped off with a three hundred man NKVD security details.

The dacha had been a hive of activity all day, as reports and briefings went on from breakfast until late afternoon.

The full extent of the Baltic fiasco was now laid open for all to see, and yet still the General Secretary had not spilt blood on the matter.

Nazarbayeva had briefed the whole GKO, starting with the loss of her prized RAF asset, whose nonsense message bore every break in code form possible, as well as his distress tag.

She brought proof, undeniable proof, that the new Army group was a fake, a maskirovka, the same trick the Allies had played on the Nazis in France during 1944.

Beria let her speak, knowing full well that she was wrong.

In truth, she had been right, but Comrade Philby had come through, his latest report indicating that the formation would be 'accidentally' revealed as false and, when the Soviet High Command had swallowed the bait, it would be properly constituted in secret.

It was a thing of beauty as far as Beria was concerned.

His pleasure in the duplicity of his former allies only overtaken by his complete joy for the embarrassment he inflicted upon Nazarbayeva.

It was but the first move in a day that would see Stalin's birthday made special for him in so many ways.

Nazarbayeva had seemed to take it in her stride but he knew… he **knew** that he had hurt her pride badly.

The GRU General continued with an assessment of Allied casualties during the failed offensives, one that, in Beria's opinion, overstated by nearly 10%.

When he questioned the woman he found that she still had teeth, and that his own information was incomplete.

Nazarbayeva finished with an upbeat assessment of the balance of forces, with a GRU assessment that Allied ground forces were incapable of launching any substantial action in the prevalent weather conditions and, in any case, had supply difficulties and personnel problems of their own.

The Soviet Academic who presented the forecast for Europe, both in the short term and over an extended period, rumbled and coughed his way through his presentation, but was undoubtedly a man who knew his business.

"So, Comrade Academician, you are telling us that the temperatures could be as low as minus fifty in places?"

"Yes, Comrade General Secretary."

Stalin quickly continued.

"And that this weather could extend well past the end of January?"

"That is our middle estimate, Comrade General Secretary."

Such a happening would give the Red Army time to rebuild its supply base and rest the exhausted units on the German front.

Of course, the same would apply to their adversaries,

The rest of the day moved between reports on production, transport, and manpower availability, and came to a natural end at 3pm exactly.

The evening was set aside for a celebration of the Leader's birthday, and most of those present left to prepare.

Nazarbayeva was on her way out when Molotov, directed by Stalin, caught her arm and told her to remain.

Gestured to a chair, she sat with Bulganin, small talking about classical music and the ballet, whilst Beria and Molotov listened to the hushed whispers of Malenkov. Stalin pleasured himself with his pipe until the room was brought to order by an urgent knocking.

In walked six men, some of whom Nazarbayeva knew, some of whom she didn't, particularly those from Japan, and one 'Hero' she thought she should know by name. The faces were lighting up her memory, but the lost names avoided detection for now.

The matter was soon made irrelevant in any case.

Admiral of the Fleet Hovhannes Isakov did the introductions, starting with the head of Naval Planning, Rear-Admiral Lev Batuzov.

Next in line was a civilian, one she had seen before.

"Comrade General Secretary, Director Kurchatov."

*'The head of our Atomic programme?'*

"May I introduce Director Nishina, director of His Imperial Majesty's Nuclear Weapon research programme."

*'What?'*

"Leytenant General Takeo Yasuda, director of the Imperial Japanese Air Force's Scientific and Technological development team."

Many thoughts whirled in Nazarbayev's mind, but none were particularly clear until the final introduction, the man in naval uniform whom she really knew she should recognize.

"Comrade General Secretary, Kapitan third rank Mikhail Kalinin."

The medals hanging from the submarine commander spoke more eloquently than words.

His presence clarified matters for Nazarbayeva, her mind coming to an inescapable solution in an instant.

*'We are building a bomb for a submarine.'*

A gentle kock on the door broke her concentration, and also rubbished her thoughts.

The door opened and admitted an Army general.

"Comrade General Secretary, my apologies. Comrade Marshal Beria asked me to obtain some production figures, and I knew you'd want the most up to date I could obtain."

Beria had already tipped his leader off, so there was no anger at the Army officer's late arrival.

Everyone took up a seat around the table.

"My apologies, Comrades."

Isakov had realized his omission and stood up again, pointing at the most recent arrival.

"Comrade Polkovnik General Boris Vannikov, People's Commissar for Ammunition."

Kurchatov sat down as Nazarbayeva mentally added, *'also Minister of Middle Machinery... and Beria's man.'*

Few outside the walls of the Dachas of Kuntsevo understood that 'Middle Machinery' was the Soviet term for Atomic Weapons.

---

Nazarbayeva had contributed nothing to the technical briefing, for that was what it was. There was no argument or discussion, just a procession of facts, schedules, needs, wants, and projections. The Japanese conversed with Kurchatov in English, their only common language. Some of what they said might as well have been in Swahili, for all the good it did to the listeners, the technicalities of the task ahead wasted on men whose intellect normally only ran to organizing a little internal genocide, or executing political opponents who were too powerful.

Stalin made it clear that the GRU's role was to help acquire missing information, as requested by the men around her, and in that regard, she was required to place GRU's resources at the disposal of Colonel General Vannikov, as required.

She accepted a numbered copy of the secret file for Project Raduga, hers being number thirty-six of thirty-seven.

She did not, could not, ask why the GRU had been excluded to this point. At least, not at the moment.

The briefing broke up at 5.30pm and, again, Nazarbayeva found herself beckoned to stay.

"Comrade General, you look shocked."

"Comrade General Secretary, I had no idea we were so near to producing a weapon."

Stalin poured himself a tea. The orderly had only brought one cup.

"The Germans were very helpful, and our new allies have opened up their research to us. In fact, they've transferred some of their finest brains to us, and it has reaped benefits already."

Stalin did not pass on the fact that two of the three Pacific fleet submarines had been sunk, taking over twenty invaluable Japanese scientists to the bottom of the North Pacific.

He looked at the woman that he now considered his protégé.

"You want to ask why GRU has not been involved before this, Comrade Nazarbayeva."

It was not put as a question.

"I can only assume that there was good reason, Comrade General Secretary."

It wasn't meant to be sycophantic, and Stalin knew it.

"It's a State secret and, with such things, the fewer that know, the better kept the secret will be. You know this to be true, Comrade."

Nazarbayeva nodded.

"Anyway, that's not why I asked you to stay. There's a celebration here tonight," he took a gentle sip of the scalding tea, "And I'd like you to attend."

Nazarbayeva was about to swing into the standard litany of female excuses that every woman can peel off when caught on the hop for such events.

Stalin chuckled.

"I hope you don't think that I lack the proper organizational skills for such an evening, Comrade General?"

The nearest thing to a laugh that had escaped from Stalin for some time, and it was accompanied by a genuine grin.

"Comrade Beria was detailed to ensure that all feminine articles necessary are at your disposal, along with a guest dacha. There are no uniforms tonight. Tonight, we forget the war and drink to happier times."

Simply put, she clearly had no choice.

"Thank you, Comrade General Secretary. I would be delighted."

"Quite so, Comrade Nazarbayeva. Seven o'clock sharp."

After a formal salute, she left the room, her plans to return to Germany scuppered without an opportunity to appeal, although the prospect of clean sheets and a quiet night was not unwelcome.

She would have neither.

### 1731 hrs, Wednesday, 18th December 1945, NKVD guest dacha. Kuntsevo, USSR.

Nazarbayeva had been escorted to her guest lodgings by two female NKVD officers, who revealed that they had been tasked with providing the GRU General with the proper accoutrements for a social evening.

Safely delivered to her dacha, Nazarbayeva was left alone with a promise that, at 1850hrs precisely, the car would be back to take her back to Stalin's quarters for the birthday party.

The dacha was simple, but reeked of wealth, the artifacts inside the plain wooden walls seemingly from the time of the Tsars. She had no idea that it belonged to the NKVD but, regardless, she intended to make sure that it was without the standard paraphernalia of bugs and listeners.

The log fire roared away and an attendant appeared to serve tea, inviting her to sit in a voluminous red leather armchair warming in its orange glow.

Despite the relatively short time until the festivities, Nazarbayeva welcomed the relaxation on offer, and felt the warmth of the aromatic tea fill her belly as she stretched her legs, easing the boot from her damaged foot without attempting to conceal the manoeuvre.

After informing the GRU General of the location of her bedroom, and offering to be on hand if needed, the orderly slipped quietly from the lounge and left her to herself.

The silence was like a drug, filling her senses with a wonderfully relaxing nothingness that she could barely recall from before the war.

Nazarbayeva had to force herself from the chair and into the bedroom, where the products of the two NKVD women's efforts were laid out like a fashion presentation.

Quickly, she slipped around the room, checking all the usual haunts of the electronic surveillance equipment.

She found none. and there were none to find. Well, maybe just one.

The large mirror on the wall was perfectly positioned for a fashion parade, and she swiftly slipped out of her uniform and went through the selection process.

Firstly, she started with the underwear.

None of it was 'dramatic', to say the least, but the choice came down to one of two, both matching sets, one in black, the other red.

Slipping out of her own more mundane undies, she stopped to admire her nakedness.

She never really looked at her foot, or rather, the absence of it.

It always reminded her of its issues at a time like this, as balancing was not as easy without the metal strap.

None the less, her eyes swept over her body from toe to head, examining the legs she had always been proud of, the veritable forest of pubic hair and moving over the belly.

Whilst it was clearly one of a mother of several children, it was only slightly marked and, as a soldier, she was fit enough for the curves to be natural, rather than the result of age and excess.

Her breasts hung in splendid curves, almost perfect, the large brown nipples surmounting the soft flesh, solely scarred by the passage of the bullet fired in Pekunin's office.

She cupped them, squeezing gently and enjoying the feeling. Her mind tried to remind her of her position, and it had to battle the joy of the contact until it achieved victory.

She reached up and undid her hair, allowing the dark locks to cascade down over her shoulders and below her neck, framing her face.

Her eyes screwed up and she grabbed at the left side, examining it closely and finding grey hairs within.

*'Bath first.'*

There was no bath. There was a large shower and, after a quick 'bug' check around the tiled room, she walked into the enclosure, allowing the luxurious warmth of the water to wash over her.

Finishing her ablutions quickly, she moved back into the bedroom and selected the red set.

The knickers were a little tight, her bottom just slightly too large, but it was close enough, especially as the bra fitted her well and was extremely comfortable.

The dresses were a range from plain to flowery, from unadorned to one so laden with sequins and other paraphernalia that she immediately discarded it.

The red dress looked wonderful and she slipped into it, falling against the mirror as she overbalanced.

The glass gave a little groan but did not break and she recovered herself, buttoning the front and smoothing it into place.

Her nipples were extremely prominent and, for that reason alone, she decided against it, although she surprised herself with the thought that she should be all woman this evening. She ran a finger over the prominent left nipple, feeling little shocks as she pressed firmer.

*'Why not show them what a real woman looks like eh?'*

She shook the bizarre idea from her head. She was not to know that the tea she had drunk had a special ingredient, one that started its clandestine work on her mind from the moment her body started to absorb it.

549

Wary not to fall again, she propped herself against the wall and removed the red dress, selecting a knee length black one instead.

Repeating the performance, without the tumble this time, she ran her hands down the sheer material that hung to her body like it was tailor-made for her.

The dress was simple, with no frills, but it was of superb quality.

She selected a strappy shoe for no other reason than to assist in keeping her metal support in place.

A small white leather bag completed the ensemble and she was nearly ready.

On the dressing table were a selection of perfumes and after shaves.

She opened the cap of an American brand, liked what she sniffed at and sparingly applied the parfum to all the places that a woman does.

It smelt wonderful, and she examined the bottle more closely.

*'White Shoulder by Evyan. I shall get some of this for when I next see my husband.'*

It might prove difficult of course, but being the head of the GRU Europe was not without fringe benefits.

She closed the door and returned to the lounge. Within a minute, a knock on the door indicated that her transport had arrived.

---

Once the sound of the car had faded, the man with the camera heaved a sigh of relief.

"You know, when she started playing with those fat titties, I nearly shot in my britches."

"Fuck, yes. Mind you, when she fell against the mirror, I thought you'd shat your pants. Fancy gasping like a girl!"

"I didn't see it coming, tovarich. The camera was against my eye. Anyway, no harm done. It's very rugged."

He rapped his knuckles on the two way mirror by way of emphasising his point.

Sarkisov shook his head.

"That's some fucking woman, tovarich. I'd love a piece of her myself. Never fucked a General before... at least... not in the traditional sense."

NKVD Colonel Sardeon Nadaraia laughed a sort of laugh that was without humour of any kind.

"Perhaps you may get your opportunity, Rafael. Who knows what could happen once the party is over."

With a straight face, NKVD Colonel Rafael Sedrakevich Sarkisov delivered a telling line.

"Which party, tovarich? The General Secretary's, or the one our man has planned for the GRU bitch?"

Nadaraia laughed and slapped his fellow officer on the shoulder.

"Well, as we aren't invited to the formal ceremony, I think we'll have to do it here."

He carefully undid the camera and removed the film.

"Let's get this developed and see what delights we can set before Comrade Beria."

Sarkisov slipped out of the orderly's tunic and recovered his own jacket.

"What was that stuff anyway, comrade?"

Nadaraia spoke of the 'tea' that his counterpart had served the GRU General.

"Fuck knows, tovarich. Old Vovsi said it would prepare a woman to be more... err... amenable to suggestions of a certain kind."

Entering the main premises, Nadaraia took his leave to seek out the photographic office, whilst Sarkisov waited for the new orderly to arrive.

Sergeant Malenkov had a special physical gift that was to form part of the night's amusements, and the NKVD Colonel just wanted to check that the man fully understood what was required of him.

### 1900 hrs, Wednesday, 18th December 1945, Stalin's Dacha, Kuntsevo, USSR.

Nazarbayeva was not the only woman there, as the hierarchy had brought either wife or mistress and, in one case, both.

However, whilst she was not the thin, painted women that many of the men had their affairs with, her full and totally feminine form, for once revealed out of uniform, drew many looks.

Somehow, it didn't bother her, although part of her felt that it should.

She selected a large glass of her favourite wine, a Georgian White wine, made from the famous Rkatsiteli grape.

Beria's agents had done their research well and the Rkatsiteli was also more than it appeared to be.

Beria had planned a narcotic assault upon his nemesis, one that would end in his dominance and control.

An army of attendants fussed back and forth, bringing trays of canapés, many topped off with the finest Beluga caviar.

It was never something that appealed to her, so the tasty snacks with meat and cheese got the most attention.

"Try the beetroot and Zakusochny, Comrade Nazarbayeva. Exquisite, truly."

"Good evening, Comrade Marshal. I will."

Normally, his closeness would make her feel uncomfortable but, she conceded, the relaxed nature of the party made even his presence seem acceptable.

There was a part of her brain that railed against her acceptance, the same part that positively exploded when he grabbed her arm and steered her towards the food area, selecting one of the cheese and beetroot snacks that he had recommended.

The larger part of her brain was simply affable and accepted the man's proximity.

"That's very special, Comrade Beria."

"Indeed it is, Comrade Nazarbayeva. Now, if you will excuse me."

Beria retreated, happy that the drugs were obviously working, given the woman's tolerance of his presence.

'Good. Soon, Tatiana, soon. The Zakusochny is very special indeed.'

The evening progressed with more food and drink, punctuated by gift presentations to the General Secretary, some from fawning communist party members, some from

Ambassador's and representatives of allied states, yet more from the inner sanctum.

The latter seemed to vie with each other to present the most personal gift, something that the leader might use every day.

Nazarbayeva had not come prepared. However, she had in her possession a gift for her husband, to be given to him on his next leave.

The petrol lighter had been taken from a dead British pilot, and had found its way into her possession.

Solid silver and heavy to handle, it lit every time.

What made it eminently suitable was the inscription that was heavily inscribed on both sides.

'Chivas Regal.'

It was the dictator's favorite tipple, and was presently half-filling the old tin cup that he used for serious drinking.

Tied in a white cloth handkerchief, Nazarbayeva waited her turn.

"Thank you, Comrade Nazarbayeva. A splendid gift. I shall treasure it."

Hardly pausing for breath, Stalin leant forward and whispered in a conspiratorial fashion.

"The Bulgarian ambassador can't take his eyes off you, Comrade General. His wife's back in his country and his girlfriend is heavily pregnant. He looks fit to bust but, please..." he looked across at the aging man and smiled disarmingly, "If he does do anything foolish, please try not to break him. I've need of his cooperation soon."

"I'll avoid the man, Comrade General Secretary. I hope your birthday is enjoyable, Sir?"

Stalin snorted, aware that a group including the ambassador from Yugoslavia was approaching with intent.

His voice dropped to a conspiratorial whisper as he leant in towards Tatiana's ear.

"I'd rather have a straightforward affair, but the requirements of the Rodina override my own simple peasant wishes, Comrade Nazarbayeva. Now, I must do my duty."

Stalin accepted the hand of the Yugoslavian, and both men retreated to a corner by the fireplace to discuss Tito's position on the present de facto cease-fire across Europe.

A strange pang filled her stomach, almost as if something was about to rebel against the food and drink she had recently consumed.

Her system seemed dulled, slowed, almost disconnected, and growing worse by the minute.

Miron Vovsi, Stalin's personal physician, noticed something about her from across the room, and made his way over.

"Comrade Nazarbayeva, are you unwell?"

"I think I'm unused to this fine wine and rich food, Comrade Doctor. It will pass."

"Excuse me please," the Doctor's hands taking first her wrist and, satisfied with her pulse, pressed his hand to her forehead.

"I think that you have a fever developing. Comrade."

Given the illness that had incapacitated her earlier in the year, such a statement was bound to get Nazarbayeva's full attention; as had been the plan.

"Might I suggest that you have an early night tonight and rest for a day?"

Normally, she would have refused the advice on the spot, but now she felt she could only agree.

The stealthy, but purposeful approach of the Bulgarian Ambassador, clinched the decision.

"Could I ask you to accompany me to the car please, Comrade Doctor?"

"Of course, of course."

Offering up his arm, he assisted the GRU General towards the exit, his eyes holding those of Beria for only the briefest of moments.

The NKVD Marshal smiled and determined to spend his next thirty minutes attending to business before he left the party to attend to 'business'.

Savouring the pepper vodka and ice, he started counting down the minutes until his revenge was complete.

The KIM 10-52 car, used to move dignitaries around the Kuntsevo complex, pulled up at the NKVD guest dacha, not that Nazarbayeva had any idea that was what the building was.

Dr Vovsi leapt out and moved round to open the other passenger door, before assisting Nazarbayeva out.

An orderly appeared, but Tatiana declined his offer of assistance, preferring to steady herself on the shoulder of her fellow passenger.

"Make sure the car waits, orderly."

The orderly moved to do as he was asked, and Vovsi helped Nazarbayeva inside.

She made her way to the comfortable armchair and collapsed into it.

Again, Vovsi examined her pulse, temperature and produced a stethoscope, which he warmed before listening to her inner sounds.

"You need a day of bed rest, Comrade General, no arguments."

He moved to his medical bag and rummaged, quickly finding the required item.

"Your temperature's raised and your pulse is up on earlier. Breathing seems fine. I want you to go to bed now. Take this…" he passed her a phial of orange liquid, "Mixed in with water, but only once you're under the covers."

She looked at the phial and asked a silent question.

"It's a sedative, but also has powers that will address your fever. You'll sleep like a fallen tree. Take it before you're in bed and you risk a night lying on the carpet, Comrade General."

He slipped his stethoscope back into the bag and closed it with a snap.

"I will return at," he checked his watch, "Eleven in the morning to check on your condition. If you need me before then, just tell the orderly and he can contact me."

"Thank you, Comrade Doctor."

"The pleasure is mine, Comrade General. Now, to bed with you… and have a good night."

555

The orderly moved to open the front door.

"Thank you, but I can see myself out, Comrade Serzhant."

---

Nazarbayeva moved unsteadily towards the bedroom, her mind not working as she would expect.

The orderly brushed past her to open the door.

"Thank you, Comrade."

Once she was inside, he turned up the slumbering oil lamps and turned down the heavy bedding.

"So many lamps, Comrade Orderly?"

"Some of our guest like enough light to make the room as day, Comrade General."

A fair reply, she thought.

"Please turn them all back down, Comrade. I need my bed."

"As you wish, Comrade General."

Each of the lamps was reduced to next to nothing, providing sufficient light for undressing.

*'I'll turn them up later, you GRU whore!'*

The orderly came to attention.

"If there's nothing else, Sir?"

"No, thank you."

"The Comrade General can reach me by pressing the button on the bedside table, should she require any service."

She missed the edge completely.

"Again, thank you, Comrade Orderly."

NKVD Serzhant Ruslan Spartakevich Stranov nodded and closed the door, before proceeding to the telephone and reporting in as ordered.

---

Sarkisov replaced the receiver and checked his watch.

"The Boss'll be ready by now. Warm up the car and we can get the fun started."

Nadaraia looked sternly at his colleague.

"You start the fucking car. I'm senior Polkovnik remember!"

The battle over seniority was permanent and would never be resolved, but it had never really mattered, and was always done in humour.

Sarkisov conceded.

"Well, I suppose it's my turn anyway."

---

The Packard car was warm and inviting.

Lavrentiy Beria dropped onto the wide back seat and tackled his Colonels immediately.

"Report."

Sarkisov passed on all that he had gleaned from Stranov, Nadaraia added the facts he had been given by Doctor Vovsi.

"Excellent. Let's pay her a visit then. No need to rush though."

Beria wanted to savour the build-up for as long as possible.

### 2100 hrs, Wednesday, 18th December 1945, NKVD guest dacha. Kuntsevo, USSR.

Switching off the engine, NKVD Colonel Sarkisov extracted the bag from the glove box. Nadaraia got out and opened Beria's door.

The three quickly made their way inside.

Stranov took all three men's coats and then offered up the drinks that he had already prepared.

Still holding the paper bag, Sarkisov passed on his instructions from Dr Vovsi, who had been very keen that they should be understood by all.

"Comrade Marshal. Vovsi has one more dose in here, to be administered by syringe. He suggests between the toes, so as to mask the entry site."

Beria listened patiently, although both Colonels knew that it would fall to one of them to do the deed.

"2330hrs and no sooner. He suggests concluding our business by 0220 at the latest. The residual effects will last through until morning, but only if the patient is left undisturbed, Comrade Marshal."

"The effects will be as described. She may have some feeling of the experience, but will have no control and will not be conscious. None the less, he still advises taking the precautions you both discussed, to be on the safe side."

Beria laughed, a throaty genuine laugh, taking all three NKVD men by surprise.

"The bitch won't see my face unless she's eyes in the back of her fucking head!"

They all shared the joke and understood the full meaning of Beria's words.

"Now, let's start…" his eyes shone brightly as he sought out a response from both Colonels, "And no cameras until young Stranov's called into action."

## 2111 hrs, Wednesday, 18th December 1945, NKVD guest dacha. Kuntsevo, USSR.

Like a scene from a horror movie, the defenceless woman lay in bed whilst anonymous men with intent in their hearts stood over her, assessing her, making decisions as to how to proceed.

Sign language was now required, at least until they were certain, so Sarkisov responded to the physical instruction and pulled down the covers.

Nazarbayeva had left the underwear in place and so her curves were still encased in red material as they came slowly into view.

Nadaraia pulled down on the other side and soon the sleeping woman was exposed all the way to her feet.

Beria nodded and Nadaraia extended his hand, gently grazing the soft flesh of Tatiana's left breast.

There was no reaction.

He squeezed gently.

She lay still, untroubled, breathing gently.

He squeezed harder.

A light snoring commenced.

With encouragement from Beria, he used his other hand to liberate the sleeping woman's breast, exposing a nipple.

He needed no encouragement to play with it.

Beria whispered and pointed.

"Them."

The two Colonels took hold of the red panties and, in an excellent display of gentle teamwork, removed Nazarbayeva's underwear, leaving her naked under their collective gaze.

"Slide her over," Beria indicated the left side of the double bed and moved out of the way.

He considered removing the cloth balaclava from his head, but resisted the temptation, just in case.

Having positioned the sleeping body on the edge of the bed, both Colonels stood back. Both eased their own headwear in order to see everything properly.

Beria unbuttoned himself and moved forward.

"For all the times you have fucked with me, and tried to embarrass me, you fucking bitch."

He pressed the tip of his penis against Nazarbayeva's mouth and pushed it inside, feeling the scrape of her half-open teeth as he moved deeper.

The moment almost proved too much for him, such was his sexual excitement.

He withdrew hastily, for fear of choking the woman as she slept.

"Revenge is certainly sweet."

His whispers drew smiles from his men.

He squeezed her breasts hard, the now erect nipples standing proud.

"Fine titties, at least the best I've seen on a General!"

Neither Sarkisov nor Nadaraia offered any argument.

"Turn her."

Beria dropped his trousers and climbed on the bed.

He tried to enter her but nature fought back.

Saliva helped win the battle and he slid himself inside her anus before pushing himself slowly into her depths.

A soft female moan made the three of them freeze, but nothing came of it, so Beria started a steady rhythm, thrusting himself in and out of the woman he hated.

As his passion grew more and more, he became noisier, and both NKVD officers watched Nazarbayeva closely for any reaction.

Sarkisov could see her mouth open, but that was it.

Beria approached his moment, ramming harder and harder into Tatiana's body, causing the bed to rock and noisily protest.

"Have this, you fucking bitch whore fuck!"

He exploded inside her, continuing to fuck her as he deposited his cum.

He rolled off, panting for breath, driven from his torpor by a wish to complete his revenge.

Her open mouth provided the final ignominy that he had planned to visit upon her personally.

"Comrades, now you can have your fun. Once you've administered the next dose," and with intended humour, Beria resorted to the NCO's nickname, "Comrade Serzhant Mamont can play his part."

Beria redressed as he spoke and produced a handkerchief with which to wipe his brow.

"Enjoy yourselves, Comrades, you've earned it."

Beria went to leave and then turned back.

"So which of you won the draw?"

Sarkisov looked triumphantly at his master.

---

Just before 2300 hrs, the door opened and the two NKVD Colonels entered the lounge, still tucking in shirts and playing with ties and buttons.

Beria looked over the rim of his glass of pepper vodka and found no need to ask the question.

They had well and truly fucked the bitch and it was written all over their faces, as well as reflected in their movements, the aches and pains of a full-on session being most apparent.

His mind turned to the next part. Almost too delicious for him to wait for, but wait he would, for now.

"Get yourselves tidied up. You look like you've spent the night with a two rouble whore."

The clock chimed eleven in a soft way, not enough to wake the sleeping, just enough to inform those already awake.

"Administer the final dose as directed and then let our Mamont know the love of his life is ready and willing."

The two men left in search of refreshment, and an opportunity to discuss the delights of the sleeping woman, before ensuring that 'Mamont', so called because of his unnaturally large endowment, was ready for his part in the humiliation and neutralization of GRU Major General Tatiana Nazarbayeva.

---

"By the Motherland!"
Nadaraia could only manage that small exclamation.
Sarkisov took it a little further.
"Now that's what I call a fucking cock!"
Nadaraia nodded at the film camera.
"Have you got the wide-angle lens?"
Sarkisov guffawed softly.
Beria said nothing, although he felt just the smallest pang of jealousy at the apparition.
The second dose had been administered, and the three NKVD officers had taken their station in the secret room that looked out onto the guest bedroom.
The wide two-way mirror afforded each a full view of events.
Nadaraia had his Leica, its precise lenses ready to capture more moments in the sexual history of Comrade Nazarbayeva.
Sarkisov manned the movie camera, with which he would record the licentious behaviour of the GRU General... and with an enlisted man to boot!
Beria held the folder containing the developed photographs that Nadaraia had shot that early evening, preferring to keep them for later, as he watched in nervous anticipation of the Mammoth's employment.

---

He turned the oil lamps up and looked at the sleeping woman.
To be honest, Stranov had been ordered to more worrying duties, such as when he was called upon to seduce a homosexual diplomat, or respond to the advances of some visiting dignitary whose love for his fellow man was well known to the NKVD.

Performing for the camera was as natural for him as the act itself.

Tonight, however, he felt that he would enjoy his work.

Whilst the woman was old, she had a beauty that could not be challenged, and her body offered nothing but the promise of pleasure.

As the camera whirred and the Leica clicked, he rolled onto the bed and ran his hands over the curvaceous form, lingering on her breasts, and examining the secrets hidden within her pubic hair. He was surprised to find her moist and ready, even though the Doctor had told him that her female responses would not all be inhibited.

Another thought also occurred, and he withdrew his fingers. He did not know of the violations that had already taken place, but he considered that, perhaps, the wetness had a different source.

He leant forward and sucked her thick nipple into his mouth, ensuring that her face was away from the camera, hiding the fact that she was not a willing participant.

Stranov had already pulled the bedclothes off to unmask the damaged foot, as he had been told to do, so that there could be no mistake who was being fucked before the camera.

His hands worked between her thighs, and he was rewarded as Tatiana opened legs wider.

The NCO looked quizzically at the mirror, not seeing the shrugs by way of response.

"That can be edited out later, Comrade Marshal."

Beria merely hummed a response, his own pleasures a receding memory as he started to become more aroused at what he was observing.

Believing in never looking a gift horse in the mouth, Stranov rolled on top of Nazarbayeva and slid easily inside her, despite the huge girth of his penis.

There was no lack of moisture.

Nadaraia could only admire the woman's capacity.

"Fucking hell, but she took that without a wink. Is her old man a mamont too?"

"How the shit should I know, but judging by the way he parked his fucking bus, it would seem to be a possibility.

Mind you, if he isn't, it'll be like throwing a sausage down Dzerzhinsky Street for him after Stranov has had his way."

Even Beria snorted at that one.

The three returned to concentrate as Stranov pumped in and out of the drugged woman.

His width was not the only abnormal quality of his penis and he knew that he was reaching into the very depths of the woman, and the thought spurred him on.

Sarkisov quickly played with the audio setting, ensuring that the script would be recorded.

"Ah, I'm coming, Tatiana, my darling woman. Oh my love, how we fuck... how we fuck so well... I'm coming darl... ahhhhhhhh."

Whilst it wasn't what he normally did, for the camera it was expected, so he withdrew his huge penis and the camera recorded it depositing its contents forcefully over Tatiana's pubic hair, on her belly, and reaching the underside of her breasts.

"Blyad! The boy has many talents, tovarich."

Sarkisov couldn't disagree, the efforts not yet complete as Stranov milked more from his organ.

Beria had seen the boy at work before, so wasn't surprised. Given the sensitivity of this mission, the two NKVD Colonels were his fresh film crew, their exposure to the talents of 'Mamont' Stranov being new; they found it seriously impressive.

In the bedroom, Stranov knelt either side of her head and used her mouth as he had used her vagina, careful to hold her head level with his right hand for the benefit of the camera.

He had retained his erection and slowly approached another orgasm.

"Fucking hell! He needs fucking caging!"

"Shut up!"

Beria called a halt to the exchange, his own excitement reaching the level where he needed to become involved.

Stranov repeated the cries of love as he proceeded to repeat the visual experience, showing no less a quantity of fluid than before, except ensuring that he covered Tatiana's face and hair before ensuring a sufficient deposit was given to her breasts.

Tatiana started coughing and everyone froze.

The obstruction was soon cleared, and she continued with her drugged slumber.

This time, Stranov needed a few minutes of rest before he was able to resume his violations.

Now the finale commenced, one that was not without risk, but one that Beria had specifically choreographed to produce a fitting end to his production.

The script required a different approach this time and Stranov's acting skills came to the fore.

He swept Nazarbayeva up in his arms, feigning passionate kissing and intimate contact, done so well that the watchers were all impressed.

Even though vertical, she remained in her comatose state.

Side on to the camera now, the men behind the mirror had a close up view of a lover's embrace, the woman's legs wrapped around her sweetheart as he plunged inside her, pulling her up and down with his hands on her buttocks.

Slowly.

It had been agreed that it would be slow and brief because of the additional risk, a risk that the Colonels and Stranov had questioned, but Beria really wanted the shots of the proceedings, and so it was risked.

The final stage commenced.

Whilst the act of placing her on the bed, head away from the camera, was imperfect, no-one who saw what followed would be in any doubt that it was Tatiana Nazarbayeva who was being violated by the huge cock.

He spent a moment squeezing her breasts, remembering to ensure that the scar of her most recent wound could be seen and recognized.

As Beria watched Stranov drive himself into the same place he himself had orgasmed some while beforehand, the moment overtook him and his own gentle strokes produced a wonderful repeat, brought to a full intensity by watching the woman anally raped before his eyes.

The act was prolonged and brutal, the huge cock driving as deep as Stranov could manage.

Even though that was what his orders directed, he would have anyway, so sweet was the sensation.

The camera and the Leica both worked hard, catching every thrust, and every bead of sweat.

As he came close to his end, Stranov swore he felt a response, a gentle rising up of the woman's rear, almost as if beckoning him further inside.

He exploded and, this time, remained inside her, filling Tatiana with his remaining cum.

His words of love rang clearly through the room, the tape preserving every syllable for whatever audience would have the pleasure in the future.

He rolled off, totally spent, permitting the close-up shots to be taken; close enough to see the product of his labours exit her body.

The curtain came down on the play that Beria had directed, and the three men exited the secret room to take some refreshment before, finally, the encore commenced.

### 0837 hrs, Thursday, 19th December 1945, NKVD guest dacha. Kuntsevo, USSR.

In the manner of those waking from a deep sleep, Tatiana started to come alive by section, feeling the aches and pains of her body, some familiar, some the things of memory.

The covers were soft and warming, the itch in her non-existent foot ever-present.

The smells of...?

*'Eh?'*

The cock...?

*'Cock?'*

Her eyes flicked open and she made herself lie still, realising that there was the sound of gentle breathing by her side.

In her hand was something that she instantly recognised by touch alone, although it should not have been there.

She risked a look and found the orderly fast asleep beside her, his huge flaccid penis held firmly in her grasp.

Her senses then lit off with aches and pains from parts that should only have been available to her husband.

She touched her hand to her vagina, feeling both the moisture and raw flesh, immediately knowing that the cock she held had taken her.

She sat up carefully, suddenly aware that the huge penis had done much more than that, the sharp stabs of pain reminding her of the first time that she had surrendered herself completely to the love of her life.

Automatically, she ran her hands over her breasts and knew what it was that made them sticky.

The hint of bruising tainted them, indicating rough handling.

She looked into the big mirror and her hair told its own story.

There was pain now, real pain.

A hint of blood on her nipple betrayed a bite that had exceeded the necessity of passion.

She touched her vagina, and the rawness was almost too much, the very pressure of her fingers bringing tears to her eyes.

Looking at her breasts, the residue was obvious, silvery and shimmering in the lamp light.

But it was her back passage that screamed the most. Inside she felt battered and she understood why. She looked at the sleeping man, and knew that he had been inside her very depths with his monstrous appendage.

Reaching round her sex and down to her anus, the pain was very real. The mixture of semen and blood upon the sheet beneath her proved her violation.

If she needed proof.

*'What have I done? Oh, my husband, what have I done!'*

As if on cue, Stranov awoke and cupped her breast playfully.

She pushed his hand away and got out of bed.

Naked.

Her ravaged state was recorded in still and movie formats. Clearly the participant in a sexual adventure of some sort, the GRU officer looked like she had been through a hurricane, which, in some ways, she had. But, each man conceded to himself, she had lost none of her sexual charm.

"Comrade General... Tatiana, my love..."

She turned on him, her eyes flashing with anger.

"What has happened here, Comrade Orderly? Tell me truthfully."

Stranov gave his best hurt and puzzled look.

"My Princess, my Tanyushka, wh…"

His use of the endearment blew her fuses.

"Silence! I want to know what happened here!"

Feigning more confusion, Stranov stumbled through a brief résumé.

"You came back early, feeling unwell, Tan… Comrade General. You went to bed and I left you alone."

He rolled over, revealing his continued and growing interest in the woman in front of him.

Tatiana snatched a curtain off the pole and wrapped herself in it.

"Show's over," she said emphatically.

"Show's over," agreed the cameraman.

"Maybe. Keep the thing running, just in case, tovarich."

Sarkisov adjusted the focus, now that natural light was filling the room.

"Carry on," Tatiana demanded.

"Well, you rang the bell for my attention. It was my fault, I suppose, Comrade General. I had no time to dress properly and, as I knew you were unwell, I came as quickly as I could. I was wearing only my underwear."

"What did I want?"

"Water. You said you were thirsty and wanted water."

"And?"

"I filled a glass for you… and then it happened."

"What happened exactly, Comrade Orderly?"

"You grabbed me, Comrade General."

"Go on."

"You grabbed me and pulled me towards the bed… I didn't know what to do, Comrade General."

He lowered his voice, acting his heart out, portraying a mind that had been caught between a rock and a hard place.

"You're a General... I'm a Serzhant. I didn't know what to do; you wanted to suck me, so I let you. I don't see that I had any choice, Comrade General."

Those secreted in the special room were glad that they had continued filming, the celluloid preservation of Nazarbayeva's look being priceless beyond measure.

"Go on."

"You were wonderful, Tat... Comrade General, truly you were... are! What a woman! Your brea..."

"Shut up! Shut up!"

She now fully understood that the aches and pains she felt had been earned in close coupling with the hugely endowed orderly.

She slipped into language normally beneath her.

"So we fucked. You fucked me?"

"No, no, Comrade General. It was lovemaking. You were wonderful, so passionate, so responsive."

Nazarbayeva's mind was spinning, partially as a result of the narcotic residue in her system, partially because she would never do such a thing. But Tatiana could not deny the evidence offered by her aching and battered body.

"Enough, Comrade Orderly. I do not remember any of this," she held up her hand to silence his protestations.

She gathered her thoughts, dealing with it as best she could.

"I do not remember this... but it has happened... and I'm sorry for it. I will always be sorry for it."

She shook her head, speaking in a way as if she was almost trying to convince herself.

"Maybe it was the drugs and the alcohol?"

More than one eyebrow rose in agreement.

"Possibly I drank too much, maybe the food was off... but for you and me it never happened, nor as far as anyone else is concerned. I must make that clear, Comrade Orderly."

Stranov's wounded face was worthy of an Oscar.

"But our love? What we had last night?"

"We had nothing last night, nothing at all, am I clear? It never happened... and it will never be spoken of."

She took the plunge.

"My position offers some advantages, and I can be of use to you after this war has concluded. Your silence will ensure my support. Are we agreed?"

"If there's no chance for our love t…"

"None. Never, Comrade Orderly. There's no future in this. I have a husband."

Behind the mirror, there were smiles, as the husband might one day have a front seat at a special film show, depending on how his wife responded to certain suggestions in the future.

"Then I agree, Comrade General, but I wish it was otherwise, for I've never made love with a more desirable woman."

"Enough. Now, get out and never speak of this."

Stranov couldn't resist a sneaky look towards the mirror as he left the room, pausing only to pick up his shreds of clothing.

Truly, the show was now over and the three NKVD officers removed themselves and the equipment as Nazarbayeva showered, painfully scrubbing away the residue of her night of 'passion'.

In the confines of the bathroom, she cried. Tears of anger for the abuse she had suffered; tears of hurt for the pain that wracked her every movement; tears of grief for the husband whose trust she had dishonored.

And then she cried no more.

## 0801 hrs, Saturday, 21st December 1945, US 130th Station Hospital, Chiseldon, England.

"Good morning, boys."

The nurse's smile always brought joy to the small ward simply known as number twenty-two. It was her domain, eight beds filled with what was left of men retrieved from the horrors of the front.

Not a man was intact, with wounds ranging from single amputations up to the loss of three limbs.

Chiseldon Camp's medical facilities had been established in 1915, to help deal with the huge influx of battered soldiers from the Great War.

In the Second World War, it became a focus for US units training to join the fighting in Europe and, on 7th June 1944, the 130th arrived and set up a receiving station for battle casualties that were to be flown in from the Normandy beaches.

The arriving wounded were assessed, treated, stabilized, and sent on, if it was safe to do so, a string of hospitals in and around the area set up to receive men for specialist treatments.

Most of the camp had been returned to civilian use after May 1945, but the 130th remained in its base, expanding again when the violence recommenced.

Ward twenty-two had started as an experiment, providing early intervention in amputation cases, dealing with the mental, as well as physical, aspects of the injuries.

The experiment had been successful, and there were three other such wards on the site, each with a dedicated team of nurses to bring the wounded through the traumas of their loss.

Twenty-two was now an 'Officers only' unit, and the nurse who they all called 'Florence' was a Major with a bedside manner similar to an unsympathetic poor house manager, an attitude that her patients all saw through.

Her first port of call was the man who had only lost one leg; an artillery major who had just stepped on the wrong piece of Germany and detonated a mine.

The explosion had 'only' removed his foot, but the explosive blast had done awful work, travelling up inside his leg and degloving the bone, forcing gaps in the tissue all the way to the  thigh, gaps which accommodated the expanding explosive gases.

The chances of saving the limb had been next to nothing, but that had not stopped the130th trying.

Major Jocelyn Presley administered the pain relief and checked the dressings on the Artilleryman's leg, knowing that the efforts had failed. She wrote her findings on the chart in the clipped non-descript words that clinicians always use around bad news.

The doctor's rounds would confirm her fears soon enough and the middle-aged national Guardsman from Virginia would lose his limb all the way to the hip.

Moving on, she found the armless bomber pilot still asleep. The rules of Ward 22 were to let people sleep unless the medication was time critical, so she marked the chart that the pain relief had not been administered.

As always, the eyes of patient three burned brightly.

"Good morning to you, Major."

"Good morning to you to, Florence."

She feigned anger.

"How often do I have to tell you guys? It's Major Presley to you. Strictly formal, no nonsense, even for our British cousins!"

Ramsey grinned, understanding that the normal morning routine would not be the same without the 'name game'.

"So, how are the twins this morning?"

It was part of the psychology of the ward that the loss of limbs was dealt with up front, without avoiding the issue. Ramsey called his stumps the twins as, after skilled work by the surgeons at an anonymous casualty clearing station in Holland, the remaining parts of his legs were identical in every way.

"Well, I know they are there, Major Presley."

By Ramsey's standards, that was almost a desperate cry for pain relief.

Presley prepared some oral analgesia.

"Your wife is coming to visit today. I thought you would like to know so you can tidy up a bit."

Ramsey's smile almost needed stitches, it was so wide.

"She badgered the War Department apparently. Didn't take no for an answer."

Ramsey choked and spluttered as he consumed the pain killer.

"That would be her for sure, Major Presley."

Making more notes on Ramsey's sheet, Jocelyn Presley cracked one of her rare grins, as she was truly happy for the delightful English officer.

"Well," she made a deliberately studious examination of his paperwork, "Soon enough, you'll be able to go home to her and leave this horrible war behind you.

Ramsey looked at her in a way that made her wonder exactly what she had said.

"Major Presley, nothing could be further from my mind. I **will** walk again, and I **will** contribute again… and there'll be no argument on the matter either!"

The grin was there, but she could see his eyes.

Normally full of mischief, they were now hardened, and she knew that behind them lay a brain resolved to somehow return to the war.

She returned the silent stare, sending her own message to the Black Watch officer.

*'You're a goddamn solid gold hero, man! You've done your bit and paid a heavy price, John Ramsey. Please, let it go now and return to your loved ones, eh?'*

His eyes sent back a silent reply.

*'I've lost my legs, not my mind. There's work I can do… and I **will** do it!'*

The medication started to kick in and he felt drowsy.

"Sleep well, Major Ramsey."

Nodding at 'Florence', he fell asleep.

Presley dwelt by the bed for just a moment, looked at her sleeping charge and whispered her thoughts to sleeping ears.

"Actually, I don't doubt that you will, John. Wouldn't bet against it, and that's a fact."

Which, for Jocelyn Presley, was actually quite sad.

*We draw our strength from the very despair in which we have been forced to live. We shall endure.*

*Cesar Chavez.*

# Chapter 124 - THE ROLLCALL

They had been arriving for the past two days, trains and trucks bringing the rag-tag assembly of men together in the one new facility.

Actually, facility was an overstatement.

The handful of huts, each built to house forty men, thus far contained an average of one hundred and ten souls each. Simple maths brought the number of POWs to at least seven-hundred and fifty, and the new guests were arriving every hour.

Old tents were available for the late-comers, and these were pitched, despite the best efforts of the growing storm.

The NKVD officer in charge of camp security sat on his verandah, rocking backwards and forwards absent-mindedly as the vodka seared his throat, his eyes seeking out every detail of the panorama laid out before him.

Out of the corner of his eye, he saw the previous commander approaching.

"Comrade Kapitan Durets, to what do I owe this pleasure?"

"Comrade Mayor, the latest transport has deposited two hundred and three prisoners here. This brings the number assigned to this camp to…" he checked the figure to get it absolutely right, "Nine hundred and seventy-three."

"Excellent, Comrade Kapitan."

The look on the man's face told the security commander that was not necessarily the case.

"Go on, Comrade."

"Even with our present arrangements in the huts... and the old tents you were able to secure, we will come up short on accommodation... by my calculations... by forty-three places, Comrade Mayor."

Skryabin gave the matter a moment's thought, grimacing as an icy blast hit both men full on.

"Then we must either find more places, or fewer bodies to fill them."

Another draught of warming vodka hit the spot and his face creased in genuine mirth before becoming business-like again.

"Seeing as I cannot produce more tents out of my arse, then I shall have to whittle away at the bodies. Roll call parade, Comrade Kapitan," Skryabin checked his watch and made a mental calculation.

He drained the last of the vodka and set the glass down hard, the rifle shot sound making more than Durets jump.

"Six minutes."

The NKVD Captain threw up a salute and trudged back through the snow and icy water to get the guard prepared for a spot roll call.

Skryabin's reputation had come before him; both that of the bravery, as well as that of the cruelty, and it appeared to Captain Durets that it would be the latter on display today.

---

"Attention!"

The tired and freezing men made a valiant effort to present themselves as a group of soldiers, but the cold cut through their rags like a knife and they soon hunched or grouped again, driven apart or upright only by the butts of rifles as the Guards counted them off.

After eleven minutes the figure came back.

*'Nine hundred and seventy.'*

"Incorrect. Do it again."

The counting resumed, hand in hand with an increase in the cut of the wind, with those on the northern edge of the assembly area worst affected.

Skryabin looked on in satisfaction as two men dropped into the slush.

*'Nine hundred and seventy-one.'*

"Wrong, you fucking oaf! There's two of the bastards lying dead there. Did you count them? Well? Did you?"

The Senior Sergeant overseeing the roll call turned to get the answer from one of his subordinates, but Skyrabin was on a roll.

"Right! Enough of this shit. Comrade Captain. Name and rank parade, left to right. No-one leaves the parade ground until it is correct. Understand?"

The NKVD officer did and the guards herded the miserable prisoners to one side of the parade area whilst the Captain and Senior Sergeant oversaw the setting up of two tables and chairs.

"Begin."

The prisoners lined up in two separate columns, pressing closely together to reduce their exposure to the killing wind.

Skryabin, drinking from a recently filled hip flask, drew closer to the Captain.

Pencil poised over the paperwork containing the prisoner details, he looked up at the first man.

"Name and rank?"

"Schwartz. Major."

It took a minute to find the name, on the last but one sheet.

A head gesture moved the suffering Schwartz on, the frozen man still wrapped in the summer tunic he had been wearing when taken prisoner on the 7th August.

"And you?"

"De Villiers, Flight Lieutenant."

The South African pilot's name was on the first sheet.

"Next."

"Jus' there, man."

The Scottish soldier tapped the paper hard, causing a small tear at the side.

"See there. It says 'Kiss ma fucking chassis, ye commie wanker'. Just there."

McLinden laughed.

De Villiers laughed.

Collins laughed.

Skryabin certainly didn't.

No-one laughed as the top of McLinden's head disappeared, and those nearest got a spray of blood and brains as Skryabin's bullet smashed a path through the NCO's head.

Returning his pistol to the soft leather holster, Skryabin leant forward, speaking over the shoulder of his Captain, who had received an exaggerated share of the detritus from the dead McLinden.

Indicating the body, the warm blood steaming in the freezing temperature, Skryabin shouted at the next prisoner in line.

"Now. What was that's name?"

Julius Collins looked long and hard at the sneering NKVD officer and debated his options.

*'You'll fucking keep, you commie son of a fucking bitch. But you an' me'll dance soon enough.'*

"Maclinden, Lance-Corporal."

The NKVD Captain re-established himself.

"And yours?"

"Collins, Master Sergeant."

A head gesture sent Collins limping on his way as McLinden's body started to stiffen in the cold.

An American officer strode up to the table, pushing others aside in his anger.

"Who the fuck is in charge of this... this...," his finger pointed at the corpse, his anger leaving him unable to speak.

"I am. Who are you?"

"I'm Colonel Lee," the ex-commanding officer of the 317th US Infantry Regiment leant over the table, using his scarred face and huge frame to try and intimidate the two enemy officers, "And who the hell are you? Shooting prisoners is murder, you sonofabitch. When this is over, there'll be a reckoning."

Skryabin also leant forward and encouraged Durets to find the name.

Once it was located, the pencil did its work.

The Tokarev was out of the holster and had put the first of two bullets into Lee before anyone had a chance to move.

Skryabin, his face lightened in amusement, tapped Durets on the shoulder.

"Amend your records, Comrade Kapitan. They are incorrect."

Converting the tick into a cross, Durets steadied himself with a deep breath.

Skryabin walked down the line of waiting men, seemingly indifferent to the naked hate that emanated from each set of eyes, although those that looked saw a purposeful grip maintained on the unsheathed pistol.

Back at the desk, Dryden and Hamouda tended to Lee, trying to stem the flow of blood.

The Colonel, shock removing his capacity for coherent speech, started to moan louder and louder.

Anxious to avoid any further attention from the psychopath NKVD commander, Hamouda clamped his hand over Lee's mouth, stifling the sounds of a man in the extremes of pain.

Skryabin, hearing the moans, turned back, but was intercepted by the arrival of one of his soldiers.

The salute was text book and extremely impressive, something all the Major's team had found to be necessary to avoid a beating, or worse.

577

"Comrade Mayor. General Lunin is on the phone. Guard hut Seven."

As Skryabin stalked off towards the nearest guard post, Dryden appealed to Durets.

"Please, Captain… if I don't get him in the warm and work on these wounds, he will die."

English simply wasn't Durets strong point, but he understood what the naval doctor wanted.

However, his language skills were up to a response.

"No."

To punctuate his response, Durets continued with the next in line.

---

It was twenty past eight in the evening by the time the Allied prisoners were permitted to move off the assembly ground, by which time forty-nine more men had succumbed to the effects of the Soviet winter.

By some miracle, Dryden and Hamouda had managed to keep the wounded Lee alive.

In hut two, a space was created close to the single stove, and the two men went to work.

All around them, men huddled together on solid bunks, six to a space meant for one, some watching, others drifting off into a sleep of sorts, all just thankful to be alive.

At nine o'clock the two electric lights went out, the normal routine for the camp, had they but known it.

"No! Get them back on!"

Dryden fumbled around solely by touch, desperate to find the blood vessel that was still causing Lee problems.

"I need light!"

A movement of a finger brought some, as Julius Collins flicked his contraband lighter into life, although it was weak and flickering.

Another , then another joined, but the combined light was still less than ideal.

Dryden probed with his finger, feeling a pulsing flow.

All of a sudden that flow became a geyser, squirting Lee's blood straight at his face.

"Shit! More light!"

Two more lighters added to the array.

The geyser subsided, but not because the blood vessel had been found.

"No! No! No! Hany!"

Standing ready with the twine, Hamouda could do nothing but check the colonel's vital signs.

"Weak, racing."

He laid his hand on Dryden's, the one deep inside the main wound.

"Lieutenant Commander, there is nothing you can do now."

Lee died, one final prolonged exhalation marking his end.

"Bastards! We could have saved him, Hany! Bastards!"

The lighters clicked out one by one, until the glow of the wood stove provided the only illumination.

Kevin Roberts, a young Canadian Major, lit two cigarettes from one of the pieces of red luminous timber and passed one to the naval man.

"You gave it your best shot, Commander. It just wasn't enough today."

Dryden looked at him in anger, and then he slumped in resignation.

Hamouda stayed silent, but he was also obviously feeling the loss.

Roberts slapped both men on the shoulder and spoke with conviction.

"There will be other days."

---

Huts one, two, and three contained the Senior NCO's and officers from amongst the prisoners, men whom the NKVD reasoned would be of higher intelligence, and therefore more capable of the later tasks that would be demanded of the workforce.

Until that time came, all prisoners cut wood, mixed concrete, carried stone, or dug as best they could in frozen soil, often prepared by explosives,.

Much as the Germans had brought together their most troublesome prisoners in one place, a move that concentrated the most devious minds in one camp, the Soviet focus on huts one, two and three also meant that they created a rod for their own backs, as subtle moves, planned discretely round the hut stoves, spelt delay for the project over the coming weeks and months.

*It is not a field of a few acres of ground, but a cause that we are defending, and whether we defeat the enemy in one battle, or by degrees, the consequences will be the same.*

*Thomas Paine.*

# Chapter 125 – THE QUIET

### December 1945, the European Front

Across Europe the major battles had all ended, and even the small ones had all but ceased, so bad were the conditions.

Rivers normally running freely in winter became nothing but solid walkways and, in a few instances, commanders launched their men across the ice.

Supply issues hounded both sides, and it almost seemed that an agreement was reached between opposing forces.

*'If you keep out of my way, I'll leave you alone too.'*

There were no recorded instances of cease-fires, no sign of a reoccurrence of the First World War camaraderie between opposition troops.

It was not the Soviet way, and the Allies seemed less inclined than had been the case in the past.

None the less, unspoken agreements reduced the fighting to a minimum, unless stirred by some interloping officer from a higher command.

In both armies, casualties caused by bullet, bomb and shell declined, whilst those caused by the extreme cold rose.

Men from sunnier climes suffered the most.

Above the frozen ground the aircraft still flew, but cold weather missions were not without risk, and accidents rose.

The Allied Bomber force continued to pound anything that could be of use to the Red Army, which found much of its new supply of men and materiel could not move forward because the infrastructure was being dismantled by Allied high-explosives.

Choke points then attracted more attention from bombers, and trauma casualties behind the lines exceeded those at the front, often by considerable distances.

Bridges meant for the Army were needed at points where men and supplies were choked up, so the vital equipment never reached the engineers who would need it when the thaw came.

The war at sea was virtually over, the occasional Mediterranean scuffle with a submarine from the Black Sea Fleet normally resulted in the Soviet craft remaining underwater permanently.

The political and military hierarchies on both sides concluded that it was in their best interests to use the big freeze to rebuild, rest, plan, and prepare for the thaw.

On each side there were individuals who counseled otherwise, stressing that the enemy would be doing likewise.

None of their voices were heard or, if they were, their argument was ignored in favour of the enticement of an extended spell of peaceful time.

Perhaps the Soviet dissenters were more correct, in that the mighty industrial power of the United States would not stop for snow, the convoys that plied the Atlantic, no longer troubled by the small but effective Elektroboote force, would go on through storm and ice, and the build-up of men, weapons, and ammunition, would continue unhindered by air attacks, the Red Air Force being spent as an offensive arm for the foreseeable future.

The GKO had other thoughts, perhaps they were blinded by the dazzling possibilities of the Atomic programme's progress.

The Allies, perhaps also enchanted by their own programmes, almost seemed to forget the resilience and come-back capabilities of their enemy, capabilities that had drawn many plaudits when they all sat on the same side of the table.

From SHAEF's headquarters in Versailles, to that of the Red Banner Forces of Europe under the rock of Nordhausen, the military commanders had curtailed their plans in favour of renewal and rest.

Their political masters, Churchill aside, had concurred, and supported the unofficial cease-fire. Churchill's desire to strike hard was considered unrealistic, but he was right in some of what he said, as the advantages of Spectrum Red were slowly eaten away by the lull.

When Eisenhower went for a walk, or when Konev ventured from his underground tunnels, both found the air so cold that it hurt to breathe, and the ground covered with snow, sometimes above the height of the tallest of men.

The weather forecast predicted more of the same, without thaw, well into the New Year.

A Europe filled with armed men was relatively quiet, but the plans were being laid for when they could start killing each other again.

## 1051 hrs, Monday, 23rd December 1945, Headquarters of SHAEF, Trianon Place Hotel, Versailles, France.

Bedell-Smith settled into his chair, the one normally occupied by his commanding officer.

Eisenhower was thousands of miles away, enjoying a well-earned leave at his home.

Staff in the headquarters had been on the same flight, the situation enabling others who had been in Europe since 1943 to go home and spend Christmas with their loved ones.

Not that the Allied Armies would be repeating the errors of 1944, when the German attack had caught them badly unprepared. Once is a mistake, twice is unforgivable.

The situation map was quiet, the last reports he had seen were those detailing aircraft casualties from the night's raids, and assessments of damage caused by their bombs. There were also personal messages from him, messages of encouragement and congratulations requiring his signature, due to the units that had carried out the missions.

The ever-present Colonel Hood broke his reverie.

"Sir, the meeting. It's nearly eleven."

"Thank you, Thomas."

Bedell-Smith stood and stretched, and walked crisply to the conference room, meeting Major Goldstein en route.

"How's your German today, Major."

"Well I've been practicing some, General. I've a hunch that Speer's briefing's gonna get all technical on me today, so I've brushed up on some big words."

He held out a book.

"Also I brought this, just in case."

Bedell-Smith grinned.

"Very wise, Major, very wise indeed."

### 1100 hrs, Monday, 23rd December 1945, the conference room, Headquarters of SHAEF, Trianon Place Hotel, Versailles, France.

"Good morning, gentlemen. Please sit."

The sound of chairs scraping as they responded to Bedell-Smith's invitation echoed around the large room, eventually dying away as the last of the men made themselves comfortable.

Bradley and De Lattre sat on one side of the large table, opposite Bedell-Smith and Goldstein.

Devers had sent his apologies, but the weather had socked his area in completely.

To their left, Generals Robertson, Simpson and Horrocks, the latter acting as McCreery's eyes and ears until the Denmark situation subsided. The two vacant seats were left for Tedder and Patton, should their respective aircraft be able to land on time.

To their right sat Von Vietinghoff, Guderian, and Speer, all for the German Republic, and it was they who had requested this extra meeting. The empty seat belonged to Von Papen, who had been taken ill that very morning.

Bedell-Smith took the lead in Tedder's absence.

"Well, gentlemen," he directed his comments at the German leadership contingent, "What is it that has caused such a stink?"

He omitted the word 'panic', despite it being used freely around SHAEF when the request had been sent in.

Von Vietinghoff took up the baton.

"Our forces have suffered heavily in the failed assault on Cologne. We can bring our units up on manpower without problem or loss of time. In fact, we will be able to

584

increase our number of units in the field if we can resolve the equipment issue."

"Equipment issue?"

"General Smith, our units are equipped with German tanks and weapons, most of which have been supplied from 1944/1945 stocks."

The Allied officers in the room read that as 'captured', which was correct.

"Our munitions level is good, as is the morale of our troops. But we now see a shortage of the vehicles, particularly tanks and personnel carriers."

Bedell-Smith had heard there might be a problem in the future, but clearly it was here and now, and of sufficient concern to force a meeting just two days before Christmas.

"I assume that you have a solution, General?"

Von Vietinghoff cleared his throat, looking at De Lattre, before starting.

"The Legion Korps seems to consume huge amounts of every asset, particularly tanks and personnel carriers, many of which are being used to increase the size of the unit. Our French Allies are," the exact terminology had been agreed beforehand, but he momentarily paused as he tried to recall it, "Are restricting our access to items stockpiled in France, which is affecting our ability to maintain strength, even without operations such as Spectrum Blue."

Again, he sought some reaction from De Lattre, and found none.

"We must have access to the stocks that the French Army control, or we will not have full offensive capability when the thaw comes, even with Herr Speer's plan."

All eyes swivelled to De Lattre, who certainly did not enjoy being the centre of attention.

"Monsieurs, the Legion Corps is one of our most effective units. If you deprive it of assets then it will lose its power and eventually leave a hole in our forces. France cannot permit one of its units to suffer in such a fashion."

A sharp exchange took place between Guderian, Von Vietinghoff, and De Lattre, the voice of Goldstein getting gradually louder as he strove to translate some of the increasingly harsh language.

Bedell-Smith had rapidly realized that this decision was well above his pay grade.

Like a cross schoolmaster, he slapped the table with the palm of his hand.

"This decision cannot be made here. It is for our political masters to make. For now, I would ask the French authorities to release some equipment," De Lattre puffed himself up before Bedell-Smith raised his hand in a calming gesture, "As a show of good faith, as we are all in this together."

The Frenchman settled down and nodded.

"I will suggest it to De Gaulle, immediately following this meeting."

"Thank you, General. Will that be sufficient for now, gentlemen?"

Grudgingly, Guderian accepted the modest concession.

Bedell-Smith thought quickly and made his own play.

"I will pass on this conversation to the President, and I will recommend that he presses for the release of the French stocks."

The German contingent brightened as much as De Lattre sank, both sides knowing that such political weight would be certain to ensure that the Germans got their equipment, to the detriment of a unit that, even though it fought extremely well, still did not have the support of many of the Allied hierarchy.

"Now, I believe that Minister Speer has some requests to make?"

Goldstein played with his technical terminology book in anticipation.

Speer could speak very passable English, but had a habit of slipping into his native language just for comfort, and certainly did so when speaking on technical matters.

He stood to address the group.

"Meine Herren, as the military men have informed you, our army is short of certain resources. The solution we have set in motion is temporary, particularly if this war moves on as we expect. Even the stockpiles and the skill of our recovery troops will be overcome by the needs of our front-line soldiers."

He took a sip from his water and ploughed on.

"My job within… sorry… one of my jobs within the new government is to address production capability, and to see how Germany can start contributing to the war effort in ways other than the blood of her young men."

Having waxed lyrical for a few seconds, Speer then got down to business.

The facts and figures flowed freely.

*Resources available in the Ruhr and Germany.*

*Resources available in other Allied-held parts of Europe.*

*Resources that are critical and not available.*

*Available manufacturing that is undamaged.*

*Available manufacturing that is capable of partial production.*

*Available manufacturing that is repairable.*

*Skilled manpower available or needed.*

*Unskilled manpower available or needed.*

Even though he was brief, the mountain of information overwhelmed the listeners.

Horrocks, once commander of British Thirty Corps during the Arnhem debacle, found it necessary to interject.

"Err, I say, Herr Speer, but this is all mumbo-jumbo to me."

Neither Goldstein's translation skills nor his technical book were up to the task of translating 'mumbo-jumbo' into German, so he plumbed for something more direct.

"If you are saying that you can start bunging out some of your tanks and vehicles in the near future, then I'm sure we're all delighted, truly."

He waited whilst the translation was done, taking his own water on board.

"I'm a soldier, not an engineer. Would you please be awfully kind and just let me have the bottom line of what you want and what you can do, old chap?"

The German contingent might well have taken offence had it been anyone but Horrocks, but his credentials were well-known, and his eccentricities were accepted as part of the man that he was, for Horrocks was a general with an enviable reputation amongst his peers and former enemies.

"Herr General, as you say, cut to the chase, yes?"

Horrocks laughed, and the modest amount of tension in the room vanished instantly.

"If you'd be so kind, Sir."

"If we can have the raw materials, the manganese, aluminium, iron ore, tungsten..." the generals started to shift uneasily and Speer got the message, "Everything on the list, then I have the tooling, the power supply, the workforce and the capacity to produce vehicles and munitions sufficient to maintain 130% of the German forces presently in the field."

That was a bombshell and a half, and one that screamed for clarification.

Simpson was first in.

"Hold on there, Mister Speer. Are you telling me that you can cobble together enough capacity to keep... what is it... best part of seven divisions supplied, plus thirty percent?"

"No, General. I am including the units in Italy as well."

"Bullshit, if you don't mind me saying, Mister Speer."

Wisely, Goldstein remained silent.

"If the resources are made available, and no further German and Austrian territory is lost to the Communists, then it will be so, General Simpson."

Speer felt he needed to say more.

"Meine Herren, keeping hold of the Ruhr was absolutely vital. Many, but not all, of the facilities I have visited and assessed are there, or nearby."

Again, this was a political decision, but the group would put their names to it when it went forward.

Given the quiet nature of the winter war, there were very few other matters to air, so the meeting broke up less than an hour after it had commenced.

### 1238 hrs, Monday, 23rd December 1945, Headquarters of Command Group Normandie, Pfalzburg, France.

Knocke and Bittrich shared a quiet exchange whilst Lavalle was engrossed in his telephone conversation.

Knocke's hand was wrapped in bandages, the injury self-inflicted.

When dismounting from his command tank he had slipped on the icy top plate. He slid off the turret, grabbing desperately for a handhold, finding one on the cupola.

For the briefest of moments his whole weight had been supported by one hand, specifically his ring finger which was kept in place by his wedding band.

The ring had cut straight through to the bone.

To add to his misery, when he took the weight off the wound and dismounted, he sliced the back of the same hand on one of the damaged track guards.

Bittrich was merciless in his ribbing.

Both men suddenly realized that the phone call had come to an end, mainly because Lavalle was clearly on the point of meltdown.

Bittrich poured another coffee for Normandie's commander and set it before him.

"We've been stabbed in the back."

Such a comment needed more explanation, and both officers waited for the next line.

"That was Général De Lattre, calling from SHAEF in France."

That they already knew.

*'Get on with it, Christophe!'*

"The German Army has asked that all ex-German Army stocks in France are turned over to them, as a lot of their armour and half-tracks were lost in the Cologne offensive."

Both Knocke and Bittrich understood the implications of that.

"He thinks that it will be after Christmas before the decision is made."

Lavalle acknowledged Bittrich's efforts by raising the cup in salute, before emptying half of the contents in one gulp.

"He suggests that we consider making the most of the interim period to stockpile what we can. Ammunition for our weapons should be fine, but I don't think we'll take the chance, eh?"

He got no argument.

589

"It is the armour, guns, and vehicles, where we're definitely going to suffer. So we get what we can as quickly as possible."

A plan was forming in his mind.

"I'll get onto Sassy and make sure that they know to grab what they can and keep it inside the perimeter. I'll also speak to Plummer."

He started writing a list.

"Willi, organize a group to sweep through the area, find the locations of all the dumps and vehicle graveyards. Anything and everything that we might need, they grab it."

Bittrich understood perfectly.

"Map."

Lavalle was on a roll, and his clipped tones were not meant to be rude, just indicated that his mind was in gear.

The three moved to the map table, and Lavalle swept it with his eyes, seeking the perfect spot.

"Here!"

His triumphant tone was accompanied by a tap of his finger.

Both German officers leant forward.

"Le Forêt Domaniale. Perfect. oui?"

"Jawohl."

He made a further note.

"We shall amass our own dump in the woods there, away from prying eyes from all sides. I'll speak to Beveren, and see if he can provide the security for it."

Knocke and Bittrich couldn't get another word in, so fired up was Lavalle.

"Ernst, I need you to go through the runners and wrecks in our positions; German, French, Russian, I don't care, just get your workshops units to recover them and make something of them."

More furious scribbling.

"De Lattre wants me to inform the other group commanders. He said he will inform Molyneux when he rings him Christmas day, which gives us two days grace."

Despite his improved performance, Molyneux was still deeply mistrusted throughout the Legion Corps D'Assault.

"Oh, Ernst, have a chat with Montgomerie, see what Deux can offer by way of assistance."

Lavalle suddenly became aware of the two grinning faces opposite him and he immediately understood their mirth.

"Shut up you swine! I'm getting old, and if I don't spit it all out, I'll forget!"

The grins remained, as both Germans were at least a dozen years his senior.

"Alright, alright, so I got excited," his face went serious for the moment, "But the decision, when it comes, will leave us without the tools to fight, and that is to be avoided."

Both Knocke and Lavalle held their breath as Bittrich froze, his face screwed up prior to a monumental sneeze.

"Make sure you stay wrapped up warm, Willi. Now, no time to waste. Let's make a start."

Knocke brought them back to the subject they had been discussing before the phone call.

"And Uhlmann?"

Lavalle sighed, but held firm.

"We can do no more than we are doing, Ernst. The enquiry is lodged with the Red Cross. If he's dead, we'll do all we can do to get his body back. If he's a prisoner, then we must hope they don't realise who he is… and if he's alive and still out there somewhere… well… he's escaped from hell once before, hasn't he?"

## 0401 hrs, Tuesday, 24th December 1945, Maaldrift airfield, Holland.

As is typical in war, supreme acts of bravery most often go unseen and unrecognised, the gallant man or woman doing what they did without subsequent recognition for their ultimate sacrifice.

Such was the case at Maaldrift.

The young Dutchman had been born to a family of communists. He served his time in the Resistance, killing Nazis, and attacking the infrastructure that maintained the German forces in his country.

His political affiliation had long since been forgotten, at least by those with whom he served, not by him.

591

When he saw the eleven silver-plate B-29's being fuelled and bombed up, he knew his moment of destiny had arrived.

These new Allied bombers were special, and he believed that they would only be employed on missions of supreme importance.

His job as interpreter gave him access to the entire base and, so trusted was he, that he was permitted to carry the Sten gun that had been his companion through the years of occupation.

He had thought and thought over the weeks since the huge planes arrived, just how he could do the job of destroying them.

His mind kept coming back to just one way, and so it was that he found himself in the base transport office, taking the spare set of keys for fuel bowser six, the fully loaded spare set aside in case of problems.

Henk Hoosen slipped inside the vehicle and keyed the ignition.

Initially refusing to fire, the engine then burst into life with a sound like an artillery barrage, or at least that was how Hoosen heard it.

He beckoned one of his helpers forward, and the man slipped into the passenger seat.

Dropping into first gear, he eased the truck forward slowly, wishing to avoid inquisitive eyes.

He reasoned that switching the lights on was more likely to avoid such attention than moving blacked out, and the decision seemed to bear fruit as the working men spared him hardly a glance.

He drove out to the field and parked up by the control trailer. One of the ground crew was up on the top, sweeping the snow off the Perspex dome.

The Sten gun chugged three times, the silencer containing most of the sound of the cartridges propelling the projectile. The man fell into a pile of snow by the side of the trailer.

A USAAF officer stuck his head, wondering what the odd sound was. He died still wondering.

The other three airmen in the trailer grabbed for their pistols but, before they could even get their holsters open,

Hoosen's companion had made it to the door and shared his own magazine between them.

He reached inside the door to pick up the object that five men had just been killed for. Almost as an afterthought, he grabbed some spare flares, just in case.

Within a minute, the fuel bowser was off on its final journey.

Hoosen stopped the articulated vehicle just short of the dispersal area, where the eleven fuelled and bombed-up aircraft stood ready, ground crews polishing the skin and completing the final preparations for the bomber's mission.

He opened the fuel discharge valve and ran to the cab.

The vehicle moved off, leaving a stream of aviation spirit in its wake.

---

"What the fuck is that goddamned idio..."

The heavy vehicle crushed the USAAF officer into the concrete, the flat of his hand no defence against the solid metal.

The bowser swung around the first B-29 and Hoosen slowed deliberately, bashing the cab into the lower propeller blade on the port outer before going hard right and bending the inner engine's propeller too.

Another airman disappeared under his wheels as he moved on to the next revetment.

Emboldened, Hoosen decided to swipe the nose of the Superfortress, and increased his speed accordingly.

The aircraft shuddered with the impact and moved a few feet to the left as the heavy bowser dragged it.

He moved away in search of other targets and found them without too much trouble.

His windscreen shattered where bullets struck the glass, his cheek wet and sticky as a shard sliced him through to his teeth.

His compatriot smashed the rest of the windsfreen out with the butt of his Sten and fired a burst without result.

The next B-29 lost two propellers and had a bath in aviation fuel before the bowser moved on.

The whole base was alive now and Hoosen could sense the indecision in those responsible for security. Most held their fire, conscious of the huge bomb that was driving around the base. Some made the decision that if it blew, it blew, but maybe there was a chance to save something.

Hoosen's three other communist fighters started firing from different positions around the perimeter, adding to the confusion.

Back at the second aircraft, one of the wires damaged by the crash dropped and shorted, creating a small set of sparks. Where the fuselage had ripped the top of the tank, a small amount of fuel had slopped inside and it was this that hungrily welcomed the ignition source.

The nose of the B-29 started to burn.

The instruction booklet for the bombsight, normally kept in a pocket on the sight's mount, had been displaced and, soaked in fuel, it started to burn.

It was balanced on a damaged aluminium strut and, as the flames consumed one side, the weight and gravity combined to make it fall from to the ground, where the puddles of fuel lay waiting their turn.

The fire developed at a terrific rate, the fumes almost creating a cloud of orange and red as they ignited.

Much of the fuel trail had fumed off, but sufficient remained for the fire to spread in two directions and, within a minute, aircraft one and three were also alight.

Hoosen increased speed, driven as much by a need to fulfill his task as by the thought that he was still spilling aviation spirit and that fire can spread pretty fast when the circumstances are right.

The concrete aprons and runways had been cleared of snow and the soft joints between the heavy pads proved inviting for the fuel to flow into, creating large rectangles of fire.

Someone, somewhere, gave the order and return fire started slamming into the bowser.

A rear tyre went and, even though he was slowing to take out his fifth aircraft, Hoosen nearly lost control.

The B-29 succumbed to the bowser's attention and he moved on, smashing into jeep containing three MPs, crushing them and their vehicle without losing an ounce of momentum.

The jeep caught fire and ignited fuel spilling from the bowser.

His comrade took a round in the shoulder, dropping his sten on the floor of the bucking vehicle. As the man bent to retrieve it, he was hit half a dozen times.

Hoosen, suddenly terrified, increased his speed and sped towards the next target.

A bullet clipped his hand; a second entered the door and stuck in his calf.

From the other side, two bullets smashed the side window, one of which grazed the back of his head.

He yelped in pain, but held the bowser steady, despite the growing orange fire in his side mirrors.

Up on the control tower, the base commander watched as the extremely valuable silverbird squadron was destroyed one by one, by nothing more complicated than man's old adversary; fire.

The tender bore a charmed life, as did Hoosen.

Four more bullets had struck him, but none vitally so, his ability to steer intact, although his clutch leg now felt too numb for words.

---

Whatever it was that was going on, off-duty or not, Riley wanted a piece of it.

Rousing his ten man section from their pits, he got them into order and deployed them in defence of their small building.

Nipping up onto the roof, he was able to observe the destruction of the Superfortresses and, more importantly to him, what it was that seemed to be causing the mayhem.

Almost like a cartoon, the Grenadier Guardsman looked at the moving bowser, then at the B-29 nearest him, the last in the line and, as yet, untouched

Looking back at the weaving fuel bowser, Riley made a decision.

"Right lads! Push up to the apron there, next to the marker."

Faces were raised and they noted where the big Sergeant was pointing.

"You two," he selected Jones and Newton, "Grab the Vickers and get it set up on that small rise to the side. You, get the daisy chain. Now move!"

The section moved as swiftly as they could and deployed towards the apron, setting themselves between the end B-29 and the now fiery bowser.

---

Hoosen saw that the fire had followed his progress like a faithful dog, the early morning sky and its snow filled clouds orange in reflected light. Everything was on fire; aircraft, men, the very earth itself.

His breathing was labored now; a single bullet had taken him under the rib cage and hammered the breath from him.

'One more, just one more."

He pushed the bowser on, cornering on the point of the revetment and turned hard left towards the final bomber.

He screwed his eyes up, his vision impaired by fumes, by smoke and by blood loss.

"Fire!"

The Vickers started lashing the bowser with .303s, the front tyres simultaneously giving up the ghost.

Perhaps if they had done so independently, the result might have been different but, with the destruction of both came a sort of balance to the steering that enabled even the weakened Hoosen to control.

The radiator suffered under a number of hammer blows, and steam and scalding water spurted from the holes.

A single rifle bullet struck his shoulder, wrecking the ball joint and making him scream in agony.

The vehicle lurched and a stream of .303 bullets wrecked the passenger side, visiting more damage on the corpse by his side.

But Hoosen's luck was holding out until the last.

The lurch took the bowser away from the daisy chain of mines that would have stopped it dead.

The lurch also took the bowser straight up and over the small rise on which the Vickers was positioned.

596

Newton and Riley were pulped in the blink of an eye.

The trailer bounced up and over the hump, coming down with such force that it split at two of the numerous damage points, allowing a greater flow, almost emptying the few gallons still left behind in an instant.

Unable to control the vehicle, Hoosen just did what he could with the steering wheel, now unable to see anything but a hazy shiny shape some distance away.

The front wheels, devoid of rubber, struck the concrete of the slipway and generated enough sparks to light a thousand fires.

Only one was needed.

The trailer disintegrated with explosive force, the fireball shooting out the ruptured rear end like a flamethrower, removing Riley and his men in an instant.

The momentum of the bowser carried it forward and it closed the small remaining distance to the surviving silverbird.

Hoosen coughed clots of blood and his eyes went glazed, the totality of his wounds meaning that he did not survive to see the bowser come to rest against the bomber.

Nor did he live to hear the first of many huge explosions, as bomb loads cooked off.

All but one of the communists guerrillas was killed, the wounded survivor taken prisoner. His captors assured of the most horrible existence until they knew all that he knew. He lasted two hours.

By the end of the incident, Maaldrift was wrecked, its silverbirds were all destroyed, and over four hundred casualties were either in the morgue or being cared for in the makeshift hospital, set in one of the hangars.

### 1107 hrs, Tuesday, 24th December 1945, RAF St Angelo, Northern Ireland.

"Top of the morning to you, Sam."

"Merry Christmas to you, Dan."

The two shook hands and moved off to the warmth of the staff car, the RAF marked Hudson already on its way to a hangar where its doubtful parentage could not be noticed.

"So, what brings you all the way here on Christmas Eve?"

"I'll save it for the group, Sam. But it's a bloody can of worms and no mistake."

The car arrived at Rossahilly House, the normal venue for the clandestine meetings of the shadier arms of the Allied forces

Percy Hollander was away in Cambridgeshire with family but, as always, he placed the house at the disposal of the Intelligence services.

Major Generals Colin Gubbins and Kenneth Strong were absent, but Sir David Petrie was there on behalf of MI5.

Colonel Valentine Vivian of the SIS had made it, although his vehicle had been involved in an accident en route from RAF Belfast.

Only Bertram Leonard had made it on time, the rest of the normal attendees either away on leave or unable to answer Bryan's call in time

The smells of their dinner pervaded the smoky atmosphere, making them hungry, although the greater hunger was to find out what had so exercised the head of the Irish Army's Intelligence Service that he had summoned the group to a meeting this close to Christmas.

Bryan stood on cue and walked to a board and easel, producing a map and pinning it in place.

The four pairs of eyes took it in, the roads, the sea and the buildings.

Bryan walked to the map that had been positioned on the wall long before he arrived.

Selecting the target carefully, he pressed the pointer to the north-west part of Éire and spoke but one word.

"Glenlara."

They all got it immediately.

"You've confirmed it. We've found the bastards!"

He nodded at Vivian in acknowledgement.

"Indeed we have. Your submarine base... and more besides, I think... it's all here...at Glenlara."

The rest of the meeting and the luncheon that followed was occupied by the nature of the response, the timing of the response and the depth of the response.

By the time the cigars were lit, the answers had been found.

Land forces, as soon as practicable, and total annihilation.

Sam Rossiter, USMC, came up with the solution on all three counts, with the assistance of some underhand thinking by Dan Bryan, and the expectation of some assistance from a Squadron Leader who had recently lost a brother.

## 2239 hrs, Tuesday, 24th December 1945, Frontline position, 400 metres north of Hinteregg, Austria.

To Leander, it must have seemed like a lifetime since his platoon had been butchered by silent Soviet ski troopers.

For many soldiers on both sides it had indeed been a lifetime, terminated in blood and darkness, as their commanders, keen to appear active and full of fight, ordered their frozen men to cross the no man's land and kill, sometimes seize, occasionally destroy, but always kill.

The boy had become a man in those handful of days, going from the platoon's worst soldier, to the platoon's only soldier, and finally to the platoon's Sergeant. All in seven weeks of enduring the unendurable.

And for what?

King Company's position was the same one he had been in that night. Third battalion had not advanced one yard; nor had it conceded one either.

The 370th Regiment sat on the same line it had occupied seven weeks ago, as did the entire 92nd Colored Infantry Division.

The only things that had changed were the faces.

Men came and went, sometimes alive, often dead. After the incursions, snipers started to play their part, claiming the unwary and the unlucky.

Mortars joined in, adding their tree bursts to the litany of exciting ways to die during an Austrian winter.

And then the cold decided to make its presence felt, making all that had gone before a walk in the park.

The Sergeant's eyes were fixed on the tree line ahead, watching, waiting, and prepared, his Garand on the trench parapet in front of him, covered with a white blanket, two grenades placed ready for use to the right of the rifle.

His eyes saw nothing and his ears detected no sounds.

The forest was silent.

No mortars came, no artillery, and no snipers.

The enemy had attacked stealthily, just after 2000hrs, and the work had been hot but brief. They went as quickly as they came, leaving a dozen bodies behind in the crimson snow.

Leander had done the rounds, organized the removal of their five dead and the evacuation of the eight wounded.

His work done, he returned to his position, now occupied by him alone, his terrified partner shot down as he turned and ran during the attack.

The blood had stopped flowing from his own wounds; wood splinters in his shoulder and back, the slightest graze from a rifle bullet across his arm.

He did not complain, just maintained his silent vigil whilst his men, boys like he had been but a few weeks beforehand, nestled low in their holes and did all they could to keep the chill from their bones.

Leander had no greatcoat, just a padded jacket, a thick jumper, and a scarf round his neck, but he stood to his post, defying the cold.

The company commander, Captain Forbes, moved carefully through his positions, surprising some who had fallen asleep, welcomed by others who had managed a small triumph over winter in the form of a warm coffee.

To the left of Leander's position one such victory had brought forth coffee for the four men in the hole, plus enough for more besides.

Accepting a cup for himself and Sergeant Leander, Forbes worked his way round to the front of the Sergeant's position, making sure he could be seen by the veteran NCO.

Holding the two mugs, Forbes moved forward and then stopped.

The coffee makers watched, wondering why until Forbes sat on the parapet to drink the hot liquid, merely setting the metal mug in front of the ever-vigilant Leander.

The answer to that was simple.

Frederick Lincoln Leander had long since frozen to death.

He had spent fifty-two days in the front line, seen combat on twenty-nine of those, during which time he had metamorphosed from boy to man. Promotions had come, from Pfc to Platoon Sergeant, mostly via dead men's shoes. Conservatively, it was estimated that he had killed twenty Soviet troopers, taken five prisoners and wounded countless more. For his troubles, his superiors had sent back recommendations for both the Bronze and Silver Stars, as yet to be confirmed or rejected.

On New Year's Day 1946, the Leander family was celebrating until the news was delivered by a family friend… and then they celebrated no more.

## 2342 hrs, Tuesday, 24th December 1945, the Wilders Estate, Rottelsheim, Alsace.

Artur Wilders had not always been a farmer. Indeed, the absence of his left ear, the eye patch and stiffened left arm would give away that once he had been a soldier; a German soldier.

He had been a member of the 320th Infanterie Division, fighting on the steppes of Russia. Accidentally wounded by a German grenade, he risked being swept up in the Soviet advance, but the SS had come to the rescue and extracted his division, leading them to the comparative safety of the German front line.

Wilders owed the Schutzstaffel his life.

Hiding the ex-SS legionnaires came easy to him, an honour debt to be repaid.

He hid the two men in plain sight, as farm hands on the large estate. That both were wounded gave them the limps necessary to make their presence believable, as relics from the Patriotic War, as the hated Russians called it.

It had not occurred to the occasional Soviet visitor that the wounds were more recent and still healing.

The large hall that Wilders had added to the main building was filled with his staff and their families, all good Germans first and foremost.

They all knew the two men were not what they were presented as. Some knew exactly what they were, some even knew what they had once been, depending on the level of confidence they enjoyed with Wilders, or his wife, for that matter.

Tonight was Christmas Eve, a time when Germans find a soulful depth not normally on display.

The cold was offset by beer, wine, and brandy, all washing down plates of steaming pork, potatoes and cabbage.

The two fires were tended as the meal was cleared away, permitting tradition took over.

It fell to the master of the house to talk about the year past, and the year ahead, thanking those who had excelled, and mapping out the course for the estate over the coming twelve months.

Wilders, without notes, went through 1945 and the joys and horrors it had brought, but only relative to the estate.

There was silence for the son of his Head Gardener, killed by a strafing Soviet fighter some months before.

His description of the year ahead could only be his hopes; the war would not stop and accommodate the needs of an agricultural community.

After seventeen minutes of hopes, fears, thanks, acknowledgements, and inspiration for the future, he finished and reached for his drink.

Raising his glass, he toasted his workers, their families, and Germany.

The hour left, a new one came, and with it came Christmas Day.

He then departed with tradition, as he had been asked to do.

The room fell silent as the two 'new workers' stood.

"Kameraden. We thank you for helping us. You have saved our lives, and we are very grateful. One day, we will be able to repay you all. Until then, please accept this gift."

The younger man surprised everyone by starting to sing.

*"Stille Nacht, heilige Nacht,*
*Alles schläft; einsam wacht..."*

His voice was a like a dream, every note precise and with the feeling required of the German's most favourite Christmas song.

Eyes moistened, the wonderful voice bringing every colour and emotion ever necessary to the carol.

When the older man joined in, the harmony brought the song to a higher level.

*Nur das traute heilige Paar.*
*Holder Knabe im lockigen Haar,*
*Schlaf in himmlischer Ruh!*
*Schlaf in himmlischer Ruh!*

No-one else sang until the two Legionnaires encouraged them to join in.

It was a magical time that none present would ever forget.

The whole hall reverberated with the wonderful carol, rising voices bringing it to a worthy conclusion.

*Jesus der Retter ist da!*
*Jesus der Retter ist da!*

There was silence, all save the occasional crack as heated wood spat its resin. The tears fell silently.

Caporal Fritz Zenden, until recently a driver of a Panther tank, nodded to the assembly and sat down, leaving his commander to speak.

"Thank you all and Merry Christmas."

He sat down and raised his glass to Wilders, both men understanding that the tears in their eyes were for other times and other people, now long gone.

"Thank you, Artur. Merry Christmas."

"And to you, Rolf, and to you."

### 2343 hrs, Tuesday, 24th December 1945, One kilometre southeast of Zittersheim, Alsace.

This was always going to be the trickiest part, and the Russian carefully surveyed the ground and positions with his damaged field glasses, the single intact lens finding the weakness he sought almost immediately.

He checked his watch, immediately understanding that his period of grace would soon be over.

Twelve minutes to get across and identify himself before some sentry took a pot shot at him.

He made his calculations.

'Two hundred metres, possibly two-ten."

The opposing positions were one hundred metres behind him, containing men who had been told not to fire at anything until 2345hrs precisely.

A flare rose up and he froze.

As it sank to earth, all he could think of was the time.

In his badly weakened state, even covering the two hundred metres might prove too much, as his guides had now left him, their support and steadying hands having got him this far on the coldest night of the year so far.

The raggedly dressed man lunged forward, his initial approach masked by a drift.

On he went, his breathing seemingly loud enough to waken the dead, but nothing; no reaction at all.

In good time, he made the position he had spotted earlier, and nestled between the two rocks.

Checking his watch, he found that five minutes remained, five minutes in which he had to convince the soldiers in the position adjacent to him that he was a friend, not a foe.

He had decided on his method and started into the famous Simonov poem, speaking as loudly as caution permitted.

**"Wait for me and I'll come back.**
**Wait with all you've got.**
**Wait, until the dreary yellow rains**
**Tell you, you should not."**

The rising sound of voices encouraged him and his volume rose.

**"Wait when snow is falling fast,**
**Wait when the summer is hot,**
**Wait when our yesterdays are past.**
**And others are forgot."**

The duty officer had been summoned and arrived quickly but, for some reason, let the unknown voice finish the first section of the poem to Valentina Serova.

**"Wait, when from that far-away place,**

604

Letters don't arrive.
Wait, when they with whom you wait
Doubt if I'm alive."

"Shut the fuck up, you shithead!"

The Senior Lieutenant had been warm in his bed and was in no mood to play games, no matter how well the soldier recited the famous poem.

"I'm a Red Army soldier. Help me!"

"Move this way, quickly, No tricks or you'll be shot like a fucking dog. C'mon, move your fucking ass. It's too cold for... what the fuck is that?"

The apparition that scrambled over the top of the trench seemed like it had come from another world.

On top, the vestiges of some sort of heavy duty civilian coat, tied together with something that could have once been strips of animal skin. Whatever it was, it had an odour all of its own, even in the freezing cold of Christmas Eve 1945.

On the 'thing's' head was a cap that might once have looked like a Soviet officer's side cap.

The light of the brazier did little to aid investigation, so the officer decided to take the problem into somewhere lighter and, for his own comfort, much warmer.

"Yefreytor Amanin. Two men, search this... person... and then bring whatever it is to my bunker immediately. Serzhant Kremov, send a runner to Captain Arganov. Tell him what we have caught. Move."

The party moved swiftly, the guards and prisoner also encouraged to speedier movement by the promise of warmth.

Sitting on the table, swinging a booted leg, Senior Lieutenant Chamanov wished he had just shot the man out of hand and not wasted his time.

When the bundle of rags arrived, Chamanov was surprised to find that he was not held firm, neither was he restrained in any way.

"What is the meaning of this, Amanin?"

He extracted his pistol, intent on getting rid of the problem.

"Comrade Starshy Leytenant."

Amanin held out a disheveled identity card.

Chamanov read it in the candle light, a sense of foreboding spreading across his chest and into his heart.

"Attention!"

He sprang to parade attention, along with the rest of the escort. Only the raggedy man remained at ease.

"Sir, my apologies but… what… how… where've you come from? Why are you in this state? What the…"

"Calm yourself, Comrade Chamanov."

Ex-Polkovnik Atalin had told the man all he wanted to know about the penal unit officer.

"One question at a time. Now, can I have a drink, something to eat, and some room by that fire?"

Chamanov leapt aside like a supercharged deer, opening the way for the raggedy man to gain a seat near the warming flames.

One of the soldiers hesitantly offered up his canteen and it was gratefully accepted. The new arrival took a deep draught.

His mind immediately leapt back to another time, when vodka had tasted really good, and his soldiers were still alive, before this abominable war started all over again.

"Thank you, Comrade."

Chamanov had an idea.

"Atalin, fetch my greatcoat."

"Sir."

He found it easily and held it out, but Chamanov directed him to the figure by the fire.

"Sir, can I relieve you of your… coat and replace it with this one?"

The grunt was clearly one of agreement, the new arrival standing immediately and shedding his rags.

Beneath them, tired, dirty, and incomplete, were rank markings still identifiable as those of a Red Army Major General.

The blanket covering the door flew open and in burst an extremely irritated Captain Arganov.

"What the fuck is this all about, Comrade Chamanov. This better be fucking good or you'll… err… I… Blyad! Who the hell's that?"

"Comrade Kapitan," Chamanov quickly checked the pass he still held in his hand, "May I introduce Mayor General Ivan Alekseevich Makarenko, commander of the100th Guards Airborne Rifle Division 'Svir'."

**Perhaps <u>this</u> is the end of the beginning.**

# Table of Figures

# Glossary

| | |
|---|---|
| .30cal machine-gun | Standard US medium machine-gun. |
| .45 M1911 automatic | US automatic handgun |
| .50 cal | Standard US heavy machine-gun. |
| 105mm Flak Gun | Next model up from the dreaded 88mm, these were sometimes pressed into a ground role in the final days. |
| 128mm Pak 44 | German late war heavy anti-tank gun, also mounted on the JagdTiger and Maus. Long-range performance would have made this a superb tank killer but it only appeared in limited numbers. |
| 50mm Pak 38 | German 50mm anti-tank gun introduced in 1941. Rapidly outclassed, it remained in service until the end of the war, life extended by upgrades in ammunition. |
| 6-pounder AT gun | British 57mm anti-tank gun, outclassed at the end of WW2, except when issued with HV ammunition. |
| 6x6 truck | Three axle, 6 wheel truck. |
| 92nd Colored Infantry Division. | The US Military used to distinguish between units of different ethnic backgrounds, such as Nisei, Puerto Rican and, in this case, Coloured soldiers. Racism was rife in the WW2 US Army, something which is not widely known or accepted. Black soldiers were mainly employed on pioneer or transport duties and not permitted near the front for some time. However, the shortage of manpower following the Battle of the Bulge created a vacuum the black soldiers could fill. The 92nd developed a reasonable combat reputation. other units such as tank-destroyer, tank and artillery units gained very good reputations |

| | |
|---|---|
| Achgelis | The Focke-Achgelis Fa223, also known as the Dragon. One of the first helicopters. |
| Achilles | British version of the M-10 that carried the high velocity 17-pdr gun. |
| Addendum F | Transfer of German captured equipment to Japanese to increase their firepower and reduce logistical strain on Soviets |
| Adin | In Russian, the number one. |
| Airspeed Oxford | Twin-engine Allied transport aircraft. |
| Aldis | A signal lamp used for communications consisting of a fixed light with a shutter on the front that was opened and closed to produce morse code messages. The lamp referred to by the Sunderland crew would not have been an Aldis but the word became synonymous with signal lamps of all types. |
| Archer | Valentine chassis developed to house the 17pdr gun. Unusual as it pointed backwards in a fixed mount. |
| Ashita | Tomorrow [Japanese] |
| ATPAU | Army Tank Prototype Assessment Unit. As far as I am aware, this is a figment of my imagination. |
| AVRE | Armoured vehicle, Royal Engineers. |
| B-29 | The American Superfortress, high-altitude heavy bomber. |
| BA64 | Soviet 4x4 light armoured car with two crew and a machine-gun. |
| Baka | Fool [Japanese] |
| Balebetishen | Roughly means respectable or respectable person. |
| Bali radar | German Ant3 Radar Detector. |
| BAR | US automatic rifle that fired a .30cal round. It was an effective weapon, but was hampered by a 20 round magazine. Saw service in both World Wars, and many wars since. |

| | |
|---|---|
| Battle of the Bulge | Germany's Ardennes offensive of winter 1944 |
| Bazooka | Generic name applied to a number of different anti-tank rocket launchers introduced into the US Army from 1942 onwards. |
| Beaufighter, Bristol | British twin-engine long-range heavy fighter, saw extensive service in roles from ground attack, night fighter, to anti-shipping strikes. Also served in the USAAF in its night fighter role. |
| BefehlsPanther | Command version of the German battle tank, equipped with extra radios. Most versions retained their 75mm gun whereas, a few others, converted from Beobachtswagen, did not. |
| Beobachtungspanzer Panther | Observation vehicle, with main gun removed and a ball-mounted MG34 in the turret front. Its main purpose was as an artillery vehicle but could be used as a mobile command post. |
| BergePanther | German Panther tank converted or produced as a engineering recovery vehicle to service Panther Battalions in combat. |
| Bianchi | Italian motorcycle |
| Blau Division | Designated the 25oth Infanterie Division in the German Army, the Blau Division was made up of Spanish volunteers who signed up to fight the communists. |
| Bletchley Park | Location of the centre for Allied code breaking during World War two. Sometimes known as Station X. |
| Blighty | British slang term for Britain. |
| Blue and Grey Division | The nickname of the 29th US Infantry Division. |
| Boyes | .55-inch anti-tank rifle employed by the British Army but phased out in favour of the PIAT. |
| Bren Gun | British standard issue light machine-gun. |

| | |
|---|---|
| Browning Hi-Power | 9mm handgun with a 13 round magazine, used by armies on both sides during WW2. |
| Brylcreams | Slang expression for RAF aircrew. |
| Buffalo | British term for the LVT or Amtrak, the amphibious tracked vehicle which became a mainstay of the Pacific War, and featured in all major Allied amphibious operations from Guadalcanal onwards. |
| Buffalo Soldiers | The 92nd Colored Division was sometimes referred to as the Buffalo Division |
| C47 | US development of the DC3, known in British operations as the Dakota. Twin-engine transport aircraft. |
| Calliope | Also known as the Sherman T34, the tank was fitted with 60 4.5" rocket tubes, mounted on a frame over the turret and aimed by a simple arm attached to the main gun. Other combinations of rocket tubes existed. |
| Cavalry | The German army had cavalry until the end, all be it in small numbers. The SS had two such divisions, the 8th and 22nd. |
| Centauro tank division | Officially, the 131st Armoured Division 'Centauro', this Italian formation surrendered in Tunisia during May 1943. |
| Centurion I | British heavy tank, equipped with the 17pdr and a Polsten cannon. |
| Challenger | The British Challenger [A30] was mounted on an altered Cromwell chassis and equipped with a 17pdr gun. |
| Chekist | Soviet term used to describe a member of the State Security apparatus, often not intended to be complimentary. |
| Chesterfield | American cigarette brand. |
| Chickamauga | A battle in the American Civil War, fought on 19th to 20th September, 1863. It was a Union defeat of some note, and second only to Gettysburg in combined casualties. |

| | |
|---|---|
| Chikushou | Damn it or Fuck [Japanese] |
| Churchill IV | 6pdr equipped version of the British heavy tank, some of which fought with the Soviet Army at Kursk. |
| Churchill VII | Much improved version of the Churchill tank, equipped with a 75mm gun and uparmoured. |
| Colloque Biarritz | The fourth symposium based at the Château du Haut-Kœnigsbourg. |
| Combat Command [CC] | Formation similar to an RCT, which was formed from all-arms elements within a US Armored Division, the normal dispositions being CC'A', CC'B' and CC'R', the 'R' standing for reserve. |
| Comet | British medium tank armed with a 77mm high-velocity gun. |
| Contraband | Derogatory name applied to black escapees from the Southern States, originating from General Benjamin Butler's declaration that he would treat runaway slaves like 'contraband of war.' |
| Corvette | Small patrol and escort vessel used by Allied navies throughout WW2. |
| Court of Bernadotte | The Court of the Swedish Royal Family. |
| Crusader III | British cruiser tank that saw a great deal of action in the Desert Campaign. With a 6pdr gun it was superior firepower wise to the PzIII and PzIV it encountered there. |
| Dacha | A country cottage, but has become synonymous with a retreat for Soviet ruling classes. |
| Deuxieme Bureau | France's External Military Intelligence Agency that underwent a number of changes post 1940 but still retained its 'Deux' label for many professionals. |
| Douglas DC-3 | Twin-engine US transport aircraft, also labelled C-47. [Built by the Russians under licence as the Li-2] |

| | |
|---|---|
| DP-28 | Standard Soviet Degtyaryov light machine-gun with large top mounted disc magazine containing 47 rounds. |
| Dva | In Russian, the number two. |
| Easy Eight | An M4A3E8 Sherman tank, derived from the E8 designation. |
| EBW | Explosive bridge-wire detonators. |
| Elektroboote | A Type XXI U-Boat |
| Falke | Infra-red sighting system, installed on some German vehicles, especially useful for night fighting. |
| Fallschirmjager | German Paratroops. They were the elite of the Luftwaffe, but few Paratroopers at the end of the war had ever seen a parachute. None the less, the ground divisions fought with a great deal of élan and gained an excellent combat reputation. |
| Fanculo | Italian expletive meaning 'Go forth and multiply' |
| Fat Man | Implosion-type Plutonium Bomb similar in operation to 'The Gadget'. |
| FBI | Federal Bureau of Intelligence, which was also responsible for external security prior to the formation of the CIA. |
| FFI | Forces Francaises de L'Interieur, or the French Forces of the Interior was the name applied to resistance fighters during the latter stages of WW2. Once France had been liberated, the pragmatic De Gaulle tapped this pool of manpower and created 'organised' divisions from these, often at best, para-military groups. Few proved to be of any quality and they tended to be used in low-risk areas. |
| FG42 | Fallschirmgewehr 42, a hybrid 7.62mm weapon which was intended to be both assault rifle and LMG. |
| Firefly, Fairey | British single-engine carrier aircraft, used as both fighter and anti-submarine roles. |

| | |
|---|---|
| Firefly, Sherman V | British variant of the American M4 armed with a 17-pdr main gun, which offered the Sherman excellent prospects for a kill of any Panzer on the battlefield. |
| Flak | Flieger Abwehr Kanone, anti-aircraft guns. |
| FUBAR | Fucked up beyond all recognition. |
| FUSAG | Acronym for the First US Army Group, a phantom formation set up to mislead the Germans for the Invasion of France. |
| G2 | Military Intelligence branch of the Irish Army. |
| Garda | The Garda Síochána, the Irish police force. |
| GAVCA | Grupo de Aviação de Caça [Portuguese] Translated literally means 'fighter group', the 1st GAVCA serving within the Brazilian Expeditionary Force. |
| GAZ | Gorkovsky Avtomobilny Zavod, Soviet producers of vehicles from light car through to heavy trucks. |
| Gebirgsjager | German & Austrian Mountain troops. |
| Gestapo | GeheimeStaatsPolizei, the Secret Police of Nazi Germany. |
| Gewehr 43 | Sometimes known as the Kar43 or G43, it was the German Army's automatic rifle. Some were modified to accept ST44/MP43 magazines. |
| GKO | Gosudarstvennyj Komitet Oborony or State Security Committee, the group that held complete power of all matters within the Soviet Union. |
| Grease gun | US issue submachine gun, designated the M3. Cheaper and more accurate than the Thompson. |
| Green Devils | Nickname for the German Airborne troops, the Fallschirmjager. |
| Greenhorn | An inexperienced soldier |

| | |
|---|---|
| GroßDeutschland | German Army unit, considered to be it's Elite formation. Sometimes mistaken for SS as they wore armband, although on right arm, not the left as SS formations did. |
| GRU | Glavnoye Razvedyvatel'noye Upravleniye of Soviet Military Intelligence, fiercely independent of the other Soviet Intelligence agencies such as the NKVD. |
| Haft-Hohlladung magnetic mine | Often known as the Panzerknacker, this was a hollow charge magnetic AT mine. |
| Halifax, Handley Page | British four-engine heavy bomber |
| Hauptmann | Equivalent of captain in the German army. |
| HEAT | An anti-tank shell, High-Explosive Anti-Tank. |
| Hellcat Tank-Destroyer, M18. | US tank destroyer armed with a 76mm gun. Capable of high speed. |
| Hero of the Soviet Union award | The Gold Star award was highly thought of and awarded to Soviet soldiers for bravery, although the medal was often devalued by being given for political or nepotistic reasons. |
| Hetzer | Jagdpanzer 38t was a light tank destroyer with a 75mm gun on a fixed mount. Highly successful vehicle on the proven Czech 38t chassis. |
| Hispano | Swiss in origin, the full name is Hispano-Suiza 404 autocannon. It fired a 20mm shell, increasing aircraft firepower over the normal machine-guns. |
| Hitler Youth [Hitler Jugend] | Young males organisation of the Nazi Party. |
| HNoMS | His Norwegian Majesty's Ship. |
| Horsch 108 | German transport that served throughout WW2 in a variety of roles from officer's car to ambulance. |
| HVAP | High-velocity armour piercing. |

| | |
|---|---|
| IL-4, Ilyushin. | Soviet twin-engine medium bomber. |
| IR | Infra-red, a technology that the Germans pursued late in the war. |
| IRA | Irish Republican Army |
| IS-II | Soviet heavy tank with a 122mm gun and 1-3 mg's |
| IS-III | Iosef Stalin III heavy tank, which arrived just before the German capitulation and was a hugely innovative design. 122mm gun and 1-2 mg |
| ISU152 | Using the chassis of the IS-II, the ISU152 could serve as either mobile artillery or a heavy tank-destroyer. The shell had the capability of removing the turret from any vehicle in the German inventory just by its kinetic value alone. |
| JagdPanther | SP version of the Panther tank, armed with the 88mm gun. |
| JagdPanzer IV | SP version of the Panzer IV, armed with the 75mm gun. |
| Jeep | ½ Ton 4x4 all terrain vehicle, supplied in large numbers to the Western Allies and the Soviet Union. |
| Job tvoyu mat | With apologies, this is translated in a number of ways, and can mean anything of the same ilk from 'Gosh' through to 'Fuck your mother." |
| Kai | Sometimes known as Kye, the drink has many different recipes. Generally speaking, it had a base in bars of chocolate to which boiling water was added. Certainly, many recipes add condensed milk, sugar when it was available and Pusser's, a very alcoholic Naval rum. |
| Kandra | Knife, sometimes double-edged, originating in Siberia. They had various forms but many resembled the Kurki of the Nepalese hill men. |

| | |
|---|---|
| Kangaroo | Allied infantry carrier, either converted from a tank, mainly M4 Shermans and M7 Priest SP's, or purpose built from the Canadian RAM tank. |
| Kar98K | German standard issue bolt action rifle. |
| Katorga | Soviet penal system, also accepted as a noun for a place of hard servitude. |
| Katyn | 1940 Massacre of roughly 22,000 Polish Army officers, Police officers and intelligentsia perpetrated by the NKVD, Site was discovered by the German Army and much propaganda value was made, although in reality there was no sanction against the USSR for this coldblooded murder. |
| Katyusha | Soviet rocket artillery weapon capable of bringing down area fire with either 16, 32 or 64 rockets of different types. |
| Kavellerie | German translation of Cavalry. |
| Kerch | Soviet peninsular that juts out into the Black Sea, known in English as the Crimea. |
| Kilmainham | Prison located in Dublin, Eire. |
| King Tiger tank | German heavy tank carrying a high-velocity 88m gun and 2-3 machine guns. |
| Kingdom 39 | The Fairytale Kingdom in Russian Folklore. |
| Kradschutzen | Motorcycle infantry, term also applied to reconnaissance troops. |
| Kreigie | US slang for a German prisoner of war. |
| Kreigsmarine | German Navy |
| Kriegsspiels | Wargames |
| Kukri | The curved battle knife of the Gurkha soldier. |
| Kuso | Shit [Japanese] |
| LA-7 | Single-engine Lavochkin fighter aircraft, highly thought of despite poor maintenance history. |
| Lavochkin-5 | Soviet single-engine fighter aircraft. |

| | |
|---|---|
| Leutnant | German Army rank equivalent to 2nd Lieutenant. |
| Lightning, Lockheed, P38 | US twin-engine fighter, most successfully used in the Pacific Theatre. |
| Lisunov Li-2 | Soviet licenced copy of the DC-3 twin-engine transport aircraft, |
| Little Boy | Uranium based fission bomb. |
| Lockheed Hudson | US built aircraft, originally designed as a light bomber. It found usefulness as a Coastal Command patrol and anti-submarine aircraft, a transport, a trainer and even for clandestine missions into Occupied Europe. |
| Luftwaffe | German Air Force |
| Lysander, Westland. | British single engine monoplane designed for Liaison activities, but best known for its use in ferrying agents into Occupied Europe. |
| M-10 | Known as the Wolverine, this US tank destroyer carried a 3" gun with modest performance. It was subsequently upgunned in British service, and the more potent 17-pdr equipped vehicles became known as Achilles. |
| M13/40 | Italian light tank with a 47mm gun and 3-4 machine-guns. |
| M-16 half-track | US half-track mounting 4 x .50cal machine-guns in a Maxon mount. For defence against aircraft at low level it was particularly effective against infantry. |
| M18 Hellcat | US tank destroyer armed with a 76mm gun. Capable of high speed. |
| M1Carbine | Semi-automatic carbine that fired a .30 cal round, notorious as being underpowered. |
| M20 | US 6x6 Armoured utility car, which was basically an M8 without the turret. |
| M20 Utility Car | turretless conversion of the M8 Greyhound, with a .50cal in a ring mount and with the hull .30cal removed. Used mainly in Td battalions as a command vehicle or cargo carrier. |

| | |
|---|---|
| M21 | M3 halftrack with an 81mm mortar mount, providing mobile fire support. |
| M24 Chafee | US light tank fitted with a 75mm gun and 2-3 machine-guns. |
| M26 Pershing | US Heavy tank with a 90mm gun and 2-3 machine-guns. Underpowered initially, it had little chance to prove itself against the German arsenal. |
| M3 Halftrack | US standard half-track normally armed with 1 x .50cal machine-gun and capable of carrying up to 13 troops |
| M36 Jackson | US tank destroyer armed with a lethal 90mm gun. |
| M37 HMC | Expected to be a replacement for the M7, the M37 was a 105mm Howitzer mounted on a converted M24 Chafee chassis. |
| M3A1 submachine gun | Often known as the Grease Gun, issued in .45 or the rarer 9mm calibres with a 30 round magazine. |
| M4A3E2 Jumbo | Additional armour version of the M4A3, occasionally upgunned to the M1 76mm but mainly equipped with the standard M3 75mm. Vehicle was slower because of the extra weight. |
| M4A3E8 | M4 Sherman armed with the 76mm HV gun. |
| M4A4 | US medium tank, last of a number of developments, Armament ranged from 75mm through 76mm to 105mm Howitzer. |
| M5 HST | US fully-tracked high-speed artillery prime mover. |
| M5 Stuart | US light tank equipped with a 37mm gun, and capable of high speed. |
| M8 Greyhound | 6x6 Armoured car with 37mm main gun and 1-2 machine-guns. |
| Maior | German Army rank equivalent to Major. |
| Mamont | Russian word for Mammoth. |

| | |
|---|---|
| Manhattan Project | Research and development project aimed at producing the first atomic bomb. |
| Marmon-Herrington | Built in South Africa, this vehicle went through a series of upgrades, from Mk I to Mk IV and carried a range of weapons up to and including a 2pdr main gun. |
| Maskirovka | Soviets have a fondness for deception and misdirection and Maskirovka is an essential of any undertaking. |
| Matrose | German naval term for a common sailor. |
| Maxon mount | A single machine gun mounting which could be installed on a half-track [such as the deadly M16 halftrack], or a trailer, by which means 4 x .50cal were aimed and fired by one man. |
| Maybach | German vehicle and parts manufacturer who produced the huge Maybach engines inserted in the Tiger I tank. |
| Meteor F3, Gloster | British twin-engine jet fighter, which first flew in 1943. |
| Metgethen | Scene of a successful German counter-attack in 1945, where evidence of Soviet atrocities against the civilian population was uncovered. |
| MG.08 | German WW1 machine gun. Many survivors were employed during WW2. |
| MG34 | German standard MG often referred to as a Spandau. |
| MG42 | Superb German machine gun, capable of 1200rpm, designed to defeat the Soviet human wave attacks. Still in use to this day. |
| Midori Takushi | Green taxi [Japanese] |
| Mikoyan-9 | The first turbojet fighter developed by the USSR. [It's first flight was in 1946 but I have brought that forward in the belief that the war would have spurred the Soviets on.] |
| Mills Bomb | British fragmentation hand grenade. |

| | |
|---|---|
| Molotov Cocktail | Simple anti-tank/vehicle weapon, consisting of a bottle, a filling of petrol, and a flaming rag. Thrown at its target the bottle shattered on impact and the rag did the rest. |
| Moscow Crystal Vodka | Highest quality triple distilled vodka. |
| Moselle | Mainly white wine originating from areas around the River of the same name. |
| Mosin-Nagant | Russian infantry rifle. |
| Mosquito | DH98 De Havilland Mosquito was a multi-purpose wooden aircraft, much envied by the Luftwaffe. |
| Mosquito Mk NF30, De Havilland | British twin-engine night fighter. |
| Mosquito Mk VI, De Havilland | British twin-engine fighter-bomber. |
| Mosquito Mk XXV, De Havilland | British twin-engine light bomber. |
| MP18 | A WW1 design submachine gun, often known as the Bergmann. |
| MP40 | German submachine gun. |
| MP-40 | German standard issue submachine gun. |
| MTB | Motor Torpedo Boat, armed with 2 or 4 torpedoes, plus machine-guns and Oerlikons. |
| Mugalev | Soviet heavy mine roller gear, normally attached to T34 tanks. |
| Mustang | P51 Mustang, US single seat long-range fighter armed with 6 x .50cal machine-guns. |
| Nagant pistol | Standard Soviet revolver, very rugged and powerful using long case 7.62mm ammunition. |
| Natzwiller-Struhof | Concentration camp in Alsace. |
| Nebelwerfer | German six-barrelled mortar weapon, literally translated as 'Smoke Thrower' and known to the Allies as the Moaning Minnie, ranging up to 32cms in diameter. |

| | |
|---|---|
| NKVD | Narodny Komissariat Vnutrennikh Del, the People's Commissariat for Internal Affairs. |
| Normandie Squadron [Normandie-Niemen Regiment] | French Air force group that grew to three squadrons and served on the Russian Front throughout WW2. |
| Oerlikon | A 20mm cannon, originally German in design and still in use today. Used by all participants, the Oerlikon could be found in aircraft and ships from both sides. |
| OFLAG XVIIa | Offizierslager or OfLag No 17A, prisoner of war camp run by the Germans for officer detainees. |
| Opel Blitz | German medium transport lorry. |
| Operation Kurgan | Soviet joint-operation to employ paratroopers, Naval Marines, NKVD agents and collaborators to attack and neutralise airfields, radar, communications and logistic bases throughout Europe. Subsequently enlarged to include assassinations of Allied senior officers. |
| Operation Sumerechny | Soviet plan to remove German leadership elements from their prisoners. All officer ranks from captain upwards were to be executed. |
| Operation Unthinkable | Study ordered by Churchill to examine the feasibility of an Allied assault on Soviet held Northern Germany. |
| Operation Varsity | The largest single airborne operation of WW2, undertaken in in March 1945, Varsity involved dropping over 16,000 paratroopers to the east of the Rhine. |
| OSS | US Intelligence agency formed during 2, The Office of Strategic Services was the predecessor of the CIA, and was set up to coordinate espionage activities in occupied areas. |
| P.O.L. | Petrol, oil and lubricants. |

| | |
|---|---|
| Panther | German medium tank, considered by many to be the finest tank design of WW2. Armed with a high-velocity 75mm, it could stand its ground against anything in the Allied arsenal. |
| Pantomine | Operation Pantomine was part of the Spectrum original planning but was allocated its own codename when the scope of the operation expanded. |
| Panzer IV | German tank, which served throughout the war in many guises, mainly with a 75mm gun. |
| Panzer V | See Panther Tank |
| Panzer VI | See Tiger Tank |
| Panzerfaust | German single use anti-tank weapon. Highly effective but short ranged. |
| Panzerjager | Antitank troop[s] [German] |
| Panzerkanonier | Tank gunner |
| Panzertruppen | The German tank crews. |
| PanzerVIb | See King Tiger Tank |
| PE-2 | The Soviet Petlyakov PE-2 was a twin-engine multi-purpose aircraft considered by the Luftwaffe to be a fine opponent. |
| PEM scope | Soviet sniper scope for Mosin and SVT rifles. |
| PIAT | Acronym for Projector, Infantry, Anti-tank, the PIAT used a large spring to hurl its hollow charge shell at an enemy. |
| Plan Chelyabinsk | Soviet assault plan utilising lend-lease equipment in Western Allies markings. |
| Plan Diaspora | Soviet overall plan for assaulting in the East and for supporting the new Japanese Allies. |
| Plan Kathleen | IRA plan for the German invasion of Ireland combined with an Irish uprising. Sometimes referred to as the Artus Plan, Stephen Hayes, the IRA Chief of Staff, arranged for it to be drawn up in 1940. It was military unfeasible. |

| | |
|---|---|
| Plan Kurgan | Soviet joint-operation to employ paratroopers, Naval Marines, NKVD agents and collaborators to attack and neutralise airfields, radar, communications and logistic bases throughout Europe. Subsequently enlarged to include assassinations of Allied senior officers. |
| Plan Zilant | The Soviet paratrooper operations against the four symposiums, detailed as Zilant-1 through Zilant-4. |
| PLUTO | Acronym for 'Pipeline-under-the-ocean', which was a fuel supply pipe that ran from Britain to France, laid for D-Day operations and still in use at the end of the war. |
| PPD | Soviet submachine gun capable of phenomenal rate of fire. Mostly equipped with a 72 round drum magazine but 65 rounds were normally fitted to avoid jamming. It was too complicated and was replaced by the PPSH. |
| PPS | Simple Soviet submachine gun with a 35 round magazine. |
| PPSH | Soviet submachine gun capable of phenomenal rate of fire. Mostly equipped with a 72 round drum magazine but 65 rounds were normally fitted to avoid jamming. |
| Pravda | Leading newspaper of the Soviet Union, Pravda is translated as 'Truth'. |
| PS84 | Passenger Aircraft built at factory 84, the initial designation of the Li-2 transport aircraft. |
| PT-34 | Soviet T34/76 with mine clearing Mugalev attachment. |
| PTAB | Each Shturmovik could carry four pods containing 48 bomblets, or up to 280 internally. Each bomblet could penetrate up to 70mm of armour, enough for the main battle tanks at the time. |

| | |
|---|---|
| PTRD | Protivo Tankovoye Ruzhyo Degtyaryova, or simply put, the Degtyaryov anti-tank rifle, which fired a 14.5mm AP bullet. Amazingly, they were still being produced in 1945. |
| PU scope | Soviet sniper scope for Mosin and SVT rifles. |
| Puma | German eight-wheel armoured car with a 50mm and enclosed turret. |
| Pumpkin Bomb | Replica of the Fat Man bomb, produced with the same handling and ballistic characteristics, to permit aircrews and ground crews to practice without using actual atomic devices. They were produced in both inert and HE versions. |
| Pyat | In Russian, the number five. |
| RAC | Royal Armoured Corps |
| RAG | Rumanian Armoured Group |
| RAMC | Royal Army Medical Corps |
| RCT | Regimental Combat Team. US formation which normally consisted of elements drawn from all combatant units within the parent division, making it a smaller but reasonably self-sufficient unit. RCT's tended to be numbered according the Infantry regiment that supplied its fighting core.[See CC for US Armored force equivalent.] |
| Red Devils | Nickname for the British Airborne troops, the Red berets. |
| Red Star | Standard issue Soviet military cigarettes. |
| Rodina | The Soviet Motherland. |
| RPG-6 | Soviet anti-tank grenade with a HEAT warhead, a shaped explosive charge. Could penetrate 100mm of armour |
| SAAF | South African Air Force |
| Schmuck | A Jewish insult meaning a fool of one who is stupid. It also can literally mean the foreskin that is removed during circumcision. |

| | |
|---|---|
| Schnorkel | Equipment on a submarine that enables it to 'breathe' underwater, performing things like battery charging without exposing itself to danger. |
| Schürzen | Side armour, most often solid sheet metal but occasionally mesh, designed to prevent HEAT shells from striking the main tank, instead making them detonate against the stand-off barrier. |
| Schutzstaffel | The SS. |
| Schwalbe | German for Swallow, it was the name of the ME 262. |
| Schwere Panzer Abteilung | Heavy tank battalion [German] |
| SDKFZ 234 | German eight-wheel armoured car equipped with a range of weapons, the most powerful of which was a 75mm HV weapon. Of the four variants, the Puma with its 50mm and enclosed turret is probably the most well known. |
| Seagulls | Affectionate nickname for the Fleet Air Arm of the Royal Navy. |
| Sexton | A Sherman chassis based SP gun equipped with a 25pdr piece. |
| Shaska | A Cossack's curved sword. |
| Sherman [M4 Sherman] | American tank turned out in huge numbers with many variants, also supplied under lend-lease to Russia. |
| Shtrafbat | Soviet penal battalion. |
| Shturmovik | The Ilyushin-2 Shturmovik, Soviet mass-produced ground attack aircraft that was highly successful. |
| ShVAK | Soviet 20mm auto cannon that equipped aircraft, armoured cars, and light tanks. |
| Skat | German card game using 32 cards. |

| | |
|---|---|
| SMLE | Often referred to s the 'Smelly', this was the proper name of the Short, Magazine, Lee-Enfield rifle. |
| SOE | British organisation, Special Operations Executive, which conducted espionage and sabotage missions throughout Europe. |
| Spectrum Black | The Black plan was a diversion originating in Alsace, designed to draw down units from the Armies around the Ruhr, where a subsequent ground offensive would be staged. |
| Spectrum Blue | The Blue plan was the main ground offensive's first stage, in which Patton's Third Army and Guderian's 101st Korps would launch a pincer attack, intended to take Cologne and isolate large enemy forces to the west, where another phase of Spectrum Green had been designed to recreate the 1944 Falaise extinction. |
| Spectrum Green | The Green plan dealt with the responsibilities of the Air Forces, from the Baltic Trap [conjoined with Spectrum Red] to the overall heavy bomber plan to denude the red Army of its resources and infrastructure. |
| Spectrum Red | The Red plan dealt with the Baltic Foray in December and planning for subsequent operations there. It also encompassed the use of the Carrier force in other operations in support of the European War |
| Spectrum White | During the D-Day preparations, the Allies had fooled the Germans with a fictitious Army, known as FUSAG, Spectrum White was an attempt to recreate that confusion by indicating the existence of ASAG, the Allied Second Army Group. |
| Spitfire, Supermarine. | British single-engine fighter aircraft. |

| | |
|---|---|
| SS-Hauptsturmfuhrer | SS equivalent of captain. |
| ST44 [MP43/44] | German assault rifle with a 30 round magazine, first of its generation and forerunner to the AK47. |
| Standard HDM .22 calibre pistol | Originally used by OSS, this effective .22 with a ten round magazine is still in use by Special Forces throughout the world. |
| Starshina | Soviet rank roughly equivalent to Warrant Officer first Class. |
| Station 'X' | See Bletchley Park entry. |
| STAVKA | At this time this represents the 'Stavka of the Supreme Main Command', comprising high-ranked military and civilian members. Subordinate to the GKO, it was responsible for military oversight, and as such, held its own military reserves which it released in support of operations. |
| Sten | Basic British submachine gun with a 32 round magazine. Produced in huge numbers throughout the 40's. |
| Straipach | An Irish whore or prostitute |
| Studebaker | US heavy lorry supplied to the Soviets under lend-lease, or built in the USSR under licence, often used as the platform for the Katyusha. |
| Stuka [Junkers 87] | Famous dive-bomber employed by the Luftwaffe. |
| SU-100 | Self propelled gun on the T34 chassis equipped with the lethal 100mm. Its armour left it vulnerable but the gun had excellent penetrative qualities. |
| SU-76 | 76mm self-propelled gun used as artillery and for close support. |

| | |
|---|---|
| SU-85 | 85mm self-propelled gun that was quickly discontinued once the T34/85 came out, thee being no point in having the disadvantages of having an SP mount whilst carrying the same gun as the main tank. |
| Suka | Russian word for bitch. Also the nickname for the SU76. |
| Sunderland | British four-engine flying boat, used mainly in maritime reconnaissance and anti-submarine roles. |
| SVT40 | Soviet automatic rifle with a 10 round magazine. |
| Symposium Biarritz | Utilisation of German expertise to prepare wargame exercises for allied unit commanders to demonstrate Soviet tactics and methods to defeat them. |
| T.O.E. | Table of Organisation and Equipment, which represents what a unit should consist of. |
| T/34 | Soviet medium tank armed with a 76.2mm gun and 2 mg's. |
| T/34-85 [T34m44] | Soviet medium tank armed with an 85mm gun and 2 mg's. |
| T-44 [100] | Soviet medium tank, produced at the end of WW2, which went on to become the basis for the famous T54/55. Armed mainly with the same 85mm as in the T3485, a few were fitted with the devastating 100mm D-10 gun. |
| T54 | Medium battle tank that became the mainstay of the Red Army and the most produced tank in history. Equipped with the 100mm D-10T gun and fender mounted machine guns, analysts believe it would have made a fearsome opponent. The first prototype was built in March 1945, so I have advanced its progress as I felt the war would encourage progress. |

| | |
|---|---|
| T-70 | Soviet light tank with two crew and a 45mm gun. |
| Ta-152 | Focke-Wulf Ta 152 was a high-altitude fighter interceptor. Too few were made to impact on WW2. |
| Tacam R2 | Rumanian SP anti-tank gun on the R2 tank chassis equipped with a captured Zis-3 76.2mm gun. |
| Tallboy | British designed earthquake bomb, containing 12,000lbs of high explosive. It weighed five tons and proved effective against the most hardened of targets. |
| Thompson | .45 calibre US submachine gun, normally issued with a 20 or 30 round magazine [although a drum was available.] |
| Tiger I | German heavy battle tank armed with the first 88mm gun, capable of ruling any battlefield when it was introduced in 1942. |
| TOE | Table of Organisation and Equipment. |
| Tokarev | Soviet 7.62mm automatic handgun [also known as TT30] with an 8 round magazine. |
| Trimbach | Quality Alsatian wine. |
| Trunnion | Heavy metal mounts either side of a gun barrel. |
| TU-2, Tupolev | Soviet twin-engine medium bomber. Extremely successful design that performed well in a variety of roles, the TU-2 is considered one of the best combat aircraft of WW2. |
| Type XXI submarine | The most technologically advanced submarine of the era, produced in small numbers by the Germans and unable to affect the outcome of the war. |
| Typhoon, Hawker. | RAF's most successful single seater ground attack aircraft of World War Two, which could carry anything from bombs through to rockets. |

| | |
|---|---|
| U-Boat Type XX | 30 such U-Boats were planned, but none produced during WW2. They were intended as pure supply boats, shorter than the Type XB but with a wider beam. |
| U-Boat Type XXI | Advanced U-Boat design capable of extended underwater cruising at high speed. |
| UHU | German 251 halftrack mounting an infra-red searchlight, designed for close use with infra-red equipped Panther units. |
| USAAF | United States Army Air Force. |
| Ushanka | Fur hat with adjustable sides. |
| Vampir | German term for the ST44 equipped with an infra-red sight, also used to refer to the operators of such weapons. |
| Venona Project | Joint US-UK operation to analyse Soviet message traffic |
| Vichy | Name of the collaborationist government of defeated France. |
| Vickers Machine-Gun | British designed machine-gun of WW1 vintage. Extremely reliable .303 calibre weapon, standard issue as a heavy machine-gun. |
| Wacht am Rhein | Literally, 'Watch on the Rhine', a codename used to mask the real purpose of the German build-up that became the Ardennes Offensive in December 1944. |
| Walther P38 | German 9mm semi-automatic pistol with an eight round magazine. |
| Wanderer W23 Cabriolet | German vehicle designed for civilian use, sometimes pressed into military service, particularly as a staff car. |
| Wehrmacht | The German Army |
| Welrod | British silenced pistol that was magazine fed and primed by a bolt action. Used by SOE, OSS and resistance groups throughout Europe. The weapon remains in service to this day. |
| Winnie | Slang term for a British Churchill Tank. |

| | |
|---|---|
| Yak-6 | Twin engine aircraft that could be either a light bomber or light transport. |
| Yakolev-9 | Soviet single-seater fighter aircraft that was highly respected by the Luftwaffe. |
| Yakolev-9U | Soviet single-engine fighter aircraft, probably the best Soviet high-altitude fighter. |
| Zakusochny | Russian soft blue cheese |
| Zilant | Legendary creature in Russian folklore somewhat like a dragon |
| Zimmerit | Anti-magnetic paste applied to the side of German vehicles. |
| ZIS3 | 76.2mm anti-tank gun in Soviet use. |
| Zrinyi II | Hungarian assault gun equipped with either a 75mm or 105mm gun. |
| ZSU-37 | Soviet light self-propelled anti-aircraft vehicle, mounting a 37mm gun. |

# The full text of the poem 'Wait for me' by Konstantin Simonov.

*to Valentina Serova*

*Wait for me and I'll come back !*
*Wait with all you've got !*
*Wait, when dreary yellow rains*
*Tell you that you should not.*
*Wait when snow is falling fast,*
*Wait when summer's hot,*
*Wait when yesterdays are past,*
*Others are forgot.*
*Wait, when from that far-off place,*
*Letters don't arrive.*
*Wait, when those with whom you wait*
*Doubt if I'm alive.*

*Wait for me and I'll come back !*
*Wait in patience yet*
*When they tell you off by heart*
*That you should forget.*
*Even when my dearest ones*
*Say that I am lost,*
*Even when my friends give up,*
*Sit and count the cost,*
*Drink a glass of bitter wine*
*To the fallen friend -*
*Wait ! And do not drink with them !*
*Wait until the end !*

*Wait for me and I'll come back,*
*Dodging every fate !*
*"What a bit of luck!" they'll say,*
*Those that would not wait.*
*They will never understand*
*How amidst the strife,*
*By your waiting for me, dear,*
*You had saved my life.*
*Only you and I will know*
*How you got me through.*
*Simply - you knew how to wait -*
*No one else but you.*

[Courtesy of www.simonov.co.uk, with my thanks.]

# Bibliography

Rosignoli, Guido
The Allied Forces in Italy 1943-45
ISBN 0-7153-92123

Kleinfeld & Tambs, Gerald R & Lewis A
Hitler's Spanish Legion - The Blue Division in Russia
ISBN 0-9767380-8-2

Delaforce, Patrick
The Black Bull - From Normandy to the Baltic with the 11th Armoured
Division
ISBN 0-75370-350-5

Taprell-Dorling, H
Ribbons and Medals
SBN 0-540-07120-X

Pettibone, Charles D
The Organisation and Order of Battle of Militaries in World War II
Volume V - Book B, Union of Soviet Socialist Republics
ISBN 978-1-4269-0281-9

Pettibone, Charles D
The Organisation and Order of Battle of Militaries in World War II
Volume V - Book A, Union of Soviet Socialist Republics
ISBN 978-1-4269-2551-0

Pettibone, Charles D
The Organisation and Order of Battle of Militaries in World War II
Volume VI - Italy and France, Including the Neutral Conutries of San Marino,
Vatican City [Holy See], Andorra and Monaco
ISBN 978-1-4269-4633-2

Pettibone, Charles D
The Organisation and Order of Battle of Militaries in World War II
Volume II - The British Commonwealth
ISBN 978-1-4120-8567-5

Chamberlain & Doyle, Peter & Hilary L
Encyclopedia of German Tanks in World War Two
ISBN 0-85368-202-X

Chamberlain & Ellis, Peter & Chris
British and American Tanks of World War Two
ISBN 0-85368-033-7

Dollinger, Hans
The Decline and fall of Nazi Germany and Imperial Japan
ISBN 0-517-013134

Zaloga & Grandsen, Steven J & James
Soviet Tanks and Combat Vehicles of World War Two
ISBN 0-85368-606-8

Hogg, Ian V
The Encyclopedia of Infantry Weapons of World War II
ISBN 0-85368-281-X

Hogg, Ian V
British & American Artillery of World War 2
ISBN 0-85368-242-9

Hogg, Ian V
German Artillery of World War Two
ISBN 0-88254-311-3

Bellis, Malcolm A
Divisions of the British Army 1939-45
ISBN 0-9512126-0-5

Bellis, Malcolm A
Brigades of the British Army 1939-45
ISBN 0-9512126-1-3

Rottman, Gordon L
FUBAR, Soldier Slang of World War II
ISBN 978-1-84908-137-5

Schneider, Wolfgang
Tigers in Combat 1
ISBN 978-0-81173-171-3

Stanton, Shelby L.
Order of Battle – U.S. Army World War II.
ISBN 0-89141-195-X

Forczyk, Robert
Georgy Zhukov
ISBN 978-1-84908-556-4

# List of units mentioned within 'Red Gambit' that have been awarded the Presidential Unit Citation since 6th August 1945

| | |
|---|---|
| 100th [Nisei] Infantry Battalion | Germany |
| 101st US Cavalry Group | Germany |
| 11th US Armored Division | Germany |
| 16th US Armored Brigade | Alsace |
| 1st GAVCA, Forca Aerea Brasileira | Germany |
| 1st Provisional Tank Group | China |
| 26th US Infantry Division | Germany |
| 2nd Ranger Battalion | Alsace |
| 312th Fighter Wing USAAF | China |
| 416th Night-Fighter Squadron USAAF | Germany |
| 4th US Armored Division | Germany |
| 501st Parachute Infantry Regiment | Germany |
| 501st Parachute Infantry Regiment | Holland |
| 506th Parachute Infantry Regiment | Germany |
| 63rd US Infantry Division | Germany |
| 712th US Tank Battalion | Germany |
| 736th US Tank Battalion | Germany |
| 808th US Tank-Destroyer Battalion | Germany |
| 83rd US Infantry Division | Germany |
| 90th US Infantry Division | Germany |
| 94th Combat Bombardment Wing | Germany |
| 9th US Infantry Division | Germany |

Fig#116 – Impasse paperback end cover.

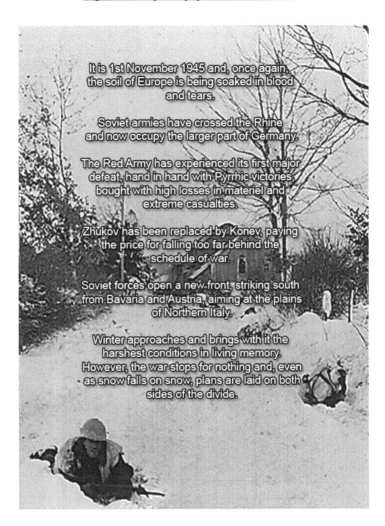

It is 1st November 1945 and, once again, the soil of Europe is being soaked in blood and tears.

Soviet armies have crossed the Rhine and now occupy the larger part of Germany.

The Red Army has experienced its first major defeat, hand in hand with Pyrrhic victories, bought with high losses in materiel and extreme casualties.

Zhukov has been replaced by Konev, paying the price for falling too far behind the schedule of war.

Soviet forces open a new front, striking south from Bavaria and Austria, aiming at the plains of Northern Italy.

Winter approaches and brings with it the harshest conditions in living memory. However, the war stops for nothing and, even as snow falls on snow, plans are laid on both sides of the divide.

# 'Counterplay' - the story continues.

Read the opening words of 'Counterplay' now.

*God rest ye merry Gentlemen*
*Let nothing you dismay*
*Remember, Christ, our saviour*
*Was born on Christmas Day*
*To save us all from Satan's power*
*When we were gone astray*
*O tidings of comfort and joy*
*Comfort and joy*
*O tidings of comfort and joy.*

*Anon.*

# Chapter 126 - THE ANNIHILATION

## 1317 hrs, Wednesday, 25th December 1945, airborne above North-West Éire.

Smoke poured from the two outboard engines, leaving parallel lines in the sky as the crippled B24 Liberator tried to make the nearest friendly territory.

Despite the obviously fraught situation, everyone aboard the Coastal Command aircraft was calm, and there was even laughter amidst the serious activity of their real mission.

It fell to the navigator to bring failure or success, for his skill would bring the Liberator directly to the precise point where they would achieve the task set them… or they would fail.

There could be no repeats, so it was imperative that the B24 hit its mark right on the button.

He thumbed his mike.

"Navigator, Pilot. Come left two degrees, Skipper, course 89°."

"Roger, Nav."

After a short delay, the navigator, sweating despite the extremely cold temperatures, spoke again.

"On course, Skipper. Estimate seven minutes to game point."

"Roger, Nav. Bombs?"

"I'm on it, Skipper."

The bombardier shifted to one side of the modified nose and checked for the umpteenth time that the internal heating circuit was functioning.

"Bombs, Pilot. Ready."

The pilot looked across to his co-pilot.

"Time for you to play."

---

It was Christmas Day, and most of those still asleep bore all the hallmarks of heavy encounters with the local brews, Russian and Irishmen alike.

A few, an unlucky few, had literally drawn short straws and found themselves sober and alert, providing the security whilst others spent the day acquainting themselves with their blankets or, in the case of a few, the latrines.

Seamus Brown was one of the selected few, and it was he who first heard the sounds of an aircraft in trouble.

The staccato sound of misfiring engines and the drone of their fully working compatriots mingled and grew loud enough to be a warning in their own right.

The camp was occasionally overflown, so there were procedures for this moment, and Brown instigated them immediately.

A large bell was rung, only a few double blows from a hammer were needed to warn the base what was about to happen. It was a question of keeping out of sight for most, but balancing that with having a few bodies in sight so as not to make the place seem deserted which, quite reasonably, they had all agreed might make the camp suspicious, even though half of it could not be seen from the air.

Brown dropped his rifle into a wheelbarrow and started to move across the central open area, his eyes searching the sky for the noisemaker.

---

"Nav, Pilot. Twenty seconds."

"Roger. Bombs, over to you."

643

The Bomb Aimer looked through the unfamiliar sight and decided that he could proceed.

The finger hovered above the button, pressed down hard, and the shooting commenced.

---

Brown kept walking, his eyes taking in the smokey trails from two of its engines, his ears adding to the evidence of his eyes.

*'The fucking bastards are in trouble'.*

"Crash, you fucking English shites! Go on! Merry fucking Christmas, you bastards!"

A couple of his men chuckled and shared the sentiment, although not quite as loud as Brown.

His raised voice brought a response from some of those aching from the night's exertions and windows were opened, the oaths and curses directed his way not always in Irish brogue.

He heard the window open behind him and knew the stream of Russian was for his ears, but he kept his attention firmly on the dying aircraft, shouting louder to make sure his new allies were even more agitated.

"Die, you fucking bastards, die!"

The Liberator, for he was sure that was what it was, kept dropping lower in the sky, and eventually flew below his line of vision.

In his mind, he enjoyed the image of the mighty aircraft nose-diving into some Irish hillside and promised himself that he would find out what happened at some time.

Turning to the nearest open window, that of a small hut hidden under a camouflage of turf roof and adjacent shrubs, Brown tackled the verbal aggressor.

"I don't know what the fuck you are saying my little Russian friend, but if you don't fuck off, I'll shoot you in the fucking balls."

The words were said as if he was apologising for waking the Soviet marine; his smile was one of sincere regret.

The Matrose nodded and closed the window, happy that the stupid Irishman would not repeat his error.

---

The Liberator continued on for some miles before the navigator gave another change of course, this time turning northwards and out to sea.

Once clear of land, the smoke generators were turned off, the flight engineer corrected his engine settings, and the B24 resumed its journey to RAF Belfast. There it was met by two members of the SOE Photo interpretation section, specially flown in from the Tempsford base to look at the stills and movie footage shot by the special duty crew as they passed precisely over the IRA base at Glenlara.

## 2002 hrs, Thursday, 26th December 1945, Camp 5A, near Cookstown, County Tyrone, Northern Ireland.

Wijers helped the female officer carry her equipment from the car into the lecture room.

Section Officer Megan Jenkins, and one assistant, had been rushed from RAF Tempsford to RAF Belfast, where they joined up with the film produced by the B24 Liberator pass over Glenlara.

The stills were easier to produce quickly, so Megan Jenkins had already examined them and found a great deal of information that would be of use to those present.

She had not waited to view the film footage before she left for Camp 5A so, once everything was set-up and introductions were made, the movie footage from the fly by was shown for the first time.

The others in the room looked at surprisingly good clarity work and were surprised, allowing that surprise to mask their disappointed reaction as to what the film contained.

Not so Jenkins and her assistant, who made notes and, when the short film had ended, compared them.

The assistant, a male Sergeant, removed the film from the projector and took it away to make some copies of still frames that they had selected during the show. A small suitcase contained everything they would need, and Wijers showed the sergeant to a suitable dark place.

The main room had been set up to her requirements, so Jenkins moved across to the table, spread with white paper and set with rulers, protractors and pencils.

She started to draw her map.

The others in the room gathered round, careful not to get between her and the maps and photos.

A special scale ruler flitted from photo to paper, the maths of the photographing height to ground scale tumbling from her brain with the ease of a Cambridge maths professor.

The speed and accuracy with which she worked was seriously impressive and, before their eyes, a scale map of the whole IRA camp started to appear.

The Sergeant reappeared, holding some of the images selected from the movie. In the manner of specialists throughout the services, he enjoyed his moment in the limelight, taking the main map and annotating it with the number of one of the new pictures.

Two in particular were of great note and Jenkins moved between her hand drawn map and the new photographs, comparing and adjusting.

Wijers was the first to voice doubts.

"Officer Jenkins, these two positions here... and here... the new ones... they are not in these photographs."

Megan smiled, knowing that not everyone could grasp the science of photo interpretation.

"Here, Sir, these are from the movie. When we watched," she indicated the smug looking Sergeant, "Both of us saw a flash, small, but there for sure. The new pictures prove it. The flashes were caused by reflections... something moving in the light, such as a window, a mirror, a glass, anything like that."

She moved back to the original photos and selected one that covered the new 'position' nearest the water's edge.

"Here. If you look carefully, that flash would come from this point here. See?"

He didn't.

"Look here, Sir. Here is a shadow band. The sun is to the south east, so this shadow is on the northern edge of the position. The bushes muddy the waters a little... and I will have to study them a lot closer, but my experience tells me that this position is roughly eleven foot tall from ground level."

Wijers looked at her and the photograph without comprehension.

"To be honest, Sir, I'm a little annoyed that I didn't see it first time. Still, got it now."

The Dutchman still didn't see it.

Neither did Sam Rossiter, Head of SOE.

Michael Rafferty, top man in Northern Ireland's Special Branch couldn't either.

Much to his surprise, the last officer in the room could see it perfectly.

Turning his attention back to the hand drawn plan, he found himself well satisfied.

"Offizier Jenkins, can you put everything down on this map here. Find every position and put it here?"

"Yes, of course, Major. You tell me what you want, I will put it there.

De facto Sturmbannfuhrer and leader of the SOE's Special Ukrainian force but, for the purposes of Megan Jenkins, Major Shandruk of the US Army, nodded to Rossiter.

"More than enough, Colonel."

He turned his eyes back to the plan, his mind already assessing how the job would be done and how, at the end of the operation, Glenlara would be nothing but a wasteland.

*-To be continued-*

Made in the USA
San Bernardino, CA
14 February 2014